François Couperin
and the French Classical Tradition

A portrait of François Couperin le Grand by André Bouys, engraved by Filibert in 1735, two years after the composer's death.

François Couperin

and the
French Classical Tradition

New Version, 1987

Wilfrid Mellers

faber and faber

LONDON · BOSTON

First published in 1950 by
Dennis Dobson Limited

This new and revised edition first published in 1987
by Faber and Faber Limited
3 Queen Square London WC1N 3AU

Photoset by Parker Typesetting Service, Leicester
Printed in Great Britain by
Redwood Burn Ltd Trowbridge Wiltshire
All rights reserved

Music examples drawn by Paul Courtenay

British Library Cataloguing in Publication Data

Mellers, Wilfrid
François Couperin and the French classical
tradition. – 2nd rev. ed.
1. Couperin, François – Criticism and
interpretation
I. Title
780'.92'4   ML410.C855
ISBN 0–571–13983–3

*To my (past) students
and to my (present) teachers:
Davitt Moroney and Jane Clark*

Contents

List of Illustrations

Preface to First Edition, 1950

So far as I am aware, this is the first book on Couperin le Grand in English; indeed it is possibly the first comprehensive study of his work in any language, for of the three French books on him known to me, that of Bouvet is purely biographical while those of Tessier and Tiersot do not claim to be more than introductory monographs. (As such, they are both admirable.)

I have divided this study of Couperin into three sections. The first gives the facts of his life and some account of the nature, values, and standards of his community. Of the facts of his life, little is known, and I have not indulged in speculation. For most of the information contained in my introductory chapter I am indebted to the biographical sections of the previous books on Couperin referred to above, with the addition of some documentary evidence more recently published by M. Paul Brunold.

The chapters on the values and standards of the *grand siècle* do not pretend to offer a revolutionary approach. My general attitude to the period is influenced by the miscellaneous writings of Mr Martin Turnell, published in *Horizon*, *Scrutiny*, and elsewhere[1] – especially those on Racine, Molière, Corneille, and *La Princesse de Clèves*, and by a most interesting essay by Mr R. C. Knight also published in *Scrutiny*, which was in part a criticism of Turnell's account of Racine. I have also found many hints worth following up, and much useful information, in Mr Arthur Tilley's two books, *From Montaigne to Molière* and *The Decline of the Age of Louis XIV*. Most of the information in my chapter on the court theatre music is derived from the writings of the recognized authority on the period, M. Henri Prunières. These books are listed in the bibliography. In this chapter, as in the others, I am of course responsible for the critical comments

---

[1] Much of Mr Turnell's work on the period is available in book form. (*The Classical Moment*, 1948.)

on the music and for the various analogies between Lully and other artists.

In general I have tried where possible to base my remarks on contemporary documents, creative or critical, and perhaps I may claim as original my attempt to state and interpret the relationships between the various facets of *grand siècle* culture in manners, philosophy, literature, painting, architecture, and music. I am aware that comparisons between the arts are sometimes considered dangerous, but I cannot see that, providing some technical basis is given to them, they can be other than illuminating. One would certainly expect artists working in different media but in similar conditions, with a similar philosophical background, to have much in common. In any case my whole approach presupposes an interrelation between the arts, as manifestations of the human spirit, and life; and I have taken pains to establish by frequent cross reference the close dependence of the second part of the book on the first.

This second part includes some comment on everything Couperin wrote. Even at the risk of monotony, I wished the book to serve as a work of reference as well as a critical study. This section thus stands in lieu of a thematic index. But of course the primary intention of this part is not merely informative but also critical. It aims to assess Couperin's achievement in relation to his social and musical background.

In such an attempt it is always difficult to decide how a book may be most profitably arranged. Even if the dates of composition of Couperin's works were all definitely established, a chronological method would hardly be feasible if adequate consideration is to be given to the various styles and conventions which Couperin employs. I have thus dealt in separate chapters with Couperin's contribution to each of the genres current in his time, preserving some hint of chronological sequence in so far as I deal with each genre at the time in the composer's career when he showed most interest in it. Thus I discuss the violin trio sonatas after the organ masses because it was at that stage in his work that Couperin was most preoccupied with the problems of the sonata convention. But he wrote other violin sonatas late in his life, and these I have discussed in the same chapter, since only as a whole can one assess Couperin's contribution to this convention.

x   From some points of view it would have been more con-

venient to the reader if I had discussed Couperin's predecessors –
not merely the theatre music but all that he owed to the past – in a
preliminary chapter, instead of scattering the information
throughout the chapters on each genre of his work. For instance,
the reader who knows something about the lutenists is in a better
position than the reader who knows nothing to approach any
aspect of Couperin's music. Yet an account of them undoubtedly
fits most cogently into the chapter on the keyboard music which
thus views the evolution of the clavecin school as a continuous
process from the early years of the *grand siècle* to Couperin le
Grand. Moreover, by inserting a proportion of general information and theory into the chapters on particular branches of
Couperin's work, I hope I have to some extent palliated the
monotony of many continuous pages of technical comment and
analysis. If in this arrangement some duplication and cross reference between the chapters is unavoidable, I do not think this is
necessarily a liability.

For Part II my main sources are of course Couperin's music, in
the Oiseau-Lyre text (whose spelling and accentuation of titles is
adopted in this book), and the music of other relevant composers
in editions specified in the Bibliography. But I should mention
that for much of the information contained in the chapter on the
secular vocal works I have drawn on Théodore Gérold's study of
Le Chant au XVIIième Siècle; and that I have found Paul-Marie
Masson's comprehensive work on the operas of Rameau
especially helpful with reference to the dances and the social
background of the Regency.

On the third section of the book no comment is necessary
except to remark that even in dealing with matters of theory and
practice I have tried not to forget their relation to aesthetic and
social values. One need hardly add that anyone who writes on
eighteenth-century musical theory owes much to the work of
Arnold Dolmetsch and to Dannreuther's book on ornamentation.

Many people have helped me with comment and discussion. In
particular I must mention Mr R. J. White of Downing College,
Cambridge, and Mr Alan Robson of Oxford University, who
have made many useful suggestions about the first part of the
book. Mr Felix Aprahamian has lent me music from his library
and has discussed seventeenth-century French organ music with
me; Mr Eric Mackerness has made various incidental criticisms.   xi

But most of all I must pay a tribute to Mr C. L. Cudworth, of the Pendlebury Library, Cambridge, and to Mr R. C. Knight, of the French Department of Birmingham University. Mr Cudworth has put his extensive knowledge of early eighteenth-century music at my disposal and has unerringly directed my attention to music in the Pendlebury, Rowe, and University Libraries which seemed, however remotely, relevant to my subject. He has also read the whole of the manuscript, making many pertinent criticisms; and has compiled the catalogue raisonné of Couperin's music. I cannot too strongly express my gratitude both for his erudition and for his enthusiasm.

Mr Knight has undertaken the arduous task of reading and checking the proofs, especially the French quotations. He has corrected me on several points of fact, and has discussed with me many of my opinions. Both his knowledge and his sympathy have proved invaluable.

Finally I must convey my thanks to my publisher for his unfailing courtesy and generosity in dealing with more than two hundred music type quotations and many not easily accessible illustrations, at a time when even the simplest kind of book production is beset with difficulties.

W.H.M.

CAMBRIDGE, *August* 1949

Preface to New Version, 1987

My book on Couperin was written between 1945 and 1949, immediately after the Second World War; perhaps I was sub-consciously making a retrospective comment on civilization in the aftermath of its disintegration and near destruction. The original edition, published in 1950, has been out of print for many years, though it had a reprint in the admirable American Dover Press paperbacks. Rather surprisingly, the book has not been superseded by a bigger and maybe better book on the subject; so I have accepted my original publisher's suggestion that a revised and updated edition is due. How best to accomplish this called, however, for careful consideration, for the ways in which I think and write today cannot be readily accommodated to my literate identity of thirty-five years back. Though I still hold by most (not all) of the critical judgements I made in the late forties, the book as first published has inevitably become, at least in some aspects, obsolete. In those days one couldn't take it for granted that baroque music, especially in its hyper-sophisticated French manifestations, would be performed with any approach to authenticity either in the choice of instruments or in deference to what we now know of performing techniques and stylistic conventions. My warnings against the horrid ineptitude of pianos, romantic organs and modern strings, and my regrets about the scarcity of competent players of lutes and viols, now read somewhat comically; still quainter seem references to the paucity of recordings now that not only the music of Couperin le Grand, but also that of contemporaries as unambiguously minor as Bodin de Boismortier, is copiously available on disc and tape. True, Couperin's church music, apart from the *Leçons de Ténèbres*, is less adequately represented than it was in the forties, since the recordings of the various *Versets* and the *Motet de Ste Suzanne* have been deleted. This lacuna is no more than temporary, however, for the French company xiii

L'Astrée is issuing a 'total' recording of Couperin's works, in celebration of the two hundred and fiftieth anniversary of the composer's death.

After some reflection I decided that an attempt to rewrite a book written so many years ago wouldn't be successful: so I have left the text substantially as it was. I have made minor revisions of tone where the text seemed incompatible with our approach in the 1980s; I have deleted references to recordings and to modes of performance that are outdated; I have corrected the odd passage – the most notable instance is the section on the music of Jacques Duphly – wherein I now think I made a critical misjudgement; and all the music examples have been re-edited by Davitt Moroney and completely redrawn. The substantial new material I have to offer I've presented in a series of Addenda and Periphera, except for the discussion of Couperin's resources and the problems involved in performing his works today.

This topic was covered originally in Chapter 13 – which has dated so damagingly that it had to be totally rewritten, after the introductory historical section. I have incorporated into this revised chapter comparative comments on contemporary recordings, since such comment may be generally as well as specifically illuminating. I have included here some discussion of tuning and temperament, a theme little explored forty years ago, though it is important and of far more than academic interest. I have also commented on the 'authentic' use of voices, string and wind instruments – about which much more is known now than then. Again comparative consideration of recordings may provide glosses on technical matters, such as fingering, which are more abstractly discussed in Chapter 12. Now that the music has been more widely and frequently performed, we know more about how theory is translated into practice. I have observed that today's students, even quite young ones, 'take to' the malleabilities of unequal notes and the expressivity of ornamentation as naturally as ducks to water, whereas in my student days we tended to be stiff with self-conscious intellectuality, making the grade (or not) by trial and error.

While commenting in the new Chapter 13 on current recordings I have omitted a discography *per se*; there is now too much material, ephemerally in and out of the catalogues. The original Chapter 14, which was in effect a list of editions of Couperin's music, I have deleted, replacing it with a catalogue prepared by

David Griffiths, Music Librarian of the University of York, who also helped me with a revised bibliography. These are now placed at the end of the book.

The first five appendices are unchanged. I considered omitting Appendix A on the grounds that Couperin's authorship of the organ masses is no longer disputed. But I decided that it was worth preserving for 'documentary' interest. The preface to the revised Oiseau-Lyre edition by Kenneth Gilbert and Davitt Moroney gives a definitive account of the matter. Appendix F I have scrapped since its material, corrected and enlarged, is now incorporated in Addendum III.

I toyed with the idea of inserting the addenda intermittently throughout the book, after the chapters to which they are most pertinent. On reflection, however, I decided that this would impair the original unity and that the addenda work better in retrospect, to some degree modifying the original perspectives. The addendum on the 'new' motets simply extends the chapter on vocal church music to embrace music that has been redis-covered since the first publication. The essay on Watteau, Couperin and the Theatre and the analysis of the trio sonata *La Visionnaire* are, however, a different kind of writing from any-thing in the original book – to which they add, I hope, a relevant dimension.

By far the most substantial of the addenda is the Handbook to Couperin's pieces for harpsichord (which, incidentally, I now prefer to call a harpsichord rather than a clavecin, as I somewhat preciously termed it in the original edition). This began as a revision and extension of Appendix F on the titles of Couperin's harpsichord pieces, but turned into a much more comprehensive survey, no less 'central' than the original Chapter 9 itself. Chap-ter 9 and the addendum overlap to a slight degree, but the original chapter still seems right in the original context: to which the addendum is a supplement, serving as a commentary for the use of players and students. Some of the fresh information included came to light through the researches of Jane Clark, who has generously allowed me to make use of her findings. She has demonstrated that the musical and the anecdotal aspects of Couperin's harpsichord pieces are interdependent; the titles often have implications far wider and deeper than tittle-tattle. To this section I've added, since it is meant to serve as a working compendium, the catalogue raisonné of the harpsichord pieces,   xv as it appeared in the 1950 edition. The rest of the original catalogue raisonné I have omitted since it is now covered by David Griffiths's catalogue of works.

To the acknowledgements in the preface to the 1950 edition I must add others: to David Griffiths for his bibliographical contribution; to Jane Clark not only for the research material she offered me but also for pleasant and profitable hours of talk about and around Couperin; to Kenneth Gilbert, master player of and authority extraordinary about Couperin's harpsichord music, for conversation and for reading and commenting on my new material; to Davitt Moroney, also distinguished as a performer and scholar of Couperin, for re-editing the music examples and much other help; to Margarita Hanson for permission to publish the music examples which conform to the new Oiseau-Lyre edition; to Sir Sacheverell Sitwell for permission to quote extensively from his writings about Watteau; to Faber and Faber Ltd and Harcourt Brace Jovanovitch Inc. for permission to reproduce lines from 'Burnt Norton' in *Four Quartets* by T. S. Eliot, copyright 1943 by T. S. Eliot, renewed 1971 by Esme Valerie Eliot; to Lewis Jones, one-time student at York, for checking technicalities in the new Chapter 13; and to the York students who attended the project on Couperin which I gave as, appropriately enough, my last official assignment as a university teacher. Slightly to my surprise, they responded with extreme enthusiasm to Couperin's music as well as to my enthusiasm about it. From their intelligent comments and probing questions, and still more from their performances of the music, I learned as much or more as I hope they learned from me. The original edition of this book was my academic initiation; it seems fitting that I should dedicate this New Version to my students.

W.H.M.

LONDON, 1986

xvi

Part I

Life and Times

Rien n'est beau que le vrai.

BOILEAU

We Polish one another, and rub off our Corners and Rough Sides, by a sort of *Amicable Collision*.

SHAFTESBURY

I think, moderately speaking, that the Vulgar are generally in the Wrong.

SHENSTONE

GENEALOGICAL TABLE OF THE COUPERIN FAMILY

CHARLES COUPERIN

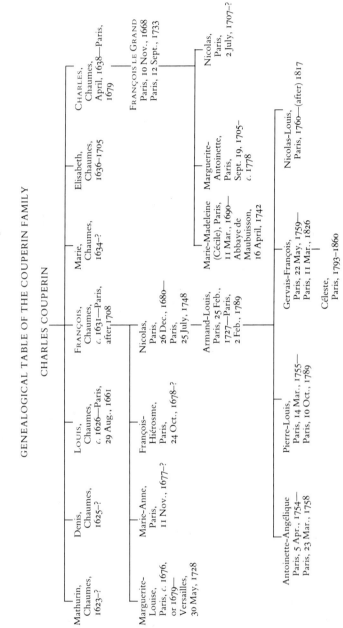

Chapter One

The Life

After the Bach family the Couperins are probably the most distinguished of all musical dynasties. Little is known about their origin though it is rumoured that there was foreign blood in their veins some time in the sixteenth century. At the beginning of the seventeenth a Mathurin Couperin was village lawyer at Beauvoir, in Brie. His son Denis succeeded him and eventually advanced to become a royal notary. Another son, Charles, set up as a tradesman in the neighbouring town of Chaumes. He was an amateur musician of some ability, playing the organ at the parish church and also at the Benedictine abbey in the town. He was the grandfather of Couperin le Grand. Three of his eight children became professional musicians, laying the foundations of the Couperin 'dynasty'. These three were Louis, born in about 1626, François I, born in 1631, and Charles, born in 1633.

The story of how the Couperins entered the fashionable musical life of Paris is well known, picturesque, and authentic – since it comes from the reliable contemporary chronicler Titon du Tillet. We may leave him to tell the tale in his own words:

> Les trois frères Couperin étoient de Chaume, petite ville de Brie assez proche de la terre de Chambonnière. Ils jouoient du violon, et les deux ainez réussissoient très bien sur l'orgue. Ces trois frères, avec de leurs amis, aussi joueurs du violon, firent partie, un jour de la fête de M. de Chambonnière, d'aller à son chateau lui donner une aubade; ils arrivèrent et se placèrent à la porte de la salle où Chambonnière étoit à la table avec plusieurs convives, gens d'esprit et ayant du goût pour la musique. Le maître de la musique fut surpris agréablement de même que tout la compagnie, par la bonne symphonie qui se fit entendre. Chambonnière pria les personnes qui l'exécutoient d'entrer dans la salle et leur demanda d'abord de qui étoit la composition des airs qu'ils avoient jouez; un d'entre eux lui dit qu'elle étoit de Louis Couperin, qu'il lui présenta. Chambonnière fit aussitôt son compliment à Louis

3

Couperin, et l'engagea avec tous ses camarades de se mettre à table; il lui temoigna beaucoup d'amitié, et lui dit qu'un homme tel que lui n'étoit pas fait pour rester dans un province, et qu'il falloit absolument qu'il vint avec lui à Paris; ce que Louis Couperin accepta avec plaisir. Chambonnière le produisit à Paris et à la Cour, où il fut goûté. Il eut bientôt après l'orgue de St. Gervais à Paris, et une des places d'organiste de la Chapelle du Roi.

The year of this musical tribute is not specified, but it was probably about 1650, or earlier.

The post of organist at St Gervais was one with which the Couperin family became intimately associated. Louis also played the viol and violin in the ballet music of the court. When the great Chambonnières incurred the King's displeasure, reputedly because he would not play *basse continue*, Louis was offered the much coveted post of Joueur de l'Epinette de la Chambre du Roi. He declined it out of a sense of delicacy, but that the offer was made testifies to the esteem in which he was held; he seems to have been affluent and highly successful. He was studying the work of Chambonnières and Gaultier, and composing energetically himself when, on the crest of his fortunes, he died. This was in 1661, in his thirty-fifth year.

The second son, the elder François, came to Paris a few years after Louis. He too became an organist and music teacher, but he does not seem to have shared either the talent or the fame of his brothers. He lived in the parish of St Louis en l'Ile and there is no evidence that he was ever organist of St Gervais, though he may have helped out occasionally during the interim period after Charles's death, when the busily fashionable La Lande was *locum tenens*. It is certain that he never occupied the St Gervais organist's house. ★

Charles, the third son, followed Louis to Paris after an interval of a few years. He too became a protégé of Chambonnières, and one of the King's violinists associated with the ballet. When Louis Couperin died he succeeded to the organ of St Gervais, married, and installed himself in the ancient organist's house overlooking the graveyard. Here, after seven years, a son, François, was born on the tenth of November 1668. Eleven years later Charles, like Louis, died at an early age. The little François,

---

★ The question of the attribution of the great François's organ masses to the elder François is discussed in Appendix A.

although only a child, inherited the organist's post from his father, and continued to live with his mother in the old house in the rue de Monceau. The church authorities arranged that until François grew up the brilliant La Lande should deputize for him on the organ, simultaneously fulfilling the duties of his two other Parisian churches. Meanwhile François had received a thorough musical training from his father, with some help perhaps from his uncle at St Louis en l'Ile and from the renowned organist, Jacques Thomelin. After Charles's death, Thomelin became, according to Titon du Tillet, a second father to François. He could not have been in better hands. It was undoubtedly from Thomelin that François learned the firm contrapuntal science, the mastery of the old technique which is conspicuous in his first work, the organ masses.

The contract made with La Lande had specified that he should carry out the organist's duties until Couperin was eighteen. Owing to the pressure of his commitments at court, La Lande was only too pleased to leave St Gervais somewhat before the stated date; he can have been in no doubt about the young François's proficiency either as an executant or theoretical musician. Couperin took over the St Gervais organ in his eighteenth year, in 1685 or early in 1686. Four years later he married Marie Anne Ansault, of whom little is known. In 1690 were born both his first child and the first fruits of his musical creativity. He obtained a *privilège du Roi* to enable him to publish, with La Lande's recommendation, his organ masses; he had several manuscript copies made, and bound them with an engraved title page saying that they were composed by 'François Couperin de Crouilly, organiste de St. Gervais'.

About two years later, François thought he would show his mettle as a fashionable composer by writing some sonatas in the Italian manner. Many years afterwards, when he published the works with some new sonatas, Couperin revealed an innocent deception he had practised. The passage from the preface to the sonatas is worth quoting, if only because the prose has so Couperin-like a flavour:

La première Sonade de ce Receuil fut aussy la première que je composay et qui ait été composé en France. L'histoire même en est singulière. Charmé de celles de signor Corelli, dont j'aimeray les oeuvres tant que je vivray, ainsi que les ouvrages françaises de M.

5

de Lully, j'hasarday d'en composer une, que je fis executer dans le concert où j'avais entendu celles de Corelli. Et me defiant de moi-même, je me rendis, par un petit mensonge officieux, un très bon service. Je feignis qu'un parent que j'ay, effectivement, auprès du Roi de Sardaigne, m'avoit envoyé une Sonade d'un nouvel Auteur italien: je rangeay les lettres de mon nom, de façon que cela forma un nom italien que je mis à la place. La Sonade fut dévorée avec empressement; et j'en tairay l'apologie. Cela cependant m'encouragea, j'en fis d'autres. Et mon nom italianisé s'attira, sous le masque, de grands applaudissements. Mes Sonades, heureusement, prirent assez de faveur pour que l'équivoque ne m'ait point fait rougir.

It is clear however that by this time François was becoming famous in his own right, without recourse to anagrams; for in 1693 he entered the King's service as one of the organists of the Chapelle du Roi, having been chosen by Louis himself as 'le plus experimenté en cet exercice'. Four organists shared the royal chapel between them, officiating for periods of three months yearly. Couperin succeeded his old master Thomelin; his colleagues were Le Bègue, Buterne, and Nivers. Once he had established this link with the court, François progressed rapidly. In 1694 he was appointed Maître de Clavecin des Enfants de France, teaching the Duke of Burgundy and almost all the royal children, at the same time as Fénelon. He must by now have been in very comfortable material circumstances; he was also gaining confidence in his creative work which, although conceived in the Italian fashion, had already revealed a decisive personality.

About this time, probably in 1696, Louis paid a tribute to Couperin's distinction and celebrity by ennobling him. It was an honour that was well deserved, for no man has had a more innate aristocracy of spirit than François le Grand. Characteristically he showed a touchingly innocent delight in the compliment, and was still more overjoyed when, a few years later, he was made a Chevalier of the Lateran order. He devised a coat of arms for himself, incorporating a golden lyre as a symbol of his muse, and signed himself, with a flourish at once baroque and precise, Le Chevalier Couperin, at the baptism of his daughter Marguerite-Antoinette in 1705.

During the first decade of the eighteenth century he was 6 engaged on the production of music which would soothe the

King's increasing melancholy. A considerable part of his output was church music written for Versailles. In much of it, very high and delicate soprano parts were written for his cousin Marguerite-Louise, a daughter of François the elder, who must have been a singer of remarkable accomplishment, if we are to judge from the words of Titon du Tillet:

> Une quantité de Motets dont douze à grand choeur ont été chantés à la Chapelle du Roi, devant Louis XIV, qui en fut fort satisfait de même que toute sa cour. La Demoiselle Louise Couperin, sa cousine, musicienne pensionnaire du Roi, y chantait plusieurs versets avec une grande légèreté de voix et un goût merveilleux.

The motet *Qui dat Nivem* was the first of Couperin's works to be published except for a few slight *airs de cour*. It appears that at this period he also wrote some secular cantatas, including one on the theme of *Ariane abandonée*, but these are lost.

In addition to the church music Couperin also regularly produced chamber music for the *concerts du dimanche*. Couperin's position as a court musician is not very clear, for the Ordinaire de la Musique at the beginning of the century was officially d'Anglebert the younger, and François did not succeed him until 1717. It is certain however that Couperin was virtually in charge long before that date, and probable that he presided at the clavecin from 1701 onwards. D'Anglebert's ill-health and defective eyesight are possible reasons for his failure to fulfil an office he ostensibly held. In any case Couperin had some of the most celebrated musicians of the day in his charge. Forqueray the violist and Rebel the violinist were among those who played with him at the *concerts*, and it may have been at these entertainments that Marguerite-Louise sang the lost cantatas. We know too that at this period of his life Couperin became the intimate friend of the organist Gabriel Garnier, to whom one of the loveliest of his early harpsichord pieces is dedicated.

By 1710 Couperin was already known to his contemporaries as Le Grand. Monteclair, Siret, Dornel and many other disciples dedicated works to him, expressing their recognition of his pre-eminence. François himself seems to have been serenely conscious of his powers, though this does not mean that his urbane irony, as revealed in his prefaces, did not extend to himself. He had the true humility of genius, and was always 7 willing to pay deference to others when he recognized genius in them. He had a profound respect for La Lande, and in the case of the great Marin Marais went so far as to hold up the production of one of his works because, 'ayant tous deux le même graveur', the publication of his work would have interfered with the publication of Marais's. The only two musicians of consequence who seem to have distrusted François were Lecerf de la Viéville and Louis Marchand. Lecerf de la Viéville, author of a famous book on the conflict between the French and Italian styles, suspected Couperin of a dangerous partiality for Italianism – a rather unreasonable charge when one recalls Couperin's often reiterated desire to mate the two styles, and his many tributes to his 'ancêtres' and to the incomparable Lully, 'le plus grand homme en musique que le dernier siècle ait produit'. Marchand seems to have been a difficult person on any count. He was hostile to Couperin not because he regarded him as a fanatical adherent of any musical cause but through jealousy, partly professional, partly personal. The legend that there was a woman in the case, recounted by the unreliable son of d'Aquin de Château-Lyon, is not otherwise authenticated. Significantly, if the stories about him are true, Marchand seems to have felt about Bach very much as he felt about Couperin. A man of remarkable talent★ and orginality, he wrote music which is in some ways frustrated and unresolved; it may well have been the lucidity, the objectified quality, of Bach's and Couperin's music that so exasperated him. Most probably his exasperation has been grossly exaggerated with the passing of the years.

During the period of his court activities Couperin returned to Paris periodically to teach and to direct the services at St Gervais. He had moved from the old organist's house as early as 1697 and lived in a succession of Parisian houses up to 1724, each dwelling growing more majestic as his reputation advanced. On the fourteenth of May 1713, he took out a *privilège du Roi* to publish his work, and this time was able to carry it through. He first printed his first book of clavecin pieces, which had been written inter-

---

★ Cf. Dr Burney: 'Marchand was one of the greatest organ players in Europe during the early part of the present century. Rameau, his friend and most formidable rival, frequently declared that the greatest pleasure of his life was hearing Marchand perform; that no one could compare with him in the management of a fugue; and that he believed no musician ever equalled him in extempore playing.' (*A General History of Music*.)

mittently over the last ten or fifteen years; in the next year he began to publish his *Leçons de Ténèbres*, but this project was unfortunately never completed, so that only three out of nine survive. In 1716 appeared his theoretical work, *L'Art de toucher le Clavecin*; and the second book of harpsichord pieces in 1717, in which year, on the fifth of March, he at last officially acquired the post of Ordinaire de la Musique. He was still writing concert music for the king's evening entertainment during these years, and after Louis's death continued to act as Maître de Clavecin aux Enfants de France. (He taught the little princess, the wife-to-be of Louis XV, from 1722 to 1725.) Couperin was forty-seven when Louis XIV died. During the Regency he published his third book of clavecin pieces, and some of the *concerts*, under the title of *Les Goûts Réünis*. The success of these encouraged him to publish some of his early Italian violin sonatas, adding a 'French' suite to each of them to redress the balance and incorporating one completely new work. The whole collection, called *Les Nations*, appeared in 1726.

For two years the Couperins had now been settled in a beautiful new house in the rue Neuve des Bons Enfants. We know almost nothing about the last ten years of his life. In 1728 he published the suites for viols and also a *Benedixisti* which seems to have been a revival of a work dating from 1697. The fourth book of clavecin pieces, put together with the help of his family, was published in 1730. Never very strong, he was intermittently ailing from his early forties; the preface to the fourth book is valedictory in tone:

> Il y a environ trois ans que ces pièces sont achevées, mais comme ma santé diminue de jour en jour, mes amis me conseillent de cesser de travailler et je n'ay pas fait de grands ouvrages depuis. Je remercie le Public de l'aplaudissement qu'il a bien voulu leur donner jusqu'icy; et je crois en mériter une partie par le zèle que j'ai eu à lui plaire. Comme personne n'a guères plus composé que moy, dans plusieurs genres, j'espère que ma Famille trouvera dans mes portfeuilles de quoy me faire regretter, si les regrets nous servent à quelque chose après la vie, mais il faut du moins avoir cette idée pour tâcher de mériter une immortalité chimerique où presque tous les Hommes aspirent.

The tinge of irony in this gravely measured prose only makes its cadence the more poignant; in much of the music which follows 9 this preface we may find a comparable union of melancholy with an objectified precision, a detachment from the merely personal. The last two clavecin *ordres*, perhaps the most civilized music that even Couperin ever wrote, are his farewell to civilization and the world. In 1723 he had handed over the St Gervais organ to Nicolas, a son of François l'aîné; in 1730 he relinquished his remaining posts, his daughter Marguerite-Antoinette becoming Ordinaire de la Musique for the interim period until d'Anglebert died.

Couperin died on the twelfth of September 1733, in the big, elegant house in the rue Neuve des Bons Enfants. Another daughter, who was also a musician, became a nun. A son, Nicolas-Louis, born in 1707, presumably died in infancy, for nothing is known of him. Six months before his death Couperin had taken out a second *privilège du Roi*, on the expiration of the period of twenty years covered by the *privilège* of 1713. His intention, referred to in the preface to his fourth book, that his wife and relations should undertake the production of his unpublished works, was not fulfilled. His wife, a shadowy figure throughout, possibly had little business sense or initiative; his nephew Nicolas, to whom the task was entrusted, seems to have been irresponsible. Whatever the reason, nearly all Couperin's music apart from that which he himself published is lost. The missing manuscripts include a considerable amount of church music and 'occasional' concert music, but probably not any important harpsichord works.

After François's death the musical direction of St Gervais remained in the hands of the Couperin family for several more generations. Nicolas's son Armand-Louis, and then his grandsons Pierre-Louis and Gervais-François, followed in the succession. They were all reputable musicians, both as executants and composers, but their distinction declines progressively with the civilization that produced them. The Revolution meant the end of the world that had made the glory of the Couperins possible; perhaps they were ill-adapted to survival in the strange new world which was inevitably emerging. Gervais-François died in 1826 in circumstances that were a bathetic reversal of the great days of the first Louis or of François the great. His daughter Céleste was given the thorough musical education habitually accorded to members of the family and seems to have been a competent organist. But her father was the last of the Couperins

LE PORTAIL DE S.^T GERVAIS.

I. The Church of St Gervais, the dynastic church of the
Couperin family. The classical façade to the Gothic building was
designed by De Brosse in 1616, and was greatly admired in the
age of le Roi Soleil.

to officiate at St Gervais; Céleste declined to the status of a
second-rate piano teacher. In 1848, in indigence, she was obliged
to sell the family portraits to the state; the Couperins had
become a museum piece. She never married; and that was the
end of the Couperin dynasty. At least it would have been the end
had not the Couperins of the *grand siècle* and the age of the Roi
Soleil left an imperishable monument to their name in their
music.

We have little direct evidence as to the kind of man the great
François was. No correspondence survives – a regrettable fact
since we know that Couperin had a long correspondence about
musical matters with Bach; the letters not unnaturally disappeared after being used as lids for jam-pots.* We know that
Bach copied out several of Couperin's scores for himself and
Anna Magdalena, and admired him above all French composers
for 'l'élégance et la mélancolie voluptueuse de certains motifs, la
précision et la noblesse dans le rythme, enfin une sobriété qui
n'est pas toujours forcée, mais témoigne parfois d'une louable
discrétion' (Pirro). From his prefaces and other writings one
gathers that Couperin was, as one might expect, habitually
courteous and urbane though capable of an acidulated irony.
Clearly he suffered fools, but did not suffer them gladly. The
beautiful portrait by André Bouys gives to Couperin a characteristically compact and neat appearance; it does not surprise us
that this man wrote the music he did, or that he should have
taken such scrupulous pains over the engraving of his works and
have left such detailed instructions for their correct performance.
In particular, Couperin's hands seem appropriate to the delicately lucid appearance of his printed scores. But of course there
is more to the portrait than this; the essence lies not in the
precision which belies any hint of ostentation in the Louis XIV
perruque, but in the large, rather melancholy eyes, at once
intelligent and sensitive. It is here that we see the real Couperin,
who is not so much a representative of his age as its moral and
spiritual epitome.

We know very little about the facts of Couperin's life. There
are speculations in plenty which can all be read in the largely

---

* This story was related to Charles Bouvet by Mme Arlette Taskin, who
claimed that it was handed down in her family from an ancestor who was a
relative of Couperin.

hypothetical biography of Bouvet. But the essential facts I have given, and they are not many. When one has said that, one has only to look at Couperin's portrait to realize that the chain of facts, the sequence of events, is not very important. We may have little evidence as to what, on any specific occasion, was going on in Couperin's mind, what he said or thought on this occasion or the other, what other people said to him. But if we have little particular information, we have a great deal of *general* evidence. As M. Tiersot has pointed out, in the *concerts* and clavecin *ordres* we have Couperin's memoirs, a microcosm of the world in which he lived. There are movements, such as *L'Auguste* or *La Majestueuse*, which reflect the gallant bearing of the King himself, and an easy familiarity with the great ones of Society. There is the gracious gallery of portraits of noble ladies, proud, tender, languid or coquettish. There are pieces, such as *Les Plaisirs de St. Germain-en-Laye*, which tell of the exquisite pleasures of the *fête champêtre*. Other movements reflect the sights of the Parisian streets which Couperin observed from his window in the rue Neuve des Bons Enfants – the martial glitter of soldiers (*La Marche des Gris-vêtus*), the comic antics of acrobats and strolling players (*Les Fastes de la Grande et Ancienne Ménestrandise*). Other movements again tell of his love, as urbanely civilized as that of La Fontaine, for the country, with memories of days spent in his youth in the pastoral gentleness of Crouilly (the piece with that name, *Les Moissonneurs*, *La Muséte de Choisi*). And yet all these reflections of a world which to Couperin was immediate and actual, are universalized in the pure musicality of his technique. A world of life has become a world of art.

For it is not the surface of the pictures that matters; it is the moral and spiritual values which the pictures represent. Though we know little about the facts of Couperin's life, we know much about the ways people living in his society felt and thought; similarly we know a good deal about the ways *he* felt and thought if we can listen intelligently to his music. Knowledge of the values and standards of his time will help us to listen intelligently; conversely, listening to his music is one of the ways, together with reading Corneille, Racine and Molière and looking at the pictures of Poussin and Claude, whereby we learn what the values of his time were. In any case we do not listen to Couperin's music merely to re-create the past; we re-create this aspect of the past because we believe that it is of significance for

13

us. Apart from Racine and Molière, no artist presents the values of his time, purified of all merely topical pomposity, with as much precision as Couperin. If we can listen to his music adequately we shall experience one of the most profound conceptions of civilization which music has to offer. It can hardly be disputed that, the conditions of the contemporary world being what they are, anything which helps us to understand what the term Civilization might mean is worth investigation.

It may be that Couperin's civilization seems hopelessly remote from the problems with which we are preoccupied. If so, that is not anything for us to be proud about. He still stands as a criterion; he serves as a reminder of things we are rapidly forgetting. That we shall be any the wiser for the loss of them, few would have the temerity to claim. For myself, I do not even believe that we shall be any the 'freer' or the happier.

Couperin's culture was a minority culture, and it was doomed from the start; many things about it were foolish, and some were wicked. This does not alter the fact that it entailed values and standards which no serious conception of civilization can afford to ignore. In the first part of this book we shall discuss in general terms what these values and standards were. In the second part we shall discuss their manifestation in the technique of Couperin's music.

Chapter Two

Values and Standards in the Grand Siècle

Chaque heure en soi, comme à notre égard, est unique: est-elle écoulée une fois elle a péri entièrement, les millions de siècles ne la rameneront pas: les jours, les mois, les années, s'enfoncent et se perdent sans retour dans l'abîme des temps; le temps même sera détruit; ce n'est qu'un point dans les espaces immenses de l'éternité, et il sera effacé. Il y a de légères et frivoles circonstances du temps, qui ne sont point stables, qui passent et qui j'appelle des modes: la grandeur, la faveur, les richesses, la puissance, l'autorité, l'indépendance, le plaisir, les joies, la superfluité. Que deviendront ces modes, quand le temps même aura disparu? La vertu seule, si peu à la mode, va au delà des temps.

Les extremités sont vicieuses, et partent de l'homme; toute compensation est juste, et vient de Dieu.

LA BRUYÈRE

There would nowadays, one imagines, be few dissentient voices to the suggestion that the France of Louis XIV is one of the supreme glories of European civilization. Yet if this opinion is now a commonplace, it was not such at the end of the last century. To artists and critics of the nineteenth century, Versailles was anathema. The romantics loved solitude, bosky nooks, and nature picturesque because confused: the people of Versailles liked company, were apt to be afraid of solitude, and regarded the *confusion* of nature as an unmitigated evil. They would do what they could to mitigate it; they would chop down trees, open up vistas, clip lawns, marshal avenues, arrange their gardens and houses with geometrical precision. Since the King was the Sun, they must see that their world rotated around him. In a very literal manner, they planned the axis of the park and gardens of Versailles so that it should run from the Avenue de Paris in the east, through the centre of the Palace, through the 15 middle of the King's bedchamber, out at the Parterre d'Eau to Latona, and from there through the Tapis Vert to the Fountain of Apollo. They knew that nature had dark corners, and they knew that there were dark corners in the mind. But they believed, with all the conviction of which they were capable (and they were nothing if not self-assured), that the dark corners, where possible, should be illuminated; and where that was not possible, should be left alone.

The romantics loved shadowy corners and regarded order as suspect. It is therefore not surprising that they saw, in the attempt of the *grand siècle* to order and illuminate, nothing but the superficies. The elaborate code of values which Versailles evolved to regulate human behaviour was to them always silly and inhumanly obstructive; to them the whole of life at Versailles seemed to *périr en symétrie*, to use the phrase which Mme de Maintenon permitted herself, thinking petulantly of the draughts which whistled through the carefully balanced windows. The finical code of manners which involved such unjustifiable emotion, such petty jealousy and such obsequious flattery (for instance the business of the King's *lever*) was to them merely absurd. The geometrical plan of the gardens was to them not the consummation, but the denial, of art. The ceremonial stylization of the literature, painting, sculpture, architecture and music was to them a confession of bankruptcy, as frigid and 'artificial' as the menageries, the grottoes, the fountains, the temples *à l'antique*, the hydraulic organs that imitated the carollings of birds.

It is only with the passing of the 'romantic' attitude to life that we have been able once again to see what is there, in the art of the *grand siècle*. And the renewed response to the art has brought with it a revaluation of the society that produced it; for we are not naïve enough to suppose that this remarkable crop of artists in almost every medium – Corneille, Racine, Molière, La Fontaine, Le Nôtre, Poussin, Claude, Watteau, Lully, La Lande, Marais, de Grigny, Couperin, to mention merely the more obvious names – occurred together by accident. If we admit the greatness of the art, we must look with a modified eye on things that in social intercourse might otherwise appear pernickety, affected, foolish. We come to see that when the men of the *grand siècle* referred to an entertainment as 'galant et magnifique' they meant something that had a whole philosophy – a view of the

COSTUME D'APOLLON.

II. God, Sun and King: 'Costume d'Apollon', an engraving by
Delpeck, 1720. Louis XIV himself often danced Apollo in *ballets
de cour*, moving – as he played billiards – like a Master of the
World; which he was.

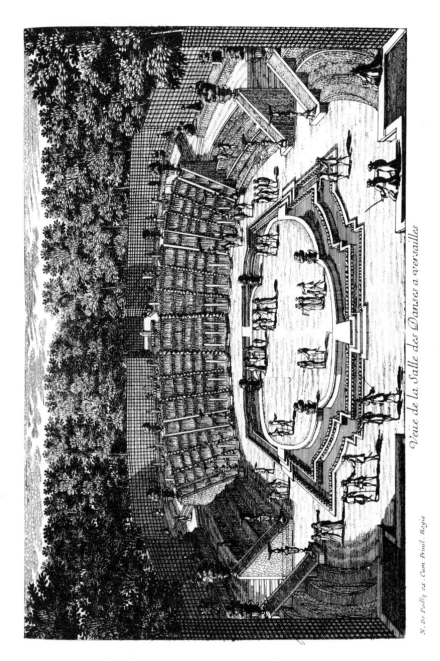

N. De Poilly ex. Cum Privil. Regis.

Veüe de la Salle des Danses a versailles

III. Versailles: the Green Room, with gardens and water theatre designed by Le Nôtre. The Green Room was so called because it was green, and because music and theatre were performed in it.

nature and destiny of man – behind it. We see that the unity with which artists in different media worked together is a factor of profound social significance; we see, from many a passage of Saint-Simon for instance, that even the insistence on deportment may not be a trivial thing:

> Jamais homme si naturellement poli, [he is speaking of Louis] ni d'une politesse si fort mesurée, si fort par degrés, ni qui distinguât mieux l'âge, le mérite, le rang, et dans ses réponses, quand elles passoient le *je verrai*, et dans ses manières. Ces étages divers se marquoient exactement dans sa manière de saluer et de recevoir les réverences, lorsqu'on partoit ou qu'on arrivoit. Il était admirable à recevoir différemment les saluts à la tête des lignes à l'armée ou aux revues. Mais surtout pour les femmes rien n'étoit pareil. Jamais il n'a passé devant la moindre coiffe sans soulever son chapeau, je dis aux femmes de chambre, et qu'il conoissoit pour telles, comme cela arrivoit souvent à Marly. Aux dames, il ôtoit son chapeau tout à fait, mais de plus ou moins loin; aux gens titrés, à demi, et le tenait en l'air ou à son oreille quelques instants plus ou moins marqués. Aux seigneurs, mais qui l'étoient, il se contentoit de mettre la main au chapeau . . .

One can well believe, with Mlle de Scudéry, that Louis played billiards with the air of a master of the world.

In English Augustan civilization too we can observe how standards of correctness may be inseparable from standards of value. Though the romantics did not like Pope any more than they liked Corneille and Racine, it is clear that when Pope and his contemporaries talked about Reason, Truth and Nature they were speaking of socially tested values which their readers would immediately recognize as such. And it is an inestimable advantage for an artist if he can accept the sanctioned values of his time without being ashamed of them; for although, if he is a good artist, he will lend an additional depth and subtlety to the conventional valuations, he can always be sure that what he says will be the richer for having the endorsement, not merely of his own convictions, but of a civilization. Moreover, he will have the advantage that the terms he uses will mostly be comprehensible to his audience.

If the Augustan civilization of Pope and Johnson was a fine one it had, however, obvious limitations; significantly it 19 produced no vital tragic poetry and no great music.★ Though Reason, Truth, and Nature were values that meant much to Augustan society, to the society of Versailles, or at least to the more sensitive spirits in it, *raison, honneur, honnêteté, le galant, la gloire* meant rather more. They were perhaps a series of counters; but the counters mattered because they were imbued with moral significance. Naturally, the balance was precarious; the code was always in danger of becoming divorced from its moral implications. But this society was great because at its best the code was an incarnation of life, not a substitute for it; because it was related to the complex of human passions, desires and fears; because it referred not only to the formal integration of society but also to the integration of the individual as a part of that society. The simultaneous preoccupation of the *grand siècle* both with *Caractères* (human nature) and with *Maximes* (behaviour and morality) is not an accident.

It is hardly too much to say that seldom if ever in a civilized, as opposed to a primitive, society has 'living' been so highly developed an art, and art and life more closely connected. And almost all the significant art of the period, in social intercourse as well as in poetry, theatre, music and painting, depended on the moral tension involved in, on the one hand, feeling deeply, and on the other hand preserving that self-control which, through reference to an accepted standard, makes civilization possible. Nothing could be more beside the mark than to accuse the people of the *grand siècle* of a deficiency of passion; the evidence of passion is there not only in Racine and Couperin but everywhere throughout the copious memoirs of the period. When they proclaimed as their ideal the *honnête homme* they did not mean that they advocated that last refuge of the spiritually craven, indifference; they did mean that the individual ought to realize that his own passions are not the be-all and end-all of existence. Probably, in the long run, it was best for his own spiritual health, as well as society's, if he admitted that he had obligations to the people among whom he lived. So the creed of *bienséance,* in the heyday of the Hôtel de Rambouillet, maintained that the *honnête homme* should have *un cœur juste* and *un esprit bien fait.* He should be considerate of other people's *amour-propre*, solicitous for their pleasure, alert to spare them pain or

★ For note, see page 39.

distress, prompt with his sympathy if pain cannot be avoided; and he should never impose his personality on others. To these people , *Raison* was both a personal and a social virtue; both an intellectual ideal and an emotional attitude of poise and moderation. They were far too intelligent to imagine that *la raison* could necessarily be equated with *la verité*; they knew that falsehood and wickedness and egoism would exist as long as man remained fallible and a sinner. But they believed that these evils were more manageable if one acted reasonably; and that one's chance of acting reasonably was better if one acted in accordance with the tested wisdom of civilization than if one trusted implicitly to one's own whims and fancies. This is why *le moi est haïssible*.

This moral tension between passionate feeling and personal self-control, with its attendant social implications, functions at widely different levels. At a fairly frivolous level we may cite Mme de Sévigné's description of how one behaves at the end of a love affair. The Chevalier de Lorraine visits a one-time mistress of his, La Fiennes, who promptly plays the forsaken nymph for him. Is there anything extraordinary in what has happened? he asks. Please let us behave like ordinary people, in a grown-up fashion. And as a final comment he adds, That's a pretty little dog you've got there. Where did you get it? Mme de Sévigné adds that that was the end of that *grand amour*. The story of course is funny; but there is no need to depreciate the girl's feeling, or the sincerity of the Chevalier's desire to put her at her ease. And the remark about the little dog is an achievement of civilization.

Similarly Bussy-Rabutin's comments to Mme de Sévigné on the war of the Fronde are not only brilliantly witty; they place the war in the perspective of civilization. It is odd to think, he says, that we were on different sides in this war last year, and are so still, even though we have both changed over. But your side seems to be the better one, because you manage to stay in Paris. I've come from St Denis to Montrond, and it looks as though I'll end by going from Montrond to the devil. Keep gay and lively, he says, and never take things too solemnly; then you will live at least another thirty years (they were both quite advanced in years when he wrote this), and I can talk to you and write to you and love you. After that, I shall be happy to wait for you in Paradise. He says he is never serious; yet beneath the poised 21 urbanity with which he says it, we feel the affection which, despite many violent upheavals, must have existed between these two. The passion is there, though it is not expatiated on. It is interesting to note that the only passion which Mme de Sévigné seems to have been unable to cope with was her love, almost pathological in its intensity, for her daughter.

A more subtle case is the celebrated affair of Vatel, on the occasion of the King's visit to the Duke of Condé at Chantilly in 1671. This is worth quoting in full:

> Le roi arriva hier au soir à Chantilly; il courut un cerf au clair de la lune; les lanternes firent des merveilles, le feu d'artifice fut un peu effacé par la clarté de notre amie; mais enfin, le soir, le souper, le jeu, tout alla à merveille. Le temps qu'il a fait aujourd'hui nous faisait espérer une suite digne d'un si agréable commencement. Mais voicy ce que j'apprends en entrant ici, dont je ne puis me remettre, et qui fait que je ne suis plus ce que je vous mande; c'est qu'enfin Vatel, maître d'hôtel de M. Fouquet, qui l'était présentement de M. le Prince, cet homme d'une capacité distinguée de toutes les autres, dont la bonne tête était capable de contenir tout le soin d'un Etat; cet homme donc que je connaissais, voyant que ce matin à huit heures la marée n'était pas arrivée, n'a pu soutenir l'affront dont il a cru qu'il allait être accablé, et en un mot, il s'est poignardé. Vous pouvez penser l'horrible désordre qu'un si terrible accident a causé dans cette fête. Songez que la marée est peut-être arrivée comme il expirait. Je n'en sais pas davantage présentement; je pense que vous trouvez que c'est assez. Je ne doute pas que la confusion n'ait été grande; c'est une chose fâcheuse à une fête de cinquante mille écus . . .
>
> M. le Prince le dit au roi fort tristement: on dit que c'etait à force d'avoir de l'honneur à sa manière; on le loua fort, on loua et l'on blama son courage. Le roi dit qu'il y avait cinq ans qu'il retardait de venir à Chantilly, parce qu'il comprenait l'excès de cet embarras. Il dit à M. le Prince qu'il ne devait avoir que deux tables, et ne point se charger de tout; il jura qu'il ne souffrirait plus que M. le Prince en usât ainsi; mais c'était trop tard pour le pauvre Vatel. Cependant Gourville tâcha de reparer la perte de Vatel; elle fut reparée; on dîna très bien, on fit collation, on soupa, on se promena, on joua, on fut à la chasse; tout était parfumé de jonquilles, tout était enchanté.

This is no doubt a most amusing story; but one may observe that it involves a very complex tissue of emotions. There is of course the contrast between the tragedy of Vatel's suicide and the bathetic circumstances that occasioned it. But the real reasons for his suicide were not trivial at all; they indicate in a remarkable manner how the moral values of the society of Versailles permeated all its manifestations, from highest to lowest. On top of this there is Mme de Sévigné's attitude to be taken account of. Her appreciation of the element of the ridiculous in the situation (it was a shocking thing to happen at a fête that cost 50,000 crowns), even a suggestion of callousness in the way she seems to regard such tragedies as inevitable if unfortunate incidents in the running of an ordered society; these should not lead us to underestimate her sensibility to the issues involved. In this case, after all, the tragedy was only the result of a misunderstanding; for the fish may have arrived, just too late. It was the consequence, society decided, of too nice a sense of honour, which is a good thing. Vatel's action, some thought, showed courage; which is also a virtue. Others thought his response a little in excess of the object; and excess is bad. Even a person as exalted as the King showed delicacy in realizing that his visit was bound to cause trouble one way or another; and the pressure of feeling which poor Vatel must have laboured under can only be imagined. There is plenty of emotion all round; but the admirable maître d'hôtel is dead, and tears will not bring him back to life. Meanwhile civilization must go on; so the scent of the jonquils is everywhere, and in short all is delightful.

Some considerable space has been devoted to this apparently unimportant incident because it has so representative a value. Something comparable with its peculiar balance of feeling is observable in the most profound manifestation of the culture of the time. The writings of Saint-Simon are a case in point. He was a man whose creed was guided by *la raison* and *la loi*. However aware he may have become of the imperfections of the *ancien régime*, of its failure to live up to its standards, he none the less believed in those standards profoundly. His preoccupation with details of court etiquette may even prove exasperating to modern readers (for instance his tedious account of *l'affaire de la quête*); and yet his concern for the letter of the law and the urbanity of his mode of expression do not disguise, but serve rather to reinforce, the intensity of his loves and hates. His prose has a colloquial flexibility and sinuosity within its sophistication. The orderly precision of the words, the psychological acumen, acquire an almost reptilian venom; for all the *galanterie* and the *politesse* the words come out like pistol shots:

23

De ce long et curieux détail il resulte que Monseigneur était sans vice ni vertu, sans lumières ni connoissances quelconques, radicalement incapable d'en acquerir, très paresseux, sans imagination ni production, sans goût, sans choix, sans discernement, né pour l'ennui, qu'il communiquoit aux autres, et pour être une boule roulant au hasard par l'impulsion d'autrui, opiniâtre et petit en tout à l'excès . . . livré aux plus pernicieuses mains, incapable d'en sortir ni de s'en apercevoir, absorbé dans sa graisse et dans ses ténèbres, . . . sans avoir aucune volonté de mal faire, il eût été un roi pernicieux.

No one can say that this lacks feeling, or that the feeling is not intensified by the razor-sharp edge of Saint-Simon's mind; just as his criticism is the more valid because we know that when he speaks of *vertu, goût, choix, discernement* and so on, he is not merely using words.

The incident of Vatel is a part of contemporary life; the memoirs of Saint-Simon are perhaps half-way between life and art. With the poets we are a stage further towards the objectifying of the values of life in art, and all the significant poets show the same union of deep and delicate emotion with formal discipline. La Fontaine, for instance, has many qualities in common with Saint-Simon – the sharp intelligence, the slightly acidulated wit, the diction that is close to polite conversation, but still more tautly disciplined; and he has many qualities in common with Mme de Sévigné – the urbanity and poise, together with great nervous sensitivity. He has a sensibility to nature and a sympathy with animals such as are usually supposed to be foreign to his age; but these qualities are always subservient to his prime interest in human behaviour. The more one reads La Fontaine, the more he reveals himself as a great traditional *moral* poet. He is witty and charming, of course; but in all his most representative work (we may mention *Le Chêne et le Roseau*) his sensitivity combines with the lucidity of his mind to create a noble emotional power and grandeur. In *La Mort et le Mourant* the passion rises to the heights of tragic art.

But it is in the dramatic poets that the relation between poetic technique and moral values is most clearly indicated. In all of them the formal alexandrine, like Pope's heroic couplet, is an achieved order in poetic technique which corresponds to an achieved order in civilization. The stylized vocabulary is also, as we have seen, indicative of moral values, sanctioned by society;

and in each case, to varying degrees, the poet is concerned with the tension between this criterion and personal sensibility – with some kind of conflict between passion and social obligations.

The 'tension' is least marked in the earliest of the writers, Corneille; or at least in his work there is the minimum of ambiguity as to what ought to be the issue of the conflict. His early plays were written in the reign of Louis XIII, and represent a consolidation of values, an attempt to arrive at, to win to, a conception of order and stability:

> Je suis maître de moi, comme de l'univers.
> Je le suis, je veux l'être.

The famous lines splendidly express the connection between personal and social integration, the proud assurance with which it is held, and also the effort of will-power involved ('je veux l'être') in achieving it. But if Corneille was aware of the effort, he had no doubt as to what ought to be its outcome:

> Sur mes passions ma raison souveraine
> Eût blâmé mes soupirs et dissipé ma haine.

He never for a moment doubted that reason ought to dominate passion, and could do so. In a dedicatory epistle to *La Place Royale* he says:

> C'est de vous que j'ai appris que l'amour d'un honnête homme doit être toujours volontaire; que l'on ne doit jamais aimer en un tel point qu'en ne puisse jamais n'aimer pas; que si on en vient jusque-là, c'est une tyrannie dont il faut secouer le joug.

He is quite unequivocal; and his superb conviction echoes through the clang of his alexandrines, through the lucidity with which each word 'stays put', without emotional overtones. He did not advocate a passive acceptance of the code; but he was convinced that the code represented the wisdom of civilization, and that it must withstand all threats from within and without. It was greater than the individual; but it was for individual men to keep it alive as the safeguard of their sanity and happiness, and not to seek to destroy it. Though this was an attitude which could easily droop into complacency, within its limits its nobility, its heroic quality, was authentic.

The above is the conventional account of Corneille; it has not gone unchallenged. One interesting account of his work has suggested that his world, far from being unambiguous, is assailed by fundamental uncertainties and doubts; that his characters, particularly in the later plays, are wilfully living on error. The human will is prized for its power to impose order on chaos, independently of ethical considerations; there might almost seem to be, in Corneille's obsession with the power and the glory of absolutism, an element of psychological compensation for the timidity of his nature and the relative lowliness of his origin. If this account is accepted it gives a slightly different stress to, but does not radically alter, our case. For it would then appear that Corneille regarded order as so important that he was prepared to uphold it even if it entailed in some respects the substitution of error for truth. Such a view of the world must no doubt be considered a confession of failure, in so far as it sacrificed the *grand siècle*'s ideal of a harmonious balance between collective and individual morality. It is, however, a failure that has an element of proud and impressive greatness.

Both Molière and Racine come at the zenith of the reign of the Roi Soleil. They accept the values that Corneille lived by and helped to create, and also the alexandrine and the stylized vocabulary that help to express them; but the tension between these values and the demands of personal sensibility is now more complex. This is demonstrated in the *use which they make* of the alexandrine. Their language has not the ceremonial precision of Corneille's, the rhythms are more flexible, the imagery 'suggests' more; just as, in the paintings of Poussin and Claude, the precise architecture of the proportions, the grouping of tones, the sculpturesque treatment of the figures with their stylized heroic gestures, are enriched by the sensuously evocative quality of the colour. In Molière's case this increased flexibility goes alongside the fact that he wrote comedy rather than heroic tragedy; the language, though still urbane, is less consciously stylized, more close to *galant* conversation. We may observe in this connection that the conversation of so ordered a society slides into art almost without one noticing at what point the metamorphosis happens.

This great plasticity of rhythm and metaphor parallels a deeper psychological interest in the workings of the mind – of the personal consciousness. In Corneille the insistence is primarily on the moral *order*; in Molière the stress is on the complexity of the relations between the moral order and the personal sensibility. This tendency reaches its climax in Molière's greatest play, *Le Misanthrope*, in which the balance betweeen the two groups of interests is maintained with consummate subtlety. To a degree, we are clearly meant to sympathize with Alceste in his attack on the idiocy and potential wickedness of *empty* social conventions; in so far as Célimène represents them they are obviously unsatisfactory. But on the other hand we are clearly meant to feel that the intensity with which Alceste denounces is not altogether admirable; that it springs from a lack of 'integration' in his own personality, and is in a sense adolescent. The poise is held by Philinte, the *honnête homme*, who continually brings Alceste's transports to the bar of *raison*:

> *La parfaite raison fuit toute extrémité,*
> *Et veut que l'on soit sage avec sobriété.*

When Alceste breaks out desperately:

> *Et parfois il me prend des mouvements soudains*
> *De fuir dans un désert l'approche des humains,*

Philinte replies:

> *Mon Dieu, des mœurs du temps mettons-nous moins en peine,*
> *Et faisons un peu grace à la nature humaine.*

All the satire of the frivolous time-serving courtiers, the play seems to say, is justified, and the imperfections of society are manifold. But society *is* human life, and it is for human beings to make it work; running away into deserts is no answer at all. In no play of Molière, however, is the difficulty of the issues more subtly indicated. Mr Turnell has even suggested that Molière himself was beginning to grow doubtful about his positives; for nobody in the play seems to find Philinte's reasonable advice either helpful or convincing. This is a point to which we shall return later.

Molière was less roughly handled than Corneille by nineteenth-century critics because he wrote comedy rather than tragedy, and therefore had more excuse for not being sufficiently 'poetic'. Racine is a heroic writer, like Corneille; but his verse, which is tragic in a sense which the earlier poet did not attain to, has emotional overtones in plenty. Perhaps the nineteenth-century critics vaguely realized this when they invented the legend of the 'tender' Racine; though in some ways this may have been an even more damaging misrepresentation. Couperin, as we shall see, has suffered from something similar.

In Racine, as in Molière, the stress is centred on the threat to organized society occasioned by the unruly impulses of the individual. But whereas Molière emphasizes the folly involved in submission to the passions, so that his work is both serious and funny, Racine emphasizes the evil. The intensity of passion in his characters, especially Phèdre, sometimes breaks down the conventional norm; but it is only because of the existence of the norm that the effect of the passion is overwhelming. The sudden glimpses of an unsuspected world in the dark reaches of the mind which the imagery and movement reveal to us, are the more terrible because they appear against the background of 'les bornes de l'austère pudeur'; we have learned afresh in the last forty years that in a world of violence, violence may cease to shock. Racine's psychological penetration and his poetry are one and the same. They suggest that he is a greater poet than Corneille not because he believed less in Corneille's positives, but because he relates these positives to so very much wider a range of experience.

Phèdre is an analysis of evil – or of the effects of evil – more comprehensive and profound than anything attempted by Corneille, who was not much interested in evil as a problem of the individual. But Racine's greater subtlety is revealed still more remarkably in his last play *Athalie*, which deals not only with the consequences of sin in relation to man and society, but for the first time with the relation between man and God. That this play can so identify *la loi* with spiritual sanctions is a testimony to the greatness of his civilization; it is paralleled only in the greatest work of Couperin and La Lande. But while this spiritual interpretation of *la loi* was a possible one, it was not habitual. It was also possible for *la loi* to become synonymous with brute force; it was possible for it to destroy the very things it had been intended to preserve.

La Bruyère cynically remarked that a *dévôt* is a man who under an atheist king would be an atheist; and Mazarin advised his nieces to hear Mass for the world's sake, if not for God's. Yet although there was, particularly in the latter part of the reign after Louis's conversion, a good deal of purely fashionable religion, one would not say that the average religion of the time was insincere. If there was an increasing tendency for convents to become homes for the unmarriageable but unvicious, and if there was a large number of priests, like Cardinal de Retz, who were really politicians, there were also good priests like the Jesuit Bourdaloue, who with genuine piety stressed the potential ethical significance of the values of the time. In the sermons of Bourdaloue and Bossuet and in the writings of Fénelon, there is a mixture of qualities – of imaginative passion, psychological penetration and abstract logical argument – very similar to that in the higher manifestations of the poetry and drama. But perhaps one could say that it was the mastery of logical argument, among these qualities, which excited such remarkable enthusiasm in congregations during the great days of the classical epoch, and in this connection we may note this significant comment of Mme de Sévigné: 'Le maréchal de Gramont était l'autre jour si transporté de la beauté d'un sermon de Bourdaloue, qu'il s'écria tout haut, en un endroit qui le toucha, *Mordi, il a raison!*'

The religion of the age, that is, did not normally signify much in purely spiritual terms. It is certainly legitimate to suggest that Racine's *Athalie* entailed a conception of spiritual, even of mystical values which, although not unique, was exceptional. It is probable that Racine saw some analogy between the persecution of the Israelites and that of the Jansenists in his own day. And although there is no *necessary* connection between the spirituality of *Athalie* and Racine's conversion to Jansenism, none the less *Athalie* does help us to appreciate the significance of the Jansenist movement in the world of the Roi Soleil. Corneille's heroic plays suggest that through reason and the human will order may be attained and preserved; Racine's tragic plays suggest that reason and the human will are helpless without the intervention of God's grace. Whereas the Cornelian hero believes that he is 'maître de moi comme de l'univers', Racine's heroine says 'je crains de me connoître en l'état où je suis'. Implicitly, Racine makes the same point about the corruption of the world in which he lived as Mme de Maintenon makes when she says:

Otez ces filles qui ne respirent que le monde. . . . Otez ces beaux esprits qui dédaignent tout ce qui est simple, qui s'ennuient de cette vie uniforme, de ces plaisirs doux et innocents et qui désirent de *faire leur volonté*. (My italics.)

Implicitly, Racine offers a criticism of the Cartesian view of the destiny of man to which Corneille in the main adheres.

Descartes's mechanical view of nature, his belief in the sovereignty of reason as the only means of obtaining knowledge of material things, presented the *grand siècle* with a philosophical formulation of the values it lived by. 'The whole is greater than the parts' is a creed reflected no less in social behaviour than in the administration of Colbert, the gardens of Le Nôtre, the theatre music of Lully, the buildings of Mansart, the decorations of Lebrun; and the aesthetic theories of Boileau are an exact counterpart of Cartesian philosophy, for both attempt to interpret nature through reason, deprecate enthusiasm, start empirically from the present moment, and are completely non-historical. (To Molière, Gothic cathedrals were odious monstrosities of the ignorant centuries.) Moreover, like most of the people of his time, Descartes reconciled his instinct for rationality and order with a profound interest in the workings of the human mind, expressed in the *Traité des Passions de l'âme*. Here he demonstrates that the passions are good in themselves; that evil consists in the wrong or immoderate use of them; and that only through reason can one decide which use is justified, which is not. Descartes, like Lully and Corneille, remained formally a Catholic, and his theories of the absolute and infinite Thought which our individual thoughts presuppose were much exploited by Catholic theologians as a 'rational' proof of God's existence. Even the Jansenists found in the pre-determinist aspects of his thought something which seemed superficially to support their beliefs. But in the most important respects Descartes's thought was fundamentally non-religious. Bossuet, the exponent of Catholic orthodoxy, perceived that the insistence on the pre-eminence of reason inevitably led to free thought; Pascal, more profoundly, realized that Descartes's teaching was inimical to the concept of Grace.

In some respects a man of the new world, a brilliant mathematician imbued with the spirit of scientific curiosity, and at first himself a Cartesian, Pascal was at the same time of a fervently religious temperament rather alien to the outlook of his age. It was his intellectual equipment that disposed of the Cartesian proof of God's existence; it was his religious temperament that, when once he had exposed the fallacies which in his opinion made Cartesianism not a bulwark of Christianity but its potential destroyer, led him to develop his notion of the dual reasons of heart and mind. The heart has its reasons, of which *raison* knows nothing. Descartes, he said, would much have preferred to have dispensed with God in the whole of his intellectual system, but had to bring Him in to set his mechanistic universe in motion; that done, Descartes had no further use for Him. But to Pascal, whose natural proclivities were encouraged by the Jansenist preoccupation with St Augustine and by his long brooding over the stoicism of Montaigne, the opposition between good and evil cannot be explained in purely rational terms; and the proof of the existence of God lies in the misery of man without Him.

Such an attitude goes to enforce a peculiar gloom. The proofs of Original Sin and of the Fall are all around one in cynicism, scepticism and folly; only through the crucified Christ can sin be redeemed. Crucifixion, in one form or another, is the only hope of life to come, and by inference the only tolerable form of life here and now. Beneath the suave lucidity which characterizes not only the prose of the *Lettres Provinciales* but even the casual epigrammatic jottings of the *Pensées*, the mystic's ecstasy of self-immolation burns with unquenchable passion. We can see something similar in the tautness of line which gives such tension to the apparently tranquil paintings of Pascal's and Arnauld's friend, Philippe de Champagne.

Naturally, the group of Solitaries who met and meditated at the Cistercian nunnery of Port-Royal did not normally carry their religious fervour as far as Pascal's Augustinian abnegation; but their outlook did have a two-fold relation to the life of the time. In a positive sense it was a recognition that there were aspects of experience which the values of the contemporary world were apt to neglect. From this point of view it is not, of course, to be considered in narrowly sectarian terms. Jansenism did not necessarily involve religious partisanship. The Jesuit Bourdaloue and people such as Mme de Maintenon and Mme de Sévigné who were the intimates of Jesuit circles were impregnated with Jansenism; just as the cleric Fénelon, who took the 31 side of the Jesuits in the controversy over efficacious grace, could support the case of the later quietist sect in the affair of Mme Guyon.

And then in a negative sense, it was a reaction from the world of Versailles, with its absolute identification of Church and State; it was not so much a search for new values as an admission that the vitality of society depended on a balance between organization and human impulses which seemed in danger of growing lop-sided. So elaborately organized a world, calling for so much unity and conformity, could exist only under a despotism. Racine had dreamed that that despotism might be the rule of the Holy Spirit; Saint-Simon, looking back, saw clearly that it had become the despotism not of God, but of an arrogant man, self-deified, so afraid of *la vérité* that he had to surround himself with an army of sycophants who would tell him what he wanted to believe, and nothing else. In Racine's attitude there was still something of mediaevalism; the course of history represented the triumph and the tragedy of the Cornelian ideal of 'maître de moi'. The identification of King and God is revealed in a famous passage from La Bruyère:

> Qui considérera que le visage du prince fait toute la félicité du courtisan, qu'il s'occupe et se remplit pendant toute sa vie de le voir et d'en être vu, comprendra un peu comment voir Dieu peut faire toute la gloire et tout le bonheur des Saints;

while in a sermon on the occasion of the Dauphin's birth, Senault compared Louis with God the Father and the Dauphin with Christ. Louis himself said, 'Celui qui a donné des rois aux hommes a voulu qu'on les respectât comme ses lieutenants'. We must remember however that the King's absolutism obtained an enormous popular support; and this was partly due to the fact that the peasants and bourgeoisie felt that the only alternative was the anarchy of the nobility and the horrors of the Fronde.

It is easy to exaggerate the degree to which the court culture was removed from everyday life; we shall later note plenty of evidence that it preserved some contact with popular elements. Most of the great artists of the time were not professional courtiers, and many of them never even visited Versailles. Yet there is some truth in the conventional account that the artificial removal of the court from the centre of French life in Paris has a quasi-symbolical significance. In a sense, it was only because the court was self-enclosed and homogeneous that it could evolve such lucid moral values, and achieve such subtlety and depth within them. But it is interesting that a person of such exquisite nervous adjustment as Mme de Sévigné can write with callous indifference of the sufferings of people outside her circle; that she can cheerfully describe the breaking on the wheel of an itinerant musician involved in a provincial rebellion, casually remark that the hanging of sixty scapegoats is to begin tomorrow, and conclude with the pious reflection that this will no doubt serve as a lesson to any others who might be thinking of throwing stones into their betters' gardens. Significantly, it is only after the midsummer of the culture that a humane sympathy with other spheres of life begins – in the painting of Chardin for instance – to manifest itself. As we shall see, there is perhaps an anticipation of this in some of Couperin's later harpsichord pieces.

Towards the latter end of the reign the appreciation of the dangers latent in it autocracy assumed, in many of the most acute minds of the time, the proportions of a social conscience. Saint-Simon criticized the absolutism of the King, the cult of *la gloire* and war, the misery it brought in its wake, and the ultimate stupidity of it:

> C'est donc avec grande raison qu'on doit déplorer avec larmes l'horreur d'une éducation uniquement dressée pour étouffer l'esprit et le cœur de ce prince, le poison abominable de la flatterie la plus insigne, qui le déifia dans la sein même du christianisme, et la cruelle politique de ces ministres, qui l'enferma, et qui pour leur grandeur, leur puissance et leur fortune l'enivrerent de son autorité, de sa grandeur, de sa gloire jusque'à le corrompre, et à étouffer en lui, sinon toute la bonté, l'équité, le desir de connôitre la verité, que Dieu lui avoit donné, au moins l'émoussèrent presque entièrement, et empêchèrent au moins sans cesse qu'il fît aucun usage de ces vertus, dont son royaume et lui-même furent les victimes.

Fénelon is no less severe:

> Quelle détestable maxime que de ne croire trouver sa sûreté que dans l'oppression de ses peuples. . . . Est-ce le vrai chemin qui mène à la gloire? Souvenez-vous que les pays où la domination du souverain est plus absolue sont eux où les souverains sont moins puissants. Ils prennent, ils ruinent tout, ils possèdent seuls tout

l'Etat; mais tout l'Etat languit. Les campagnes sont en friche et presque désertes; les villes diminuent chaque jour, le commerce tarit. Le roi, qui ne peut être roi tout seul, et qui n'est grand que par ses peuples, s'anéantit lui-même peu à peu par l'anéantissement de ses peuples dont il tire ses richesses et sa puissance. . . . Le mépris, la haine, le ressentiment, la défiance, en un mot toutes les passions se réunissent contre une autorité si odieuse.

This sombre vision is reinforced by La Fontaine's moving fable of *La Mort et Le Bûcheron*, and by La Bruyère's terrible picture of life in the country districts:

L'on voit certains animaux farouches . . . répandues par la campagne, noirs, livides, et tout brûlés de soleil, attachés à la terre, qu'ils fouillent et qu'ils remuent avec une opiniâtreté invincible. . . . Quand ils se lèvent sur leurs pieds, ils montrent une face humaine; et en effet ils sont des hommes. Ils se retirent la nuit dans des tanières où ils vivent de pain noir, d'eau, et de racines;

though we must remember that conditions in the countryside varied enormously, and that in many parts a rural folk culture was still very vigorous. We must remember too that the mere fact that Saint-Simon, Fénelon, La Bruyère and many others can write such astringent criticism is itself testimony to the intellectual honesty which their society permitted them. Their account must be qualified by the manifest achievements of Versailles, which they not only appreciate, but represent. None the less, the weakness is there; and how inseparably it is linked with the virtues is demonstrated most subtly in Mme de La Fayette's great novel, *La Princesse de Clèves*.

The world here described by Mme de La Fayette is one in which the existence of absolute values is accepted as unquestioningly as are standards of manners; the characters speak of *la vérité*, *l'honneur* and so on without any conscious ambiguity. The theme of the book is the analysis, within this scheme of values, of the passions of personal relationships, particularly sexual passion. With great subtlety we are shown how, in such a closely ordered society, personal life is inevitably mixed with public; how *amour* merges into *intrigue*, and that into *affaires*. Between private and public life a balance ought to be maintained. But what in fact seems to happen is that *amour* reveals a fatal disparity

34 between public affairs and the ideal absolute values that are

supposed to give them meaning. Order is meaningless apart from what, in human terms, is ordered; yet in practice society does not regulate *amour*, but *amour* proves that the pretensions of society are not what they seem. It destroys tranquillity of mind, and ultimately, therefore, civilization:

> L'ambition et la galanterie étoient l'âme de cette Cour (the book is ostensibly set in the court of Henri II, but this is no more than a tactful disguise for the contemporary court) et occupoient tous les hommes et les femmes. Il y avoit tant d'interêts et tant de cabales différentes, et les dames y avaient tant de part, que l'amour étoit toujours mêlé aux affaires, et les affaires à l'amour. Personne n'étoit tranquille ni indifférent; on songeoit à s'élever, à plaire, à servir, ou à nuire; on ne connoissoit ni l'ennui ni l'oisivété et on étoit toujours occupé des plaisirs ou des intrigues.

This attitude is similar to that expressed in more dolorous terms by La Bruyère:

> Il y a un pays où les joies sont visibles, mais fausses, et les chagrins cachés, mais réels. Qui croirait que l'empressement pour les spectacles, que les éclats et les applaudissements aux théâtres de Molière et d'Arlequin, les repas, la chasse, les ballets, les carrousels couvrissent tant d'inquiétudes, de soins et de divers intérêts, tant de craintes et d'espérances, des passions si vives et des affaires si sérieuses?

and broadly parallel to that expressed by Molière in *Le Misanthrope*; and while possibly Molière and certainly Racine would have said that the remedy was not to have less love but to have more wisdom in dealing with it, there is here a paradox by which many sensitive and intelligent people of the time must have been bewildered. There is no easy solution to it. The end of the book, the woman's entry into the convent, is as much an evasion of the issues as Alceste's threat to run off into the desert, since there is no evidence that the Princess has experienced any spiritual conversion. Such a religious solution almost certainly calls for some special aptitude, and a type of mind similar to that of Racine, Pascal or Couperin. The Jansenists, one imagines, must have been composed partly of people like Pascal, partly of people whose motives resembled those of the Princesse de Clèves; and there can be no doubt that in the society as a whole the Princesses de Clèves must greatly have outnumbered the Racines and the Pascals.

35

In some ways comparable with the entry of Mme de La Fayette's heroine into the convent is Louis's own belated religiosity – as opposed to the religious emotion of the Jansenists, whom the God-King persecuted as being rebellious to the State Church and to his absolute authority. The great age of the Roi Soleil was over, internal corruption was increasing, *la gloire* was not what it had been. The succession of military triumphs began to be succeeded by an equally monotonous series of defeats. Despondency echoed hollowly through the corridors of Versailles, and the King pathetically pretended, perhaps even believed – for he was not consciously insincere – that *la gloire* was not what he had lived for; that his nature, at least under the influence of Mme de Maintenon, was essentially religious; that he liked nothing so much as to be alone with God. So this King of the Sun, who abhorred limited horizons, retired to a damp, forest-enclosed house in a mean valley at Marly ('un méchant village, sans clôture, sans vue, ni moyens d'en avoir, un repaire de serpents et de charognes, de crapauds et de grenouilles', Saint-Simon called it); rather like – to descend from the sublime to the tawdry – another addict of power, Henry Ford, who in his old age became a passionate antiquarian, buying up quaint old pubs, rebuilding the old farm homestead just as it was when he was a lad, trying to put everything back, as Dos Passos put it, 'as it was in the days of horses and buggies'. It almost seems that Louis himself came to accept the irony of La Bruyère; 'Un esprit sain puise à la cour le goût de la solitude et de la retraite'. The deeper irony of the position is that Louis could not escape his self-imposed destiny. He ended by transforming his successive retreats from pomp and circumstance into the very thing he had been seeking to avoid. Marly grew into a miniature Versailles; just as Ford's rural homesteads glittered with Every Modern Convenience.

It was in the more melancholy latter end of Louis's reign that Couperin's genius matured. Of course the gradual changes cannot have been very perceptible to someone working within that self-enclosed circle; and it would be utterly erroneous to find anything valedictory in Couperin's classical, positive, and on the whole serene art. But we might be justified in saying that the conditions under which he worked influenced his outlook in two unobtrusive, connected ways. They imbued some of his music with a sensuous tenderness and wistfulness beneath its elegant bearing which, like the comparable quality in the painting of his great contemporary Watteau, spring from an apprehension of transience; from a recognition that all this graciousness and beauty must pass away, perhaps quite soon. And they encouraged him to develop the religious aspect of his genius which produced his greatest work and is as much more 'spiritual' in conception than Lully's ceremonial art, as Racine's late work is more spiritual than that of Corneille. (I shall hope in the course of this book to demonstrate, in terms of the technique of music, what I mean by these generalizations.)

Couperin's music thus gives an oddly subtle impression of being simultaneously of his world, and not of it; just as the world of Watteau's pictures is simultaneously the real world, and a golden Never-never-land of the spirit. In one sense, Couperin may still be the *galant homme*, the symbol of civilization painted competently if not very profoundly by men such as Mignard and Hyacinthe Rigaud. In another sense, he is the black-robed figure who, in some paintings of Watteau, beside the merry throng discoursing and flirting with such gracious urbanity, stands quietly in his corner, seeming to suggest not that the junketings are meaningless, the gestures empty, the urbanity a sham, but that, though the company may be delightful, one may be lonely, still. This is something much more complex and valuable than the emotion of nostalgia; it is an achieved equilibrium which, for being sensitive, is no less strong. It was because Paris, 'le théâtre des scènes tendres et galantes', seemed to be becoming a place where 'chacun y est occupé de ses chagrins et de sa misère', that many sensitive spirits sought in a mythical Ile de Cythère a civilization that was not subject to calumniating Time, where age and bitterness and the complexity of human emotions did not destroy the qualities that make civilization possible:

> *Venez dans l'île de Cythère*
> *En pélerinage avec nous,*
> *Jeune fille n'en revient guère*
> *Ou sans amant ou sans époux,*
> *Et l'on y fait sa grande affaire*
> *Des amusements les plus doux.*

This was not merely an escape. It was an attempt to achieve in art something which the real world could not give. The world   37 which Watteau and Couperin present to us is one in which the codes and the values of the time are not frustrated – as they so painfully were in real life – by people's wickedness or stupidity; in which there is no disparity between intention and realization. In this connection it seems to me no accident that in the last years of the seventeenth century appeared the work of the King and Queen of fairy-tale writers, Charles Perrault and Mme d'Aulnoy. It is important to remember that, at their very much slighter level, these tales are not unallied to the religious aspects of the art of Couperin and Racine.

The society of Louis XIV was not unique in producing some of its most consummate artistic manifestations when its end was near; one could say almost as much of Shakespeare's society. But in approaching Couperin it is not the decline we should think of; we should remember the beauty and magnificence of the achievements of this society rather than the gossip and intrigue, and the more idiotic affectations of court etiquette.* It was in the walks of the Tuileries that Racine absentmindedly declaimed his tragedies to a group of labourers on the waterworks; it was in the theatres and salons of this community that Lully and Molière talked over their latest enterprise, that La Fontaine told his immortal fables, and Perrault his no less immortal tales. Make all the qualifications you like, but how many times has there been a better environment for an artist to be born into? Perrault was justified when he said of Versailles:

> *Ce n'est pas un Palais, c'est une ville entière,*
> *Superbe en sa grandeur, superbe en sa matière,*
> *Non, c'est plutôt un Monde, où du grand Univers*
> *Se trouvent rassemblez les miracles divers.*

---

* It was a popular saying that courtiers had three things to remember: speak well of everyone, ask for everything that is going, and sit down when you get the chance.

Note to p.20

This is to discount Handel as a non-English composer, though a case might be substantiated that Handel became so intrinsic a part of Augustan England that minor composers imitated him rather than their English predecessors; and that this was not merely because his genius was irresistible but also because he had absorbed and brought to consummation our cultural values. Certainly he was himself influenced by Purcell, and his collaboration with John Gay in *Acis and Galatea* effects an English, relatively demotic, remoulding of the heroic theme which is at once witty and profound. Similarly his re-creations of Milton in *L'Allegro* and *Il Penseroso* are in tune with what cultured Englishmen of his time found in this poet; and there are deep affinities between Handel and the greatest poet among his contemporaries, Alexander Pope. The values implicit in Pope's *Essay on Man* might be described as Handelian; and there are parallels between Pope's use of the heroic couplet and Handel's disciplined symmetries. Just as there are often tragic intensities hidden beneath Pope's satiric surface, so there are often ironies latent beneath the pompous Handelian façade. Handel's 'English' manner, even in purely instrumental works like the greatest of the concerti grossi, sometimes attains a tragic–ironic grandeur that may be directly related to the Pope of the *Epistle to Boyle*. I have written of these matters in my book *Harmonious Meeting:* a study of the relationship between English poetry and music *c.* 1600–1900.

Chapter Three

Taste during the Grand Siècle

La belle Antiquité fut toujours vénerable,
Mais je ne crus jamais qu'elle fust adorable.
Je voy les Anciens, sans plier les génoux,
Ils sont grands, il est vray, mais hommes comme nous:
Et l'on peut comparer sans craindre d'être injuste,
Le Siècle de Louis au beau siècle d'Auguste.
PERRAULT: *Le Siècle de Louis le Grand.*
Parallèle des Anciens et des Modernes

In the last chapter we have tried to give some idea of the values and moral concepts of the world which Couperin inherited. In a general sense these values conditioned the ways in which he felt and thought, and therefore the nature of his music; but we can adequately assess their influence on his art only if we supplement our general remarks on the values of the time with some more particular comments on the evolution of taste and on the relation between the artist and the *grand siècle* audience. For it is not too much to say that the taste of Couperin's day was the consequence of a long maturing which had gone on more or less continuously since the beginning of the seventeenth century. Only against this background are some aspects of Couperin's art intelligible.

The classical conception of a lofty, noble, and heroic art, apposite to a heroic mode of life, was originally associated with the Renaissance attempt to establish a finer discrimination in social tone. The civilizing influence of women in the early years of the century did more than create a taste for the exquisite. The tremendous vogue for Honoré d'Urfé's interminable pastoral romance *L'Astrée* was attributable not so much to its literary merits – though it was not devoid of graciousness – as to the fact that it offered a primer of good manners; a chivalric code going back not only to French, Spanish and Italian pastoral romances of the sixteenth century, but still more to the troubadours. 41

Women, the ornaments of the world, were to be served and worshipped; and in the pages of *L'Astrée* men could learn how to serve them, the phrases to use, the gestures to indulge in, the refinements of approach and response. If at one level this seemed frivolous enough, it offered opportunities for civilized inter-course which the more intelligent and sensitive were quick to seize upon. Soon Mme de Rambouillet's Blue Room was pro-viding an environment in which men and women could meet together to discuss seriously, within a scheme of conventional courtesies, not only the etiquette of love, but all aspects of human behaviour and psychology, the values and standards of art, even grammar. The Hôtel de Rambouillet offered a series of rules for living, and a rallying point where artists could meet to discuss their work, as members of society honoured by virtue of their calling. Moreover, it provided for those artists an audience which, though not large, had high discrimination and an adult morality. Mme de Scudéry's fictional description of such a society was not so far from the reality in its heyday:

> On y voit sans doute, comme ailleurs, des gens qui ont une fausse galanterie insupportable; mais, à parler généralement, il y a je ne sais quel esprit de politesse, qui regne dans cette cour, qui la rend fort agréable et qui fait qu'on y trouve effectivement un nombre incroyable d'hommes fort accomplis. Et ce qui les rend tels est que les gens de qualité de Phénicie ne font pas profession d'être dans une ignorance grossière de toutes sortes de sciences, comme on en voit en quelques autres cours où on s'imagine qu'un homme qui sait se servir d'une épée doit ignorer toutes les autres choses; au contraire il n'y a presque pas un homme de condition à notre cour qui ne sache juger assez délicatement des beaux ouv-rages, et qui ne cherche du moins à se faire honneur en honorant ceux qui savent plus que lui.

This was not a society of specialists, but of people whose 'educa-tion' covered every aspect of their lives.

From the early years of the century, the civilizing tendency in social behaviour is accompanied by a civilizing classicism in literature. Both the salon of Mme de Rambouillet and the aes-thetic of Malherbe banned 'low' words and provincialisms; and Malherbe's insistence on lucidity and purity of style in poetry was influenced by the growing tendency for men of fashion, the representatives of the *salons*, to intermingle with the professional men of letters. The nobility increasingly dabbled in literary and musical composition, and the professional writers and musicians were increasingly accepted in aristocratic society; most of the leading artists in the great classical period were to come from bourgeois stock, later to be ennobled by Louis. In general, Malherbe's critical aesthetic is a remarkable anticipation of full-flown classicism, as is Richelieu's transformation of a polite literary circle into the Académie française. Balzac's polishing of the cadences of his prose, and Vaugelas's work on the dictionary and his *Remarques sur la langue française*, aimed to regulate language not in accordance with an abstract system of rules, but with the usage of 'la plus saine partie de la cour et des écrivains du temps'. We may note as an example of the centralizing tendencies of the time that whereas Malherbe had said that the language of poetry ought to contain no phrase that an educated Parisian could not understand, in Vaugelas's prescription the model is narrowed to that of the court.

None of these men was himself remarkable for creative genius; their formalizing influence was, however, of as great an importance as was that of Mme de Rambouillet in the field of social conduct. In the works of the minor but truly creative poets who, though they jeered at Malherbe, would not have written as they did but for his work, we can find a combination of exquisite sensibility with nobility of bearing which is the product of a high degree of civilization. And this is something which survives in La Fontaine and, despite many cultural upheavals, well into Couperin's day. We can trace some relation between the simultaneous exquisiteness and gravity of one of Couperin's pastoral pieces and, say, a lyric of Tristan l'Hermite, for 'exquisiteness' is not a characteristic of the classical age itself. Perhaps, too, the measured nobility of the great chaconnes of the clavecinists has something of the lofty purity of the odes and elegies of the early years of the century.

The society of the Blue Room had created a public with standards both of technique and morality. It was perhaps inevitable that as it grew in size it should decline in quality. The great days of the salon were over by 1650; its material growth outpaced its moral growth, and its standards were overlaid by a veneer of immature sophistication. Something of this is expressed in a passage from La Bruyère:

Voiture et Scarron étaient nés pour leur siècle, et ils ont paru dans un temps où il semble qu'ils étaient attendus; s'ils s'étaient moins pressés de venir, ils arriveraient trop tard, et j'ose douter qu'ils fussent tels aujourd'hui qu'ils ont été alors: les conversations légères, les cercles, la fine plaisanterie, les enjouées et familières, les petites parties où l'on était admis seulement avec de l'esprit, tout a disparu. Et qu'on ne dise point qu'ils le feraient revivre; ce que je puis faire en faveur de leur esprit est de convenir que peut-être ils excelleraient dans un autre genre; mais les femmes sont de nos jours ou dévotes, ou coquettes, ou joueuses, ou ambitieuses, quelques-unes même tout cela à la fois; le goût de la faveur, le jeu, les galants, les directeurs, ont pris la place, et la défendent contre les gens d'esprit.

Of course the excesses of the *précieuses* – the ultimate inability to call a spade a spade – were the development of elements which were present in the society of Mme de Rambouillet. In the salons of Mlle de Scudéry and of the other successors of the original Hôtel de Rambouillet, however, the conventional stylizations of language and behaviour gradually came to have a less intimate relation to life. Mlle de Scudéry's super-subtle attempts to define *la galanterie* are an indication of the atmosphere of the precious mid-century:

Cependant cet air galant dont j'entends parler ne consiste point précisément à avoir beaucoup d'esprit, beaucoup de jugement, et beaucoup de savoir, et c'est quelque chose de si particulier et de si difficile à acquerir quand on ne l'a point, qu'on ne sait où le prendre ni où le chercher. Car enfin je connois un homme que toute la compagnie connoît aussi, qui est bien fait, qui a de l'esprit, qui est magnifique en train, en meubles et en habillements, qui est propre, qui parle judicieusement et juste, qui de plus fait ce qu'il peut pour avoir l'air galant, et qui cependant est le moins galant de tous les hommes. . . . Je suis persuadé qu'il faut que la nature mette du moins dans l'esprit et dans la personne de ceux qui doivent avoir l'air galant une certaine disposition de le recevoir; il faut de plus que le grand commerce du monde et de la cour aide encore à le donner; et il faut aussi que la conversation des femmes le donne aux hommes . . . je dirai encore qu'il faut même qu'un homme ait eu, du moins une fois de sa vie, quelque légère inclination amoureuse pour acquérir parfaitement l'air galant.

The epics and romances of such writers as Chapelain and Madeleine de Scudéry, with their jargon of *galanterie*, their ludicrously flattering portraits of commonplace people, were an inflation beyond the bounds of sense of qualities which had once been admirable. They were the result of the too rapid growth of a reading public, for they appealed to a public which was educated enough to toy with the externals of the *galant* conventions, without being sufficiently educated to understand what, for the original circle, those conventions had stood for. La Bruyère gives a trenchant account of this bogus education:

> Avec cinq où six termes de l'art, et rien de plus, l'on se donne pour connoisseur en musique, en tableaux, en batîments, et en bonne chère; l'on croit avoir plus de plaisir qu'un autre à entendre, à voir, et à manger; l'on impose à ses semblables et l'on se trompe soi-même. La cour n'est jamais dénuée d'un certain nombre de gens en qui l'usage du monde, la politesse ou la fortune tiennent lieu d'esprit et suppléent au mérite; ils savent entrer et sortir, ils se tirent de la conversation en ne s'y mêlant point, ils plaisent à force de se taire, et se rendent importants par un silence longtemps soutenu, ou tout au plus par quelques monosyllables; ils payent de mines, d'un geste, et d'un sourire. Ils n'ont pas, si je l'ose dire, deux pouces de profondeur: si vous les enfoncez, vous rencontrez le tuf.

The members of Mme de Rambouillet's society wanted to purify language as well as behaviour, but they did not deliberately put the stress on the *difference* of their language from that of ordinary people, as did the *précieuses* of the mid-century, according to Somaize's *Grand Dictionnaire de Précieuses*, published in 1661. Moreover, the very last thing that members of the Blue Room would have said was that, even in matters of pleasure and entertainment, they valued imagination more than truth.

At the same time we cannot regard the *précieux* phase of the middle years of the century merely as the decline of a highly developed civilization. The cheaper sophistication prevalent during the early years of the Fronde, after the retirement of Mme de Rambouillet and of Julie d'Angennes, was an inevitable consequence of the expansion of a homogeneous group, and the part it played in moulding the taste of the time was far from ephemeral. At its best the *précieux* vocabulary was as much a part of Corneille's moral code as was the neo-Platonic conception of love he inherited from *L'Astrée*. Even Molière, who delivered a frontal assault on the affectations of the *Précieuses Ridicules*, 45 assimilated much of the love-etiquette of *préciosité* and employed its stylized vocabulary not only in verse but in prose as well. In a musical form it appears, we shall see, in the technique of the lutenists, and Chambonnières' ornamentation may be considered a manifestation of it. Even as late as Couperin's day its influence is still discernible.

One literary form which the cult of *préciosité* assumed was a consciously naïve, archaizing, pseudo-popular style of occasional poetry, invented by the celebrated wit of Mme de Rambouillet's salon, Vincent Voiture. About the middle of the century, this type of 'marotic' verse – so called because of its deliberate introduction of archaisms mostly taken from the work of Clément Marot – became highly fashionable, and it was perfected by La Fontaine in the early part of his career. The work of the Jesuit Du Cerceau, one of the most admired humorous poets of the day, proves that in Couperin's time the marotic line was still vigorous; Du Cerceau wrote a preface to the first re-edition of Villon in 1723, in which he treats Villon as a forerunner of the marotic vein. Certainly there is an aspect of Couperin's work – a consciously popular manner, a sophisticatedly naïve interest in 'old' French things which are regarded as at once *naturels* and *ingénieux* – which relates back to this tradition: and we may mention too the elegantly rustic *galanteries* which Bodin de Boismortier composed for flutes, bagpipes, and hurdy-gurdy.

Closely associated with this type of occasional verse was the burlesque tradition, an outpouring of sophisticated high-spirits which were irresponsible because uncritical. Practised mainly by Scarron and d'Assoucy, burlesque was a travesty of classical literature in an affectedly 'low' language, a smart game intentionally inverting the precepts both of Malherbe and of Mme de Rambouillet.★ Spanish and Italian drama and literature, particularly Marini, were absorbed into a local convention, devised to meet a popular demand. The nobler spirits protested against it; Poussin for instance dismissed Scarron's *Typhon* as 'dégoûtant'. None the less, the burlesque manner influenced the outlook

---

★ The burlesque tradition is later found in theatre music, as well as in literature and the drama. A parody of the Lully–Quinault opera *Phaéton* was extremely popular in Paris, towards the end of the century. It may have had some bearing on the growth of the English ballad opera.

of the century. Couperin's pieces 'dans le goût burlesque' are not unrelated to it; certainly they have an oblique connection with it through the *commedia dell'arte*.

The Italian players, with their stylized and yet improvisatory art, had been cultivated in France all through the sixteenth and early seventeenth century. There is a reference to a 'Maistre André italien' and his company as early as 1530, the celebrated Gelosi troupe was in France in 1571, and Isabella Andreini, as cultured and distinguished as she was beautiful, died in France in 1604, her memory being fêted all over Europe. During the first half of the seventeenth century, the companies of the Accesi and the Fedeli were in repeated demand in France. But it was not until the mid-century that the vogue reached its height, and until 1660 that the Italian players, at the instigation of Mazarin, founded a permanent Parisian group. The great Scaramouche Fiorilli at one time lodged and worked in collaboration with Molière himself, at the Petit Bourbon; the story of the friendship between them, and of the way Molière incorporated many aspects of the Italian theatre into the French comedy, is well known. Other celebrated Italian players, including Biancolelli as Harlequin, were intermittently in the French company, and the conventional *commedia* characters soon became a part, not only of the French theatre, but of French popular culture. As Louis, swayed by Mme de Maintenon, grew more sober-minded with advancing years, the vogue of the Italian players declined, until in 1697 they were expelled for having made some tactless witticism at the expense of *la fausse prude*. But their reign had lasted long enough to make a profound impression on the sensibilities of the young Couperin and Watteau. There is a moving picture of their farewell by Watteau; and in all his work, and in Couperin's pantomime, harlequin and other pieces *dans le goût burlesque*, the old stylizations are rarefied and immortalized. Here we can gain some notion of the beauty, pathos and wit that the improvisation of such highly cultured and imaginative artists as Isabella Andreini, Fiorilli, and Biancolelli must have given to the conventional framework, in the heyday of the *commedia*. Like Shakespearean tragedy, the *commedia* appealed at a number of different levels. It was of course a popular entertainment; but for those who had eyes to see and ears to hear, that was not the whole story.

Here however we are not concerned with what the *commedia*   47 meant to a Couperin or a Watteau; we are concerned with it as an aspect of taste during the middle years of the century; and in this respect one might legitimately correlate the hardening of the official attitude to its frivolity with Boileau's attack on the various facets of *préciosité*. There are certainly many signs, round about the sixteen-sixties, that a fresh start was considered necessary; we may perhaps best appreciate the significance of, for instance, La Rochefoucauld's rather sentimental (*mélancolique*) cynicism if we see in it a recognition that the conventional counters of etiquette were becoming divorced from their moral implications, so that *la vérité* began to look suspiciously like self-interest. Within the narrow range of experience which he allowed himself, La Rochefoucauld had an acute insight, typical of his time; none the less he is, despite the metallic precision of his comments, the product of a phase of relative decadence. The Great Age might have countered his arguments with the words of Vauvenargues: 'Le corps a ses grâces, l'esprit a ses talents; la cœur n'aurait-il que des vices, et l'homme capable de raison, serait-il incapable de vertu?'

Boileau has been much castigated for his inadequate appreciation of the great poets of his time, yet his pedestrian approach has value in so far as it sums up ideals and opinions from which even the greatest, consciously or unconsciously, profited. His critical aesthetic had two main, interlinked purposes. One was to establish a criterion of naturalness and lucidity, in opposition to the unreality of *préciosité*; in this he was the climax of the tradition which had been established by Malherbe. The other was to insist on the relationship between aesthetic and moral standards. He wanted to give the growing and comparatively irresponsible reading public a standard of reference by reminding it of classical achievements. Roughly speaking, this phase lasted from about 1660 to the publication of the *Art Poétique* in 1674, when it attained a resounding European success.

We have seen in the last chapter that Boileau's aesthetic was in some ways a reduction into literary terms of the Cartesian philosophical outlook, and thus a seminal creation of the time; and we have seen that most of the great writers show some kind of conflict between Boileau's ideal of Nature ordered by Reason, and the complexity of human passions. What ultimately matters is how the great artists use the conventional framework; but in this chapter, concerned as we are with the fluctuations of taste, it is the nature of the framework itself that interests us. Boileau did not object to the *précieux* style *per se*; he accepted it, with reservations, in Corneille for instance. He objected to it only in so far as it had become, in such works as Mlle de Scudéry's novels and Scarron's plays and burlesques, frivolous and irresponsible. This is why he insisted on themes of a high moral elevation and of general, as opposed to topical and local, interest; and the best way to achieve such a generalized significance seemed to him to be through the imitation of classical antiquity. He did not advocate pastiche; he recommended the use of a convention which liberated the author from the ephemeral. The artist should aim to interpret man in his general and eternal, rather than in particular, aspects. He should exercise his powers of selection in determining what is important, what is not, remembering always that 'tout ce qu'on dit de trop est fade et rebutant'. Above all he should avoid triviality, even in comedy.

While Boileau's attitude is in some respects so closely rooted in the Cartesian outlook, in others it is clearly irreconcilable with Cartesianism. For if one fully accepts the supremacy of reason and the irrelevance of history, art, like human nature, ought to be growing progressively less imperfect, so that to study the ancients, even in order to reinterpret them, would be absurd. This latent paradox became more evident in 1688, in the famous quarrel of the Ancients and Moderns, in which Fontenelle, Perrault (the author, strangely enough, of the fairy tales), and Malebranche took the progressively 'modern' scientific view, whereas the leading artists on the whole defended the Ancients. Boileau himself was reduced to a feeble compromise, maintaining that perhaps the Ancients were better at some things, the Moderns at others. But even this confusion is a part of Boileau's representative significance, for a mingling of reverence for antiquity with a progressive modernism is found repeatedly in the outlook and culture of the time. The classical ideal came to have a very direct bearing on contemporary life, as we may see from, among many possible examples, this passage in which Fénelon recommends

aux jeunes filles la noble simplicité qui parait dans les statues . . . qui nous restent des femmes grecques et romaines; elles y verraient combien des cheveux noués négligemment par derrière, et des draperies pleines et flottantes à longs plis sont agréables et

49

majestueuses. Il serait bon même qu'elles entendissent parler les peintres et les autres gens qui ont ce goût exquis de l'antiquité. . . . Je sais bien qu'il ne faut pas souhaiter qu'elles prennent l'extérieur antique; il y aurait de l'extravagance à le vouloir; mais elles pourraient, sans aucune singularité, prendre le goût de cette simplicité d'habits si noble, si gracieuse, et d'ailleurs si convenable aux mœurs chrétiennes.

Here we see Boileau's literary precepts translated into terms of social etiquette. The rational belief in their own standards gives to these people their self-confidence; their habitual reference to a criterion outside themselves – in this case antiquity – preserves their humility, their sense of the mean. It is this union of self-confidence with humility which is so impressively demonstrated in La Bruyère's essay *Des Jugements*. It still survives in Couperin's attitude to his art, and the part played by the classical ideal in achieving it should not be lightly estimated.

Classicism begins and ends with the distinction of genres which is an expression in art of a refinement of social approach. Everything is well in its proper place; 'tout poème est brillant de sa propre beauté'. The generation that lived on after Boileau's death into the Regency marked in some ways a return once more to the precious, a softening of the outlines, a loosening of the tension between etiquette and morality. And yet all this veering and tacking between the noble and heroic, the naïve and ingenious, the archaic and popular, the pompous and intimate is a part of the gradual maturing of public taste. If the values and standards are becoming less clearly defined, they are also becoming operative for a wider public. The autocracy of Versailles is decaying and the life of Paris is beginning to take its place. A tendency towards decentralization is manifested in every branch of social entertainment. Art, expressing the ideal of *douceur de vivre*, becomes easier and more familiar. Architecture changes from the 'official' grandeur of Mansart to the style of a Robert de Cotte, which preserves something of the external magnificence, but inside is gracious, elegantly ornamented, comfortable, suited to the intercourse of a more amiably intimate society.* In

---

* For a minor but very revealing illustration of the changing cultural atmosphere compare the grandly proportioned case of the *buffet* of the St Gervais organ, which dates from the great age of Louis XIV, with the more graciously elegant case of the Versailles organ, which is the work of Robert de Cotte. See pages 311 and 312.

painting the propagandist Lebrun is succeeded by the more personally emotional Watteau; in music Couperin follows Lully. The history of the opera and ballet during the last years of Louis's reign and the early years of the Regency reveals the changing outlook most clearly. But this is a subject of such crucial importance for the understanding of the musical culture that Couperin inherited that it must be dealt with in a separate chapter.

Chapter Four

Music, the Court, and the Theatre

On trouve dans ses récits, dans ses airs, dans ses Chœurs, et dans toutes ses Simphonies, un caractère juste et vrai, une variété merveilleuse, une mélodie et une harmonie qui enchantent, et il mérite avec raison le titre de Prince des Musiciens François, étant regardé comme l'inventeur de cette belle et grand Musique Françoise.

TITON DU TILLET (*of Lully*)

So far we have tried to give some account of the values and the taste of the society into which Couperin was born, mainly through reference to the memoirs, literature, and painting of the period. The musical counterparts of these fluctuations in taste will be discussed in detail when, in Part II of this book, we examine the various branches of Couperin's musical activity. There is, however, one aspect of court music – the ballet and opera – which Couperin did not touch upon, but which none the less influenced profoundly both his sensibility and his technique. In this chapter we shall therefore give some general account of the rise of a courtly musical-theatrical art in France during the *grand siècle*, and suggest some reasons why Couperin did not make any specific contributions to the theatrical genre, even though the whole temper and character of his work is impregnated with the Lullian spirit.

In order to understand French theatrical music in the seventeenth century it is necessary to consider briefly the relations between French and Italian culture during the period and, to a lesser degree, during the preceding century. There is nothing surprising in the fact that Italy should have evolved a sophisticated secular art, founded on aristocratic patronage, earlier than any other European culture. The breakdown of the social and economic framework of the Middle Ages occurred in Italy sooner than elsewhere; indeed the fifteenth and even the fourteenth century are often referred to as the 'Italian renaissance', rather than as the end of the Middle Ages. And although Burck-hardt's tendency to attribute everything vital in the Middle Ages to a premature renaissance is to be deprecated, it is true that the brilliant fifteenth-century Florentine culture in some ways anticipates developments normally associated with the next century. It demonstrates that, while the church had always provided opportunities for spectacle of a ritualistic order, a relatively unstable economy is apt to encourage a heightened humanism, to give a vigorous impetus to the instinct for rhetoric and dramatization. In the Florentine cities, as later in Elizabethan England, feudalism was dying and a national, commercial outlook was becoming more obtrusive. Both because man's economic position was more precarious, and because his relation to a universal Order was less clearly defined, the claims of the individual seemed more important, and the relation between the individual and the community more complex. This heightened personal and social consciousness found expression in a great outburst of pageantry and spectacle; we may note that it was the guild movements that brought pageantry out of the aegis of the church. This pageantry in turn gave a fillip to the theatrical aspects of the arts attendant on it. It is no accident that it was in Italy, which already had so long a tradition of spectacle and theatre, that the tremendous humanistic passion of the chromatic madrigal and of early baroque opera was first manifested.

When the musical-spectacular dramatic art of the Italian renaissance spread to France in the sixteenth century, it was rapidly modified by the native French tradition. Considerably before the full flowering of Italian baroque opera, the sophisticated court society of Henry II saw in the Italian masquerades, intermedii, and balletti a type of entertainment which could be adapted to local court functions. *Mascarades à grand spectacle*, held in the open air on a lavish scale, and *mascarades de palais*, held less magnificently in a room or small garden, became the customary accompaniment to the complimentary speeches to the King and nobility which graced all court festivities.

French composers had no difficulty in providing a stream of dance movements for these entertainments. The French tradition had always been rich in dance music. The folk music is itself remarkable for its sense of physical movement; and although men such as Josquin and Lassus exhibit in their religious polyphony a rhythmic variety no less subtle than that of Byrd or 53

Victoria, there flourished too, all through the sixteenth century, an elegant homophonic choral tradition which is linked to folk dance. The symmetry and precision of this secular line, from Adam de la Halle to Jannequin, to Guillaume de Costeley, gives to French folk dance a super-civilized reincarnation. The combination of melodic and rhythmic simplicity with a delicate economy of craftsmanship give the music a quality, at once naïve and sophisticated, which is not paralleled by the English madrigalists, who are either more complex and profound, or else less sophisticated, more directly in touch with a folk culture. Even some sixteenth-century French religious choral music, for instance the Psalms of Mauduit, uses a technique of homophonically built-up choral masses which almost anticipates the majesty of Lully.

Now the instrumental dance music is complementary to this elegant choral homophony. Many of the dances were published in the famous collection of Attaignant in 1557. Some were modelled on imported Italian dances, for instance the corantos, though the French soon developed their own version of the dance also. Others, such as the various types of branles, were a direct transference of folk dances, indicating that the sophisticated court culture had not yet lost contact with 'the people'. Others again, such as the pavanes and galliards, were a compromise between sophisticated and popular elements. The music, scored for strings, oboes, bassoons, and *cornets à bouquins*, had similar qualities to the vocal chansons; the implicit connection with a vocal tradition lent the rhythm plasticity, without any sacrifice of verve. The clarity of texture, the sharp definition of line and rhythm and orchestration, make the music still entrancing to listen to; it is entertainment music which is admirably designed for its function, and is also an enlivening of the spirit. The string parts probably included violins rather than viols, for a version of the violin more resembling the Italian *lyra da braccia* than the modern violin was introduced in France as early as 1530, well before the appearance of violins in Italy. The characteristic tone colour of the instrument must have enhanced the music's vivacity and *allure*. The following quotation from Philibert Jambe-de-Fer, dated 1556, would seem to indicate that in the mid-sixteenth century the attitude of cultivated musicians to the violin was still somewhat patronizing:

Le violon est fort contraire à la viole. . . . Il est en forme de
corps plus petit, plus plat, et beaucoup plus rude en son. . . . Nous
appellons *violes* celles desquelles les gentilz hommes, marchantz, et
autres gens de vertu passent leur temps. L'autre sorte s'appelle
violon, et c'est celui duquel en use en dancerie communement et à
bonne cause: car il est plus facile d'accorder pour ce que la quinte
est plus douce à ouyr que n'est la quarte. Il est aussi plus facile à
porter, qui est chose fort nécessaire, mesme en conduisant quelques noces, ou mommerie. . . .

But by the early years of the seventeenth century violins had
become the rule in court festival music, having lost much of the
social stigma attached to them. That their theatrical glamour
was clearly recognized is attested by the appearance in the score
of Monteverdi's *Orfeo* (1607) of *violini piccoli alla francese*; and by
this passage from Mersenne's *Harmonie Universelle* of 1636:

Et ceux qui ont entendu les 24 Violons du Roy, aduouent qu'ils
n'ont jamais rien ouy de plus rauissant ou de plus puissant; de là
vient que cet instrument est la plus propre de tous pour faire
danser, comme l'on experimente dans les balets, & partout ailleurs. Or les beautez et les gentillesses que l'on pratique dessus sont
en si grand nombre que l'on le peut préférer à tous les autres
instrumens, car les coups de son archet sont par fois si rauissants,
que l'on n'a point de plus grand mescontentement que d'entendre
la fin, particulièrement lors qu'ils sont mêlez des tremblemens &
des flattemens de la main gauche. . . .

The brilliant French dance orchestras soon became famous all
over Europe; some of them travelled to Germany, England, and
even as far as Poland and Sweden.

The greater importance of the dance in art music was, however, only one aspect of the influence in France of the Italian
renaissance. In both countries – and many Italian musicians
were, in the second half of the sixteenth century, resident in
France – it was felt that the figured dances of the court entertainments contained latent aesthetic possibilities which had not been
adequately explored. Just as Peri and Bardi tried to combine the
arts of music, dancing, painting, and poetry into an organized
whole, in a manner which they imagined to be a marriage of
modern civilization with the principles of classical antiquity, so,
in France, Ronsard and the poets of the Pléiade group collaborated with the musicians to work out similar theories. From 55

the start, the Italians had the drama in mind; the French, to begin with, were content to insist on the interdependence of music and poetry. Music was to be 'la sœur puisnée de la poésie'. Without it, poetry is 'presque sans grâce, comme la musique sans la mélodie des vers, inanimée et sans vie'. (Ronsard.)

The first product of this experiment was the *airs de cour* for solo voice and lute. A more detailed account of these will be given in the chapter on Couperin's secular vocal music. Here it is only necessary to say that, unlike the finest songs of the English Dowland, these airs have lute parts which were increasingly divested of polyphonic elaboration and reduced to a series of continuo-like chords. Le Roy interestingly contrasted the *airs de cour* with the chansons of Roland de Lassus, 'lesquelles son difficiles et ardues'. In England, this desire for the simple and tuneful develops very much later.

It is hardly just, however, to suggest that the early *airs de cour* were lacking in subtlety. If they had a less delicate balance between melodic and harmonic elements than the English ayres, they were no less subtle in the way in which the extraordinarily free rhythm of the solo line reflected the slightest nuance of the text. Jodelle said 'Même l'air des beaux chants inspirés dans les vers/Est, comme en un beau corps, une belle âme infuse'. In the hands of a composer such as Claude Le Jeune, who is also a superb contrapuntist in his church music, these songs may achieve a limpid beauty which is a fitting complement to the poetry of Ronsard that Le Jeune so frequently set. Occasionally, through the introduction of the intense chromaticisms of the Italian arioso technique, the songs may rise to a considerable passion. Normally, however, such humanistic drama was left to the Italians; the effect of the *airs de cour* as a whole – we may take Du Caurroy rather than Le Jeune as typical – is of a witty entertainment of the spirit, or of a gently nostalgic melancholy that is somewhat emasculating. Mersenne, writing during the height of the fashion, summed up adequately both the airs' virtues and their limitations:

> Il faut avouer que les accents de la passion manquent le plus souvent aux airs français parce que nos chants se contentent de chatouiller l'oreille et de plaire par les mignardises sans se soucier d'exciter les passions de leurs auditeurs.

Nothing could be further removed, both in intention and effect, from the Italian arioso at its best.

The French tradition of courtly theatre music developed through the mingling of these *airs de cour* with the instrumental dances discussed previously. In 1571 the poet Antoine de Baïf and the musician Thibault de Courville founded under royal patronage the *Académie Baïf de Musique et de Poésie*, to practise and propagate the new theories about music and prosody, to combine music and poetry with the dance by creating ballets based on Greek metres, and to circulate ideas among performers and audience. (There was often no sharp distinction between the two.)

> *L'entreprise*
> *D'un ballet que dressions, dont la démarche est mise*
> *Selon que va marchant pas à pas la chanson*
> *Et le parler suivi d'une propre façon*

was, with its insistence on Greek metres, perhaps a rather coldly academic prescription, but it was not rigidly adhered to. By the time the work of the *Académie* was interrupted by the Wars of Religion, it had impregnated French culture so deeply that its influence was felt for the next hundred and fifty years.

In 1581 Charles IX commissioned Ronsard, Baïf, and Le Jeune to produce *mascarades* to celebrate the marriage of the Duc de Joyeuse and Mlle de Vaudemont. Stung to emulation, Catharine de Medici ordered Balthazar de Beaujoyeulx to arrange an even grander affair, and although the King had already obtained the most distinguished artists, Beaujoyeulx compensated for the lack of glamorous 'names' in his production by an element of novelty. He created *Circé, ballet comique de la reine*, which although not in any way profound, for the first time made a conscious attempt to link dance, music, and spectacle into a coherent whole through the introduction of a slender story. 'Je puis dire avoir contenté en un corps bien proportionné l'œil, l'oreille, et l'entendement'. *Circé* immediately created a furore. The *ballet comique* superseded the casual *mascarade* as the recognized entertainment for all big court festivities; even the smaller *mascarades de palais* were influenced by it, introducing more developed literary and musical elements.

The history of the French ballet through the seventeenth 57

century is described in detail in Prunières's fascinating book on the subject, to which the reader is referred. Briefly, the ballet fluctuated between a literary and musical approach, the element of the dance remaining constant throughout. During the early years of the century, the presence of Rinuccini and Caccini at the French court encouraged a development of the musical elements; with the production of the *Ballet d'Alcine* in 1610 the dramatically inclined *ballet comique* reasserted itself. A new form, embracing dance, song, spectacle, pantomime and gesture, was created, and flourished from 1610 to 1621, when the Constable de Luynes, who had been in charge of it, died. Prunières refers to this type as the *ballet mélodramatique*. De Luynes's successor as master of the revels, the Duc de Nemours, had a partiality for the grotesque *ballet mascarade*; and the classical form of the *ballet de cour* was the offspring of a liaison between the *ballet mélodramatique* and the *ballet mascarade*.

The classical ballet was usually in five sections, each divided into several subsections. It opened with the dedicatory chorus to the King and court ladies, which was followed by a number of entries with characteristic dances, often of a grotesque nature. Then came the entry of quaintly masked musicians with lutes and viols to play instrumental interludes and to accompany the recitative and airs. Next came the climax with the entry of the King and nobles, masked; and the ballet concluded with a general dance and chorus. The songs included *airs de cour*, and *vaudevilles* or adaptations, some satirical, some amorous and pastoral, of popular songs and carols; another indication of the popular affiliations of this esoteric art. The one new element was the recitative, and this was a natural evolution from the freer type of *air de cour*, from which it differed only in being more consistently narrative and declamatory. One cannot say that this recitative is in the least dramatic; rather flat and characterless, it hardly attempts to solve the difficult problem of the relation between speech and lyrical song. But at least it was a step *towards* the opera; it was something that Lully could start from.

Musically, the most interesting section of the ballets would seem to be the *entrées de luth* which preserved some connection with the old polyphonic technique. They are not brisk like the conventional fanfares, but emotional and melancholy, dreamy and relaxed, obviously related to the elegiac tone of the lutenist music of the salons and *ruelles*. The other instrumental sections were not much more distinguished than the vocal parts – the recitative, solo airs, and choruses. Before Lully, the overtures do not extend beyond a few conventionally imposing gestures; and the dances appear to have been less rhythmically alert than those of the sixteenth century. Prunières warns us, however, that we have imperfect evidence as to the nature of the original ballet scores. Comparison of Philidor's early eighteenth-century transcriptions with the few examples which have survived in contemporary transcriptions for the lute, indicates that Philidor has emasculated the dances. In any case they must have been, in their original orchestration, a bright and colourful addition to the spectacle.

The dances made animated play with decorative and descriptive details; soldiers, battles, cock-crows and other bird-calls, 'national' dances, the more outlandish the better, were especially favoured. Ornamentation and the French dotted rhythm (which was not an invention of Lully), were employed to give vigour and point to physical gestures. Moreover, a case can be made out that the French were justified in putting the stress on the dance rather than the drama in creating a musical-theatrical art, because music and dancing are natural allies which move at the same speed. Music, on the other hand, is bound to take longer than poetry to make its emotional effect, and thereby produces a tricky technical problem which few opera composers have adequately solved. However this may be, the architectural quality of the French *ballet de cour* made an immense impression on foreign artists. It greatly influenced the later masques of Ben Jonson. Rinuccini studied it in detail, and determined to introduce it into his own country on his return; Monteverdi's magnificent *Ballo delle Ingrate* is one of the fruits of the French influence. If the French theatre music had originally sprung from Italian sources, it had certainly developed a character of its own which the Italians, among other European musicians, were eager to emulate.

During the early years of the seventeenth century the ballet had one composer of character, Pierre Guédron. His dances have unusual virility, and his *airs de cour* a genuine pathos and dramatic power. One cannot say, however, that Guédron is the representative composer of the ballet of the *grand siècle*. It is his successor Antoine Boësset who, as the most fashionable ballet composer, was universally honoured and fêted; whose work 59 was studied by Heinrich Albert, one of the leading German composers for the solo voice, and, according to St Evremond, by no less a person than Luigi Rossi, the Italian opera composer esteemed in France above all others. Boësset is a real composer, with a personal melodic gift, but he lacks – and would not, one imagines, have desired – Guédron's tautness and sinew. He is a 'génie de la musique douce', writing music that is sweetly mellifluous and often subtle. But the soft fluidity of his rhythms and the elaborations of his ornamentation get increasingly out of touch with the prosody they had originally been designed to illustrate. They are indulged in for their own sake, and become in the long run wearisome and enervating. By the time of the Roi Soleil the ballet appeared to be in decline. What was needed to weld its constituents into a musico-dramatic convention of classical maturity was an artist of commanding authority. He came in the person of Jean-Baptiste Lully.

Lully was, interestingly enough, himself an Italian, and the son of a miller. Born in Florence in 1632, he was brought up in the humanistic traditions of Italian music. At the age of fourteen he came to France as *garçon de chambre* and unofficial instructor in Italian to Mlle d'Orléans; by the time he was twenty his precocious musical gifts and headstrong temperament had carried him into the court ballet, where he excelled both as dancer and musician. He acquired a thorough grounding in the French traditions of composition from two men of the old school, Roberday and Gigault, and was himself soon composing, with equal fluency, ballet music in the French style, and Italian airs in the manner of Rossi and Carissimi. A brilliant fiddler, Lully had little use for the famous Vingt-quatre Violons du Roi; indeed of them he 'faisait si peu de cas qu'il les traitait de maîtres aliborons et de maîtres ignorants', in particular protesting against their habit of introducing unauthorized ornamentation into their parts. Lully's appeal for naturalness and simplicity applied of course to his vocal writing as well as to his instrumental. Lecerf de la Viéville reports him as saying: 'Point de broderie; mon récitatif n'est fait que pour parler, je veux qu'il soit tout uni.' It is worth noting that Lully's first appeals for dignity and lucidity in performance and composition correspond in date with Boileau's attack upon the excesses of *préciosité*.

That Lully's personality had remarkable power is indicated by the fact that the King listened to his complaints even though, at the time, Lully was not a person of much consequence. Louis put him 'à la tête d'une bande de violons qu'il peut conduire à sa fantaisie'. Lully soon proved that the King's confidence in him was not misplaced; according to Lecerf de la Viéville, the new band, called Les Petits Violons, 'en peu de temps surpassa la fameuse bande des Vingt-Quatre'. Lully introduced many improvements into string technique, mostly for the purpose of achieving greater brilliance and more incisive rhythm. There can be no doubt that his experience of playing string music as an accompaniment to physical movement was of great value to him in his subsequent career as a theatre composer.

When Lully, with his Italian background, first came to France, Italian music, and in particular the opera, was in vogue among the French intelligentsia, largely because of Mazarin's insatiable passion for it. Mazarin's vindication was that he 'ne faisoit pas ces choses tant pour le public que pour le divertissement de leurs Majestés et pour le sien, et qu'ils aymoient mieux les vers et la musique italienne que la française'. (Perrin.) It was at his invitation that Luigi Rossi and Carlo Caproli spent long periods in France, and through his efforts that in the sixteen forties Rossi's opera *Orfeo* was given a sumptuous Parisian production. It enjoyed a considerable *succès d'estime*, or possibly *succès de scandale*, among the dilettanti; and undoubtedly the aristocratic refinement and hyper-subtlety of both Rossi's and Caproli's music must have appealed to an audience which admired the sophistications of the lute music and the *airs de cour*. But it cannot be said that the perfervid Italians made any lasting impression on the French temperament. If the French liked the Italians' emotional subtleties, they distrusted their violence; the dolorous intensity of Rossi's music, its vehement chromaticisms, were admired less than its languishing elegance. On the whole the Italian musicians were regarded with suspicion. After Mazarin's death it was inevitable that the Italian influence should decline.

The much heralded visit of the great Cavalli in the sixteen sixties was thus somewhat of an anti-climax. His opera *Serse* passed, musically speaking, almost unnoticed, and when, a little later, his *L'Ercole Amante* was produced, it was the additional ballets written by Lully that aroused all the enthusiasm. Not unnaturally Cavalli was piqued that a composer of international celebrity such as himself should be ousted by a composer of pleasant dances – which were almost all Lully had to his credit at 61 that date. He returned to Italy, leaving Lully in full musical possession of the country of his adoption. But although opposition to things Italian was temporarily so strong that Cavalli's music was not generally appreciated, Lully himself was not slow to recognize its virtues.. He was aware that, though the French might not know it, there were things in Cavalli's theatre music that the French tradition could use to its own advantage.

For while Cavalli could employ a passionate Italian chromaticism when he wanted, as in the famous lament from *Egisto*, the general tendency of his work was towards balanced periods founded on the integration of melody and bass, and simple diatonic harmony of the type that reaches its culmination in Handel. Rossi and Caproli were transitional composers in the sense that their dramatic harmonic audacities and sensuous glamour still have contact with the polyphonic methods of the past. Cavalli differentiates much more sharply between his supple but highly stylized declamation, and his formal arias. He has not Rossi's baroque imaginativeness, but he has dramatic power combined with a sense of architectural order and of the alternation of mood. Cavalli deliberately avoids the subtle harmonic effects of false relation and appoggiatura that Rossi delighted in; avoids, too, Rossi's contrapuntal complexities in choral and instrumental part-writing. He aims at a broad effect; and this was just what Lully wanted if he was to establish a criterion of order in music, as Boileau established it in poetic technique; if he was to discipline the floridity of *précieux* line and harmony, as Mansart regulated and stabilized the proportions of baroque architecture. After the production of *L'Ercole Amante* all Lully's ballets show an expansion of the traditional French technique (which he had helped to formulate with his *Ballet de la Nuit* of 1653) by means of the sense of harmonic proportion he had learned from the Italians, and from Cavalli in particular. This debt remains, even though Lully, having thrown in his lot with the French cause, came bitterly to resent any Italian interference.

To the traditional French methods Lully added, at the start, little that was new. But he gave the ceremonial dances and cortèges on the classical model a more organic unity with one another, and a more intrinsic elegance and zest. Early on he showed a clear understanding of the tonal principles on which a convincing homophonic architecture was to depend; and he developed the ground-bass technique of the chaconne, that most primitive expansion of a symmetrical figure through the simple process of repetition, into a medium capable of an intense emotional expressiveness, exploiting the possibility of tension between the regularly repeated bass and the varied groupings of the melodies above it. This development of the chaconne is an example of how the seventeenth-century composer turned to his advantage a practical necessity – namely, the repetition of the symmetrical ballet tune as long as the dancers wished to go on dancing. The somewhat later development of the rondeau with couplets is a further example, as we shall see, of a technique of expediency turned to an expressive purpose. Both techniques are a compromise between a dance music for practical use and the *melodically* generative technique of the sixteenth century. Though the rhythmic conception is now more accentual, there is still a link between the chaconne and rondeau technique of Lully and Couperin respectively, and, for instance, the variation technique of the Tudor virginalists.

Important as was Lully's work in developing the dance element in the ballet, still more significant is his transformation into the theatrical overture of the formal introductory fanfares heralding the arrival of the maskers. This reconciles all the transitional elements of the technique of composition which were then current. The slow majestic opening harks back to the polyphony and false relations of the instrumental fantasia, the bouncing dotted rhythms and the ornamentation deriving from Lully's knowledge of the physical movements of the ballet, acquired when directing Les Petits Violons; while the quick fugal section is a compromise between polyphonic procedure and the regular rhythms and simple harmonies of the dance. If the Lullian overture is a transitional technique, it is none the less mature. It is not surprising that its influence spread far beyond the confines of the French court.

In addition to his expansion of the symphonic aspects of the ballet, Lully developed the vocal elements. His interest in vocal music was considerably encouraged when, in 1664, he entered into collaboration with Molière and produced a long series of *comédies-ballets, Le Mariage Forcé, La Princesse d'Elide, L'Amour Médecin, Le Sicilien, Le Ballet des Muses, Le Grotte de Versailles, George Dandin, Les Amans Magnifiques, Monsieur de Pourceaugnac, Le Bourgeois Gentilhomme*, and, to complete the cycle, *Psyché*, in collaboration with Pierre Corneille. In all these, care is taken to   63 relate the musical interludes to the action. Some of them, *La Princesse d'Elide*, *Les Amans Magnifiques*, *Psyché*, were heroic works in the grand style, with considerable choral passages, treated vertically in massive homophony, and with elaborate stage machinery; they were almost grand operas, but for the absence of dramatic recitative. The lighter works, on the other hand, *Le Mariage Forcé*, *L'Amour Médecin*, *Le Bourgeois Gentil-homme* and *Pourceaugnac*, led on to the French comic opera. Here, in the dance movements we find a crispness and bubbling zest which is enhanced by the scrupulously clean orchestration, a vein of exquisite pastoral elegance (*Le Sicilien* is the loveliest example), and a lyrical idiom sensitively moulded to the inflexions of the French language. The line is unbroken from *Pourceaugnac* to Chabrier's *Le Roi Malgré Lui*. Moreover, in *Le Grotte de Versailles*, *George Dandin*, and *Les Amans Magnifiques*, Lully has gone far towards creating a recitative as well as a lyrical style which is a musical incarnation of the French language. All these *bergeries* and *comédies-ballets* are full of intimations of the later operas. The gay satirical scenes of *Pourceaugnac* and *Le Bourgeois Gentilhomme*, with their extravagant local colour, their serenades, drinking-songs and descriptive details, are already the creation of a mature comic genius which M. Prunières relates to Rossini. In *Les Amans Magnifiques*, the *sommeil* of Caliste and the scene of the *Jeux Pithiens*, with its ceremonial dialogues between choir and resplendent orchestra of trumpets, flutes, oboes, strings, and percussion, give a foretaste of some of the most impressive moments of *Cadmus* and *Thésée*.

The creation of *ballets comiques* continued from 1664 to 1671, the date of *Psyché*. In the following year, after complicated and unscrupulous legal negotiations, Lully obtained an exclusive privilege of founding an *Académie Royale de Musique*. As a result of this, he established a school of opera centred at the Palais Royal, and between 1673 and 1686 produced his famous series of operas, twelve of them in collaboration with Quinault, three with Campistron and Thomas Corneille, the brother of Pierre. If Lully had been fortunate in having the wit and urbanity of Molière at his disposal for his *ballets comiques*, he was hardly less fortunate in having for his tragic operas the services of a poet who, though not a genius, had habitual distinction and good taste. We have already referred to the rewarding collaboration between artists in different media as being indicative of the cultural unity and vitality of Versailles; in this case the collaboration appears to have been especially intimate, for Quinault was much influenced by Lully's ideas and allowed the composer a considerable share in the shaping of the librettos.★ The plan of the operas was highly stylized. After the overture, a more spacious version of the ballet overture already described, came the prologue with complimentary speeches to the King and allusions to the latest victories, followed by choruses and dances of patriotic intent. All this was a direct survival from the masque. Then followed the tragedy, usually concerned with sexual passion, and involving supernatural agencies which provided opportunities for complicated stage mechanism.

The centre of interest, the unfolding of the story, lies in the recitative; this is the principal difference from the ballets. This recitative is far from the perfunctory declamation of the old ceremonial addresses. Lully modelled it with the greatest care, studying the inflexions of the great Racinian tragedians such as La Champmeslé, trying to create a line which should be scrupulously attentive to the effect of the spoken word, while at the same time having sufficient musical interest to stand on its own feet. There is a good deal of evidence, as Romain Rolland has shown, that Racine's own notion of declamation was close to song: leaps in pitch as great as an octave were encouraged in the more passionate passages. It is probable, therefore, that Lully's recitative reflects fairly accurately the contour of Racine's declamation. The latter was closer to song than are our notions of declamation, whereas Lully's recitative was closer to speech than our, or at least nineteenth-century, recitative. If today Lully's recitative sounds dull, it is usually because it is sung too stolidly and formally. It should have the flexibility of animated, if always elegant, conversation; contemporary opinion insists repeatedly not only on its majesty, but on its liveliness and naturalness. If Lully studied the tragedians as a model for his recitative, it is equally true that they in their turn studied his recitative as a model for their declamation. It may have been the decay of this relation between the dramatic and operatic traditions that led to the widespread misunderstanding of Lully's idiom.

★ A most interesting account of Lully's method of work and of his association with Quinault is given in Bonnet's *Histoire de la Musique*, vol. iii, p.95 *et seq.* (1725 edition.)

Though never, like that of the Italians, dramatically violent, Lully's line attains a convincing Cavalli-like balance between melodic interest and harmonic elements, exemplified for instance in the line's use of diminished fifths and sevenths. Since the French language perhaps does not naturally lend itself to musical expression, Lully's achievement was, even on purely technical grounds, of no mean order; but what is most remarkable is the range of emotional expression he compasses within his restrained utterance. The use of melodic intervals is carefully graded according to the intensity of the emotion to be expressed; but the fact that the idiom is stylized, as are the values of Lully's civilization, does not mean that it is insincere. As he matures, Lully tends to make his recitative more lyrical without sacrificing its fluidity, while he tends to submerge his arias in the recitative. In the last operas he almost discards the late baroque differentiation between aria, arioso, and recitative in favour of the early baroque's continuous arioso which absorbs into itself both recitative and lyrical song. The arias now give the impression of being merely the overflow of the recitative's more passionate moments. They are infrequent – not more than two or three marking the high points of the opera; when they do occur, they are sometimes derived from the *air de cour* (and therefore still fairly close to speech), sometimes brief strophic melodies with refrain. In no case are they allowed to assume a self-subsistent importance or to interrupt the flow of the voice's intimate relation to the poetry and the orchestra.

The orchestra on the other hand is given a more independent function. The stylized action offers plenty of opportunities for the introduction of *bergeries*, dances, and interludes, treated in an expansive style by both chorus and orchestra. The vocal and symphonic elements are clearly differentiated in the early operas; through the succession of *Alceste* (1674), *Thésée* (1675), *Atys* (1676), and *Isis* (1677) we can observe that the recitative acquires a more lyrical swell and continuity, while the symphonic elements are more closely linked to the recitative.

With the great operas of the last years of the Lully–Quinault collaboration, *Proserpine*, *Persée*, *Phaéton*, *Amadis*, *Roland*, and *Armide*, the French classical tradition comes musically to fruition. The heroic parts of the central characters are not only more lyrically rich, but roles of some psychological power. Moreover, while formal ballets, *bergeries* and marches in the line of the

66

Mlle. CHAMPMELEE.

dans Iphigenie en Aulide.

IV. Mme de la Champmeslé as Iphigenia, an engraving by
Delpeck, 1675. Lully's operatic recitative was directly influenced
by her vocal declamation – and perhaps by her deportment.

ballet de cour are still introduced these symphonic elements begin, too, to acquire psychological significance – to have bearing on the dramatic situations, on the desires and fears, joys and despairs, of the characters. Lully now frequently employs recitative accompanied by the orchestra, making the instruments underline the emotional implications of the scene; the battle pieces, thunderstorms and the like become less decoratively descriptive, more descriptive of 'states of mind'. In particular, the *sommeil* scenes in *Armide*, *Roland*, and *Amadis*, with their vague, vaporous murmur of muted violins, are almost impressionistic in effect, though the texture and structure remain meticulouly clear and the effect does not depend on the confusion of line and timbre, as does late nineteenth-century impressionism.

The combination, in passages such as these, of grand symmetrical architecture in the *symphonies*, with intimacy in the inflexions of the vocal line and the harmony of the inner parts, suggests some analogy with the gardens of Le Nôtre. For the broad, clear horizons of Le Nôtre's gardens are planned with geometrical precision, while within that lucid framework the detail is of extraordinary complexity; the total impression owes something to both the lucidity and the elaboration. A similar but still more significant analogy may be established between Lully's music and the painting of Poussin and Claude. Poussin, of course, died in 1665, before the great days of Louis XIV, and both he and Claude spent most of their careers in Rome – another instance of the relations between French and Italian culture in the seventeenth century. But we can regard them as more imbued with the Racinian spirit than the conventional court painters like Lebrun, who see only the surface *grandeur*; and Poussin at least was much admired at Versailles – Le Nôtre had a fine collection. Just as Lully groups his periods with ceremonial equilibrium, so the architectural proportions, the relations of part to part, in Poussin's classical mythology and Claude's landscapes are calculated with mathematical exactitude. On the other hand, the quality of the colour has sensuousness and translucency, just as has Lully's harmony in such things as the *scènes de sommeil*. But these colours are placed in balanced groups, put on smoothly, with no gradations, no impressionist flowing of one shade into another; the colours, even the sharply defined shadows, are part of the architecture. We remember Louis Testelin's remark which became one

68 of the key-phrases of the period – 'Le dessin est intellectuel, tandis

V. The Orangerie at Versailles, with horticultural arabesques by
Le Nôtre.

VI. The gardens and cascades at Sceaux, designed by Le Nôtre
for Colbert in 1673. Sceaux was later the seat of the Duc et
Duchesse de Maine. Couperin knew them well and was
intermittently a resident musician there.

que la couleur n'est que sensible'; and Poussin's statement of principle, which stands as an epitome of the ideals of the *grand siècle*: 'Mon naturel me contraint de chercher les choses bien ordonnées, fuyant la confusion qui m'est aussi contraire et ennemie comme est la lumière des obscures ténèbres.'

Exactly comparable with Poussin's architectural use of colour is Lully's use of the sensuous colour of his harmonies and orchestration. These elements he employs not in the intentionally blurred manner of the nineteenth-century orchestra, but in clearly defined groups, as part of his tonal architecture. The effervescent and resilient orchestration of Lully and La Lande, even in merely occasional works like the latter's *Simphonies des Noëls* or the in the strict sense superb *Musique pour les Soupers du Roi*, is the polar opposite of Wagner's 'harmonizing with the orchestra'. The spare linear texture, together with the sonorous brilliance which should characterize the chamber-music combinations of the time, has been buried as deeply beneath the incrustations of nineteenth-century academic convention as the luminosity of Poussin and Claude was buried beneath the incrustations of begrimed varnish. The re-created classical mythology, the heroic gestures in the painting, seem to have as great a weight of traditional experience behind them as does the stylized vocabulary of the dramatic poets. If Lully's last operas were produced with a sensitive appreciation of his idiom and with adequate resources, it is possible that we should find a comparable sublimity in his heroic gestures and noble perorations. The argument which maintains that Lully's operas are impractical for modern performance because they depend on out-moded fashions, does not seem to me impressive; so do the plays of Corneille, and even Racine. A producer and audience that cannot appreciate a sense of stylization are not worth their salt. The plots of the operas, *qua* plots, are, like the plots of Shakespeare's drama, of little consequence; what matters is what the music, or the poetry, does to them. It is interesting that the most remarkable instrumental and colouristic development in Lully's work coincides with the flowering of his lyrical speech. Compared with the Italians, the lines in the last operas are still quiet and close to speech; but we can hardly deny to the composer of the famous *Bois épais* the command, when he wanted it, of a melodic line of distinction.

Despite its restraint the work of Lully was considered, by the   71 contemporary opinion of Bonnet's *Histoire de la Musique* of 1715, to be moving enough to melt hearts and to make the very rocks groan with him; while speaking of *Alceste* Mme de Sévigné remarked 'On joue jeudi l'opéra qui est un prodige de beauté, il y a des endroits de la musique qui ont mérité des larmes. Je ne suis pas seule à ne les pouvoir soutenir, l'âme de Mme de la Fayette en est alarmée.' It is also worth noting that when the last great operas were presented in Paris at the public theatre they enjoyed a spectacular popular success; *Phaéton* was even called '*l'opéra du peuple*'.* This certainly suggests that the court culture was not as out of touch with French life as is sometimes suggested; if it had been, it could hardly have given so triumphant a manifestation of vitality. It is precisely this zest combined with elegance that Lully expresses in his last work, *Acis et Galathée*, a return, after the cycle of tragic operas, to the pastoral convention. This beautiful work, the most obvious candidate for revival, unites the rhythmic exuberance and melodic *allure* of the early ballets with the linear subtlety and architectural gravity of the late operas. It is the ripe fruit of a great civilization; and it suggests the direction in which the opera is to tend after Lully's death. In its more amiable and intimate atmosphere it is also of all Lully's works the closest to Couperin.

From the start the opera had not been without opponents. To the logical French mind, absurdities which might be tolerated in a superficial entertainment were inappropriate in a music drama which purported to be a representation of life. La Bruyère, Boileau, and St Evremond, among other celebrated people, deplored the frivolity of the spectacles, the incredibility of the recitatives. Yet in many ways, as we have seen, Lully's aesthetic was complementary to Boileau's; and in general the classical stylization vindicated itself. Marmontel's defence that 'la musique y fait le charme du merveilleux; le merveilleux y fait la vraisemblance de la musique', seemed convincing so long as the opera dealt with themes parallel to those of the classical drama. Lully's triumph was complete; even the acid St Evremond made an exception in his favour:

---

* 'Et je vous apprends, mon petit cousin, qu' *Armide* est l'opéra des femmes; *Atys* l'opéra du Roi; *Phaéton* l'opéra du peuple; *Isis* l'opéra des musiciens. Mais enfin revenons au recitatif. C'est principalement par là que Lully est au dessus de nos autres musiciens . . .'

Would you know what an opera is? I'll tell you, it is an odd medley of Poetry and Musick, wherein the Poet and Musician, equally confined one by the other, take a World of Pains to compose a wretched Performance. . . . It remains that I give my advice in general for all Comedies where any singing is used; and that is to leave to the Poet's discretion the management of the Piece. The Musician is to follow the Poet's direction; only in my opinion, Lully is to be exempted, who knows the Passions and enters further into the Heart of man than the Authors themselves.

When the opera finally fell out of favour it was not because it was stylized but because the stylization ceased to have a purpose. In the last years of Louis's reign, *la gloire* was in decline, festivities were no longer officially in fashion. In the circumstances the patriotic celebrations with which the opera had always been associated were hardly in the best of taste. Mme de Maintenon encouraged Louis to regard the opera as frivolous; it became so when it no longer had the backing of the quasi-religious cult of the state.

As soon as the King had definitely thrown over the opera, the rationalist Boileau and the devout Arnauld and Bossuet came out into the open with their moral denunciations of it. Despite its generic and structural relation to the noble classical tragedy, the opera was regarded with disapproval by these men because it tended to idealize love at the expense of duty. The main theme was considered to be lubricious; while the incidental divertissements were condemned because they were frivolous and trivial. Ironically enough, when the opera decayed with the *grand goût* of the Roi Soleil, it was precisely the divertissement that once more took its place. As culture became more decentralized, the divertissement became more a private party than a state function; entertainments were less sumptuous, but more exquisite. The revival of the opera-ballet, instead of the tragic opera, 'sympathise', as a contemporary writer put it, 'avec l'impatience française';* the 'moral' implications of the theatre music of the classic age had been lost because 'le public n'est plus ouvert à une certaine

---

* Roy: *Lettre sur l'opéra*, in *La Nouvelle Bigarrure*, quoted by Masson in *L'Opéra de Rameau*.

With reference to the changing cultural atmosphere, the title of one of the *entrées* in Campra's delightful *Fêtes Vénitiennes* of 1710 seems especially significant; it is called *Le Triomphe de la Folie sur la Raison*.

73

sensibilité et il est bien plus flatté des choses agréables à ses yeux que de celles qui touchent le cœur.'

Yet this new phase is not simply, or at all, a decline, as the above rather extravagant quotation from Destouches would suggest. For it goes together with the other manifestations of a more intimate and familiar culture which we mentioned in the last chapter; if it means a loss in some of the virtues of Versailles's autocracy, it is also a gain in so far as it applies to a wider, more centrally Parisian, public. So the vivacious pastoralism of the opera ballet of Campra, Mouret and Destouches is the link between the court opera of Lully and the next great opera composer Rameau who, in the early part of his operatic career at least, wrote for the Parisian public.

Campra is especially interesting from this point of view, for although his music has plenty of aristocratic finesse it has also a popular *allure*, a sun-baked vitality, which seems to spring from his Provençal origin. His exuberant sense of physical movement and of orchestral colour makes him perhaps the most enchanting of all dance composers. Something of this resilience is found even in his fine religious motets, which resemble Couperin's in mating the French and Italian *goût*. Mouret, 'musicien des Grâces, si gai, si vif,' as Daquin said, was also a Provençal and manifests, in his *Divertissements pour la Comédie Italienne* and his *Suites des Simphonies pour des violons, des hautbois et des cors de chasse*, a comparable popular buoyancy of rhythm and glittering clarity of orchestration. De Noinville, in his *Histoire de l'opéra en France* of 1767, said that 'tant des ouvrages de Mouret ont un goût de légèreté qui semblent répondre à son tempérament, et ils ont toujours plu extrèmement aux connoisseurs.'

Destouches has less vigour, but the seductive emotionalism of his harmonies likewise testifies to the more relaxed atmosphere. His originality is his charm, though his unconventional harmonic progressions may often be due to his technical inexperience. He was a rich dilettante and a pupil of Campra; his work shows a slender but remarkable talent exactly suited to the temper of his age. These three composers have an easy geniality which is seldom found in the music of the great days of Louis XIV's reign; and of Couperin, as of Rameau after him, we may say that the highest point of French musical culture since the late Middle Ages comes at a time when it is not too late to remember

and live by the old classical virtues while avoiding, in the new more intimate environment, the dangers of autocratic rigidity.

The first twenty years of Couperin's working life correspond with the last twenty of Louis's reign. During this period, therefore, he was called upon to provide music that could soothe in the relative quiet of chamber or salon, that could enliven the ceremony of eating, that could elevate or inspire in the ritual of the church. Thus he did not follow Lully in composing ballets and operas. He concentrated on domestic music, concert music, and church music, fields which had been cultivated in Lully's day only as accessories to the all-important theatre music. By the time of the Regency he had discovered that the forms of chamber music suited him best, for he made no attempt to follow Campra and Destouches into the more relaxed delights of the ballet-opera. It is hardly necessary to add that, while Couperin did not write any theatre music, all his musical thought is influenced both by the divertissement and by recollections of Lully's art. Couperin's library included no fewer than twenty scores of contemporary operas. The pastoral and mythological subjects, the dances, the sonorous texture of Lully's orchestra, Lully's combination of architectural dignity with subtle sensuousness of detail – all these are latent in Couperin's work. The harpsichord *ordres* might even be considered as a series of miniature ballets, expressed in absolute instrumental form.

But the change from a technique of theatre music to a chamber-music idiom involved certain developments which Lully had not fully anticipated. The elder man had shown how it was possible to weld the heterogeneous elements of a theatre music into a convincing organism. He had created the structure of the operatic overture, and shown a grasp of tonal relationships, somewhat before the comparable work of Alessandro Scarlatti; his influence is unmistakable both in the early overtures of Scarlatti and in those of Cesti. But it was the Italians again who, at the end of the century, were to make the classically final reconciliation of Italian harmonic drama with the French sense of physical movement and architectural proportion. It was the Italians who were to indicate with classical economy how dances could be imbued with intense emotion, how dramatic harmony could be given formal discipline, and how the two could be combined in an entity which could stand by itself as 'absolute' music without reference to a theatrical framework.

Here we see the significance of the vogue for the Italian violin 75 sonata, which was at its height when Lully's death in 1687 removed the main impediment to a renewed enthusiasm for things Italian. For the Italian sonata might be said to summarize in instrumental microcosm the technique of baroque opera. It is fitting, therefore, that our survey of the position as Couperin found it should close with this brief reference to a convention to which composers all over Europe felt obliged to pay homage. For the moment the reference must suffice. We shall have occasion to discuss the technique in detail when we come to Couperin's own experiments in the idiom. His first work, on the other hand, does not greatly depend on this 'modern' Italian technique. It is rather a tribute to his forebears, a recognition of the nature of his inheritance.

Part II

The Work

Mon naturel me contraint de chercher les choses bien
ordonnés, fuyant la confusion qui m'est aussi contraire
et ennemie comme est la lumière des obscures ténèbres.

POUSSIN

La clarté orne les pensées profondes.

VAUVENARGUES

Polissez-le sans cesse et le repolissez: soyez-vous à
vous-même un sévère critique.

BOILEAU

Chapter Five

The Organ Masses

Starting just after the heyday of French classical civilization, and in his youth at least unaware of the impending collapse, Couperin can never have been in any doubt as to the kind of music he wanted to write. His first work, however, partly owing to the circumstances in which it was written, pays a tribute to the long tradition which lay behind him by being deliberately an exercise in a manner of the past. The two organ masses were published when Couperin was twenty-one, four years after he had become organist of St Gervais. The first of them, *À l'usage ordinaire des paroisses pour les fêtes solemnelles*, was presumably employed by Couperin at St Gervais; the other, *Propre pour les Convents* (sic) *de Religieux et Religieuses*, was probably written for some specific community. These works do not betray much conscious modernism; but like Purcell's string fantasias, composed at the same age, they reveal more about their creator and the society he lived in than he may have realized. Though their modernism is implicit rather than explicit, it is none the less real.

Like most of the work of the seventeenth-century organ schools, the masses were intended as music for religious ritual. Yet as far back as the early years of the century we are aware of a gradual change in instrumental church music. The supreme figures of the baroque organ school, Titelouze, Sweelinck, Frescobaldi, Bull, and Gibbons, all follow Cabezon in starting from the vocal conventions of sixteenth-century polyphony. But their use of a keyboard, and of a technique derived from the fingers, suggests harmonic and figurative developments which, despite the experiments of a Gesualdo, were beyond the scope of the human voice. Bull, Frescobaldi, and Sweelinck exhibit this passionate intensity in harmony and figuration more consistently than Gibbons or Titelouze; they are closer in spirit to the violent humanistic genius of Monteverdi. But all the early baroque 79 organ composers used this technique because the impulses behind them were changing. The crowning glory of European organ music – the line stretching unbroken from the early baroque composers to Buxtehude and Bach – appeared when vocal music was forced to learn a new technique. Though they did not know it, the early organists were on the way from a religious outlook to the ethical humanism of the eighteenth century; from polyphony, to diatonic harmonic structures founded on the dance, not the voice. And beyond those harmonic structures lies the instrumental 'drama' of opposing key centres, and the great world of classical sonata music.

If one compares Gibbons's fantasias with those of Purcell, which are in the same tradition, one may observe a clear example of this tendency. Gibbons's harmonies are often audacious enough; but he remains sixteenth-century in approach in that he is primarily interested in the flow of his lines and regards the harmonies as a consequence, albeit not a fortuitous one, of that flow. Purcell tends to use shorter, more easily memorable, phrases so that the grouping of his themes in sequence produces a more rhetorical effect. The fourth four-part fantasia creates, through its chromaticisms, dissonant suspensions and overlapping false relations, a more directly 'personal' and dramatic effect than anything in Gibbons. It might be a lament from one of Purcell's operas; it has even been called Wagnerian! The balance between melodic and harmonic organization, characteristic of sixteenth-century polyphony, is being superseded by a preoccupation with the poignant phrase and expressive harmony *per se*. These harmonic elements could be given coherence only through some new type of organization, such as we discussed in general terms in the last chapter, involving the dance and the stage.

Purcell did not succeed, for reasons for which he was not personally responsible, in establishing such a system. When Couperin started work in Paris the form had already been developed in the opera of Lully. Purcell's fantasias represent the more or less unconscious emergence of impulses which the composer, during the remainder of his short life, must attempt to subdue and organize. Couperin's organ masses may start from a similar point, but they contain other elements that help us to understand why, in France, a great classical and operatic tradition survived; whereas, after Purcell, the English tradition withered.

Besides containing much lovely music, the two organ masses

are thus a case-book demonstrating the growth of the French classical tradition. They amalgamate, without any immature experimentalism, the many different tendencies observable in seventeenth-century French organ music. Basically, there is the austere, religious polyphonic technique of the plainsong fantasia, inherited from the great Titelouze; it was from the German Protestant complement to this tradition that J. S. Bach started. Then there are passages which use chromaticism and dissonant suspensions to convey a peculiar impression of the dissolution of the senses. This technique is more extremely employed by Gigault and Marchand, and we have already referred to its appearance in Purcell. It is significantly used by the subjective and emotional Frescobaldi to accompany the most mystical moment of the Catholic ritual, the Elevation of the Host. The greatest and most celebrated of all examples of the technique is, of course, the Crucifixus of Bach's B minor Mass.

At a further extreme from these chromatic passages there are movements showing a lively sense of physical movement, which Couperin learned from the ballet. This links up with the more naïve popular type of *air de cour* such as the *vaudevilles*; as one may see more obviously in the relatively unsubtle work of Nicolas Le Bègue. From the more sophisticated aspects of the *air de cour*, and from the clavecinists and lutenists, Couperin and the other organ composers derived a symmetrical graciousness in their melodies and some conventions of ornamentation. And over all there is a concern for the proportions of the whole which he learned from the theatre music of Lully. Most of these contributory features will be discussed in more appropriate contexts in later chapters of this book. In this estimate of Couperin's start, it is the synthesizing process that we are most interested in.

The form of the masses is simple. Since they were intended for liturgical use, any elaborate musical development would have been unsuitable. The Catholic Church in France did not allow the organ the musical importance it came to have in Protestant Germany; liturgically, it had to fill in any gaps in the service with brief comments or variations on the important plainsong motives.★

★ This convention still survived in 1770, as we may see from Dr Burney's patronizing description of a service at Notre Dame: 'Though this was so great a festival, the organ accompanied but little. The chief use of it was to play over the chant before it was sung, all through the Psalms. Upon enquiring of a young abbé,

Couperin's couplets on the Kyrie, Gloria, Offertory, Benedictus, Elevation, Sanctus, and Agnus Dei have, like those of his contemporaries, mostly lost their connection with the plainsong base; they are short pieces, identified by a phrase of the Latin text, some in the old fugal idiom, others more operatic in technique. Most of the couplets in the minor end on the dominant, suggesting their functional position as a preparation for some part of the service. We may note that Couperin and his contemporaries usually employ the term couplet for the episodes of the rondeau. The use of the term in the organ masses reflects their function in an *alternation* liturgical performance, with organ and plainsong alternating. The (normally unstated) theme is the plainsong melody.

In discussing the music we shall in the main follow the catalogue of its constituent elements, given earlier in the chapter. All the real plainsong fantasias, those directly rooted in the old technique, occur in the grander work, the *Messe Solemnelle*. Of course, Couperin's plainsong pieces are not monumental music like the tremendous hymns of Titelouze. Those are the culmination of a great religious age; their polyphonic embroideries around the plainsong stem attain great intensity, but even at their most baroque they remain cathedral music as much as the masses and motets of Lassus, with never a hint of theatricality. Some of the finest movements in Titelouze's *œuvre* (and he seems to me one of the most profound and noble of all keyboard composers) have a pure, other-worldly suavity in the vocal contours of their lines which is almost medieval in feeling, closer to Josquin than to anything in the later sixteenth century.† We may mention as one

---

whom I took with me as a nomenclator, what this was called, "C'est proser" ('Tis prosing), he said. And it should seem as if our word prosing came from this dull and heavy manner of recital.' (*The Present State of Music in France.*)

† From this point of view, it is interesting that Titelouze deprecated modal alteration and encouraged rhythmic freedom as a means of achieving variety: 'Quant au changement du mode, je croy qu'il faudroit plustot changer de mouvement, haster aux paroles voilentes et furieuses et tarder aux tristes et pesantes, car pour le changement de mode il est défendu par les lois musicales en même ouvrage, et le changement de mouvement est permis et a un grand effet par la variété qu'il y apporte.' (Correspondence with Mersenne, 1622.)

Titelouze must have acquired a thorough grounding in the old style vocal polyphony of the Franco-Flemish school at the Walloon Jesuit College of St Omer, where he received his elaborate education. On the other hand he would also have become familiar with more advanced instrumental techniques. The college was much frequented by English Catholics escaping persecution, and it seems reasonably certain that Titelouze must have met Bull and Peter Philips.

instance a truly celestial fantasy on *Ave Maris Stella*, which employs a more or less continuous pedal point:

Nowhere does he indulge in the chromaticisms and recitative-like rhapsodic passages that we find in, say, Frescobaldi's toccata elevations. It is noteworthy, however, that although Titelouze adheres always to the medieval plainsong-variation convention, and theoretically at least to the scholastic basis of the church modes, his concern for an effective keyboard technique constantly leads him into devices (chains of suspended sevenths, for instance), which give a curiously rich and 'modern' tonal impression:

Now it is this polyphonic-harmonic aspect of Titelouze's technique which Couperin develops in a more extreme form in his plainsong pieces and fugues. The rich sequential sevenths in the last few bars of the tiny *Deo Gratias* that forms the epilogue to the *Messe Solemnelle* are a beautiful example of this; and the yearning upward lift of the diminished fourth in the little fugato motive illustrates the more 'harmonic' nature of Couperin's linear writing:

83

A comparable and highly impressive example of this harmonic-contrapuntal technique is contained in the five organ fugues on one subject, by d'Anglebert, with their powerful false relations, parallel sevenths, and appoggiaturas:

Another composer who was partial to the sequential technique was the organist of Chartres, Giles Jullien, who employed it sometimes with nobility, as in the *Prélude du Premier Ton*, sometimes with a rather cloying pathos:

Couperin, however, never loses his balance. Later, a merging of this harmonic-contrapuntal idiom with the overlapping suspensions which he learned from the Italian violin sonatas is to produce beautiful results not only in chamber music but also in church motets and elevations.

These passages represent the basis of Couperin's technique in organ music; and they are, as we have seen, half-way between polyphony and harmonic thought. We next come to the passages and movements which are ostensibly harmonic in effect, depending mainly on chromaticisms and dissonant suspensions. They are perhaps best regarded as an intensification of the basic contrapuntal-harmonic technique, since although they are not usually fugal, they are always the product of fluent part-writing. The point of departure is the same; only the harmonic impact of the passage takes the centre of the stage, ousting the linear element.

The *Premier Couplet du Gloria* is a fine example from the *Messe pour les Convents*, almost identical with a passage in one of Purcell's fantasias; one chromatic chord resolves on to another until they sink to rest on a serene major third:

Still more remarkable is the whole of the Elevation from the same mass. There is nothing here which is astounding in the manner of the contemporary organist Louis Marchand, whose suspended dissonances are so elliptical as to produce an almost Tristanesque dissolution of tonality, paradoxically violent in its emotional effect, considering that the piece is so consistently quiet:

But Couperin's idiom is as a whole more coherent and mature. Though Couperin's dissonances are intense, there is nothing emotionally virulent in his style, as there is in the work of Marchand and Gigault, or in the earlier generation, Bull, Sweelinck, or Frescobaldi. The acridity of Couperin's dissonances is rounded off in the flow and the warm spacing of the parts. Those of Gigault are uncompromising, and at times even ferocious, as witness this coruscation of sevenths, ninths, and seconds:

Other powerful composers such as Boyvin, or elegiac ones such as Dumont, occasionally have a similar muscular quality:

What counterbalances the emotional harmonies in Couperin's organ music is the lucid diatonicism of his melodies, which have a simplicity and freshness perhaps derived, deep down, from French folk song and its relation to the French language. The elegance of the clavecinists here meets the austere passion of the organ composers, so that the 'linked sweetness' of the double suspensions is reconcilable with the sonorous simplicity of a piece like the sixth couplet of the Gloria, *Dialogue sur la Voix*

86

humaine. The poise of this – the pure yet flexible line, the clear yet fluid part-writing – gives the music a luminosity which is, if possible, a refinement on the most fragrant triple-rhythmed melodies of the lutenists and Chambonnières. The tender strophic tune and the diatonic harmonic period appear to be related to the Italian operatic aria; yet how completely different is its mood from that of the slow airs of Handel:

This music has a spring-like innocence, a *premier matin du monde* atmosphere which is also supremely civilized; we may compare it, perhaps, with Racine's *Esther*. The couplet is interesting, too, in that it shows how Couperin's voluptuous delicacy, which like Lully's is capable of a theatrical interpretation, is not irreconcilable with the religious roots of his art in sixteenth-century polyphony. Both spiritually and technically he stands between the melodically (and religiously) founded Titelouze and the harmonically (and socially) centred Rameau. We shall note a more significant instance of this compromise when we examine Couperin's vocal church music.

The chromatic harmonic technique of emotional drama, in the organ pieces of Marchand no less than in the madrigals of Gesualdo, had been disruptive of the old conception of tonality rather than re-creative. It was assimilated into a coherent form of theatre music only through a preoccupation with harmonic clauses based on the symmetry of the dance such as we find principally in the works of Rameau and Handel. Couperin is neither Handelian, nor disruptively baroque. His methods of achieving a balance between melodic flexibility and harmonic symmetry are more mature than those of Purcell, and in some ways comparable with those of Bach.

Some couplets, particularly the trumpet pieces like the 87

delightful fourth couplet of the Gloria of the *Messe pour les Convents*, are simply symmetrical in their dance rhythm, although their lucid harmonic periods are enlivened by contrapuntal treatment. But more subtle pieces, for instance the beautiful eighth couplet of the same Gloria, achieve an equilibrium between the calm fluidity of the part writing, the melancholy of the chromaticisms which the flexible parts create, and the regularity of the underlying metrical pulse. As in so much of Bach, the level flow of the rhythm and the tranquil arching of the lines 'distances' the melancholy of the chromaticisms, divests them of any subjective emotionalism which would be inapposite to a music conceived for religious ritual:

In other pieces the symmetry of the pulse is counteracted by the unmetrical flow of a baroquely ornamented solo line, the ornaments playing an integral part in the line's expressiveness. (See the Elevation of the *Messe pour les Convents*.) In the complementary movement from the other mass, both elements, fluid chromaticisms and ornamented solo part, are combined together with a regular rhythmic pulse:

This method is more maturely developed in many of the greatest of Bach's choral preludes and in the finest of Couperin's later church music. Significantly the technique is less used during Couperin's most Italianate period.

The way in which these elements can be brought together to make a musical-theatrical form on a fairly extensive scale is revealed in the two *Offertoires*, the biggest pieces in the collections. That of the *Messe pour les Convents* is especially remarkable. It is modelled on the operatic overture, with a massive introduction embodying chains of harsh suspensions, rooted in vocal technique but much more aggressive in their instrumental form; a plaintive fugal section, with piquantly dissonant entries; and a virile, contrapuntally treated gigue to conclude. This last movement uses clear dominant-tonic key relations, but its contrapuntal treatment of them is less harmonically formalized than the dance movement structure of the eighteenth-century suite. In this respect the piece as a whole is closer to the keyboard suites of say, Kuhnau, which resemble Lully's overture in that they occupy with dignity and beauty a position somewhere between fugal polyphony, operatic lyricism, and the dance. It lives without confusion in both a religious and an operatic world.

Nicolas de Grigny, the greatest of Couperin's contemporaries in the French organ school after Titelouze, shows the same compromise between religious polyphony, fluid baroque ornamentation, and clear architectural period; so does the powerful if less profound Du Mage, and the subtly refined Roberday. It is interesting that the organ composers who come out 'progressively' on the side of the new, secular, dance-like elements are musically the least satisfying. They have relinquished the old tradition without having learned how to deal adequately, in a purely instrumental form, with the new. Even a composer with a boldly experimental talent such as Marchand displays in the slow chromatic piece previously referred to, or in the richly 89 dissonant *Plein Jeu* with the double-pedal part, fails on the whole to achieve a coherent idiom; while Gigault, who has a really impressive technique and a vigorous personality, makes no attempt to reach the paradoxical mingling of voluptuousness and spirituality which is the subtlest feature of the work of Couperin and de Grigny. The lesser men, such as Le Bègue, can substitute for the old polyphonic craftsmanship nothing but sequences of (often very charming) dance tunes. The final secularization of the tradition occurs in the Noëls and other pieces of Claude Balbastre, which although often in two parts are unequivocally dances built on symmetrical harmonic periods, with figuration and ornamentation as appropriate to the harpsichord as it is inapposite to the organ. The lutenist school declined when the harpsichord composers took over many of the essentials of lute style. The harpsichordists absorbed some features of organ polyphony also, but in this case there was little direct continuity because the technique of the organ, unlike that of the lute, is fundamentally opposed to that of the clavecin. Thus Couperin is the climax to the classical French organ school and even he wrote all his work for the instrument in his early twenties.

But Couperin was a man of the future as well as of the past. It was for him to show what the dance tune could be made to yield, for him to develop his work towards a classical stability. It was with this in mind that he turned, after the composition of the organ masses, to a deliberate study of the technique of the Italian trio sonata for violins and continuo.

Chapter Six

The Two-Violin Sonatas

Il faut écouter souvent de la musique de tous les goûts. . . .
Embrasser un goût national plutôt qu'un autre, c'est prouver
qu'on est encore bien novice dans l'art.

RAMEAU

At the end of the seventeenth century the Italian trio sonata was
accepted everywhere as the supremely fashionable musical convention. If it was 'modern', however, it was not revolutionary.
There was no element in it that was altogether new; its importance lay in the fact that it provided a synthesis of tendencies
which had been developing all though the century. These trends
towards technical lucidity accompany, of course, the trend
towards an autocratic, highly stylized order in society.

There were two types of instrumental sonata, the sonata da
chiesa, and the sonata da camera. As its name suggests, the
former had the closer links with the past. It was normally
written for violins, lute, and organ, and comprised a slow prelude, a fugal *allegro*, a lyrical *grave*, and a more dance-like *presto*.
All the movements inclined to imitative treatment; and the very
fact that the composers favoured the two-violin medium rather
than the solo violin suggests a reluctance wholly to relinquish
polyphonic methods in favour of the homophonic continuo.

There are still frequent passages, in the classical Corelli as well
as the more intrepid Purcell, in which the lines produce the most
dramatic intensity through chromaticisms, false relations, and
overlapping figurations, similar to those in the toccata technique
of the brilliant Frescobaldi or Gabrieli. In general, however, the
tendency which we have already noticed in the organ masses, for
the polyphony to be ordered by harmonic considerations rather
than itself producing the harmony, is here more explicit. The
polyphonic element is represented by the solo instruments, the
homophonic element by the continuo which articulates the 91

harmonic periods not, as in the opera, in accordance with a series of events on a stage, but with a musical logic of its own. This logic graded all diatonic chords in accordance with their distance from a tonic centre, distance being measured by reference to the cycle of fifths. Certain harmonic procedures – such as the use of chains of suspended sevenths and to a lesser degree 6 : 3 chords, or the use of the dissonant diminished seventh chord to gather tension before the resolving dominant-tonic cadence – gradually became accepted methods of defining tonality. To this definition the soloists' polyphony had to be adjusted.

Gabrieli had used a melodically generative technique whereby the initial subject grows into other themes, so that the movement often ends with five or six related motives. The sonata composers employ a basically similar technique, but seek for greater unity and cogency, usually restricting themselves to a mono- or bi-thematic treatment. It is true that they sometimes, when they use two themes, suggest a contrast of mood between them, thus remotely anticipating the development of 'shape' music in the second half of the eighteenth century. They never attempt, however, to investigate the possibilities of contrasted tonalities. Even to music of the late baroque period the dramatic tonal contrasts associated with the Viennese sonata are entirely foreign. The late baroque sonata still functions by way of a continual melodic generation and expansion; it differs from the early baroque principle of *division* and variation mainly because the continuous expansion of the initial motive or motives is now ordered by the scheme of tonal relations based on the cycle of fifths. The growth of the figuration moves through a series of fresh starts in different keys, usually the dominant, sub-mediant, sub-dominant, super-tonic, and relative minor or major, the dominant having an importance equal with but not greater than the other keys. The structure is essentially architectural rather than dramatic.

The other type of sonata, the sonata da camera for one or two violins usually with harpsichord continuo and string bass, was not radically different from the current dance suite. This will be discussed in detail in a later chapter; here we must note that the dance movements in the sonatas showed an increasingly mature understanding of the principles of tonal relationship and, as a corollary, an increasing independence of the dance itself. In achieving this independence the sonata da camera borrowed

many characteristics from the sonata da chiesa, into which convention it in turn introduced a more dance-like secularity. The
two types soon became but vaguely differentiated. The sonata da
chiesa acquired airy dance elements and lyrical passion from the
theatrical inclinations of the sonata da camera, and the latter
stiffened its backbone with some of the contrapuntal vitality of
the sonata da chiesa; just as baroque opera incorporated many
elements of religious polyphony and was then reabsorbed into the
church. By Corelli's time the two sonata conventions, though
still flexible, had more or less settled down as follows: Sonata da
chiesa; slow overture (majestic and inclined to the polyphonic),
free fugal movement (canzona), slow air (usually in 3 : 2 with
some imitation and smooth chordal progressions), and finally a
fugued dance. Sonata da camera; slow overture, canzona or
allemande or coranto (the dance, particularly if an allemande,
inclining to contrapuntal treatment), slow air or sarabande, quick
dance (often a gigue, and often quasi-fugal). In his works for solo
violin Bach applies the term sonata only to the sonata da chiesa;
the da camera sonatas he describes as partitas. His solo violin
works thus offer a neat illustration of the difference between the
two types.

As the two kinds of sonata merge into one another, one sees
that the sonata owes its historical importance to the fact that it
mates the technique of voice and dance. The violin can do things
which the voice cannot, yet it is not anti-vocal in conception. The
violin line modifies the traditional vocal phrases by the introduction of intervals, such as the diminished seventh or augmented
fourth, which have a high degree of tension and passion; but it
does not deny vocal principles. All the contemporary com-
mentators refer to the cantabile character of Corelli's playing;
Martinelli points out in his *Lettre familiari e critiche* of 1758 that
Corelli's unenterprising partiality for the middle register of his
instrument was due to his desire to preserve a singing sweetness
and naturalness of tone. He wanted his violin to sound like
someone singing with ease and purity; the very high and very low
registers of the instrument were used only rarely and for some
special effect, as an opera composer might, in exceptional circumstances, demand from his singers a shriek or a growl. One might
also say that during the later baroque period the violin became the
moulding influence on operatic vocal line itself. In the operatic
arias and the bel-canto-like slow movements of the violin sonatas, 93

the ornaments with which violinist and virtuoso singer embellish their lines both counteract the rigidity of the harmonic periods and help to build up the climax in the line itself; there is a beautiful example in the largo of Handel's D major sonata.

Only gradually did the violin composers overcome a deep-rooted distrust of the simple symmetrical 'tune', which had for so long been regarded as unworthy of inclusion in a serious composition. But even in fugal movements a more dance-like symmetry becomes noticeable. Fugal entries increasingly concentrate on a simple metrical motive with clear harmonic implications, and there is a leaning towards the 'thematic development' of a pithy phrase in place of the technique of lyrical growth. This procedure may have been suggested by the operatic splitting up of words for dramatic effect. On the other hand, the violin composers of Corelli's school do not approach the harmonically systematized fugue of the middle eighteenth century. Their fugal subjects are 'harmonic' in character, but their method of treating the subjects preserves much of the seventeenth-century freedom. Perhaps one might say that there is about an equal proportion of old-fashioned, quasi-vocal fugues 'instrumentalized', and of bright symmetrical dances 'fugued'.

Formally, as we have seen, the sonatas usually start from the old method of melodic generation and expansion. The influence of the dance, however, leads to frequent phrase-groupings in sequence, to repetitions of phrases in related keys, and, still more important, to a repetition of material at the ends of the sections. From this point of view there is an interesting development in the dance forms. The majority are in binary structure, state their melodic material and develop it with contrapuntal passage-work to a close in or 'on' the dominant, thus concluding the first section. The second section repeats the material in the same order, only starting from the dominant and working back to the tonic. On the other hand, a later type of dance movement, much favoured by Domenico Scarlatti, has a similar first section, then a section of development or mild contrast in related keys, then a restatement of the original material in the original key at the end. This is a remote anticipation of the 'inveterately dramatic' sonata form of Haydn and Mozart. In both Bach and Couperin the more archaic convention still holds its own with the new. This latter type of ternary structure should not be confused with ternary *da capo* form, which has a first section ending in the *tonic*, middle section of development in related keys, and restatement of the original material in the original key. The conclusion of the first section in the tonic deprives the *da capo* form of any sense of progression, and makes it more suitable for reflective and meditative than for dramatic expression; many of Bach's arias in the cantatas are a case in point. The sonatas have a few movements constructed on this relatively static principle, but they are not frequent.

The technique of the violin sonata is usually associated with Corelli, though he did not 'invent' it. It was rather an autonomous growth, fine sonatas of the da chiesa type having appeared many years before Corelli's volumes were accepted as the classical prototype. Continuity with the earlier tradition, as represented by composers such as Marini and Mezzaferrata, as well as musicians of other nationality such as the brilliant Biber and Rosenmüller, is a matter of some significance: for one cannot perform baroque trio sonatas convincingly unless one remembers that, stemming from the melting pot of baroque adventure and enterprise, they fuse conventions which are richly disparate. Rosenmüller's superb E minor sonata, for instance, illustrates all the features of the early baroque sonata: a massive slow introduction, a second movement half-way between vocal polyphony and the operatic aria, a transitional movement derived from operatic recitative, and a fugued dance to conclude. The soaring polyphony of the violin lines complements the stability of the continuo's harmony; the theatrical gestures of operatic arioso balance the gravity of contrapuntal discipline. Simultaneously, trio sonatas are successors to the archaic convention of the contrapuntal fantasia and miniature operas in instrumental form. They are at once consolidatory and embryonic, in ways demonstrated in my analysis of Couperin's *La Visionnaire* sonata (see Addendum I).

If Corelli did not invent the sonata, however, there is some excuse for associating it with his name in that he did, in his scrupulously pure and polished examples, give it its classical form. His work has both lyrical ardour and incisive precision; and this union of qualities prepares the way for the great classical baroque composers whose work for his instrument and in an idiom in part derived from him, may be said to surpass his work in sublimity and power. These composers are Vivaldi, J. S. Bach, Leclair, and the Couperin of *L'Impériale*.

There were three main reasons why Corelli's sonata attained so remarkable a popularity in France. One reason, as we have seen, was that its technique could not be ignored by any European composer who wished to create a vitally 'contemporary' music. Another reason was intellectual snobbery, for even people who could not understand the implications of the sonata realized that so advanced and sophisticated a society as the French could not afford to be musically behind the times. And the third reason was that there was much in Corelli's sonatas that the French could recognize as a native product. It is hardly surprising, considering the high point to which Lully had developed the forms of theatre music, that Corelli should have made use of many facets of Lully's work in his classical sonata. Many of Corelli's gavottes and minuets have a flavour of the French theatre, and, particularly in the concerti grossi, there are movements – for instance the largo and allegro of the third concerto – which derive directly from the Lullian overture. Corelli acquired a thorough knowledge of Lully's work from the francophile Muffat, and cannot himself have approved of the animosity which was later shown by the partisans of both the French and Italian cause.*

We have seen that during the *grand siècle*, in France as in England, the violin had been regarded as a somewhat ribald instrument; as Peter Warlock pointed out, the attitude of cultivated musicians to the violin was similar to the attitude of such people to the saxophone today. The viol, lute, and clavecin were the instruments of polite society; the violin, could be used for dance music, on festive occasions, and in operatic tutti when a considerable noise was required. But even as late as 1682 Father Ménestrier referred to the violin as 'quelque peu tapageur', while six years earlier, in England, Mace had written: 'You may add to your Press a Pair of Violins to be in Readiness for any Extraordinary, Jolly and jocund Consort Occasion: *But never use them, but with this Proviso.*' We should remember, of course, that Mace was a valetudinarian in his attitude to contemporary music.

---

* It can, however, have been only in his late work that Corelli was *conscious* of the influence of Lully. We remember the well-known story of Handel's exasperation with Corelli, when the Italian performed with inadequate passion one of Handel's works – Handel is said to have snatched the fiddle out of Corelli's hands; whereupon Corelli, retorted, 'Ma, caro Sassone, questa musica è nel stilo francese, di ch'io non m'intendo.'

It was by way of the church that the violin became respectable in France; for an instrument that could be used to accompany the cantatas of a Carissimi was clearly worthy of serious attention. The cantata was related to the sonata da chiesa, which could also be performed in church; when once the French public had observed the dignity which Corelli could give to the instrument there was no more ground for suspicion. Then, in 1705, even Lecerf de la Viéville, the bitterest opponent of Italianism, could admit that although the violin 'n'est pas noble en France, mais enfin un homme de condition qui s'avise d'en jouer ne déroge pas'. The vogue spread with phenomenal vigour. 'Quelle joie, quelle bonne opinion de soi-même n'a pas un homme qui connoît quelque chose au cinquième Opera de Corelli,' complained Lecerf de la Viéville, in despair. Couperin's innocent deception in producing his early sonatas under an Italian name, as described previously, had shown which way the wind was blowing. Soon, 'cette fureur de composer des sonates à la manière italienne' obsessed almost all French composers, and from 1700 a continuous stream of sonatas appeared, culminating in the four volumes of the great Leclair's sonatas from 1723 to 1738, the last two violin works of Couperin in 1724–6, and the noble sonatas of Mondonville in 1733.

About 1692, two years after the publication of the organ masses, Couperin wrote four sonatas in the Italian da chiesa manner. In 1695 he added two more. Some thirty years later, in 1726, he added to three of the original four sonatas sets of dances or suites in the French manner, thus producing a series of diptychs analogous to the Bach violin sonatas and partitas. He then rechristened them; (*La Pucelle* became *La Françoise*, *La Visionnaire* became *L'Espagnole*, and *L'Astrée* became *La Piémontoise*); added another double sonata called *L'Impériale*, the da chiesa part of which may have been written about 1715; and published them all together under the title of *Les Nations*. In these double works we can thus see the Italian and French manners placed side by side. In the two *Apothéose* sonatas which he published in 1724 and 1725, we can see the two manners mated. We shall examine these works more or less in chronological order, first dealing with the Italian sonatas of *c.* 1692 and 1695, then with the partitas added to them, then with the two parts of *L'Impériale*, which are both manifestations of Couperin's maturity, and lastly with the two *Apothéoses*.

97

As though to emphasize its experimental nature at this stage of his career, *La Steinquerque*, one of the earliest of the first group of sonatas, is the work that most reminds us, not only of Corelli, but also of Handel. In these sonatas Couperin is investigating some of the possibilities of the harmonic 'shape', as opposed to the melodic texture; so, whereas the organ masses had been to a considerable degree polyphonic in impetus, he here produces a work which relies mainly on the balance of spacious harmonic clauses, in which even the fugal subjects are, like so many of Handel's, built largely out of the notes of the common triad. The result is an Italianized version of Lully's battle musics, a work in the grand manner, befitting a ceremonial occasion – the piece is in honour of the victory at Steinkerque. But compared with the mature reconciliation of polyphonic and harmonic principles which we find in Couperin's later work, or in Bach, or even in the earlier organ masses, its spaciousness is achieved at the expense of subtlety. Being in some ways a ceremonial piece, and in others a technical experiment, the music lacks personality; it has few of the unmistakable Couperin touches.

Its form is a free descriptive version of the sonata da chiesa, with a strong dance influence. It opens with a vigorous overture constructed out of the martial fanfares of the introductory flourishes to the ballet; the interest centres almost entirely in the massive march of the harmonies. This is followed by a simple symmetrical air, on the model of the airs of Lully, though perhaps with a slightly Handelian solidity. A powerfully harmonized *grave* – musically the most interesting section of the sonata – makes extended uses of overlapping suspensions and leads to a jaunty, but not very sustained, fugue. An interlude of military fanfares, a perky tribute to the battle the sonata celebrates, introduces a swinging theme in 3 : 2, fugally treated, but harmonic in character. There is a further *grave* passage, and then the movement bounds in triple rhythm to a joyous close, the violins playing in consistent homophony in thirds and sixths.

The E minor sonata, finally called *La Françoise*, is of deeper musical interest than *La Steinquerque*, but it is still hardly representative of Couperin's intrinsic quality. This time it is closer to Corelli than Handel, though the opening *grave* displays an almost lush 'Italian' indulgence in chromaticisms, such as the classical Corelli himself did not often sanction. Though short, the movement rises to a most impressive climax:

The atmosphere is refined, elegant, and *mélancolique*; it has possibly something of the elegiac self-indulgence of La Rochefoucauld. The briskly contrapuntal second movement is quite elaborately developed, and makes jocular use of a little descending scale passage. Here too the atmosphere is highly charged and emotional; the brisk rhythm is counteracted by some extraordinary passages in dissolving sequential sevenths:

The other movements are not at the same level as these two. A simple, quasi-operatic air half-way between Lully and Corelli, two measured *grave* interludes, and a couple of very Corellian gigues (the second of which has an agile bass viol part), are all beautifully made but compared with Couperin's finest work are lacking in character.

L'Espagnole sonata, in C minor, opens with a very fine *grave* which produces a dark sonority through frequent use of augmented intervals, and dissonant appoggiaturas and suspensions: 99

The quick section into which the *grave* leads also has tension and excitement, and mounts to its B flat climax in the first-violin part, with inevitable momentum. The air in siciliano rhythm makes fascinating use of the opposition of solo voices and a quasi-tutti effect. It often uses a falling scale passage, diatonic or chromatic, in the bass, grouping above it melodic patterns, decorative figurations, and seductive harmonies of sevenths and ninths:

The feeling, at once noble and pathetic, suggests a French *air de cour* crossed with seventeenth-century baroque opera; one is reminded of Purcell, or even of the airs on a chromatic bass in Monteverdi. A merry canzona is notable for the whirling descending scale passages in the bass part, combined with chains of suspensions in the violins and continuo. A brisk, rather 'harmonic' and Handelian gigue is followed by a chromatically accompanied air, and the work concludes with a powerful double fugue on a diatonic theme, with a chattering countersubject.

The opening *grave* of *La Piémontoise* sonata, in G minor, is perhaps the most Purcellian movement in Couperin's work. In this passage it is not merely the chromatically moving bass, but the long arch of the lines, the habitual syncopations, the augmented fourths and diminished fifths, which remind us of Dido's lament:

Something of this operatic passion is preserved in the elaborately syncopated quick fugal movement, where the part-writing has an agility and rhythmic independence which is common in Bach, but rare in Handel or Corelli; in this respect it presages Couperin's most mature work. The next *grave* is in the mood of the opening, and has some acute dissonant suspensions. Here, too, the level flowing movement, the dissonances, and the sudden change to the major anticipate some of Couperin's most characteristic effects in later work. The delicate canzona is based on two instrumental figurations derived from the common triad and the major scale. Two quasi-operatic airs, one in the major, the other in the minor, are gently symmetrical and have a more personal voice than the similar movements in the other sonatas of this group; the suspensions and ornamental resolutions in the inner parts suggest the influence of the clavecinists, and may be compared with the similar devices in the sarabande of Chambonnières, quoted on page 179. A return to Purcellian intensity occurs in the brief *grave*, with its chromatic progressions and energetic *marqué* dotted rhythm, in ascending and descending scales. It leads without break into a simple Corellian gigue, charming, but not especially significant.

The two 1695 sonatas, *La Sultane* and *La Superbe*,★ use the same idiom as the first group, but within their deliberate Italianism they allow for a much freer expression of Couperin's sensibility. Here Couperin absorbs the Italian convention into the French tradition as consummately as Purcell adapted it to the linear and harmonic vigour of the English. *La Sultane*, in particular, is conceived on a grand scale, and is remarkable not only for its extensive development but also for the fact that it includes two more or less independent bass viol parts. It thus has four free string parts in all; the first bass viol sometimes, but by no

---

★ For note, see page 117.

means habitually, doubles the bass of the continuo.

The first *grave* is on a much bigger scale than any of the overtures to the earlier sonatas. It is more than twice as long, and, over a level flowing crotchet pulse, imitatively develops proud, spacious themes in overlapping suspensions which reinforce the majestic progression of the harmonies. In passages such as this:

persistent suspended seconds have a sinewy power, balancing the richness of the harmonies, which we meet with for the first time in Couperin's work – for the comparable passages in the organ masses have not this linear vigour. It is the first intimation of that union of solidity with subtlety which relates Couperin's finest work more closely to Bach than to any other composer. This controlled but highly emotional prelude also includes a remarkable, dark-coloured passage for the two bass viols, over long-sustained dominant and tonic pedals.

The second, quick contrapuntal, movement is thematically related to the *grave* and is also designed on a broad scale. It is notable for its close, Bach-like rather than Handelian, texture, both in its harmonic progressions:

and in its linear organization:

The *air tendre* is a dialogue between the two bass viols, dark-hued in the minor, and the two violins, softly glowing in the major. It leads into a *grave*, built on drooping appoggiaturas, wherein Couperin, for the first time in his Italianized music, recovers the quintessential Couperin of the finest movements of the organ masses. Predominantly harmonic in effect, the chains of appoggiaturas are suavely sensuous, and yet paradoxically create an unearthly feeling that the ego (*le moi*) and the will (*la volonté*) are dissolving away. Note the insistent dotted rhythm; the caressing ninth; and the augmented fifth chord which almost suggests that the tenderness of the emotion is about to break into tears:

The words of Fénelon – 'C'est dans l'oubli du Moi qu'habite la paix' – are relevant to this aspect of Couperin's music. We shall discuss it in detail in the chapter on the church music, and shall then have occasion to note many examples of the technical features referred to above. The two remaining fast sections of 103 this sonata are less personal, though the gigue has some typical harmonic acridities and rhythmic surprises. It provides, in any case, an appropriately festive note to conclude this most beautiful work.

The A major sonata, *La Superbe*, though this time for the normal resources, also has a certain *ampleur* of conception. It opens with a *grave* and canzona which have a maturely experienced majesty comparable with Handel's finest work, and far removed from the more naïvely noble gestures of *La Steinquerque*. None the less, these movements are not among Couperin's most representative work. The next section, *très lentement*, is, however, one of his finest inspirations, combining the *superbe* Handelian manner of this sonata with a subtle use of false relation reminiscent of the organ masses. Through the dotted rhythm and the hushed progression of the harmonies it evokes a tremulous quietude similar to that of the *grave* interlude of *La Sultane*. The harmonies are often of a most unconventional nature – for instance, this 'sobbing' use of the diminished fifth in an interrupted cadence, followed by the melting sequence of seventh chords; the last of them produces one of those 'catches in the breath' that we have had occasion to refer to once or twice before:

The canzona and final gigue are sprightly and well developed, but have not the closely wrought texture of Couperin's best work in this manner. The *air tendre* is one of the simplest and most beautiful of Couperin's pieces in the triple-timed *brunette* convention.

The dance suites which Couperin added to three of the sonatas of *c.* 1692 are identical in technique with his *Concerts Royaux*, published about the same time. In some ways it would thus be logical to discuss them together with the *concerts*, as the most central expression of the French instrumental tradition. By considering them beside the sonatas to which they were attached, however, one can understand more clearly how the classically developed form of the French suite approximated to the binary convention of the Italian partita or sonata da camera. We shall therefore leave detailed consideration of the suite until the chapter on the *concerts*; and in this context we shall say on the subject only so much as is necessary to indicate the relationship between the French and Italian genres. The two-violin suites all date from the last years of Couperin's life, and may stand with Bach's cello, violin and keyboard partitas as examples of an apparently limited convention used with the maximum of imaginative significance.

As with Bach – and in conformity with tradition – the allemandes are, apart from the chaconnes, the most musically extended movements, and often have considerable polyphonic complexity. Couperin's more discreet sensibility does not often call for the whirling linear arabesques typical of Bach's most baroque work, as exemplified in the great allemande from the D major cello suite, or those from the D major and E minor harpsichord partitas; but there is something of Bach's disciplined melodic profusion in the treatment of the aspiring scale passage in the allemande of the first (E minor) suite. The C minor allemande is less free melodically, but more involved harmonically; it is at once richly chromatic and gravely elegiac. This quality is found, too, in the allemande of the G minor suite, perhaps the finest of the three, very subtle in its phrase groupings.

Each suite has two courantes, the first of which (the French type) carries the traditional rhythmic ambiguity of the dance to an extreme point. Couperin rivals Bach in the complexity of the alternations and combinations of 3 : 2 and 6 : 4 which he extracts from his material. These movements are usually highly ornamented, the ornamentation being an integral part of the line and harmony:

These rhythmic and harmonic elaborations of a simple dance structure testify to the high degree of sophistication in Couperin's community. The second courante is usually more airy and flowing, more dance-like; though Couperin does not confine himself to the 6 : 4 Italian form, and never gives the courante the straightforward harmonic treatment of Handel.

Couperin writes two types of sarabande. One (like that of the G minor suite; it is actually in the major) is *tendre* and *cantabile* in character, of exquisite refinement and fragilely ornamented, in the manner of the theme of Bach's Goldberg Variations. This type of sarabande, as we shall see in a later chapter, is a part of Couperin's legacy from Chambonnières, who in his turn inherited it from the lutenists. The other type is grave and powerful, congested in harmony, like that of Bach's E minor partita; it often uses dissonant appoggiaturas and acciaccaturas, and employs a slow but strenuous dotted rhythm, conventionally performed with the dots doubled.

Couperin's gigues are sometimes of the amiable Italian type in a lilting 6 : 8 (that for instance from the G minor suite); sometimes of a French type in 6 : 4, more complicated rhythmically than those of Corelli or Handel. This type of gigue Couperin derives from Chambonnières and the lutenists; he treats the dance with a tautness which is again suggestive of Bach, though his gigues are usually slight and rather frothy. They are scherzo movements, and he has no crabbed, almost ferocious gigues such as Bach writes, in a contrapuntal style, in the E minor partita. The little gavottes, bourrées and minuets are not much more than occasional music, and do not call for comment in this chapter.

The crowning glories of the suites are the rondeaux and the chaconnes – both being a further development of Lully's treatment, which we have already discussed, of the ballet dances. The rondeau of the C minor suite is suavely melancholy but not especially remarkable; the rondeau in G, from the fourth suite, is on the other hand a delightful example of Couperin's sophisticated-rustic manner, producing a silvery flute-like sound through canonic overlapping and dulcet thirds:

This mode is even more beautifully expressed in the rondeau of *L'Impériale*, which we shall describe shortly.

In the chaconnes, the regular flow of the repeated bass (with the accent on the second beat of the traditional 3 : 4) provides a foundation over which the lines and figurations grow cumulatively more impassioned until they break into quicker movement. The opening suspensions across the bar, in the E minor chaconne, have a tone of noble melancholy; the level crotchet pulse splits into quaver movement, then into a vigorous dotted rhythm with great animation in the bass part, and finally into resplendent staccato descending scale passages combined with extended trills. The chaconne of the C minor suite is an even grander work. The opening statement (*noblement*) is itself massively harmonized, with appoggiaturas suggesting an anguish almost comparable with that of the great B minor clavecin *Passacaille*. There is an exquisite couplet for the two violins unaccompanied, in canon, and then the movement begins to build up a remorseless crescendo of excitement. A *vivement* couplet is founded on trumpet fanfares and castanet rhythms; the bass acquires greater animation, while the violins chant long chains of suspensions. Tentatively, the bass introduces chromatic elements, and the climax is reached in the mingling of the chromatic version of the bass with triple suspensions in the continuo and a powerful duo in double-dotted rhythm for the two violins:

The Bachian quality which we have noticed in our account of the suites finds its most consistent manifestation in the two parts of *L'Impériale*, a work in which both the da chiesa and da camera sections have an equal maturity. The classical ripeness is demonstrated most clearly in the power and length of the melodic structure. The opening *grave* has a melodic span that one finds but seldom outside Bach's work; its amplitude of structure is combined with subtlety in its linear and harmonic details:

The contrapuntal movement that follows is fiery, with acute dissonant suspensions. The second three-time *grave* is a *galant et magnifique* piece over a pulse in dotted rhythm. Its subsidiary chromaticisms have a dignified restraint, compared with the more fervid chromaticisms in the first two movements of the early *La Françoise*. This piece is in the relative major, as is the next, a gracious minuet in rondeau. A return to the triple rhythm provides a lyrical transition back to D minor, and the

sonata ends with a vigorously developed fugue on this muscular
subject, with its prominent tritonal sequences:

This is music of tremendous power, even ferocity, with a Bachian closeness of texture. This one movement is sufficient to
dispose of the legend of Couperin the 'exquisite'.

The sonata da camera has a deliciously tenuous gigue and a
massive sarabande, but is notable chiefly for its two big movements, the rondeau and chaconne. The rondeau has a theme of a
tender diatonic simplicity which, in conjunction with the level
rhythm, like a quietly breathing pulse, suggests a sense of light,
space, and tranquillity comparable with the emotional effect of
the ordered landscapes of Claude:

Like so much of Couperin's finest work, this music sounds as
though it was written to please, to entertain, and yet is at the
same time, in its purity, a spiritual rejuvenescence. The mood of
the chaconne is similar, though the piece is on a grander scale.
The broken rhythm and violently contrasted sonorities of the
couplet in the minor key have an unexpected dramatic force,
and, as in the graver C minor chaconne, the gradual introduction of chromatic elements gives the piece a cumulative
momentum:

It ends, however, in happy tranquillity.

Couperin's last word in the sonata convention is contained in the two *Apothéoses*, dedicated to Corelli and Lully respectively; and there is no more effective demonstration of the distance Couperin has travelled than to compare the prelude of the Corelli *Apothéose* of 1724 with that of *La Steinquerque* of *c.* 1692. In the late work there is no sacrifice of majesty in the proportions. The balance of the movements as wholes is preserved, as is the lucid sequence of tonalities which do not adventure far beyond the dominant, sub-dominant, sub-mediant, and relative major and minor. But the incidental vitality and subtlety of melodic life have increased enormously. The lines are more nervously sensitive, so the polyphony is more flexible; and, as a consequence of this flexibility, the harmony has an added richness. Such a passage as this, with its eloquent augmented and diminished intervals, indicates admirably this interior vitality, which is on the one hand so much more supple than the rather beefy homophonic texture of *La Steinquerque* and is on the other hand so much more mature than the chromaticisms of *La Françoise*:

Something of this quality is found, too, in the fugal movement that expresses Corelli's joy at his reception on Parnassus; the tight harmonic texture is enhanced by fascinating syncopations. In such passages – we shall meet them throughout Couperin's work – the music, like the painting of Watteau, achieves a moving union of strength with sensitivity. The sensuous quality of the harmony parallels Watteau's glowing use of colour, which he in part derived from Rubens, and to a lesser degree from Titian and Veronese; the supple precision of the three string lines parallels Watteau's nervous draughtsmanship, the most distinctive quality of his genius, which he in part inherited from the Flemish and Dutch genre painters; while the stable sense of tonality in the movements as wholes corresponds to Watteau's instinct for proportion and 'composition', which was in part encouraged by his study of the noble serenity of Giorgione and the Venetians.★

The tranquil movement describing Corelli drinking at the spring of Hypocrene is one of those quintessential Couperin pieces which, however often one hears them, strike one anew with their freshness. The material – a level quaver movement proceeding mainly by step, accompanying serene minims which form quietly dissonant suspensions – is simple; yet the result has a spirituality which is perhaps Couperin's unique distinction. The piece is a still more rarefied distillation of the serenely 'dissolving' movements in the early *La Sultane* and *La Superbe* sonatas. It

---

★ This account of Watteau's work indicates how he reconciles the two opposing parties of the *Poussinists* and the *Rubenists*. The conflict between the two schools, led by Felibien and De Piles respectively, was not dissimilar to the quarrel between the Ancients and the Moderns. In the contending factions, Poussin stood for draughtsmanship and the classical ideal, Rubens for colour and a 'modern' sensuousness. Both Watteau and Couperin – and for that matter Poussin himself – showed that the two conceptions need not be opposed, but could mutually enrich one another.

See Addendum IV.

produces the same feeling of the dissolution of the ego and the
will, and thus may, not altogether extravagantly, be termed
'paradisal'. In particular we should mention the modulation to A
minor which comes at the end of the movement after two pages of
unsullied D major. In the fluidity of the harmonic transitions
here, we have a reminiscence of the technique of the organ masses
– the paradox of a voluptuous purity. Note for instance the
heart-rending false relation in the penultimate bar, before the
tender resolution on to the major third:

The reminiscence of the earlier technique in no way compromises
the music's integrity. Couperin no longer feels it necessary, as he
did in *La Steinquerque*, to insist on his command of modern
homophony.

Another movement in this radiant manner is the *sommeil* music,
one of the few intrusions into this Italianate work of an element
intimately associated with Lully, even though originally derived
from the Italian opera. It is remarkable for its delicately
intertwined figuration. The progression of the lines by conjunct
motion, in even quavers with a crotchet pulse, was the accepted
musical stylization of the idea of repose. The two sections flank-
ing it, describing Corelli's enthusiasm and his awakening by the
Muses, have a gaily glittering texture. In the first, Corelli's
happiness bubbles and swirls in rapid scale passages and florid
arabesques for the violins unaccompanied; in the second, the

French dotted rhythm bounces through some closely wrought modulations from D to A, to F sharp and C sharp minor. The work concludes with an elaborately developed fugue on this excitingly syncopated subject:

This also breaks into florid passages for the violins towards the end. We are a long way from the rather perfunctory, chordally dictated fugato passages of *La Steinquerque*.

Despite the interpolation of descriptive movements suggested by the ballet, the structure of the Corelli *Apothéose* is basically that of the sonata da chiesa; or it is the Italian sonata modified by Couperin's long experience of the French tradition. In the Lully *Apothéose* Couperin first gives, as it were, a summing up of the tradition on which he had been nurtured; and then demonstrates how he has, through his career, managed to incorporate the Italian sonata into it. The *Apothéose* begins with a suite of pieces which are a microcosm in instrumental form of Lullian opera; only when Corelli appears on the scene in the second part does sonata technique become obtrusive. Then it is not merely in such superficialities as the quaint device of making Lully and Corelli fiddle in the 'French' and 'Italian' clefs respectively that we see how their two idioms have merged into one another.

Couperin's preface explains that the work is not conceived for violins exclusively; indeed one of the parts includes a low F sharp not playable on the violin. The piece may be played on any appropriate melody instruments, or on two harpsichords. This is true to some extent of all the sonatas; but it is interesting that it should be this explicitly theatrical work which prompts Couperin to say so. The Overture (Lully in the Elysian fields) moves with grave simplicity in a regular crotchet pulse, achieving a noble pathos through groupings of a falling scale passage. It is a theatre piece which is more consistently homophonic than the Corellian da chiesa prelude usually is, but the relationship between the two types is clear enough. The airs of the *ombres liriques*, the *Vol de Mercure*, the *Descente d'Apollon* (contrapuntal but dance-like), and the *Rumeur souteraine* of Lully's contemporaries and rivals, are all chamber music versions of operatic devices. The *Tendres Plaintes* of Lully's contemporaries, which

113

Couperin specifies should be performed by flutes or by *violons très adoucis*, is a beautiful instance of Couperin's rarefied sensuousness, built on a faux-bourdon-like procession of 6 : 3 chords. Again it differs from the 'rarefied' movements in earlier sonatas in being entirely homophonic. The *enlèvement de Lully* to Parnassus for the first time introduces the contrapuntal method of the Italian canzona, and makes fascinating play with a syncopated rhythm.

When Lully reaches Parnassus he is met by Corelli and the Italian muses who greet him with a *largo* strictly in the da chiesa manner, majestically proportioned, with acrid augmented fifths:

The *Remerciement de Lulli à Apollon* is a symmetrical operatic aria which illustrates the absorption of the Lullian air into the tonally more developed Italian arias of Handel; note the solid sequences and the figuration. The ornamentation remains, however, more French than Handelian:

Next Apollo persuades Lully and Corelli that the union of *Les Goûts françois et italiens* would create musical perfection; so the two muses sing together an *Essai, en forme d'ouverture*. This opens with a brilliant fanfare in dotted rhythm, which is followed by a 3 : 4 tune in flowing quavers, making considerable use of arpeggio figures. Then come two little *airs légers* for the violins without continuo; in one of them Lully plays the tune and Corelli the accompaniment, in the other the roles are reversed. And the whole work is rounded off with a full-scale sonata da chiesa, in which Lully and Corelli play together, the Italian technique being finally, as it were, translated into French.★

Musically, this sonata is the finest part of the Lully *Apothéose*. The *grave* is in the main Italian, with astringent augmented intervals and a Bachian closeness of texture. But the canzona, *Saillie,* is French in spirit and worthy to be put beside Couperin's best pieces in the burlesque vein. (We shall discuss this in detail in the chapter on the harpsichord pieces.) The 3 : 2 *grave, rondement,* recalls the fragrance of the *Messe pour les Convents,* though it has now a more Italian amplitude. The last movement combines a Corellian contrapuntal technique with the dotted rhythm of the French theatre, and includes some interesting modulations, such as this from G to the minor of the dominant:

Although the Lully *Apothéose* is one of the most important of Couperin's works from a documentary point of view, it seems

---

★ For an interesting anticipation of this mating of a 'French' and 'Italian' melody, see J. J. Fux's *Concentus Musico-instrumentalis,* published at Nuremburg in 1701. The seventh Partita of this work includes a movement in which an *aria italiana* in 6 : 8 is played simultaneously with an *air françois* in common time. Most of the pieces have French titles (*La joye des fidèles sujets, Les ennemis confus,*etc.); the *Sinfonia* combines a French triple rhythmed middle section with an Italianate contrapuntal opening. See Chapter 11 for a general account of the French influence in Germany.

to me musically inferior to the Corelli *Apothéose*. The latter work, with the *Impériale* sonata, perhaps represents the highest level of Couperin's achievement in this convention; and both impress by their Bachian maturity. From this point of view, Couperin offers an interesting comparison, and contrast, with Purcell. Both experimented in the Italian sonata technique in the early sixteen-nineties, and for the same reason – they knew that if their country's music was to have a future, they had to take account of the new directions which the Italian sonata stood for. When they started to compose their sonatas, Purcell had behind him the Tudor tradition and the seventeenth-century baroque polyphonists such as Lawes and Jenkins; Couperin had behind him the organists, the lutenists, the ballet, and the theatre music of Lully. Purcell's more direct relation to the 'inflectional' methods of the sixteenth century was in some ways an advantage, for through it he was able to create those bold modulatory and harmonic effects which are the glory of his finest sonatas, such as the F minor or A minor. But if Couperin's early sonatas have not Purcell's fiery originality, their relatively polite urbanity brings its own reward. Purcell, without a developed theatre music behind him, was unable to establish an English classical tradition; Couperin, with Lully behind him, had merely to modify in a contemporary manner a tradition that was already there.

This is why Couperin was able in later years to create sonatas, such as *L'Impériale* and the Corelli *Apothéose*, which in their classical poise are beyond anything which Purcell attempted in this style; this is why Couperin was able to produce music that can seriously be related to the work of Bach. It is not so much a question of the comparative degree of genius with which nature endows a particular composer; this is always difficult to estimate, since so many contributory factors have to be taken into account. It is a question of the value of a tradition; and while Couperin, like Bach, could have made nothing of the tradition without his genius, it is possible that, without the tradition, his genius might have been frustrated.

Note to p. 101

The date of 1695 for these two sonatas, established by Tessier, was accepted without quibble at the time I was working on the book, but has since been challenged by Pierre Citron, echoed by others. He gives a date between 1710 and 1714: first on interior evidence, because the style of the sonatas is said to be more mature than that of the works of *c.* 1692; and secondly on the historical evidence that the vogue for orientalism, which may bear on the title of *La Sultane*, was at its height around 1710. (The sonata may be an act of homage to the Dauphin's wife, Marie-Adelaide, Duchesse de Bourgogne, who gave a ball at Marly in 1700, at which she appeared, according to the Marquis de Sourches, 'exquisitely disguised as a Sultana'. The Duchess died in 1712.) I don't find this argument entirely persuasive. Admittedly, the two sonatas are very fine and *La Sultane* in particular betrays some of the 'spiritual' qualities of the *Leçons de Ténèbres*, which were composed 1712-14. On the other hand the highly polyphonic texture is seventeenth century in flavour, comparable with Purcell's most profound exercises in the genre, and the matter of the Dauphine's party cannot be regarded as conclusive; there must have been many masking sultanas in the divertissements in which court life abounded.

Chapter Seven

The Secular Vocal Works

In discussing Couperin's concern with 'les Goûts réunis', we have broadly equated the French 'goût' with the style of Lully. This style, however, incorporated a number of elements from French traditions of domestic music for the solo voice; and to these traditions Couperin himself made a modest contribution. Intrinsically his secular vocal music is of little importance; but the conventions which he employed in it have a direct bearing on his church music, and an implicit bearing on almost everything he wrote. In this chapter we must therefore offer some account of French conventions of solo vocal music in the seventeenth century, in order that we may understand how, in his church music, Couperin was able to translate Italian techniques into French terms; in order that we may have a more adequate appreciation of the native traditions to which he belonged.

During the *grand siècle* there were in French song two main lines of evolution, which are not always sharply differentiated. The first of these is the sophisticated *air de cour*, on which a few preliminary remarks have been made in Part 1; the second is the more popular *chansons à boire, vaudevilles,* and *brunettes*. In the early years of the century there was not much difference between the two lines. Both were variations of the simpler homophonic madrigal in which the melodic interest was centred in the top line, so that the under parts could be with equal effectiveness either sung or played upon instruments; and both were associated with the dance, whether folk dance or the sophisticated ballet. The collection of *airs de cour* made by Adrien le Roy in 1597 makes no attempt to delineate the characteristics of the genre, beyond indicating that simplicity and a gentle graciousness were prerequisites of it.

Under the influence of *précieux* society, the *air de cour* became explicitly monodic and more sophisticated. It was not an attempt to embrace Italian humanistic passion, but the deliberate creation of a refined, virtuoso stylization. It is true that the finest of the early *air de cour* composers, Pierre Guédron, showed, under the influence of the *ballet mélodramatique*, some influence of the methods of Caccini, and in some of his airs attained to an almost operatic fervour:

Que je puis___ bien souf-frir mais, mais que je n'o - - se di - re

but such passages are exceptional. In general the *air de cour* composers remained recalcitrant to the Italian style not because they were ignorant of it – they themselves composed 'Italian' settings of Italian words – but because they sought a different effect. Like every artist of the salons, they wanted a certain proportion and refinement combined with a highly charged emotionalism of a sweetly '*mélancolique*' order. The atmosphere is indicated by this quotation from Sorel's novel *Francion*:

> Alors il vint des musiciens qui chantèrent beaucoup d'airs nouveaux, joignant le son de leurs luths et de leurs violes à celui de leurs voix. Ah, dit Francion, ayant la tête penchée dessus le sein de Laurette, après la vue d'une beauté il n'y a point de plaisir qui m'enchante comme fait celui de la musique. Mon cœur bondit à chaque instant; je ne suis plus à moi; les tremblements de voix font trembler mignardement mon âme.

The date of this passage, 1663, places it in the second flore-scence of the *air de cour*; it is quoted here because it demonstrates so clearly the impulse from which the *air de cour* grew. The concentration on an esoteric emotionalism, the deliberate cultiv-ation of sensuous subtleties, is found also in the contemporary lutenists; it produced a kind of escape art which links up with the pastoral convention of the highly fashionable *Astrée*. This pas-toralism had itself been borrowed from Italian sources – from Guarini, Tasso, and Sannazar; it was not surprising that it prospered in the hyper-sophisticated French community. The pastoral life became an ideal because it was supposedly free of complications, free of *intrigue*; because it seemed to offer, regressively, a simpler mode of existence. From this point of view we can see the significance of Mersenne's remark:

Il faut premièrement supposer que la musique et par conséquent les airs sont faicts particulièrement et principalement pour charmer l'esprit et l'oreille, et pour nous faire passer la vie avec un peu de douceur parmi les amertumes qui s'y rencontrent.

This is an ambiguous attitude which we have met before – in La Rochefoucauld, for instance. The self-protective irony should not lead us to underestimate the degree to which the authors meant what they said.

In terms of musical technique, the sense of proportion was realized in the very simple formal structure which the composers adopted – the strophic tune in two parts, both with repeats (AA, modulation to dominant; BB, return to tonic). The emotionalism and sensuousness within this formal framework were achieved partly by the incidental rhythmic subtleties, suggested by the text and by the composers' experiments in Greek prosody:

Ces Nymphes hos-tes-ses des bois,   Bravant les a - mou-reu - ses loix

and partly by the ornamentation which, with increasing complexity, embellished the vocal line. The elegant emotionalism was thus almost entirely a rhythmic and linear matter; the composers were not greatly interested in the Italian harmonic audacities, and were content if their lute parts 'accompanied' with flatly homophonic chords.

Even in the early days of the *air de cour*, the ornamentation was thus an integral part of the *préciosité*, of the *mignardise* which all the artists of the salons cultivated. It gave the line its suppleness of nuance; it made hearts tremble. Some of the ornaments were suggested by sixteenth-century conventions, particularly those of a descriptive nature. Thus references in the text to upward or downward movement, to flight, to flames literal or metaphorical, to pain or distress, are accompanied by appropriate melodic stylizations:

si   la   mort _____ flé - chi - - - roit

and there is some approach to a scheme of musical symbols, analogous to the conventional vocabulary of the poems of a

Tristan l'Hermite. There was, however, a growing tendency to indulge in ornamentation for its own sake – as a virtuoso exhibition of *mignardise*. Formulae such as the following were sometimes appropriate to the words:

Que n'es - tes vous las - sé - es,

at other times purely conventional:

D'un _____ si doux trait,

In either case they rubbed any sharp corners off the lines and provided some compensation for the melodies' unenterprising range, which seldom exceeded an octave, was often restricted to a fifth, and, except in the case of Guédron, avoided leaps with any degree of harmonic tension. The ornaments helped to create a stylization suitable for the expression of *douceur* and *mollesse*.

Between 1630 and 1640 the *airs de cour* seemed to be in decline. A new impulse came from Pierre de Nyert, a wealthy dilettante, born in 1597 and educated in musically 'progressive' circles. He lived in Rome for a while, and made a study of the Italian theatre and Italian song: Maugars tells us that de Nyert himself announced that he wished to 'ajuster la méthode italienne avec la française'. He must have been a singer of virtuoso accomplishment; Bacilly remarks that the great Luigi Rossi 'pleuroit de joie de luy entendre exécuter ses airs'. He must also have been a man of some force of character, for all the composers followed his lead in attempting to reconcile the French and Italian techniques. La Fontaine's famous epitaph:

> Nyert, qui pour charmer le plus juste des Rois,
> Inventa le bel art de conduire la voix,
> Et dont le goût sublime à la grande justesse,
> Ajouta l'Agrément et la Délicatesse,

does not seem hyperbolical when compared with the mass of contemporary tributes to de Nyert's 'génie prodigieux, discernement merveilleux', and so on. His schools for singers, teaching voice production, pronunciation, style and gesture, soon became nationally celebrated: and it was partly through de Nyert's work, which encouraged a more declamatory technique and a more systematized harmonic sense, that the *air de cour* became one of the constituents of the classical opera.

Perhaps the most impressive evidence of de Nyert's influence is the re-emergence of Antoine Boësset, after a silence of some years, during which he was presumably studying the new techniques. The work of Boësset's old age has a lyrical vitality which cannot be found in the cloyingly 'sensitive' music he wrote in the first part of the century; we may note, for instance, his use of melodic progressions which have a clear harmonic basis:

It is also worth noting that the final volumes of Boësset's work are still published with lute tablature. Henceforth, the songs are published occasionally with lute tablature, more often with an instrumental bass, sometimes with a bass intended to be sung. The more modern methods increase at the expense of the old.

The leaders of the new movement were men of a later generation than either de Nyert himself or Boësset. Le Camus, de la Barre, and Michel Lambert (whom Lecerf de la Viéville called 'le meilleur maître qui ait été depuis des siècles') wrote their airs consistently with figured bass, and are more interested in problems of form and proportion than were the composers of the first half of the century, though they preserve much of the traditional rhythmic freedom. Their *air sérieux* is the old *air de cour*, modified by Italian harmony and virtuosity. None of them has a talent of the order of Guédron, but they can create melodies which have a genuine dignity and pathos, as we may see from Lambert's setting of Jacqueline Pascal's poem, *Sombre désert, retraite de la nuit*. Although Mazarin imported Italian singers, and encouraged Italianism in every way, the native tradition was not swamped. Italianate violence was never allowed to imperil propriety, good taste, and *mignardise*. The distinction made by J. J. Bouchard, in a letter to Mersenne, was still upheld:

Que si vous voulez sçavoir mon jugement, je vous dirai que,
pour l'artifice, la science, et la fermeté de chanter, pour la quantité

de musiciens, principalement de chanteurs, Rome surpasse Paris autant que Paris fait Vaugirard. Mais pour la délicatesse et une *certa leggiadira e dilettevole naturalezza* des airs, les François surpassent les italiens de beaucoup.

Mersenne himself makes the same point:

> Les Italiens . . . représent tant qu'ils peuvent les passions et les affections de l'âme et de l'esprit, par exemple la colère, la fureur, le dépit, la rage, les défaillances du cœur et plusieurs autres passions, avec une violence si extraordinaire que l'on jugeroit quasi qu'ils sont touchez des mêmes affections qu'ils représentent en chantant, au lieu que nos Français se contentent de flatter l'oreille et qu'ils usent d'une douceur perpetuelle dans leurs chants, ce qui en empesche l'énergie.

Even the Italians themselves seem to have been susceptible to the virtues of the French idiom, while recognizing its limitations, if we may judge from J. B. Doni's *Traité de la Musique* of 1640:

> Où est-ce que l'on chante avec tant de mignardise et délicatesse et où entend-on tous les jours tant de nouvelles et agréables chansons, même en la bouche de ceux qui sans aucun artifice et étude font paroistre ensemble la beauté de leurs voix et la gentillesse de leurs esprits; jusqu'à tel point qu'il semble qu'en autres pays les musiciens se font seulement par art et exercice, mais qu'en France ils deviennent tels de nature.

It may seem a little odd that Bouchard should break into Italian in attempting to describe the characteristics of the French style, and that Doni should find this most highly stylized technique remarkable for its naturalness. But all the authorities are agreed as to the general character and value of the French convention; and it is interesting that Cambert, who of all French composers approached most nearly to the Italian cantata technique, was considered crude compared with the most civilized French standards. 'Les sentiments tendres et délicates lui echappaient,' said St Evremond; and a disciple of *préciosité* could hardly make a more damning comment than that.

The second generation of *air de cour* composers not only systematized the formal and harmonic structure of the genre, they also organized the haphazard decorative techniques of the early part of the century into a fine art. The elaborate system of 123 ornamentation which they evolved was partly an extension of traditional practice – the *port de voix*, the *coulé*, the *flexion*, the descriptive vocalise and the *tremblement* had all appeared in the airs of Guédron and Boësset. But now the various resources are systematized, and the system is more or less synonymous with the invention of the *double* or *diminution*. This ornamentation was the basis of the ornamentation of Couperin and the clavecinists, and it is therefore important that we should have some notion of what it was like, and of what the composers thought they were doing when they used it. A detailed account of Couperin's own ornamentation will be reserved until our consideration of his theoretical work, in the third part of this book.

The origins of the *double* are obscure. It is said that Bacilly may have invented it, through singing embroidered versions of airs by earlier masters such as Guédron and Boësset, though in so doing he may merely have been imitating an Italian fashion. Titon du Tillet seems to suggest that Lambert – celebrated equally as composer and singing teacher – was responsible for the development of the technique:

> On peut dire qu'il est le premier en France qui ait fait connoître la beauté de la Musique et du Chant, et la justesse, et les grâces de l'expression; il imagina aussi de doubler la plus grande partie de ses airs pour faire valoir la légèreré de la voix et l'agrément du gozier par plusieurs passages et roulades brillantes et gracieuses, où il a excellemment réussi.

In any case, it soon became the custom to compose and to sing one's airs more or less 'straight' in the first stanza, adding increasingly complex passage work in subsequent verses. Bacilly himself offers a somewhat unconvincing analogy with painting as an explanation of the method:

> Tout le Monde convient que le moins qu'on peut faire de passages dans un premier Couplet c'est le mieux, parce qu'assurément ils empeschent que l'on entende l'Air dans sa pureté, de même qu'avant d'appliquer les couleurs qui sont en quelque façon dans la Peinture, ce qu'est dans le Chant la Diminution, il faut que le Peintre ait premièrement désiné son ouvrage, qui a quelque rapport avec le premier Couplet d'un air.

124   The strophic build of the air is, as it were, the draughtsmanship;

the ornamented couplets are the sensous elements of colour applied to the linear structure.

The *port de voix* was the simplest and most common of the ornaments. It was an upwards appoggiatura, a slide up a major or minor second, or sometimes a third, fourth, or even a fifth; it was widely employed for 'les finales, médiantes, et autres principales cadences'. An extremely complicated set of rules conditioned its employment: its purpose was to enhance the plasticity and delicacy of the line, and its correct application called not only for a sound technique but also for good taste. As Bacilly said:

> Que le port de voix soit le grand chemin que les gens qui chantent doivent suivre, comme estant fort utile, mesme pour la justesse de la voix . . . mais . . . il y a des coups de maistre qui passent par dessus le règle, je veux dire que les sçavans par une licence qui est en eux une élégance du chant, obmettent quelquefois de jetter le note basse sur la haute par un doublement de notte imperceptible.

A hardly less important grace was the *tremblement*, by which the composers meant a rapid alternation of two notes, corresponding to the Italian *tremolo*. (The Florentines' *trillo* consisted of rapid repetitions of the *same* note.) More complicated was the *cadence*, 'un des plus considérable ornamens, et sans lequel le chant est fort imparfait'. This took the form of a variously elaborated preparation, followed by a *tremblement*, followed by a resolution:

que   j'at - tends

Another ornament was the *tremblement étouffé*, in which 'le gosier se présente à trembler et pourtant n'en fait que le semblant, comme s'il ne vouloit que doubler la notte sur laquelle se devoit faire la cadence'. This appears to correspond with the Germans' *Pralltriller*. *La flexion de voix* was a quick mordent.

All these ornaments and many subsidiary divisions of them were executed on the long syllables. Another group of ornaments, called *accents* and *plaintes*, was used on the short syllables. Bacilly defines them as follows:

> Il y a dans le Chant un certain ton particulier qui ne se marque
> que fort légèrement dans le gosier que je nomme accent ou aspir-
> ation, à qui d'autres donnent assez mal à propos le nom de plainte,
> comme s'il ne se pratiquoit que dans les endroits où l'on se plaint.

Mersenne also speaks of the 'accent plaintif' performed 'sur la
notte accentuée, en haussant un peu la notte à la fin de sa
pronunciation et en lui donnant une petite pointe, qui passe si
viste, qu'il est assez difficile de l'apercevoir'. All the ornaments
were sung with considerable rhythmic freedom; groups of decorative notes were conventionally sung in a *pointé* dotted
rhythm, not liltingly in the manner of the gigue, but 'si finement
que cela ne paroisse pas, si ce n'est en des endroits particuliers
qui demandent expressément cette sorte d'exécution'.

The performer was thus called upon for a considerable degree
of creative artistry, if he was to interpret sensitively the ornaments which the composer had marked in the score, and at the
same time to know where to add ornaments which the composer had not troubled to indicate because he regarded them as
conventionally understood. For both performers and audience,
the ornaments are introduced partly to enhance the music's
expressive *préciosité,* partly to show off the skill which made
these people a musical, as well as a social, elect. The ornaments
make the music more subtle and *tendre*, and less approachable by
the common rank and file. While some of the ornaments are
suggested by the words in the manner of the sixteenth century:

it is significant that this realism is less in evidence than in the
early part of the century. Bacilly insists on the importance of
stylization for its own sake and pokes fun at the exponents of
descriptive realism, which he considers childish and unsophis-
ticated:

> De dire que par exemple sur le mot *onde* ou celui de *balancer* il
> faille expressément marquer sur le papier une douzaine de nottes
> hautes et basses pour signifier aux yeux ce qui ne doit s'adresser
> qu'à l'oreille, c'est une chose tout à fait badine et puérile.

Lully himself disapproved of the hyper-subtle ornamentation of the *doubles* as being of Italian extraction and inimical to the French tradition of naturalness and grace. He underestimated the degree to which the ornamentation had become a local product; in any case he is to Lambert and Le Camus a direct successor. They had written much music, both vocal and instrumental, for the ballet, and it is their sense of proportion and of harmonic progression that Lully, in his theatre music, more impressively developed. In his work, the esoteric *air de cour* meets the popular elements in French song which complemented it.

Before we turn to examine this more popular tradition, however, we should note that French religious song, during the *grand siècle*, became virtually indistinguishable from secular song; a fact which is sociologically as well as musically interesting. The *chants religieux* of a man such as Denis Caigret, who started from the lute song convention of Le Jeune and Mauduit, are relatively simple and homophonic in technique, since they were intended for amateur performance; but in essentials they are the same as the secular pieces. Of the religious songs of the mid-century Bacilly roundly declares that 'Il faut que ces sortes d'airs soient si approchés des airs du monde pour être bien reçus, qu'à peine on en puisse connaitre la différence': and Gobert's preface to his settings of versified psalms takes care to warn the performer not to 'obmettre à bien faire les ports de voix, qui sont les transitions agréables et les anticipations sur les notes suivantes. On doit observer à propos les tremblements, les flexions de voix . . . etc.' De Gucy, in his settings of psalm-paraphrases published in 1650, wrote fully developed *doubles* to the psalms, and blandly admitted that one had to 'faire des chants sur le modèle des airs de cour pour estre introduits partout avec facilité'.

Both in the music and in their words the *airs de cour* were a sophisticated art form. Bacilly, in his *Remarques*, describes songs of the *air de cour* type as *airs passionés* (he means that they are full of feeling, not passionate in the modern sense). His other main division of *airs de mouvement* includes all the more 'popular' types of seventeenth-century French song. During the second half of the century, the sophisticated and popular elements tended to become more sharply differentiated; Perrin, after defining the *air de cour* as a song which 'marche à mesure et à mouvement libres et graves', adds that 'la chanson diffère de l'air en ce qu'elle suit un mouvement réglé de danse ou autre'. All the lighter songs – 127 *chansons, vaudevilles, airs à boire, brunettes,* and *airs champêtres* – had some affiliation with the dance and were, as Lecerf de la Viéville says, 'articles considérables et singulières pour nous'. Most of them fall into one of two groupings; songs in which both words and music have a popular character, and those in which sophisticated words are adapted to popular or quasi-popular tunes.

The songs which are popular in both words and music are comparatively few, and are almost all *chansons à danser,* survivals from the sixteenth-century technique of homophonic sung dances. Their technique and purpose had not greatly altered since Mangeant's description of them in 1616:

> Il n'est point d'exercice plus agréable pour la jeunesse, ny qui soit plus usité en bonnes compagnies que la danse; voire en tel sorte que le plus souvent au défaut des instruments l'on danse aux chansons.

Another charming contemporary account suggests that they were sometimes preferred to instrumental dance music:

> Il y avait des violons, mais ordinnairement on les faisait taire pour danser aux chansons. C'est si joli de danser aux chansons.

The chansons were symmetrical in construction, 'simples et naturelles'.

Much more frequent, in Ballard's collections of the airs, are the songs in which sophisticated words are written to popular tunes. Some of these are in dance rhythms. It became a fashionable pastime to write verses in sarabande, gavotte, and bourrée form, and so on. Normally, however, the songs are not meant to be danced to, and the more serious ones such as the sarabandes are often indistinguishable from the simpler *airs de cour.* More characteristic of the sophisticated adaptations of popular tunes are the *vaudevilles* (or *voix de villes*); it is interesting that in defending them against the charge of vulgarity, Bacilly points out that popular tunes are in essence *naturels,* 'qui est une qualité fort considérable dans le chant'. 'Les François sont à peu près les seuls qui aient entendu cette brièveté raisonnable qui est la perfection des vaudevilles et cette naïveté qui en est le sel.' De Rosiers, in the preface to his collection *Un Livre de Libertés,* explains why he

thinks *vaudevilles* are an important part of *musique de société*:

> Un homme toujours sérieux serait insupportable et sa conversation ne serait bonne que quand l'on est endormi; le rire dissipe l'humeur mélancolique, c'est pourquoi la pratique en est nécessaire;

and he goes on to say that though his music may appear somewhat frivolous, none the less to compose it calls for considerable cunning:

> Ceux qui font profession de mettre au jour quelque musique sçavent bien que la naïveté des chansons à danser ne demande point l'artifice et l'étude des airs de cour; néanmoins s'ils considéront bien mes chant ils verront que ma plume les fait voler assez haut pour en acquérir le titre.

We may note that, just after the middle of the century, when the *air sérieux* was reaching its highest point of esoteric elaboration, there was a complementary increase in the numbers of trivial and facetious *chansons* and *vaudevilles*. At the same time, sophisticated ornamentation was tentatively introduced into the more popular songs, 'qui veulent estre exécutées avec plus de tendresse', as Bacilly characteristically put it. This desire to 'get it both ways' – to enjoy the advantages of a civilized society while avoiding social responsibility through a consciously naïve retreat to a simpler mode of existence – also connects up with the pastoralism of *L'Astrée*.

A more extreme instance of this is provided by the *chansons à boire*, which also flourished most vigorously during the period of the *air de cour*'s greatest refinement. (We may compare the development of the English tavern catch, during the reign of Charles I, beside the highly sophisticated music of Jenkins and William Lawes.) The phenomenon of the *chanson à boire* parallels the growth of burlesque literature. At the beginning of the century, the *chansons à boire* are not distinct from other chansons of a light character; they fall into a period of triteness and vulgarity, and then, in the second half of the century, gain a more self-conscious elaboration, ultimately becoming songs which demand considerable virtuosity from the performer:

où soir et ma - tin l'on dé - - - - char - ge du vin

Prosp: du Cours de La Reyne Mere

'Dans le Goût Pastoral': Cours de la Reine Mère

Nature, low life and majesty on the periphery of the Court.
VII. 'Dans le Goût Pastoral': Cours de la Reine Mère, from the
Topographia Galliae of 1655.

VIII. Musette-playing pseudo-shepherd, an engraving by
Mariette.

The *chansons à boire* were more often for two voices, in canon, accompanied by two violins as well as continuo; though examples for a single voice and for various other combinations with continuo are plentiful. Lully composed some sprightly examples in the classic form with violins, and approved of them strongly because they 'sont des pièces propres à la France que les Italiens ne connoissoient pas – l'art de faire des jolis airs, des airs d'une gaîté et facilité qui cadrent aux paroles est un point que l'Italie ne nous contestera pas'. (Lecerf de la Viéville.) Despite its bacchic and dionysiac associations, the *chanson à boire* was not remote from the other popular manifestations of the air. The *air tendre et à boire* was a frequent compromise, the implication being that the wine would titillate the amorous palate, leading it not to intenser passion, but to greater subtlety and *préciosité*.

The *brunette* did not materially differ from the *vaudeville*, except that it tended to use less spicy texts, and a more elegantly Platonic version of the love theme. The proportion of pseudo to real folk songs was also rather larger. Some of the more melancholy brunettes thus merge into the *airs sérieux*, and Ballard reprints the simplest *airs de cour* in his *brunette* collections. *Brunettes* were for one, two, or three voices, accompanied by theorbo lute, or sometimes sung unaccompanied. The singers took great pride in singing the songs unaccompanied, *à la cavalière*, with the appropriate ornamentation and nuance; the habit also had practical advantages:

> On sçait que l'accompagnement aide et adoucit la voix: cependant une belle voix, qui n'est point accompagnée, ne devient pas insupportable . . . il y a des moments où l'accompagnement est presque incommode. La conversation languit; on prie quelqu'un de chanter un Air, on l'écoute et on recommence à causer. S'il avait proposé d'envoyer chercher une basse de viole, on se seroit separé. A la fin du repas, dans l'émotion où le vin et la joie ont mis les conviez, on demande un air à boire à celui qui a de la voix; l'accompagnement aurait là quelque chose de gênant, qui serait hors de saison . . . Nos François les plus amoureux de leurs voix ne font pas non plus difficulté de chanter sans théorbe et sans clavescin et . . . c'est faire le précieux ou la précieuse de se piquer de ne point chanter sans Théorbe. (Lecerf de la Viéville.)

These little pastoral songs – called *brunettes* after the pseudo-shepherdesses who sang them or about whom they were sung – enjoyed a phenomenal popularity throughout the seventeenth century, and it was a song of Lully in this manner (*Sommes-nous pas trop heureux*), which inverted the normal relation between folk music and art music, and entered French folk song as a carol.

Lully also carried the *brunette* into the opera where, under the title of *air tendre*, it preserved its national identity, 'ce caractère tendre, aisé et naturel, qui flatte toujours sans lasser jamais, et qui va beaucoup plus au cœur qu'à l'esprit'. Not *too* much to the heart, however, for it is only 'un *peu* d'amour' that is 'nécessaire' and 'un charmant amusement'. Here, as always, one must preserve a balance between emotion and a sense of propriety, if only because it is more comfortable to avoid emotional complications. By the early eighteenth century the term *brunette* was being used rather indiscriminately to cover most varieties of the pastoral. But it was still a living reality, and perhaps more than anything, preserved the French tradition from the encroachments of Italianism. In Couperin's work it was a counterpoise to the Corellian sonata; he must have felt about it much as did Lecerf de la Viéville when he wrote:

Et toutes ces Brunettes, toutes ces jolies airs champêtres, qu'on appelle les Brunettes, combien ils sont naturels. On doit compter pour de vraies beautés la douceur et la naïveté de ces petits airs – les Brunettes sont doublement à estimer dans notre musique, parce que cela n'est ni de la connoisance, ni du génie des Italiens, et que les tons aimables et gracieux, si finement proportionnés aux paroles, en sont d'un extrême prix.

It is rather surprising that Couperin's specific contributions to the *brunette* collections are so few. If we discount the numerous arrangements of his harpsichord pieces in vocal form, we have left only three *airs sérieux*, and half a dozen or so songs in the semi-popular, semi-sophisticated vein. The earliest of the *airs sérieux*, *Qu'on ne me dise plus*, is dated 1697. It is a gravely melancholy piece in E minor, with first section ending in the relative major. The groupings of the melodic clauses are varied, and the line mounts to a quite impressive climax:

The second *air sérieux*, *Doux liens*, was published in 1701, and the words are a French translation of an Italian poem already set by Alessandro Scarlatti. The music, however, is French in its rhythmic fluidity, and is perhaps closer to the *air de cour* of the first half of the *grand siècle* than is the more architecturally balanced *Qu'on ne me dise plus*. The third *air sérieux*, explicitly called *Brunette*, is dated 1711. The most developed piece in Couperin's secular vocal music, it is an *air de cour* with five *doubles* or couplets. The air itself is in the usual two sections, with repeats, the first section modulating from G to the dominant with some piquant intimations of D minor. Exquisitely stylized, the melodic arabesques of the *doubles* have no obvious descriptive intent, although the pliancy and *douceur* which they give to the line are a part of its expressiveness. As in the earlier *airs de cour* the convolutions of the ornamentation counteract the rigidity of the harmonic structure:

The harmonies remain constant while, through the succession of couplets, the complexities of the ornamentation increase. However much the influence of de Nyert may have encouraged the French to experiment with this kind of melodic filigree, the soft fluidity of the line is germane to the French tradition. One can observe reflections of it all through Couperin's work. As a whole, this song is a most beautiful example of musical *préciosité*.

These three songs are sophisticated pieces in the esoteric

134

manner of the *air de cour*. Another sophisticated song, of a simpler, more harmonic type is *Les Solitaires*, a piece of amicably self-indulgent melancholy, written for two voices, moving note for note, and continuo. Then there are a few songs in the semi-popular vein, *La Pastourelle, Muséte, Vaudeville,* and *Les Pellerines*, all published in 1711 or 1712. The *vaudeville* is for three voices and bass, the other songs for two voices, the parts in every case moving note for note. *Les Pellerines* also exists in a harpsichord version in Couperin's first book of keyboard pieces. Despite their popular flavour, the tunes seem to be original, not adaptations of folk songs. They are all charming, but indistinguishable from innumerable other songs in the *brunette* tradition; Couperin here makes no attempt to use the *brunette* convention, as he does later, for his own ends.

More interesting than these pastorals is Couperin's *air à boire*, a setting of La Fontaine's *Epitaphe d'un Paresseux*. The two vocal parts follow convention in being freely canonic; there are some contrapuntal jokes on the words *Deux parts en fit*, and the canonic parts are throughout neatly dove-tailed. Finally, there are three unaccompanied songs in three parts. Two of them are canons, the second being an entertaining *chanson à boire, A moi, tout est perdu,* which parodies operatic recitative. The declamatory theme gives prominence to the notes of the major triad. Appoggiaturas in the ornamentation create some effectively odd parallel seconds:

The three-part unaccompanied parody, *Trois Vestales champêtres et trois Poliçons,* is one of the most personal secular pieces, and suggests the kind of modification of the pastoral convention which Couperin introduces into his most significant work. There may not be much in a passage such as this: 135

to indicate that it is by an important composer, but it is illuminating to consider it in relation to, say, the quick sections of the *Leçons de Ténèbres*.

For clearly, our account of the *brunette* tradition, comparatively detailed as it is, could not be justified simply as an introduction to Couperin's few exercises in this style. We need to understand the pastoral tradition because it is one of the points from which Couperin starts. His contributions to the idiom are insignificant; what is important is the manner in which he uses elements of the *brunette* in all his most important work. We shall find subtle transmutations of the *brunette* repeatedly throughout his harpsichord music and *concerts*; while in the relatively Italianate period of the church music, it is the *brunette,* even more than the opera of Lully, which stands for Couperin as the central line in the French tradition.

Chapter Eight
The Church Music

La Musique d'un Motet, qui en est, pour ainsi dire, le corps, doit être expressive, simple, agréable. . . . La Musique de l'Eglise doit être expressive. Les régles que nous nous sommes établies la mènent là bien certainement. N'est-il pas évident que plus ce qu'on souhaite est doux, plus ce qu'on craint est terrible; et plus nos sentiments veulent être exprimez d'une manière vive et marquée? Or où est-ce qu'on craint et qu'on souhaite de si grandes choses? Les passions d'un Opéra sont froides, au prix de celles qu'on peint dans notre Musique de l'Eglise.

BONNET, *Histoire de la Musique,* 1725

The secularization of church music during the seventeenth century was not an isolated phenomenon, but a part of the drift of European culture from the church to the stage. Secular music evolved from Orazio Vecchi's latently operatic treatment of the madrigal, to Monteverdi's explicitly narrative and dramatic version with soloists and instrumental ritornelli; and thence to the solo cantata itself. (For instance, such works of Monteverdi as *Il Combattimento di Tancredi*, and the baroquely emotional cantatas of Rossi.) Similarly, in the field of ecclesiastical music, the monumental polyphony of the Venetian school of Giovanni Gabrieli gave to the religious technique a glamour which almost suggested the humanistic passion of the chromatic madrigal. When once the chromatic idiom entered the church, it was only one step further to introduce the operatic aria and recitative.

The first years of the century show an extraordinarily rich fusion of techniques. The Vespers and Magnificat and other church music which Monteverdi composed for St Mark's, Venice, have a grounding in the old counterpoint, combined with monumental colouristic effects, brilliant instrumentation, baroque figuration, madrigalian chromaticism, and passages of operatic aria and recitative. And there is a mature fusion, not a   137 confusion, of styles. Even when the homophonic theatre style had been unequivocally accepted in the church, there are still traces of continuity with the old methods. Ecclesiastical motets and solo cantatas of Schütz, who was briefly a pupil of Monteverdi, often incorporate juxtapositions of unrelated triads similar to those in the chromatic madrigal; no less common are fugato passages which, being chromatic, have become mainly harmonic in effect.

But the key-figure with reference to the future of church music is not Monteverdi, nor Schütz, but the Italian Carissimi. His life stretches across the century from 1605 to 1674, and his work is intimately linked with the religious life of Rome. No doubt the enthusiasm of Pope Urbino VIII for the new monodic style encouraged Carissimi to develop Cavalieri's attempt (in his *Rappresentazione di anima e di corpo*) to adapt the operatic technique to a religious use; but in so doing he was following the direction in which his sensibility led him. In 1630 he was appointed musical director of the Jesuit college of St Apollinaire, for German students, and it was in this environment that he composed his long series of sacred histories and oratorios. He accepted in his technique the operatic recitative and aria, madrigalian chromaticism, and the 'monumental' homophonic style of choral writing; his music is by no means devoid of the Bernini-like qualities, the declamatory passion and emotional chromatic progressions which characterize the secular cantatas of Rossi.

The essence of his achievement, however, lies in the more sober stylization of baroque exuberance which he introduces. Like Cavalli in the opera, he employs an almost consistently homophonic style in his large-scale choruses; in his solo cantatas he is as much interested in the balance of clauses, the alternation of mood, as in lyrical expressiveness. In these smaller works he substituted for the glittering baroque orchestra the more intimate combination of solo voices, with two obbligato violins, and a rich but subdued continuo of organ, harpsichord and theorbo lute. There is thus some analogy between the chamber cantata and the baroque violin sonata.

Some of Carissimi's arias have a lyrical suavity and balanced elegance which reminds one of Lully, or even Handel; and there is a very moving passage of choric lamentation at the end of

Jephtha which anticipates the technique of tranquilly sensuous suspensions in dotted rhythm which we have already observed in some of the slow movements of Couperin's violin sonatas. In any case, it is not difficult to understand why Carissimi's music, with its aristocratic disciplining of baroque passion, made so immediate an appeal to his contemporaries who were in search of an autocratic stylization; the virtues of his work were such as were bound to interest, in particular, the adherents of the Roi Soleil. By the time of Lully, Carissimi's influence on French church music was of an importance which was hardly to be exceeded even by Corelli's influence on the instrumental school. Lecerf de la Viéville, who was the last person to flatter an Italian, said:

> Quoique Carissimi soit antérieur à cet age de la bonne musique italienne, j'ai toujours été persuadé qu'il est le plus grand musicien que l'Italie ait produit et un musicien illustre à juste titre, plein de génie sans contredit, mais de plus, ayant du naturel et du goût; enfin, le moins indigne adversaire que les Italiens ayent à opposer à Lully.

It seems probable that at the height of his popularity this 'homme d'un mérite extraordinaire s'était longtemps formé en faisant chanter ses pièces aux Théatins de Paris.'

In 1649 a French youth of fifteen, Marc-Antoine Charpentier, went to Rome to study painting. He seems to have had precocious musical gifts also, for, hearing some of Carissimi's sacred histories, he decided that his life's work must be to create music such as that. The legend has it that he memorized several of Carissimi's works and carried them back to France in his head. However this may be, there is no doubt that his efforts and those of Michel Farinel did much to encourage the vogue for Carissimi in France. Most of Charpentier's own work is sacred music in Carissimi's convention; though his *Médée* suggests that he might have been a successful opera composer also, but for Lully's monopoly. His compositions include masses, psalms, and *leçons de ténèbres* for the Dauphin's private chapel, sacred histories and motets for the Jesuits of the rue St Antoine, and even a few small works for Port Royal. In Charpentier's music, the lyrical suavity and architectural gravity of Carissimi acquire a rather more pathetic and introspective tinge, as they merge into the French line of Lullian recitative. The declamation itself is a compromise between Lully and the Italian baroque flourish:

Per-cu-ti-am pas-to-rem, per-cu-ti-am pas-to-rem   et dis-per-

- gen - - - - - - - - - - - - - tur
etc.

and the tone of his work has an elegiac quality comparable with
that of the lutenists. If he has less power and variety than
Carissimi, he has possibly greater subtlety and depth, and certainly he preserves a closer contact with the polyphonists; Titon
du Tillet called him 'un des plus sçavants et des plus laborieux
Musiciens de son tems'. In the wonderful closing section of his
cantata *Le Reniement de St Pierre*, he attains to a sustained purity
of line, mated with a dissolving sensuousness of harmony,
which rivals the finest work of Couperin himself:

There is nothing that more recalls Couperin's flavour, unless it
be a few passages in the cantatas of Henri Dumont.

Of all the church composers of the *grand siècle* Henri Dumont
has perhaps the closest link with the polyphonic art of the
previous century. Indeed he continued to compose contrapuntal
music in the old *a cappella* tradition until the end of his life in
1684, and he was the only composer of his time to write masses
directly based on plainsong themes, even though these themes
were mensurated and tonally modernized. He is, however,
chiefly remembered for his fine motets in the new style for solo
voices and continuo, many of which date from the middle of the

century. These have a sinewy power which is at once fervent
and devotional. They suggest a development which was finally
consummated in the work of La Lande, unquestionably one of
the greatest religious composers of the seventeenth century,
though his work is, in this country at least, little known. With
his habitual good taste Louis personally chose La Lande to be Du
Mont's successor★ as Superintendent of the Royal Chapel. He
had picked a man who was able to create in church music a
worthy counterpart to the grandeur of Lully's achievement in
secular music. The general tenor of La Lande's work is noble and
Handelian, but the contrapuntal vitality of his lines gives great
nervous force to his rich and sonorous harmonies. We cannot
deny that a work such as his *De Profundis* conveys a spiritual
illumination which makes it perhaps the most impressive musical instance of the strain of mysticism that we have seen to be
latent in this ostensibly hedonistic society.

Now while Couperin in his church music does not attempt to
emulate La Lande's massive dignity he rivals, perhaps even
excels him in the ability to express an intimate spirituality, a
purity of feeling and a sense of wonder which are the prerequisites of a religious view of experience. From this point of
view both Couperin and La Lande differ essentially from Lully.
Sometimes, it is true, there is an unexpected tenderness, as well
as nobility, in the drooping suspensions of Lully's motets:

and the magnificent early *Miserere* (1664) that so moved Mme de
Sévigné achieves its lacerating intensity by a La Lande-like fusion of harmonic and contrapuntal elements. His more typical,
later church works, however, such as the *Te Deum* or even the
nobly passionate *Dies Irae*, are massive, ceremonial, festive,

---

★ 'Le Roi qui se connoissait parfaitement en Musique goûta fort celle de La
Lande, il lui donna successivement les deux charges de Maître de Musique de la
Chambre et les deux de Compositeurs, celle de Surintendant de la Musique, et
les quatre Charges de Maître de la Chapelle.' (Titon du Tillet.)

deriving not from the intimate sacred histories of Carissimi but from his homophonic choral pieces. There is nothing specifically religious about these bold lines and monumental harmonies, any more than there is about Corneille's ostensibly Christian play *Polyeucte*. Some analogy may be established between Lully's harmonic and architectural majesty, and the noble resonance of Corneille's heroic couplet. They both have few emotional overtones; they deal in the social values of civilization.

Compared with Lully's ceremonial homophony, the church music of Couperin, like that of La Lande, shows a greater fluidity of line and freedom of harmony; we see in his finest religious music perhaps the most remarkable demonstration of his compromise between polyphonic and homophonic technique. If Lully's homophony may be related to Corneille's alexandrine, perhaps we may see, in the more flexible line and harmony of Couperin, some analogy with the depths of meaning which imagery and rhythm reveal beneath Racine's ostensibly conventional language. Ultimately, this plasticity corresponds to a deeper interest in the workings of the human mind and to a more spiritual conception of values than is common to the gallantry of Lully and Corneille. We can adequately understand Couperin's Molière-like sanity and humour only if we realize that it is modified by a tragic sense of the implications of *Le Misanthrope;* we can appreciate his classical poise only if we see it in relation to the ferocity of *Phèdre*; and we can most clearly understand his spiritual radiance if we see it in relation to the *extrême douceur* of Racine's *Athalie*.★

For central representative of the *grand siècle* though he is, Racine has, especially in *Athalie*, a spiritual purity which seems to refer back to the great days of French medieval civilization. Couperin's church music has a similar quality. He accepts the Italianized, secularized convention of the motet and cantata in the manner of Carissimi, but he manages to reconcile this with a purity and simplicity of technique and feeling which reminds one of Josquin, or even Dufay. In this he more maturely develops an element which we shall later note in the work of

---

★ The music for the choruses in Racine's *Athalie* and *Esther* was in fact composed by J-B. Moreau, who also set three of Racine's *Cantiques Spirituels*. While not in the class of Couperin's finest work, his music has an exquisite grace which is worthy of *Esther*, if not of *Athalie*.

Chambonnières. Of course, apart from the linear nature of his idiom – closer to Bach than to Lully or Handel – there is in Couperin's work no direct technical heritage from the fifteenth and sixteenth centuries. But there is a certain temperamental affinity, and it is this which gives him so central a position in the French tradition. While he belongs without ambiguity to the age in which he lived, and cannot be said to live, like Bach, culturally in the past, none the less he has something of Bach's transitional significance. What was clearly true of the organ masses is more subtly true of all his representative work. He looks backwards rather than forwards; he stands between the medieval and the modern world.

The church music of both Couperin and La Lande was composed between 1695 and 1715, during the last melancholy years of Louis's reign, and for that reason it is perhaps understandable that a more intimately spiritual tone should be discernible in it, if it be compared with Lully's worldly splendour. This more spiritual quality is not, however, present in the earliest example of Couperin's work for the Chapelle Royale, the motet *Laudate pueri Dominum*, dated 1697. This is an exercise in Carissimi's cantata technique, comparable with the experiments in Corellian sonata technique which Couperin had made a few years previously. Although an impressive piece, it is not a work of mature personality.

The 'Symphony' is designed in the Carissimi manner for two violins and continuo, though Couperin is not specific about the instruments to be employed. The melodic parts are freely canonic, with many overlapping suspensions, as in the two-violin sonatas. The solo instruments anticipate the material of the vocal sections, but are used only during the interludes or ritornelli, not in conjunction with the voices. The next movement, *Sit nomen Domini benedictus*, uses voices and violins together in imitation, in a solemn 3 : 2 pulse. The piece corresponds to the *grave* sarabande of the da chiesa sonata. The harmony is rich and massive, though not especially personal.

A solis ortu is a brilliant virtuoso section in the Italian fashion, a fugal movement on a 'harmonically' centred subject incorporating a rising arpeggio and falling scale passage:

A so - lis or - tu us - que ad oc - ca - - sum

Here the two instrumental parts have a continuously animated share in the counterpoint, and include much glittering passage-work in thirds. The *Excelsus super omnes gentes* section is in a simple symmetrical rhythm resembling the French *air tendre*. Echo effects are obtained in dialogue between voices and violins, and the gentle rhythm and limpid diatonicism provide the first intimation of an effect which Couperin is to develop in later church works:

et su - per coe - los glo - ri - a e - jus

Then follows a passage of arioso, making use of sequential figurations:

in coe - lo et in ter - ra, in coe - lo et in ter - ra, in

A charming Lullian dance in a dotted triple rhythm accompanies the words *Suscitans a terra inopem*, and leads into an Italianate arioso duo on the words *Ut collocet eum*. The work concludes with a long canzona on a brisk dance tune:

involving the two violins and three voices in continuous contrapuntal dialogue. The voices are called upon for considerable virtuosity; Handelian baroque passages in the bass are frequent:

lae - tan - - - - - - - - - - - - - tem, Qui ha - bi - ta - re fa - cit

The movement is brilliant and effective, if not very typical of Couperin.

144   The *Quatre Versets d'un Motet chanté à Versailles*, 1703, to

words from the psalm *Mirabilia testimonia tua*, marks the emergence of the authentic Couperin manner in Latin church music. It opens with a remarkable arioso passage (*Tabescere me fecit*) for two unaccompanied sopranos, treated in free imitation. The tenuous purity of the two voices, pitched high in their register, evokes the atmosphere of the whole work, which is of a 'celestial' radiance such as we have met before in parts of the violin sonatas and organ masses. The unaccompanied opening – Couperin's direction that it 'se chante sans Basse-Continuë ny aucun Instrument' is unequivocal – has flexible lines and subtle effects of ellipsis. The instruments enter with a delicate theme embracing a rising fifth and a little repeated falling scale figure in quavers. The texture resembles that of the gayer, more ballet-like fugal sections of the organ masses, though when the voice appears it exploits a more Italian technique, with long roulades suggested by the words:

The quaver scale passage is used here sequentially to the *doux* accompaniment of drooping octaves on the violins. It appears fairly consistently throughout the movement; towards the end, a more emotional chromaticism is introduced into the bass.

The next verse, *Adolescentulus sum*, is in the major, scored for soprano, two flutes, and continuo played on violins. This limpid sonority accords with the innocent diatonicism of the lines, with the caressing passing notes, and with the simply symmetrical rhythm. This conscious naïveté could not have been created but for Couperin's relation to the *brunette* tradition. It is, however, much more than that, for it is in such effects as this intertwining of soprano and flute that we may find a spiritual innocence more 145 reminiscent of Josquin and Dufay than of the sensual emotion of Carissimi and the *grand siècle*. In this instance we may even see some slight technical similarity between the dissolving effect of the passing notes in the Couperin:

and those in some of the simpler, more homophonic work of Josquin.

This movement leads into a lightly dancing setting of *Justitia tua* for two sopranos, with a continuo of violins. The leap of a tenth gives the theme a lilting airiness:

There are piquant canonic entries producing dissonant suspensions:

The last section, *Qui dat nivem*, is scored for the same combination as the *Adolescentulus sum*, and likewise proceeds in a gentle crotchet pulse. Passing notes and appoggiaturas again create a 146 glowing, radiant quality:

At the end the voice and flute dissolve away in triplets and then semiquavers in silvery thirds. Throughout, the texture of the work has a filigree-like delicacy, and no one but Couperin could have written it.

After this ethereal work, the *Sept Versets du Psaume Benedixisti Domine* of 1704 strike a different note. This piece has grandeur and intensity. The first section is a bass aria with flute obbligato. Although meditative and withdrawn, with a quiet regular pulse like some of Bach's Passion arias, it is remarkable for its spacious proportions, linear complexity, and powerful sense of climax. The vocal phrases are of great length, with Italian descriptive flourishes:

Chromatically rising figures create a sense of urgency and pleading, but the emotion is always controlled by the even pulse, and by the grave proportions of the whole. Note for instance how in this passage the upwards aspiring line is counterbalanced by the falling sequences of the last two bars:

The texture has here a Bachian richness. The flute is subtly used both in imitation of the voice and, in a highly effective passage, 147

in unaccompanied duplication at the tenth.

The next section, in the relative major (B flat), is a duo for tenor and bass with independent obbligato parts. The words *Numquid in aeternum irasceris nobis* suggest a contrapuntal treatment, highly baroque and Italianate, though with a French graciousness. The vocal parts indulge in rapid scale passages and virtuoso roulades. A passage of arioso for the *Ostende nobis Domine* leads into one of Couperin's hushed, contemplative movements in a swaying triple rhythm, for tenor with instrumental obbligato, probably flute. An atmosphere of naïve wonder is obtained through some odd processions of unresolved 6 : 4 chords:

The tonality changes to a clear G major and a passage of recitative flows into a gentle aria on a crotchet pulse. Sometimes the part-writing creates tender dissonances similar to those in the *sommeil* movements of the *Apothéose* sonatas:

more commonly the texture is as transparently diatonic as that of the organ *Messe pour les Convents*:

The next verset is a duet for two tenors, again in the minor, and elegiac in tone, with Italian arabesques, mainly in thirds. *Veritas de terra* is a brief *da capo* aria in D, with ritornello. The theme starts with the notes of the major triad ascending, and again the solo line has an Italian floridity. The harmonies, however, attain a certain acerbity, during a prolonged modulation to the minor of the dominant. This motet ends quietly with a duet between two pairs of oboe and flute in unison without continuo; after the instrumental prelude, the voices double the first oboe and flute parts. As in the Versets of the previous year, this tenuous finale seems to suggest that the worldly glory of the Roi Soleil is dissolving away into eternity. In this sense, it is not altogether extravagant to say that Couperin's delicate sensuousness has merged into an attitude that can be called transcendental. To this music, as to the hushed, dissolving passages in the violin sonatas, the massive Handelian full close would be inappropriate.

The *Qui regis Israel* versets of the next year, 1705, show a further development of the graver Bachian manner of the 1704 work. A triple-rhythmed prelude exploits echo effects between the solo instruments and the continuo instruments. The two voices, haute-contre and bass, move mainly note for note in a nobly cantabile manner. The *Excita potentiam tuam* is one of Couperin's jaunty 3 : 8 movements, with the voices this time treated imitatively. The main theme has a sprightly rising scale figure:

The *Vineam de Aegypto* section is a bass aria in B flat, with a Lullian dance lilt underlying its Italianism. It leads into a lively 3 : 8 air for bass and double chorus, accompanied by groups of oboes and flutes, and violins. All these quick movements are of a somewhat secular frivolity. An altogether deeper note is sounded with the two magnificent arias for haute-contre with obbligato flutes. These are in F minor – according to Rameau the conventional key for *chants lugubres*. The *Operuit montes umbra ejus* section employs wild, whirling scale passages in the instrumental parts, similar to those adapted from Lully's overture by the violists and lutenists in their *tombeaux* movements. The piece as a whole has a most impressive union of the violist's ceremonial grandeur with Monteverdian dramatic fire – note for instance the big leaps, the diminished sevenths and tritones in the proudly declamatory line:

The second air, *Extendit palmites suos*, is in a steady triple rhythm, warm in its harmonic texture. It includes extended passages for voice with flutes and violins unaccompanied by the continuo. Here again we find the characteristically disembodied, unearthly effect.

The last section returns to C minor for a grave aria for haute-contre with flute and viol obbligato. The regular rhythm and independent part-writing once more suggest a more ethereal Bach, especially in certain sequential effects in the obbligato parts:

The harmony, however, often inclines to an un-Bachian, if delicate, voluptuousness.

With the *Motet de Ste Suzanne* we reach one of the peak points of Couperin's church music. Here the paradox of a sensuousness of harmony that is united with a virginal spirituality of line finds its loveliest expression. The opening is Italianate and Handelian, yet the impression it produces is remote from Handel's solidity. The material is founded almost entirely on this little phrase:

The expressive wriggle on *coronaberis* later attains a lilting exuberance:

and is bandied about between the haute-contre and obbligato violins. Couperin's sensuous sevenths and ninths introduce a more introspective tinge into the minor episodes, but the movement never loses its innocently smiling, almost playful, quality.

This playfulness is a part of the music's innocence and there is nothing superficial or irreverent about it. The seriousness of the work is revealed in the following duo for haute-contre and 151 soprano, *Date serta, date flores,* one of the most fragrant of all Couperin's movements in this manner. We may compare its ninth chords and melting suspensions with those in the *sommeil* movements of the *Apothéose* sonatas, or with the less mature examples in the organ *Messe pour les Convents*:

Nowhere does Couperin more cunningly exploit the effect of voices in thirds and sixths, high in their register. This air leads into a chorus, *Jubilemus, exultemus,* transparent in sonority, though gay. There are some exquisite overlapping scale passages, and naïve arpeggio figurations and chordal effects at the words *resonet coelum plausibus.*

The 3 : 2 aria, *O Susanna, quanta est gloria tua,* is related to the *grave* sarabande of the Italian violin sonata. It is superbly moulded in the Carissimi or Handelian manner, but voluptuously tender. We may regard it as the consummation of the little *Qui tollis peccata mundi* couplet of the *Messe pour les Convents* referred to in the chapter on the organ works. It has the same spiritual fragrance, but has too a classical amplitude in its proportions, particularly in passages in which the two obbligato violins sing in company with the soprano. This quotation gives an idea of its calm lyrical beauty, its richly tranquil harmony:

A change to two rhythm introduces the *Voluit Dominus sacrificium* for bass, obbligato instruments and continuo. This is a harmonically treated fugal movement in which voices and instruments use an imitative technique more or less consistently. The theme makes play with an octave leap, and the soloist has some eloquent descriptive flourishes:

After a repetition of the *Jubilemus* chorus comes a duet for soprano, bass, and continuo, the two voices being treated canonically. The gently rising theme, with its elliptical entries, and the suspended sevenths and ninths of the continuo again suggest an emotional warmth, mingled with naïve wonder:

Here too the feeling resembles that of the *Messe pour les Convents*. A brief ritornello and a passage of not particularly distinguished recitative is then rounded off by a second repetition of the *Jubilemus* chorus.

Probably Couperin would have claimed no more for the *Ste Suzanne* motet than that it was a simple, sensuous act of veneration, dedicated to a saint who was also a pretty girl. Yet in the 153 very simplicity of the sensuousness – the candour of the feeling – a spiritual experience is involved. The *douceur* and quietude of this music touch on a realm of emotion which we find in all Couperin's most significant work, and which has perhaps been most adequately described in verbal terms by Fénelon:

> L'état passif est celui où une âme, n'aimant plus Dieu d'un amour mélangé, fait tous ses actes délibérés d'une volonté pleine et efficace, mais tranquille et désintéressée. Tantôt elle fait les actes simples et indistinctes qu'on nomme quiétude ou contemplation; tantôt elle fait les actes distinctes des vertus convenables à son état. Mais elle fait les uns et les autres également d'une manière passive, c'est à dire, paisible et désintéressée. . . . Cet état passif ne suppose aucune inspiration extraordinaire; il ne renferme qu'une paix et une souplesse infinie de l'âme pour se laisser mouvoir à toutes les impressions de la grâce. . . . L'eau qui est agitée ne peut être claire, ni recevoir l'image des objets voisins; mais une eau tranquille devient comme la glace pure d'un miroir. . . . L'âme pure et paisible est de même. Dieu y imprime son image et celle de tous les objets qu'il veut y imprimer; tout s'imprime, tout s'efface. Cette âme n'a aucune forme propre, et elle a également toutes celles que la grâce donne. . . . Il n'y a que le pur amour qui donne cette paix et cette docilité parfaite.

The phrase 'tranquille et désintéressé' is the key to all Couperin's most characteristic music, and, indeed, to the most significant art of his time. It is not a matter of any 'inspiration extra-ordinaire'; it is a matter of simplicity and honesty of response, and if one can achieve that, says Fénelon, the grace and the peace of God will be added unto one. It is purity of heart that leads to a *docilité parfaite*, which is greater than *le moi* or *la volonté*. We may recall also a passage from one of Fénelon's letters to the Com-tesse de Montbaron:

> L'amour-propre malade, et attendri sur lui-même, ne peut être touché sans crier les hauts cris. L'unique remède est donc de sortir de soi pour trouver la paix.

There is no more beautiful testimony to this than Couperin's music; and even in the nineteenth century we can, from this point of view, see Gabriel Fauré as Couperin's successor. His music, too, has purity of line, combined with a subtle sensu-ousness of harmony; and his *Requiem,* like Couperin's *Ste*

Suzanne motet, is 'so near to God that it is without revolt, cry, or gesture'.

The motets which we have so far considered are all constructed on a plan similar to that of Bach's cantatas, with arias, recitatives of a lyrical arioso character, instrumental ritornelli, and obbligato parts. Unlike Bach and unlike Lully, Couperin makes little use of the chorus. When he does employ it, as in the *Ste Suzanne* motet, it is with discretion. The series of *Elévations* that follow the 1705 versets are all essentially music for soloists, with organ continuo. With one exception, they have no solo obbligato parts. Their form, like that of Carissimi's cantatas, is closely related to the sonata da chiesa. They are, as it were, 'chamber' cantatas, and in writing them Couperin was following the lead given by the beautiful *Elévations* of Lully.

The first elevation, *O Misterium ineffabile*, is the only example of Couperin's church music which was published in a modern edition before the issue of the Oiseau-Lyre edition. It sets the temper of most of the elevations; a flexible vocal line flows over smooth harmonic progressions, in an even crotchet pulse. Some rather surprising modulations give the piece a restrained fervour:

This quality is particularly noticeable in the 3 : 2 aria, in which long sustained suspensions on the exclamation 'O' combine with chromatic progressions and false relations to convey a quietly ecstatic yearning:

The second elevation, *O amor, O gaudium*, is for three male voices, and is in a similar mood. The opening 3 : 2 *grave* is not remarkable; an *affetuoso* 3 : 4 is a delightful air with cross-rhythmed exultations in the solo part:

The return to 3 : 2 takes us richly through the relative minor, and includes some imitative treatment of a *tendre* phrase built from descending fourths.

The third elevation, *O Jesu amantissime,* for haute-contre and continuo (called *Aspiratio mentis ad Deum* in one source and in the new Oiseau-Lyre edition) is perhaps the finest in this elegantly fervid manner. Its 3 : 2 aria has a spacious gravity, with effective melisma on the word *aeternitas.* It is chiefly notable, however, for its intense arioso – note this treatment of the word *crudelis*:

The triumphant aria in the major provides a florid Italianate conclusion, but is hardly an adequate resolution of the more melancholy parts.

The *Venite exultemus Domino* elevation is more strenuous, and tauter in harmony. Its rising scale opening phrase expresses a more active yearning, compared with the relaxed emotion of the preceding works:

A more vigorous homophonic treatment is also given to the ecstatic exclamations in the phrase *O immensus amor*:

The final 3 : 4 aria has some chains of suspended sevenths. This more powerful manner is developed further in the next elevation, *Quid retribuam tibi Domine*, which is also in E minor. Here even the bass line has considerable rhythmic animation. The haute-contre's arioso line is ardently lyrical, and the words' reference to the perils of material existence suggests some exciting roulades:

Later the words *crudelis* and *salvasti* produce a plaintive chromaticism and melisma:

With the *Audite omnes*, also for haute-contre, we come to the only elevation which has a 'symphonie' of obbligato parts. The instrumental lines are in the main restricted to echo effects in dialogue with the voices. The final 3 : 2 aria uses sequential sevenths in a way that recalls the *Ste Suzanne* motet; but as a whole the work is not very interesting. This is the last of the pieces specifically called *Elévation*. The other motets in the collection are not substantially different in form, though they possibly cover a wider range of feeling. The first of them, *Motet pour le Jour de Pâques*, at once strikes a new note, being one of the most brilliant works Couperin ever wrote. Its florid theme is developed with Handelian exuberance, with many resonant 157 thirds between the two voices. The *Christo resurgente* section is ripely harmonized, and has elaborate descriptive arabesques:

in qua sur- re - - - - - - - - - - - - - - - xit

The change to a four pulse brings some powerful Handelian decorated suspensions to *Alleluya*. Throughout, the alterations in rhythm for the different sections build up a cumulative sense of climax. The concluding alleluyas in 6 : 4 are a paean of triumph, again with effective syncopated suspensions:

The lengthy Magnificat also has some rousing exultations in 6 : 4, and some typically sensuous seventh chords:

A brief passage marked *Lentement*, to the words *Suscepit Israel puerum suum*, introduces one of Couperin's sudden shifts from major to minor, followed by dissolving sevenths; and an aria of glorification powerfully exploits a sprightly rising scale figure.

The next two motets are also pedestrian. The triumphant flourishes of the *St Barthélemy* motet have little of Couperin's imprint; though a reference to the Cross leads to some lovely drooping dissonances:

and the victorious conclusion interestingly reiterates its conventional penultimate suspended fourth. In the *Motet de Ste Anne* the regularity of the rhythm is not used to much expressive purpose. The *Memento O Christe* section has, however, an agile arioso line, and there is some neat contrapuntal writing for the three soloists in the final setting of *concedat nobis filius gratiam et gloriam*.

After these two works, we come to two which are, in different ways, among the finest. The *O Domine quia refugium*, (called *Precatio ad Deum* in one manuscript and in the new Oiseau-Lyre edition), for three basses and continuo, is a dark-coloured, majestic piece, though without, perhaps, the sinewy vigour of the E minor *Quid retribuam*. The opening 3 : 2 *grave* is in C minor. A noble homophonic movement with modulation to the relative major and simple return to the tonic by way of G minor, it contains no surprises, but impresses as being the opening of a work of some grandeur and solemnity. The change to a four pulse brings a more contrapuntal treatment, and the words *Dum turbabitur terra et transferentur montes in cor maris* suggest a semiquaver melisma, and then a surging arpeggio figure which is echoed between the three voices, to the accompaniment of a sustained major triad:

The *Propterea in Deo laudabo* shifts to the major and has an animated bass in quavers, reinforcing the soloists' laudatory flourishes. At first, the treatment is homophonic, interspersing a solo line with passages of three-part note for note writing. Later there is some close canonic imitation, and the parts demand an increasing virtuosity. The growth of contrapuntal elements and 159 of lyrical decoration builds up an imposing climax, until the motet ends in a blaze of diatonic counterpoint to the words *psalmos cantabimus.*

The *Motet de St Augustin* is in A, and returns to the radiant manner of the tribute to Ste Suzanne. The opening phrase, with its tenderly resolving 6 : 4 chord, has a soft glow which, if most un-Augustinian, is quintessentially Couperin. The resolving 6 : 4 is later developed into this delicious lilting phrase, with the persistent A as pedal in the bass:

A fine passage of arioso in the minor has a highly decorated solo line, with a flexibly melodic bass which occasionally introduces chromaticisms. The return to the major again brings one of Couperin's smiling diatonic phrases, imitatively treated:

The words *coronatus immortali gloria* are set to quietly rising scale passages in imitation, combined with a sustained pedal E. The conclusion has some of Couperin's warm suspensions in dotted rhythm.

The *Accedo ad te (Dialogus inter Deum et hominem)* is one of the most successful of the longer motets, and like the Versets of 1705 and 1706 offers some comparison with the technique of Bach. The opening aria is unpretentious, but the *Accede fili mi ad fontem* section, which changes the tonality to the major, is conceived on a grand scale. Much use is made of sequential figures, and the haute-contre's line has a baroque luxuriance. A passage of arioso is interesting both melodically and harmonically, and the next 3 : 4 aria, in the minor, combines the grace of the *air de cour* with a Bach-like closeness of texture. A rising scale figure in the continuo gives the air a sense of urgency which is counterbalanced by the fact that the scale passage is grouped in *falling* sequences:

The last section, *Totum ardeat et consummatur flamma*, is a magnificent piece of baroque contrapuntal writing over a steady crotchet beat. The melismata suggested by the word *flamma* gather momentum, and linear arabesques combine with sustained minims to create processions of suspended sevenths:

None of Couperin's motets has a more organic sense of growth to an inevitable end.

With the three *Leçons de Ténèbres* for one or two voices with organ and viol continuo we reach the highest point of Couperin's church music, and one of the peaks of his music as a whole. They were written between 1713 and 1715, possibly at the request of a convent. These are the works which justify the tentative comparison, made early in this chapter, between Couperin's achievement in church music and Racine's *Athalie*. While always preserving a civilized decorum, they attain to an intensity of passion which Couperin attempts but seldom. The Latin words of the prophet Jeremiah are interspersed with ritualistic Hebrew phrases which are used by Couperin as an excuse for vocalises of remarkable elaboration. Here the Italian aria technique is reinterpreted in terms of the French tradition; the *port de voix, tremblement*, portamento and other ornamental devices of the *air de cour* lose their fragility and enervating nostalgia, and are transformed into a line which reconciles subtlety with strength.

The opening of the first *Leçon* indicates admirably this breadth of line, and also shows how the ornamentation is both an expressive part of the line's contour, and a concomitant of the harmony:

In the first arioso passage, the freedom of the lines creates supple key changes, for instance this transition to E minor:

The ornamentation of the *air de cour* is again in evidence, with great lyrical intensity. At the end of this section there is a beautiful instance of Couperin's progression to the flat seventh, followed by the rise to the sharp seventh to form the cadence. We are here in the re-created world of the organ masses.

The second section of vocalise is even more elaborate than the first. Long held suspensions are resolved ornamentally, and there is a subtle use of false relation in the cadence. The minor passage of arioso, *Plorans ploravit in nocte*, is one of the most extraordinary and poignant pieces in the whole of Couperin's work. The vocal line is an impassioned lament, in which dissonant *ports de voix* convey a heart-rending sorrow. Both the contour of the lines, and the harmonies, are of extreme boldness:

163

A little chromatically altered phrase for the word *lachrymae*, accompanied by suspended sevenths, is simpler, but hardly less moving.

The second passage of recitative-arioso, *Migravit Juda*, is also powerful. Here the chromatically rising phrase, followed by a falling fifth, is particularly expressive; so is the characteristic cadence to the major.

Double appoggiaturas and diminished intervals are conspicuous in the F minor arioso, and the last passage of recitative introduces some painfully dissonant *ports de voix* and some chromatically ornamented resolutions in which the emotionalism is balanced by the *grave* arch of the line:

This 'weeping' chromatic resolution is then taken over by the continuo, becoming the main motive in the concluding aria. The swaying chromaticism imbues the line with a yearning quality, comparable with that of the earlier *Elévations*. Here, however, the lilting line is never limp, but has great nervous vitality. And this vitality is enhanced by the supple interplay between the voice and the continuo:

As a whole, the work seems to me one of the most impressive examples of linear organization and harmonic resource in late baroque music.

The second *Leçon* is also for one high voice, with organ and viol continuo. Again it opens with a rhapsodic vocalise in D major. The first recitative has drooping suspended sevenths; the second vocalise, in triple time, flows mainly in conjunct motion with *air de cour* ornamentation. Acute double suspensions and chromatic progressions in the bass occur in the second arioso, in the relative minor. Again the ornamentation of the vocal line increases the dissonance, while the balance of the phrases guards against any emotional instability – note the mingling of conjunct motion with figures built from the minor triad:

The subsiding chromaticisms of the conclusion have a Purcellian pathos, though the air as a whole is more classically 'objective'.

The next two passages of vocalise are nobly diatonic, with suspensions in the continuo. Some effective portamento falling sevenths are grouped in sequence, in the *Peccatum peccavit* arioso. A change to the minor occurs for the *Sordes ejus in pedibus ejus*, a section having considerable dramatic power, with tritones prominent in the vocal line, and harsh dissonances in the continuo:

The work concludes with an extremely beautiful aria, also in the minor, *Jerusalem convertere ad Dominum.* It is built on a simple phrase rising up a fifth, and then serenely falling. *Ports de voix* are again used to give harmonic intensity and at the same time to smooth off the contour of the line. The final statement of the theme is in an ornamented version. The subtlety and sensitivity of the ornamentation never destroys the music's architectural quality, while the noble architecture gives power to the sensitivity:

If the third *Leçon* impresses one as being the greatest, it is largely because, being conceived for two voices instead of one, it offers opportunities for a combination of the vocalise technique with polyphony. The opening vocalise uses the familiar soaring line in effective dissonant suspension, after the manner of the two-violin sonata. Here the winged, disembodied lines, moving mainly by conjunct motion, are vocal in conception, while the terseness of the dissonances is instrumental; this is the representative compromise between religious and secular technique:

166

The vocalise is repeated in artfully varied forms between each arioso section.

The first arioso incorporates Couperin's favourite modulation to the minor of the dominant; the second begins with a strange chromatic deliquescence:

The chromaticism is, however, defeated by the trumpet-like call of the voices in dialogue on the words *Vide Domine*; and the duo flows without break into a supple ornamented version of the vocalise in canon.

The *O vos omnes* section of recitative also balances a speech-like freedom of line and acute dissonances in the continuo, against trumpet-like phrases in rising fourths and sixths on the word *Attendite*. The tonal transitions still have a seventeenth-century plasticity:

The pace quickens on the words *Quoniam vindemiavit me*, and the voices proceed note for note until, with the words *irae furoris sui*, a climax is reached on a diminished seventh chord.* The section concludes with a beautiful version of the vocalise, even freer in rhythm and longer in melodic span:

The next section of recitative is notable for its dramatic falling sixth and even more vehement falling diminished octave, the latter being an emendation incorporated into the new Oiseau-Lyre edition. The passage, which thrusts forward from the descent into a dissonant *rising* appoggiatura, makes 'incarnate' the words *posuit me desolatam*:

---

* Such a use of the dramatic diminished seventh is not common in Couperin's work. The French were inclined to regard the chord with suspicion as being essentially Italian.

The following vocalise has one of Couperin's pathetic false relations:

An arioso on *Vigilavit jugum* leads to another homophonic section in quicker movement; this has a delicate grace which reminds one, even in this spiritual work, of Couperin's relation to the *brunette* tradition:

The work ends with a full-scale statement of the vocalise, developed canonically, but now adapted to the Latin text of the *Jerusalem convertere*. Over a level crotchet movement, the aria evolves with conventional architectural modulations to the dominant and sub-dominant. The contrapuntal writing is of great purity, and uses a phrase – a rising fourth followed by a descending scale – which had been common property among the sixteenth-century polyphonists. This clear counterpoint, mated with this equally lucid tonal architecture, shows us that in his last and greatest church work Couperin is still, like Bach, poised between two worlds, and making the best of them both.

It should perhaps be mentioned that the three surviving *Leçons de Ténèbres* are part of a projected set of nine. The other six seem to have been lost, or perhaps were never completed. Titon de Tillet also tells us that Couperin wrote twelve motets 'à grand choeur'. If so, they would be the only works of Couperin in the style of the monumental baroque. In any case, they are lost.

Chapter Nine

The Clavecin Works

In Tudor England, the relation between the secular and ecclesiastical keyboard schools was always intimate, and Bull and Gibbons are equally remarkable as composers of polyphonic organ fantasias and as composers of virginal pieces which, however complex they may become, at least start from secular song and dance. This close connection between the religious and the secular was one of the secrets of the extraordinary richness of English music at the turn of the century; and we have already seen that something rather similar was true of contemporary French musical culture. But whereas the French were aware of the implications of the 'modern' elements in musical style, and were prepared to sacrifice the old to the new, the English accepted the old and the new on equal terms. They were hardly aware, perhaps, that they had to make a choice; and their relative lack of self-consciousness is their strength. But it also means that their keyboard music – which is of a variety and subtlety not exceeded by any period of European history, and certainly not by the contemporary French schools – is an end as much as a beginning. Byrd, Gibbons, Farnaby, and Bull were not followed by a 'classical' keyboard composer, as Titelouze was followed by Chambonnières, and Chambonnières by Couperin. Between sixteenth-century polyphony and the classical age, there was a break in England's cultural continuity; and this break has, of course, social and economic causes which are summed up in the phenomenon of the Civil War. In French culture there is no such break in continuity. For the clavecinists the connecting link between sixteenth-century polyphony and the classical age is the work of the lutenist composers.

All through the sixteenth century, in France as in England, the lute had been a musical maid-of-all-work analogous to the modern piano. It had been used as a makeshift, for playing polyphonic vocal music in transcriptions that were literal apart from 171 slight modifications and decorations suggested by the nature of the instrument; it had been used for playing homophonic dance music – pavanes, galliards, branles and so on – usually as an accompaniment to the dancing. In this way, it was in close touch with both the social and religious aspects of sixteenth-century music, and beyond them with many of the traditions of folk art; so that when the lute composers began to grow into an independent school, they had behind them a consciousness of many centuries of French musical history – religious polyphony, secular harmonized chansons, court dances, and the dances of the people.

It was in the later years of the sixteenth century that a personal, expressive element became noticeable within music that had previously been of an 'occasional' order. In the dances of a man such as Antoine Francisque, a vein of sophisticated sensuousness appeared parallel to the growth of *précieux* elements in the verse of a St Amant or Théophile. The influence of the passionate Spanish vihuela music of Luis Milán may have encouraged this development of an expressive, rather than a purely functional, dance music. Certainly the connections between French and English culture were a contributory factor, for Dowland himself had a brilliant continental reputation, and at one time stayed at the court of Henri IV; while it was common for French musicians to visit England, some of them, such as Jacques Gaultier the elder, for considerable periods. Possibly the dolorous nature of Dowland's temperament encouraged a comparable gloom on the part of the French composers; possibly an elegiac quality native to the Frenchmen was reinforced by the development of the lute with eleven strings instead of the traditional nine, for the additional strings gave increased opportunity for a grave solemnity of harmony and for richness of part-writing. In any case, outside influences and material circumstances did no more than intensify a development which was native to French culture.

The English lutenists were highly developed art composers who were still related to a folk culture; there was with them no sharp division between esoteric and popular elements. The French lutenists, on the other hand, soon began to lose contact with their popular origins, becoming an autonomous school associated with the *précieux* movement in society. In the first generation of lute composers – the adventurous Bocquet, the virtuoso Vincent, the fragrant Mézangeau, Jacques and Ennemond Gaultier, Etienne Richard and Germain Pinel – there was something of the freshness and spontaneity of the English composers, if not their comprehensive power. But the second generation of lutenists – the great Denis Gaultier, Jacques Gallot, and Charles Mouton – were artists of high sophistication, the leading musical representatives of the *ruelles* and salons. Like the *air de cour* writers and the other mid-century exponents of *préciosité*, they strove, in their ornamentation, their stylized refinement, even their methods of fingering their instrument, to become a musical Elect, preserving their music from popular contagion. They even invented a semi-private language for the fanciful and cryptogrammatic titles of their pieces; the tradition survives in Couperin's work. At the same time, the stylization did not imply any emotional frigidity. The pictures in the beautiful contemporary edition of Denis Gaultier's *La Rhétorique des Dieux* that describe the relation of the various modes (the sixteenth-century terminology is somewhat incongruously adhered to) to different passions, are a further indication of the interest in subtle states of feeling which this society cultivated. Charmé even added quasi-psychological descriptive comments to some of Gaultier's pieces.

There is nothing in the lute music of this hyper-civilized society as passionately lugubrious as the wonderful chromatic fancies of Dowland; but the tone of the pieces, though always restrained, is elegiac, tenderly melancholy or dreamily noble, comparable with that of the *airs de cour*, only less enervating. Passages of ripe chromatic harmony such as this:

are fairly frequent in the work of Mouton, while the dissonant suspensions, sequential sevenths, and false relations of this passage are typical of the work of Jacques Gallot:

This composer is also enterprising in the matter of tonality, having some powerfully gloomy pieces in F sharp minor, a key known to the lutenists as *le ton de la chèvre*. The pieces of the greatest of the lutenists, Denis Gaultier, show a similar union of a polyphonic inheritance with an interest in the sensuous implications of harmony; but it is significant that it is he who most puts the stress on the moulding of his line and the balance of his clauses. The lovely *Tombeau* or memorial piece for the uncle of the famous Ninon de l'Enclos illustrates this clearly; note how the soprano line leads up – intensified by the chromatic progression of the bass – to the climax of a modulation into E minor, only to resolve into a cadence in C:

from which point the lines and harmonies subside to their source. All Gaultier's pieces have this instinct for dignity and proportion. Not only the grand *tombeaux* and sarabandes, but also the subtle-rhythmed courantes, are pervasively melancholy. Even the canaries, gigues, and galliards are more wistfully fanciful than joyous.

But Gaultier's expression of the aristocratic values of his community is revealed most remarkably in the cantabile character of his line. His rhythms have not the rather insensitive symmetry of some eighteenth-century music; but he does sometimes achieve a measured gravity of line, involving clearly defined modulation, which almost suggests Italian bel canto, or a

fresher, more delicate Handel:

That is one aspect of Gaultier, which we shall see echoed in Chambonnières, and later in Couperin himself. A more adequate notion of his genius will be given if we quote, before leaving him, the end of the *Tombeau* which he wrote for himself:

Here we may call attention to the noble span of the line; the caressing suspensions; the occasional tense diminished interval; the resonant spacing of the parts, derived from lute technique; and the sombre repetition of the Bs, and of the grave minor triad, in the last bar.

The most distinctive feature of lute technique – clearly revealed in most of the foregoing examples – is what one might call simulated polyphony. The broken arpeggio technique is used to create an illusion of part-writing which both preserves the sense of movement in the composition (despite the short sustaining power of the instrument), and at the same time establishes a solid harmony. The skill called for in interpreting the polyphony latent in the lute tablature was what principally gave its highly virtuoso character to lute technique. Only very sensitive and resourceful players were capable of an inadequate 'realization'.

Further evidence of this virtuosity both of technique and feeling is found in the ornamentation which was often not indicated in the text. This ornamentation was adapted to the lute 175 from the embellishments of the *air de cour*, and Jehann Basset's *L'art de toucher le luth* of 1636 indicates that in employing orna-ments the lutenists were inspired by similar motives as were the composers of *airs de cour*; 'de là vient que le jeu de nos devanciers n'avoit point les mignardises et les gentillesses qui embellissent le nostre par tant de diversitez'. The ornaments, which were an integral part of both line and harmony, included all kinds of slide or portamento, the sudden damping of strings, the *ver cassé* or vibrato, and various kinds of *tremblement* – for instance a rapid tremolo on a single string or an alternation of two notes coupled with a sighing diminuendo. The subtlety of these ornaments came from the direct contact between the string and the human agency of the finger. We must remember that the Gaultiers in France, like Dowland in England, were composers who were usually their own performers. Through their music they spoke intimately to their friends of *La Rhétorique des Dieux*, inculcating musical values that were also moral and spiritual: as we hear from the performances of their music, and that of Charles Mouton, by Walter Gerwig, included in Archiv's monumental series of recordings. Still more revealing is the recording of Dowland's lute music made by five lutenists for the Consort of Musicke's issue of Dowland's complete works: not only because Dowland is the greatest, the most varied and the most profound of lute masters, but also because modern recording techniques and performing expertise are now adequate to his subtleties. Most of Dowland's greatest music was written in the Jacobean era; the esoteric culture of the succeeding court of Charles I suggests that the English lutenists might have developed in a stylized fashion similar to the French, had not the tradition been interrupted by the Civil War. In any case the preoccupation of French harpsichord composers from Chambonnières to Couperin with delicacies of rhythm and ornamentation was in part a search for the lute's immediate relationship between the finger and the sounding medium. A relatively mechanical con-trivance had to be rendered humanly expressive.

Of the forms which the French lutenists adopted, the prelude was closest to the improvisatory style of the lute air. Written in unmeasured notation, to be interpreted by the performer, it was a more organized development of the preliminary flourishes in arpeggios and other obvious instrumental techniques which the player might improvise to a song. In a more measured form, the technique survives in both Louis and François Couperin, particularly in the pieces explicitly called Prelude, and in the most famous of all examples, the first prelude of Bach's Forty-Eight. The dances themselves, pavane (and later allemande), courante, sarabande, and gigue, preserve the features of the ballet dances, but, as with the bigger galliards and pavanes of the Tudor virginalists, the original character of the dance may sometimes be submerged in the melodic and figurative developments. This is not often the case, however, with the slighter dances, such as bourrées, canaries, and branles.

All these forms, and many of the techniques implicit in the nature of the lute, were taken over by the first composers for clavecin, who often wrote in a more or less identical manner for the lute or keyboard instrument. To them the clavecin was a kind of mechanized lute, and spread chord formations, plucked string effects, and overlapping canonic entries were all elements of lute technique which survived, or were modified, in the technique of the keyboard instrument: indeed simulated polyphony survived even though a naturally polyphonic instrument made deceit unnecessary. Almost from the start, however, the harpsichord strove to develop the formal aspects of the convention – as hinted at by Denis Gaultier – at the expense of the improvisatory elements. They belonged more to the new age of the mid-baroque. Possibly the best way to demonstrate this is by way of a comparison between the work of Chambonnières and that of his pupil, Louis Couperin.

Like Gaultier, Chambonnières was a product of *précieux* society, a leading musical representative of the Hôtel de Rambouillet, and later court clavecinist to Louis XIV. In most ways it is legitimate to regard his work as an extension of that of the lutenists, who were emulated as much for social as for musical reasons, the lute being the traditional instrument of nobility. His finest pieces derive from the polyphonic elements of the lute idiom. The three big G minor pavanes, with their contrapuntal entries, false relations, and rhythmic flexibility, can even be connected with the more massive polyphony of the religious choral and organ schools:

We can here see Chambonnières exploiting the traditions of the sixteenth century, together with luxuriant ornamentation, and with a richness of harmony encouraged by the spacing of the lute parts. The warm sound of the tenth and of the dominant seventh is especially attractive to him: he will dwell on the chords, revelling in their sensuous appeal:

These pieces, like the lute *tombeaux*, often attain a surprising grandeur and power.

Then there is a range of pieces analogous to the delicately proportioned sarabande of Gaultier which we have already quoted. Within their sophisticated symmetry, these pieces have a conscious naïveté which seems to entail a civilized reincarnation of the fragrance of French folk song; or we may relate it perhaps to French art song in the Middle Ages, to the troubadours' mating of innocence with sophistication. At the same time, the suave progression of the harmonies, with the sonorous spacing and fragile ornamentation, are the product of a courtly society:

We have already observed a development of this manner in some of Couperin's work, other than his keyboard music. In the following passage, the effect of the rising sharp seventh, succeeded by the flat seventh in the descent, is analogous to the Couperin of the organ *Messe pour les Convents*:

An even subtler case is this little sarabande in F, which combines its diatonically innocent air with inner parts in which ornamentally resolved suspensions create tender augmented and diminished intervals and other dissonances; we may note also, in the first section, the slightly disturbing effect of the modulation to D minor, before the conventional resolution in the dominant:

A further anticipation of Couperin's early work is found in the warm, quietly flowing gigue in G (No. 55 in the new Oiseau-Lyre edition, 1987).

Some of Chambonnières's quick pieces, such as the delightful *Gigue bruscambille* – built on an irregular rising scale passage in imitation – afford similar delight; and a few pieces, such as the B flat galliard with its *double* in clattering semiquavers, have an unexpectedly manly vigour. In general, however, his best movements are those which are in direct contact with the polyphonists, or with the lutenists, or with both. They tend, like Gaultier's work, to the elegiac and contemplative, without reaching, perhaps, the sombre refinement of Gaultier's best music. When Chambonnières attempts to build his pieces not on latently polyphonic principles, nor on the simple dominant-tonic basis of the G major sarabande, but on a more developed scheme of tonal relationships, the result is not very convincing. The larger allemandes, though interesting for their flexible part-writing, have not the balance between polyphonic vitality and harmonic architecture which marks the mature allemandes of Couperin and Bach. From this point of view, this normally impeccable artist suggests a development which he did not live to fulfil. The rather gauche allemande, *La Loureuse*, may be referred to as an illustration.

Comparatively, Chambonnières's pupil, Louis Couperin, is a much more vigorous personality: the Abbé Le Gaulois said that his playing was 'estimé par les personnes sçavantes à cause qu'elle est pleine d'accords et enrichie de belles dissonances, de dessins et d'imitations'. His pieces show a sturdy contrapuntal technique and an aggressive use of dissonance alien to the refined discretion of his master – witness this opening of a D minor sarabande:

More interesting, however, is the increasingly mature command of tonal organization which he manifests. He writes grandly expressive sarabandes which, even more than the 'exquisite' sarabandes of Chambonnières, provide some anticipation of

Handel; and his control of incidental modulation, within the tonic-dominant-tonic or minor-relative major-minor framework, gives no impression of the tentative or experimental. The E minor sarabande (No. 65 in the new Oiseau-Lyre edition, 1985), is an imposing example, and we may mention the Handelian D major (No. 60), and the canonic sarabande in D minor (No. 47). The polyphonic-homophonic compromise suggested by this last-mentioned sarabande is especially impressive, since the canonic entry starts on the last beat of the sarabande rhythm, so that the counterpoint consistently negates the bar measure. The most significant of the allemandes also preserve the linear independence of Chambonnières and the lutenists while achieving a satisfying tonal order; in this respect they anticipate the finest allemandes of Bach and Couperin le Grand. We may instance the slow rhapsodic allemande in D No. 58, the E minor No. 63, and the gentle G major No. 82, which recalls the silvery sound of the baroque organ.

Even the pieces of Louis Couperin which incline to the old polyphonic methods show this more vigorously organized quality. The famous *Tombeau de M. de Blancrocher* is in the tradition of the resplendently decorated *tombeaux* of the lutenists, but it intensifies the conventional improvisatory effects and dissonances to a pitch of dramatic passion that is almost operatic; consider the odd grinding noise of the unresolved sevenths at the end of this passage:

A comparable piece is the big pavane in F sharp minor – a key which crops up intermittently in the clavecin music, being a survival from the lutenists' *ton de la chèvre*. This pavane is again founded on lute technique; its chromatic alterations give it a remarkable pathos. The classical stability of its proportions, 181 together with the sensuous, melodically derived augmented intervals of the incidental harmonies, might even be compared with the elegiac late nocturnes of Fauré:

Another piece looking back to the false relations and polyphony of the lutenists is the G minor allemande, No. 93:

More startling is the G minor fantasia which begins contrapuntally in the manner of the organ fancy, and then develops by widely skipping arpeggio figurations, without any return to the fugal principles of the opening. The new age of the dance and the theatre has here routed the old world of the church, in a manner as original as it is convincing.

This is probably an organ piece, related to the work of a man such as Nicolas le Bègue. The lively sense of the keyboard which it displays is more convincingly demonstrated in the *Duo*, perhaps the finest of Louis Couperin's more animated movements, notable for the variety of its linear patterns, and for the surprising richness and piquancy of the harmony produced by the movement of the two parts:

But the most impressive of Louis Couperin's pieces, as well as the most 'modern' in effect, are those using the transitional technique of chaconne or passacaglia, which we have already discussed with reference to Lully. Louis Couperin's chaconnes proceed with relentless power, and are usually dark in colour and dissonant in texture; consider the spiky clash in the first bar of No. 55:

Here again Couperin introduces a bold modification in the chaconne-rondeau technique, since he occasionally allows the modulations of the couplets to be continued into the repetitions of the theme, thereby making a compromise between the traditional static technique and the new sense of tonal relationship. The G minor chaconne, No. 121, is also remarkable for its dramatic use of diminished seventh chords.

Among the passacailles, the G minor No. 96 is characterized by a rhythmic freedom in line and ornamentation which reminds one of operatic recitative. This is a fine piece, but still finer are Louis Couperin's two masterpieces, the C major passacaille No. 27, and the passacaille in G minor and major, No. 98. The C major is a gravely massive piece which uses ornamentation, dotted rhythms, and scale passages to build up a cumulative power almost comparable with the chaconne of Couperin le Grand's C minor violin suite, or with the grand choral chaconnes in Lully's last operas. It ends in evocative solemnity with a repetition of the *grand couplet* in the minor instead of the major, a reversal of the normal procedure such as one occasionally finds in Purcell. The great G minor passacaille No. 98 is Louis   183

Couperin's biggest piece in every sense. It is built over a falling scale bass, and employs every device afterwards used by Couperin le Grand to build up an overwhelming climax – dissonant suspensions, more animated movement, flowing scale passages in parallel and contrary motion. There is a wonderful modulation into the major, incorporating richly spaced suspensions, and a chromatically modified version of the bass which is balanced by soaring diatonic scale figures:

The final couplet keeps the chromatic bass but returns sombrely to the minor.

Two other pupils of Chambonnières should be mentioned among Couperin's predecessors – Jean Henri d'Anglebert and Gaspard le Roux. D'Anglebert represents perhaps the culmination of the mid-baroque period that preceded Couperin le Grand. He transfers to harpsichord idiom much of the contrapuntal power and harmonic luxuriance which we observed in his organ fugues, a quotation from which was given in Chapter 5. His clavecin work has a remarkable grandeur, whether it be in a brilliantly expansive piece such as the long variations on *La Folia*, a grave, austerely wrought movement such as the G minor allemande, or a spaciously serene piece such as the D major chaconne, which has a Claude-like quietude fully worthy of comparison with the rondeau from the *Impériale* suite of François Couperin himself.

Le Roux's *Pièces pour Clavecin*, although not published till 1705, were written considerably earlier. With d'Anglebert he is the last representative of the *grand goût* of the mid-century, and his music has much of the valedictory nobility of Denis Gaultier. But if he is less of a modernist than Louis Couperin, he is a more mature and developed artist than Chambonnières; his work is remarkable for the lyrical contour of its melody, and for the richness of its balanced sequential writing, as we may see from this passage from a courante:

184

We may mention also the beautiful suite in F sharp minor, which may be compared with Louis Couperin's movements in the same *ton de la chèvre*; the F major chaconne which deserves to keep company with the grandest pieces in this contemporary form; and the long sarabande with variations in G minor. This last sarabande is really an elaborate chaconne, and although less remarkable musically than the other pieces mentioned is interesting for its unexpectedly progressive treatment of keyboard technique. Its use of arpeggio and scale figurations almost suggests the Handel of the harpsichord passacaglias. An appendix includes a second clavecin part for five of the pieces. These are included in the excellent modern edition, and make a fascinating contribution to the restricted range of music for two keyboards.★

Behind composers such as Chambonnières, Louis Couperin, d'Anglebert and Le Roux was the school of lutenist composers; and behind them in turn were, as we have seen, generations of French musical tradition, from folk song and troubadours, to the polyphony and harmonized dance music of the sixteenth century. Interacting with these traditional French elements were Italian influences: the implicit presence of the operatic aria and occasionally of the dramatic harmonic formulae with which the continuo accompanies recitative; the influence of Italian dance music and the popular culture of the *commedia dell'arte*, linking up with the French popular culture; and the influence of Corelli and his conception of the tonal formalization of dance movements. In the work of all Chambonnières's successors, one can observe these French and Italian elements slowly merging into

---

one another, whether it be at the level of the finest work of Louis Couperin or of d'Anglebert or at the level of the unpretentious dances of Nicolas le Bègue. The fusion is consummated in the harpsichord music, as in the concerted music, of Couperin le Grand. In the first book of his clavecin pieces we are most conscious of the constituent materials, French and Italian, as such; in the fourth they are so completely assimilated into an idiom of classical maturity that we are conscious of the perfect proportions of the whole building, rather than of the richness of detail that goes to make it up.

Some dance movements of the lute suite Couperin takes over as they stand, though he presents them in a more lucidly diatonic form. The gigue and sarabande survive in their Italianized version; the pavane is replaced by the allemande, as it was tending to be in the work of Chambonnières and Louis Couperin. These dance rhythms are all absorbed into the binary principles of the baroque sonata, with the first section ending in the dominant or relative major, the complementary second section returning to the tonic (the dances and their structure will be discussed in detail in the next chapter). All the pieces which are not basically dance movements of this type are rondeaux or chaconne-rondeaux – an extension of the old technique of dance tune with couplets, whereby the symmetrical theme is stated, followed by a short episode of allied but distinct material possibly involving a simple modulation, followed by a restatement of the tune in its original form always without modulation, followed by another episode, and so on, *ad libitum*. Both techniques were, as we have seen, in the first place functional, arising out of the practical exigencies of the dance; and both, especially the rondeau, may seem to be extremely limited. But Couperin le Grand – like Bach and Scarlatti, and like Louis Couperin before him – shows how the limitation may be used to convey an intensity of experience such as can be achieved only in the full maturity of a civilization. We may compare Corneille's, Racine's and Pope's use of the alexandrine and heroic couplet.

Although the plan of Couperin's movements is harmonically dictated he still, like Bach and Scarlatti, occupies a transitional position between polyphony and homophony, in so far as his music normally entails a dialogue between melody and bass; the latter nearly always has melodic significance. Implied polyphony exists alongside the ripest development of tonal harmony; the lucid harmonic scheme both moulds, and is moulded by, the dialogue of the parts. Like Bach, Couperin borrows vitality and subtlety from the polyphonic tradition, and from the homophonic a classical objectivity. Not only the violin sonata which we have already discussed, but also the gigue of the keyboard suite had long manifested this harmonic-contrapuntal fusion, since its clear harmonic basis was combined with fugal treatment 'inverted' in the second half of the structure, the inversion of the themes corresponding with the inversion of the sequence of keys. But the melodic-harmonic fusion is much subtler than this in Bach's and Couperin's conception of keyboard technique, reaching its most profound expression in their more baroque movements (such as the allemandes of Bach's E minor and D major partitas, or a piece of Couperin such as *Les Langueurs-Tendres*). Here the symmetrical harmonic periods are no more than implicit beneath the continuous, unmetrical flow of ornamented lyricism. This is the consummation of a technique which we have already observed in a tentative form in some movements of the organ masses.

Couperin's first book of harpsichord pieces was published in 1713, though many of the pieces had been written much earlier. If the 'Bachian fusion' is least evident in this volume, one can perhaps find here the various types of piece which Couperin is subsequently to develop, in their most accessible form. Firstly there are, particularly in the second *ordre*, a number of simple undeveloped dances, more or less the same as those which were actually danced to in the ballets. These are often charming and are interesting as one of the roots from which Couperin's art grew, but are not otherwise remarkable. Secondly there are, closely related to these dances, slightly more sophisticated dance pieces in which the influence of Corelli's tonal plan is more perceptible; *La Milordine*, *La Pateline*, and *La Florentine* are obvious examples. These are staightforward movements in Italian binary style, though with a gallic delicacy in the texture. Then, thirdly, there is a class of pastoral pieces which are ostensibly French in manner, related to the *brunette* tradition and the ballet. Some of these are charmingly personal in flavour; the idiom of a piece such as *La Fleurie ou la tendre Nanette*, though more harmonic, resembles the chansons of a Guillaume de Costeley in its combination of sophisticated ornament with a melodic and harmonic naïveté which has the spiritual innocence of folk song. Others (*La Tendre Fanchon*, *La Bandoline*, *La Flore*) link this innocence of melody with a technique of figurative sequences built on seventh chords, thereby creating a delicate voluptuousness which we have seen to be one of the most typical features of Couperin's sensibility:

This is the kind of technique, reconciling a mannered 'social' artificiality with a latently personal emotion, in which it is possible to trace some analogy with the painting of Watteau. Beneath the apparently passive acceptance of the courtly convention there is an intense apprehension of the loneliness of the individual consciousness.

A somewhat different aspect of the Watteau-like manner is shown in the fourth group of pieces – those exploiting the arpeggio figurations of lute technique. *Les Idées Heureuses* has a tranquil flow of arpeggio figuration which, by means of tied notes and suspensions, creates a quasi-polyphonic effect. Both the melodic interest and the harmonic subtlety of the piece profit from this treatment. The movement also includes a touching passage built over a descending chromatic bass in a manner much favoured later by Couperin himself, and by Bach. *La Garnier* is another beautiful piece in the lute tradition, exploiting the resonance of the clavecin's overtones in a way that might almost be called impressionistic. This too is a style that Couperin develops in later work.

The fifth group of pieces comprises those influenced by the more powerful aspects of lute technique – bigger movements in the tradition of the *tombeau*. The finest examples are the allemande and sarabande, *L'Auguste* and *La Majestueuse* in the G minor *ordre*, and the comparable movements, *La Ténébreuse* and *La Lugubre*, from the *ordre* in C minor. These are magnificent pieces, using massed broken chords, passionate ornamentation, lute-like percussive effects and harmonic acridities, and revealing a closeness of texture which rivals the graver suite movements of Bach. Such a passage as this from *La Ténébreuse*, almost as much as the larger contrapuntal movements in the late violin sonatas, at once reveals the absurdity of the account of Couperin – at one time current – as a hot-house composer:

The courantes, too, have a rhythmic and contrapuntal virility that makes them more comparable with Bach than with any other exponent of the late baroque.

The last group of pieces includes the most mature movements in the first volume – those which already illustrate what we have called the Bachian compromise. The allemande *La Logiviére* is a splendid example, reconciling its architectural structure and latent dance rhythm with a continuous stream of baroque melody, powerful dissonances in the inner parts, and some characteristically 'impressionistic' drone effects. *La Laborieuse* is a similar piece, with strange, melodically derived modulations; and another remarkable movement is *Les Regrets*, in which the pathos is attained by means of suspensions continuously hovering over a bass which proceeds with measured gravity. But the finest piece in the book is the C minor chaconne *La Favorite*, which is in duple time instead of triple.★ This is a work which, even by Bach's standard, one may call great. There is nothing outside Bach which has such massive dignity of workmanship, and yet it is quite unlike Bach, and could have been written by no one but Couperin. This piece demonstrates superbly how Couperin's technique depends on a dialogue

---

★ 'Autrefois, il y avait des chaconnes à deux tems et à trois; mais on n'en fait plus qu'à trois.' (Rousseau's *Dictionnaire*.)

between soprano melody and bass, for the bass line is throughout of a wonderfully cantabile character, always balancing the sombre articulation of the main melody:

With the B minor *Passacaille*, the piece is also perhaps the most impressive instance of Couperin's ability to extort a monumental power from the very rigidity of the chaconne-rondeau convention. Its disciplining of intense passion is again both a personal achievement and an achievement of civilization.

From the second volume onwards, each *ordre* begins to acquire a definite character of its own. Since we have now dealt in general terms with the main classes into which Couperin's pieces fall, it will be simplest if henceforward we deal with each *ordre* as we come to it in sequence. The second volume appeared in 1716/17, and the first *ordre* in it (the sixth of the whole series) is tender and delicate in mood. It contains one of Couperin's most beautiful works from the linear point of view – *Les Langueurs-Tendres*, a piece we have already mentioned as an example of the reconciling of a highly ornamented, rhythmically fluid line with a latently regular pulse and harmonic development. The ornamentation, inherited from the *air de cour*, smooths all angles off the line, gives it a caressing flexibility which suggests some kinship with the ordered plasticity of Racine's rhythm. Here the ornamentation is not, like much of Handel's ornamentation, something applied to a symmetrical harmonically conceived melody, but a part of the melodic contour, a means of achieving nuance and gradation:

While the method is the same as that of Bach in, say, the theme and some of the slow movements of the Goldberg Variations, Couperin's flavour, his radiance, is unique. It may be partly
attributable to the covert relation of his line to the French lan-

guage, which certainly influenced the line of the *air de cour*. Such a relationship need not manifest itself as patently as in the case of Lully's recitative.

A simpler, more homophonic piece in the same mood is *Les Bergeries*. This is melodically of great distinction, wistfully sophisticated like Watteau and yet not altogether remote from French folk song. The second couplet of the rondeau makes an impressionistic use of the bagpipe drone effect, an evocative, summer-like noise on the harpsichord, which cannot be translated into pianistic terms:

Nothing could more effectively illustrate how Couperin's melodic grace and economy of texture can invest stock ingredients of the *brunette* tradition with a personal and subtle poetry. This *ordre* also includes another evocation of the countryside, the gay rondeau *Les Moissonneurs*; a very famous piece in lute figuration, with chains of resonant suspensions, *Les Baricades Mistérieuses*; and a number of witty pieces written with characteristic precision in two parts, of which both the subtlest and the funniest is *Le Moucheron*, an 'Italian' gigue in which the line exasperatingly dances round itself.

The next *ordre*, the seventh, is in G, and is also mainly pastoral in mood. It is on the whole less distinguished than the previous (B flat) *ordre*, but contains some interesting harpsichord writing in syncopation in the first part of *Les Petits Ages*. *La Ménetou* is a lovely piece combining baroque line with 'impressionistic' suspensions; *Les Délices* is especially rich in sonorous sequential writing:

In contrast, the eighth *ordre*, in B minor, is almost uniformly serious, even tragic, in style; and while as a whole the second book cannot compare with the fourth in maturity, a good case can be made out for the eighth as the greatest individual *ordre*. It opens with a magnificent allemande, *La Raphaéle*, which in complexity of rhythm and harmony and in architectural power can be justly compared to the analogous movements in Bach. A quotation will indicate its intensity, the dissonances over a pedal point, the lute-like suspensions, the disciplined chromaticisms:

Equally majestic is the sarabande, *L'Unique*, with its dramatically percussive harmonies and violent changes of rhythm. The two courantes are among the most tightly wrought of all Couperin's dance movements, while the allemande *L'Ausoniéne*, though simpler in texture, has dignified Bachian sequences and suspensions over a regular metrical pulse.

But the climax of the *ordre* – unquestionably the greatest single piece in Couperin's clavecin music and one of the greatest keyboard pieces ever written – is the terrific *Passacaille*. The tragic effect of this movement is attributable to the tension between the audacious fluidity of the harmonies, and the rigid repetition not merely of the bass, but of the whole opening period at the remorselessly regular intervals demanded by the chaconne-rondeau convention:

Each couplet adds to the intensity – even the quiet episodes such as the third, with its sparse texture and drooping, weeping suspensions contrasting with the chromatic sonority of the harmonization of the theme – until a shattering climax is reached in the seventh couplet with its great spread discords, and anguished suspensions percussively exploiting the whole range of the instrument:

Although the passion increases cumulatively, the unaltered repetition of the opening clause gives the music a timeless, implacably fateful quality. It is astonishing that the composer of this terrifying music could ever have been regarded as exclusively amiable and elegant; we may compare the nineteenth-century legend of the 'tender' Racine. Certainly there is no music which has a more profoundly Racinian quality than this *Passacaille*, in which the rigidity of a social and technical convention (having reference to accepted standards in social intercourse), only just succeeds in holding in check a passion so violent that it threatens to engulf both the personality and the civilization of which that personality is a part. Just as we are conscious of Racine's alexandrine holding in control the wayward passion of *Phèdre's* rhythms and metaphors, so we are aware of the severe chaconne-rondeau form damming the flood of Couperin's chromaticism and dissonance. Rather oddly, after the *Passacaille* this B minor *ordre* is rounded off with an amiable Corellian gigue, *La Morinéte*; as though Couperin wished to reassert the validity of social elegance after his incursion into the merciless psychological and spiritual terrors that surround our waking lives.

The ninth *ordre* in A is again gentle, Watteau-like in tone. It contains one supremely lovely, and quite well-known piece, the rondeau *Le Bavolet-Flotant*. This is a melody of the simple *brunette* type; and the two-part texture is airy and luminous. There is also a subtle movement, *Les Charmes*, using suave, overlapping lute 193

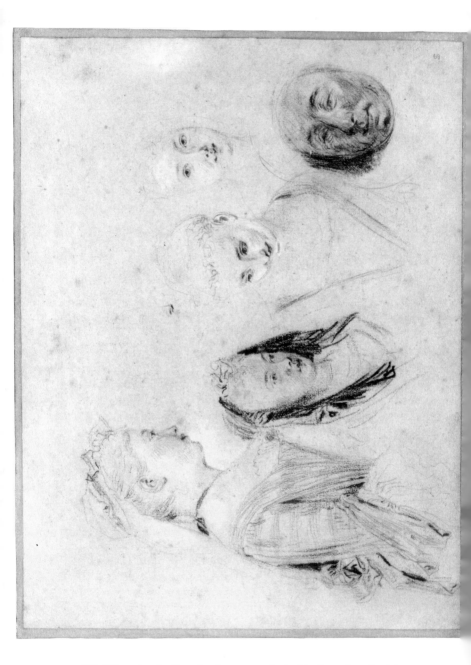

IX. Watteau: *Le Bavolet flotant*, study in black, red and white
chalk. The *bavolet* was a peasant's cap also worn by fashionable
young women.

figurations, and introducing a radiant change from minor to major in the second section. *La Séduisante* and *La Rafraîchissante* make effective use of sequences and of the sonorous registers of the keyboard, and the *ordre* opens with a fine polyphonic allemande for two harpsichords, which provides evidence of what one might call the interior density of Couperin's style. As with Bach, the expressive quality of the harmonies is here largely the result of the flexibility of the lines within a clearly ordered harmonic framework. The *Passacaille* represents an extreme manifestation of this.

The next *ordre*, the tenth, in D, is musically less interesting, though it is interesting historically because it contains some fairly developed examples of descriptive music – an aspect of Couperin's work to which the conventional account devotes a disproportionate attention. The first three pieces are battle pictures, cleverly exploiting the metallic, percussive features of the harpsichord. The battles are not to be taken seriously, though the second piece, *Allégresse des Vainqueurs*, is fine music, expressing an extreme degree of youthful buoyancy by the simplest of means – an engaging 6 : 8 lilt, with melodic sequences phrased across the beat, and making brilliant play with extended trills:

La Mézangére, in the minor, is a more concentrated movement, using lute technique with the dotted rhythm of the Lullian overture. *Les Bagatelles* is an effective piece for two keyboards, depending more on the metallically glinting sonority of the crossed parts, than on melodic appeal. The other pieces are of slighter interest.

The eleventh *ordre*, in C, is notable mainly for another biggish descriptive work, this time of considerable musical value. *Les Fastes de la Grande et Ancienne Mxnxstrxndxsx* demonstrates to a remarkable degree the influence on Couperin of popular music; we find here not merely a general relationship to folk-song such as we have often referred to before, but the direct presence of the 'low' music of the towns. Couperin's love for and understanding

195

of popular music – bagpipes, fiddlers, street-songs, rarefied in the economy of his technique – suggests that although he was, like Racine, an artist who worked for an aristocracy, he none the less embraced an unexpectedly comprehensive range of experience. There is about some of these pieces a quality almost comparable with the painting of Chardin – a tender sympathy for the things of everyday life, together with a technical delight in problems of balance and form, whereby these things are objectified, released from the temporal and local. The subtle precision of Couperin's and Chardin's technique gives to things that are mundane a quality that seems eternal, and by inference divine.

Thus the popular element in Couperin's work is reconcilable with its more serious aspects, just as Lully's aristocratic tunes were whistled by errand boys, and found their way into folk-song. Couperin's wit belongs without incongruity to the salon, the fair, the street, the village green, and the cathedral. If less obviously than an Englishman of Jonson's time, Couperin still worked before head and heart, laughter and tears, were divorced, and one can listen to a frivolously impudent piece such as *Les Jongleurs et les Sauteurs* from this *ordre* immediately after, say, the noble chaconne *La Favorite*, without experiencing any emotional jolt; there is clearly the same sensibility behind the clarity of the texture. We are not therefore surprised that this work in five *actes* should include, side by side with comic drum-and-fife pieces like those about drunkards, bears, and monkeys, a grave, stately movement such as *Les Invalides*; and should also in one movement use a popular technique – a wailing, monotonous air of *Les Viéleux et les Gueux*, over a plodding *bourdon* – to produce an effect not merely lugubrious, but unexpectedly pathetic:

This piece, as well as the brisk musette-like movements in the popular vein, needs the nasal tone of the harpsichord if its poetry is to be realized adequately.

The last *ordre* in the second book (No. 12 in E), is comparatively slight. It includes a charmingly suave courante, a most polite *La Coribante*, and a delightful piece, *L'Atalante*, in running semiquavers, over a quaver pulse.

Five years were to elapse before the appearance of Couperin's third book. But in the same year as the second volume he published his theoretical work, *L'Art de toucher le Clavecin*, and incorporated in it, for illustrative purposes, a series of eight preludes and one allemande. The allemande is a solidly made two-part invention with a good deal of canonic imitation, but is not especially interesting. The preludes, however, contain pieces which must rank among the finest examples in Couperin's work of the 'Bachian compromise' between harmonic proportion and melodic independence.

Couperin explains that though he has 'measured' them for the convenience of performers, these pieces are preludes and therefore, in accordance with the lutenist tradition, should be played with the utmost freedom:

> Quoy que ces Préludes soient écrits mesurés, il y a cependant un goût d'usage qu'il faut suivre. Je m'explique: Prélude est une composition libre, où l'imagination se livre à tout ce qui se présente à elle. Mais comme il est assez rare de trouver des génies capables de produire dans l'instant, il faut que ceux qui auront recours à ces Préludes réglés les jouent d'une manière aisée, sans trop s'attacher à la précision des mouvements, à moins que je ne l'aye marqué exprès par le mot *Mesuré*. Ainsi, on peut hasarder de dire que dans beaucoup de choses la Musique (par comparison à la Poésie) a sa prose, et ses vers.

The connection with the lutenists is explicit in the first prelude in C, since this depends almost entirely on spread chord formations in suspension (cf. Bach's C major prelude). The second prelude, in D minor, uses a similar technique, only with a more independent and rhapsodic line. The conventional dotted rhythm appears more or less consistently, and some of the sweeping scale passages suggest the influence of Italian recitative effects similar to those found in the *tombeaux* of the lutenists and violists; dissonant appoggiaturas are frequent:

The third prelude, in G minor, is a courante, lucid in its part-writing. No. 4, in F, returns to the suspensions and decorative arabesques of lute technique, and may be compared with Louis Couperin's *Tombeau de M. de Blancrocher*. No. 5, in A, is one of the finest pieces in which a metrical beat is dissolved in a supple, delicately ornamented line. The B minor, No. 6, is an invention again notable for the way in which the bar-metre disappears in the ellipses of the counterpoint:

Like the fifth, the seventh prelude, in B flat, has a highly ornamented baroque melody in which the convolutions of the line create some peculiar harmonic effects:

and the last prelude, in E minor, is an elegant piece with a typical undertone of wistfulness, using beautifully wrought figurations in sequence.★

Couperin intended his preludes to be used as 'loosening-up' exercises before any group of his pieces in the appropriate key; they were conceived with particular reference to Books I and II. It was in 1722 that the third volume of clavecin pieces appeared, and this time it opens with an *ordre* which is among the peak points of Couperin's keyboard music. It is in B minor again, a key which seems to have had a significance for Couperin analogous to Mozart's G minor; and it starts with a tender movement, *Les Lis Naissans*, in melodically grouped arpeggios. This is followed by a rondeau, *Les Rozeaux*, which ranks with *Les Bergeries* and *Le Bavolet-Flotant* as one of the loveliest of his works in a simple melodic, homophonically accompanied style. The balanced rise and fall of the opening clause is subtly underlined by the harmonies; here once more we can see how a poise which in one sense is a virtue of Society, may in another sense become a moral and spiritual quality:

<hr />

★ Here we may mention also the *Sicilienne* published as an appendix to the Oiseau-Lyre edition of the first volume of harpsichord pieces. This was first published anonymously by Ballard in his collection of *Pièces Choisies . . . de différents Auteurs* (1707.) It seems to have been popular, for it appears in several MSS. all anonymous with the exception of one inscribed *Sicilienne de M. Couperin*. The question of the authorship is not of much importance. It is an amiable, undistinguished little product of the *brunette* tradition with Italian influence, such as might have been written by Couperin in his youth or by any minor clavecin composer of the period.

X. Watteau: *Les Confidences d'Arlequin*, drawing. Both Couperin
and Watteau were intimately acquainted with the *commedia
dell'arte*, whose mythical characters transformed the indignities
of life into 'something rich and strange'.

But most of the *ordre* is taken up by the big chaconne *Les Folies Françoises ou les Dominos*. This is a series of variations on a ground bass, on a principle analogous to that of Bach's Goldberg Variations, without the strict contrapuntal movements. Though the *Folies* are, of course, on a much smaller scale than Bach's work, their emotional range is wide, extending from the melting harmonies of the variation called *La Langueur*, to the powerful internal chromaticisms of *La Jalousie taciturne*; from the simplicity of *La Fidélité* to the vigorous dotted rhythm of *L'Ardeur* and the ponderous tread of *Les Vieux Galans*; from the rhythmic whimsicalities of *La Coquéterie* to the whirling figuration of *L'Espérance* and *La Frénésie*. The work is a microcosm of Couperin's art, its tragic passion, its witty urbanity, its sensuous charm. Whereas the earlier B minor suite had been rounded off with a piece of inconsequential gaiety, Couperin adds as an epilogue to this *ordre* a short movement, *L'âme-en-peine*, which, apart from the *Passacaille*, is perhaps his most impassioned utterance. It is composed of almost continuously dissonant, drooping suspensions, including a high proportion of strained augmented intervals:

Although short, it produces an impression of grandeur and tragedy; just as *Les Folies Françoises*, though its duration in time is not long, seems – through the variety of its mood and the architectural precision of its structure – to be a work of imposing dimensions.

The next *ordre*, No. 14 in D, is mostly of the pastoral type. It opens with one of Couperin's most exquisite pieces of decorated melodic writing, *Le Rossignol-en-amour*, in which the line can be related to his baroque method of treating the human voice in parts of the *Leçons de Ténèbres*, and still more in the *Brunette* of 1711. *Les Fauvétes Plaintives* is plaintive indeed, with its tremulous treble registration, its chromaticism, and its tender appoggiaturas in dotted rhythm. *Le Carillon de Cithére,* again 'scored' in the high registers of the instrument, is among the most beautiful of all bell pieces; and *Le Petit-Rien* is a nimble two-part invention.

From the fifteenth *ordre* onwards, the level of the movements remains almost uniformly high. This A minor *ordre* begins with a noble allemande, *La Régente*, combining irregular baroque lines with great richness of texture and harmony; this use of the chord of the ninth is representative:

The lullaby that follows, *Le Dodo*, is a tender and civilized re-creation of a popular nursery song – a simple melody phrased across the bar, accompanied by a rocking figure. Again a most touching effect is achieved by the simple contrast between major and minor in the complementary sections. The two *Musétes* are in the popular drum-and-fife style, with short, excitingly irregular periods over the drone, and some clattering trills. *La Douce* is a sophisticated-naïve piece in the folk-song manner, and *Les Vergers Fleüris* perhaps the most remarkable of all Couperin's impressionistic pieces, creating an effect of heat and summer haze through a line which seems to be gradually dissolving into its suave ornamentation, and through the use of protracted suspensions which seem only to resolve on to other suspensions, over a sustained drone:

Here again the sensuousness of the harmony and ornamentation is disciplined by the symmetrical form in a way which recalls Watteau's structural disciplining of his idealized vision of the hues of nature.

In the sixteenth *ordre* the finest piece is *La Distraite*, which
preserves a civilized symmetry beneath its 'distraught' scale

passages. *L'Himen-Amour* uses widely skipping leaps and arpeggio formations; *Les Vestales* is a charming rondeau with a folk-
song-like melody. Both the seventeenth and the eighteenth *ordre*
contain magnificent pieces of a Bach-like polyphonic texture (*La
Superbe* and *La Verneüil*), brilliant movements in harpsichord
figuration of a quasi-descriptive order (*Les Petits Moulins à Vent,
Les Timbres, Le Tic-Toc-Choc*), and a fine piece (*Le Gaillard-
Boîteux*) 'dans le goût burlesque'. But more outstanding still is
the nineteenth *ordre* in D minor, which begins with one of the
very finest pieces in the popular manner, *Les Calotins et les
Calotines*, includes a piece, *Les Culbutes Ixcxbxnxs,* in which
irregularly grouped clauses and abrupt leaps are combined in
sequences to produce at times a quasi-polytonal effect:

and has penultimately a lilting movement over a gently chromatic bass (*La Muse-Plantine*) which simultaneously demonstrates Couperin's sensuousness and his classical detachment:

Another eight years elapsed before, in 1730, Couperin published his fourth book of harpsichord pieces. Though it contains
no piece on the scale of the *Passacaille*, it must on the whole be
regarded as the culmination of his achievement in keyboard
music. It is also one of his last works, for he died in 1733, and
owing to ill-health composed nothing during the last few years
of his life. In his preface, Couperin explains that the pieces in the
fourth book had mostly been finished some three years previously; this would place them more or less contemporary with
the great suites for viols.

The volume opens unpretentiously with an *ordre* which is 203 pervasively witty in tone. *La Princesse Marie, Les Chérubins,* and *Les Tambourins* all use very short phrases, in unexpectedly irregular groupings, often based on a syncopation of the phrase rhythm against the bar rhythm. The suaver movements, *La Croûilli* and *La Douce Janneton,* are also habitually phrased across the bar, the falling sevenths of the last named being typical of Couperin's late work. The next *ordre,* the twenty-first, in E minor, is mainly grave and serious. *La Reine des Cœurs* has a proud nobility, conveyed through balanced sequential sevenths, in a sarabande rhythm:

La Couperin, a large-scale allemande, is one of the most magnificent of all Couperin's Bach-like pieces, with superbly devised keyboard polyphony in three parts:

Lute figurations and internal chromaticisms give to *La Harpée* and *La Petite Pince-sans-rire* a surprising harmonic piquancy.

The twenty-second *ordre* in D is the climax of Couperin's urbane wit. Almost all the pieces have some elegantly comic feature; *L'Anguille* in particular is a brilliant two-part invention, in which the abrupt harmonies and reiterative figuration convey as appropriately as musically the eel's writhings.

A *galant et magnifique* opening to the twenty-third *ordre* is provided by *L'Audacieuse,* a piece consistently in the dotted rhythm of the Lullian overture. *Les Tricoteuses* is a descriptive piece suggested by the metallic rustle of the harpsichord in quick semiquaver movement; it makes an impressionistic, homophonic use of the chord of the diminished seventh. Still more extraordinary harmonically is the next piece, *L'Arlequine,* which, in the tradition of the *commedia*, has some exciting percussive effects, and some startlingly modern progressions of seventh and ninth chords:

The passage is a fine example of Couperin's ability to attain to great sonorous richness with the minimum of means; it is this kind of effect which made so deep an appeal to Debussy, and still more to Ravel, since they found in its emotional quality something that was not irrelevant to their position in the modern world. This quality is extremely subtle. A little swaying figure, oscillating between the fifth and sixth, opens the piece with an air of wide-eyed diatonic innocence which is belied by the artificial symmetry of the clauses, by the witty major and minor seconds, and by the melancholy of the sequential harmonies. As a whole, the piece is balanced between a bumpkin simplicity and a sophisticated hyper-sensitivity, in a manner that almost justifies a comparison with Watteau's wonderful painting of Gilles. Both Watteau and Couperin seem, in works such as these, to be attempting to transmute a personal loneliness or distress into the world of the *commedia*, precisely because the theatre can idealize the crudities and indignities of everyday life into 'something rich and strange'. It is the tenderness of the feeling – the sympathy with the outcast – that is so remarkable in Watteau's pictorial, and Couperin's musical, representation of the Fool. We may relevantly recall that at the time they created these works both Watteau and Couperin were sick men.

In *Les Satires*, another movement *dans le goût burlesque* in this *ordre*, we may find similar qualities. The tenderness is here less 205

XI. Watteau: *Portrait of Gilles*, the most famous of the artist's *commedia* pictures. The young man portrayed may be a professional actor, or may be a friend of Watteau, dressed up.

evident; but the weird dissonances, the percussively treated diminished seventh chords, are never crudely obtrusive. They give a sudden ironic twist to an apparently innocuous phrase:

here again the Harlequin resolves his spiritual gaucherie into a world of exquisite artifice.

The twenty-fourth *ordre*, in A, is distinguished by one of the longest and noblest of Couperin's clavecin pieces, the *passacaille L'Amphibie*. This is not in the chaconne-rondeau convention of the more intense B minor *Passacaille*, but is a series of variations on a ground bass which is itself treated very freely. It is the only movement in Couperin's keyboard works that can be compared with the big chaconnes from the two-violin suites, and it uses similar technical methods to build up an increasing momentum. Lute-like suspensions, virile dotted rhythms, flowing triplet figures are all employed in a technique which covers the whole range of the keyboard. As in the violin suites, the bass itself shares in the growing excitement by acquiring more animation and by introducing chromaticisms. The piece concludes with a massive statement of the theme in its original form. *Les Vieux Seigneurs* is a sarabande, also in the old *grand goût*. It is comple-mented by a piece called *Les Jeunes Seigneurs, cy-devant les Petits Maîtres*, in a perky 2 : 4 with semi-quaver figuration phrased across the beat; again, a witty use is made of diminished seventh effects. Couperin possibly intends some satirical reference to the new, exquisite style of the *divertissement* in the manner of Mouret – compared with the old-style Lullian majesty of *Les Vieux Seigneurs*. In *Les Guirlandes* we come to one of the finest pieces using lute arpeggios in a sonorously impressionistic manner. Played on a big, resonant harpsichord, this piece rivals *Les Vergers Fleüris* in its richly atmospheric effect.

The twenty-fifth *ordre* is possibly the most technically experi-mental of all. The first piece, *La Visionnaire*, is a Lullian overture in miniature, with a slow, powerful introduction which mingles the intense recitative-like line and surging portamentos of the 207 violists with very dramatic harmonies, in a manner that recalls the sarabande of Bach's E minor partita:

The quick section, though in two parts throughout, produces an energetic effect through the vigour and complexity of its rhythms. The next piece, *La Misterieuse*, is centred in C major, in contrast to the overture's E flat; its mysteriousness seems to consist mainly in its abstruse transitions of key. A passage such as this dissolves the sense of tonality almost as remarkably as does Bach's B minor fugue from Book I of the Forty-Eight:

But Couperin never obscures his tonal sense as completely as does Bach in the twenty-fifth of the Goldberg Variations; he remains too much a part of a civilized aristocracy. *Les Ombres Errantes* depends mainly on the insistent syncopation of its phrasing, and on 'weeping' internal suspensions which create a fluid chromaticism in the inner parts. Despite the emotional harmony, the impression is throughout one of dignified refinement. As in so much of Bach, the figuration is consistent from start to finish; the expressive quality arises out of the subtleties of phrasing.

The twenty-sixth *ordre*, in F sharp minor, is possibly – with the B minor *ordre* from Book II – the finest. If it has no movement of such overwhelming intensity as the B minor *Passacaille*, it has perhaps greater variety than the earlier suite, and has such consummate lucidity and economy in its technique that it is a joy

to look at, as well as to play and listen to. This is immediately apparent in the opening allemande-like movement, *La Convales-cente*, with its beautiful suspensions over a chromatic bass:

its rich harmonic sequences:

and in its coda, which almost rivals Chopin in its disciplined sensuality, while preserving a Couperinesque spiritual poise. Equally lovely is the rondeau, *L'Epineuse*, in which tied notes and suspensions combine with melodic figuration to produce an effect as of part-writing. The third couplet uses a simple lulling rhythm across the bar-line, recalling the earlier *Dodo*; and the fourth couplet introduces one of those radiant transitions to the major which give intimation of how Couperin's civilized deportment is not merely a social virtue, but is, as it were, a spiritual illumination. In this passage, the texture luminously 'glows'; and the gentle yearning of the rising melodic figure is counterpoised by the symmetrical grouping of the clauses:

The last piece in this *ordre*, *La Pantomime*, is a superb example of Couperin's *commedia dell'arte* style, using percussive guitar-like effects and brusque dissonances of minor and major ninth with an irresistibly witty vivacity:

209

The twenty-seventh and last *ordre*, in B minor again, is in the
same mood as the F sharp minor, and is hardly less beautiful.
The allemande, *L'Exquise*, has the same serenity and plasticity of
part-writing as *La Convalescente* – a keyboard technique comparable with that of Bach's most mature works, though more
delicate in texture. *Les Pavots* evokes an impression of heat and
languor through broken chords and appoggiaturas in an even
crotchet rhythm in the high register of the instrument. A very
French *Les Chinois* is remarkable for its rhythmic surprises; and
the last piece, *Saillie,* has a Bach-like technique of neat imitative
writing which on the last page dissolves into quintessential
Couperin – a simple repeated figure involving a falling fourth.
The peculiarly disembodied feeling which this figure, in conjunction with the level flowing movement, gives to the music is
enhanced by the fact that the figure does not occur in the first
half of the binary architecture (which ends in the dominant and
starts off again in the relative major). In its softly floating repeti-
tiveness the figure has an eternal quality that is at once elegant
and wistful; we may note too the touching Neapolitan sixth
effect of the flattened C in the last few bars:

Despite its ostensible limitations compared with, say, the *Art of Fugue*, the Mass in B minor, the Jupiter Symphony, the Hammerklavier sonata, or Byrd's five-part Mass, Couperin's fourth book of clavecin pieces seems to me to be among the most remarkable feats of creative craftsmanship in the history of music. If we have understood the significance of its lucidity aright, we shall have no difficulty in appreciating how the exquisite Couperin could on the whole have more than any other composer has in common with Bach. Nor shall we have any difficulty in understanding how the composer of a funny piece about monkeys, or a charming piece like *Le Bavolet-Flotant*, could also create, in the *Passacaille* and the finest of the church works, music in which a tremendous tragic passion, revealed in a tautness of linear and harmonic structure, should hide beneath the surface elegance; in which Couperin's habitual preoccupation with social values and 'states of mind' receives what it is hardly excessive to call a spiritual re-creation.

Like Bach, Couperin preserves a delicate balance, perhaps peculiar to his epoch, between the claims of the individual personality, of society, and of God. Though the Phèdre-like vehemence of the *Passacaille* may endanger his formal lucidity, though the melancholy that lurks in the eyes of Watteau's harlequins is perceptible beneath even his most witty moods, Couperin never forgets that he is the *honnête homme*, living by a code of values which, if they are more than personal, are, in the conventionally accepted sense of the term, more than social too. And in his greatest work he seems to indicate – as does Racine in *Athalie*, and as does Bach, who lived much more directly in contact with a religious community, through the whole of his career – that in the long run such values are meaningless unless one accepts the notion of an absolute, or God.

Note to p. 185

There is also a distinguished woman composer among Couperin's immediate predecessors – Elisabeth Jacquet de la Guerre.

Born in 1659, she came of a family of musicians, her father and brother being organists; and she married another organist, Marin de la Guerre, who officiated at Ste Chapelle. According to Titon du Tillet, she 'showed extraordinary talent from the earliest years', appearing at court at the tender age of fifteen. Louis XIV greatly admired her ability as harpsichordist and as improviser; 'a person of her sex,' Titon adds, 'has never before had such great gifts for composition and for amazing performance upon the harpsichord and organ'. That a woman should excel in music, in this refined society which produced so many women of literary distinction, is not altogether surprising; if we think of Elisabeth Jacquet in comparison with Couperin we will find that he shares something of her feminine sensibility, while she has something of the strength that supports his elegance. Like Couperin, she is a linear composer who thinks in terms of two polyphonic voices, one for each hand; their interplay creates, as in Couperin, surprisingly dense harmonic implications. A first volume of four suites appeared in 1687, and has been recently rediscovered. A second volume was published in 1707 – from which Kenneth Gilbert has recorded the D minor suite. Especially beautiful are *La Flamande* (really an allemande) and its *double*; the tender sarabande, which shifts dreamily between major and minor; the chromatically witty gigue; and the grandly pathetic chaconne-rondeau. Elisabeth Jacquet's range is more limited than Couperin's; her music lives and breathes in her aristocratic salon and does not, like his, evoke a multifarious world. None the less, within her salon live and breathe she certainly does; and the parallel between her and Couperin suggests how inseparably, in this society, masculine and feminine elements of the psyche were interlinked.

When Couperin le Grand started to compose harpsichord music he had the music of Chambonnières, Louis Couperin, d'Anglebert, Le Roux and Elisabeth Jacquet de la Guerre to work from, not to mention the great Rameau, whose first volume appeared as early as 1706, and Clérambault who, although not primarily a harpsichord composer, published some fine pieces in the years 1702–4.

Chapter Ten

The Concerts Royaux and Suites for Viols

Le goût Italien et le goût François ont partagé depuis
longtemps (en France) la République de la Musique; à mon
égard, j'ay toujours estimé les choses qui le méritoient sans
acception d'Auteurs, ni de Nation; et les premières Sonades
Italiennes qui parurent à Paris il y a plus de trente années ne
firent aucun tort dans mon esprit, ny aux ouvrages de monsieur de Lulli, ny à ceux de mes Ancêtres.

FRANÇOIS COUPERIN, *Les Goûts Réünis*, 1724

Couperin's *concerts* were published in two volumes in 1722 and
1724. The first volume of four suites was entitled *Concerts
Royaux*; the second collection of ten *concerts*, with the addition of
the first *Apothéose* sonata, was given the generic title of *Les Goûts
Réünis*. The suites were written for the court, after the last of the
church works, the *Leçons de Ténèbres*; their composition therefore dates from 1714 onwards. Composed to soften and sweeten
the King's melancholy, they are conceived in a style more
French than Italian. They are not concertos in the Italian sense of
the word but simply concerted music in dance form scored for
an ensemble group. None the less the music throughout, as well
as the titles in the later volume, indicates how deeply Couperin's
French idiom is impregnated with Italianism.

No particular medium is specified for the pieces. They were
usually printed on two staves, as though for harpsichord, and in
this medium are mostly effective. But Couperin remarks in his
preface that 'ils conviennent non seulement au clavecin, mais
aussi au Violon, à la flûte, au hautbois, à la viole, et au basson';
and it seems clear that it was on some such combination of
instruments that the works were performed at court. Couperin
says that they were originally played by Duval, Philidor, Alarius, and Dubois, with himself at the clavecin. Duval was a
celebrated violinist, Alarius a violist, and Philidor and Dubois
were virtuosos on the oboe and bassoon. The ideal arrangement 213

would thus seem to be for two stringed instruments, two wind instruments, and continuo, the strings and wind playing either together or alternately. The choice of instruments should depend on the expressive qualities of the movement in question. Thirty years later opinion associated particular instruments with specific passions, as we may see from this passage in Avison's *Essay on Musical Expression* (1752):

> We should also minutely observe the different qualities of the instruments themselves: for, as vocal Music requires one kind of Expression, and instrumental another, so different instruments have also different expression peculiar to them.
>
> Thus the Hautboy will best express the Cantabile or singing style, and may be used in all movements whatever under this denomination, especially those movements which tend to the Gay and Chearful.
>
> In compositions for the German flute is required the same method of proceeding by conjunct degrees or such other natural intervals, as, with the nature of its tone, will best express the Languishing, or Melancholy style.

In general oboes and bassoons are suitable for merry movements such as rigaudons and bourrées, perhaps because of the instruments' rustic associations; flutes are appropriate to tender and melancholy movements such as the sarabandes. Violins, in Couperin's *concerts*, are essentially lyrical and noble, though less pathetic than the flutes. A more specifically instrumental character is discernible in the later volume, in which Couperin expressly states that some of the pieces are to be played on unaccompanied viols.

Almost all the *concerts* are in the form of dance suites; and like the suites of the lutenists and clavecinists, they adapt their movements from the dances of the ballet and theatre. The only movement which is an exception to this is the Prelude, which is usually related to the *grave* opening of the Italian sonata da chiesa. It is always a more formal piece than the improvisatory prelude of the lutenists.

Many of the dance forms have already been briefly described in other contexts in this book; since, however, Couperin's *concerts* are his apotheosis of the contemporary dance, this seems an appropriate place to attempt some more systematic catalogue. We must remember that, deriving as they do from the theatre, the opera, and the ballet, these dances have all an expressive intention. All the theorists insisted that 'la première et la plus essentielle beauté d'un air de ballet est la convenance, c'est à dire le juste rapport l'air doit avoir avec la chose représenté' (Noverre); that 'chaque caractère et chaque passion ont leur mouvement particulier; mais cela depend plus du goût que des règles' (Rameau). Moreover, although taste may have been more important than rules, this does not mean that rules were non-existent. The relationships between different passions and different physical movements were as rigidly classified as were the possible relationships between passions and pictorial formulae in the painting of Lebrun. 'La danse est aujourd'hui divisée en plusieurs caractères . . . les gens de métier en comptent jusqu'à seize, et chacun de ces caractères a sur le théâtre, des pas, des attitudes et des figures qui lui sont propres.' Of course, there was not any 'psychological' intention in the dances; they did not deal in individual passions. But they had a general relation to types of experience and types of people. They were musical and terpsichorean Humours, and as such were carefully graded and differentiated.

The first dance in the suites, the allemande, had gradually displaced the pavane which, some authorities suggest, had been metamorphosed into the slow section of the French overture. Couperin uses two types of allemande. One, which he called *allemande légère*, is in four time, light and flowing, but unhurried; this is probably a survival of the popular allemande which was a sung dance. The other type of allemande, of a more grave character, is an instrumental sophistication of the original dance, and is of all the dance forms except the chaconne the most musically developed. Rousseau says that it 'se bat gravement à 4 tems', and Mace describes it as 'heavie . . . fitly representing the nature of the People whose Name it carryeth, so that no Extraordinary Motions are used in dancing it'. The titles of Couperin's most typical pieces in allemande form make clear that he associated the dance with a certain seriousness and dignity, though the pace should never be sluggish. Even his *allemandes légères* incline, as we have seen, to contrapuntal treatment. Both kinds are regarded as highly wrought instrumental compositions, bearing out Mattheson's comment that between allemandes danced and allemandes played there is as much difference as there is between Earth and Heaven.

The differences between the two types of courante, French and Italian, have been discussed previously. Originally a very quick dance, as its name suggests, it must, by Couperin's day, have become considerably slower. A steady minim pulse is essential if the cross rhythms and other metrical complications are to be intelligible. Rousseau describes the dance as being 'en trois tems graves', while D'Alembert, in 1766, even goes as far as to call it 'une sarabande fort lente'. Both writers, however, remark that the courante 'n'est plus en usage'. Most contemporary indications of tempo give the courante and the sarabande the same speed (see Appendix D). On the whole, however, the evidence indicates that played, as opposed to danced, sarabandes were slower and more noble than courantes; despite their rhythmic complexity courantes preserved something of the quality referred to by Mace when he described them as being 'commonly of two strains, and full of Sprightfulness, and Vigour, Lively, Brisk, and Chearful'. Quantz says that courantes should be played with vigour and majesty, at a speed of approximately a crotchet for one beat of the pulse. Some such combination of stateliness with energy seems an appropriate speed for courantes, and Quantz's suggested pace seems reasonable for Couperin's courantes in the French manner, in which the animation depends so much on cross accents between 6 : 4 and 3 : 2. The smoother 3 : 4 Italian courantes may be taken slightly faster, though even in these movements Couperin is apt to spring disconcerting rhythmic surprises on the performer. According to P. Rameau's *Maître à danser* of 1725 even the danced courante was, by that date, a very solemn dance with a nobler style and a grander manner than the others. The subtlety of its danced rhythm depended on the fact that only two steps were danced for each three beats of the music, the first of the steps taking up two parts in three of the measure. (Feuillet's *Choréographie ou l'art de décrire la danse,* 1700.)

The sarabande was one of the oldest of the ballet dances, having been introduced into France from Spain in 1588. Transplanted into England in the seventeenth century, it became a rapid and skittish dance, as we may see from the sarabandes of the Jacobean virginalists. During the seventeenth century it progressively slowed down, culminating in the powerfully pathetic sarabandes of Couperin, Bach, and Handel. The mature form of it is characterized by a slight stress on the second beat of a slow

triple rhythm, and Brossard defines it as 'n'étant à la bien prendre qu'un menuet, dont le mouvement est grave, lent, sérieux
etc.' Grassineau adds that it differs from the courante in ending
on the up beat instead of the down. Lacombe also described the
sarabande as 'une espèce de menuet lente'. Rémond de St Mard
remarked in 1741 that the sarabande, 'toujours mélancolique,
respire une tendresse sérieuse et délicate', and this elegiac languishing mode must for long have been typical of the sarabandes
of the ballet. Couperin frequently composed sarabandes of this
type, sometimes specifying them as *sarabande tendre*. But, as we
have observed, he also writes sarabandes in a *grave* style, which
although melancholy, are anything but relaxed in effect. Even
more than the lutenists, Couperin reserves the *grave* sarabande
for many of his most passionate utterances.

Rivalling the sarabande in grandeur is the chaconne, which
also came from Spain and was widespread throughout the
seventeenth century. This dance too was in triple time, with a
slight stress on the second beat, though it was less ponderous in
movement than the sarabande. Its formal structure over a
repeated bass makes it perhaps the most important of all the
dances from a musical point of view; for it offers opportunities
for musical development on a more extensive scale than the
other dances. Originally chaconne basses had taken the form of
the descending tetrachord, major, minor or chromatic. By
Couperin's time the range of possible basses was more extensive; nor was it necessary for the bass to be preserved unaltered
through the whole composition. For Couperin, the bass may be
a linear ground; or it may be merely an ostinato harmonic
progression, as it is in the gigantic chaconne of Bach's Goldberg
Variations. D'Alembert adequately defines the chaconne as 'une
longue pièce de musique à trois tems, dont le mouvement est
modéré et la mesure bien marquée. Autrefois la basse de la
chaconne était une basse contrainte de 4 en 4 mesures, c'est à dire
qui revenoit toujours la même de 4 en 4 mesures; aujourd'hui on
ne s'astreint plus à cet usage. La chaconne commence pour
ordinaire non en frappant, mais au second tems'.

The growth of the music over the regular bass called for
considerable skill on the composer's part if a satisfactory sense of
climax was to be obtained; we have repeatedly noticed that this
was a challenge to which François Couperin, like Lully and
Louis Couperin before him, responded with enthusiasm.

Couperin writes two types of chaconne, corresponding with his two types of allemande and sarabande. The *chaconne grave* is in 3 : 2 or 3 : 4 and is derived from the ceremonial chaconnes of the operatic finales. The *chaconne légère* is normally in 3 : 8, more moderate in movement and slighter in texture, though still rather serious in temper. Chaconnes are most commonly in the minor mode, but often have a series of variations or couplets in the major in the middle of the composition. In the biggest pieces this may paradoxically suggest the effect of a ternary structure, despite the essentially monistic nature of chaconne technique.

The passacaille may be taken as identical with the chaconne. Quantz maintains that its tempo is slightly faster than that of the chaconne, Rousseau and D'Alembert say that it is 'plus lente et plus tendre'. Some authorities suggest that the chaconne has the syncopated sarabande rhythm whereas the passacaille has a smooth three beats in a bar. Modern musicologists have attempted to establish a distinction between the passacaglia as a composition on a linear ground and the chaconne as a movement built on a harmonic ostinato. The exceptions are so numerous and the evidence so conflicting that it would probably be equally easy to make out a case for the opposite view. The above remarks apply to real chaconnes and passacaglias, not to the hybrid chaconne-rondeau, which will be referred to later.

The gavotte is a dance in 2 : 2 time, beginning on the second beat. Its movement was moderate, and its mood usually that of 'une gaieté vive et douce'. It was, however, susceptible of somewhat varied interpretations. Rousseau says that it is 'ordinairement gracieux, souvent gai, quelquefois aussi tendre et lent', and Lacombe defines it as 'quelquefois gai, quelquefois grave'. In general – like Couperin, and his civilization – it avoids extremes. If gay, it is never rumbustious; if sad, it is never oppressively so: or in the words of D'Alembert it is 'tantôt lent, tantôt gay; mais jamais extrèmement vif, ni excessivement lent'. Perhaps its dominant characteristic is an amiable wistfulness.

Also in 2 : 2 or 2 : 4, but beginning on the last quarter of the bar, is the rigaudon, 'composé de deux reprises, chacune de 4, de 8, de 12 etc. mesures' (D'Alembert). This dance was especially popular during Couperin's time, and was very merry, with a popular flavour. It is robust and simple in rhythm, having an open-air jauntiness. The tambourin (used by Couperin only once under this title) and the bourrée are similar to the rigaudon, except that the tambourin, with a drone bass, is still more rustic in flavour, while the bourrée often has a syncopation on the first half of the bar. Another dance in 2 : 2 of a popular and rustic type is the contredanse, the name of which is a corruption of the English country-dance; we may see in this further evidence of the self-conscious interest of a sophisticated society in the naïve and 'primitive': 'les choses les plus simples sont celles dont on se lasse le moins', as Rousseau said. Contre-danses are symmetrical in melody and rhythm and were employed in the joyous finales of operas. Despite their popular virility, they are not in any way wild, as are the tambourins. They begin on the second beat of the 2 : 2 rhythm, and may thus be regarded as a racier, less civilized version of the gavotte.

Three related types of quick, triple-rhythmed dance are the loure, gigue, and canarie. The loure is usually in 6 : 4, some-times in 6 : 8, and is always lilted, in a dotted rhythm, with a slight 'push' on the short note. Its movement is flowing, but dignified and graceful. The gigue, which came from England, is 'vive et un peu folle', in the words of Rémond de St Mard. Some gigues, in 12 : 8 or 9 : 8, are in equally flowing quavers, after the Italian manner; others, in the French style, are in a skittish dotted rhythm; this type of gigue 'n'est proprement qu'une loure très vive' (D'Alembert). The gigue was extremely fashionable in Couperin's day. The French form of it is indistinguishable from the canarie, a farouche dance performed in the ballets by pseudo-Canary Islanders, and other exotics. The same rhythms are found at a more moderate tempo in the sicilienne and forlane. Not all Couperin's siciliennes are in the conventional dotted rhythm; some are in level quavers, like a slower Italian gigue. Couperin's one lovely example of the forlane is in the dotted rhythm. Rousseau, in his *Dictionnaire*, says that the forlane 'se bat gaiement, et la danse est aussi fort gaie. On l'appelle forlane parce qu'elle a pris naissance dans le Frioul, dont les habitants s'appellent Forlans'. D'Alembert says that it has 'un mouvement modéré, moyen entre la loure et la gigue'. The dance flourished especially during the Regency.

Like the sarabande, the minuet seems progressively to have slowed down in tempo. In Couperin's time it was written in 3 : 4 or 3 : 8, and had 'une élégante et noble simplicité; le mouvement en est plus modéré que vite, et l'on peut dire que le moins gai de tous les genres de danse usités dans nos bals est le 219 minuet. C'est autre chose sur le théâtre'. (Rousseau.) Couperin's minuets would seem to be closer to those of the theatre than to those of the ballroom. They are graceful, but should flow along quite speedily. The passepied is similar, and still faster. 'Une espèce de minuet fort vif', it is usually in 3 : 8, beating one a bar. Unlike the minuet, it begins on the third quaver, not the first, and introduces frequent syncopations. Both are sophisticated dances, with regional origins.

The musette is much favoured by Couperin, and has been admirably described by Rousseau: 'Sorte d'air convenable à l'instrument de ce nom, dont la mesure est à deux ou trois temps, le caractère naïf et doux, le mouvement un peu lent, portant une basse pour l'ordinaire en tenue ou point d'orgue, telle que la peut faire une musette, et qu'on appelle à cause de cela basse de musette. Sur ces airs on forme des danses d'un caractère convenable, et qui portent aussi le nom de musettes'. Here the dance is derived from the music, instead of – as is more usual – the music from the dance.

It is possible that the order in which the dances were arranged in instrumental suites was not entirely arbitrary. In Renaissance masques and the seventeenth-century *ballet de cour* the initial dance, the pavane, was the grandest, accompanying the entry of kings, queens, and the most important people. The allemande was slightly less grand but still noble; the courante moderate paced; the sarabande quicker; gavottes, minuets, bourrées etc., faster still; gigues or canaries at the end positively skittish. There may have been a hierarchical procession from High Life to Low. One cannot, however, apply this gradation convincingly to the mature suites of Couperin, Bach or Handel. By their time the dances had acquired more 'absolute' musical values; the sarabande, for instance, greatly slowed down, had become the suite's centre of emotional gravity and the pavane had been replaced by the Prelude, essentially a personal, sometimes even an improvised, music. The grandly 'public' pavane had turned into the heroically slow opening section of the Lullian overture.

In addition to these specific dance forms, Couperin also uses, as do the opera and ballet composers, the term *air* to describe dance pieces of a variously characteristic nature. The term no doubt comes from the 'air de symphonie par lequel débute un ballet'; Couperin always qualifies it adjectivally – *air tendre, air gracieux, air grave*, and so on.

All these dances are treated either in some type of binary form, or in rondeau. If in binary form, the second section, after the modulation to the dominant or relative, may start off with the original theme in the new key, reflecting the material of the first section in the same order; or it may start off with subsidiary material, returning to the original ideas towards the end; or it may include no thematic repetition at all, achieving unity rather by the balance of keys and the grouping of figuration. The second sections, incorporating the modulations, tend to be longer than the first. Most of the more serious binary pieces depend on the growth of linear figuration and harmonic pattern, rather than on the easily recognizable tune. When Couperin writes simple dance *tunes*, he tends to treat them *en rondeau;* they are then self-enclosed periods in one section, interspersed with contrasting episodes. Gavotte, minuet, forlane, rigaudon, passe-pied – all the lighter, more tuneful dances are thus often treated *en rondeau*; and the connection of the rondeau with the round suggests a popular origin for this sophisticated technique. Significantly, the more complicated dances, allemandes, sarabandes, and courantes, are never 'rondeau-ed'. The one exception to this is the chaconne; but although the chaconne-rondeau has ceased to be a chaconne, it remains distinct, in its majestic power, from all the more customary, frivolous types of rondeau. Something of the remorselessness of the chaconne's repetitions is transferred into the more lyrical repetitions of the rondeau.

Two or more of the smaller dances are sometimes linked together – gavottes and bourrées in major and minor, for instance, or any of the rustic dances in the minor with a musette in the major. In these interlinked pieces the musette with drone is a prototype of the trio section of what later became the sonata scherzo. As in the classical scherzo, the first dance of the pair is often repeated after the second, making a primitive ternary or 'sandwich' form; this, however, did not become obligatory till some time after Couperin's day.

The first four *concerts*, Couperin says, are arranged *par tons*, beginning in G, and proceeding up the cycle of fifths to the key of the dominant – to D, A, and E. Like most of the Preludes, that to the G major *concert* is influenced by Italian models. Though an elegant piece, light in texture, it has a modulation to A minor, incorporating some abstruse dissonances and a cadential false relation, in a style which is familiar to us from the grander preludes to the violin sonatas:

The allemande is of the *léger* type, in the usual binary structure, with neat imitative writing but without much polyphonic complexity. Towards the end of the second section a gently rocking figure suggests an undercurrent of wistfulness:

The sarabande, in the minor, is a simple, noble piece with drooping sevenths in sequence. The remaining movements, gavotte, gigue, and minuet, are slight. The gigue has some amusing repeated scale figures, and the minuet uses floating scale passages in contrary motion.

The second *concert* is in D. The prelude is gracefully pathetic, with soft appoggiaturas and ornamented suspended sevenths over a chromatic bass. The *allemande fuguée* is again of the *léger* variety but, as its title implies, gives a quite elaborate contrapuntal development to this perky theme:

In the second half the theme is very freely inverted. The *air tendre* is in the minor, in the style of the *air de cour*, with portamentos and intermittent canonic entries:

The *air contrefugué* is a counterpart of the allemande, with a similar jaunty subject. Its second section has some wittily unexpected harmonies, similar to those in the Harlequin clavecin pieces:

For the last movement of the *concert* we have an extremely beautiful rondeau in the *Echo* convention, comparable in mood with the rondeau of the *Impériale* sonata in the same key. Symmetrical clauses, a tranquil rhythm, and a 'luminous' diatonicism produce a Claude-like effect of pastoral serenity:

A couplet in the minor develops a richer harmony. The later statements of the theme are ornamented in the *brunette* fashion.

A more serious style and more extended developments are observable in the third *concert*, in A. The prelude, with its *contre-partie* for viol, violin, flute, or oboe, has a Bachian polyphonic texture; the sense of metre disappears in the interlappings of the lines:

Though lighter in character, the allemande uses a similar technique, and has a typical passage of 'aspiring' chromatic sequences. The courante, in the minor, is more complicated, both rhythmically and harmonically. Although ostensibly a quick piece, it uses diminished intervals with a Purcellian pathos.

With the *sarabande grave*, we come to a movement which looks far beyond the normal confines of entertainment music; which stands with the greatest sarabandes in the clavecin *ordres* and violin sonatas. Again it. has an additional *contre-partie*, and the intensity of its polyphony is reinforced by elaborate ornamentation, often producing incidental dissonances, and by considerable rhythmic variety. These points are illustrated in the following quotation; note the stress on the chord of the augmented fifth, on the accented second beat of the sarabande rhythm:

In the second half, the dissonances are even more abstruse, and the piece has a monumental power worthy of comparison with the greatest dance movements of Bach:

Founded on a little figure in rising thirds, the gavotte is unpretentious, but still somewhat melancholy in tone – 'quelquefois gai, quelquefois grave'. The musette, in two sections, one in the major and one in the minor, is a 6 : 8 pastoral over a *bourdon*, elegant, but still with a flavour of folk-song. Its coda is especially beautiful, floating in a summer haze between the major and minor third:

We may compare such an effect as this with the tremulous haze into which, in the background of many of Watteau's *fêtes champêtres*, two lovers are strolling.

This large-scale suite ends with a chaconne of the *léger* type. While this is not a piece of the monumental order of Couperin's *chaconnes graves*, it is of considerable dimensions, and fine polyphonic workmanship. In the chaconne-rondeau convention, it makes repeated use of dynamic contrasts of *fort* and *doux*. The mood again is of pastoral wistfulness. A couplet in the major, with a drone accompaniment, has a 'glow' comparable with the preceding musette; the main theme, in the minor, is given a tersely linear treatment.

The fourth *Concert Royal*, in E minor, maintains the high level of the third; indeed it is possibly the finest of the group. The prelude is a noble piece of polyphonic writing which invites comparison with the prelude of the Corelli *Apothéose*. The ornamented lines are superbly moulded, over a bass which is as much melodic as harmonic in significance. Though a slighter 225 movement, the allemande contains some fascinating imitative treatment of the little rising scale figure with which it opens. The *courante française* changes the tonality to the major, and rhythmically and harmonically is even more complicated than the A minor courante. Much of the part-writing depends on opposition between 3 : 2 and 6 : 4 rhythms, occurring simultaneously in different lines; passages of elliptical harmony, created by the movement of the parts, are frequent:

The *courante à l'italiéne* returns to the minor and is rhythmically more straightforward. On the other hand, it is possibly the biggest of Couperin's courantes, the second section being developed at more than usual length, with relatively complex modulations. Here the part-writing is fluid, and the harmonies rich. At times there are acute dissonances, and ripe sequential writing:

The trills at the seventeenth, at the end of this passage, are further developed in a longish coda. As a whole, the piece is remarkable for its cantabile lyricism and sonorous harmony.

The sarabande, in the major, has an independent *contre-partie*, and is in Couperin's *très tendrement*, serenely diatonic vein. The second section involves a pathetic modulation to the minor of

226

the dominant, proceeding by way of a flattened seventh in the bass:

The melodies have a Chambonnières-like fragrance, but are developed with greater architectural control. Also in the major, the rigaudon is a perky dance in binary form with a pseudo-contrapuntal treatment of a little rising fourth motive, which is inverted in the second half. After the entry, there is little pretence of counterpoint. The last movement, *Forlane*, is in rondeau, and is one of Couperin's most personal conceptions. The tranquilly gay tune again suggests an exquisitely civilized re-creation of a folk-dance:

In the couplets the warm harmonies suffuse the music with a mellow Watteau-like sunshine. The last couplet, in the minor, achieves a touching unexpectedness by the simplest of means – a melody lilting between the interval of a second and a fourth, with a drone accompaniment rocking on the interval of a sixth:

The E minor is the last of the *Concerts Royaux* collection. No. 5, the first suite in the volume which Couperin called *Les Goûts Réünis,* is in F major, and is slight in texture and character. Its prelude is marked *gracieusement,* instead of the customary *grave;* it is a charming piece in 3 : 8, with falling scale figures neatly imitated in two parts. The *allemande légère* is also freely contrapuntal in technique, with a theme leaping up a fifth, and then a sixth, to a tied note. The motive is often imitated in stretto, thereby creating some elliptical phrases across the bar-line:

Majestically in the minor, the *sarabande grave* has not the passionate and personal tone of the A minor sarabande; but its phrases have a Handelian grandeur, especially in the final clause, when the line mounts by way of a trill to A flat, and then subsides. Also in the minor, the gavotte is a wistful piece in quaver movement, *coulamment.* The *Muséte dans le Goût de Carillon* is a lovely bell piece with the flavour of a *vaudeville.* It would sound well on a small baroque organ.

The prelude of the sixth *concert* in B flat is constructed almost entirely out of a tied crotchet, followed by a semiquaver figure, usually treated as a resolution of the suspension. The allemande, *à 4 tems légers,* is quite a big movement, contrapuntally developed. Delicately dancing, it tosses a little scale figure to and fro between the parts:

Marked *noblement,* the *sarabande mesurée* lives up to its pretensions, though it is among the more simply euphonious, and 228 less passionate, of Couperin's sarabandes. Subtle effects of cross-rhythm are obtained by the concurrence of an appoggiatura-ornamented main melody, with a triplet figure in the bass:

In the next piece the Devil makes an amiable appearance. This mephisto, though fiery, is as well mannered as the devils in Lully's operas. Electrically shooting scale passages, and the discreet introduction of that *diabolus in musica*, the tritone, do not substantially modify this *Air du Diable*'s urbanity:

Its mood and technique may be related to the harlequin and pantomine pieces for clavecin; there is a devil-may-care jauntiness, rather than a dæmonic quality, about the persistent leaping sixths. The last movement of this B flat suite is a sicilienne, a smooth 12 : 8 pastoral with a few dissonant canonic entries.

With the seventh *concert*, we return to a more serious tone. The prelude is both *grave* and *gracieuse*. Its lines are beautifully rounded, and repeated entries in stretto give to the level movement a subdued melancholy:

The allemande is gay, its perky theme being treated in unusually sustained canon. Bachian harmonic sequences occur in the piece's extensive development:

The sarabande returns to the mood of the prelude; the theme, again imitatively treated, incorporates a rising minor sixth which droops back expressively to the fifth. A relaxed melancholy, derived from the lutenists, is suggested by the chromatic harmony, and by the drooping phrases, sometimes ornamented with appoggiaturas, sometimes built on arpeggio figures:

The *Fuguéte* has this interesting, rather spiky subject:

Despite its title, it is an extensively developed movement, in a compromise between fugal technique and harmonic binary form; and despite its feathery texture, it shows a Bach-like contrapuntal solidity. After the first section has ended in D, the second half starts off in B flat – the relative major of the original G minor – with a modified version of the theme inverted. The development of the scale passage and the leaping figure create an exciting animation; on the last page a telling climax is reached by stretching the scale passage through an eleventh. The gavotte also uses a rising scale figure, and contains much canonic writing, while the graceful sicilienne has some tritonal progressions in the bass.

This last piece is Italianate in style. The next *concert*, with the sub-title *Dans le Goût Théatral*, is ostensibly French, a miniature Lullian opera in instrumental form, without the recitative. The overture has the familiar ceremonial opening in dotted rhythm, followed by a quick fugal section in triple rhythm. Here the nature of the theme and the texture recalls the French Couperin of the organ masses. The piece rises to a sonorous climax with the appearance of the theme in thirds:

In the coda, there is a characteristic false relation. The *Grande Ritournéle* is a stately curtain tune; the opening illustrates the measured dignity, and the powerfully dissonant texture obtained by the use of passing notes and appoggiaturas:

A section in four time leads into a Lullian aria in 3 : 2, of a type which had orginally been modelled on Carissimi. This piece is imposing, but not among the most interesting of Couperin's movements in this style.

The heroic manner is continued in a French air in 2 : 2, with chromatic progressions and much gallic ornamentation. The *air tendre* is a sweetly melancholy *brunette*; the *air léger*, in the major, another *brunette* in Couperin's vein of limpid diatonicism. A naïve–sophisticated spirit pervades, too, the loure and the next *air tendre*, in which an appealing use is made of repeated detached minims. The *sarabande grave et tendre* is more *tendre* than *grave*, halfway between the manner of Chambonnières and of Handel. The groupings of the phrases, in their level rhythm, are of some subtlety; note how in this passage the rising scale of the third and fourth bars counteracts the falling sequences of the scale figure of the first two bars:

The poised serenity of the clauses places this among the loveliest of Couperin's spacious, Claude-like movements. Then follow two *airs de cour*, the second of which has some charming echo effects in false relation. An *Air de Bacchantes*, in the conventional 6 : 4 of the operatic bacchanal, brings the work to a rousing conclusion.

In contrast to the *Concert dans le Goût Théatral*, the next *concert*, No. 9 in E, has an Italian title, *Ritratto dell' Amore*. None the less, though a more Corellian technique is noticeable in the fugal movements, the work is still French in feeling; indeed, the pieces have French sub-titles, like the clavecin *ordres*. The French and Italian styles are now equally, and unselfconsciously, a part of Couperin's sensibility. As a whole, this suite is both one of the most representative, and most beautiful, of the *concerts*.

The first movement, *Le Charme*, is more *gracieuse* than *grave*, though it is marked both. Its pellucid polyphony often creates an impressionistic sonority:

L'Enjouement is an *allemande légère* in fugal binary form, with the theme inverted in the second half. Suspensions, syncopations, and stretti suggest a delicate impudence. *Les Graces* is a *courante françoise*, and one of the most complex of this type in rhythm, ornamentation and harmony. It is a revealing instance of the way in which Couperin's harmonic surprises are often the result of linear independence:

The *je-ne-scay-quoi* is based on a cheeky triadic figure which is later wittily treated in stretto:

In the same mood is *La Vivacité*, but the canonic passages are here more consistently developed, exciting use being made of scale passages travelling both ways. In the minor key, the sarabande, *La Noble Fierté*, opens with a magnificent phrase, involving a falling tenth, which fully lives up to the piece's title:

In the second section a long *falling* scale passage in *rising* sequences builds up a climax of a paradoxically passionate sobriety. The minor key is retained for the next piece, *La Douceur*, one of Couperin's intimate linear movements in a quiet 3 : 8. The ornamented flow of the lines and the use of sequences produce some piquant harmonies and modulations:

233

L'et Cœtera is a rustic 6 : 8 movement, with a rising third and falling scale passage in canon. The second part, in the minor, is atmospheric, a repeated phrase droningly revolving on itself.

Of equally fine quality is the next *concert*, No. 10 in A minor. The prelude is one of the most concentrated examples of Couperin's polyphony, in which the lines create the intense harmony – note, for instance, the Neapolitan sixth effect in the penultimate bar:

The 4 : 8 *Air tendre* is also meditative in tone; and here too the economical part-writing leads to some acute dissonances. *Plainte*, the next movement, is for two viols and string bass without continuo. The viols play mainly in dotted rhythm, in thirds and sixths, while the bass reiterates a pedal note; the effect is sensuously rich:

A change to the minor is made for the second part, which is more linear and austere. The last movement, *La Tromba*, is a jaunty binary piece built on a 6 : 8 trumpet arpeggio; at the end, some imitations in stretto are irresistibly comic:

A somewhat sombre temper characterizes most of the eleventh *concert*, in C minor. A longish 3 : 2 prelude in consistent dotted rhythm has power and dignity. The allemande, marked *fièrement*, is in fugal binary form, with an angular, instrumental subject such as one frequently meets with in Bach's work:

The second allemande, *plus légere*, is smoother, containing a higher proportion of conjunct motion; the theme is freely inverted after the double bar. Both the courantes, one in the major and one in the minor, are of the French type. The first is particularly free in its rhythmic ellipses between soprano and bass, combined with much ornamentation. In the second courante trills are used in animated ascending sequences.

The *Sarabande, très grave et très marquée*, is one of the most notable of Couperin's pieces in the *tombeau* convention. The lines use energetic dotted rhythms and a plethora of tremblements, mordents, and portamentos; these elements, however, serve to reinforce phrases – usually built on spread chord formations – which are at once violent and monumental. The tonal sequences and harmonies are exceptionally bold, even including a cadential chord of the thirteenth:

The *gigue lourée* is a fascinating piece of contrapuntal writing, phrased, like so much of Bach, across the bar lines, with frequent dissonant appoggiaturas. Such appoggiaturas play an 235

important part, too, in the line of the concluding rondeau. This is a dialogue between melody and bass, a quiet 3 : 8 built mainly from semiquavers grouped in pairs. While having no outstanding feature, it is one of those movements, *léger et galant*, to which one must be able to respond if one is fully to appreciate Couperin's savour.

The next two *concerts* are for two viols, mostly unaccompanied. They belong to the great French tradition of viol music, which we shall refer to in greater detail later. Although not musically among the most interesting of the *concerts*, the economy of their part-writing is a delight throughout. The prelude to the A major suite is in a *pointé* 3 : 2, and, as so often occurs in the prelude of the da chiesa sonata, it repeatedly employs trills, with turns, on the second beat of the sarabande rhythm, sometimes in ascending sequences. *Badinage* is a quick contrapuntal movement, with a brilliant conclusion in thirds. It is separated from the final air by a short slow recitative section, again on the analogy of the sonata da chiesa. This is marked *patétiquement*, and is a very emotional piece with whirling portamentos and grinding appoggiaturas:

The air is suave, in regular semiquavers, moving mainly by step.

If the twelfth *concert* had affinities with the Italian sonata, the thirteenth is again unambiguously in French suite form. The prelude, on a little arpeggio figure, is consistently canonic. The air, *agréablement* in the minor, uses an imitative technique in 6 : 8, with interestingly irregular phrase grouping – the first section contains eleven bars, and is answered by a section of fifteen. Calm and warm in its diatonicism, the sarabande returns to the major. Finally the *chaconne légère* is based on a brief rising scale figure and leaping fourth, with a rather odd ambiguity between major and minor third. The figure is later presented in a modified form inverted, and developed in free fugue.

The fourteenth and last *concert*, in D minor, is a fine one. The *grave* prelude is powerful in its harmonies, both those contained in the continuo, and those produced by the lines' complex ornamentation:

Here the French dotted rhythm is used within an Italian move-ment; while the climax has a Bach-like combination of discipline with emotion. The same architectural logic is found in the allemande's development of an arpeggio-founded figure; Bach-ian sequences and syncopated phrase-groupings show a fine mastery of instrumental technique. A nobly drooping figure characterizes the theme of the sarabande; note how the falling interval contracts in the first four repetitions, and expands in the following three:

In the second half, the interval is stretched to a sweeping seventh, conveying a sense of emotional liberation.

The last movement, modestly called *Fuguéte*, is a fully developed contrapuntal piece. The 6 : 8 theme, again phrased across the bar, is closely wrought, with syncopations and sequential chromaticisms:

A second subject in semiquavers, founded on arpeggio figuration, is later introduced and cunningly combined with the first theme. As a whole, the piece is a splendid example of classical counterpoint and a fitting conclusion to the whole series.

We have now finished our survey of Couperin's concerted music; but there is one more work – or rather a group of two works – which may conveniently be dealt with at this point, since it is conceived in the same form of the French suite, and since its date is contemporary with the last *concerts*. The suites for two viols were Couperin's last published work, apart from the fourth book of harpsichord pieces. The title-page of this publication, which was rediscovered by Bouvet early in the twentieth century, runs 'Pièces de viole, avec la Basse Chiffrée, par M. F. C. Paris, Boyvin, 1728'. The identification of this M. F. C. with Couperin is open to no doubt. It is supported not only by stylistic considerations and by the fact that the suites contain many signs and phrase markings which were used by no other composer, but also by the *privilège du Roi* which accompanics the publication, and by Couperin's own catalogue of 1730, which mentions some suites for viols appearing, in his *œuvre*, between *Les Nations* and the fourth book of clavecin pieces. The date 1725, given in the catalogue of the *Mercure de France* in 1729, is supported by no other contemporary document, and is presumably false.

These two suites, coming at the end of Couperin's life, are also the end of a great tradition. The midsummer of the French solo viol music lasted from about 1660 to Couperin's death. If it seems odd that the full flowering of this music should occur at a time when the viol was being superseded by the violin, we must remember that there was still a tendency for the most sophisticated members of this hyper-cultivated society to regard the violin as a rather low and undignified instrument. Hubert le Blanc's *Défense de la Basse de Viole* repeatedly points out that the veiled tone and the nature of the bowing of the viol gave it a superior subtlety in the conveyance of emotional nuance; while Rousseau, speaking of the 'Pièces d'Harmonie réglées sur la viole' says:

> La tendresse de son Jeu venoit de ces beaux coups d'archet qu'il animoit, & qu'il adoucissoit avec tant d'adresse et si à propos, qu'il charmoit tous ceux qui l'entendoient, & c'est ce qui a commencé à donner la perfection à la Viole & à la faire estimer préferablement à tous les autres instruments.
>
> (*Traité de la Viole*, 1687.)*

By Couperin's time, as we have seen, the violin had occasioned a fashionable furore, and Couperin made his own impressive contribution to its literature. But it is possible that, even in his day, in the innermost circle of the Elect, the old instrument was still more fashionable than Fashion.

During the *grand siècle*, as the violin had replaced the viol as the stock instrument for dance and other occasional musics, the older instrument had begun to develop a virtuoso tradition. Like the lute, it had become an instrument of the *ruelles* and salons. Maugars and the other early violists had been in the main occasional composers, as were the early lutenists; Marin Marais and Forqueray and the other composers of the solo viol's heyday were, like the later lutenists, the product of an intellectual and emotional esotericism. We may compare them with the English violists of the court of Charles I and the Interregnum, such as William Lawes, Jenkins, and Simpson. Though the English composers remained more conscious of their polyphonic ancestry, it may have been merely the Civil War that prevented them from developing the virtuoso solo aspects of their tradition – as represented by Simpson's *Divisions* – into a classical Augustan homophony.

The nature of this virtuoso music was in part conditioned by the physical nature of the viol, a six-stringed instrument with a flat back and a flat bridge, which made chord playing relatively easy. The tuning, like that of the lute, was in fourths, with a

---

* Cf. also, Mersenne: 'car le Violon a trop de rudesse, d'autant que l'on est contraint à le monter de trop grosses cordes pour esclater dans les suiets, auxquels il est naturellement propre.' (*Harmonie Universal*, 1636.)

Pierre Trichet, in his Traité on viol playing, praises the instrument for its 'mignards tremblements' and the 'coups mourants de l'archet'.

third between the third and fourth strings – D,G,C,E,A,D; Marin Marais, following the invention of his teacher Sainte-Colombe, used a viol which had a seventh string, the low A in the bass. In the preface to his *Pièces de Viole* of 1685, de Machy explains that the viol may be used simply as a melody instrument, accompanied by continuo, or it may be used as a bass for one's own singing; but its most characteristic activity is as a solo instrument playing both melody and harmony. It is possible, he points out, to make a pleasing sound by playing a tune with one hand on the clavecin, but nobody would call that real clavecin playing. Similarly, the viol can play a single melody very agreeably if need be, but the instrument fully reveals itself only when it is played solo, its melodies being harmonized with rich chords and arpeggio devices, often involving big leaps. It is this manner of treating the solo viol which was adapted to the violin by German composers such as Biber, Baltzar, and J.S. Bach. If one objects that in this style it is impossible to play cantabile, and with an expressive use of ornaments, the answer is that everything depends on the skill of the player. It is true, too, that the range of tonalities in which one can play fluently in the harmonized style is limited – D,G,A, and E minor are the keys most convenient to the tuning, in which sextuple stopping is easily practicable on the D major triad. Composers trained in the old linear traditions would not, however, find this lack of tonal variety cramping.

The French violists have left fewer works for unaccompanied viols than their English predecessors. But it is clear in most of their works for one or two viols and continuo that they habitually thought of the viol as a solo harmonizing instrument. The richness of the chords and the mellowness of the tone enhance the elegiac quality of their lyricism. Thus the feeling, as well as the technique and tuning, is close to the tradition of the lutenists; most strikingly of all, the viol composers resemble the lutenists in the way they reconcile their ripe harmonic technique with an extreme delicacy and sophistication of ornament. The basis of this ornamentation and of certain rhythmic conventions is identical with that of the lute music of the court. *Ports de voix, tremblements, pincés,* and *batteries* abound, while the technique of the stringed instrument encourages the use of exaggerated portamento effects. In some of the later viol composers, even so fine a one as de Caix d'Hervelois, the ornamentation is apt to get out of hand; the hyper-sophistication of the music seems somewhat precious, just as the degenerated vocal tradition relapses into an excessive finickiness. In the work of the masters of the medium, however, notably Marais and Forqueray, the subtleties of ornamentation intensify the grand pathos of the lyrical line; and Marin Marais, Lully's pupil in composition and Couperin's almost exact contemporary, must be accounted an artist of Racinian power in his music's fusion of dignity and lyrical ardour. His variations on *La Folia* are, for instance, more nobly distinguished than Corelli's famous set. Forqueray's work is scarcely inferior in grandeur, while being harmonically even more audacious.

Not even Marais or Forqueray, however, achieved a work of such ripe beauty as Couperin's two suites which, like so many aspects of the work of Bach, are the last word, and the most significant, in a particular language. They may not have the nervous virility of the B minor *Passacaille*, or the subtle energy of the Corelli *Apothéose* or *L'Impériale* sonata, Couperin's finest contributions to the more modern violin medium; but on the whole they are possibly Couperin's greatest instrumental work.

The suites are written for two viols, one of them figured. In the original editions there is some confusion between singular and plural on the title-page, for the works are variously described as 'Pièces de violes' and as 'Suites de viole'. This confusion has led to some speculation about the manner in which Couperin intended them to be performed. The most probable explanation is that Couperin had in mind two alternatives. The pieces could either be played by two viols unaccompanied; or the first viol part, which is of a highly virtuoso character, could be played by a soloist, while the second part was played as a bass in conjunction with a harpsichord continuo. The prevalence of multiple stopping and the extraordinary richness of the texture suggest that Couperin regarded the unaccompanied version as aesthetically the more satisfying. As unaccompanied pieces they would be completely in accordance with the viol tradition.

The E minor suite has a Handelian grandeur together with a personal harmonic complexity. In the *grave* prelude, the solo or virtuoso viol part is characterized by its sweeping phrases, swirling portamentos, and passionate ornamentation. The harmony, enriched by the double and triple stopping of the solo-part, has tremendous resonance – for instance this use of the chord of the ninth:

The allemande is as complicated, linearly and rhythmically, as the most abstruse examples of Bach; the leaps and phrase groupings of the solo part produce a quasi-polyphonic effect comparable with that of Bach's suites and sonatas for a solo stringed instrument:

The sonorous chord of the ninth is again in evidence. Similar effects are obtained through big leaps in the energetic courante, which also has powerful chromatic progressions in double stopping:

The sarabande is one of Couperin's noblest movements, again very rich in harmony, making a majestically strenuous use of the French dotted rhythm. The gavotte and gigue are somewhat less remarkable, but have a tautness of line and harmony which is unexpected in these dances. The gavotte flows in a quiet quaver movement, with melancholy, drooping appoggiaturas.

The final *Passacaille ou Chaconne* is in the major, and for the first time lets the sun into this majestically gloomy work. The diatonic radiance of the lines and harmonies is familiar to us from some

242

movements in the violin sonatas and harpsichord pieces; in the viol *Passacaille* it acquires a dynamic drive which we do not normally associate with Couperin. As the couplets evolve trills and turns, bouncy dotted rhythms and flowing scale passages, the music becomes a joyous carillon. The minor couplets enhance the passion with sonorous double stoppings and sequential sevenths:

and the return to the major, *Gay*, brings the work to a virtuoso conclusion in a blaze of baroque ornamentation, repeated notes and arpeggios.

This glowing resonance is the dominant feature of the whole of the A major suite. The prelude has not the E minor's ordered dolour, but a ceremonial splendour. Long curving lines polyphonically treated, luxuriant ornamentation, ripe sequences, double stoppings, and flexible, strong rhythms combine with a dignified exuberance. The *Fuguette* is in fact a fully developed polyphonic movement of over six pages, going through a wide range of keys, with exciting syncopations and a lucidly flowing texture.

The *Pompe Funèbre* is the most magnificent of all pieces in the *tombeau* tradition. It has a Racinian gravity and power; one can appreciate its background more adequately if one relates it to the rhetoric of the funeral orations of Bossuet or to the wonderful *Pompe Funèbre* scene in Lully's *Alceste*:

> Troupes de femmes affligées, troupes d'hommes désolés, qui portent des fleurs et tous les ornamens qui ont servi à parer Alceste. Un transport de douleur saisit les troupes affligées; une partie déchire ses habits, l'autre arrache les cheveux, et chacun brise au pied de l'image d'Alceste les ornamens qu'il porte à la main.

Within the majestic lines of the simple binary structure, the details of ornamentation and harmony are exceptionally rich; 243

there is a still greater profusion of double stoppings and chromatic harmonies – notice in this passage the abrupt transition to the G major triad, and the repeated trills and turns:

After this tragic funeral fresco, the work ends with a typical Couperin *jeu d'esprit*, with the enigmatic title of *La Chemise blanche*. This has a virtuoso first viol part in a chattering moto perpetuo. The second section, in the major, though still impudent, recovers enough of the gallantry of the earlier movements to make the piece a convincing epilogue to the whole work.

The suites for viols, and a few movements in the *concerts*, stand among the very greatest of Couperin's achievements. Normally, however, it is not for profundity or tragic passion that we go to these pieces; we find in them rather the most beautiful and civilized occasional music in European history. To them the definition of Descartes – 'la fin de la musique est de nous charmer et d'évoquer en nous de diverses sentiments' – is peculiarly appropriate, and we remember that Couperin himself said, 'J'aime beaucoup mieux ce qui me touche que ce qui me surprend'. This is music of 'les charmes de la vie', as witty and exquisite as the conversation of the young ladies and gentlemen in the paintings of Watteau.★ But, like the paintings of Watteau, it repeatedly gives one a glimpse of unsuspected horizons, and it is in no way inconsistent with the most profound aspects of Couperin's work. There is no music that demonstrates more clearly how narrow, in a civilized society, is the line between art and entertainment; we may learn from it how the music of the casual glance, the fortuitous conversation, may imperceptibly

★ Cf. M. de Grenailles, *L'honneste Garçon ou l'art de bien élever la noblesse*, 1642: 'Quant à l'adresse aux honnestes exercices, il faut qu'un jeune homme sache chanter et danser autant qu'il en faut, cela veut dire qu'il prenne ces divertissements pour les ornamens de la vie commune plustôt que pour des

occupations continues.'

XII. Watteau: *Les Charmes de la Vie* – 'L'amour et la musique, en
plein air.'

merge into one of the noblest manifestations of European culture. It is apposite that we should end our survey of Couperin's work with music that has such direct social validity, that so intimately reminds us of those values and standards from an examination of which this book began. No aspect of Couperin's work reveals more lucidly that those values and standards depended, not on the denial of the life of the individual member of society, but on a profound appreciation of the issues involved in his relation to the community. These works are not, with the exceptions already mentioned, the greatest of Couperin's creations; but they are perhaps the most essential for an understanding of his work's nature and significance.

Chapter Eleven

Chronology, Influence, and Conclusions

In this book we have devoted separate chapters to each genre of Couperin's work and have made little attempt to discuss the evolution of his music chronologically. This method seemed, on the whole, the least unsatisfactory, particularly since Couperin is not the kind of composer whose work undergoes any startling transformations or changes of front. But of course his music does develop. Innately lucid of mind, he writes with a progressively increasing precision; and the greatest precision entails the greatest subtlety.

The organ masses (1690) present us with most of the essential materials – the symmetrical diatonic melodies, related both to folk-song and to the sophisticated *air de cour*; the baroque ornamentation of this melody, tending to dissolve the rigidity of the metre; the transparent texture of a polyphonic technique inherited from the seventeenth-century organists; the Purcell-like harmonic flexibility; the formal proportions derived from the theatre music of Lully. The early violin sonatas (*c.* 1692 to 1695) bring a more lyrical and operatic type of melody; a compromise between the soloists' polyphony and the homophony of the continuo; and a growing sense of harmonic order learned from Corelli in particular. Certain recognizable Couperin traits begin to appear – a fondness for rich spacing and harmonies, especially ninth chords, disciplined by the economy of texture; a peculiar melting effect produced by hushed suspensions in dotted rhythm; a partiality for the 'touching' effect of the sharp seventh in the ascent, followed by the flat seventh descending; many abstruse dissonances created by appoggiaturas and other ornaments derived from the *air de cour*; and a favourite modulation to the minor of the dominant.

The period of the church music and the early harpsichord pieces (1697 to 1715) blends these French and Italian elements in forms adapted from the church music of Carissimi, Charpentier, 247 and Lully. During the period of *Les Goûts Réünis* (1715 to 1730), the *Concerts Royaux*, the later clavecin pieces, and the last violin sonatas make use of all these elements, but tend to encourage the French elements at the expense of the Italian. Certain dissonances, spread chord effects, dotted rhythms and portamentos suggested by the lutenists and violists help Couperin to achieve some of his grandest creations, particularly in sarabande form. And although he is beginning to relinquish his seventeenth-century-like compromise between polyphony and homophony in favour of a balanced harmonic architecture, it is during this period that we become most clearly aware that his technique is founded on a dialogue between soprano and bass. Here, too, we find his most contrapuntally taut and powerful work, that which most invites comparison with the lucid complexity of Bach. We may refer especially to some of the allemandes, and to *L'Apothéose de Corelli* and *L'Impériale*, music in which, as in Bach's work, vertical harmonies are given density and virility through the independence of the parts that make them up, while at the same time the contour of the lines is conditioned by a clearly defined scheme of tonal order. Finally, in the precision of workmanship in his last compositions, such as the fourth book of harpsichord pieces and the suites for viols, all suspicion of influences, French or Italian, has vanished. He has created an idiom which we can regard both as a triumph of the declining civilization in which he lived, and as perhaps the most central expression of the French tradition.

In 1733, the year in which Couperin died, Rameau, who had been Couperin's neighbour in the rue des Bons Enfants, produced his first opera. The association of the French musical tradition with the theatre was re-established; it was to continue, more or less unbroken, down to our own day. This renewed association was a further growth of the less autocratic culture we have already noticed in Couperin, and it is ironic that the emergence of a more 'popular' culture should – as the level of taste declined – eventually lead a sensitive spirit, such as Claude Debussy, to the Ivory Tower. Couperin's work, however attains the perfect equilibrium between an aristocracy of form and an intimate emotion; he could have occurred only at that precise moment in French history. In the work of a Lebrun, the formal gesture defeats the artist's integrity; in the work of a 248 Boucher, emotional indulgence reduces the art to (very charming) sensory titillation, without – in the widest sense – any moral implications. But in Watteau we find emotional intimacy together with a formal control which reflects a moral and spiritual order. Couperin's relationship to most of his disciples seems to me exactly to parallel that of Watteau to Boucher.

With the great exceptions of Rameau and Leclair, and to a lesser degree Mondonville and Clérambault, Couperin's disciples are musical Bouchers. They write to please; and please they do, for one could scarcely imagine a more deliciously sensuous entertainment music than the *Conversations Galantes et Amusantes* of Dandrieu, Dornel, Duphly, and Daquin in clavecin music, of Guillemain, Mouret, Blavet, Corrette, and Bois-mortier in concerted music for strings and wind instruments. Their work implies an instinct for social elegance; their indul-gence of their emotions never prevents them from raising their hats and making their bow in the appropriate places. But they have forgotten *why* they raise their hats. The gesture is auto-matic; they act from habit, having lost their guiding sense of a moral order.

The best of Couperin's minor disciples, Dandrieu and Dagin-cour, are thus, despite great sensibility and charm, derivative in a bad sense; and they are essentially miniaturists, which Couperin, *essentially*, was not. Even Rameau, Couperin's peer in the French classical tradition, does not achieve in his keyboard music the close texture of Couperin's finest work. His is more harmonic, less linear in lay-out, more virtuoso and theatrical in treatment. It is more brilliant, and more immediately emotional than Couperin's work; but it is not therefore more profound. Perhaps Rameau's very finest pieces, such as the superb A minor allemande and in a quieter vein *Les Tendres Plaintes*, are an exception to this, having much of Couperin's sombre dignity. But they are less characteristic of his work than an audaciously imaginative, 'colouristic' piece like *Le Rappel des Oiseaux*; a grand Handelian piece like the *Gavotte* with variations or the A major *Sarabande*; or an expansive virtuoso piece such as *Les Tourbillons*, *Les Cyclopes*, with its non-melodic Alberti bass, *La Dauphine, La Triomphante,* or the exciting rondeau *Les Niais de Sologne*. All these, in the Handelian fashion, are based more on arpeggio formations than on scale-wise motion:

Couperin, like Bach, on the whole favours conjunct motion rather than arpeggio figures.

Rameau, unlike Couperin, looks forwards rather than backwards. There are passages in his clavecin works – which were all written early in his career, before he began to take himself seriously as an operatic composer – which already give intimation of eighteenth-century sonata style. *La Poule* is a genuine harpsichord piece in the classical baroque tradition; yet towards the end, just before the coda, there is a passage, harping on the chord of the dominant seventh, which has in miniature the structural and harmonic effect of the cadenza to the Mozartian concerto:

There is nothing comparable with this in Couperin. Similarly one of the most remarkable of Rameau's pieces, *L'Enharmonique*, is deliberately a study in tonal relationships. It has a diminished seventh cadence which is not produced by linear movement, but which is harmonic in its own right, marking a rhetorical or dramatic point in the structure, as do the cadences in the

250 eighteenth-century sonata:

Rameau's delightful *Pièces de clavecin en concert*, cast in the three-movement Italian form of allegro-andante-allegro, illustrate this progressive 'modernism' even more clearly. Their keyboard part is not a continuo part like that of Couperin's trio sonatas, nor a piece of polyphonic writing like that of Bach's sonatas. The keyboard is treated as a virtuoso solo instrument, in a way that suggests Haydn and Mozart's treatment of the combination of piano with strings. The relation of the string writing to the new bourgeois rococo style becomes patent in the version for string sextet which some disciple made after Rameau had deserted chamber music for the theatre.

Perhaps the most interesting instance of the twilight of the French clavecin school is provided by the four volumes of pieces by Jacques Duphly, engraved by Mlle Vendôme and published by Boyvin in 1755 and subsequently.* Duphly has two disparate manners, most evident respectively in his first and fourth books, though the sequence is not strictly chronological. In the first book especially, the allemandes, courantes and some of the rondeaux preserve the linear gravity of the classical style as manifest in Couperin, and some of them – for instance the D minor allemande and courante – are exceptionally beautiful. At the

---

* No modern edition of Duphly's music existed when I wrote the book. Heugel has now issued one edited by Françoise Petit. Several recordings have also appeared. Especially interesting is music from the first and fourth books, played by Françoise Petit on a softly sonorous instrument built to a classical specification by Gérard Fonvielle in 1971. The performances are worthy of the lovely instrument; if they're occasionally a little quirky, that seems in keeping with the music.

opposite extreme are pieces from the fourth book, such as *La de Sartine* and *La de Juigne*, which are fully fledged rococo movements relying on simple chordal progressions rather than line, with tunes like baby Mozart, and with fill-in scales and arpeggiated Alberti basses which would sound as well, perhaps better, on the fortepiano as on the harpsichord. Somewhat paradoxically, Duphly exploits these modern techniques even within the old-fashioned convention of the chaconne, for he has a very long chaconne in F containing Alberti figurations – a device that Couperin, as a linear composer, regarded with suspicion. Even in the first book he gives us a piece, *La Cazamajor*, which exploits arpeggio and scale figurations in a manner that in virtuosity, if not in intensity, rivals Rameau and even Scarlatti. Still more dazzling is a piece appropriately titled *La Victoire*.

Duphly's 'modern' and/or 'decadent' characteristics should not necessarily be regarded as loss. He is a real composer who profited from, rather than being inhibited by, his transitional position: if he surrenders some of Couperin's civilized elegance, he is alertly responsive to a mutable world. Even in a formal dance piece like *La Boucon*, a courante dedicated to a famous harpsichord virtuoso, there may be a nervous, slightly febrile quality testifying – in this case by way of rootlessly sequential diminished sevenths and weird passages based on rapid finger alternation – to an underlying insecurity. Similarly the first minuet of the C major Suite opens in polite conventionality, only to titillate with metrical surprises; while the second minuet, shedding aristocratic finesse, sidles into the domesticity of a rococo drawing room. A piece like *La Larare* may owe its title to the fact that two worlds – those of Couperin's aristocratic grace and of the rococo symphony's democratic ebullience – are juxtaposed within one number. Throughout, Duphly's vacillations between the high and low, both socially and spiritually speaking, stimulate and disturb. Far from being a weathercock passively veering to social change, he is a barometer who helps us to understand the human motives that had made climatic change obligatory. Such compromising pieces are most prevalent in the third book. *La de Villeneuve*, for instance, preserves the authentic Couperin fragrance in its arching melody, while reconciling it with an urban rococo vivacity in the broken arpeggios of the second half. *La Forqueray* gives a more popular flavour to traditional F minor grandeur, in an arpeggiated technique recalling Couperin's *Les*

Baricades Mistérieuses. La Medée, also in the key of *chants lugubres*, is genuinely powerful, attaining a ferocity worthy of its subject, with operatic gestures resembling the theatre music of Rameau and even prophetic of Gluck; the form expands Scarlatti-style binary structure towards the sonata, with a development section beginning in the relative major.

Even in the fourth book, alongside pieces like *La Du Drummond* which charm through the gaucherie of their approach to the rococo symphony, Duphly still produces a chaconne-rondeau such as *La Pouthouin*, which recalls Couperin's great *La Favorite* in its rondeau tune, but intersperses it with couplets in Alberti figuration. Although or perhaps because the idiom is transitional, the effect is oddly touching; Duphly's pathos, like his occasional feverishness, is testimony to his vulnerability, which is also his sensitivity, to a world in uneasy transition. Only occasionally are the new elements in his music unassimilated into the old. There is an example, oddly enough, in the first volume, which ends with a piece in C major, marked *légèrement*, built out of more than usually footling scales and arpeggios rounded off, after a double bar, by a reiterated Handelian full close: a musical method of saying The End which is almost comically simple-minded.

Born in 1727, nine years later than Duphly, Claude-Benigne Balbastre also displays the directionless vigour of a composer responsive to an age in transition. His quick pieces often have impressive rhythmic impetus, combined with a Scarlattian sense of startlement, so that they seem to herald a new age; the extravert *La Monmortel* may be cited, and still more *La Lugeac*, with its bounding arpeggiated theme, its fragmented cadenza, and its near-hysterical rising chromatics over a pedal point. Such exuberance is positive yet also a shade desperate, perhaps because he was still deeply aware of the virtues of the Old World. Balbastre has many pieces – we may mention *Le d'Hericot* and *La Segur* among the selection superbly recorded by Gustav Leonhardt – which recall the pastoral conventions of Couperin le Grand, but imbue them with a dark broodiness that may derive from an intuitive recognition that they belonged to a society soon to be destroyed and already half forgotten. Even a composer as strong as Balbastre has lost his centre, and cultivates a *'variété des goûts'* instead of the one *goût* which all civilized people knew to be *bon*. Though he survived the 253

Revolution by ten years it was, materially and spiritually, the end of him. He was stripped of his court appointments, and not even his pathetic attempts to curry favour by writing variations on the Marseillaise could save him from ignominy and misery. The pieces on revolutionary tunes have some intrinsic interest, for the perky, rhythmically vivacious arrangements of the military airs are interspersed with couplets that are often chromatically melancholy. The music hopes for the best from the new world but doesn't rate its chances highly; the chromatic interludes tell us that revolution cannot be taken at its face value since it is bound to hurt, and the victors suffer along with the victims. But they may not suffer very much, being top dogs who have surrendered the old world's capacity for feeling. When Balbastre's pieces were published in 1759 *Mercure de France* rather condescendingly praised them for being 'felicitous and diversified' in manner, 'pleasant' to listen to, and 'free of irritating and unnecessary technical difficulties'. This underestimates the qualities of Balbastre's music, but is a significant straw in the wind. *Hoi polloi* takes over.

Born in the same year as Balbastre is the last of the Couperins to establish a reputation as a professional composer as well as performing musician. Though Armand-Louis Couperin is not as good a composer as Duphly or Balbastre, he is historically fascinating; and his fascination is inseparable from his instability. A collection of his harpsichord pieces was published in 1751, when he was a young man of twenty-four; not surprisingly, much of the music is rooted in the old world. The opening allemande, for instance, is grave, spacious, nobly sonorous in its regularly flowing figuration: simpler in texture than an allemande of Couperin le Grand, but undeniably in the same tradition. The courante that follows, *La de Croissy*, abruptly whisks us into another world. Bounding in rhythmic *élan*, it is formally and texturally a cross between a Scarlatti bipartite sonata and the demotic style of the new rococo music; it was about this time that the works of the Stamitz family began to take Paris by storm. The piece is both comic and startling: genuinely exciting yet, in comparison with François Couperin's wit, a little crude. *L'Affligée* exactly complements this in 'tragic' terms, the inverted commas being called for, but in no spirit of condescension. Built, as one might expect, on sobbing, often acutely dissonant appoggiaturas, it is beautiful and, indeed, moving; compared with François's *L'âme-en-Peine*, however, its pathos seems a rhetorical gesture. The simpler the texture, the more calculated the 'effects' seem: especially when the 'affliction' proves so overwhelming that the music momentarily collapses in silence. If this suggests the chromatic Style of Sensibility explored contemporaneously by C. P. E. Bach, it too is experienced at a rather obvious level. Armand-Louis's contribution, as successor to the French harpsichord tradition in which his family had been so illustrious, is epitomized in a piece with the quintessentially Couperinesque title of *Les Tendres Sentimens*. The music has charm – which is on the surface in that tender sentiment has become expressively as well as technically rudimentary. In metrical regularity an upbeat lands on a gently dissonant appoggiatura which resolves in a slight sigh, in the tempo of a slow minuet with perhaps a distant prophecy of a post-Revolutionary valse. That's all there is to it, except for some faint dubieties in a minor episode and some briefly tremulous chromatics towards the close. There are no inner polyphonies, and the inward-looking tension of François Couperin's *tendres sentiments* has evaporated. The charm that is left, however pleasurable, had little chance of surviving the revolutionary holocaust. Armand-Louis's charm, in his early music, bypasses the sense of threat that a disintegrating society carries with it.

As Armand-Louis grew older, however, he was by no means impervious to the winds of change; on the contrary he scurried, wildly buffeted by them, in several contradictory directions. He was unafraid of adventure and experiment but, less durable than Balbastre, found himself at sea or in limbo, bewildered because he didn't know where his explorations were leading him. Only recently have we became aware of this extraordinary aspect of Armand-Louis's work, with the discovery and publication of the music for two harpsichords, edited by David Fuller in 1975. With William Christie, Fuller has recorded the surviving member of the two *Quatuors* for two harpsichords (so titled in reference to the two players' four hands), and the *Simphonie de Clavecins*, both works dating from the early seventeen-seventies, twenty years later than the solo harpsichord pieces.

The music looks, in score, like rococo symphonic music, bearing the conventional Italian tempo directions, and being littered with crescendos, diminuendos and expression marks such as would seem alien to the harpsichord. It is clear that this 255 was deliberate: Armand-Louis consciously exploits sundry gadgets which harpsichord builders were experimenting with, in an attempt to rival the excitations of the Mannheim-style orchestra. The effects he achieves by using the two instruments antiphonally, in a wide range of contrasted dynamics, are genuinely orchestral and demonstrate a vivid aural imagination. The 'steam-roller' crescendo in the last movement of the *Simphonie* is technically dazzling; and technical audacities are often informed too by emotion, as is the beautiful passage in the first movement when the first harpsichord plays *pianissimo* on the *buffles*, while the second harpsichord resounds *fortissimo*. Still more imaginative is the slow movement of the *Quatuor*, which extracts bell-like sonorities from ostinato-like repeated notes. This music, economic in texture and figuration, attains true personal identity, being delicately sensuous in a manner quite distinct from Couperin le Grand, yet distinct too from the affability of routine rococo charm. For the rest, however, Armand-Louis Couperin's 'symphonic' harpsichord music succumbs not to routine but to randomness. Musical events of Scarlattian trenchancy and C. P. E. Bachian sensibility make decisive impacts, only to dissipate them, for Armand-Louis didn't have the emotional stamina, nor perhaps the technical ability, to establish command over the fresh fields into which he'd courageously ventured. Old French manners are in desuetude in his work; but though he is both vigorous and provocative in exploring 'modern' ideas, he is insufficiently directed to forge them into an Austro-Italian symphonic allegro, and is more convincing in the jig-style finale of the *Quatuor* than in the enterprising first movement of the *Simphonie*. David Fuller reports that at his death Armand-Louis Couperin owned two harpsichords (one with modern gadgets), two spinets, a clavichord, a piano, two organs and a regal. Clearly he wasn't going to miss out on any sonorous possibilities which keyboards offered; equally clearly, he hardly knew where he stood among them.

Though this is more obvious in the late pieces for two keyboards it was already implicit in the Janus-like qualities we remarked on in the early solo pieces. As fill-ups on the disc of two harpsichord works William Christie appends two movements from the collection called *Les Quatre Nations*, dating from around 1750. The juxtaposition of the 'French' with the 'Italian' piece points the contrast between the old and the new *goût* extravagantly, for whereas the French piece uses consistent figuration in the low register to create a gravity simpler than, but recognizably within, the old tradition, the Italian piece sounds almost like a parody of fashionable modernities. Sudden silences, 'licentious' modulations, hammered repeated notes and an outrageous cadenza carry baroque rhetoric to the brink of absurdity; yet the new, experientially valid drama of the Classical Age doesn't crystallize out of it. Though Armand-Louis doesn't exactly fall between stools, he straddles them uneasily. *

It is clear that Couperin stood for something which, by Duphly's time, already belonged to a past world. Apart from Rameau, only the great Leclair came close to Couperin's elegiac aristocracy, and even he developed a more symphonic and harmonic style. Although like Rameau he favoured a monothematic as much as a bithematic technique, in his work too the suite is superseded by the Italian concerto and the classical triptych of allegro-andante-allegro. Couperin stood for something from which the French tradition was turning away. His influence survived in France for barely twenty-five years after his death. By 1771 Grimm was able to say: 'il y a deux choses auxquelles les François seront obligés de renoncer tôt ou tard, leur musique et leurs jardins'. The noble architectural symmetry of the classical tradition had perished. †

Couperin had an enthusiastic Belgian disciple in J. H. Fiocco. Some of his pieces make a genuine attempt to reproduce both Couperin's complexity of line (*L'Inconstante* or the dotted rhythmed allemande from the D minor suite), and his serene naïveté (*La Légère,* the two gavottes from the D minor suite). *Les Promenades de Bierbéeck ou de Buerbéeck* is a very close imitation of one of Couperin's gentle flowing 3 : 8 movements with consistent semiquaver figuration. The pieces are not, however, very distinguished, and are all disfigured by clumsy passages of

---

* For note, see page 267.

† An interesting gloss on the inability of the Handelians to appreciate Couperin's linear idiom is provided by Dr Burney's comments on his ornamentation: 'The great Couperin . . . was not only an admirable organist but, in the style of the times, an excellent composer for keyed instruments. His instructions for fingering, in his *L'Art de toucher le Clavecin*, are still good; tho' his pieces are so crowded and deformed by beats, trills and shakes, that no plain note was ever left to enable the hearer of them to judge whether the tone of the instrument on which they were played was good or bad.' (*A General History of Music.*)

parallel octaves which betray Fiocco's inability to maintain a consistently linear style. Even in these his most Couperin-like pieces he seems in danger of falling into the easy homophonic *style galant*; in pieces such as *La Fringante* or *L'Anglaise* he quite explicitly writes straightforward arpeggiated movements in the Italianate Handelian style. Most of the other Belgian clavecinists, such as Boutmy and Gheyn, also use the Italian technique. Such relations as they have with Couperin are superficial.

In England and Italy the music of Lully had exerted a most powerful influence, but the influence died with the culture that produced it, if we except the reminiscences of Lully in Handel's English work. Only in Germany was the French spirit deeply entrenched.

Because of the time lag occasioned by the Thirty Years War Germany was culturally somewhat behind the times, so that the French vogue in Germany came to its height after *la gloire* had decayed. Communications between France, Belgium, and southern Germany were stimulated by the Bavarian alliance, and French culture became the accepted criterion of taste. In the last decade of the seventeenth century German composers were as eager to emulate Lully as were their aristocratic patrons to emulate Lully's master the Roi Soleil. French musicians such as Buffardin frequently visited Germany, castles were built in Germany on the model of Versailles, and a movement that had started in the Catholic south soon spread to Prussia and the north. Frederick the Great was to entertain Voltaire, and to speak French more graciously than German.

Even before Lully's triumph composers such as Rosenmüller and Bleyer had been influenced by the French ballet. By the end of the seventeenth century many German composers had gone to Paris to study the French methods under Lully himself. Possibly J. J. Froberger was a copyist in French employment; he wrote harpsichord works – including an impressive piece which may have been a model for Louis Couperin's *Tombeau de M. de Blancrocher* – which derive from the lute-like French keyboard style. Erlebach and Mayr were for a time among Lully's pupils, writing quantities of dance suites in the French manner; while in 1682 J. S. Cousser published in Stuttgart his *Composition de musique suivant la méthode française, contenant six Ouvertures de Théâtre accompagnées de plusieurs Airs*. A little later appeared Johann Kaspar Fischer's *Le*
258 *Journal de Printemps consistant en Airs et Balets à 5 parties et les*

Trompettes à plaisir, entrancingly fresh occasional music modelled on the *Musique pour le Souper du Roi* of La Lande and others. The first volume of Fischer's harpsichord music was published in 1696. Most of the little dances are a more muscular version of those of Chambonnières, though some of the big chaconnes, notably the G major, are worthy of Lully himself.★

The most notable of all Lully's German pupils and disciples was, however, Georg Muffat, whose *Florilegia* suites were published in 1695. Muffat, who came from Passau, had at one time played in Lully's orchestra. In his preface to the *Florilegia*, he maintained that of Lully's work he had 'fait autre fois à Paris pendant six ans un assez grand Estude . . . à mon retour de France je fus peut-estre le premier qui en apportay quelque idée assez agréable aux musiciens *de bon goût*, en Alsace'. (My italics.) He can hardly have been justified in claiming to be the first German composer to use the French style, but it is true that he offers an example 'd'une mélodie naturelle, d'un chant facile et coulant, fort éloigné d'artifices superflus, des diminutions extravagantes', and that for solidity of part-writing and richness of harmony his example could hardly be improved upon. Each suite has a title referring to some human quality (Gratitudio, Impatientia, Constanzia, etc.), and the titles of the individual pieces that make up the suites are in French. Some are dances – allemandes, bourrées, sarabandes, canaries, ballets, airs, passe-pieds, and so on; others are of a descriptive nature – *Les Gendarmes, Ballet pour les Amazones*, even *Gavotte de Marly*. Each suite is prefaced by a full-scale Lullian overture, complete with double dotted rhythm, the familiar crotchet tied to a semiquaver figuration ♩♪♫♫ , and a triple-rhythmed fugal section often with a rousing conclusion in parallel thirds. These overtures, and the other big movements such as the passacailles, are exceptionally fine, with all Lully's sonorous grandeur and, in addition, a certain Germanic sobriety. One may mention, in particular, the G minor overture, and the *Passacaille* in A minor. Like Couperin, Muffat was later much influenced by Corelli as well·

★ The most interesting pieces in the collection are not, however, in the French style, but in the German development of Italian toccata technique which Bach was to use with wonderful effect in such things as the Chromatic Fantasia. Some of Fischer's preludes, for instance the D major, are remarkably bold experiments in harmonic progression.

as Lully, and published a series of Italianate concerti grossi.

By the time Couperin had become a musical celebrity, the taste for things French was thus well established in Germany, and it is not surprising that he too became a dominating force in German music, particularly keyboard music. Fux and Telemann copied not only Couperin's titles, but also his airy texture, and the more percussive features of his style. Telemann was especially Francophile; 'les airs françois', he said, 'ont replacé chez nous la vogue qu'avaient les cantates italiennes. J'ai connu des Allemands, des Anglais, des Russes, des Polonais, et même des Juifs, qui savaient par cœur des passages entières de *Bellérophon* et d'*Atys* de Lully.' He was fortunate enough to have his quartets for flute and strings played by such distinguished performers as Blavet,★ Guignon, Forqueray, and Edouard, while in 1728 a psalm and cantata of his composition were performed with considerable success at a Concert Spirituel. He published a work called *Musique de table, partagée en trois Productions, dont chacune contient l'Ouverture avec la suite à 7 instruments.* The dances include such typically French forms as the forlane, passepied, loure, chaconne, musette, and rondeau, and the titles suggest a complete Watteau décor, with Réjouissance, Allégresse, Badinerie, Flatterie, and even Bergerie, Harlequinade, and La Douceur. Telemann's treatment of the style is, however, more unambiguously homophonic than Couperin's; for his sympathies, as J. S. Bach realized, were associated as much with the new kind of symphonic music as with the old linear style of the classical baroque.

A more significant mingling of French and German styles is provided by the most distinguished of Couperin's German disciples, Georg Muffat's son Gottlieb, and Johann Mattheson, who in his *Kernmelodische Wissenschaft* of 1736 recommended the

---

★ Blavet admired Telemann's work greatly, and, as Lionel de Laurencie has pointed out, his own music betrays Telemann's influence, both in some of its ornamentation and in certain pedal effects – for instance, the tonic pedal for the flute in the Prelude to Blavet's *Nouveaux Quatuors* of 1738. In general, the German composers had a slight reciprocal influence on their French hosts. It is noticeable as late as 1768, in Corrette's *Cinquante Pièces ou Canons lyriques à deux, trois, ou quatre voix,* which are modelled on Telemann's canons. In 1746 an article on *La Corruption du Goût dans la Musique Française,* published in the Mémoires de Trévoux, mentions Telemann among other baleful foreign corruptions, such as

Vivaldi, Locatelli, and Handel.

French style to young composers, because 'Frankreich ist und bleibt die rechte Tanzschule'. This verdict on the 'claire et facile' melody of the French, as opposed to Italian complexity, was endorsed by the theoretician Quantz, after he had spent several months in Paris in the late seventeen-twenties. Like that of Telemann the musical thought of Muffat and Mattheson is more consistently homophonic than Couperin's, and their texture is thicker; but they discover a common denominator between the French and German styles, and one may regard them, perhaps, as a cross between Couperin and Handel. Mattheson's allemandes are often quite involved, in the manner of Couperin and Bach – for instance that from the C minor suite:

His more customary manner is represented by the air with doubles in arpeggio accompaniment, from the same suite, or by the melancholy sarabande with variations from the F minor suite, Handelian in technique, but more austere in feeling:

Muffat, on the other hand, with his south German Catholic background, has all Handel's Italianate flamboyance, and writes movements, such as the big prelude and fugue of the B flat suite, in a rhetorical toccata style which Couperin never attempted:

261

Some of his finest pieces are chordally accompanied airs in Handelian style, rather more abstruse harmonically – for instance the B flat minor sarabande from the same suite, with its poignant Neapolitan sixths:

and throughout Muffat thinks more 'chordally' than Couperin. He has, however, some fine linear pieces which resemble Bach if not Couperin (the G major, E minor and D minor sarabandes, and the allemandes in D major and D minor); and something of the authentic Couperin spirit still survives in the sprightly courantes, with their contrapuntal entries; in the cross rhythms of the B flat Hornpipe; in the audacious portamentos of *La Hardiesse*; in the grandly rigid rhythm of the G major chaconne; and especially in the flowing lilt and dissolving harmonies of the G major gigue. Here too, the technique depends on harmonic progression rather than linear movement; Couperin does not use the Neapolitan sixth effect in this explicitly chordal form:

But the grace of the movement, with the undercurrent of wistfulness, recalls Couperin, Watteau, and the world of the *fête champêtre*, and Muffat must have been one of the last composers to understand, intuitively, what the *fête champêtre* had stood for in spiritual terms. Some of Muffat's suites – for instance, the C major and D minor – have an orthodox Lullian overture instead

262

of the toccata prelude. He is a highly impressive keyboard composer whose work ought to be more widely known.

Some of Handel's dances were published in Paris in 1734 by Antoine Bretonne, and were frequently played during the following decade. Reciprocally, both Handel and Bach studied Couperin's work. Although Couperin's influence on Handel, who is temperamentally closer to Lully, can have been merely superficial, we have repeatedly mentioned that Bach found in Couperin a spirit with whom he could sympathize. His own ventures into the French style, in keyboard and orchestral suites, have little of Couperin's *galant* finesse, but bring to his linear draughtsmanship an austerely powerful German contrapuntal science. We have frequently discussed the general similarities between Bach's technique and Couperin's.

Even in the work of Bach's sons, the influence of Couperin is still discernible, though the use which they make of him differs from their father's. J. S. Bach found in Couperin a composer whose technique was basically linear, like his own; Carl Philipp Emanuel, in his many pieces with French titles,★ such as *La Caroline*, adapts the binary structure, the airy texture, the staccato arpeggio figuration and the sequential passage-work typical of Couperin's lighter movements:

But the form is now harmonically and metrically dictated, in a way which suggests Haydn and the early symphony; witness the pause followed by a Neapolitan sixth in the coda, a device which, depending on harmonic and dynamic *contrast*, is

---

★ Many of C.P.E. Bach's pieces with French titles appeared in Marpurg's *Raccolta delle più nuove composizioni di clavicembalo* (Leipzig, 1756-57), and thus belong to the middle years of C.P.E. Bach's career. The titles include such characteristic formulae as *L'Auguste*, *La Bergins*, *La Lott*, *La Glein*, *La Prinzette*, *La Complaisante*, *La Capricieuse*, *L'Irrésolue*, *La Journalière*, *La Xenophon*, *Les Langueurs Tendres*. Some of the pieces are reasonably convincing imitations of Couperin; we may mention *L'Irrésoluse* and *La Journalière*, especially the latter, with its habitually syncopated phrasing and its characteristic breaks in rhythm. In all, there are twenty-four of these 'French' pieces. On Marpurg, see below.

essentially dramatic and symphonic, rather than a product of linear movement:

A passage such as this seems to invite orchestral treatment.

Similarly, some of Wilhelm Friedemann Bach's 'French' sarabandes revealingly illustrate the transformation of the sarabande into the slow movement of the eighteenth-century symphony; and although G. M. Monn has a movement with the authentic-sounding *grand-siècle* title of *La Personne Galante*, it is hardly possible to see any affinity between his music and Couperin, beyond a few skipping staccato figures based on triads. His work, composed about the middle of the century, depends on the tonal principles of the diatonic sonata, and from it to the Mannheim symphonists is but a step. It is no accident that the elder Stamitz first achieved fame, in the seventeen fifties, before a middle-class audience in France, as *chef d'orchestre* to the enterprising Le Riche de la Pouplinière; and that the symphonic works of the younger Stamitz and the others Mannheimers were first published in Paris. The age of classical aristocracy, of the late baroque, is outmoded by the age of the rococo. If we take Johann Stamitz and C. P. E. Bach as representative of the two main strands of the new period, we may say that in Stamitz we find the deliberate cultivation of a bold popular style, designed to have a commercial appeal to a relatively wide audience; while in C. P. E. Bach's later work we find a romantic individualism, a preoccupation with *sensibilité*, expressed not only in the almost lushly harmonic nature of the slow movements, but even in his dedication of his volumes to '*Kenner und Liebhaber*'. Since 1750, these two elements, the popular and the personal, have drifted gradually further apart.

Probably the latest examples of Couperin's influence in Germany are to be found in the keyboard work of Graupner, Krebs, Kirnberger, and Marpurg. Graupner has a rather beautiful *Sommeil* movement; Krebs, a duller composer, has a piece called *Harlequinade* which is, however, already more Mozartian than

264

Couperinesque in style and feeling. Some pieces of Kirnberger, such as *Les Complimenteurs* and *Les Carillons*, have more of the authentic manner, and his D major chaconne is interesting as a transition between the *galanterie* of Lully and Couperin, and the new, Mozartian *galant* convention. But most striking is the *Clavierstücke* collection of Marpurg, published in Berlin in 1762. Into this volume Marpurg has transcribed Couperin's *Le Réveil-matin*, and pieces by other clavecinists such as Clérambault, and has added pieces of his own which not only have characteristic titles (*La Badine, Les Fifres*, etc.), but which are closer to the linear style of Couperin than are most of the Germanic versions of his idiom mentioned in this chapter. The pieces are not, however, much more than pastiche. The Couperin tradition is no longer a living reality; it has been engulfed by the symphony, as was the tradition of Bach.

And so, as the Viennese symphony prospered, Couperin was forgotten, both in Germany and in his own country. The revival of interest in him has more or less coincided with the revival of interest in Bach; and his position in French musical history is comparable with that of Bach in the history of *European* music. Just as Bach sums up the evolution of European music down to his time, and suggests potentialities which have only recently been investigated; so Couperin, in his less comprehensive way, has the whole of French musical history implicit in him, and hints at later developments in Fauré, Debussy, and Ravel. The two latter played a considerable part in the re-establishment of Couperin and their attempt, in their later work, to reinstate the French classical tradition in place of their earlier 'nervous' intros-pection is significant – particularly in view of their preoccupation with the world of Watteau and the Harlequin. But still more important is the comparison with Fauré, because Fauré's tech-nique, as has been pointed out, has a similar combination of harmonic subtlety in the inner parts with solid line drawing between melody and bass. Fauré, too, is a guardian of civilization and tradition. His civilization, however, has a less direct relation to a real world than Couperin's; it is an idealization, in an art form, of his response to the French tradition. For this reason, perhaps, his enharmonic fluctuations give to his urbanity a certain precariousness. He cannot aspire to that proud serenity and mastery of stylization which was natural to Couperin because he lived in a society which believed in itself, was confident of its values. 265

Couperin's civilization, as we have previously suggested, was both real and ideal at the same time. It was real in the sense that it existed outside his music in the world in which he lived; it was ideal in the sense that, in his music, he presented the values of his society in a form distilled of all merely topical and local dross. We have no real parallel to this in English music. In some ways the civilized quality of Couperin's music is, in its finest moments, not incomparable with the urbanity of Ben Jonson. That magnificent poem, *To the World, A Farewell for a Gentlewoman, Virtuous and Noble*, mates courtly elegance with earthy vigour, urbanely balanced movement with tragic passion, in a manner similar to that which we have noticed in Couperin's greatest achievements. The exquisiteness of the courtly lyrical poets, the spirituality of the seventeenth-century devotional poets, and the immediate vitality of the dramatists and the Donne tradition meet in Jonson's work; Couperin, too, shows that urbanity, wit, and courtly grace may exist together with a deeply serious, even religious, attitude to life. And if we feel that in Couperin there is more exquisiteness and less earthy vigour, that should not lead us to underestimate the vigour that is certainly there. Nor is it at all surprising, making allowances for the difference in date and environment, that Couperin should have many temperamental affinities with Jonson. During the latter part of Jonson's life, English Caroline culture was developing in a manner closely parallel to French culture. Had it not been for the Civil War, it is at least feasible that Dryden or some other successor to Jonson might have been as convincing in his heroic work as he was in his critical and satirical; that we might have produced something closer to Racine than in fact we did. In that case, it is possible that the masque might have developed into the mature opera; and that Purcell, as successor to Jenkins and William Lawes, might have been, not a greater genius, but a composer more aristocratically elegant, more precise, more Couperin-like. By the time England had evolved her Augustan civilization she seemed for the most part to have lost an awareness of tragic issues. Apart from a few passages in Pope, our Augustan age has nothing comparable with the greatest things in Couperin and Racine.

Couperin is not, of course, a composer whose outlook on life is fundamentally religious, even mystical, as is Bach; nor has he Bach's comprehensiveness. In some obvious respects, Alessandro Scarlatti, La Lande, Handel, and Rameau are all classical baroque composers on a grander scale than Couperin. None of them, however, comes as close to Bach as does Couperin in his finest work; none of them has anything as aristocratically noble as *La Favorite*, as spiritual as the *Leçons de Ténèbres*, as tightly wrought as *L'Apothéose de Corelli* or *L'Impériale*, as tragic as the *Passacaille*, as civilized as *La Convalescente*. No doubt Rameau is the key figure with reference to the future of French musical culture, since his passionately disciplined theatrical art looks forward to the next supremely great figure in the French tradition, Berlioz. Yet Couperin himself is not as remote from Berlioz as one might superficially imagine; and, unlike Rameau, he also looks back, beyond Lully, to the sixteenth century and even the Middle Ages. It is hardly too fanciful to suggest that Couperin is a central link between Lassus, the richest and most multifarious of the Franco-Flemish sixteenth-century masters, and Berlioz, the man who, despite his much vaunted romanticism, is the greatest aristocratic master of linear draughtsmanship in the nineteenth century.

And then, by way of Fauré, Couperin establishes a link with the modern world. Perhaps the nature of this connection is indicated if one remarks, in conclusion, that the relation of the classicist Valéry to Racine resembles the relation of Fauré's last works to Couperin.

Note to p. 257

There is, it would seem, a gulf between the real composer, be he major or minor, and the higher well-meaner, such as Armand-Louis was. We may learn from his failure, recognizing that only a composer of genius could have assimilated the radical transformations through which Armand-Louis lived. There is a certain allegorical significance in the fact that he turned ecclesiastical music into fairly big business, officiating at no fewer than eight churches; and there is certainly allegorical appropriateness in the manner of his death, killed by a runaway horse in the streets of Paris, as he scurried from Ste Chapelle to St Gervais, hoping to arrive in time to finish off the service launched by his son as surrogate! This was in 1788, on the eve of the Revolution. Perhaps it is fortunate that he didn't survive it, for one doubts whether he, less tough than Balbastre, would have been able to take the humiliations it would have inflicted on him.

Part III

Theory and Practice

De tous les dons naturels le Goût est celui qui se sent le mieux et qui s'explique le moins; il ne seroit pas ce qu'il est, si l'on pouvait le définir; car il juge des objects sur lesquels le jugement n'a plus de prise, et sert, si j'ose parler ainsi, de lunettes à la raison. . . .

Chaque homme a un Goût particulier. . . . Mais il y a aussi un Goût général sur lequel tous les gens bien organisés s'accordent; et c'est celui-ci seulement auquel on peut donner absolument le nom de Goût.

ROUSSEAU, *Dictionnaire*

Une Musique doit être naturelle, expressive, harmonieuse. . . . J'apelle à la lettre *naturel* ce qui est composé de tons qui s'offrent naturellement, ce qui n'est point composé de tons recherchez, extraordinaires. . . . J'apelle *Expressif* un Air dont les tons conviennent parfaitement aux paroles, et une Symphonie qui exprime parfaitement ce qu'elle veut exprimer. J'apelle *harmonieux, mélodieux, agréable,* ce qui contente, ce qui remplit, ce qui chatouille les oreilles.

BONNET, *Histoire de la Musique,* 1725

Ce bel Art tout divin par ses douces merveilles,
Ne se contente pas de charmer les oreilles,
N'y d'aller jusqu'au cœur par ses expressions
Emouvoir à son gré toutes les passions:
Il va, passant plus loin, par sa beauté suprême,
Au plus haut de l'esprit charmer la raison même.

PERRAULT, *Le Siècle de Louis le Grand*

Chapter Twelve

Couperin's Theoretical Work

The theoretical writings of Couperin comprise a small treatise called *Règles pour l'Accompagnement*; a larger work entitled *L'Art de toucher le Clavecin*; and miscellaneous passages in the prefaces to his published compositions.

The first of these, the *Règles pour l'Accompagnement*, is an early work, probably dating from the last years of the seventeenth century. Known from only two manuscript copies, it is a straightforward account of the methods of treating discord current in Couperin's day, and is interesting mainly because it indicates Couperin's familiarity with the most advanced Italian techniques. We may observe that Couperin here, early in his career, gives theoretical backing to the abstruse dissonances of eleventh and thirteenth, such as we have called attention to in our discussion of his music.

The important treatise on harpsichord playing was first published in 1716, before the second book of clavecin pieces, and was re-issued shortly afterwards. In the preface to the second book of clavecin works Couperin explains that he had written his didactic book because it was 'absolument indispensible pour exécuter mes pièces dans le Goût qui leur convient'. It is not a systematically planned work, but rather a series of random reflections which Couperin puts down as they occur to him. Here it will perhaps be best not to attempt to summarize the contents in the order in which they appear. Instead, we will arrange Couperin's opinions under a series of headings, supplementing what he says in *L'Art de toucher le Clavecin* with such comments from the Prefaces as seem relevant.

A. Hints on Teaching Methods

Couperin begins by explaining his intention in writing his *Méthode*. Playing the clavecin, he says, is not merely a matter of digital facility; it is a question of learning how to interpret, with sympathy and taste:

271

> La Méthode que je donne icy est unique. . . . . J'y traite sur toutes choses (par principes démonstrés) du beau Toucher du clavecin. . . . Je ne dois point craindre que les gens éclairés s'y meprennent; je dois seulement exhorter les autres à la docilité. Au moins les dois-je assurer tous, que ces principes sont absolument nécessaires pour parvenir à bien exécuter mes Pièces.

He then goes on to discuss the most suitable age to start learning the instrument:

> L'âge propre à commencer les Enfans, est de six à sept ans; non pas que cela doive exclure les personnes avancées; mais naturellement, pour mouler et former des mains à l'exercice du Clavecin, le plus tôt est le mieux.

The player should be seated so that his elbows are approximately level with the keyboard, and his feet resting gently on the floor. In the case of small children whose legs are too short, it is wise to give their feet some support, so that they may be securely balanced. The body should be seated about nine inches from the keyboard.

Little movement of the body is called for in playing the clavecin, and the beating of time with the head or feet should be avoided. 'A l'égard des grimaces du visage, on peut s'en corriger soy-même en mettant un miroir sur le pupitre de l'épinette.' In general one's posture should be attentive but easy. Couperin remarks that, in the early stages, children should not be allowed to play the harpsichord except in the presence of their teacher or some other responsible person, because left to themselves they can 'déranger en un instant ce que j'ai soigneusement posé en trois quarts d'heure'. He also offers the sensible advice that it is profitable for children to learn several pieces by ear and memory before studying notation. Thus they can early acquire some command of musical expression without being troubled by the mechanics of music. A very typical touch occurs in a passage wherein Couperin advocates humility on the part of the teacher:

> Il serait bon que les parents, ou ceux qui ont l'inspection générale sur les enfans, eussent moins d'impatience, et plus de confiance en celui qui enseigne (sûrs d'avoir fait un bon choix en sa personne) et que l'habile Maître, de son côté, eût moins de condescendance.

He further insists that a spinet or single manual harpsichord is sufficient for children, and that it should always be 'emplumé très faiblement', so that little muscular force is needed to press down the keys. Only thus can suppleness and independence of the fingers be developed; and these qualities are more important than strength. *Douceur de toucher* depends on keeping the fingers as close to the keys as possible: 'La souplesse des nerfs contribue beaucoup plus au bien jouer, que la force.' This point leads to our second heading:

B. *Remarks on the Nature and Technique of the Instrument*

Les sons du clavecin étant décidés, chacun en particulier, et par conséquent ne pouvant être enflés ni diminués, il a paru presque insoutenable jusqu'au present qu'on pût donner de l'âme à cet instrument; cependant, par les recherches dont j'ai appuyé le peu de naturel que le ciel m'a donné, je vais tâcher de faire comprendre par quelles raisons j'ai su acquerir le bonheur de toucher les personnes de goût.

Il faut surtout se rendre très délicat en claviers et avoir toujours un instrument bien emplumé. Je comprens cependant qu'il y a des gens à que cela peut être indifférent, parce qu'ils jouent également mal sur quelque instrument que soit.

The quotations indicate how Couperin regarded the harpsichord as an instrument capable of conveying great emotional sensibility; the technique of fingering and ornamentation which he describes later is the means whereby this sensitivity is realized. The French style is essentially a clavecin style, the Italian a violin and sonata style. 'Les personnes médiocrement habiles' prefer the Italian manner because it is more obvious, less dependent on subtleties of phrasing and ornamentation. But the clavecin 'a ses propriétés, comme le violon a les siennes. Si le clavecin n'enfle point ses sons, si les battements redoublés sur une même note ne lui conviennent pas estremement, il a d'autres avantages, qui sont la précision, la nétété, le brillant, et l'étendue'.

With this passage from *L'Art de toucher* we may correlate two passages from the preface to the first book:

L'usage m'a fait connoître que les mains vigoureuses et capables d'exécuter ce qu'il y a de plus rapide et de plus léger ne sont pas toujours celles qui réussissent le mieux dans les pièces tendres et de

sentiment; et j'avoueray de bonne foy que j'ayme mieux ce qui me
touche que ce qui me surprend;

and

> Le clavecin est parfait quant à son étendue et brillant par luy-
> même; mais, comme on ne peut enfler ny diminuer ses sons, je
> sçauray toujours gré à ceux qui, par un art infini soutenu par le
> goût, pourront arriver à rendre cet instrument susceptible d'ex-
> pression; c'est à quoy mes ancêtres se sont appliquées, indépen-
> damment de la belle composition de leurs pièces; j'ay tâché de
> perfectionner leurs découvertes; leurs ouvrages sont encore du
> goût de ceux qui l'ont exquis.

Couperin concludes this part of his treatise with some advice
which we have seen to be admirably demonstrated in his own
practice:

> Pour conclure sur le toucher du clavecin en général, mon senti-
> ment est de ne point s'éloigner du caractère qui y convient. Les
> passages, les batteries à portée de la main, les choses lutées et
> syncopés, doivent être préférées à celles qui sont pleines de tenues,
> ou de notes trop graves. Il faut conserver une liaison parfaite dans
> ce qu'on exécute; que tous les agrémens soient bien précis; que
> ceux qui sont composés de batemens soient faits bien également, et
> par une gradation imperceptible. Prendre bien garde à ne point
> altérer le movement dans les pièces réglées; et à ne point rester sur
> les notes dont la valeur soit pincé. Enfin former son jeu sur le bon
> goût d'aujourd'hui qui est sans comparaison plus pur que l'Ancien.

This last sentence is sociologically interesting with reference to
the values of Couperin's society and eighteenth-century notions
of Progress and Perfectability. The rest of the quotation provides a transition from Couperin's consideration of the nature
and technique of his instrument, to the first of the means
whereby the instrument is rendered 'susceptible d'expression'.

C. Comments on Tempo and Rhythm

Couperin's comments on rhythm and movement are of great
importance, being one of the sources for our knowledge of the
rhythmic conventions of the early eighteenth century. He
274 explains that the French style has been underestimated in other

countries – he is thinking, mainly, of Italy – because our pieces are not played as they are notated, whereas 'les Italiens écrivent leur musique dans les vrayes valeurs qu'ils l'ont pensée'. Since our pieces have a descriptive intent, they are played freely; we use words, such as *tendrement* or *vivement*, to indicate the mood of the piece, and it would be helpful if these words could be translated for the benefit of foreigners. Moreover, we differentiate *mesure* from *mouvement*, whereas the Italian sonatas 'ne sont guères susceptible de cette cadence'. 'Mesure definit la qualité et l'égalité des temps, et Cadence est proprement l'esprit et l'Ame qu'il y faut joindre.' 'La cadence et le Goût peuvent s'y conserver indépendamment du plus ou du moins de lenteur.' Here the term *cadence* seems to mean lilt and subtlety of movement; we may compare the definition in Rousseau's *Dictionnaire*:

> Cadence est une qualité de la bonne Musique, qui donne à ceux qui l'exécutent ou qui l'écoutent, un sentiment vif de la mesure, ensuite qu'ils la marquent et la sentent tomber à propos, sans qu'ils y pensent et comme par instinct. . . . 'Cette chaconne manque de Cadence.'

This use of the term should not be confused with its significance in the *air de cour*, where it means a trill preceded by an appoggiatura, usually occurring in a cadential phrase.

But although the French pieces are free in movement, there is nothing haphazard about them. Even the *tendre* pieces should not be played too slowly, owing to the short sustaining power of the instrument. *Mesure* (metre) must always be respected; *esprit* must be obtained through *goût* and *cadence*. The correct interpretation of these irregularities of movement is one of the most difficult of all the problems involved in early eighteenth-century music.

Dolmetsch's discussion of the conventional alterations of rhythm seems to me the least satisfactory part of his invaluable book, because he does not explain the complicated conditions which regulated the employment of these effects. These conditions are, however, described in detail in E. Borrel's article on 'Les notes inégales dans l'ancienne musique française', published in the *Revue de Musicologie* of November 1931. Borrel's case is based entirely on contemporary documents, so by supplementing Couperin's own very ambiguous pronouncements on the subject with the testimony of the other seventeenth- and eighteenth-century authorities quoted by Borrel, we may hope to obtain some coherent notion of the correct interpretation of Couperin's rhythms.

The tradition of *notes inégales* goes back, in French music, as far as the early years of the sixteenth century, but the first important and detailed statement on the subject is that of Loulié in 1696. According to him, in any time, but especially in triple rhythms, there are three possible ways of playing notes of half-beat value. Firstly the notes may be all played equally. This method is called *Détacher*, and is used in passages which proceed by *degrez interrompus* (i.e. by disjunct motion). In passages moving by conjunct motion, when a *détacher* effect is intended, it is customary to place dots over the notes; these dots do not indicate staccato, but merely the rather more weighty effect which even playing gives to the notes, in contrast with the habitually flexible treatment.

Secondly, the first note of each pair may be played slightly longer than the second. This effect is known as *Lourer*, and is used in passages which proceed by conjunct motion. Thirdly, in passages in which the first note of a pair has a dot affixed to it, the first note should be *very much* elongated; this effect is called *Pointer* or *Piquer*. The terms *pointer, piquer, marteler, passer* and *lourer* later became more or less synonymous; where dots are included in the written score a more exaggerated effect is of course intended. The whole of the passage from Loulié described above is so important that it is perhaps worth quoting in his own words:

> Dans quelque Mesure que ce soit, particulièrement dans la Mesure à trois tems, les demi-tems s'exécutent de deux manières différentes, quoy que marquez de la même manière.
> (1) On les fait quelquefois égaux.
>   Cette manière s'apelle détacher les Notes, on s'en sert dans les chants dont les sons se suivent par degrez interrompus, *et dans toute sorte de Musique étrangère où l'on ne pointe jamais, qu'il ne soit marqué*. [My italics.]
> (2) On fait quelquefois les premières demytems un peu plus longs.
>   Cette manière s'apelle *Lourer*. On s'en sert dans les chants dont les sons se suivent par degrez non interrompus.
> (3) Il y a une troisième manière, où l'on fait le premier demi-tems beaucoup plus long que le deuxième mais le premier demi-tems doit avoir un point.
>   On apelle cette 3 manière Piquer ou Pointer.

In 1702, St-Lambert explains that these inequalities of rhythm are introduced 'parce que cette inégalité leur donne plus de grâce'. All the authorities insist that the purpose of the rhythmic alterations is to add subtlety and nuance, and point out that the correct application of them depends ultimately on *le bon goût*. St-Lambert goes on, 'Quand on doit inégaliser les notes, c'est au goût à déterminer si elles doivent être peu ou beaucoup inégales; il y a des pièces où il sied bien de les faire fort inégales, et d'autres où elles veulent l'être moins; le goût juge de cela comme du mouvement'. Later, in 1775, Engramelle remarks that it is left to the performer to decide in what proportions the long and short notes shall be played: 'Il est bien des endroits où les inégalités des notes varient dans le même air; quelques petits essais feront recontrer le bon et le meilleur ou pour l'égalité ou pour l'inégalité; l'on verra qu'un peu plus ou un peu moins d'inégalité dans les notes change considérablement le genre d'expression d'un air'. Choquel says that the inequality of rhythm 'lie le chant et le rend plus coulant'. Emy de l'Ilette suggests that 'inégalités' serve to 'donner de l'élégance à l'exécution de la musique', adding that they should be used only in the melodic parts ('parties chantantes'), not in 'l'accompagnement'.

The fundamental rule in the interpretation of unequal notes is stated by Monteclair: 'En quelque mesure que ce soit, les notes dont il faut quatre pour remplir un temps sont toujours inégales, la première un peu plus longue que la seconde'. Duval makes the same point in saying, 'On fait inégales toutes les notes de moindre valeur que celles qui sont indiquées par le chiffre inférieur'; except that in 2 : 4 only semiquavers and demi-semiquavers are played unequally; in 3 : 2 only crotchets, quavers and subdivisions of quavers; in 3 : 4, 6 : 4, 9 : 4 and 12 : 4 only quavers and subdivisions of quavers; in 3 : 8, 6 : 8, 9 : 8 and 12 : 8 only semiquavers and demi-semiquavers. Some theorists maintain that 'les notes inférieures aux notes inégales sont aussi inégales'; others maintain that when notes of smaller value than the unequal notes, as indicated by the time signature, occur in profusion, they are played unequal, while what would have been the unequal notes become equal. For instance, Corrette says, 'A 3 on fait les croches inégales, mais on les joue quelquefois égales, quand il y a des doubles croches, ce qu'on peut voir dans la passacaille d'*Armide* de M. de Lully et dans la chaconne des *Indes Galantes* de M. Rameau.'

277

All these devices refer mainly to notes grouped in fours or sixes. When quavers, semiquavers, and sometimes crotchets are phrased in twos, with a slur over them and a dot above the second note, a different kind of inequality is implied. In this case, the second note is played slightly longer than the first; a modern interpretation of this notation would probably be directly contrary to eighteenth-century practice. This effect, which Couperin terms *couler*, occurs most frequently in passages involving 'drooping' pairs of quavers. A very slight rest is made after the second quaver.

We may summarize Borrel's conclusions as follows:

(1) There are two kinds of *notes inégales* in use in French music of the period. The most common concerns groups of four or six notes, in which the first note of each pair is elongated; the contrary effect is occasionally found in quavers slurred in pairs.

(2) The following notes are treated in the unequal manner:

In 3 : 1 time	minims.
In 3 : 2 time	'white' crotchets and quavers.
In 2, 3, 3 : 4, 6 : 4, 9 : 4, 12 : 4 and C time	quavers.

If the sign C represents two slow beats the quavers are unequal; if it represents four quick beats the quavers are equal and semiquavers unequal.

In 2 : 4, 3 : 8, 4 : 8, 6 : 8, 9 : 8, 12 : 8 and C time	semiquavers.

Some authorities say that semiquavers, but not quavers, are played unequally in allemandes. Couperin seems to favour this, since he often tells the performer to use the *pointé* effect in an allemande, implying that without this direction it would normally be played equally.

In 3 : 16, 4 : 16, 6 : 16, 9 : 16 and 12 : 16 time	demi-semiquavers.

(3) Notes that would normally be played unequally, in accordance with the rules outlined above, are played equally in the following circumstances:

(*a*) When they are interspersed with notes of shorter value. (As we have seen, however, this exception is not upheld by all theorists, some of whom maintain that in such cases, *all* the smaller valued notes are unequal.)

(*b*) When the lines move by disjunct motion; (and especially, therefore, in arpeggio figuration).

(*c*) When the words *Notes égales*, *Détachez*, or *Martelées* are written on the score, or when the tempo is marked *Mouvement décidé* or *marqué*.

(*d*) When there are dots or short lines above the notes which would otherwise be unequal.

(*e*) When the notes which would otherwise be unequal are interrupted by numerous rests.

(*f*) When they involve syncopations.

(*g*) When they involve repetitions of the same note.

(*h*) When they occur in accompanying parts.

(*i*) When they occur in the music of other countries. For instance, quavers are played equally in the 3 : 4 sarabande of the Italians, whereas they are unequal in the French sarabande.

(*j*) In very quick tempi, when the even method of playing semiquavers, with a slight stress on the first of each group of four, is the only practicable method.

(*k*) When there is a slur over a group of four, six, or eight notes.

The last two points are not mentioned by the French writers, but occur in Quantz. It seems clear that the *lourer* effect cannot have been employed in very rapid passages.

(4) In passages in which dotted notes occur, the dot is always elongated, the short note played with a snap. In passages in which a dotted note is followed by a group of very rapid notes, the value of the dot is variable. The quick notes should take exactly as long as is indicated by the number of 'tails' affixed to them, the dot being stretched out, or contracted, in order to regularize the measure. In the following rhythm ♪♫♫♪ , the demi-semiquavers are played very quickly and brightly, never slurred.

(5) Triplet figures are always played equally.

279

(6) In recitative in duple or triple time, quavers which would normally be unequal are often sung equally; while in four-time recitative quavers which would normally be equal are often unequal. No rules can be established with reference to recitative, for here the rhythmic inequalities are dependent on 'l'expression de la Parole et le goût du Chant'.

(7) The proportionate lengths of the long and short notes in unequal groups depend on the character of the music. The correct interpretation can be achieved only through *le bon goût*, which D'Alembert's *Encyclopédie* of 1757 defines as 'Le talent de démêler dans les ouvrages de l'art ce qui doit plaire aux âmes sensibles, et ce qui doit les blesser'.

Since the original edition of this book was published, much work has been done on rhythmic inequality, some of which modifies, though it does not supersede, the findings of Borrel, on which my discussion was largely based. Jacques Chailley's writings, published in 1960, wisely discourage any attempt to systematize *degrees* of inequality. The ratio of inequality might be 1 : 2, 2 : 3, 3 : 4, 3 : 5, 5 : 7, and so on, according to the character of the piece; hardly ever will it be identifiable with the regular proportion of 3 : 1: ♪♩ . Chailley suggests that there may be a connection between musical *notes inégales* and the declamation of the French language, especially since most contemporary theorists encouraged instrumentalists to emulate singers. Rhythmic irregularities, no less than ornaments, sought the human expressivity of spoken and sung language; interestingly enough, Rameau notated irregularities in instrumental parts whereas in vocal parts, singing the same phrases, he often considered notation unnecessary. When Couperin spoke of *le bon goût* in reference to these matters he was implying that inequality was not a question of knowing how many parts the beat should be divided into, but of representing 'the proper expressive declamation – which is only approximately three or four, both for the voice and for the instrument.' (Chailley.) There is a useful if superficially improbable analogy between rhythmic inequalities in French eighteenth-century music and those which may still be heard in the improvised arts of rural Irish (and other) fiddling and in urban jazz, in which irregularly loping lilts and boogie rhythms and vagaries of melodic accentuation (and for that matter of pitch) are not only unnotated, but

unnotatable. Such parallels seem improbable because French

eighteenth-century civilization was a 'high' culture, supremely sophisticated, whereas the Irish peasantry and the Negroes of New Orleans and Chicago were as 'low' as they were instinctual. None the less the improbability is superficial because the metrical irregularities in Irish folk fiddling and in jazz derive, as do those in French classical music, from vocal declamation – as one may recognize if one listens to the great Tommy Potts fiddling his version of an ancient Irish air, or if one listens to Louis Armstrong heroically trumpeting permutations of phrases he has sung in his gravelly voice. One would hardly be tempted to describe in mathematical terms the variations of pulse and pitch that Tommy and Louis introduce, and the same principle applies to the apparently less spontaneous Couperin. If I now comment on three of his works from the point of view of metrical irregularity, it is not with the intention of offering definitive instructions, but rather of giving pragmatic extension to the information presented above.

Let us consider first the E minor *Concert Royal*, fourth of the group published in 1722. The prelude is in **C** time, marked *Gravement*. At this tempo quavers are habitually equal and semiquavers unequal: but here not very unequal, since in so dignified a piece they should serve merely to render the line smoother and more gracious; a proportion of longs and shorts around 7 to 5 would probably be appropriate. Similarly the dotted quavers followed by semiquavers should not be mathematically precise; the duration of the dots will vary in accord with the speaking expressivity of the line.

The allemande is also in **C** time, but is quicker because marked *légèrement*. Again quavers are equal and semiquavers unequal, producing an effect rather sprightly but gentle; a proportion of around 3 to 2, or possibly 2 to 1, seems apposite. The *courante française*, being in 3 : 2 time, is more complicated. According to Hotteterre, writing in 1719, crotchets in 3 : 2 are unequal when they are the smallest note value, but quavers only are unequal when they are prevalent. In this piece there are many quavers, and the tempo, marked *galament*, is flowing but not very fast. So the stepwise-moving quavers – probably in subsidiary parts as well as in the main melody – should be unequal, but flexibly so. The graciousness of these metrically complex French courantes depends on their malleability; mathematical precision would be fatal to the genre. The *courante à l'italiéne*, on the other hand, is 281 simply notated in three time, common in French airs and dances and usually slightly faster than 3 : 4. Semiquavers are not often found in it; quavers are usually unequal. In this case Couperin makes assurance doubly sure by adding the words '*Pointé – coulé*, thereby encouraging both long–short and short–long inequalities. The stepwise-moving scales should trip fleetly as well as *gayement* (as indicated), with considerable distinction between the sharpest and the gentlest *pointé* effect. The *coulés*, mostly in appoggiaturas, should as usual be tranquil, perhaps suggesting a transition to the middle section which introduces octave leaps and should probably be played equally, thereby affording contrast and relief. The occasional bars incorporating trills and turns are equal because Couperin slurs them.

The *sarabande*, in the major, is marked *tendrement*, and is also in three time. Normally, the quavers would be unequal; but there are few of them. The recurrent figuration is of dotted quaver followed by semiquaver, in which the proportions should never be mathematical but always flexibly expressive, as though words were being sung in this tenderest of love songs. The elaborate ornaments also create their own rhythmic inequalities. The quavers phrased in twos in the *contre-partie* should probably be short–long rather than long–short, but very discreetly so.

The rigaudon is in 2 : 4, which was usually quicker than 2 and, according to Hotteterre, was suitable for airs that are light and (on wind instruments) tongued. Quavers are equal and semiquavers unequal, unless the tempo is very fast. The character of this piece, *legèrement et marqué*, suggests that the semiquavers should be rather grotesquely unequal ('dans le goût burlesque'), except when Couperin slurs them. The forlane is in 6 : 8, a fastish compound time in which quavers are normally equal, semiquavers unequal. But here there are no flowing semiquaver passages, so performance should be virtually as notated, unless the bucolic character be stressed by a slight elongation of the dots. The fourth couplet in the minor is marked by Couperin '*Notes égales et coulées*': a precaution hardly necessary since the arpeggiated figures would be equal in any case, and the stepwise figures are all slurred. Presumably Couperin is encouraging us to play the couplet *very* smoothly and suavely, in contrast to the perky rondeau tune.

282   The *Concerts Royaux* are concerted music, in which the one or

two players of melody instruments, the harpsichordist and the gambist engage in '*conversations galantes et amusantes*', each preserving independence while showing deference to the others. Couperin's solo harpsichord music lends itself still more readily to expressive flexibilities, since only one player is involved; he is responsible mainly to himself, though he will of course think of himself as 'conversing' with whomever is around to listen. I will take as example one of the most intimate and personal of the *ordres*: the thirteenth, in B minor, from Book III – music that is probably directly associated with the sadly desperate life of the Regent (see Addendum III). The first piece, *Les Lis Naissans*, is in two time, but the speed is mollified by the direction *Modérément et uniment*. In this tempo quavers would normally be unequal; but here are mostly equal since they flow in broken chords rather than in scales. Although basically equal, the quavers shouldn't be played rigidly; they should sway and bend like the lilies they depict; the dots on the quavers in bars 3 and 7 should be lingeringly elongated. The quaver appoggiaturas in bar 15 should be short–long, caressingly, the inequality slight. In bar 23 the scalewise-moving quavers should be long–short, again very gently so. In the *petite reprise* rubato, or inequality, may be a little more exaggerated.

Les Rozeaux is a pastoral in 6 : 8, marked *tendrement, sans lenteur*. At this tempo quavers would normally be equal, semiquavers unequal; but here most of the semiquavers in the left hand will be *more or less* equal, partly because they are accompanying figuration, partly because they are arpeggiated chords rather than scales. The dotted quavers in the tune might be slightly elongated, so that the melodic semiquaver doesn't coincide with the accompanying semiquaver. Thematic semiquavers slurred in pairs (bars 13 and 17) should be equal or with the first note almost imperceptibly shorter than the second, effecting a caress. The thematic semiquavers in bar 25 should follow the normal ruling in being long–short in a suave proportion of around 2 to 1: contrasting with the slurred semiquavers in bar 26 which will be short–long or nearly equal. The second half of bar 38, when both hands move in parallel scale semiquavers, could be gently long–short, or could be more or less equal to produce a quasi-allargando effect before the final statement of the rondeau tune.

L'Engageante is also in 6 : 8, this time *Agréablement, sans lenteur*. The normal ruling about semiquavers applies in this portrait of a 283 sprightly young woman; they should be fairly consistently long–short, though the inequality should vary around a basic proportion of 2 to 1. The slurred semiquavers in bars 9, 23, 24, 28 and 32 should be equal, veering towards short–long. The left hand semiquavers in the falling figure first heard in bar 3 could mingle equality with inequality.

The chaconne, *Les Folies Françoises*, provides a neat compendium of Couperin's metrical devices, as it does of his aesthetic characteristics. The theme, *La Virginité*, is in the French three time, marked *gracieusement*. The norm of inequality is the quaver; those slurred in pairs in bars 3 and 11 should be equal, veering to short–long; the descending scales in bars 6 and 14 should be gently long–short. The second couplet, *La Pudeur*, is marked *tendrement* and should probably be slightly slower than the first statement. The crotchets, though equal, are often slurred in pairs: so their phrasing should be exaggerated and, in effect, wayward even to the point of quasi-inegality. The descending quaver scales, which in three time would normally be long–short, are slurred in sixes and should flow equably. Against this the rising scale quavers in the left hand of bar 13 should probably be slightly long–short, while the dotted quavers in bar 15 should approach double dottedness. The next couplet, *L'Ardeur*, is still in three time, now marked *Animé*. Given the subject of the variation, this is a simple case of double dotting, which gives the music spring and elasticity, appropriate to a 'Domino incarnat'. *L'Espérance*, in 9 : 8 marked *Gayement*, is also unambiguous. This time, uncommon in French music, always calls for equal quavers if the speed is brisk, though semiquavers may be unequal at slower tempi. Here quavers clatter consistently throughout, summoning Hope with, perhaps, a hint of desperation. The fifth couplet, *La Fidélité*, is notated in 'white' quavers in 3 : 2, and is marked *Affectueusement*. The 'white' notation★ implies considerable freedom; the dots

---

★ Flagged white notes date back as early as the fourteen-twenties, and have their origins in medieval proportional mensuration. No such significance survives into the baroque period; when Couperin and other French composers employ white quavers, usually in 3 : 2 time, it seems to be mainly a matter of notational convenience. Crotchets cannot be flagged and so cannot be easily grouped in flowing figuration. The white quavers here and elsewhere in Couperin are more readily intelligible in musical terms than crotchets would be. The texts of secular cantatas suggest that French composers may have associated white-note figuration with languorous introspection.

should be elongated, the white quavers short, but smooth and suave, not (as in *L'Ardeur*) sharp and precise. In bar 6 only, Couperin slurs the melody's falling scale. I am not sure what this means; perhaps the inequality should be somewhat ironed out, so that the rhythm would be played more or less in proportions as notated. *La Persévérance* returns to three time, at about the original speed, *tendrement, sans lenteur* – for at this point the music seems to 'try again', after that slightly frantic assertion of Hope and that somewhat sickly expression of Fidelity. The left hand quavers in bars 1, 4, 6 and 12 should be slightly long–short, while the right hand's quaver appoggiaturas in bar 14 should be sighfully short–long.

The seventh couplet, *La Langueur*, is weirdly notated in 1 : 2, with four 'white' quavers to the bar. Since Couperin marks it *Egalement*, however, it is not metrically problematical. It should move languorously, the white quavers dragging heavily but more or less equally, sometimes across the beat, which should be felt as a slow 2. *La Coquéterie* makes an overt, notated use of inequalities in that the speed fluctuates between *Gayment, Modéré* and *Légèrement,* and the time signatures between 6 : 8, 3 : 8 and 2 : 4. This coquettish waywardness is not, however, arbitrary. We should probably think of the *gay* 6 : 8 as a brisk tempo. Though conventionally faster 3 : 8 need not necessarily be so, and here isn't, since Couperin adds the direction *Modéré*. Perhaps he changes the time signature in order to differentiate between the varieties of coquettishness; the 3 : 8 introduces semiquaver triplets along with quavers. The shift to 2 : 4, *légérement,* certainly implies an increase on the original (6 : 8) tempo; and here unnotated inequalities are also called for, the semiquaver scales being long–short, probably quite perkily so. The ninth couplet, depicting *Les Vieux Galans et les Trésorieres suranées*, is an ironic reversal to old-fashioned pomp and circumstance. The dotted quavers are here extremely elongated, the semiquavers short and snappy, as in a Lullian theatrical overture. The quavers with dots over them, on the other hand, are played evenly, heavily and detached, emulating the ancient galants' arthritic stomping. The tenth couplet about the benevolent cuckoos is metrically ambiguous. Couperin slurs the cuckoo-calls, which isn't strictly necessary, since being arpeggiated they would be played equally anyway. He gives no tempo direction apart from the time signature of 3 : 8, which is normally faster than 3. But if one plays 285 the couplet fast the figure doesn't sound very cuckoo-like. A moderate speed makes the cuckoos sound coolly indifferent; a slow speed – which is occasionally admissible in 3 : 8 – renders them sad. Either way makes a point.

The eleventh couplet, *La Jalousie Taciturne*, is again in 3 : 2 with 'white' quavers that really have the duration of crotchets. As with the other white-note pieces, movement is here very flexible. The *'mesuré'* in the directive applies, I think, to the dragging, 'taciturn' minims, while the descending scales in white quavers oscillate between long–short, equal, and short–long (when phrased in pairs). The inequalities should all be slight, the movement, in its low tessitura, gloomily undulating. The final couplet, *La Frénésie, ou le Désespoir*, offers no metrical problems. Back in three time, it is marked *Tres vite*, so the semiquaver scales are all equal, aggressively so. The left hand quavers with dots over them are heavily marked; the dots in the penultimate bar are doubled. The wonderful little epilogue, *L'âme-en-Peine*, is at the opposite pole to the last couplet's regularity. Anguish erodes the triple beat; the commas suggest a cessation of breath; the appoggiaturas lean on the beat, the first quaver slightly shorter than the second, while the dots in the dotted quaver figure are lingering. After the double bar the appoggiaturas on the second beat should resolve before the third beat in order to preserve the sighful augmented fifth; but the resolution should be painfully delayed, and never susceptible to mathematical proportion. There is no finer example of the relation between rhythmic inequality and human expressivity than is offered by this piece, in which a plucked string instrument speaks and sighs as well as sings.

For my third example I choose a piece of vocal music, the second *Leçon de Ténèbres*. Comparatively little comment is called for since, as explained in the section on Couperin's vocal resources, the 'rules' governing *inégalité* did not strictly apply to vocal music, in which rhythmic inflexion derived directly from the words. Sing the words expressively and sensitively and the rhythms will be right; and will indeed have much to tell us about rhythmic flexibility in purely instrumental music. In Couperin's more Italianate motets *inégalités* will be discreet, more or less analogous to those in his Italianate instrumental works, notably the trio sonatas. The *Leçons de Ténèbres*, scored merely for solo voices and continuo, allow for greater flexibility, in ways that

286

parallel the secular convention of the *air de cour*. Even so, the words remain the arbiter, except in the melismatic vocalises on a single syllable.

The second *Leçon* opens with a vocalise on the letter *Vau*, noted in $\math\mathbb{C}$ time, which was conventionally quicker than **C** but slower than 2. Quavers were unequal, and can be so here so long as they are sung very smoothly, inducing the appropriate trance-like state. Inequality will be slight, if used; both Kirkby and Deller float the quavers more or less equally, with exquisite effect. The first recitative is also notated in $\mathbb{C}$, but should certainly move faster, driven by the urgency of the words. Here irregularities will derive directly from verbal stress, though a gentle inequality in the quavers of the continuo part helps to carry the music forwards. The second vocalise is notated in 3 : 2, in 'white' quavers. The movement is mostly by step, and a discreetly lilting inequality is appropriate; again, equal values may enhance the vatic quality. The *Recordata est* arioso, being riddled with sobbing appoggiaturas and chromatic passing notes, is dependent on verbal inflexion even more overtly than the first recitative. Notation is again in 'white' 3 : 2. The notated dots should probably be somewhat elongated, the white quavers slurred in twos either equal or slightly short–long. Nine bars before the end of the arioso Couperin slurs the white quavers in groups of six. This suggests that he intends them to be smoothly equal here, distinguished in style of performance both from unslurred quavers and from quavers slurred in pairs. Throughout, of course, the white quavers are of crotchet duration

The *Heth* vocalise is again notated in white 3 : 2, and flows almost entirely by step. Any inequality should be almost imperceptible; the mood is rapt. A beautiful effect may be made by changing from a very slight inegality to equal notes when the stepwise movement changes momentarily to undulating thirds.

The next recitative, *Peccatum peccavit*, is again notated in $\mathbb{C}$ time, and should again be sung, Italian-style, more or less as written, modified by how one would speak or declaim the words; the ornamentation – especially the '*chutes*' of drooping sevenths and fifths – is overtly rhetorical. The succeeding vocalise, on *Teth*, is notated in two time: which should perhaps be slightly faster than the $\mathbb{C}$ of Vocalise I. The rising scales suggest *inégalité*, about in the proportion of 7 to 5. The remaining recitative and aria are the most operatically dramatic 287 music in the work, passionately dissonant and almost 'physical' in ornamentation. Again inequalities will be a matter of expressive verbal inflexion rather than of metrical convention. In the *Jerusalem convertere* aria the scale passages in the continuo part give a dancing momentum to the passion if they've a slight boogie lilt, though it would be a mistake to 'apply' this consistently.★

C. Comments on Ornamentation

As with rhythm, so with ornamentation; this too, as has already been pointed out with reference to Couperin's music and that of his predecessors, is an intrinsic part of the subtlety of both line and harmony. The most important ornament is undoubtedly the *port de voix*, or appoggiatura. Couperin's explanations of the *port de voix* (for he adopts the terminology of the lutenists and the *air de cour* composers) are very inaccurate:

Here the pure form of the *port de voix* is the second cited. What Couperin calls the *port de voix simple* is really the *port de voix pincé* (i.e. with a mordent); and in the *port de voix double* it is not the appoggiatura, but the mordent, which is doubled. Couperin makes the important point that in all *ports de voix* the ornamental notes must be struck *with* the harmony note; and that the length of the ornamental notes must be proportionate to the value of the note to which they are attached. As Dolmetsch remarks, however, he does not tell us what this proportion is. According to C. P. E. Bach, the *port de voix* takes half the value of the harmony note in duple times, two-thirds in triple times. It is always slurred to, and played slightly louder than, the note of resolution. The ornamental notes must never anticipate the beat, because then the effect of discord is ruined; on the other hand, harmonic considerations frequently lead to modifications in the normal treatment of the appoggiatura. These are not dealt with by Couperin, but are covered by Dolmetsch, on the evidence of other contemporary authorities. Again, in difficult cases the player must make his own decisions, in accordance with *le bon goût*; he will usually find some special case, cited in Dannreuther or Dolmetsch, which is relevant to any problem Couperin's work may offer. (See Appendix E, Section II.)

Couperin's treatment of the mordent or *pincé* is more straight-forward. These tables from the 1713 book of clavecin pieces, and from the *méthode* of 1716, offer no difficulty:

Mordents on long notes should be more extended (*doublé*) than those on short notes. The *pincé continu* is a shake on the note *below* the main note. *Pincés* always end with the note which they decorate.

Couperin gives the following table of *tremblements*, or *cadences* (not to be confused with the rhythmic device referred to above), in the 1713 edition:

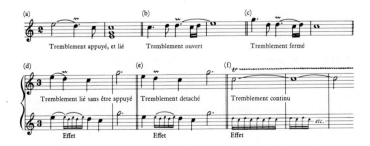

Here again there is some confusion over terminology. The *tremblement ouvert* and the *tremblement fermé* seem to differ only in that the former resolves upwards and the latter downwards; and the shake in (*d*) appears to be as much prepared (*appuyé*) as the shake in example (*a*). In his *Méthode*, Couperin explains that there are three stages in the shake: the preparation on the note above the given note; the shake itself; and the resolution on to the essential note. Shakes *always* begin on the tone or semitone above the essential note, and, where they are of any considerable length, should begin slowly and grow gradually quicker. In rapid passages, the shake – or half-shake, as it is sometimes called in such circumstances – has no time to establish its three stages; it differs from the *pincé double* in beginning on the note above the essential note, instead of on the note below it.

Most of the long shakes end with a turn; this Couperin indicates by the follow sign: **S** . He does not devote much attention to the turn itself, giving only these two examples, which seem to be identical except for pitch:

Sometimes he places the turn sign after the essential note; in that case, it is played after the principal note has been sounded. Usually it takes half the principal note's value in duple time, a third in triple time.

Couperin gives two examples of the slide:

Here again his notation suggests that the ornament anticipates the beat; but his verbal description is unambiguous. What Couperin calls the *Accent* is distinct from the accent of Bach, which is an appoggiatura. Couperin's ornament is derived from lute technique, being orginally the stopping of an auxiliary note on the lute without actually plucking it. The effect is similar to the use of sympathetic vibrations in modern piano music, and would be more adequately described by Rousseau's term *l'aspiration*, were it not that Couperin uses the term *aspiration* for a completely different ornament. The effect, whatever one calls it, cannot really be translated into terms of the harpsichord; the player approximates to it by playing the auxiliary note, usually a tone above and in dotted rhythm, as faintly and vaguely as possible:

This is identical with one variety of Bach's *Nachschlag*.★

Two examples of *batteries*, or upward and downward arpeggios, are given in Couperin's 1713 collection:

Here too the first note of the arpeggio should come on the beat. These arpeggios are much employed in pieces influenced by lute technique. The dash over a note does not indicate a real staccato, but a more emphatic, *détaché* treatment.

Some very beautiful effects of rubato may be obtained through the use of what Couperin calls the *aspiration* and the

---

★ In many respects Bach's ornamentation seems to derive from that of Couperin and d'Anglebert. His *Trillo* is the same as Couperin's *tremblement détaché*; his *Mordant* is Couperin's *pincé simple*; his *Cadence* Couperin's *double*; his *Accent steigend* Couperin's *port de voix*; and his *Accent und Mordant* Couperin's *port de voix simple*. There is no evidence that Bach was acquainted with Couperin's *L'Art de toucher le Clavecin*. But of course he knew Couperin's clavecin music, and copied out *Les Bergeries* in Anna Magdalena's *Notenbuch*. He acquired a fairly extensive knowledge of French music at Celle, about 1700; it was probably at this time that he copied out Nicolas de Grigney's fine *Livre d'Orgue*, and two harpsichord suites of Dieupart, with their table of ornaments as appendix. He may also have known the keyboard music of Gaspard le Roux, since Pirro tells us that pieces by this composer are found in a notebook of Bach's pupil Krebs.

suspension. These terms should not be confused with the *aspiration* of Rousseau and other authorities previously referred to, nor, of course, with the normal harmonic suspension. Couperin notates them thus:

and describes them in these words:

> Quant à l'effet sensible de l'aspiration, il faut détacher la note sur laquelle elle est posée, moins vivement dans les choses tendres et lentes, que dans celles qui sont légères, et rapides.
>
> A l'égard de la suspension, elle n'est guères usitée que dans les morceaux tendres et lents. Le silence qui précède la note sur laquelle elle est marquée doit être réglé par le goût de la personne qui l'exécute.

Employed with taste and feeling, by 'personnes susceptibles de sentiment', these ornaments can greatly enhance the music's expressiveness. But it is important that the slight catch in the breath of the ornaments should not disrupt the flow of the lines. Once more, their purpose is to impart nuance and sensitivity, without harming the architectural proportions. Couperin adds that effects of *aspiration* and *suspension* may be effectively combined with the *tremblement*, though only, one imagines, in rather slow pieces. He also claims to be the first to use these ornaments. He may have been the first to develop them extensively in keyboard music, but similar devices must have been in common use among the lutenists.

As *suspensions* and *aspirations* may be combined with *tremblements*, so most of Couperin's ornaments are compound ones. He seems to have considered it accepted procedure that the *port de voix* should be rounded off by a mordent; and that the *tremblement* should be prepared by an appoggiatura. He makes no reference to the acciaccatura, which is less congenial to his idiom than to the more percussive style of Scarlatti. Couperin's most important pronouncement on the general significance of the ornamentation in his music occurs in the preface to his third book of clavecin pieces, when he protests against performers who have not taken the ornaments seriously enough:

> Je suis toujours surpris, après les soins qui je me suis donnés pour marquer les agréments qui conviennent à mes pieces, d'entendre les personnes qui les ont apprises sans s'y assujettir. C'est une négligence qui n'est pas pardonnable, d'autant qu'il n'est point arbitraire d'y mettre tels agréments qu'on veut. Je déclare que mes pièces doivent être exécutées comme je les ai marquées et qu'elles ne feront jamais impression sur les personnes qui ont le goût vrai, tant qu'on n'observera pas à la lettre tout ce que j'ai marqué, sans augmentation ni diminution.

Here again we have the insistence on the connection between ornamentation and sensibility; and the suggestion that the ultimate judge must always be, in the self-assured phrase of the period, 'le goût vrai'.

D. Comments on Fingering and Phrasing

In the *Méthode* Couperin gives copious examples of his methods of fingering which, he claims, constitute a new system. They do not, perhaps, seem very new to us, being closer to the methods of the sixteenth and seventeenth centuries than to modern technique. But though they concentrate on the second, third, and fourth fingers and share the old music's distrust of the thumb, they anticipate the modern method of playing parallel thirds smoothly and they establish the principle of finger-substitution to secure a legato. Moreover, we must remember, as Dolmetsch has demonstrated, that the fingering and phrasing of the old music were always interdependent. It may be more difficult to play Couperin with his own than with a modern fingering; but the performer who uses Couperin's fingering can be sure that he will be phrasing the music correctly. Much the same is true of the keyboard work of Bach, whose system of fingering was directly based on Couperin's. For both composers, fingering was not a means of scampering about the keyboard with maximum facility; it was a means of revealing, as fully as possible, the musical sense of a composition. These two, among many possible, examples will make this clear without further comment:

(Les Silvains)

(L'Amazone)

The general nature of Couperin's phrasing is indicated in his own copious and accurate marking. Not only slurs, across the beat and with the beat:

but dashes, a more exaggerated effect, both across the beat and with the beat:

and commas:

and a combination of all three:

are used to make the groupings unmistakable. It is patent from all the examples Couperin gives that the continuous legato of nineteenth-century music, or even of the Viennese classics, is alien to Couperin's music as it is to Bach's. The life of the phrasing depends on the clear articulation of short clauses phrased on principles analogous to string bowing, as much across the beat as with it; and some of the most subtle effects arise from the combination of contrasting phrasings in different parts. (See Appendix E.)

What one might not gather from the phrase marks, but is clear from the fingering, is that even unimportant passages of figuration should be phrased according to the same general principles. The fingering of *Le Moucheron* provides an admirable instance:

(Le Moucheron)

while the fingering of the thirds in the *Passacaille* suggests that they should be phrased in pairs, across the beat:

(Passacaille)

It is for the light which it throws on such minute points of phrasing that Couperin's fingering should be studied by all conscientious performers of his keyboard music today.

The comma, which Couperin introduces into his later work, can perhaps best be regarded not as an authentic phrase mark, but as a rhythmic device analogous to the *aspiration* and *suspension*; Couperin's comment on it is as follows:

On trouvera un signe nouveau dont voicy la figure [ˌ]. C'est pour marquer la terminaison des chants ou de nos Pièces harmoniques, et pour faire comprendre qu'il faut un peu séparer la fin d'un chant avant de passer à celui qui le suit, cela est presque imperceptible en général, quoy qu'on n'observant pas ce petit silence, les personnes de goût sentent qu'il manque quelque chose à l'exécution, en un mot, c'est la différence de ceux qui lisent de suite, avec ceux qui s'arrêtent aux points et aux virgules; ces silences se doivent faire sentir sans altérer la mesure.

E. Comments on Continuo Playing

Couperin advocates that one should not take up continuo playing until one has become reasonably proficient as a solo performer. The reasons he gives are both intellectual and physical. On the one side, the expressive realization and performance of the bass line calls for a high degree of skill and taste; on the other side, the right hand's playing of regular sequences of chords, as opposed to the melodic style of solo harpsichord music, might have a stiffening effect on inexperienced fingers, 'la main droite n'étant occupée qu'à faire des accords'. This remark would seem to indicate that Couperin, in his realization of the continuo parts, followed a widespread convention, playing the bass line as written, in a very cantabile style, with the left hand, and filling in the chords with the right. Such a treatment would be consistent with the melodic–harmonic compromise we have frequently noted in his music, and with his tendency to base his composition on a dialogue between soprano and bass.

There are a considerable number of contemporary treatises which provide evidence as to the interpretation of the figured bass in French baroque music. The two most important are perhaps the *Traité de l'accompagnement* of St-Lambert published in 1707 and that of Boyvin published in 1705. The following comments are based largely on these two works.

Originally, when the harmony was comparatively simple, the basses were unfigured and the chords employed did not extend beyond diatonic triads on the bass note and, in certain circumstances, first inversions. Figures became necessary as harmony grew more complicated. In Couperin's day all the diatonic concords, chords of the seventh and ninth, and various dissonant suspensions were indicated by the figures. The sharp sign denoted a major or augmented interval, the flat denoted a minor or diminished interval, and the natural sign was used for a major interval that could otherwise be minor, or to indicate the return of an interval to its initial form. Used without a figure the sharp sign meant the major third or triad, the flat sign the minor.

Normally one chord is played on the continuo for each note of the bass, but where the bass line moves by conjunct degrees, or when the bass is rapid, one chord on the clavecin may serve for two or more notes on the bass line as played by the viol. These exceptions to the rule are described in detail by St-Lambert, thus:

(1) Quand les notes de Basse sont par degrez successifs on n'est pas obligé de les accompagner toutes; on peut n'accompagner que de deux notes l'une alternativement.

(2) Quand les notes marchent par degrez interrompus, il faut aussi les accompagner toutes, *excepté lorsqu'un même accord peut servir à plusieurs notes.* (My italics.)

(3) Quand la mesure est à trois temps et que l'air se joue vite, on peut se contenter d'accompagner seulement la première note de chaque mesure; pourvu que les notes marchent par degrez successifs.

(4) Quand la mesure est si pressée que l'Accompagnateur n'a pas la commodité de jouer toutes les notes, il peut se contenter de jouer et d'accompagner seulement la première note de chaque mesure, laissant au basses de Viole ou de Violon à jouer toutes les notes.

On the other hand, 'quand les basses sont peu chargées de notes ... il peut y ajouter d'autres notes pour figurer d'avantage, pourvu qu'il connoisse que cela ne fera point de tort à l'Air. ... Car l'Accompagnement est fait pour seconder la voix et non pas pour l'étouffer et la défigurer par un mauvais carillon. ... Quiconque joue en Concert doit jouer pour l'honneur et la perfection du Concert et non pas pour son honneur particulier.' Long-held pedal notes especially provide opportunities for the player to decorate the bass with chords not indicated in the figures, though of course he must take care not to ruin the harmony.

The usual convention in France was for the left hand to play the bass line alone while the right hand filled out the chords in three or sometimes four parts:

La méthode la plus ordinaire et la plus commode est de faire tous les accompagnements de la main droite. Elle fait communément trois parties, quelquefois aussi jusqu'à quatre, parce qu'on double quelque consonance, ou parfois aussi la seconde, suivant que la main se trouve disposée. Ainsi la main gauche ne joue simplement que la Basse, sinon qu'elle fait l'Octave quand la main droite tient un accord parfait. (Boyvin.)

On joue la Basse de la main gauche, et à chaque note de Basse que l'on touche, on en ajoute trois autres de la main droite, faisant ainsi un accord sur chaque note. (St-Lambert.)

If the voice to be accompanied is very slight, or if the texture of the music is thin, the notes of the right hand chord may be reduced to two. On the other hand, in powerful passages, for instance in choral or symphonic music, the left hand may double the right with three- or four-part chords also, subject to certain restrictions:

La main gauche peut aussi doubler les Sixtes et les Tierces mineures qui se trouvent sur les diézes, sur les Mi, les Si en montant, et autres, ce qui fait beaucoup d'effet dans un grand Concert. (Boyvin.)

On peut doubler de la main gauche quelqu'une des Parties que fait la main droite; on peut même doubler toutes, si les voix sont très-fortes. (St-Lambert.)

Dissonances should not be doubled, however, except the second.

Dissonance was encouraged in the continuo part, since 'une musique sans dissonance est une soupe sans sel, un ragoût sans épices, une compagnie sans femmes'. The dissonances of the continuo were treated, moreover, with surprising freedom:

Quoyque l'usage ordinaire demande que la Dissonance soit précédée d'une Consonance, on ne laisse pas de se dispenser quelquefois de cette Régle, et on en fait qui ne sont pas précedées; cela se connoit par le bon usage et le bon goût. (Boyvin.)

Eugène Borrel has demonstrated that it was customary to introduce dissonances into the continuo part even when they were not indicated by the figures. St-Lambert remarks

on peut en jouer quelquefois une quatrième [note] dans les accords prescrits par les Régles ordinaires, soit pour adoucir la dureté d'une dissonance ou au contraire pour la rendre plus piquante.

and according to this principle some remarkable effects were obtained. Not only were sevenths and ninths added where appropriate, but the texture was often surprisingly enriched with added seconds, sixths and sevenths. These were not necessarily resolved in the normal way, though they were dissolved into the flow of the chords by ties and retardations.

As a general principle it was considered advisable to preserve continuity between the chords by tying notes common to two successive harmonies:

> Quand on passe d'un accord à un autre, on doit examiner si quelques-unes des notes de l'accord dont on sort ne pourront point servir à l'accord où l'on entre; et quand cela se peut il ne faut pas changer ces notes. (St-Lambert.)
> La main droite doit toujours prendre ses accords au lieu le plus proche où ils se trouvent, et ne les aller jamais chercher loin d'elle. (St-Lambert.)

Normally the two hands should not move far apart, and should play in the middle of the keyboard, except for some special effect of sonority when they may move together to the top or bottom register:

> La Partie supérieure de l'accompagnement ne doit jamais monter plus haut que le Mi de la dernière Octave du Clavier, ou tout au plus jusque'au Fa, en passant, excepté que la Basse devient Haut Contre; car alors on monte tout fort haut. (St-Lambert.)

An excellent example of this exception is provided by the *Adolescentulus sum* of Couperin's *Quatre Versets d'un Motet*.

So long as a full and satisfactory harmony was obtained, the theorists did not severely enforce, in continuo playing, the usual rules governing consecutives. As a general principle of course 'les mains doivent toujours faire mouvement contraire'; but

> Quoique deux Octaves et deux Quintes de suite par mouvement semblable soient ce qu'il y a de plus rigoureusement deffendu en Musique, on n'en fait pas grands scrupules dans l'accompagnement,

especially 'quand on accompagne dans un grand chœur de Musique où le bruit des autres Instruments couvre tellement le Clavecin'. The progression from the diminished to the perfect fifth was even regarded as admirable.

The accepted ornaments, especially trills and the Chute, were frequently employed in continuo parts, often adding their share to the dissonance:

> On peut soit sur l'orgue, soit sure le Clavecin, faire de temps en temps quelques tremblemens, ou quelqu'autre agrément, soit dans la Basse ou dans les Parties, selon qu'on juge que les passages le demandent. On fait toujours un tremblement sur la note qui porte un accord double quand cette note est d'une valeur un peu considérable. On en fait un sur la penultième d'une Cadence Parfaite. (St-Lambert.)

In accompanying recitative, and sometimes in instrumental passages in a relatively free movement and at moderate pace, the chords should be split or arpeggiated at varying speeds and with varying degrees of violence, according to the nature of the passions the music is expressing. But

> Les harpégemens ne sont convenables que dans le Récitatif, où il n'y a proprement point de mesure: car dans les Airs de mouvement il faut frapper les accords tout à la fois avec la Basse: Excepté que quand toutes les notes de la Basse sont Noires, et que la mesure est à 3 tems, on sépare les notes de chaque accord de telle manière qu'on en réserve toujours une pour la faire parler entre 2 tems. Cela forme une espèce de battement qui sied tout à fait bien.

And

> Sur l'orgue on ne rebat point les accords et l'on n'use guère d'harpégemens: on lie au contraire beaucoup les sons en coulant les mains adroitement. On double rarement les Parties. (St-Lambert.)

The general conclusion one must come to is that the contemporary realization of the continuo was closer than one might have imagined to the interpretation which a sensitive musician of today would be likely to give, if left to his own devices. This is especially the case in the matter of the added seconds, sixths, and so on.

This free homophonic realization of the continuo should be regarded as the norm in Couperin's work. But there is evidence that Bach played continuo parts in a highly polyphonic style, and there is even a tradition that Handel's realizations involved counterpoint. St-Lambert's treatise suggests that the French were not averse to contrapuntal realizations in certain circumstances:

> Quand on accompagne une voix seule qui chante quelqu'Air de Mouvement, dans lequel il y a plusieurs imitations de chants, tels que sont les Airs Italiens, on peut imiter sur son clavecin le Sujet et les Fugues de l'air, faisant entrer les Parties l'une après l'autre. Mais cela demande une science consommée et il faut être du premier ordre pour y réussir.

Since Couperin, though not a polyphonist of Bach's kind, is in some ways the most Bach-like of late baroque composers, some such contrapuntal passages would seem to be appropriate to his continuo parts, on certain occasions, in his more linear compositions; the last page of the *2me Leçon de Ténèbres* is an obvious example. Such passages should be regarded, however, as exceptional, and the texture should never be allowed to grow crowded. Here as elsewhere the final arbiter is *le bon goût*: 'Le discernement délicat d'un accompagnateur habile pourroit peut-être lui en permettre encore d'autres dont il n'est pas aisé de parler, puisqu'elles ne dépendraient que de son bon goût; car on sait que le bon goût détermine souvent à des choses dont on ne peut donner d'autre raison que le goût même'.

All the theorists insist that the difficult task in continuo playing is not to realize the bass according to the rules – in the matter of correctness considerable latitude may be allowed; the difficulty is rather to interpret the bass in a manner which is exactly suited to the spirit – gay, fierce, doleful or languishing – of the music. If the player introduces ornaments or dissonances on his own initiative they must be appropriate to the feeling. He must alter his harpsichord or organ registration according to the sentiments expressed and according to the nature – the power or the frailty – of the resources which he is accompanying. Always he must remember that he does not play for himself alone but for 'l'honneur et la perfection du Concert'. Geminiani makes the same point in his treatise on thorough-bass:

> A good Accompanyer ought to possess the Faculty of playing all sorts of Basses in different manners, so as to be able, on proper Occasions, to enliven the Composition and delight the Singer and Player. But he is to exercise this Faculty with Judgment, Taste, and Discretion, agreeable to the Stile of the Composition, and the

Manner and Intention of the Performer. If the Accompanyer thinks of nothing but satisfying his own Whims and Caprice, he may perhaps be said to play well, but will certainly be said to accompany ill.

Couperin himself regarded sensitive continuo playing as of hardly less importance than solo playing; though amour-propre may make solo playing seem more rewarding!

> S'il était permis d'opter entre l'accompagnement et les pièces pour porter l'un ou l'autre à l'accompagnement, je sens que l'amour-propre me ferait préférer les pièces à l'accompagnement. Je conviens que rien n'est plus amusant pour soi-même et ne nous lie plus avec les autres que d'être bon accompagnateur. Mais quelle injustice! L'accompagnement du clavecin dans ces occasions n'est considéré que comme les fondemens d'un édifice, qui cependant soutiennent tout et dont on ne parle jamais.

F. Comments on Aims and Intentions

A famous passage from the Preface to the first harpsichord book (1713) merits some discussion here:

> J'ai toujours eu un objet, en composant toutes ces pièces; des occasions différentes me l'ont fourni: ainsi les titres répondent aux idées que j'ai eues. On me dispensera d'en rendre compte. Cependant, comme, parmi ces titres, il y en a qui semblent me flatter, il est bon d'avertir que les pièces qui les portent sont des espèces de portraits qu'on a trouvés quelquefois assez rassemblants sous mes doigts, et que la plupart de ces titres avantageux sont plûtot donnés aux aimables originaux que j'ai voulu représenter qu'aux copies que j'en ai tirées.

The pieces with 'titres avantageux' are, of course, those called *La Majestueuse*, *L'Auguste*, etc., and possibly those called La Belle this or the other.

It has been found surprising that so classical and 'objective' a composer as Couperin should thus confess to an expressive intention; and it has sometimes been remarked that his 'portraits', as such, are not very successful, since they mostly sound alike. This type of remark is not normally meant as a pejorative reflection on Couperin's *music*; but it does perhaps suggest an inability to comprehend what Couperin, and French classical civilization, have to offer. Couperin's stylization is, as we have seen, the reflection of the world in which he lived and worked; he could not, and would not have wished to, modify it. But, as we have also seen, the essence of that civilization was that it permitted great subtlety and variety of emotional experience within its stylization; and the variety – psychological as well as musical – is there in Couperin's portraits when one has learned to listen to them. The point is not one of much practical import-ance, since one cannot estimate Couperin's psychological acu-men, as revealed in his portraits, without personal acquaintance with the people whom he is portraying. It is probable, however, that the appropriateness of the portrait was clear enough to Couperin's contemporaries. In any case, we must remember the words of Rousseau:

> L'art du musicien ne consiste point à peindre immédiatement les objets, mais à mettre l'âme dans une disposition semblable à celle où la mettrait leur presence.

And the idea of the musical portrait links up with the preoccupa-tion of the period with psychology and 'character'.

Far from Couperin's practice being in any way exceptional, all the theorists of the classical age insist on music's expressive purpose. Lecerf de la Viéville even said that 'la science de la musique de l'Eglise, plus que de la profane, n'est autre chose que la façon d'émouvoir vraiment et à propos'; while in the suc-ceeding generation the theory of imitation became one of the basic tenets of the Encyclopaedists:

> Toute musique qui ne peint rien n'est que du bruit. (D'Alembert.)
> La musique qui ne peint rien est insipide. (Marmontel.)
> Il falloit donner aux sentiments humains plus d'expression et plus d'accent par les formes de la musique. (Perrin.)
> L'expression de la pensée, du sentiment, des passions, doit être le vrai but de la musique. (Rameau.)

So deeply engrained was the pictorial and expressive habit in the minds of musicians that pure instrumental music met with con-siderable opposition in some quarters, simply on the grounds of its purity. 'Toute cette musique purement instrumentale,' says D'Alembert, 'sans dessein, sans objet, ne parle ni à l'esprit ni à 303 l'âme et mérite qu'on lui demande avec Fontenelle "Sonate, que me veux-tu?" Il faut avouer qu'en general on ne sent toute l'expression de la musique que lorsqu'elle est liée à des paroles et à des danses.' Though one may think it odd that music such as Couperin's sonatas should ever have been considered *sans dessein* or *sans objet* one can see that D'Alembert's objection, however naïve, derives from an instinct that was healthy enough – from a belief that music ought to have a direct relation to a social function.

This preference for the opera, for music which was dependent on something outside itself, reached its culmination in the writings of Rousseau. The only eighteenth-century theorists who opposed the imitative view were the Chevalier de Castallux and Gui de Chabanon, who both maintained that music was not imitative but creative; therefore a purely instrumental music might be as significant as operatic music. Though music might not crudely imitate natural phenomena, however, it was in a deeper sense an imitation of human emotion. Both writers stressed the theory of communication.

In England a similar attitude is found in Charles Avison's *Essay on Musical Expression* of 1752. He maintained that 'the composer is culpable who, for the sake of a low and trifling imitation, deserts the beauties of Expression':

> And, as dissonance and Shocking sounds cannot be called Musical Expression, so neither do I think, can mere imitation of several other things be entitled to this name, which, however, among the generality of mankind, hath often obtained it. Thus the gradual rising or falling of the notes in a long succession, is often used to denote ascent or descent; broken intervals to denote an interrupted motion; a number of quick divisions to describe swiftness or flying; sounds resembling laughter, to describe laughter; with a number of other contrivances of a parallel kind, which it is needless here to mention. Now all these I should chuse rather to style Imitation than Expression; because it seems to me, that their tendency is rather to fix the Hearer's attention on the similitude between the sounds and the things which they describe, and thereby to excite a reflex act of the understanding, than to affect the Heart and raise the passions of the Soul.

On the other hand Avison follows the Encyclopædists in
believing that 'the finest instrumental music may be considered

as an imitation of the vocal'. Only Diderot seems to have had any appreciation of the individual techniques – as opposed to 'affections' – of instruments, and of the importance which was to be attributed to those qualities in the music of the future.

Couperin seems to have been unimpressed by the contemporary insistence on the supremacy of music which is closely related to literature. Even in the field of vocal music his work to Latin words (which as Brijon points out in his *Réflexions sur la Musique* of 1763 were often unintelligible to the audience) is both more extensive and more interesting than his work to French words; while many of his most psychologically expressive portraits dispense with words altogether. Since Couperin's position as one of the greatest masters of his time seems to have been unquestioned, it would appear that the pronouncements of the theorists on the subject of instrumental music were not taken too seriously.

Not all Couperin's portraits are of persons; some are of scenes and places (*Les Moissonneurs, Les Vergers Fleüris*). The descriptions are stylized but are, and are meant to be, atmospheric and evocative. While some of the titles are no doubt purely fanciful or wilfully enigmatic, far more have a realistic intent than one might superficially imagine. If they seem artificial it is because the world which Couperin imitates is itself so close to art, for it entailed, to a degree which is seldom found in communities, both emotion and discipline, both complexity and order.

The significance of Expression in baroque music has, I think, sometimes been misunderstood. The nature of Bach's musical symbolism of religious truths as described by Schweitzer and Pirro, and of Couperin's musical symbolism of character and place, is basically similar. In both cases there is no question of our being able to draw, as it were, a graph of the pictorial, descriptive and expressive implications which lurk beneath what may appear to be a piece of absolute instrumental music. The point is simply that certain extra-musical concepts served to release in Bach's and Couperin's mind an appropriate musical response. The analogical habit was hardly a conscious intellectual process for them, however naïve the interpretations of the theorists may have become. Bach embodied the conception of Christ on the Cross in tone as naturally as a painter would express it in visual symbols; similarly with Couperin's musical presentation of the pathos of Harlequin. And there is nothing 305 odd about this; both Bach and Couperin are, in this respect as in many others, the end of a tradition. It is almost possible to say that up to their day the dependence of music on extra-musical elements – and in particular the intimate relation between music and literature – was accepted without question. It is only because we have been brought up in a culture which takes for granted a divorce between music and literature and the other arts that we can find anything at all peculiar in their method. The divorce is a matter of some general aesthetic significance which does not work to our advantage.

All through baroque music the expressive elements really amount to a kind of musical (not literary or pictorial) stylization. Whereas the nineteenth-century composer tended to think of his work as self-expression, the attitude of the baroque composer is not less passionate but more objective. His selfhood is revealed through the expression and description of something outside himself; consider the significance of the Emblematic habit all through the seventeenth century. The Crucifixus of the B minor Mass is one of the most heart-rending pieces of music ever written; but Bach thought of it primarily as Christ's suffering, which happened also to be his own, and that of the people who listened to it. Similarly, in its smaller way, the pathos of Couperin's Harlequin is primarily Harlequin's suffering, which is also Couperin's, and which corresponds to a deeply rooted melancholy in his society. Both Couperin and Bach invented a musical myth apposite to the myths by the light of which people live. There is no egoism in their music. If Bach composed for 'the glory of God and the instruction of my neighbour' Couperin did much the same, though he would not have put it in quite those terms. He would have said he wrote for the entertainment of *les honnêtes gens*; but this would have implied both that his music was a communal activity, and that it was an act of praise to an Absolute, because he knew what *honnêteté* was.

Descartes, who so neatly summarized the consciousness of the *grand siècle*, had regarded music primarily as the creation of intellectual order. This is why he tended to suggest that simple music was *ipso facto* 'better' than complicated music; why he preferred homophony to polyphony; and why he tried to develop a rationalistic system of harmony which tabulated the emotional effects of chords as rigidly as Lebrun tabulated the pictorial counterparts of different passions. Lully was the realization of Descartes's musical theory, as he was of Boileau's aesthetic, despite the latter's strong disapproval of the opera. But his was a creative, not a text-book, realization; and he showed that the search for order and symmetry entailed a humane attitude to the problems which people have to face in living together. In Couperin's subtler style there is the same search for clarity and order, without Lully's (and Descartes's) tendency to simplify the issues. Couperin's clarity is both more hardly won and more richly satisfying. His 'philosophy of music' cannot be separated from the music itself.

Note to p.288

In this discussion of rhythmic inequalities in three works of Couperin I have frequently used the words 'should be' or 'should have' in advocating one or the other mode of performance. This means no more than that, given what one knows of the conventions and rules and of the nature of a specific piece of music, this seems a likely interpretation. It doesn't mean that such is the only possible interpretation; certainly not that recommended degrees of inequality are mensurable mathematically. One is approaching understanding when one no longer needs to think about what one is doing but acts as spontaneously as breathing – or speaking, or sighing, or smiling. One reaches this point sooner than one might expect, especially if one isn't too often diverted into the performance of other types of music that are metrically more assertive. I have been speaking, of course, of those 'expressive' rhythmic irregularities peculiarly characteristic of French classical music, not of alterations of rhythm which are purely notational and typical of all late-baroque music – such as the combination of triplets with dotted figures, the semiquaver coinciding with the third quaver of the triplet.

Chapter Thirteen

Couperin's Resources and His Use of Them
(with Notes on the Modern Performance of his Work)

In this section I propose first to attempt a brief summary of the conditions governing music-making in Couperin's day; and then to offer some more detailed and specific comments on his use of the media which were available to him.

A composer brought up in Couperin's environment would have had no need to complain of a lack of opportunity to express himself. Whatever the direction of his talents, there was plenty of demand for his work. The choices open to him may be grouped as follows:

(1) Opera and ballet.
(2) Musique de Chasse.
(3) Musique des Soupers.
(4) Musique des Soirées et des Bals.
(5) Chamber music for the concerts du dimanche.
(6) Church music for the Chapelle Royale.

The following orchestras and bands took part in these various activities:

Les Vingt-quatre Violons du Roi.
Les Petits Violons (directed by Lully and used especially for ballet music and dances).
Les Menus Plaisirs du Roi.
La Musique de la Reine.
La Musique de la Chambre du Roi (for ballets, balls, fêtes and Soupers).
Les Corps des Violons du Cabinet.
La Musique de la Chapelle Royale.
Les Bandes de la Grande et de la Petite Ecurie (for festivities, military reviews, hunting expeditions, open-air fêtes, etc.).

The ballets and even the operas sometimes took place in the open air, in specially constructed settings; the architect Vigarani, for instance, designed a 'parc' for the performance of *La Princesse d'Elide* in 1664. For these performances many of the different instrumental groups combined together. For the *Fêtes nautiques* which were staged on the Grand Canal as many as a hundred players were often employed; here the violins, viols, lutes, theorbes, guitars and clavecins of the various bands of the Chambre and Chapelle performed with the flutes, fifes, oboes, trumpets, horns and drums of the bands of the Ecuries. La Lande in particular excelled at writing grand music for these festivities.

From 1669, the operas were repeated before the public in Paris, at a theatre established by Perrin with the King's authority. Lully took over the public performance of all opera in 1672, establishing an opera house in the rue de Vaugirard. Later, operas were produced in the Salle des Tuileries.

Most of Couperin's church music was written for performance in the Chapelle Royale. Originally built in 1682, the Chapel was reconstructed in 1710 according to plans of Robert de Cotte and Mansart. In its revised form it was not only an extremely beautiful and harmoniously proportioned religious establishment, but a magnificently equipped concert hall. The four-manual organ was placed above the altar, and was flanked by terraces which accommodated the choristers, orchestra and conductor. The choir normally numbered twenty-four and the orchestra nineteen; but on festive occasions there were sometimes ninety or more performers. In Couperin's time the full complement of singers and players comprised ten sopranos, twenty-four altos, twenty tenors, twenty-three baritones, eleven basses, six violins, three continuo instruments, three bass viols, two flutes, two serpents and three bassoons.

High Mass was celebrated every day. Three motets were included; a lengthy movement lasting from the beginning of the ceremony to the Elevation (about a quarter of an hour); a short piece sung by a few picked voices during the Elevation; and the *Domine salvum fac regem* for full choir and orchestra as a conclusion. The motets were usually scored for soloists, chorus, strings and organ, with occasionally some obbligato wind instruments. The choral and string writing was commonly in five parts.

Two choirs, working in alternation, were maintained; only thus, one presumes, was it possible for the singers to keep pace with the very extensive repertory of new works. It was probably for this reason that four organist-directors of the Chapel were 309 appointed simultaneously, working in rotation for periods of three months each a year. The royal performances of church music were repeated publicly at Notre-Dame de Versailles, St Germain l'Auxerrois, and the big Parisian churches, St Jean en Grève, St Louis des Jésuites, St Paul and St Jacques de la Boucherie.

Public concerts, in the modern sense of the term, were not a conspicuous feature of musical activity in the early part of the seventeenth century. But Louis XIV's concerts du dimanche were regularly organized professional performances; and they set a fashion which rapidly increased during the latter part of Couperin's life. Mme de Montespan organized music-making at Clagny where, according to Mme de Sévigné, 'il y a concert tous les jours'; Mme de Maintenon put on regular concerts to enliven the King's *tristesse*.

In 1725 Philidor founded the institution of the Concerts Spirituels at the Salle des Suisses aux Tuileries. These were public concerts of church music, at which Italian as well as French works were frequently played. During the eighteenth century the increasingly powerful rich bourgeoisie emulated the aristocracy by encouraging and financing concerts of chamber and orchestral music. The artistic activities of Crozat (patron of Watteau) and of Le Riche de la Pouplinière, friend and patron of Rameau and later of Stamitz, were no less celebrated than those of the Duchesse de Maine, whose salon preserved, even to the point of parody, the old hermetic refinement. (See the account of her in Addendum III.)

Of Couperin's own works the organ masses were written before he received any official court appointment, as part of his duties at St Gervais. His later motets and elevations were composed mostly for the Chapelle Royale. His concerted music for instruments, in the form of sonatas, suites, and *concerts royaux*, was written for the King's concerts du dimanche. The solo harpsichord music was partly intended for these entertainments, partly for the use of his pupils and, perhaps, for private performance to the King and nobility. It will be observed that Couperin restricted himself to the more intimate forms of music-making current in his day. This, as we have suggested previously, was a matter of temperament, and does not imply any restriction on the range and nobility of his art.

310   After this brief survey of the various fields in which Couperin

From Baroque to Rococo
XIII. The organ of St Gervais, built in the early seventeenth
century by Pescheur and Thierry, redesigned in 1768 by Clicquot.

XIV. The organ of the Chapelle Royale, as rebuilt in 1710,
with case by Robert de Cotte.

Couperin played the St Gervais organ in his youth, when he
fulfilled the dynastic office of organist and choirmaster there. He
was one of the four organists of the Chapelle Royale after his court
appointment in 1697, though the organ was unfinished at that time.

might have worked, we will now examine his treatment of the media in which he chose to express himself.

A. Organ Music

Couperin's organ at St Gervais is one of the most magnificent of all baroque instruments. It was built mostly in the early part of the seventeenth century, probably by Pierre Pescheur and Pierre Thierry; additions and improvements throughout the century were mainly the work of later members of the Thierry family, and important modifications were made in 1768 by the great organ builder F. H. Clicquot. This, however, was after Couperin's day; the instrument he used must have been substantially the same as that played by his uncle Louis.

During the nineteenth century, the dust of the years and various acts of God took their toll, and the organ was repeatedly threatened with complete destruction and 'restoration'. The threats came to nothing, however, and the organ fell into a state of slow decay. It suffered severely from bombardment in the 1914 war, but what appeared to be tragedy turned out to be the organ's salvation. Something, after the bombardment, had to be done; the plight of the organ could no longer be quietly ignored. Inspection proved that the damage was not as fundamental as had been feared; and a commission, consisting of Charles Widor, Félix Raugel, Maurice Emmanuel, A. de Vallombrosé, Joseph Bonnet and Paul Brunold, was appointed to decide how the organ might best be reconstructed. Between 1921 and 1923, the reconstruction was carried out with an integrity and sympathy which would certainly have been lacking, had reconstruction been attempted in the palmy days of the nineteenth century. Unfortunately, during the Second World War the organ once more fell into decay.

The specification of the organ is given in detail in Brunold's book on the subject. Since this book is not generally accessible, we may quote the specification here, because it may be of help to modern organists who wish to play Couperin's masses in particular, and baroque organ music in general. The terms are translated into their English equivalent, where there is no possible ambiguity.

313

1st *Manual: Choir*, the pipes enclosed in a 'petit buffet', a miniature replica of the great organ, placed behind the organists' back. (See page 311.)

   51 notes, from C to A.

Diapason 8. The basses in wood. 15 pipes. 18th c.

Flute 8. 16 in wood, 8 in metal. Restored 1812.

Principal 4. 14 pipes, Alexandre Thierry, 1676, and 18th c.

Doublette 2. Pierre Thierry, 1659.

Nazard 2⅔. Pierre Thierry, 1659.

Tierce 1⅗. Pierre Thierry, 1659.

Plein Jeu, 5 ranks. Restored, 1843.

Trumpet 8. F. H. Clicquot, 1768.

Clairon 4. F. H. Clicquot, 1768.

Cromhorne 8. F. H. Clicquot, 1768.

Basson-Clarinette. F. H. Clicquot, 1768; restored, 1812.

2nd *Manuel: Great Organ*, 51 notes.

Diapason 16. Pescheur or Thierry, restored by Clicquot and Dallery.

Diapason 8. Pescheur or Thierry.

Bourdon 16. Wood and lead. Pierre Thierry, 1659.

Bourdon 8. Wood and lead. Pierre Thierry, 1659.

Flute 8. Pescheur, 1628.

Principal 4. Pierre Thierry, 1659.

Doublette 2. Pierre Thierry, 1659.

Nazard 2⅔. Pierre Pescheur, 1628.

Quarte de Nazard. Pierre Pescheur, 1628.

Tierce 1⅗. Pierre Pescheur, 1628.

Plein Jeu, 6 ranks. Restored, 1843.

Grand Cornet, 5 ranks. Pierre Thierry, 1649.

1st Trumpet 8. Pierre Thierry, 1649.

2nd Trumpet 8. Dallery, 1812.

Clairon 4. Pierre Pescheur, 1628; restored, Clicquot, 1768.

Voix Humaine. Pierre Pescheur, 1628.

3rd *Manual: Bombard*, 51 notes.

Bombard 16. Clicquot, 1768.

4th *Manual: Swell*. 32 notes, G to A.

Oboe 8. Clicquot, 1768.

Cornet, 5 ranks. Alexandre Thierry, 1676.

5th Manual: Echo. 27 notes, C to A.
    Flute 8. Built from the ancient Cornet d'echo, Pierre
        Thierry, 1659.
    Trumpet 8. François Thierry, 1714 (originally placed in the
        Choir).

Pedal: 28 notes, A to C.
    Flute 16. Pierre Thierry, 1649; Alexandre Thierry, 1676.
    Flute 8. The painted pipes from the organ of St Catherine's,
        the rest by Pierre Thierry, 1649.
    Flute 4. Pierre Thierry, 1649.
    Bombard 16. Clicquot, 1768.
    Trumpet 8. François Thierry, 1714; rebuilt by Clicquot,
        1768.
    Clairon 4. François Thierry, 1714; rebuilt by Clicquot,
        1768.

For the benefit of those not versed in organ technicalities, we
may add that the Cromhorne, like the German Krumhorn, is a
rather nasal clarinet, the clairon a trumpet, and the bourdon a
stopped diapason. The Plein Jeu is a mixture without thirds or
fundamental; the cornet is also a mixture playing a chord without the fundamental. The Nazard, Quinte, and Tierce are mutations, playing the twelfth, fifteenth, and seventeenth
respectively. A few stops seem to have disappeared; we know,
for instance, that there was a *jeu de viole* in Louis Couperin's
time. The first three manuals can be coupled. The Bombard is
always coupled with the Great.

Both in the range of its keyboards and the number of its stops
the St Gervais organ was, by contemporary standards, large.
Since it does not survive in playable condition, and did not
adequately survive forty years ago when I was working on this
book, we cannot know how Couperin's Masses sounded on the
instrument for which they were written. During those years,
however, we have become much more sophisticated about these
matters. We now know that many well-preserved old instruments appropriate to the music survive around Europe: while
many mechanically perfect new instruments have been and are
being built both in Europe and in America, not to mention
Australia, Canada and South Africa. These organs precisely
follow seventeenth- and eighteenth-century specifications and

adhere to the acoustic and mechanical principles of baroque organs; at the same time, of course, they avail themselves of the advantages of modern technology. Relevant information is presented, not altogether accurately, in Lawrence Phelps's *Brief Look at the French Classical Organ, its origins and Germanic counterpart*. He gives the specification of the St Gervais organ as it was in 1690, when Couperin's Masses were published (naturally much smaller than the specification given by Brunold, quoted above); juxtaposes it with the specification of a comparable German organ built by Arp Schnitger in 1688; and appends details of the organ of the Prediger-Kirche in Zurich, built by Th. Kuhn A. G. Mannedorf in 1970. This large instrument, combining the virtues of the French and German classical schools, is used by Gillian Weir for her recording of the Masses, to which Phelps's *Brief Look* serves as supplement.

Since Couperin follows contemporary convention in giving instructions as to registration for each section, a few comments on the implications of this registration may not come amiss. If a piece is called a *Dialogue*, the sections are to be played on contrasted manuals (*grand orgue* and *positif*). The term *cornet séparé* indicates a cornet made up of stops individually rather than a 'ready-mixed' cornet such as is available on the instrument. *Plein jeu* means what we would today call 'full to mixtures' – principals 16, 8, 4 and 2, with the *fourniture* and *cymbale* for brilliance. *Grand jeu* is not equivalent to today's 'full organ', but is made up of all the trumpets and cornets, including the *prestant*, to the exclusion of other foundation stops. *Jeux doux* means soft 8 and 4 flutes, usually accompanying a solo played by the other hand. *Tierce en taille* calls for the left hand on the *positif*, with *bourdon* 8, *prestant* 4, *doublette* 2, *nazard* $2\frac{2}{3}$, *tierce* $1\frac{3}{5}$, and *larigot* $1\frac{1}{3}$: while the *grand orgue* accompanies with *bourdons* 16, 8, and 4. The instructions as to the registration of French baroque organ music given in the new edition of Grove are comprehensive and accurate; to them the reader is referred.

On Couperin's organ, as on all baroque instruments, purity of tone and subtlety of colour are attainable because wind pressure on the tracker-action organ is low. In Gillian Weir's performance on the organ the round sweetness of the diapasons, the lucent glow of the solo stops and the metallic edge of the mutations seem made for Couperin's music, as his music was made for them. The doubling of the line by harmonics two octaves and a twelfth up sometimes creates an extraordinary sound, as of rustling tinfoil (perhaps we're meant to mistake it for the shimmer of angels' wings!). The effect of the *tierce*, which adds the major third two octaves up, is especially piquant in minor keys, since the major thirds of these distant harmonics persistently clash with the minor thirds of the notated music. The minor section of the fourth couplet of the Gloria of the *Messe pour les Paroisses* is a representative instance; in the major section the added seventeenths produce a much richer effect than the notation suggests, without harming clarity of texture. In both Masses Couperin 'features' the *Voix humaine*, a reed stop accompanied by a strong tremulant. Presumably the sound was considered 'human' because its pipe and reeds, beating very slowly in inexact unison, bleated in an extravagant vibrato that seemed endemic to the human condition! Perhaps it carries a threat, or at least a warning. Normally, it is the duty of an *honnête homme* to try to sing on the note rather than around it, using vibrato as a special effect, with the utmost discretion, like an ornament. Intermittently, however, the self-pity inherent in the human fallibility of the unison that doesn't make it may get the better of him; he abandons himself to the *Voix humaine*, whose quaverings deliciously ruffle the nerves and nauseate the stomach. Though this sounds fanciful, there is an anomaly here which needs further investigation. Why does a *Voix humaine* conflict with the standards of *le bon goût*?

Though it is still rare to find organists willing to experiment with tuning and temperament, no one today would attempt to play Couperin's Masses on an organ incapable of the range of colour and clarity of articulation typical of a French classical instrument. There are now several recordings of the Masses on several instruments all having their individually fascinating qualities. All organists now 'do their homework' in re-creating appropriate sonorities and in exploring aspects of performance practice, such as ornamentation and rhythmic inequalities. If I have mentioned Gillian Weir's performance it is because she more than anyone captures the rhythmic vivacity that matches the lucent colours. The dance is seldom far from Couperin's music, even when it seems to be rooted in plainsong intonation. Gillian Weir allows us to forget that an organ is a mechanical contraption of wind-blown pipes: as the pipes sing for her, so do our feet and bodies dance. Listening to these records we can 317

momentarily identify with Dr Burney who, during his continental travels, heard the St Gervais organ as reconstructed by
Clicquot in 1768:

> The organ of St Gervais, which seems to be a very good one, is
> almost new; it was made by the same builder, M. Clicquot, as that
> of St Roche. The pedals have three octaves in compass; the tone of
> the loud organ is rich, full and pleasing, when the movement is
> slow; though in quick passages, such is the reverberation of these
> large buildings, everything is indistinct and confused. Great lati-
> tude is allowed to the performer in these interludes; nothing is too
> light or too grave; all styles are admitted and although M.
> Couperin has the true organ touch, smooth and connected, yet he
> often tried, and not unsuccessfully, mere harpsichord passages,
> sharply articulated, and the notes detached and separated.

The M. Couperin referred to is Armand-Louis, François's
nephew.

A word should be added on the loft and casing of the St
Gervais organ. The buffet was a creation of the great years of the
Roi Soleil. The case of the Great Organ was rebuilt in the reign
of Louis XV but preserves the dignity of the classical age. One
can see in its discreetly ornamented proportions something of
the balanced gravity which one finds in such a piece of Couperin
as *La Favorite*. The two sides of the instrument answer one
another as serenely as the treble and bass parts answer one
another in Couperin's noble chaconne. The proportions of the
organ are as harmoniously resolved as the sounds it produces.

Couperin was organist of St Gervais for most of his working
life. From 1693 he was also one of the organists of the Chapelle
Royale. When he took over this post the great organ at Versailles
had not been built. It was not started until 1702, nor finished
until 1736, three years after Couperin's death. Thus, during the
early years of Couperin's duties at Versailles, the services did not
include dialogues between the organist and choir in the conventional manner of the parish service, as indicated in the structure
of the organ masses. The service was mainly vocal, and a small
positive organ, placed near the singers, was used merely for
accompaniment. Where solo instrumental parts were needed,
they were played by violins, flutes, oboes and *violes*, in the
manner of the Carissimi or Bach cantatas. Whether or not there
are obbligato instruments, the bass line should of course be

doubled by bass viol or cello. In all cases the function of the organ is quietly to fill in the harmonies, without disturbing the balance between soloists and string bass.

Although incomplete, the new organ at Versailles was inaugurated in 1710. Couperin may have played it at the ceremony, and must have used it during the remaining years of his court appointment. There is no evidence of this in his music, however. None of his motets and elevations calls for a large instrument; on the contrary, as we have seen, they suggest a positive. Couperin seldom favoured a grandiose manner in church music, or in anything else. Lully and La Lande, who cultivated the massive and imposing in church music, did so by way of relatively large orchestral resources. So the early Masses remain Couperin's only developed compositions for the instrument; and in connection with them it is of the organ of St Gervais, rather than that of the Chapelle Royale, that we must think.

B. *Instrumental Chamber Music*
Trio Sonatas and Suites, *Concerts Royaux*, Suites for Viols

In the late forties, when I was working on this book, we were not fully aware of the problematical issues involved in the performance of Couperin's, or any baroque composer's, instrumental chamber music. We knew that it should be played discreetly, without extravagant rubato, vibrato or other romantic excess; but for the most part we used modern instruments and conventions of bowing and phrasing derived at best from the classical age of Haydn, more commonly from classical style as reinterpreted by the nineteenth century. Today we use baroque violins, cellos and bass viols, or modern copies of them, tuned to a pitch somewhat lower than ours (though scholars argue cantankerously as to precisely how much lower, in precisely which French, German and Italian contexts); we rediscover or re-create baroque wind instruments; we play with deference to what we know of contemporary practice, which, after the labours of three decades of scholars, is quite a lot. Greater knowledge does not necessarily bring definitive solutions – partly because not enough good players are prepared, for understandable economic as well as aesthetic reasons, to devote most of their time to the performance of the music of one 319 period; partly because the evidence, on matters of style and interpretation, is often confused and sometimes contradictory.

None the less enough fine musicians have been performing long enough to convince us that the effort is worthwhile. Indeed with a composer like Couperin, who comes from a time and place with sophisticated codes of social and musical thinking, feeling and behaving, some attempt at authenticity has become obligatory: for when once one has heard his music in *his* phrasing and sonorities, later styles, applied to him, sound intolerably brash. The ornamentation and conventions of *inégalité* which, even in the forties, we knew to be inseparable from the heart of Couperin's music, are totally persuasive only when expertly played on the right instruments. The recordings of *Les Nations* and of the *Concerts Royaux* by the Kuijkens and the Quadro Amsterdam are assured enough to sound spontaneous in their sophistication; and demonstrate that the restricted range of sonority on the baroque violin and cello is not a musical deprivation, because the tone 'speaks' with such subtle intimacy. This was especially true of the French school. Raguenet remarks that 'our masters touch the violin much finer and with a greater nicety than they do in Italy': in which country 'every stroke of their bow sounds harsh, if broken, and disagreeable, if continued'.* Le Cerf de la Viéville also admonishes the Italians for their desire to elicit too much sound from their instruments: 'My intelligence, my heart, my ears tell me, all at once, that they produce a sound excessively shrill and violent. I am always afraid that the first stroke of the bow will make the violin fly into splinters, they use so much pressure.' (*Comparaison de la musique italienne et de la musique française*, 1705.) He tells a then well-known anecdote proving that the King rejected Corellian-style playing, and called for 'an air from *Cadmus*', played by one of his own violinists, to purge his ears. Listening to Couperin's string parts, played on something like his instruments in something approaching his style, *is* a chastening experience. Baroque phrasing, based on short bowing that 'lets in the air', reveals the heart of the music through the sonority. In this context Muffat's instructions about bowing, quoted in Appendix E, are broadly relevant to the performance of Couperin.

---

* The lively translation, used here and elsewhere, is probably by Sir John Hawkins.

One's first impression of baroque string sound, especially in the French manner, may be that it is pinched and mean rather than expressive. The impression wears off when one's ears adjust to the limited volume, as they do to that of clavichords and lutes; and when one learns to listen with ears tuned not to rhetorical gestures but to intimate conversation. The French were reticent not because they favoured a deadpan apathy, but because they believed that only through the exercise of *pudeur* could the ultimate delicacies of expression be realized. The musical dialogue in Couperin's concerted music complements the *conversations galantes et amusantes* of the lovely young people in the *fêtes champêtres* of Watteau; one has only to look at the pictures, or to listen to the music, to realize that polite persiflage and flirtatious badinage may reveal rather than disguise the depths of the human heart. This bears on the vexed question of vibrato in string playing, which is closely allied to vibrato in the human voice. Passionate excess is to be avoided: we remember that Couperin preferred 'ce qui me touche à ce qui me surprend'. None the less since expressivity is the *sine qua non* of conversational communication it is difficult to credit that string playing, even with the French, should be vibrato*less*. I shall have more to say of this in connection with the relationship between the *grande voix* and the *petite voix* in Couperin's church music.

The performances by the Kuijkens and the Quadro Amsterdam further reveal that baroque flutes, oboes and bassoons make better sense in Couperin's music than do modern wind instruments. At first the flute may seem deficient not merely in volume but also in sustaining power and therefore in line. There is no reason inherent in the instrument why this should be so; more competent players should appear as familiarity with the baroque flute increases, and we may expect them to reveal that the pearly sonority of the instrument ideally balances the baroque fiddle. The more brazen sounds of the wind instruments used on the Archiv recordings of the *Concerts Royaux*, even though they're played by such masterly executants as Heinz Holliger and Aurèle Nicolet, bludgeon the music's finesse.

The trio sonatas are string music and sound best on violins with cello or bass viol and harpsichord. But flute, recorder or oboe were often substituted for violins, and the Quadro Amsterdam sometimes makes such substitutions. Some of the early trio 321 sonatas – especially *La Sultane*, ripe in sonority because of its two bass viols – sound well with chamber organ; the dance suites and the *concerts*, however, call for the more percussive harpsichord. *L'Apothéose de Lully*, being theatrical in concept as befits its subject, profits from an interchange between string and wind instruments; in one movement Couperin specifies flutes rather than violins. This piece can be effectively performed with a small band as well as by soloists.

Couperin notated all his *concerts* as music for an unspecified solo melody instrument with harpsichord and string bass; occasionally the solo line is augmented by a *contre-partie, si l'on veut*. Since we know that the performers at the concerts du dimanche included a flautist, oboist and bassoonist along with string players and harpsichordist, one assumes that the scoring was varied according to the character of the piece. This is usually done in modern performances. All the pieces, Couperin tells us, may be played domestically as duets for one or two keyboards: 'L'exécution n'en paroistra pas moins agréable.' Played in this form they can give much pleasure to us today, being occasional music of ready adaptability.

In the original edition I wrote grudgingly of the problem of the suites for viols, on the grounds that no one could play them adequately on the right instrument and that to transcribe them for cellos involves technical difficulties, apart from the fact that cello sonority is inapposite. Nowadays no one would think of playing these works on anything other than the instruments for which they were written, and there are plenty of competent bass viol players. None the less I have still not heard an entirely satisfying performance of the suites, not even by Jordi Savall, who is a master of the instrument. His recorded version comes out as distinctly morose, like my comments in the original edition of this book, and I do not know the technical explanation of this, if there is one. Contemporary authorities on the bass viol, especially those valetudinarians who deplored its decline under the onslaught of the new-fangled violin family, always referred to the sweetness, softness, nobility and *brilliance* of its tone, the continuity of its line, the 'speaking' expressivity of its timbre. Roger North, writing in 1710, complained that:

the noble Base Viol lyes under this disadvantage, that so few understand the bow, and regular fingering, with the proper grace-ing of the Notes upon it, as one seldome hears it well used or rather not abused. Whereas in truth all the sublymitys of the violin – the swelling, tremolo, tempering, and what else can be thought admirable – have place in the use of the Base Viol, as well as drawing a noble sound; and all with such a vast compass, as expresseth upper, meane, and lower parts, and in lute way toucheth the accords, and is no less swift than the violin itself, but wonderfully more copious. This I must say in vindication of the Base Viol, and for the encouragement to use it; and let those that know it less, despyse it as they please.

The virtuoso bass viol tradition survived rather longer in France than in England, but was archaistic by Couperin's day. Though his two suites, the consummation of a long and by then nearly defunct tradition, are extremely taxing and were probably meant to be, I find it difficult to believe that contemporary virtuosi made them sound as dreary as they sound, to my perhaps jaded ears, on Savall's award-winning disc. Possibly they did, for bass viol-playing friends have suggested that Couperin's suites, though musically magnificent, are not well written for the instrument – which Couperin did not play, whereas Marais and Forqueray were celebrated as bass viol virtuosi no less than for their compositions. I can accept that the bass viol, like the lute and guitar, calls for a degree of inner knowledge, not to mention love, if its mysteries are to be fully revealed. On the other hand, I would have expected Couperin, always a perfectionist, to have acquired that knowledge. We should leave the matter open for the moment. There is no shortage of vintage instruments to restore and copy; perhaps twentieth-century virtuosi haven't lived with the instrument and its music long enough to convince us that they are past masters with a century or more of 'past' behind them. There may still be fields to conquer.

C. Vocal Church Music
Motets, Elevations and Leçons de Ténèbres

We have noted that all Couperin's church music apart from the organ Masses is scored for solo voices and continuo, with or without obbligato instruments. It is therefore vocal chamber music to which the same general principles apply as are pertinent to the instrumental chamber music discussed above. Where no solo instruments are specified, the obbligato parts should usually be played on violins, one to a part, on the analogy of the Carissimi cantata. In the *Ste Suzanne* motet, for instance, the obbligato parts are superbly violinistic, and the interweaving of voices and violins creates a richly satisfying texture. But if flute and oboe are to hand they might well alternate with, or even double, the violins. Baroque flute would sigh exquisitely in the sarabande aria, if it were well played. (Raguenet in his *Parallèle* of 1702 points out that 'great artists' have 'taught the flute to groan after so moving a manner in our mournful airs, and to sigh so amorously in those that are tender'.) Today, one has to decide whether to opt for the flute's languishment or the violin's warmth, and either serves admirably. Baroque oboe can be employed in plaintive and even passionate contexts. Raguenet describes it as 'equally mellow and piercing', and recommends it for merry movements especially, either on its own or in duplication of the violins. Similarly a bassoon can give edge to the bass line. It works well in the first aria of the *Ste Suzanne* motet, in the soprano and tenor duet, and in the brief ensemble number.

Such considerations apply consistently to the motets and elevations composed during the last decade of the seventeenth century. In the *Versets* of 1703–8 Couperin still uses the term *Simphonie* to designate violins and string bass, but is more specific in his instructions about wind instruments. When he asks for *flûtes*, *flûtes à l'allemande*, *hautbois* and *basson* we should always obey his instructions, for the effects are carefully considered, not merely in the use of solo instruments, but in piquant doublings of the voices by flutes or oboes or both. Obviously the *Adolescentulus sum* of the 1703 *Versets* is inconceivable apart from Couperin's ethereal flutes and violins, with no bass instruments; but this is merely an extreme instance of Couperin's meticulousness. In the Italianate pieces either bass viol or cello may be used for the bass line; in the more French-styled *versets*, and still more in the *Leçons de Ténèbres*, bass viol is preferable. A chamber organ, such as Couperin had at Versailles, should normally be the continuo instrument, though he had no aesthetic objection to the use of harpsichord in ecclesiastical works.

The vocal parts offer problems, some of which apply to
baroque singing styles in general, others of which are peculiar to

the French tradition. It is difficult to reconcile the conflicting accounts of singing technique offered by contemporary theorists. In the seventeen-twenties Rameau said that in singing 'the principle of principles is to take pains to take no pains'. The remark may be tinged with Rousseauistic implications; none the less Rameau's assertion that complete technical control will enable the most rapid and awkward phrases to be sung without strain or forcing is certainly relevant to Couperin. Though Rameau doesn't explain how this is to be effected, it seems obvious that both head and chest voices, well supported from the diaphragm, are essential; only thus could 'roundness and dignity of tone' be allied with flexibility and agility. Some passages in baroque vocal music seem to have been more, not less, highly dramatized than was typical of later practice; and these passages had to embrace floridities executed with legerity and ease. As Robert Donington puts it, 'The cantabile never wavered, but the enunciation was incisive, especially the consonants, and full of both musical and verbal point.' It is in this context that the matter of vibrato becomes relevant. Extravagant vibrato would obliterate delicately virtuosic passage-work; yet with no vibrato declamatory vigour would be impossible. 'What passion cannot music raise and quell?', asked Dryden; and classical baroque composers and singers looked for a voice adequate to passion yet aware of the need therapeutically to 'quell'. This is much what Couperin was saying when he advocated a fusion of the French and the Italian *goûts* in order to achieve the perfection of music; and this is why singers and violinists have much to teach one another about the performance of Couperin.

The common view was that, as François Raguenet put it, 'The French in their airs aim at the soft, the easy, the flowing and the coherent. The Italians venture at everything that is harsh and out of the way, but they do it like people who have a right to venture and are sure of success. . . . As the Italians are naturally much more brisk than the French, so they are more sensible of the passions and consequently express them more lively in all their productions.' Couperin's violin style, we've suggested, was simultaneously conversational and lyrical, French and Italian; complementarily his vocal style calls simultaneously or near-simultaneously for what Bacilly, in his textbook of singing of 1668, terms a (French) *voix petite* and an (Italian) *voix grande*. The declamation in the *Leçons de Ténèbres* cannot be negotiated   325 without vibrato, yet the vocalises in the same works must sound bodiless; and the transitions between the two modes must be effected without obvious change of gear.

Couperin's vocal church music presents some problems of a peculiarly acute nature. His soprano parts, especially those written for Marguerite-Louise Couperin, are exceptionally high and agile; and even if the music is sung at Couperin's slightly lower pitch, the difficulty is not solved, since the problem lies in the consistently high tessitura of lines melodically fragile and rhythmically complex. This applies both to works in French vein, like the 1703 *Versets,* and to Italianate pieces like the *Ste Suzanne* motet or the *Regina coeli laetare.* Both call for Bacilly's *voix petite,* '*douce, nette et claire*', and '*touchante*' rather than '*brillante*' if they are to cope with the figuration convincingly. Yet the sexless tone appropriate for the vocalises of the *Leçons de Ténèbres* is not adequate; the voice must be capable both of the *mignardise* of the *air de cour* and of the clarity, even the opulence, of Italian bel canto. Perhaps the compromise was difficult to achieve even in Couperin's day; perhaps his cousin was exceptionally gifted. Certainly it's a tradition that singers of twenty or thirty years back seemed to have lost track of, for on the long-deleted Oiseau-Lyre recording of the 1703 *Versets* even such accomplished artists as Jennifer Vyvyan and Elsie Morison levitate in anguish rather than in ecstasy. Today, however, we seem to be breeding a new race of high-pitched, pure-toned, unwobbling, agile-larynxed sopranos who should be ideal for Couperin. Emma Kirkby is the most distinguished representative, though so far she has made only one Couperin disc, and that is a little disappointing.

The altitudinous tenor parts present a problem similar to that of the sopranos, though of more general implication since the high French tenor is recognized as a genus on his own, essential for a wide range of French music. What Couperin calls a *haute-contre* is a natural tenor with an exceptionally high tessitura. Most of the parts he wrote for Du Fours, his most celebrated haute-contre soloist, fall within the range of the English counter-tenor or male alto; but modern research suggests that the Purcellian counter-tenor was indistinguishable from the French haute-contre: both, that is, were natural tenors with high tessitura and unusual agility. On the Oiseau-Lyre recording referred to above the tenor William Herbert changes gear into falsetto for the upper reaches. Light but penetrative tenors who don't need to do this are now available, and it seems probable that there will be more of them, of better quality, as demand increases.

It is slightly surprising, since the tessitura of French vocal music tends to be light and airy, that the French were very proud of their bass soloists, who were capable of giving to gods or kings 'an air of majesty quite different from that of the feigned basses among the Italians, who have neither depth nor strength'. Thus François Raguenet in his *Parallèle des Italiens et des Français* of 1702; and although Couperin wasn't a composer much pre-occupied with gods or kings he has a few motets, such as the last two from the Tenbury group, which seem to call for this sonorous nobility: as Raguenet puts it, 'the air receives a stronger concussion from these deep voices than it doth from those that are higher and is consequently filled with a more agreeable and extensive harmony'. Couperin's bass parts need voices without wobble, dead on the note and sustained in line. Such basses are today not easy to come by, but perhaps they never were.

Couperin's recitative and arioso should be sung flexibly, but without losing sense of the measure. In this respect the recitative of motets and cantatas differed from that of operas 'qui tend à se rapprocher de la parole'. None the less it is essential that 'la mesure qu'on y remarque ne s'observe pas à la rigueur' (Lascassagne, 1766). Since Couperin's recitative tends to be more lyrical and cantabile than French operatic recitative, it may introduce a richer ornamentation, for the natural inflexions of speech are less dominant. The peculiar recitative that occurs before the final chorus of the *Motet de Ste Suzanne*, accompanied by bass line only, should probably be sung more freely than Couperin's fully accompanied arioso. 'Le ¢ servent pour les récitatifs, son mouvement est arbitraire et ce sont les paroles qui le déterminent.' (Choquel.) The conventional account of *operatic* recitative is probably applicable in this case: 'Les accompagnateurs sçavants ne suivent point de mesure dans le récitatif; il faut que l'oreille s'attache à la voix pour la suivre et fournir l'harmonie au chant qu'il débite tantôt légèrement tantôt lentement, de sorte que les croches deviennent quelquefois blanches et quelquefois les blanches deviennent croches par la célérité, selon l'enthousiasme et l'expression plus ou moins outrée des personnes qui chantent.' Here the rules governing *notes inégales* do not apply, the time values being determined by the words. In this passage, 327 therefore, more is dependent on the singer's improvisatory talents than is customary in Couperin; the point is important since this recitative can seem a dead patch in a work of exceptional grace and vivacity.

The chorus plays a minimal role in Couperin's church music. The Jubilemus in the *Motet de Ste Suzanne* suggests a choric intrusion and sounds jolly with a small number of concerted voices. But since it is scored for only three voices instead of four, it may be, and probably was, sung by the STB soloists, whose homophonic congruence sounds, in context, surprisingly vigorous and triumphant. Occasionally in the *Versets* Couperin marks passages with the word *tous*, as contrasted with the passages given to designated soloists. Presumably this implies a small consort of female voices, but they are not essential and, indeed, their music is no less delicate than that allocated to the soloists.

My introduction to Couperin's church music, in the late forties, was by way of a long obsolete French HMV disc of the *Leçons de Ténèbres* which employed soprano and contralto voices, with harpsichord and quite full-sounding strings supporting the organ. The music moved me deeply and was, indeed, my first awakening to Couperin's tragic dimension. Yet today that recording sounds grotesquely blatant, partly because of the full-blooded Italianate voices, partly because of an organ part that matches them in luxuriance, at times emulating a symphony orchestra. Interestingly, it is not merely the high-flown romantic performance of a past generation that may seem comically inept, for more or less contemporary with this recording is a very curious performance by Hugues Cuénod – probably the one that fired Stravinsky's enthusiasm for the music. Cuénod is, of course, a high French tenor who has made an important contribution to the art of singing in our time; and we cannot but admire his technique when, prompted perhaps by André-Jacques Villeneuve's contemporary comment that *leçons de ténèbres* should be sung very devoutly and very slowly, he takes Couperin's *Leçons* at a funereal pace and with total metrical rigidity. His powers of sostenuto are near miraculous, but as a revelation of the inner spirit of this introverted music this performance is no less grotesque than the pseudo-romantic one, though in a contrary direction. Among modern recordings that of Alfred Deller comes closest to the heart of the music. Admittedly, the *Leçons* were intended for female, not male, voices; and

Deller's unique voice would seem to have been a variant of the male English alto, rather than a counter-tenor in Purcell's sense or an haute-contre in Couperin's.* None the less Deller's distinctive timbre, piercing as an angelic trumpet, is magically appropriate to the music. We remember that among the original performers of the Charpentier *Leçons* was a nun described as an haute-contre or tenor; Deller's voice, sensual yet asexual, could be characterized as at once male and nun-like.

The likelihood is, however, that Couperin's *Leçons* were sung by a *voix petite* – to revert to Bacilly's terminology – of the type of Marguerite-Louise Couperin; if so, Emma Kirkby's performance must be pretty near the mark. Her vocalises float ethereally, the ornamentation sounding spontaneous and at the same time technically impeccable; though the recitatives need more bite and edge than she gives them. Kirkby's performance sounds historically valid and is always supremely musical; Deller's is perhaps of dubious authenticity, but has the incandescence of genius. The intensity he achieves is partly attributable to his partiality for long appoggiaturas, which his trumpet-like sonorities can sustain effectively.

Perhaps the most persuasive of extant recordings of Couperin's church music is the most recent in date: a version of five motets sung by Anna Maria Bondi and Nicole Fallien, with organ and bass viol continuo and two recorders as obbligato instruments in *Audite omnes*. Anna Bondi sings with exquisite purity of line, both in terms of intonation and of rhythm, and yet at the same time achieves roundness, even richness, of tone; especially in the fervent *O Jesu amantissime* she approaches the fusion of French and Italian styles, of the *voix petite* with the *voix grande*, which one ideally looks for in this music. The chamber

---

* The matter of 'English' counter-tenor and French haute-contre is still extremely puzzling, however. Deller himself always insisted that he was not a falsettist and that his alto voice was 'natural'. Yet he certainly had a normal if undistinguished baritone register which he occasionally used in consort work. This may cast doubt on the generally accepted view that Purcell was a natural haute-contre. We know that he sang several of the baritone solos in his works; and also that he executed the famous alto solo "Tis Nature's voice' 'with incredible graces'. Either he had two voices, one natural, one 'false', or he practised what is now known as Extended Vocal Technique. But Deller never claimed to do that! Some scholars now question whether Purcell was an alto at all, maintaining that the punctuation of the famous phrase 'sung, with incredible graces by Mr Purcell' could imply that the 'by' refers only to the graces, not the singing.

organ used is described on the sleeve as 'l'orgue historique de Rozay-en-Brie', though no further information is offered. It makes an agreeably pungent noise; and is located in Couperin country. The bass line is sometimes unnecessarily heavy.

D. Music for Harpsichord

Apart from Scarlatti and the Bach of the Italian Concerto and the Goldberg Variations, no composer has shown so comprehensive a mastery of harpsichord technique as Couperin; the variety of his methods of treating the instrument is commented on in Chapter 9 and in the Addendum on the harpsichord pieces. The instrument he was familiar with was in the tradition that stemmed from Flanders rather than from Italy. Italian harpsichords were well adapted to dance music since, although their tone is often remarkably sweet as well as full, their action produces an initially explosive 'pop', which swiftly decays. The French harpsichord, based on Flemish models, lacks the sharp ictus that marks the start of every note on an Italian instrument, and the tone, being gentler, more subtly coloured and more sustained, is beautifully responsive to the *mignardise* and sensibility favoured by the French court. There was a rough and ready parallel between the richness of Italian harpsichords and the ripeness of bel canto singing and of Corellian violin style, except for the fact the percussive harpsichord couldn't of its nature be lyrical: whereas the Flemish harpsichord 'spoke' intimately, as did the French *petite voix* and French fiddling. French harpsichord building, based on the Flemish models, reached an apex in the work of the Blanchet family and their successors, the Taskins – who survived long enough to build fortepianos as an alternative to, not as a substitute for, harpsichords.

When Couperin died in 1733 he owned a Blanchet which is fully representative. Normally such an instrument is equipped with two keyboards with 8-foot register, plus a 4-foot register on the lower manual. The plectra are of quill; but the tone can be varied by the operation of a buff stop – little pads of leather attached to a strip of wood which can be shifted so as to mute one of the sets of strings, producing a quasi-pizzicato, lute-like sound against which the oboe-like timbre of the upper 8 foot can ring effectively. Each of the two manuals has a different plucking point and therefore a different tone quality: round and mellow on the lower manual, more piercing on the upper. By means of a device whereby the upper manual can be slid back or the lower manual forward so as to engage pieces of wood known as 'coupler dogs', the two manuals can be linked; the keys of both will then play while only the lower are depressed. Considerable variety of colour is thus available; and Taskin augmented it when, in rebuilding Flemish harpsichords or designing his own, he incorporated a fourth set of jacks for the lower 8-foot strings, with plectra made of soft buffalo leather. These yield a dulcet tone not unlike that of early fortepianos.

Except for the *mains-croisées* pieces, Couperin's harpsichord music can be played on a single manual and does not call for large volume. The fragilely ornamented linear movements need resonance and the percussive pieces *dans le goût burlesque* call for bite; the pieces with bell and drone effects require an instrument rich in overtones. But even the grandest movements, notably the *Passacaille* and *L'Amphibie*, can make their sonorous effect without recourse to loud dynamics, for volume is relative and a clotted texture, heard in the context of much thin two-part writing, will seem louder than it is: just as the finale of Beethoven's 'Moonlight' Sonata, played on a fortepiano of 1815, sounds louder, because more frighteningly intractable, than it does when played on a plummy modern Steinway. When Couperin remarked that 'il faut surtout se rendre très délicat en claviers' he did not mean that the instrument ought to sound bland or tepid. While he would have been appalled by the hubbub of the 16-foot stop popularized on modern harpischords by Landowska, he relished the plangent overtones created by the relatively light stringing of his instrument, and also the gradation of timbres between mellow and nasal which was readily available, even without recourse to special effects like the *peau de buffle*. There is a broad parallel between the 'colours' of Couperin's harpsichord and those of the French classical organ; and, hardly surprisingly, there's a ratio between Couperin's harpsichord and the French classical organ on the one hand, and on the other hand a late-nineteenth-century grand piano and a romantic organ.

Forty years ago Bach and Scarlatti were still frequently played on the piano. Harpsichordists were then a comparatively rare breed, and omnivorous pianists naturally wanted to play on their 331 instrument music as universally great as Bach's and as technically exciting as Scarlatti's, even though Bach's emotional range and Scarlatti's virtuosic wit and drama were inseparable from the qualities of the keyboard instrument they wrote for. Even in those days, however, Couperin was seldom played on the piano; the genius of his music was recognized as being inherent in the sounds of a plucked rather than a hammered string keyboard, and on such instruments Couperin's harpsichord music was played, if it was played at all. In the post-Dolmetsch years the revival of the harpsichord prospered; but makers understandably aimed at the creation of a mechanized lute that would be sturdy enough to function in the normal conditions of concert promotion. The Pleyel instrument on which Landowska used to play Couperin bears no more relation to his own harpsichord than does a modern Steinway or Bosendorfer to Beethoven's Graf. It was the Landowska 78 rpm recordings of Couperin that first captured my imagination. Being performances of genius, not just talent, they still enthrall us today; but no one would play the pieces on such an instrument nowadays, when all responsible harpsichordists know much about the instruments for which Couperin composed, and when mechancially expert replicas of them are available. And no one would doubt – certainly not Landowska, could she hear them – that through the medium of these instruments Couperin's essence may be best distilled.

These famous Landowska 78s are still available, dubbed on to an LP; dating back to 1930 and 1934, they come up fresh as daisies. ★ At first, listening to them today, one winces a little at the metallic penetration of the instrument's timbre and at the fussiness of the registration; the sheer poetry of the performances, however, soon carries all before it. And not merely the poetry: for what most impresses, after fifty years, is the seemingly inevitable 'rightness' of the proportions, of the rubato and of the ornamentation. How impeccable is the equilibrium between freedom and rigour in Landowska's handling of the noble *La Favorite* and the tragic *Passacaille*; with what sensitivity she weaves the tendrils of the vine through pastoral pieces like *Les Langueurs-Tendres* or

---

★ But this mechanically excellent reissue is lumbered with an irritatingly ignorant sleeve-note, thirty years out of date and condescending alike to Couperin and to his public, including you and me – while Landowska's always illuminating and often beautiful programme notes are deleted!

Les Bergeries, so that the radiance of the tune shines through the embroideries on it; how corporeally vigorous she makes *Les Moissonneurs*; how tantalizingly immediate is her *Le Moucheron*; how vivaciously antic are her pieces dans *le goût burlesque*, such as *Les Calotins et les Calotines*; how lugubrious are the drones of her hurdy-gurdies and how piquant the squeaks of her fifes and pipes in the rustic musettes and the urban gallivantings of her beggars, acrobats, jugglers, and monkeys. Sometimes she even convinces us that her sophistications of registration reveal the essence of the music: her *Sœur Monique*, the melody poised yet vacillating, smiles with an innocence at once virginal and seductive; her love-sick nightingale sounds as naturalistic as the warbling bird, and at the same time as preciously affected as the human bird the music also emulates. Most of all *Les Vergers Fleüris* fuses its dreamy registration with malleabilities of rhythm to evoke a paradise existent in the rural present and at the same time in magical Cytherea.★ After all these years I still find that these records are the best possible initiation into the heart of Couperin's art; no other performances bring his world so vividly alive in a past that is also an eternal present. Moreover, as the titles referred to above make clear, it would be difficult to conceive of a selection of Couperin's harpsichord pieces more representative of his range and depth. Even the occasional oddity – like the slow tempo for the benevolent cuckoos in what is *in toto* a profoundly witty *and* pathetic performance of *Les Folies Françoises* – makes its point in context. One ends up with the conviction that in the long run genius always serves a composer better than talent, however assiduous.

But of course this doesn't mean that knowledge gained the hard way, rather than by instinct, is to be despised. Landowska knew a great deal; but validated her knowledge in the fires of creation – which is not always the case with the knowledgeable. A number of 'complete' recordings of Couperin's harpsichord pieces have been made, the first of them by Landowska's pupil Ruggiero Gerlin. This has long been deleted; but contained

---

★ I suspect that Landowska's performance of this piece has coloured my response to it, down the years. I've never heard anyone play it as she did; most people take the musette section faster, as raucous peasant music. I still think Landowska's romantic ideality is inherent in the music, and that her performance is *precisely* on the mark.

magical moments in the authentic Landowska tradition. Gerlin too played a fierce Pleyel harpsichord that was certainly not authentic Couperin: whereas the four extant complete recordings all use period instruments, or copies of them. The brilliant version by the young American harpsichordist Scott Ross is not available in this country; neither is the version of Laurence Boulay. The two readily available versions are, however, both admirable; the earlier, by Kenneth Gilbert, was recorded between 1969 and 1972, the later, by Blandine Verlet, appeared in 1979–81.

Gilbert plays a harpsichord built in 1968 by the Boston maker Hubbard: an exact copy of an instrument designed by the Parisian builder Henry Hemsch, in 1750. It has the customary two 8-foot and one 4-foot stops. The sleeve-note points out that its 'conception is quite different from that of modern instruments', in that its 'light frame and exceptionally resonant sound-board give it the deep sonority of the old instruments'. The instrument is tuned slightly below modern pitch and in unequal temperament, to a formula recommended in his *Dictionnaire de la Musique* by Jean-Jacques Rousseau. It is not clear whether this tuning is used consistently throughout the *ordres*; this seems improbable, for technical reasons I shall be discussing later. As a whole Gilbert's performances reveal how a scholarly attention to authenticity may be fertile soil for musical creativity to sprout in. Before I heard his recordings I had, inspired by Landowska, loved Couperin's harpsichord music deeply, but had not fully appreciated the relationship between its range and depth and the sonorities available on a contemporary instrument.

Blandine Verlet's recording is no less sonorously seductive. For the early *ordres* she plays a superbly restored 'original' by Pierre Donzelague, now the property of the Musée Lyonnais. The virtues of the instrument, in relation to Couperin's music, are comparable with those of the harpsichord Gilbert uses; since its date is 1716 rather than 1750 it is still closer to the source. For her performance of the later suites Verlet uses a Blanchet copied by Derek Porteus, whose researches covered an investigation of the materials originally used for strings, as well as quills. Verlet employs a tuning advocated by Rameau in 1726, a date more or less contemporary with the Couperin pieces. The major thirds are true and the minor thirds and fifths less wolf-infested than was often the case. The sounds made by the instrument are beautiful, and slightly startling: plangent yet at the same time precise, even to the point of pain. Listening to this instrument we confront the immediate 'reality' of Couperin's music and cannot suspect it of old-world charm.

The American harpsichordist Alan Curtis also recorded his three-disc album on a Blanchet, this time an original which might even be the 'large harpsichord, mounted on a stand of varnished wood, value 300 livres' that Couperin owned at his death – for a Blanchet daughter married Couperin's nephew, Armand-Louis. The instrument has the same clarity of line and pungent articulation as characterizes the one used by Verlet, though it is – or appears to be as Curtis plays it – less subtle in variety of sonority. Both Curtis and Verlet demonstrate how intimately *notes inégales* are associated with the mechanical functioning of a contemporary harpsichord. The fingers – which are servants of the ears which are lackeys of the mind and senses – flow into them with instinctive inevitability. A minor asset is offered in the rapidity of articulation: the repeated octaves in Curtis's *Le Réveil-matin* sound at once alarming and hilarious.

Raphael Puyana uses for his selective recordings an instrument originally built, in Amsterdam in 1646, by the most famous of the Flemish masters, Andreas Ruckers. Such instruments became fashionable in seventeenth-century France; and eighteenth-century French builders enlarged and modified Ruckers's work. The instrument Puyana plays was 'rémis à ravalement par Pascal Taskin, Facteur de Clavecins et Garde des Instruments de la Musique du Roi'. Taskin, most celebrated of Parisian builders, made a new wrestplank and new keyboards, widened the case and added 10 centimetres to the soundboard. He also put in an 8-foot *peau de buffle* and added knee levers to change the stops – a device of his invention, which postdates Couperin. The limewood case and spruce soundboard are in the Flemish tradition, but the disposition is French, and typical of Couperin. So the instrument has a mid-seventeenth-century source and a mid-eighteenth-century apotheosis: a compromise appropriate to Couperin, whose art is both retrospective and prophetic. Puyana ravishingly exploits the instrument's potential, reconciling scholarship with the inspirational poetry characteristic of his teacher, Landowska. He takes more risks than do Gilbert and Verlet, but often justifies them.

From all the recordings referred to above, and from others, it 335 is clear that well-restored contemporary instruments or modern copies of them can alone do justice to Couperin's harpsichord music. From some of these instruments it is also evident that equal temperament is not the best tuning for Couperin's or, indeed, for most baroque music. When we say that two tones are 'in tune' with one another we mean that they are in 'just' intonation, based on the cycle of perfect fifths (ratio of 3 over 2). Just intonation remains feasible so long as music is vocal and monophonic, and the sound of melodies built from pure intervals can be a *tonic* to our jaded ears. But since God's cycle of perfect fifths curiously turns out to be imperfect (the upward and downward cycles do not exactly coincide, being separated by the notorious Comma of Didymus), 'true' tuning has always, throughout the centuries, had to be 'tempered' to some degree in any music polyphonically and harmonically conceived. The decisive change was inseparable from the evolution of keyboard instruments, which are palpably harmonic in that their simultaneous combinations of tones are patent to the eyes and tactile to the fingers as well as audible to the ears.

Up to well after 1700 variable tunings were employed. Mean tone was not a closed system like equal temperament, but rather a means whereby major thirds could be preserved in sweet perfection because minor thirds and fifths were – at best just over five cents – flat; the precise proportions were variable. Mean-tone tuning works with most seventeenth-century music; and on the whole keyboard composers were prepared to stomach the 'bad' triads because the 'good' ones were so beautiful. Indeed, they learned how to exploit the badness of bad intervals for expressive effect, modifying the intervals either in a sharpwards or a flatwards direction. We have noted that F sharp minor, the lutenists' *ton de la chèvre*, became, through its 'bad' intervals, associated with abnormal, perhaps even supernatural, states; and that at the opposite pole F minor was associated with death and darkness as much for its tuning problems as for its darkly flat appearance. Marc-Antoine Charpentier's description of F minor as 'obscur et plaintif' is echoed by conservative Burney who, although regretting the key's out-of-tuneness 'as it is usually tempered', thought that 'these crude chords may add to the melancholy of the composition'. Roger North, in 1726, offers a 'scientific' explanation for sharpwards and flatwards imperfections:

336

The defects will fall in the use of some keys, such as F with a flat
third, B natural with a sharp third, and F sharp with either sharp or
flat third, and some others, by mere out-of-tuneness, have certain
characters, very serviceable to the various purposes of Musick: as,
to instance in one for all, F with a flat third hath somewhat that
more resembles a dolorous melancholy than any of the rest, and so
others, in severall manners, well known to composers.

It will be observed that Burney, a modernist and perfectionist,
takes the view that bad intervals *are* bad, but that one must make
the best of them. Yet although later baroque composers, codifying tonality along with every other element of composition,
were irked by the bad intervals and sought ever more complex
compromises to temper them, they did not entirely abandon the
lutenists' distinctions between 'sharp' tunings, appropriate to
animated, ecstatic or anguished states, and 'flat' tunings, appropriate to moods gentle, passive or lugubrious. Kuhnau's Biblical
Sonata on the story of David and Goliath exploits the falsity of
false relations, much savager in his tuning than in equal temperament, as a dramatic device; even Bach's well-tempered clavier is
not equal tempered, but rather correctly tempered, on principles
arrived at empirically by Werkmeister and Kirkberger, to meet
the experiential need. The tuning appropriate to one group of
keys (and range of experience) is not suited to another. In equal
temperament every interval is slightly and equally 'chipped', so
that none is *damagingly* out of, but none is precisely in, tune.
Since there can be no distinctions between 'good' and 'bad'
intervals, all keys must sound alike: so any associations we make
between different equally tempered keys and different emotional
states must be psychologically subjective, and are probably conditioned by the association of particular keys with particular
compositions. In Couperin's tunings, on the other hand, and
probably in most of Bach's, different keys really do possess
different aural and therefore emotional properties. The matter is
exhaustively discussed in J. Murray Barbour's *Tuning and Temperament*, to which the reader is referred. Having sifted the
evidence, however, Barbour curiously decides that equal temperament is best for Bach and Couperin because it is in the long
run the least inconvenient method. In a sense this is true, and no
one would gainsay the advantages that equal temperament
brought to later, tonally more complex music. None the less the
decision seems to me cravenly evasive, and extremely dubious in   337

reference to early works of Bach like the F sharp minor Toccata, which is emasculated by having its tonal anomalies ironed out. Couperin's dates coincide with Bach's earlier years, and interior evidence suggests that in planning his *ordres* as wholes the composer decided on a tuning appropriate to each. Some of these tunings would entail a greater degree of compromise than others; in each case the degree would be apposite to the mood as well as the mode of the music. Today a responsible harpsichordist cannot ignore this problem. There is now no shortage of published material about tuning, and the articles in the *New Grove* are both clear and approachable. Far more important, however, is the evidence of the player's own ears as, having digested the sources, he puts theory into practice.

If Couperin used slightly different tunings for different *ordres* this suggests that, at least in the later books, he intended them to be played as wholes. Of course the pieces may be played separately, since each, however miniature, is finely structured. None the less they reflect on and illuminate one another, and their sequence, especially in the third and fourth books, is not arbitrary. The B minor *ordre* about the Regent (or Dauphin?) is only an extreme example of a general tendency; though the relationship of the pieces to one another is not evolutionary, like the movements of a Beethoven sonata, their sequence sometimes tells a story and usually implies psychological relationships, if not progression. The more one listens to and plays the *ordres* as entities the more their range impresses. Related to this is the matter of repeats. Kenneth Gilbert always plays them, and rightly so, for without them the architectural symmetry of Couperin's music and his world is impaired, and the time scale is too hurried. Couperin's music needs time for reflection – as more sublimely does Bach's in the Goldberg Variations, in which the repeats should be obligatory.

Just as some of Couperin's concerted works may alternatively be played on the harpsichord, so some of his harpsichord pieces may be played on other instruments. The linear nature of his keyboard writing translates readily into terms of wind instruments. The crossed hand pieces on two keyboards and other popular dances sound delightful on flute, recorder, oboe and bassoon in varying combinations: as Couperin liberally puts it, 'Elles sont propres à deux flûtes, ou Hautbois, ainsy que pour deux Violons, deux Violes, et autres instrumens à l'unisson.' *La*

Julliet 'se peut jouer sur différens instrumens. Mais encore sur deux clavecins ou Epinettes; savoir, le sujet avec la basse, sur l'un; et la mesme Basse avec la contre-partie, sur l'autre. Ainsi des autres pièces qui pouront se trouver en trio.' He also suggests that 'Le Rossignol réussit sur la Flûte Traversière ou ne peut pas mieux, quand il est bien joué'. His condition is interesting, for this piece calls for a Landowska-like subtlety of nuance if it is to reveal the paradox whereby it sounds simultaneously as 'natural' as the carolling nightingale and as 'artificial' as the human bird who prinks in an eighteenth-century salon.

In general Couperin, like Bach, is a linear composer, a draughtsman who is interested in tone colour as a means of making his linear structure clear, as were the great painters of the era, from Poussin and Claude to Watteau and Chardin. This does not alter the fact that there is a specific and sensuously beautiful tone colour implicit in Couperin's textures; we have noted how, when he writes for harpischord, his linearity is revealed through the rich resonances his instrument offered. But as with Bach, when the tone colours appropriate to a group of lines have been decided on, they should normally be adhered to throughout the piece. Fidgetiness of registration is no more relevant than dynamic gradations; and although oppositions of forte and piano may occasionally be used, especially in repeats, their function is architectural rather than dramatic. That Couperin had expressive intentions is implicit in the adjectival and adverbial indications of mood and tempo he gives, as well as in his titles. These intentions, as we have noted, affect phrasing, ornamentation and conventions of inequality, but they do not imply a romantic aesthetic.

Appendices

Appendix A

THE AUTHORSHIP OF THE ORGAN MASSES

The evidence pro and contra in the case for Couperin le Grand's authorship of the organ masses is given in detail in an appendix to Julien Tiersot's *Les Couperins*, and in the preface to the old Oiseau-Lyre edition of the works. On the contemporary engraved title-pages to the manuscript copies, the masses are described as being by 'François Couperin, Sieur de Crouilly, organiste de St Gervais'. The one-time conventional ascription of the works to the first François Couperin depended on two assumptions: one, that he was the Couperin who bore the title of Sieur de Crouilly; the other, that he was organist of St Gervais in 1690, when the masses were prepared for publication.

The researches of Pirro, Bouvet, Tessier, and of M. Tiersot himself have proved that the title of Sieur de Crouilly was one to which none of the Couperins had any legitimate right. There is no evidence at all that the elder François ever used it, and the identification of him with the Couperin of the organ masses dates from no earlier than the nineteenth century. There is no direct evidence that the younger François used the title either, though there is a contemporary document referring to 'Marie Guérin, veuve de Charles Couperin, sieur de Crouilly', and it would have been natural enough if François had taken over the title from his father. If it be asked why François never used the title subsequently, the obvious answer is that a few years later, probably in 1696, he acquired a legitimate title from Louis, and so was able to sign himself 'le comte Couperin'. Significantly, the old title reappears in the name of one of his last clavecin pieces, *La Croûilli ou la Couperinéte*, possibly a portrait of his daughter, or an evocation of his childhood, or both.

As for the second and more important point, there is again no evidence that the elder François was ever organist of St Gervais. A passage from the contemporary chronicler Titon du Tillet suggests that the second François, young as he was, had the post 343 reserved for him for a while, until he was old enough to succeed to his father:

> François Couperin avait des dispositions si grandes qu'en peu de temps il devint excellent organiste et fut mis en possession de l'orgue qu'avait eu son père.

That the post was so reserved for the young François is put beyond doubt by a document discovered by Paul Brunold, and published in his book on the organ of St Gervais. This proves irrefutably that La Lande was appointed deputy organist, during the interim period, in addition to his two other Parisian churches. The relevant portion of this document is worth quoting:

> Convention Messieurs les Marguilliers St Gervais pour l'orgue . . . lesquels mettant en consideration les longs services que le feu Charles Couperin et auparavant luy, feu son frère, ont rendus en qualité d'organistes de ladite Eglise, et desirant conserver à François Couperin son fils cette place jusqu'à ce qu'il ait atteint l'âge de dix-huit ans et qu'il soit en estat de rendre luy même son service en ladite année et ladite qualité Lesquels Sieurs Marguilliers ont choisy et retenu Michel de La Lande organiste demeurt rue Bailleul, Lequel par ces fins et souz les conditions cy aprez, s'est obligé et s'oblige par ces présentes envers lesdites SSr Marguilliers de jouer de ladite orgue dans tous les cours desdites années et jusqu'au dit tems . . . Ceque ledit La Lande a accepté.

The document goes on to refer to a pension given to Couperin and his mother during the period of La Lande's tenure, and establishes the fact that occupation of the St Gervais organist's house was a legalized privilege of the Couperins at this time, even though La Lande was organist. There is reasonably definite evidence that Couperin took over the duties of St Gervais in his eighteenth year. This was in 1685. It is certain that Couperin le Grand was organist in 1690, when he applied for a *privilège du Roi* to publish his organ masses. This document gives Couperin de Crouilly's address as 'rue de Monceau, proche l'Eglise'; furthermore the Carpentras manuscript also gives the rue de Monceau address. We have seen that the younger François had been living here with his mother ever since his father's death, 344 and we know that the elder François can never have been official organist at St Gervais, nor have lived in the traditional home of the St Gervais organists, since the document concerning La Lande's temporary appointment leaves no period of tenure unaccounted for. A small point of interest is that La Lande, in a written tribute to the excellence of the organ masses and their suitability for publication, omits the title of Sieur de Crouilly altogether. Taking it all round, it seems to me that there is no positive evidence whatever to support the attribution of the masses to the elder François. It cannot be more than a hypothesis, and a singularly perverse one, for all the known facts point to François le Grand.

Presumably the hypothesis was made only because the music of the masses seemed too mature to be the work of a young man. But on artistic grounds, as we have seen, the masses provide just the evidence we need to complete our account of Couperin's evolution. One would not expect music of such fine quality to come from the pen of an obscure musician who seems to have written nothing else, and never to have been referred to by his contemporaries as a creative artist.★ On the other hand, the masses are just the kind of music one would expect to be written by a young composer of genius, *coming at the end of a great and long tradition*. It is just possible to believe that someone else might have written the chromatic elevation of the *Messe Solemnelle*, since this technique occasionally leads other composers to create a rather Couperin-like texture and harmony. But it is not possible to believe that any other composer could have written the *Qui tollis* from the *Messe pour les Convents*; and we have observed how Couperin did not discard, but substantially modified, this idiom as he grew older.

Both on factual and on artistic grounds one can thus have no hesitation in regarding the masses as the first work of Couperin le Grand; and one by no means unworthy of his later accomplishment. For further details see the extensive preface to the new Oiseau-Lyre edition.

★ Titon du Tillet says of him: 'Le second des trois frères Couperin s'appeloit François; il n'avoit pas les mesmes talens que ses deux frères de jouer de l'orgue et du Clavecin, mais il avoit celui de montrer les Pièces de clavecin *de ses deux frères* avec une netteté et une facilité très grande. C'étoit un petit homme qui aimoit fort le bon vin.'

Appendix B

THE ORGANISTS OF ST GERVAIS

Antoine de Roy, 1545–1546.
Simon Bismant, ?–1599.
Robert du Buisson, 1599–1629.
Du Buisson fils, 1629–1653.
Louis Couperin, 1653–1661.
Charles Couperin, 1661–1679.
Michel de La Lande, 1679–1685.
François Couperin, 1685–1733.
Nicolas Couperin (son of François Couperin the elder), 1733–1748.
Armand-Louis Couperin (son of Nicolas Couperin), 1748–1789.
Pierre-Louis Couperin (son of Armand-Louis Couperin), 1789.
Gervais-François Couperin (younger son of Armand-Louis Couperin), 1789–1826.

Appendix C

LORD FITZWILLIAM AND THE FRENCH CLAVECIN COMPOSERS

In writing this book I have consulted the copies of the original editions of Couperin's *L'Art de toucher le Clavecin* and of the first two books of clavecin pieces which are in the library of the Fitzwilliam Museum, Cambridge. Classical French music is fairly well represented in Lord Fitzwilliam's collection: he bought the magnificent contemporary editions of La Lande's motets and of many operas of Lully and Rameau; while of the French clavecin school he acquired, in addition to the Couperin, volumes of Marchand, Dieupart, Duphly, and the Amsterdam edition of Gaspard le Roux. His library also includes a volume of clavecin pieces by Froberger published after his death; and there are manuscript pieces of Duphly and Nivers in Fitzwilliam's exercise books. Most of the volumes bear Fitzwilliam's signature on the title-page, together with the date on which he bought them during his continental travels. They were mostly acquired between 1766 and 1772.

I have already briefly discussed the musical significance of the four Duphly volumes, which are bound together, in the chapter on Couperin's influence. They have, however, an additional historical interest in that Duphly appears, from the evidence of an exercise book in the library, to have been Fitzwilliam's composition and harpsichord teacher. The volumes were presented to Fitzwilliam *de la part de l'auteur*; and on the fly-leaf of the first book are written some comments on fingering in what appears to be Fitzwilliam's hand, signed by Duphly. It is interesting to compare these remarks with Couperin's comments on fingering in the *Art de toucher le Clavecin*. Both writers stress the importance of an easy and natural finger action, of *douceur de toucher*, and of a good legato; and both advocate the principle of finger substitution. We may note that even in 1755 – or later if the inscription postdates publication – Duphly still shows the traditional distrust of the thumb and fifth finger. I quote the inscription in full:

Du Doigter

La Perfection du Doigter consiste en général dans un mouvement doux, léger et régulier.

Le mouvement des doigts se pend à leur racine: c'est à dire à la jointure qui les attache à la main.

Il faut que les doigts soient courbés naturellement, et que chaque doigt ait un mouvement propre et indépendant des autres doigts. Il faut que les doigts tombent sur les touches et non qu'ils les frappent: et de plus qu'ils coulent de l'une à l'autre en se succedant: c'est à dire, qu'il ne faut quitter une touche qu'après en avoir pris une autre. Ceci regarde particulièrement le jeu françois.

Pour continuer un roulement, il faut s'accoutumer à passer le pouce pardessous tel doigt que ce soit, et à passer tel autre doigt par-dessus le pouce. Cette manière est excellente surtout quand il se rencontre des dièses et des bémols: alors faites en sorte que le pouce se trouve sur la touche qui précède le dièse ou le bémol, ou placez-le immédiatement après. Par ce moyen vous vous procurerez autant de doigt de suite que vous aurez de notes à faire.

Eviter, autant qu'il se pourra, de toucher du pouce ou du cinquième doigt une touche blanche,★ surtout dans les roulemens de vitesse.

Souvent on exécute un même roulement avec les deux mains dont les doigts se succèdent consécutivement. Dans ces roulemens les mains passent l'une sur l'autre. Mais il faut observer que le son de la première touche sur laquelle passe une des mains soit aussi lié au son précédent que s'ils étaient touchés de la même main.

Dans le genre de musique harmonieux et lié, il est bon de s'accoutumer à substituer un doigt à la place d'un autre sans relever la touche. Cette manière donne des facilités pour l'exécution et prolonge la durée des sons.

Here the passages about legato in *le jeu françois* and about finger substitution in *le genre harmonieux et lié* would seem to be derived directly or indirectly from Couperin.

In view of Fitzwilliam's enthusiasm for French clavecin music it seemed worth while investigating whether the French composers, and Couperin in particular, left any imprint on his own amateur efforts at composition. But the earliest examples of his work I was able to find date from 1781; and while he copies out in the back of the volume a piece of Duphly (*La Victoire*) and a dance of Rameau, along with pieces by Purcell, Handel and D.

★ i.e. a sharp or flat on eighteenth-century French keyboards.

Scarlatti, his own style is by that date unambiguously Handelian. The only French element is an occasional hint of the styles of the Lullian overture and march, both of which he could have found in the music of Handel himself. One imagines that any pieces Fitzwilliam may have written in the seventeen-sixties would have been more in the harmonic manner of Duphly than in the linear style of Couperin. The rapid dominance of the Handelian fashion over Fitzwilliam's work suggests how completely the anglicized Handel routed the French – and for that matter the native English – tradition. As Handelian exercises, Fitzwilliam's pieces are competent and agreeable.

Appendix D

ON THE TEMPO OF THE EIGHTEENTH-CENTURY DANCE MOVEMENTS

The contemporary statement of tempi which is most closely relevant to Couperin's work is that of Michel d'Affilard, who based his primitive metronomic system on the earlier work of Sauveur. The tables which he published in 1705 may be summed up as follows:

Meter	Dance	Tempo
¢	Marche	♩ = 120
C		♩ = 72
2	Gavotte Rigaudon Bourrée Air gaye	♪ = 120
	Pavane	♪ = 90
3	Sarabande en rondeau	♩ = 88
	Passacaille	♩ = 106
	Chaconne	♩ = 156
	Menuet	♩. = 70
3:2	Sarabande	♩ = 72
	Air tendre	♩ = 80
	Air grave	♩ = 48
	Courante	♩ = 90
3:8	Passepied	♩. = 84
	Gigue	♩. = 116
	Air léger	♩. = 116
6:4	Sarabande	♩ = 133
	Marche	♩ = 150
	Air grave	♩ = 120
6:8	Canarie	♩. = 106
	Menuet	♩. = 75
	Gigue	♩. = 100

M. Eugène Borrel has interestingly compared these metronome marks with those of later theorists. On the whole their statements show a remarkable uniformity:

		AFFILARD 1705	LACHAPELLE	ONZEMBRY 1732	CHOQUEL 1762
Bourrée	♩	120	120	112–120	..
Chaconne	♩	156	120	156	..
Gavotte	♩	120	152	96	126
Gigue	♩.	116–120	120	112	120
Menuet	♩.	72–76	..	78	80
Passepied	♩.	84	..	100	92
Rigaudon	♩	120	152	116	126
Sarabande	♩	66–72–84	63	78	..
or	♩				

All the above figures are correlated with Maelzel's metronome.

Quantz, in his *Versuch einer Anweisung die Flöte traversiere zu spielen* of 1752, estimates tempi by the simple method of pulse-beats. His account of the French dance movements is as follows:

Entrée, Loure and Courante (played pompously, the bow being lifted for each crotchet): one pulsation for each crotchet.

Sarabande: same tempo as above, but played more smoothly.

Chaconne: one pulsation for two crotchets, played pompously.

Passacaille: slightly quicker than the Chaconne.

Musette: one pulsation for each crotchet in 3 : 4 time, or each quaver in 3 : 8.

Furie: one pulsation for two crotchets.

Bourrée and Rigaudon: one pulsation for a bar.

Gavotte: slightly slower than Rigaudon.

Gigue and Canarie: one pulsation for every bar.

Menuet (played with rather heavy, but short bowing): one pulsation for two crotchets.

Passepied: slightly quicker than Menuet.

Tambourin: slightly quicker than the Bourrée.

Marche (alla breve): two pulsations to a bar.

According to Schering, one of Quantz's pulse-beats equals about 80 on Maelzel's metronome. This gives the following table, which may be compared with those of the French theorists cited above:

Entrée, Loure, Courante, Sarabande	♩ = 80
Chaconne	♩ = 160
Passacaille	♩ = 180
Musette	♩ = 80
Furie, Bourrée, Rigaudon	♩ = 160
Gavotte	♩ = 120
Gigue, Canarie	♩ = 160

Menuet	$\bullet = 160$
Passepied, Tambourin	$\bullet$ or $\bullet\!\!\!\!\vert = 180$
Marche	$\bullet = 80$

Georg Muffat, in his *Premières Observations sur la manière de jouer les Airs de Balets à la Françoise selon la Méthode de feu Monsieur de Lully*, has some illuminating comments on the general significance of tempo indications in the classical age. According to him the sign **C** indicates four slowish beats in a bar – a largo or adagio movement, certainly not faster than andante, since if the speed quickens one would beat two in a bar and use a different time signature.

The sign 2 indicates two slowish beats in a bar, or sometimes four quick ones. It is used for a quiet allegro or flowing andante, but does not suggest a precipitate movement. Sometimes, in overtures, it may have a somewhat maestoso character: but an overture in 2 time is faster than one marked **₵**.

The sign **₵** indicates two quickish beats in a bar. Muffat implies that it is quicker than 2 time, though not all the theorists agree with him. No hard and fast rule can be decided on; composers seem to use the two signs indiscriminately in gavottes, bourrées and rigaudons, for instance, and the precise speed of each piece will depend on its character. Muffat's view of the two time signatures seems, however, to be supported by works in which the two signatures occur within the same movement, as they often do in overtures. Here the change from 2 to **₵** seems to imply a change to a faster tempo.

The sign 3 : 2 indicates 'un mouvement fort lent'. Its character is largo and maestoso rather than adagio.

The sign 3 : 4 covers considerable variety of tempi. It is always less slow than 3 : 2, but still 'un peu grave' in sarabandes and airs; 'plus gaye' in rondeaux; and gayer still in courantes, minuets and the fugue sections of overtures. In gigues and canaries it is very quick indeed. This account applies directly to Couperin's earlier work; in his later pieces he often employs the 3 : 4 sign in a *sarabande grave*, where Lully would have used 3 : 2.

Thus Muffat: but we cannot take his statements about the relative pace of 3 : 2 and 3 : 4 as definitive, since for many authorities in several countries 3 : 2, though majestic, seems to imply a slightly faster speed than (some) 3 : 4s. This may be because it is a survival of archaic alla breve notation which, as the word breve indicates, was originally quick. In general, it will be obvious from the lists above that authorities often contradict one another, even when writing at much the same date. For Michel d'Affilard a chaconne is faster than a passacaglia, whereas for Quantz a passacaglia is faster than a chaconne. Here as elsewhere there may be confusion between the tempo of the dance as danced and as played in relatively 'pure' music. Many attempts have been made to establish precise distinctions between a chaconne and a passacaglia; none of them convinces. Perhaps it is fortunate that theorists cannot always provide answers to musicological problems; if they did, we might think we knew all the answers, which is death to a musician. As things are, in the last resort, and usually considerably before that, we have to rely on the *bon goût* relevant to each musical event.

Appendix E

GEORG MUFFAT ON BOWING, PHRASING, AND ORNAMENTATION IN FRENCH INSTRUMENTAL MUSIC

Georg Muffat's *Premières Observations sur la manière de jouer les Airs de Balets à la Françoise selon la Méthode de feu Monsieur de Lully* gives a detailed and revealing account of Lully's techniques of performance. Couperin's *Concerts Royaux* are directly in the Lully tradition; so Muffat's comments on bowing may be taken as relevant to the performance of Couperin's concerted music also.

I

The rules about bowing may be summarized as follows:

1. The first note of each bar, when it falls on the beat, is taken on the down bow, *whatever its length*. This is the fundamental rule, on which most of the others depend. It is what principally distinguishes the French technique from the Italian, adding a more accentual emphasis to the dance movement.

2. In *Tems Imparfait* (binary time), of all the notes that divide the bar into equal parts the odd numbers are taken on the down bow, the even numbers on the up. The rule applies in triple time to notes of lesser value than the lower note of the time signature (i.e. to crotchets, quavers and semiquavers in 3 : 2 time). This rule is not modified by the substitution of rests for notes.

3. In *Tems Parfait* (triple time), when the tempo is slow, the first beat is taken on the down bow, the second on the up and the third on the down. The first beat of the next bar follows on the down bow again, in accordance with rule 1. But at faster tempi the second and third beats of each bar are elided on the up bow, in order to secure 'plus de facilité'.

4. In 6 : 8, 9 : 8 and 12 : 8 time (or 6 : 4, 9 : 4 and 12 : 4) the bar is divided into two, three or four groups of three notes, each

group being treated in accordance with rule 3. If there is a rest on the first beat, the second note of the group is taken on the down bow, the third on the up.

5. Several successive notes, each of which lasts a complete bar, are all taken on the down bow. In 6 : 8 or 12 : 8 successive dotted crotchets are taken on alternate down and up bows. Dotted crotchets in 9 : 8 follow the first part of rule 3.

6. Equal notes syncopated are taken on alternate down and up bows.

7. When notes of unequal value occur in the same bar, groups of notes of the same value are taken on alternate down and up bows. In fast tempi a crotchet followed by two quavers may adopt the principle of the second part of rule 3; the crotchet is then taken on the down bow, the two quavers being elided on the up. Rests count as notes of the same value.

8. In groups of three notes in dotted (siciliano) rhythm, the short note is taken on the up beat, the two longer notes on the down.

9. Single notes interspersed with rests are taken on alternate down and up bows.

10. A short note before the strong beat is always taken on the up bow. Any note following a syncopated note is elided on the up bow.

To the above rules, there are the following exceptions:

1. In courantes, owing to the animation of the movement, the first note of the second group of three may, 'par manière de licence', be taken on the up bow, providing that the first beat of the bar is always on the down.

2. In gigues and canaries the speed is often too quick for rules 4, 8 and 10 to be practicable. In these circumstances each note may be taken on alternate down and up bows. The same licence is allowed in bourrées.

3. Two short notes following a long one (for instance two semiquavers after a dotted crotchet) are usually slurred on the up bow.

Muffat finally gives an example of a passage bowed according to the French and Italian conventions. This illustrates clearly the dependence of the French rules on the association of the opening beat of each bar with the down bow; and the more crisply defined rhythm achieved by the French method. The French technique is dominated by physical movement, the Italian by lyrical grace. The Lullian principles of bowing should probably be observed in the performance of Couperin's string parts, though not too rigidly. One should remember that Lully's technique was evolved in music intended for the dance; Couperin's chamber music is in dance forms but is not meant to be danced to. Probably a mixture of French and Italian technique is appropriate to Couperin's more lyrical movements.

II

The following is the list of ornaments which Muffat gives:

1. *Pincés, simples et doubles.* His explanation of these is the same as Couperin's.
2. *Tremblements, simples et doubles.* His explanation of these is broadly the same as Couperin's.
3. *Ports de voix* and *Préoccupations* (anticipatory notes).

    In notating the *port de voix* Muffat writes the dissonant note as a semiquaver, the resolution as a dotted quaver. Couperin's notation is, as we have seen, ambiguous; but almost all the authorities, from Chambonnières and d'Anglebert in the seventeenth century to C. P. E. Bach in the eighteenth, give the dissonance and its resolution an *equal* value. Boyvin is the only authority who unambiguously supports Muffat; so it may be doubted whether Muffat has accurately transcribed Lully's practice in this matter.
4. *Coulements* – in various subdivisions:
    (*a*) *Coulement simple.* This is the same as Couperin's *coulé*. In dance music it links two successive notes in conjunct motion, slurring them on the same bow.
    (*b*) *Le Tournoyant.* A *coulement* sliding through a wider interval than the *coulement simple*, all the linking notes being slurred on the same bow.
    (*c*) *L'Exclamation.* A *coulement* introduced in the interval of a rising third. The *exclamation accessive* places the ornamental notes, slurred on one bow, before the beat; the *exclamation superlative* places them after the beat.

(d) *L'Involution*. This is the same as Couperin's *double* or turn.

(e) *Le Pétillement*. This is the same as the *tournoyant*, only in this case the ornamental notes are played 'distinctement, en les faisait craqueter sous un même trait d'archelet'.

(f) *La Tirade*. A *coulement* in which the linking notes cover a complete octave, and are all bowed *separately*. Thus this is 'la plus vive' of all the varieties of *coulement*.

5. *Le Détachement*. This is the same as Couperin's *détaché* effect.

6. *Les Diminutions*. The ornamental splitting up of long notes, in accordance with the seventeenth-century principle of division.

Lully uses only one sign, a cross, to indicate the position of an ornament, without explaining which ornament is appropriate. Muffat's account of the circumstances in which the different ornaments are to be introduced is thus important. We may summarize his remarks as follows:

1. *Pincés* may be introduced on any note that requires stress, even on two consecutive notes, so long as the speed is moderate.

2. *Tremblements* should rarely be used on the opening note of a piece or phrase, except on the major third, and on sharpened notes.

3. In rising scale passages a *port de voix*, either simple or with a mordent, may serve as an approach to the strong beat. When the tempo is slow, the *port de voix* may be combined with the *préoccupation* and the *tremblement*. Trills (*tremblements*) should not be used on the strong beat without preparation except on the third, the leading note, and sharpened notes.

4. In descending scale passages *tremblements* may be more freely introduced, especially on dotted notes.

5. In upward leaps *ports de voix* and *coulements* may be introduced, alone or in combination with *tremblements*. The *tirade* should be introduced rarely, for a special effect of vehemence. The *exclamation* can effectively be used in rising thirds, 'pour adoucir le jeu'. *Tremblements* should seldom be approached by a leap, except on the third and sharpened notes. 357

6. In downward leaps *tremblements* should never be used except after a fall of a third or a tritone, or a fall on to a sharpened note. Falling intervals may be decorated with the *préoccupation*, the *coulement*, the *pétillement*, occasionally with the *tirade*, and most effectively of all with the *coulement* rounded off by a *tremblement* on the last note of the descent.

7. In cadences *tremblements* should be used on the final note only after a fall from the third or the second to the tonic or, combined with the *préoccupation* or anticipatory note, on the major third (i.e. the ornamental resolution of the fourth).

Muffat gives a series of examples of cadential formulae and of diminutions or divisions, and concludes this part of the treatise with some remarks on the use of the *détachement* to give rhythmic animation.

Couperin uses much more precise signs for his ornaments than does Lully; it would seem that his ornamentation is broadly in accord with Lully's principles as described by Muffat. In his violin sonatas and church music he uses the cross, not in the indiscriminate manner of Lully, but to indicate *pincés* and *tremblements*; which of the two is intended depends on the context. He writes out in small notes the appoggiaturas (*ports de voix*) and the various types of *coulement* and *diminution*. Though he does not use Muffat's terminology, most of Muffat's ornaments can be found, written out, in Couperin's work. In his later music – the clavecin pieces, the *concerts*, and the last sonatas – he writes out the appoggiaturas and *coulements* and uses for the *pincés*, *tremblements* and *doubles* the specific signs which we have described in our account of his theoretical work.

In order to illustrate the correlation between Muffat's rules and Couperin's practice we may perhaps comment on the ornaments in some of the passages from the *Leçons de Ténèbres* which we have quoted previously. For instance, on page 162 the *port de voix* on the last syllable of the word 'incipit' probably follows Muffat in being short (about a semiquaver in length), for in that form it is most satisfactory harmonically. But the *port de voix* on the word 'prophetae' probably takes half the value of the main note. The crosses in this quotation all indicate *tremblements*, beginning with the 'prepared' note above. The wriggle at the end of 'prophetae' is a written-out *coulement* of the *tournoyant* type, followed by (in Muffat's terminology) an *involution* or turn, also written out. On page 163 (last example) the *ports de voix* probably have half the value of the main note. On page 164 (first example) the crosses represent mordents, which intensify the phrase. On the same page the cross on the last syllable of 'convertere' indicates a *pincé*; the *port de voix* on the last syllable of 'Dominum' takes half the value of the main note; and the cross on 'tuum' represents a *tremblement* possibly preceded by a *préoccupation*. On page 168 the first *port de voix* on 'dolor' is probably long rather than short; the second is almost certainly a quaver. The wriggles on the word 'sicut' are examples of the *exclamation accessive*, written out.

Muffat's account does not greatly help us to solve the most difficult problem of Couperin's ornamentation. This is the problem of the precise length of the appoggiaturas which, in his engraved scores, he has marked so carefully. In the many passages similar to that quoted on page 190 from *Les Langueurs-Tendres* the appoggiaturas – *ports de voix* – obviously have half the value of the main note, or perhaps slightly less than half, the notes being slurred in pairs. On the other hand the *ports de voix* followed by *pincés* in the passage quoted on page 199 would seem, from the rest that appears in the third bar, to have the value of one quaver; whereas according to C. P. E. Bach and most of the authorities except Muffat they should have two-thirds of the value of the main note. Similarly on page 201, in the quotation from *L'âme-en-peine*, the appoggiaturas should have the value of a crotchet, if one follows Bach; but their dissonance is much more poignant if they are played as quavers, on a principle analogous to Muffat's. On page 208 (first example) the *ports de voix* all seem to require half the value of the main note if the power and intensity of the music is to be adequately expressed.

The lack of unanimity among the theorists would seem to suggest that the precise interpretation was as much a matter of taste as of rule. Where there is doubt one must choose the interpretation that *sounds* right, as we have tried to do in the above examples.

Addenda, 1986

I

THE TRIO SONATA AS AN INSTRUMENTAL MINI-OPERA:
a note on *La Visionnaire*
(Addendum to Chapter 6)

In the original text of this book I spoke of trio sonatas as being 'operas in instrumental microcosm'; the notion deserves discussion in terms of what happens within a particular work. I choose the early sonata originally christened *La Visionnaire*, but retitled *L'Espagnole* at the time of publication. The music does not seem to have any discernible Spanish characteristics; nor for that matter do the other sonatas in the group seem to be specifically *françoise* or *piémontoise*, so perhaps the only point of the 'national' titles was to indicate that the music was *inter*national, cosmopolitanly embracing any *goûts* along with the fundamental French and Italian. There is however a specific point to the first title of this sonata, since it was directly inspired by Desmarets's play *Les Visionnaires*, written as early as 1637, revived in 1680, and played no less than twenty-five times between then and 1692, the approximate date of Couperin's sonata. The composer knew and loved Desmarets's plays, must have attended one or more of the revivals of *Les Visionnaires*, and may even have programmatically based his sequence of musical events on theatrical events in the play. Whether he did so or not is unimportant; but it matters very much that we as performers should think of ourselves, in playing this music, as actors singing and dancing on a stage. Though we have no words to speak, our musical phrases are gesture and communication; we converse as mimes do, if not as actors proper. Such an attitude to trio sonatas was fundamental, as Roger North makes clear when, writing in his *Musicall Grammarian* at the end of the seventeenth century, he describes a Corelli trio sonata as 'Sociall Musick', comparing the *grave* opening to 'a solemne dancer's entry, with his lofty cutts, and no trifling stepps, which soon follow after fast enough'. Similarly he says of Lully, 'the prefect of French musick, how stately are his Entrys!' And he reminds us of the   363 context in which most of Lully's music, and much of Couperin's, was performed – 'the Theater, where sits the Sovereigne authority of musick'. In the instrumental lines, he points out, no less than in 'magnifick opera entrys', '*they seem to argue and declaime*'.

According to North, the opening of a trio sonata 'ought to come forward as a noble *colonata* is seen in front of a mighty fabrick'. Though Couperin's *La Visionnaire* is a modest work befitting the discretion of his personality, it does open gravely in C minor, with a theatrical overture in which the melody instruments' crotchets, phrased in pairs, 'speak' in the spirit of baroque rhetoric. In the past thirty years we have learned a great deal about authenticity in the performance of baroque music; yet I suspect that we have still unveiled only the tip of the iceberg. We may never know what were the precise relationships between conventions of musical expression, rhetorical device and verbally intelligible language; but we do now know that there were such relationships, and the likelihood is that we will discover more about them. A trio sonata, especially a French trio sonata, performed even on only moderately authentic instruments with moderately authentic bowing and phrasing, tends to sound like conversation, sometimes elevated, sometimes flirtatious; and the relationships between the players – who are also implicitly singers, actors and dancers – are at once personal and social. This is manifest in the first bars of this sonata, wherein the appoggiaturas are sighs and the dissonant suspensions stabs, while at the same time their expressivity is not 'subjective' since the noble proportions (*gravement et marqué*) render them ceremonial. Although the music is intimate, like most of Couperin's work, it is projected outwards into theatre; it is not so much you and I weeping as generic weepers paying their tribute in some modest funeral oration. Individually, the lines 'speak' intimately; corporately, they dedicate their private identities to a public whole – as becomes patent when the lines grandly coalesce in a half-close that Couperin marks *Fort, et très lentement*, from which he moves into a three-voiced fugato, *vivement*, on a theme rising a fourth and proceeding scalewise to the minor sixth, only to descend through a *diminished* fourth.

As public music this offers a positive complement to the lamentation of the opening section: our separatenesses are subsumed into the fugal unity; we dance together to the same tune,

364

though independently in the sense that each part enters alone. And the musical unity is also social, because we are now dancing, and dance is a social act; indeed for Couperin's world it was a social philosophy. The music concerns the states of separateness and of togetherness simultaneously: each part is separate in that it dances the fugato theme in its own place and time; yet is together in that it fits in with the others and with the public dimension of the clearly defined, conventionally established proprieties of the tonal relationships, moving from tonic minor to subdominant minor, then from tonic to dominant, then briefly to the relative major before a more forcefully reiterated tonic minor close. During this close, however, all the parts break into semiquavers; the effect is gently jubilant, as though we're grateful to be together rather than alone.

Yet this is not after all a public consummation, for the small triumph of the cadence is succeeded by an *air* which Couperin marks *affectueusement*:

The convention of this new movement is not, like that of the overture and allegro, mainly Italian, but French, for it is, in its lilting louré rhythm, an *air de cour*. *Airs de cour* were essentially solo songs; though their dance movement was an attribute of civilization, implying conformity to a gracious ideal, the delicate ornamentation of the melodies and the often chromatic harmonies that accompanied them allowed scope for personal *mignardise*. There is still a social context and a stage on which the young shepherd or shepherdess sings of his or her usually rejected or otherwise frustrated love; but this is not public rhetoric in the manner of the overture, for we identify ourselves with the soloist. It is significant that in this *air* Couperin directs that the second melody instrument (violin or flute) should play '*seul*'. When the first melody instrument enters he is instructed to play *doux, affectueusement*, as '*l'Accompagnement*'. The effect of the trio of wordless voices is exquisite. The bass soberly marks its level dotted minims over which the main melody floats, so sensitively vocal in contour that we can almost imagine what he or she would be singing–speaking if the tune had a text. Meanwhile the upper part adds whispered comments in twining quavers and semiquavers. On a recorder or baroque flute, these arabesques sound like a cooing of doves or warbling of thrushes; the creatures of Nature join in sympathy with the love-lorn human's pastoral lament:

Though theatrically presented, this is an idealized private world – from which we shift back to the communal group for another fugato movement, the subject of which also begins with a rising fourth. It is marked *légèrement* and, like the earlier fugue, flows busily. What happens within it is, however, very different: having proceeded through symmetrical modulations to the subdominant minor and relative major, it returns to the tonic and unexpectedly takes off from the brief semiquaver figure that had seemed to be a very subsidiary countersubject to the leaping fourths. Little by little the semiquavers, always descending, grow into cascading scales, chattering through sequentially suspended chords of the seventh. The effect is at once hilarious and slightly hysterical; it seems that this time we are not, as in the cadential periods of the first fugato, rejoicing in our togetherness but are trying to break out of it. The music sounds inebriated, and what it is 'about', psychologically, is close to the state we're in when, at a party, we are mildly tipsy. We are grateful that euphoria should be generated; and at the same time are regretful that euphoria may threaten the rational order we value as representative of Civilization. The descending scales chase one another's tails; the bouncy rising fourth is not reinstated:

What happens next corroborates this account, for it is a short section (rather than movement) which, from a being as hyper-civilized as Couperin, might count as a Representation of Chaos. A sustained dominant triad, marked with the word *repos*, is followed by five flickeringly rapid bars of 6 : 4, based on the fourth inverted in free fugato. This is succeeded by another *repos* chord on the tonic major, which turns into a dominant leading into seven bars of the fugato, beginning in the subdominant and moving to the relative major. Six bars of coda take us back to C minor, again in free fugato, with falling octave followed again by rising fourth. The abrupt changes of mood and the flittering movement sound ghostly – especially when taken at the breakneck speed which the Quadro Amsterdam, I think rightly, adopts. It's as though the 'tipsy' fugato has resulted in disintegration – which is, however, only momentary. For the threat of chaos leads again to solo song: another *air tendre*, this time in the form of a gavotte. The first melody instrument now has the lovely tune, based on a scale gently descending through an octave, as though the crazy cascades at the end of the fugato, having been metamorphosed into personal feeling, have been reordered in the process. The second melody instrument now plays *l'Accompagnement*, thus designated by Couperin, and the bass line is sensuously chromatic. The effect is sad, despite the lyrical *tendresse*. Through the reality of personal feeling we surmount any hint of hysteria which communal togetherness (maybe with its concomitant alcoholic stimulation) may generate, thereby winning through to some calm of mind. But passion is far from spent, and the appoggiaturas, drooping from the major seventh through a noble fifth, sound, as they are repeated, lovingly nostalgic, as though seeking a lost Eden:

So this *air de cour* works at a deeper, more private level than the previous one, its theatrical dimension being less topical and local: more 'universal' in having become more 'ideal'. Something the same is true of the quick finale, by far the most extended movement in the sonata. Like the 'disintegrative' fugato it is in 6 : 4, moving *vivement* but also *marqué*. In principle, however, it is integrative rather than disintegrative, since it is a chaconne, the theme of which is not tied to the bass, as is conventional in chaconnes, but appears as a *cantus firmus* in each part. The chaconne motif itself is in dotted minims, which fall down the scale from the tonic or dominant through a fourth, and then rise from the third up to the fifth. It thus crystallizes thematic material prevalent throughout the sonata; but in each case the line, having annunciated the ostinato, breaks into flowing quaver scales. The entries of the three melodic parts are so disposed that the steady dotted minims of the ostinato are never silent. As in ordinary chaconnes the ostinato represents the Conformity without which we cannot hope to go on. It is something greater than, or at any rate beyond, the vagaries of personal passion; but in this context, after that heart-rending second *air tendre*, we respond to the ostinato not so much as an affirmation of social obligation, but rather as though it were a destiny we have no choice but to accept. The particularities of the quick-moving quavers exist against the timeless background of the ostinato – which renders them faintly melancholy in that it suggests that the private passions we cherish, as well as our everyday social (and sexual) intercourse, are mutable.

In the later, published score Couperin underlines this by adding what he calls a *badinage pour le clavecin, si l'on veut*. This is a fully notated right-hand part in chattering quavers, which gives a touch of desperation to the social persiflage with which we hope to keep our little flags timorously flying. He abandons it after the melody instruments too are launched on their quavers, while in one part or another the *cantus firmus* rigidly descends from the tonic or dominant. Perhaps the continuo player should continue to improvise a *badinage* if he wants to; perhaps on the other hand he must hold on to rhythmic and harmonic fundaments as the cross rhythms in the melodic parts grow more elaborate. The original upward-leaping fourths are obtrusive in the closing pages, still bouncy but, in the delicate hurly-burly, a trifle distraught. The coda phrase combines rising scales leaping through a fifth with fourths leaping both ways. Though still metrically complex, the upward tendency sounds modestly optimistic, and the final chord is a major *tierce de Picardie*.

So this unpretentious sonata would seem to portray a psychological drama of considerable subtlety. Like all Couperin's music, and most overtly his consort music, it tells us that being civilized must hurt even as it pleases, since there can never be total conformity between our personal desires and the interests of the whole. The boundaries between discipline and oppression are hazily defined; especially in quick fugal movements the unity of counterpoint may often be achieved only by dancing, through 369 syncopations, cross rhythms and displaced harmonies, on tight-ropes. Couperin's fast movements often recall the proverbial cat on hot bricks. For that matter it is helpful to remember the cat in any performance of Couperin, for no creature moves with more instinctive elegance, disciplining the body's latent savagery to attain to *cortesia*, which in our case (we can't know about the cat's!) is a spiritual as well as a social quality. I detect the same feline qualities in the young people in the paintings of Watteau: who, even if they aren't dancing (and many of them are), live with such grace in their shapely bodies, against the illimitable backcloths into which their *conversations galantes et amusantes* recede.

II

THE 'NEW' MOTETS
with a note on *Leçons de Ténèbres*
(Addendum to Chapter 8)

Since the publication of the 1933 Oiseau-Lyre edition of Couperin's *Collected Works*, and since this book was written, some lost motets have come to light in the library of St Michael's College, Tenbury. These manuscripts have since been acquired by the Bibliothèque nationale, Paris (*Rés F. 1679*, *Rés F 1680 a–e*); and the works will be published in a supplement to the new Oiseau-Lyre edition within the next few years. The motets found their way to Tenbury as part of a large collection of original editions of French baroque music, made early in the eighteenth century by the Comte de Toulouse. Many of the ecclesiastical pieces of Couperin included were already familiar from other sources. Details of these are given by Philippe Oboussier in the preface to his edition of nine out of twelve of the rediscovered motets (the remaining three are incomplete). This edition appears in Heugel's Le Pupitre series.

All the pieces are early works, composed during the decade beginning 1693, when Couperin took up his court appointment. Indeed all Couperin's church music, apart from the *Leçons de Ténèbres* written for a community of nuns, would seem to date from these years, for the nature of Couperin's output, like that of any baroque composer, was conditioned by the circumstances in which he worked. Seven of the pieces are scored for solo voices with continuo only. The last two have obbligato violins, as do the motets not included in Oboussier, and still unpublished. I will comment on the Oboussier motets in the order in which they have been republished.

Tantum ergo sacramentum is for two sopranos and bass. The opening is majestically homophonic in G minor; but is pathetic as well as majestic, since the texture is riddled with suspensions in parallel thirds or sixths, on the analogy of trio sonatas. Vestigial counterpoints enter the middle section, first declining canonically down the scale, then balanced by their inversion. The coda, with weeping sevenths and ninths, is especially beautiful:

Domine salvum fac regem, for soprano and bass, is in B minor, a key that here as elsewhere implies emotional intensity. The effect is the more impressive because the first half is built over nine repetitions of a ground bass declining down the scale from B to F sharp. That this is the simplest possible form of basso ostinato makes its rigour the more effective: it becomes the Rock to which we must cling as we cry to God for salvation. Were it not there, we might be swept away by the tempest of our passions – which are patent in the spacious phrases, leaping up a fifth, drooping down the scale through dissonant suspensions that grind against the ostinato. More angular intervals, such as falling sixths and tritones, impart energy as the dialogue unfolds:

The climax leads to a change to quick duple time and a theme that presses upwards instead of falling, expanding into quaver melismata. But although God seems to respond to our urgent prayers, the tonality remains severely B minor.

The elevation *Laude Sion Salvatorem* is a more substantial piece for two sopranos, often in free canon. The overlapping voices sound suavely sensuous, in a 'pathetic' G minor. The middle section shifts to Couperin's 'innocent' G major, beginning as a solo for the first soprano, in the delicately ornamented style of an *air de cour*; perhaps the words *Ecce panis angelorum* prompt this quasi-celestial pastoralism. The second soprano responds with another *air tendre*, in the minor but still more seductively ornamented. The first section is repeated da capo.

Respice in me is a solo motet for high tenor: a hymn to the Virgin which begins in innocent G major, but is tonally and rhythmically restless, thereby hinting at an eroticism that becomes overt in the triple-rhythmed *Te amo, O Mater pietatis*. A minor section, *Tu es Mater intemerata*, creates a characteristic sonority as the vocal line floats very high while the bass descends to a low, sustained dominant pedal. Another hymn to the Virgin – *Salve Regina*, for the same solo voice and continuo – is longer and more sombre, in the 'tragic' key of C minor. The invocatory section makes powerful use of diminished fourths in canon between bass viol and voice. The middle section in the major is high in tessitura and virtuosic in figuration, with exhilarating cross-bar phrasing:

It calls for brilliant singing if momentum is to be sustained, but justifies its length when the final section, back in the minor and in 3 : 2, proves even more sensuously impassioned than the first. The unexpected (momentary) modulation to F and C majors, stemming from vacillation between the minor and major third, is deeply affecting:

We are back in a delight-ful G major for another tribute to the Virgin, this time scored for two virginal sopranos. This *Regina coeli laetare* is exquisite, the key word being *laetare*. The voices start off in canon, with an arpeggio that skips into dancing scales; their Italianate alleluyas gambol like lambs on the biblical hills, twining around one another in overlapping suspensions, bubbling in parallel thirds. In the final section the rising arpeggio is replaced by repeated notes, producing a still more ecstatic effect perhaps because, taken fast, it sounds like a stutter. The end, with high tessitura in syncopation, is deliciously tipsy; these girls are now not so much biblical lambs as Watteauesque, or even Boucher-like, young women rolling in the hay!

Compared with this, *Usquequo, Domine*, again for high tenor, seems a shade too conventional to justify its length, though its A minor lyricism is noble and touching.

The two last of the motets collected by Oboussier are for bass solo and continuo plus a 'Symphonie' of two violins or flutes. *Salvum me fac Deus* is conceived on a large scale, for Couperin, and is therefore not altogether characteristic. The opening symphonie and aria in 3 : 2 exploit the powerful implications of B flat major in a way that suggests the young Handel; the 3 : 4 *Veni in altitudinem maris* is more skittishly French, but not particularly personal. *Laboravi clamans* is an aria on a ground bass in F minor, sounding remarkably like Purcell though harmonically less extravagant; the succeeding recitative and aria return to the French court, but sound more like Lully than Couperin. The *Deus tu scis insipientiam meam*, with obbligato flutes weaving in parallel thirds and sixths, has more of Couperin's flavour but little of his distinction. The return to B flat major, first in duple rhythm, then in 3 : 2, recalls the Handelian manner of the opening. It seems to go on a very long time, though we're rewarded when the coda, *Et ne avertas faciem tuam*, generates exuberance by way of an angularly bucking theme.

Ad te levavi oculos meos, though also lengthy, is more lively and more typical of Couperin. The first section has an Italianate theme resembling that of the delightful *Regina coeli laetare*, and begins in the same benign key of G major. It doesn't elicit the glee that characterizes that piece, and perhaps couldn't, since a bass voice is no rival for two sopranos in the pursuit of ecstasy; in partial compensation, two obbligato violins are brilliantly used in the *ritournelle*. A recitative section indulges in rapid changes of tempo; and leads into a *miserere nostri Domine* in 3 : 2 in the minor, with the violins in plangent suspensions. This sarabande lament alternates with rapid passages in duple time and in the process loses direction. But the final Gloria and 375

Amen, back in the major and in an infectiously consistent dotted rhythm, charms in its friskiness. The music becomes pure Couperin, as the bass voice scampers in youthful vivacity. It is like a rebirth – which is what Couperin's religious music, perhaps all religious music, is ultimately about.

Looking back on the enlarged range of Couperin's church music it seems that a number of the rediscovered pieces deserve to rank among his finest: the ripely resonant *Tantum ergo*, the ostinato-based *Domine salvum*, the delicious *Regina coeli laetare*. These are essential Couperin works which ought to be regularly performed: though there's nothing in the pieces that plumbs the heart of the Couperin experience, as does the *Motet de Ste Suzanne* – not to mention the extraordinary *Tabescere me fecit* for two unaccompanied sopranos that opens the *Versets* of 1703. Extraordinary is an appropriate adjective because although on paper the behaviour of the two voices can be given grammatical explanations that are ordinary enough, the effect in performance is indeed 'out of this world'. As the silvery voices climb higher their dissonant suspensions beat frantically, producing in the listeners and still more in the performers a physical state of dizziness. The light-headed effect is an aural equivalent for the phenomenon of levitation, and I know of nothing to compare with it except Couperin's own later *Leçons de Ténèbres*. There it weirdly and wonderfully occurs in the vocalises, in a richer context, though without the startlement occasioned, in *Tabescere me fecit*, by the total lack of instrumental support.

The *Quatre Versets* of 1703 and the *Leçons de Ténèbres* of *c.* 1715 are 'mystical' in a sense that most music of the Heroic Age, with the signal exception of Bach's, was not. Yet although Couperin seems thus to be unique in French culture, he is not quite so – as is evident now that we know more about the tradition to which Couperin contributed in his *Leçons de Ténèbres*. Over the centuries the Catholic Church has not unnaturally frowned on musical exhibitionism during Holy Week: God's death is to be experienced, rather than celebrated, in near-darkness and near-silence. Plainsong intonation describing the divine events has traditionally been minimal and of course monophonic, without instrumental distraction. During the *grand siècle*, however, the hedonistic and King-loving French found means of compromise with the world, the flesh, and by implication the Devil: for

ecclesiastical composers cannily introduced, within monodic

plainchant, conventions derived from the secular *air de cour*, and later from operatic recitative. Since the techniques of the *air de cour* were based, as we've seen, on rhythmic malleability stemming from verbal inflexion, the compromise worked well: the melodic line still resembled plainsong, though it was profusely embellished with *ports de voix* and other emotive ornaments, and was accompanied by harmonies discreetly played on chamber organ, harpsichord and theorbo. Often, perhaps usually, a string bass was added, though composers seem to have been somewhat wary of admitting openly to this operatic alignment, with its potential for harmonic luxury. Both Couperin and Charpentier say that one may add a *basse de viole*, should one be to hand.

The Church Fathers were quick to point out that the new music defiled the most sacred moments of the liturgy of Holy Week with the sensory graces (in both the emotional and the technical sense) of the *air de cour*, and rebuked the fashionable public for its reluctance to relinquish theatrical frivol even during the darkest days of the Christian year. The objection was understandable and probably justifiable in reference to work of the minor exponents of the genre. But the finest music for the Holy Week Lessons, though often performed before members of the nobility, was not originally devised for the Court but for communities of nuns; and this music demonstrates that, while the *air-de-cour*-derived idiom *might* be frivolous, it *could* become, in true Counter-Reformation spirit, a gateway to metaphysical bliss. In the writings of medieval (let alone seventeenth-century) saints, erotic and mystical images were always inextricably confused. Similarly the *Leçons de Ténèbres* which Marc-Antoine Charpentier creates from a synthesis of *air de cour* with plainchant prove to be at once sensuous and transcendent. During the forties I had a hunch that Charpentier was the greatest of Couperin's predecessors precisely because he was fundamentally a religious composer as against the prevailing secular ethos (see pages 139–40). That judgement has been amply substantiated now that Charpentier's music is much recorded and not infrequently performed; in particular, listening to his *Leçons de Ténèbres*, it is manifest that, working within this long-established convention, he had composed the most moving and distinctive church music of France's *grand siècle*. His *Leçons* have been beautifully recorded, using soprano, alto, counter-tenor and high tenor voices in alternation and occasionally together, with 377 continuo played on aurally seductive variants of chamber organ, harpsichord, theorbo and *viole*. That Charpentier's *Leçons*, probably predating Couperin's by at least twenty years, are no less erotically ecstatic yet mysteriously devout, makes Couperin's achievement less remarkable, but doesn't diminish its impact. Charpentier's *Leçons* are too long and too consistently monodic to be listened to as concert music. Sung by nuns, in the conditions they were intended for, during the liturgy of Holy Week, by candlelight in a gradually darkening church, their effect must have been overwhelming, and they can still move us as deeply as do the candlelit paintings of nuns by Charpentier's contemporary De la Tour. Couperin's *Leçons*, however, are the more viable in normal performing conditions, since they alternate melismatic vocalise with trenchant, at times startlingly dramatic, recitative. Though they sound best in liturgical conditions, they can make their effect anywhere and at any time. Couperin's musical organization is more complex and more self-subsistent than Charpentier's. Both composers employ chromaticism ballasted by vestigial canon in the *Jerusalem convertere* postludes, re-establishing order, after the chaos of lamentation, by chaconne-like ostinati; but Couperin supports his intensity by other musical rather than ritualistic or theatrical means – in the first *Leçon* by exploiting diversity of tonality between D and F majors and minors; in the second *Leçon* by metrical variety; and in the third by the diversity of texture and timbre made feasible by the use of two voices.

Charpentier belonged to an earlier generation than Couperin; La Lande was his contemporary who, as we noted in the original text of the book, normally favoured the public ceremonial style in church music. Yet he too, in making his Tenebrae settings for the same minimal forces of solo voice, chamber organ and string bass, was inspired to a Couperin-like intensity. There is no disputing the pathos of this music, which attains in its vocalises an abandon no less heart-felt than Charpentier's, while at the same time achieving in arioso a dramatic urgency comparable with Couperin's. La Lande's roulades are more extended than those of Charpentier, and more operatically virtuosic than Couperin's; fairly fast, dance-dominated sections approaching aria often hint at theatrical panache. The variety of emotional range and of technical resource does not lessen the 'inward' quality of the music, which is surely the profoundest, if not in every sense the greatest, that La Lande created. Perhaps one might say, however, that the music lacks the fervent economy that makes Couperin's *Leçons* a classic testament.

Couperin's *Leçons* were composed between 1712 and 1715. La Lande's could have been written around the same time, perhaps inspired by the death of his two daughters who succumbed to smallpox in 1711; or ten or more years later as a memorial tribute to his wife, who died, relatively young, in 1722. The latter date is the more probable since by then La Lande's official duties as court and chapel composer had terminated. Both La Lande's and Couperin's *Leçons* were composed 'for the religious ladies of L'. This is usually identified as the convent of Longchamp, where the services were of high musical distinction. Since they became fashionable with the aristocracy, celebrated opera singers were occasionally brought in to supplement the musicians; without them, La Lande's and Couperin's virtuosity would hardly have been negotiable – though Couperin does not *demand* operatic assurance, as does La Lande.

III

A HANDBOOK TO COUPERIN'S HARPSICHORD PIECES
(Addendum to Chapter 9)

Couperin is one of the most purely musical of composers in that his textures 'speak' with maximum economy: there is no romantic afflatus as each of his relatively few notes makes its point. None the less he was not so pure a musician as to believe that music has no extra-musical connotations; just as Bach related musical meaning to theology and philosophy, so Couperin related it to the psychology of the people among whom he lived and for whom he composed. In my original chapter on Couperin's theoretical work I discussed baroque theories of Expression as manifest in Couperin's music. These considerations may be advantageously and justifiably more particularized: as is evident if we recall that Couperin said that

> J'ai toujours un objet en composant toutes ces pièces; des occasions différentes me l'ont fourni. Ainsi les titres répondent aux idées que j'ai eues; on me dispensera d'en rendre compte; cependant, comme parmi ces titres il y en a qui semblent me flatter, il est bon d'avertir que les pièces qui les portent sont des espèces de portraits qu'on a trouvés quelquefois assez ressemblants sous mes doigts, et que la plupart des titres avantageux sont plutôt donnés aux aimables originaux que j'ai vouler représenter, qu'aux copies que j'en ai tirées.

If Couperin believed that he always had an aim (*objet*) in composing his harpsichord pieces, it does not seem extravagant to suspect that he thought his titles meant something. While we may enjoy the music without intellectually understanding its topical and local meanings, we'll enjoy it more if we appreciate its relevance to Couperin's life. With very great composers like Bach and Beethoven we may, though it does not follow that we should, discard the ephemeral aspects of their art since the universal aspects are patent. With a great composer like Couperin we are more likely to arrive at an apprehension of the universal *by way of* the topical and local, since the more his past comes alive to us the more vividly may it be *presented*. Having lived with Couperin's music another forty years I know its highways and byways more intimately than I did while I was writing the book; and my awareness of Couperin as a person, at his particular time and place, has made his music seem more deeply relevant to me, at my particular time and place. The alchemy of his art transmutes what was into what is alive and (however elegantly) kicking.

It is with these considerations in mind that I have expanded the notes on Couperin's titles which appeared as Appendix F to the original edition of this book. As I point out in the Preface, I am indebted to and grateful for Jane Clark's work in this field, some of which has been published in *Early Music* (April 1980). In an area where much must be guesswork, my guesses sometimes differ from hers. Right or wrong answers matter most when a title's meaning affects not merely our historical awareness, but also our interpretation of the music – as is the case with, for instance, *La Sophie* from the fourth book.

Almost all the titles of Couperin's harpsichord pieces, as of those of other composers of the classical age, are in the feminine. It used to be assumed that all the pieces were therefore addressed to women; but it is now accepted that the feminine gender is used adjectivally, agreeing with the omitted noun 'pièce'. This is clearly the case with a title such as *La Harpée* (*Pièce dans le goût de la Harpe*); and is almost certainly the case with pieces dedicated to the organist Garnier or the *viole*-player Forqueray. The implied grammatical construction of *La superbe ou la Forqueray* is *La Muse superbe, ou la pièce Forqueray*. It is difficult to credit that Couperin would habitually have portrayed the however charming wives or daughters of great musicians, rather than the men themselves.

By the eighteenth-century standards of a Telemann or Vivaldi, or even a Handel or Bach, Couperin was not a prolific composer, and the relative exiguousness of his output accords with his disposition. It is universally agreed that the four volumes of his harpsichord pieces, the production of which he himself supervised, are among the finest examples of music engraving created at any time or place; and one would not expect music notated in such exquisite calligraphy to have been hastily composed. The music looks as it sounds: a distillation of experience, 381 which is, despite its intimate relation to a specific time and place, impervious to Time. Yet the four volumes, which span Couperin's working life, manifest a creative evolution, which is also the growth of a personality. The first volume, published in 1713 when Couperin was forty-five, is the most haphazard in character, banding together pieces probably composed over a considerable period of time. The first three *ordres* alternate dances, some courtly, some popular, with character pieces and portraits without any planned sequence, though they exploit traditional baroque conventions in their key relationships, and this naturally affects the pieces' emotional impact in relation to one another.

Book I

Ordre I in G minor and major

In the *grand siècle* Couperin's predecessor Marc-Antoine Charpentier had characterized G minor as '*sévère et magnifique*', and for Couperin too it tends to be gravely passionate and melancholy – as indeed it is in most baroque and classical music (pre-eminently Bach's and Mozart's). Charpentier's G major complements the minor in being '*doucement joyeux*'; for Couperin too G major is, if not quite a key of benediction as it is in Bach, at least sweetly sensuous but innocent, and therefore appropriate to adolescent girls.

Allemande: l'Auguste is massively in the minor, and must be a portrait of Louis-Auguste, Duc de Maine, whose life-span, from 1670 to 1736, is very close to Couperin's. Temperamentally, the two men had much in common, and it is probable that Couperin knew the Duke quite well, both personally and professionally, since he was a household musician at Sceaux, the Maine estate, from 1701. Louis-Auguste was an illegitimate son of Louis XIV by Mme de Montespan. As a child he was sickly but intellectually precocious, though he did not live up to his early promise and, having attained maturity, was increasingly dominated by his minikin but redoubtable wife. Ultimately she involved him in lunatic plots against the Crown, certainly without his assent, possibly without his knowledge, for he was on balance a good as well as clever man who justly earned Couperin's respect. Mme de Maintenon was his governess when he was a brilliant boy, and may have influenced his adult qualities. Mlle de Launay, later Mme de Staël, who lived at Sceaux, describes him as a man 'of enlightened understanding, subtle and cultivated, a noble and serious character'. But she adds that his conversation, 'though solid, was at the same time lively, full of charm, and of a peculiar light and easy turn'. Even the Duchess of Orléans, who hated Maine for his long association with her arch-enemy Maintenon, whom she sportively refers to as 'the old turd', admits that the Duke was a cultured man, well versed in the arts, and with an able mind. His amateur attempts at composition include a bourrée on a theme of Couperin. This noble allemande bypasses the 'light and easy' charm, presenting Maine as 'a man who loved order, justice and decorum'. The Duchess may have been on the mark, however, in adding that he was one whom 'religion rather than nature made virtuous and kept him so'.

Sarabande: la Majestueuse. Presumably a portrait of the King himself, whose grandeur none the less allows place for the subtleties of spiritual and technical *mignardise.*

Gavotte. Simply a dance but, in view of the elaborately orna-mented *double,* presumably a slow gavotte of the type to which d'Anglebert attributed a '*noble* simplicity'. With the addition of words, these gavottes readily become *airs de cour.*

La Milordine. In 1701 Louis XIV handed over his palace at St Germain-en-Laye for the use of the exiled James II of England and his entourage. English lordlings were habitually in residence there, and Couperin must have met them, since he rented a house at St Germain in 1710. This piece is in the style of a Corellian, English-style gigue, but is subtler than its prototype. The flowing 12 : 8 periods in the minor key '*gracieusement et légérement*' imbue comedy with wistfulness, while Couperin's fingering in the fifth bar encourages the music to mince. This sounds like a specific rather than a generalized portrait – a likeness 'done from life'.

Les Silvains. The Duc de Maine married Louise-Bénédicte de Bourbon, a daughter of the fifth Prince de Condé, a Prince of the Blood who was mad as a March hare. The daughter inherited her share of pathological abnormalities, compensating for her dwarfish stature with a giganticized will and ego, and for her fear of solitude by the creation of a fabulously expensive dream-world in which she could play the role of Queen of the Fairies, under the mythic name of Lodovise. The Duchess of Orléans had even less patience with her than she had with most people: 'She is not taller than a child of ten years old, and is not well made. To appear tolerably well it is necessary for her to keep her mouth shut; for when she opens it, she opens it very wide, and shows her irregular teeth. She is not very stout, uses a great quantity of paint, has fine eyes, a white skin, and fair hair. If she were well disposed, she might pass, but her wickedness is insupportable.' Certainly her irascibility and her life of intrigue consort oddly with the fairy-tale paradise she created at the Duc de Maine's beautiful estate at Sceaux. Watteauesque *fêtes champêtres*, comedies and masques in which the Duchess herself acted and danced (badly), displays of pyrotechnics, pseudo-*naïf* games of shepherds and shepherdesses proceeded virtually without intermission from hour to hour, from day to day, from week to week. Though these divertissements didn't intrinsically differ from countless others except in their extravagance, they are scary in their continuousness. It's as though the Duchess were terrified lest, if the dream faltered, she would cease to exist. She tried to turn art into life, forgetting that the moment of paradisal vision, manifest in a landscape of Claude, a *fête champêtre* of Watteau, or a pastoral *ordre* of Couperin, can only be a victory over Time, achieved the hard way. Those works of art induce, from turmoil, calm; the Duchess's parties were acts of desperation into which the participants had to be dragooned by her indomitable will. The poor Duke retreated to his own quarters. We don't know whether on occasion Couperin was involved in the frivol vicariously; but we do know that the King's Musicians, of whom Couperin was one, sometimes appeared at Sceaux, disguised as 'sylvains'. This haunting piece reveals, as great art may, truths within and behind pretence. It is regal in bearing, and justifies its directive '*majestueusement*'; at the same time the low registration, the dark sonority and the broken-chord figuration carry us into realms of mystery. Couperin knew, as perhaps the Duchess did not, that though the forest parks of Sceaux may be gracefully ordered, disturbing presences lurk, satyrically, in the glades.

Les Abeilles. When this piece was first published by Ballard in 1707 its title was in the singular. This suggests that the Duchess of Maine might again be rearing her grotesque little head, since in 1704 she had founded her Order of the Honey Bee. Another of her pranks at Sceaux, this order of chivalry was intended to compete, in her dream-world, with the complicated codes of honour and etiquette prevalent at Versailles. Admission to the rank of thirty-nine members was avidly sought and fought for; successful applicants received a gold medal, engraved on one side with a beehive, on the other with a portrait of the Queen Bee, the Duchess. The motto of the Order was a line from Tasso, translated by the Duchess's pet poet, Malézieux: *The bee, though very small, can make great wounds.* True enough, in her case; though despite all the palaver the intrigues of the bee-addicts seem to have been trivially amorous, dedicated mainly to bolstering the Bee-Queen's self-esteem. There was an initiation ceremony, in which the elaborately robed postulant swore fidelity by Mount Hymettus, to music from a hidden, because magical, choir and orchestra. Though a vocal version of Couperin's piece was published, there is no evidence that it was used at the rites. If it has anything to do with the Order, it would seem gracefully to debunk it, for wounds inflicted by this amiable siciliano would be slight. In that case, whereas *Les Silvains* reveals depths the Duchess was unaware of, *Les Abeilles*, with a fetching tune that deservedly 'caught on', pricks one of her airier balloons. Of course we may also take the piece as being about real bees: a hazy hum on a summer afternoon.

La Nanète. The first of the portraits of girls: probably an anonymous villager, for the music, hinting at oboes and hurdy-gurdies, sounds rustic.

Les Nonètes. Little nuns, of course; but also little birds (of the tit family), and birds had a human as well as avian sense, then as now. There may be a small subsidiary joke in the fact that the piece is a canarie in two sections. The blonde girls dance, rather fraily, in the minor, the brunettes, more 385 assertively, in the major; Furetière's dictionary tells us that blondes wear less well than brunettes, and are less lively. The music is innocent enough to suggest teenage nuns, if we remember that girls seldom entered convents by vocation. Couperin's musical psychology is delicately on the mark in that the music – especially that for the blondes – sounds simultaneously frisky and wistful.

La Bourbonnoise. A daughter of the Duc de Bourbon (M. le Duc), who later married the Prince de Conti. The wide-eyed, vivacious music suggests that Couperin enjoyed numbering her among his pupils. The affectionate tune sounds appreciative of her beauty, while the fact that the melody prophetically lilts over a bass close to that of Bach's Goldberg Variations may also imply respect!

La Manon. A daughter of Couperin's playwright friend, Florent Dancourt, whom we'll often encounter. She was an actress, sister of the famous Mimi who was the subject of Watteau's *La Finette*. It would be pleasant to think that she was also the model for the Abbé Prevost's *Manon*, written twenty years later.

L'Enchanteresse. A piece in lute style, in broken chords and in dotted rhythm, low in register. If Couperin had in mind some particular enchantress, we don't know her name. In any case the seductive music recalls the sirens of classical antiquity, familiar to Couperin's public through the ballets and operas of Lully. The lute was traditionally an instrument of love. This piece might be played by one of the lutenists or guitarists posed elegantly in a Watteau *fête champêtre*.

La Fleurie ou la tendre Nanette. This may be the same Nanette who appeared earlier in the *ordre*: but she is here presented as a mythical creature combining girl, bird and flower. The melody is ornamented with blossom made audible.

Les Plaisirs de St. Germain-en-Laye. This palace was famous for its divertissements, as well as being a refuge for the English court. The pleasures sound, however, intimate, even slightly grave: so I suspect Couperin may be celebrating the delights of his own country house, which he rented from 1710 to 1716.

Ordre II, in D minor and major

Couperin's D minor tends to be serious but not particularly melancholy, which is broadly in accord with Charpentier's description of it as 'grave et dévot'. His D major, the key of baroque trumpets and open-stringed fiddles, is extrovert and on the whole merry, as it is with all baroque composers. He often uses it for relatively slight, witty pieces; if he approaches the pompous and circumstantial, it is with an undercurrent of irony, for he is unique among the baroque masters in that he is never a 'public' composer.

La Laborieuse. The word means industrious, assiduous, which the music is, rather than laborious, which the music is not. The texture is tightly polyphonic; and Couperin directs us to play the semiquavers unequally, in confirmation of the normal ruling about allemandes. These two musical facts impart a *laborieux* quality. We have no clue as to whether some industrious person is referred to.

Sarabande: la Prude. Again we don't know who this prude is. She sounds impressive – noble, and not particularly affected. One thinks inevitably of Mme de Maintenon, though there is no evidence to connect her with the sarabande.

L'Antonine. There are several Antons who might be the subject of this piece. The most likely is an actor who specialized in heroic roles – which would explain why the piece is to be played *majestueusement*.

Canaries. Niemetz, in his dictionary of 1718, defines the canaries as 'a bizarre dance'. In ballet divertissements canaries were danced by savage Exoticks purportedly from the Canary Islands. Their gestures were louche and farouche – which should affect the performance of canaries, even on delicate keyboard instruments.

La Charoloise. Another daughter of the Duc de Bourbon, fifth Prince de Condé. This is the eccentric termagant who married the Duc de Maine; her own title was Mme de Charolais, the district in central Burgundy. She too was among Couperin's harpsichord pupils and he must have written the piece for her. Its simplicity may have been appropriate to her technical limitations – as its lopsided phrasing may have been to her temperament!

COSTUME DE DIANE.

XV. 'Costume de Diane', an undated engraving by Delpeck.
Couperin's piece 'La Diane' about the Queen and Huntress is both
mythological and 'real' – a portrait of an unknown particular person.

La Diane. The Duchesse de Nevers was known as La Diane. If the piece is a portrait of her, Couperin puns on her name, for *la diane* means the reveille, and trumpet fanfares appear both in this piece and, more overtly, in its sequel, where they would seem to evoke Diana the huntress. One would expect the heroic fanfares to be at once physically descriptive and indicative of traits of character, though I don't know whether the Duchess had a reputation for Diana-like *hauteur*.

La Terpsicore. Again, the intensity of the music suggests a private as well as a public dimension, though we don't know who is portrayed. Some aristocratic *danseuse* plays the role of the muse of dancing in stylized, ceremonially double-dotted rhythm, epitomizing the spirit of classical French theatre and ballet.

La Florentine. Lully was known as *le Florentin* because he was one. But this unassuming Italianate jig can hardly be a portrait of so self-consciously grand a character. On the other hand Couperin is unlikely to have tossed off a portrait of an average Florentine, male or female: so it seems legitimate to associate the piece with Couperin's theatrical friend, Florent Dancourt. According to Titon du Tillet, Dancourt was renowned for his elegance and polished conversation; this piece babbles politely, if not eloquently. Links between Dancourt and Couperin are multiple for, as we have seen and will see, Couperin wrote pieces about Dancourt's wife and daughters also. More peripherally, a revival of Dancourt's play *Les Trois Cousins*, first produced in 1702, is said to have been the inspiration for Watteau's *L'Embarquement pour Cithère*, painted in 1717; we have noted how deep is the relationship between Couperin's music and that magical painting.

La Garnier. As was indicated in the biographical section of the book, Couperin was joint organist of the Chapelle Royale, along with Nivers, Buterne and Gabriel Garnier. The character of this music – low in register, complex in texture, rich in ornamentation – suggests that this is a portrait of Garnier himself rather than of his wife. Garnier was a friend of Couperin, and clearly a man to be reckoned with.

La Babet. This is the first of many theatrical references throughout Couperin's work. Elisabeth Dannaret, known as Babet(te) la Chanteuse, was the wife of Evaristo Gherardi, director of the *commedia dell'arte* company at the Hôtel de Bourgogne until it 389 was closed in 1697 for making scurrilous jokes at the expense of the King and Mme de Maintenon. (It was reopened by the Regent in 1717; and Watteau painted an exceptionally beautiful picture of the new group of *comédiens italiens*, who played in both Italian and French.) Gherardi had died as early as 1700, but Couperin seems to have known him well; the successful revival of the Gherardi scripts in the seventeen-twenties may have triggered off Couperin's late obsession with the *commedia*. Gherardi was celebrated for his portrayal of Harlequin – which Couperin surely recalls in the famous piece from his fourth book. After her husband's death La Babet became a member of l'Académie française, and what we would call a legitimate musician. This piece depicts her in her earlier, theatrical context. In the first section in the minor she dances *nonchallament*, an eight-bar clause being answered by one of fourteen bars. The second section is a brisk canarie in the major, very much *dans le goût burlesque*.

Les Idées Heureuses. 'Sensations rather than thoughts', one suspects, for these overlapping figurations and sequential sevenths in lute style are such as one might experience while floating on the gentle waters towards Cytherea. This piece is on the table in front of Couperin in the most famous portrait of him (see page x). This may mean that he was especially fond of it; or it may mean that he justifiably hoped that the title was relevant to his work as a whole.

La Mimi. Another actress daughter of Couperin's playwright friend, Florent Dancourt. Her sister Manon is portrayed in the previous *ordre*. The piece has a distinctively theatrical tinge, with affectedly caressing ornaments in the melodic line. There may be an ironic hint in the direction *affectueusement*.

La Diligente. The bustling scales are certainly diligent. Some specific fussy woman may be referred to; but perhaps not, since

La Flateuse, a mincing sarabande with the directive *affectueusement*, would seem to refer to the obsequiousness of courtiers in general. Similarly

La Voluptueuse may refer to their voluptuousness. The eroticism is far from brazen, for the harmony is not chromatic and the melody moves by step, except for an occasional leap of

sixth or octave. The voluptuousness, inherent in the warmly sustained texture and in the parallel sixths and tenths, is
tender rather than lascivious; and the tune is comparable
with that given to Couperin's ambiguously virginal *Sœur
Monique* or to the vernal *La Fleurie*. One of Couperin's
slyest verbal jokes is in the direction *tendrement &c.* One
remembers how in his *Musick's Monument* of 1676 Thomas
Mace, lamenting the obsolescence of the noble violes and
the austere string polyphony created for them, reviled the
'Loud Play' and 'High-priz'd Noyse' of the new fiddles and
their dancing music which, instead of 'disposing us to
solidity, Gravity and a Good Temper, making us capable of
Heavenly and divine Influences', was rather fit 'to make a
man's ears Glow, and fill his Braines full of *Friskes &c.*'

Les Papillons. The flickering 6 : 16 tune imitates the wavery
flight of real butterflies, but may also relate the insect to
giddy young humans. Hairpins studded with diamonds,
which scintillated in the coiffures of lovely ladies, were
called *papillons*; there is a reference to them in Boursault's
play, *Les Mots à la Mode*.

Ordre III in C minor and major

Charpentier had defined C minor as '*obscur et triste*'; throughout
the baroque period it was traditionally a dark, intense, even
tragic key, and remained so during the nineteenth century, as is
manifest in the symphonies of Beethoven, Brahms, Bruckner
and Mahler. It may have acquired some of these associations
through being the minor complement to the transparent simplicity of 'white' C major and the relative of 'heroic' E flat
major. Certainly Couperin exploits this opposition in this *ordre*,
interspersing some of his blackest pieces in the minor key with
others in the major which are not only merry, but even
deliberately fatuous. This ironic juxtaposition is to be subtly
latent throughout Couperin's work.

The gloom of most of the numbers in this *ordre* – and even, at
the opposite pole, the flippancy of the comic pieces – is so
extreme that one wonders whether the music may have been
affected by external events. The volume was published in 1713;
1712 had been a blackly calamitous year for the French nobility
for, as Saint-Simon put it, 'in less than a year three Dauphins had

died, one of them still a young child; and, in the space of twenty-four days, the father, mother and elder son were all dead'. Grief ravaged the court, and the sensitive Couperin who counted the Dauphin among his pupils, must have shared in it deeply. Certainly he never composed music more passionately valedictory than the first two pieces in this suite.

Allemande: la Ténébreuse. This grandly gloomy piece is tenebrous because it is in the *tombeau* convention, and is therefore explicitly funereal.

Sarabande: la Lugubre. This is also a *tombeau*, blackly majestic; and the two

Courantes, the

Gavotte and the

Menuet are far from jolly. On the other hand

Les Pélerines, in the tonic major, are happy as sandgirls. There is a version of the piece, dated 1712, in which the melodic treble and bass lend themselves readily to soprano and baritone voices. The words tell us how the female pilgrims, having set out on their journey to Cytherea in a radiant C major, pause in the minor-keyed section to beg tenderly, not unctuously, for alms: 'Soyez touché de nos langueurs.' In the third section, 'au Temple de l'Amour', they offer major-keyed Remerciements: 'Vos tendres soins, vos dons secourables Nous soulagent dans ce jour.' The parody version has been taken as implying that the girls are selling themselves, in which case their promise of a reward carries an oblique meaning. Such innuendos, if they exist, are not relevant to Couperin's original piece.

Les Laurentines. A highly ambiguous title. It's probably not to the point that *laurentine* is a flower (the bugle) and also material embroidered with flowers. It may be relevant that the Laurentines were a community of nuns, and it is possible to hear a tolling bell in the repeated Gs in the bass of the *seconde partie*; this would accord with the elegiac flavour of the suite as a tribute to the measles-obliterated Dauphin, Dauphine, and little Dauphin. But the piece is not otherwise melancholic, and it may be that the title refers to the Laurent family, theatre people well known to Couperin and, at an earlier date, friends of Molière. M. Laurent was a concierge at the Comédie-Française. After his death his wife

PELERINE

Pour le Divertissement du Voyage a Cithère.

XVI. 'Pélerine pour le divertissement du Voyage à Cithère', an engraving by Delpeck, 1725. The verses that accompany this portrait of a pilgrim–bergerette are set by Couperin in the vocal version of his harpsichord piece, 'Les Pélerines'. The 'voyage' was, of course, famously depicted by Watteau.

ran a café frequented by actors. The music could be construed in nun-like gentility or with theatrical panache. Georges Beck, in his notes to Kenneth Gilbert's complete recording of Couperin's harpsichord music, thinks that *Les Laurentines* refers to Latium, where Virgil's Aeneas disembarked. The inhabitants were called Laurentes (in French *laurentins* or *laurentines*) and, according to Beck, the music laments because it depicts the passage in Book XII of the *Aeneid* wherein Queen Amata and her daughter Lavinia (who will become Aeneas's consort) wailfully implore Turnus to cease fighting. Though Couperin had some Latin, this seems to me wildly speculative; there's nothing in the music, which is a courante, to suggest that it is tearful. It is far more probable that Couperin responded to an up-to-the-minute impulse, his friends the theatrical Laurents.

L'Espagnolète. A Spanish-style dance, with castanets; and also a tight-sleeved gown fashionable in the late seventeenth century. La Manon was famous for her performances of the dance, so this may be another portrait of her. The Spanish association bears obliquely on the Dauphin disaster, for Saint-Simon tells us that in Spain 'the grief and horror at these successive calamities was beyond belief'. The piece itself, though in the minor, is not particularly melancholic; and Couperin incorporates a subtle musical joke in punning on a subsidiary meaning of the word. An espagnolette is a window-latch: the turning of which Couperin imitates in the turns on the second quaver of the opening phrase, and in all repetitions of it.

Les Regrets. A heart-felt piece which surely mourns, in its languishing appoggiaturas, the young Dauphin. Couperin's direction *languissament* often carries an ironic overtone, but the frailty of the ornamentation here does not suggest *précieux* affectation but rather a tender regret for promise unfulfilled.

Les Matelotes Provençales. The melancholy of *Les Regrets* is abruptly deflated by this major-keyed hornpipe of female Provençal sailors: comic music-hall characters such as appeared in Lully's ballets. Again, farce provides release from grief and suffering.

La Favorite. This magnificent chaconne-rondeau reinstates and
brings to consummation the passionate C minor gravity of

the early pieces in the *ordre*; the vehemence of the allemande and sarabande is now serenely controlled. It could be a funeral lament for the Dauphin. Saint-Simon tells us that 'the people wept for one who had thought only of their deliverance; all France mourned a prince whose sole desire had been for her happiness and welfare; the sovereigns of Europe publicly mourned for one whom they had already taken as their model, and whose great merit might one day have made him an arbiter between the nations. The Pope was so profoundly moved that, unasked, he set the Roman tradition aside, and with universal approval held a special consistory at which he mourned the incalculable loss suffered by Christendom and the Church' (*Mémoires*, 1712). The music conveys all this: grief, dignity, majesty, power, and so truly effects an apotheosis to the suite. It has been suggested that the piece is so aristocratically beautiful that it could be a portrait of either of the King's most heartfelt loves, Louise de la Vallière and Françoise Athénais de Montespan. These contenders are however less appropriate to the music than the dead Dauphin; and in any case Couperin was a baby when la Vallière ceased to be the apple of Louis's eye and was only fifteen when de Montespan was exiled from Versailles.

La Lutine. Characteristically, Couperin doesn't end with his 'apotheosis' but brings us back to prankish normalcy with this little piece about sprites and goblins such as were rampant in bacchanalian revels in masques and divertissements. When beset by catastrophe we need such libidinal release in order to go on living. Though the limits of decorum should be preserved one should, in playing this piece, emphasize the angularities of the theme in slightly uncomfortable grotesquerie.

Ordre IV in F major and minor

This *ordre*, which is short, is the first to have a distinctive character; clearly it wasn't a compilation, but was planned as a whole. Its mood is comic, with theatrical associations, and its F major tonality was traditionally lightweight – and remains so in, for instance, the music of Beethoven and even Brahms. In the baroque period, and still in Beethoven, Gluck, Berlioz and many

other composers with classical affiliations, it had pastoral connotations. Couperin often used it in that context: but more
commonly (as here) for genre pieces with comic or even farcical
overtones.

La Marche des Gris-vêtus. This has nothing to do with St Francis,
who was known as St Gris, but refers to a fashionable
regiment with a distinctive grey uniform. The parading
soldiers are presented somewhat ironically, as one would
expect of Couperin. Both Beck and Citron say that a frag-
ment of Lully's march for the Turenne regiment is incorporated in the middle. I cannot spot it; but if it is there the
words to the tune – the one adapted by Bizet for the
Farandole of his *L'Arlésienne* music – underline the irony:
'Des gris-vêtus chantons la Gloire/Chantons leurs vertus
quand il faut boire/Et faisons l'honneur à leur vigueur.'

Les Baccanales. A carousel in three sections, the first of which,
Enjouemens Bachiques, does sound like a regimental drinking
song! The second part, *Tendresses Bachiques*, is in the minor,
and F minor, the flattest key in general use, was traditionally the key of *chants lugubres*. The sighing appoggiaturas are satirical, if affecting; and the medley of
ornaments creates a maudlin rhythmic confusion. Margery
Halford points out in her edition of *L'Art de toucher le
Clavecin* that this passage is about the most problematical –
the most difficult to interpret – in Couperin's harpsichord
music. When tipsy, we get our ornaments fuddled; and no
doubt the frustration prompts the third section, *Fureurs
Bachiques*, at first still in infernal F minor, like Lully's devil
musics, but clearing to F major for the final revels, with
bounding scales and double suspensions in syncopation. It
seems a little odd that F major, the benignly pastoral key,
should often also be associated in classical French theatre
music (and by imitation in Purcell) with skittish demons;
perhaps the unconscious collocation is that the 'natural'
world, unaided by human reason, may easily and arbitrarily
go to the bad. The 6 : 8 metre was traditionally associated
with an earthy corporeality. Beck again refers to the classics
in connection with this piece: this time to Horace's Nineteenth Ode, *Bacchum in remotis carmina rupibus Vidi docentem*.
I see no justification for this, except in the general sense that

bacchanalian revels in classical French opera and ballet paid deference to what people imagined to be the conventions of antiquity.

La Pateline. Patelin was a character in a fifteenth-century French farce, though this probably refers to an adaptation by Brueys and Palaprat performed in Paris in 1706. It was a hit, and must have been known to the theatre-loving Couperin. The original Patelin was suave and crafty, and so is this music, though it is gracious rather than grotesque.

Le Réveil-matin. One of the rare pieces that is directly programmatic. It sounds very like an alarm clock, if performed with brisk precision; but its wit is not merely onomatapœic. The whirring bell disrupts the cheerful clatter of the ticking mechanism, carrying with it the threat, as well as the promise, of a new day. The little piece, though risible, is disturbing to the nervous system!

Ordre V in A major and minor

This, the last *ordre* in Book I, is again long, and incorporates character pieces and portraits alongside dances. But it makes a more coherent entity than the first three *ordres*, and has a distinctive flavour related to its A major tonality. For Charpentier A major had been '*joyeux et champêtre*'; and for Couperin as for Bach (and for that matter Mozart) it is a radiant key, glowingly sensuous yet not erotic. Here the movements in the minor key (which for Charpentier was '*tendre et plaintif*') are not in ironic contrast with the major movements but rather balance them, underlining the wistfulness inherent in sensuous awareness, simply because it is subservient to Time. This is one reason why the lengthy suite preserves homogeneity.

La Logiviére. A majestic allemande which presumably portrays a noble character, though we don't know whom.

La Dangereuse. Nor do we know who is depicted in this oddly titled sarabande, which is ceremonious but hardly dangerous. There are no unexpected modulations, and the architectural proportions, the symmetries of phrase with phrase, are more not less regular than is customary in Couperin.

La Tendre Fanchon. In this case, however, we may be specific: Fanchon Moreau was a singer of the Académie Royale de Musique. Couperin must have known her well, since she is 397 identified in his slightly bawdy canon, *La femme entre deux draps*, and appears with her sister Louison in the three-voiced air, *Trois Vestales champêtres et trois Poliçons*, which is also not devoid of sexual innuendo. Most of Couperin's secular vocal pieces are occasional *jeux d'esprit*, full of in-jokes now difficult to unravel. Fanchon and Louison were frequently mentioned in scurrilous verses and lampoons, despite or because of the fact that they moved in high society. Fanchon was a mistress of Philippe de Vendôme, Grand Prieur de France, and both sisters had intermittent liaisons with the Dauphin. Fanchon seems to have been an accomplished professional singer as well as a high-class courtesan. Couperin's portrait captures her wit and whimsicality; her tender sensuality is manifest in the sequential sevenths of the third couplet. This is one of the pieces in which the minor tonality renders both wit and sensuality wistful, if not melancholy.

La Badine. A wag, a joker. Presumably a tricksy and coquettish girl, though we have no clue as to her identity. This piece was first published by Ballard in 1707.

La Bandoline. Bandoline was a hair lacquer extracted from the pips of quinces, and the *coulé* right-hand quavers, ballasted by the detached octaves in the bass, do sound a bit gooey. But the piece has a grave, rather mysterious dignity and may be a portrait of a grand lady who wears hair lacquer. Perhaps she also came from Bandol, near Toulon.

La Flore. The goddess of flowers and mother of spring – or maybe a particular spring-like girl.

L'Angélique. This was a name for a seventeen-string lute, tradi-tionally an instrument with both divine and amorous asso-ciations. But the piece is not in lute style, so an angelic young woman – possibly Angélique Baudet – may be depicted.

La Villers. A pliantly sensuous and feminine piece that must be a portrait of Anne de Mailly, wife of Christophe-Alexandre Pagot Le Villers, to whom this volume is dedicated.

Les Vendangeuses. These grape harvesters are lustily bucolic, in popular vein. Played with varying degrees of *inégalité*, as they are by Kenneth Gilbert, they sound too as though they've been imbibing of the fermented product of their labours. Perhaps they're merely drowsy-drunk on sun.

Les Agrémens. A technical term meaning ornaments, of course. But the piece is no more ornamented than most, and the title probably refers to agreeable conversation and *la politesse.* The word *agrémens* was also used of jewels, glistening on fine ladies' finer clothes.

Les Ondes. A very sumptuous piece, in the dark lower register – so it's probably about sea-nymph sirens who sport in the waters, as well as about the waves themselves.

Book II

Book II was published only four years later than Book I, in 1717; but by this time we can have little doubt that each *ordre* is conceived as an entity.

Ordre VI in B flat major

We have noted that the traditional pastoral key in baroque music was F major; B flat major, however, inherited and perhaps deepened its qualitites – as is still evident in Beethoven's Fourth and Sixth Symphonies. B flat major, subdominant to F major, is still more fascinatingly paradoxical. Though a conventional key for *le goût pastoral,* it was also, and more frequently than F major, employed by Lully for the antics of anti-masque demons and goblins. One reason for this may have been that two flats, being the flattest transposition permitted in sixteenth-century modality, acquired a taint of the 'lower' regions; another and more potent reason was that in French tunings B flat embraced a number of 'bad' intervals. (E flat major, with three flats, was *so* bad that it was normally eschewed; see the note on *La Visionnaire* from the Fourth Book). These 'negative' associations of B flat major seem to have been peculiarly French, for in his Italianate style in his early years Couperin writes B flat major movements that are unambiguously buoyant and bouncy – consider for instance *La Steinquerque* sonata and several of the rediscovered motets. In his harpsichord music, however, he usually employs B flat as a pastoral key; and although in this suite B flat is the reverse of demonic, I suspect that in celebrating nature's fruitfulness it allows for the momentary titillation of humanly fallible tuning. B flat doesn't here have the certitude and stability it acquired when, its fallibilities ironed out into equal temperament, it became for classical composers and supremely for Beethoven a key of humanly orientated power. None the less Couperin's pastoral B flat is modestly celebratory, for it here reflects the natural rhythms of the body, the spontaneity of the creatures, the human graces that distinguish us from the beasts. We are apt to forget that Couperin belonged to rural life no less than to the court and to Parisian streets. For all their artifice, Couperin's pastoral pieces wonderfully evoke the open air; the sights, sounds and smells of the country were close to him in a way that we, in our macadamized conurbations, cannot easily comprehend.

In 1714 the Duchess of Maine presented at Sceaux a divertissement populated by shepherds, shepherdesses and reapers, for which Mouret and Marchand wrote music and in which Couperin's cousin Marguerite-Louise sang. Couperin's pieces here invoke a similar landscape and introduce comparable personnel, but whereas the Duchess's dream-world was artifice that imprisoned her, Couperin's art is at once mythical and real – as is evident in the first piece –

Les Moissonneurs – which, like *Les Vendangeuses*, is open in sonority and corporeal in rhythm, making aurally incarnate the swing of the reapers' bodies and the swish of their scythes.

Les Langueurs-Tendres. One of the most justly famous of the pastoral pieces, in which the lines' intertwining ornamentation is human like a caress, natural like the tendrils of the vine. Emotional spontaneity and *précieux* artifice are in equilibrium, for Couperin's melancholy and his irony are complementary. A propos of this piece Citron appropriately quotes St Evremond: 'Languir est le plus beau des mouvements de l'amour; c'est l'effet délicat d'une flamme pure qui nous consume doucement; c'est une maladie chère et tendre qui nous fait haïr la pensée de notre guérison.'

La Gazouillement. A twittering and warbling of birds, surprisingly naturalistic, if highly civilized.

La Bersan. André Bauyn, Seigneur de Bersan, was an acquaintance, possibly a friend, of Couperin; but this is probably his daughter, for the music trips fleetly.

Les Baricades Mistérieuses. One of Couperin's technical jokes, the continuous suspensions in lute style being a barricade to the

LA SÉRÉNADE.

SCAPIN.
Le voilà, Monsieur; je ne viens
qu'à bonnes enseignes.

Scène XIX

XVII. 'La Sérénade': Emile Bayard as Scapin, an undated engraving by Follet. Such types are auralized by Couperin in his pieces about 'les calots, les gueux et les jongleurs'.

basic harmony; and this may link up with the illusory devices in a masque décor. *Barricade* had its modern sense after 1648, but if the harmonic ambiguities might be described as 'revolutionary' in the context of baroque orthodoxies, the tone of the music remains, even in its mystery, impeccably aristocratic.

Les Bergeries. Not surprisingly this haunting melody, civilized yet as beguiling as a folk song, became famous. Bach copied it into Anna Magdalena's Notebook; and in 1731 Rameau's patron, Le Riche de la Pouplinière, heard it played on a carillon at Delft. Bergeries were little curls, small locks coyly turned up with a puff, and also of course the pseudo-shepherdesses who sported them.

La Commère. The comic *naïveté* of the imitative phrases suggests that this group chatters on the village green rather than at court: so *le goût pastoral* is preserved.

Le Moucheron. Another comically illustrative piece. Couperin's fingering makes the insect hover more tauntingly.

Ordre VII in G major

This *ordre* is even more closely devoted to a single 'theme' than is the sixth, for it concerns a single character, Françoise-Charlotte de Senneterre, Mlle de Ménetoud, dancer, singer, flautist and harpsichordist. An infant prodigy, she appeared before the King when she was nine; the sweetly sensuous key of G major is here, and was often, associated by Couperin with childhood innocence, though he veers to the minor for the pangs of adolescence.

La Ménetou. Couperin opens with a perhaps slightly idealized portrait of the talented girl, singing, dancing, fluting in smiling grace. Then in

Les Petits âges he follows her career from birth (*La Muse Naissante*) through childhood (*L'Enfantine*) and adolescence (*L'Adolescente*) to sexual maturity (*Les Délices*). In the first section the texture sounds childlike, in two syncopated parts. As she grows from babyhood through childhood the music still sings sweetly, but in the minor key, aware of mutability. The fourth section, *Les Délices*, finds fulfilment in the major and is the most substantial piece, both in length

and in its relatively thick texture, with voluptuous sequential sevenths in the third couplet.

La Basque. A rondeau in two sections, first minor, then major. It
was a dance, perhaps performed by the precocious La
Ménetoud.

La Chazé. A château in the province of Maine-et-Loire. It ought
to have some connection with La Ménetoud, though we
don't know what. The next and last piece is certainly her
music, for

Les Amusemens returns to the smiling G major, the textural
simplicity and the syncopations of the early numbers of the
suite, though with enhanced sensuality.

Ordre VIII in B minor

It cannot be an accident that Couperin follows the childlike
seventh *ordre* with his grandest and most tragic statement. B
minor had always been a very special key, probably because,
being the minor relative of D major (key of natural trumpets and
of open-stringed violins and therefore apposite to human pomp
and circumstance), it became associated with suffering – with
what life is 'really' like, beneath our pretentiously hopeful
façades. Charpentier had called B minor '*solitaire et mélancholique*'; for Bach and Couperin it was a key of purgatorial suffering; for classical composers – Haydn, Mozart, Beethoven and
Schubert – it was a 'black' key, though the first three used it
infrequently, perhaps because they conscientiously supported
the optimistic ethic of the Enlightenment. Their support, however, grew progressively more desperate; and for Schubert, as
for Brahms, another romantic classicist, B minor is again a
quintessential key. Couperin's B minor mood, at least in this
crucial eighth *ordre*, offers no possibility of dreamful evasion. All
the pieces are resolutely in B minor, unalleviated by the major,
except in momentary, incidental modulation. All are gravely
impassioned, until they culminate in the famous *Passacaille*.
Playing them through in sequence makes us wonder if their
sensuous intensity, which never blurs lucidity, may have been
triggered off by Couperin's contemplation of the painting of
Raphael – for the opening allemande is called

La Raphaéle, and we know that Couperin was acquainted with
Watteau's patron Crozat, and played in the concerts he   403

sponsored in his fine mansion. This housed a celebrated collection of Raphaels.

L'Ausoniéne. A quicker allemande, without the passionate grandeur and grave opulence of *La Raphaéle*, but none the less with Italian connections, since the word is an archaic, poetical name for an Italian (after Ausonius). The Duke of Bourgogne was Seigneur d'Ausone and may well be the subject of this piece. Born in 1682, he was a talented pupil of Fénelon and, according to Saint-Simon, was 'passionné pour toute sorte de volupté', loving 'la musique avec une sorte de ravissement'. He became Couperin's pupil in 1694. A Judith Beseraige d'Ausone was a well-known amateur musician, but there is no evidence that Couperin was acquainted with her.

Courantes 1 and *2*.

Sarabande: L'Unique.

Gavotte.

Rondeau.

All these pieces adhere austerely to classical dance forms, though there would seem to be character portrayal in the one piece, the sarabande, that has a title. The oddity of *L'Unique* lies in its metrical vagaries – the intrusion within the *grave* 3 : 4 pulse of two episodes in 3 : 8, marked *vivement*. It would seem to portray someone of quixotic temperament, though we don't know whom. The sequence of dances climaxes in the

Passacaille, which we have described as Couperin's ultimate tragic testament. After this outburst, however, Couperin characteristically returns us to the polite social world, appending another little piece with a title –

La Morinéte. This is a simple Corellian gigue, to be played *lié et très tendrement*. Since it is still in dark B minor and is gently melancholic rather than boisterous, it is probably a portrait of the daughter of Jean-Baptiste Morin, rather than of this minor composer himself: though he was celebrated for his alleluya finales in gigue form!

Ordre IX in A major and minor

This suite, also on quite a large scale, has similar characteristics to the fifth suite in the same key. Here too the music is sensuous but radiant; and the same mood more pathetically colours the pieces in the minor.

La Princesse de Sens. Another daughter of the Duc de Bourbon, and therefore a sister of Mme Bourbon-Conti and of the Duchesse de Maine. She too was a pupil of Couperin, who offers her the most tenderly sensual of the pieces dedicated to the three sisters. Perhaps he is punning on her name.

L'Olimpique. A very bold lady, bounding in dotted rhythm like the heroic figure from classical antiquity. But specifically Olympe de Brouilly, wife of the Duc d'Aumont, a patron and friend of Couperin from his St Gervais days. According to Saint-Simon he had 'peu de reputation à la guerre', but was a man 'd'un goût excellent', with a passion for music. Concerts were held in the handsome Hôtel d'Aumont, built by Le Vau and renovated by Mansart; Couperin may have performed at them. The Duc d'Aumont was a close friend of La Fontaine and, since there are many affinities between the sensibilities of poet and composer, it would be pleasant to think that they may have met at the Hôtel d'Aumont.

L'Insinuante.

La Séduisante.

Again we have no clue as to whether these pieces are generalized psychological studies or portraits of individuals.

Le Bavolet-Flotant. This was a bouquet of ribbons affixed to a hat. Its effect was seductive, as is this ravishing melody, which portrays the girl beneath the *bavolet* as well as the headgear itself.

Le Petit-deuil ou les trois Veuves. Petit-deuil is half-mourning. One suspects a wry joke, for the music is graciously cheerful: though we don't know who the three widows are.

Ordre X in D major and minor

This suite exploits the martial characteristics of the major key, but does so comically, even farcically.

La Triomphante is a brilliant battle piece in three sections: *Bruit de guerre, Allégresse des Vainqueurs* and *Fanfare.* But Couperin was not a man to create massive music celebrating martial exploits, so scales shoot and arpeggios tootle ironically. One suspects that the battle is bibulous rather than military, 405 and Bacchus is a pervasive presence throughout the suite.

La Mézangére. Bacchus is not overtly present in this darkly sonorous, lute-styled piece in dotted rhythm, dedicated to Antoine Scott, Seigneur de la Mézangère and Maître d'Hôtel to the King, or to his wife, Anne-Elisabeth Conti, who was among Couperin's pupils. The male dedication seems the more likely in view of the music's powerfully complex texture. There may be a hint of inebriation in the hazily overlapping figurations and in the drooping movement; and there is more than a hint of the bacchic in

La Gabriéle, since although the dedicatee might be Jacques Gabriel, the designer of the organ-case and of other decorations in the Chapelle Royale, it is more probably the singer, Gabriel-Vincent Trévénard, who performed in most major opera productions between 1697 and 1729. In addition to his celebrity as an artist, he was a star personality, adored by women and feted by courtiers. He sang opposite the notorious Fanchon ('truly the most beautiful young lady of her time', according to Le Brisoys Desnoiresterres); and loved wine and women no less than he loved song. Campardon tells us that he 'swallowed considerable quantities of wine under the specious pretext that it strengthened his voice'. If the piece is his, it seems inadequate to his glamour, being a jolly Corellian jig, recalling the fanfares of the battle pieces. The imitative falling scales sound mildly tipsy, not wildly inebriated; but so gallant a character, with his theatrical training, would no doubt have carried his liquor well.

La Nointéle. There's a tenuous bacchic association here too, for the piece is remarkably similar to *Les Vendangeuses* of the fifth *ordre.* The Seigneur de Nointel commissioned Watteau to decorate a room in his Parisian house with murals on the theme of wine. The vinous music suggests that this is a portrait of the Seigneur, Jean de Turmenies, rather than of his wife, who was a prissier type, daughter of a wealthy banker.

La Fringante. A frisky horse, here surely identified with a young woman who prances, *vif et relevé,* in the rhythm of a canarie. She is almost as bouncily aggressive as the subject of the next piece –

L'Amazone. Almost certainly Mlle de Maupin, who was described as 'une des plus vaillantes amazones qui se pût voir'.

Both these girls could in twentieth-century terms be called militant, if not military. According to *Le Mercure Galant* La Maupin, who was an accomplished singer, worked with Couperin and his cantatrice cousin. It would seem that Couperin found her good fun: which may be why he ends the suite with

Les Bagatelles. Trifles which, scored for *mains croisées*, create a sonority that sounds like laughter, or even giggles.

Ordre XI in C minor–major

This suite is brief, and exploits the contrast between the gravity of the minor and the frivolity of the major in much the same way as the third *ordre*, but more precisely.

La Castelane. A sober allemande, dedicated to a member of the illustrious Castelane family, rather than to an anonymous castle-keeper's daughter.

L'Etincelante ou la Bontems. Dichotomy between the broody *La Castelane* and this C major jape is overtly ironic. *Bontems* means good time, diversion, pleasure, and that meaning effects the character of the music, the scales of which certainly sparkle (*étinceler*). But the specific reference is to Louis-Nicolas Bontemps, Chief Valet to the King's Chamber. Perhaps he was a sprightly character; perhaps Couperin was merely punning on his name. The sequel or '*suite de la Bontems*', entitled *Les Graces Natureles*, portrays his wife, Charlotte le Vasseur; her music, unsparkling but affectionate, suggests that she was a charming creature. Since she had died, quite young, in 1709, the piece was probably written several years before publication.

La Zénobie. An enigmatic title, with classical and possibly theatrical associations. Georges Beck suggests that she may be the Queen of Palmyra, described by La Bruyère as heroically fronting a hostile destiny, after the death of her husband. Although a gigue, the piece has both grace and gravity.

Les Fastes de la Grande et Ancienne Ménestrandise. A tragi-comedy in five acts, the most celebrated, and musically rewarding, of Couperin's excursions into low life. The *Ménestrandise* was a musicians' guild or trade union, founded in 1321. The leader was called the *roi des menétriers*. The guild was

407

Il y a environ trois ans que ces pieces sont achevées; Mais comme ma santé diminuë de jour en jour, mes amis m'ont conseillé de cesser de travailler et je n'ay pas fait de grands ouvrages depuis. Je remercie le Public de l'aplaudissement qu'il à bien voulu leur donner jusqu'icy; Et je crois en meriter vne partie par le Zele que j'ai cu à lui plaire. Comme personne n'a gueres plus composé que moy, dans plusieurs genres, J'espere que ma Famille trouvera dans mes Portefeüilles dequoy me faire regretter, Si les regrets nous serventà quelque chose apres la Vie, Mais il faut du moins avoir cette idée pour tacher de meriter vne jmmortalité chimerique ou presque tous les Hommes aspirent.

XVIII. Facsimile of Couperin's foreword to his Fourth Book of harpischord pieces.

sanctioned by Louis in 1659 and tried to establish authority over all composers, organists and harpsichordists, as well as the lower ranks of professional musicians. Only accredited members of the *Ménestrandise* were licensed to perform. In 1693 a group of composers, including Couperin, made a protest to the King: which was repeated, in aggravated circumstances, in 1707. On both occasions the *Ménestrandise* was defeated. Couperin's group of satirical pieces is part of the propaganda war against the closed shop. The irony is double-edged, however. The initial march of the *Notables et Jurés-Ménestrandeurs* is clownishly pompous: whereas the lower orders of fiddlers and beggars touch, through their whining viols and droning hurdy-gurdies, abysses of pathos as well as misery. Similarly the jugglers and acrobats with their bears and monkeys are farcical; but the duet between the two groups of cripples, *disloqués* in the right hand, *boiteux* (peg-legged) in the left, carries a joke to the brink of tragedy. Throughout this paradoxical mingle of the ridiculous and the sublime Couperin veers and tacks between the major and minor key, ending in a C major rout which is as much scary as funny.

Ordre XII in E major and minor

This, the last suite of the second book, is also short. Couperin's E major is usually a happy key, lighter, more floating than his A major. Charpentier had called it '*querelleur et criard*', but for Couperin it seems to suggest a tranquil content: upward-tending, though without the paradisal associations that E major, as the sharpest key in common use, frequently has in Bach and Handel, and later in Beethoven and Schubert. Couperin's E minor agrees with Charpentier's prescription in being '*effeminé, amoureux et plaintif*', though his E minor mood often acquires an elegiac nobility.

Les Juméles: Twins, appropriately in two parts, the first major, the second minor. In the second part the melody is in twin-like mirror inversion with that of the first part.

L'Intîme.

La Galante.

La Coribante.

These three pieces may be portraits of unidentified people   409 or may depict psychological states. *L'Intime* creates its intimacy from its irregularly related phrasing. *La Galante* is more perky than galant, which may bear on the fact that a *galante* was a mouche worn on the cheek, in a manner that was considered rather 'fast'. There may also be point in the fact that *La Coribante*, with its plunging fifths and sixths, begins like a minor-keyed parody of the major-keyed *La Galante*. Its classical allusion to the rites of Cybele may draw a wry parallel with the Duc d'Orléans's messier orgies.

La Vauvré. Jean-Louis Girardin, Seigneur de Vauvré, was one of the King's maîtres d'hôtel. This may be he or his wife and either, on the evidence of the music, must have been aimiable.

La Fileuse. A woman, who might be peasant-like rather than aristocratic, spinning away in Time-obliterating figuration and in blissful E major.

La Boulonoise. Here again the tune has a folky flavour, though the piece is probably another tribute to the Duc d'Aumont, or his wife. Their son was Governor of Boulogne.

L'Atalante. A piece rather fiercer than is habitual with Couperin in his E minor mood. Presumably the fleet Atlanta of classical antiquity is depicted, though a reference to some Atlanta-like contemporary may also be implicit.

Book III

The second book, we have seen, marks the emergence of the Couperin *ordre* as an entity, each with a distinctive character of its own: a process that the third book consolidates. It was published in 1722, when Couperin was fifty-four, and was the first volume to be published after the death of Louis XIV.

Ordre XIII in B minor

This is a tribute to the Regent in which the sequence of pieces not only makes musical sense, but is also ordered so that it tells an incidentally comic but ultimately tragic tale.

Couperin knew the Regent well, and apparently cared for him. His mother, the Duchess of Orléans, describes him with her habitual bluntness: 'From the age of fourteen to that of fifteen years, my son was not ugly; but after that time he became very much sun-burnt in Italy and Spain. Now, however, he is too ruddy; he is fat, but not tall, and yet he does not seem disagreeable to me. The weakness of his eyes causes him sometimes to squint. . . . I love my son with all my heart; but I cannot see how anyone else can, for his manners are little calculated to inspire love. In the first place he is incapable of passion, of being attached to anyone for a long time; in the second place he is not sufficiently polished and galant to make love. He does not like fine airs so well as profligate manners; the opera-house dancers are his favourites. . . . My son understands music well, as all musicians agree. He has composed two or three operas, which are pretty. When he had nothing to do he painted for one of the Duchess's cabinets all the pastoral romance of Daphnis and Chloe. He is eloquent enough and can talk with dignity. . . . He learned to cook during his stay in Spain. . . . The people of Paris do not forgive him for running about at balls, like a young fool, for the amusement of women, when he has the cares of the kingdom upon his shoulders.'

Yet although even the Regent's mother, who loved him, found as much to blame as to praise in her son, and although his profligacy and debauchery appalled even the laxest among his contemporaries, there must have been more to this man than an idle generosity of purse and spirit. He was weak but not vicious, a blackguard but not a cad; he earned respect and affection from Saint-Simon at least until the last few years of his fairly brief life, and had the courage to confess that for him religion, about which the high and mighty sanctimoniously prated, seemed a ruse of the rich and clever to ensure docility from the poor and ignorant. And perhaps his claim to remembrance is that he inspired Couperin to compose this heartfelt *ordre*: for which he called on his quintessential key of 'reality' and suffering, B minor; and told in the sequence of pieces a story that is as sadly terrible as it is terribly sad.

Les Lis Naissans. The lily was the emblem of royalty, and the nobly pathetic broken chords of this piece aspire upwards, yet bend in the breeze. Regality is nascent, yet cannot come to flower.

Les Rozeaux tells us why, since reeds are also an emblem, this time of human frailty – the Regent's, of course, but not merely his. Again the slowly unfolding phrase aspires upwards, only to fall. The piece has the melancholy of hopes unfulfilled. The main reason why they are unfulfilled is inherent in

L'Engageante, which is a knot of yellow ribbons, or deep double ruffles, worn by grand and/or gay ladies in their *décolletage*, and stands generically for the seductions to which the woman-obsessed as well as music-loving Regent succumbed. Intrinsically, the piece is once more lovely, like the young women – though in fact the Regent didn't care what they looked like, so long as they were serviceable.

Les Folies Françoises ou les Dominos is the climax of the *ordre*. Both in its title and its musical theme it recalls the most celebrated of all chaconne basses, the *Folia*, which, deriving from Spain and Portugal, was used as a fundament for variations by a succession of seventeenth-century composers, such as d'Anglebert, Marais, Frescobaldi and Corelli, whose *Folia* with twenty-three variations, published in 1700, acquired international celebrity as a virtuoso piece. Though Citron is going rather far in saying that Corelli's theme may be superimposed on that of Couperin's *Les Folies Françoises*, 'alors même qu'ils ne sont pas dans le même ton', I have little doubt that Couperin meant us to spot the reference to the earlier chaconne. On it his *Folies* make a commentary that is at once ironic and pathetic: ironic, because Corellian virtuosic grandeur is transformed into a Watteauesque masked ball such as the Regent was fanatically partial to (they were banned on account of their licentiousness); pathetic, because Couperin's music, like Watteau's painting, presents the ball in ideality, each variation being a different coloured mask which enshrines psychological truth even as it propagates illusion. Thus the sequence of dominos moves inevitably from the neutrality of the theme *La Virginité* (*couleur d'invisible* in this shady environment) to *La Pudeur* (*couleur de Roze*), to *L'Ardeur* (*sous le Domino incarnat*, in thrusting dotted rhythm), to *L'Esperance* (*sous le Domino vert*, in a desperately clattering 9 : 8), and so to a sadly wilting *Fidélité* (*Domino Bleu*, in old-fashioned, presumably near-obsolete 'white' notation). From that point there's nothing to do but to attempt a fresh start in *La Persévérance* (*Domino Gris de lin*), with the original theme at the original speed, though less hopefully – which explains the grey mask. Henceforth love and life disintegrate. *La Langueur* (*Domino Violet*) is again in white-note figuration, now not so much archaic as gelid, drained of vitality. *La Coquéterie* (*sous diférens Dominos*) relinquishes the pretence of passion to become a multi-metred tease. The young lack all conviction, while the old, the ancient galants and superannuated whores, limp and stomp behind their *Dominos Pourpres et feuilles mortes* in a farcical pretence of grandeur. True love is finally demolished with the joke about the ironically 'benevolent' cuckoos, whose musical *naïveté* spells disaster. For they lead to *La Jalousie taciturne*, in which the old-fashioned white notation has become sinister because unreal. If the *Domino gris de Maure* is a reference to Shakespeare's *Othello*, as is not impossible, this gives an additional twist to the theme of appearance and reality. 'Noble' Othello is a blackamoor, and blackness is associated with evil and sin – as becomes explicit when the chaconne explodes in its final variation, *La Frénésie ou le Désespoir, sous le Domino noir*! The effect is similar to the end of the great *Passacaille*. Couperin has revealed the blackest terrors behind the masking dominos and the ball's frivolous façade, and appends as epilogue his most concentratedly tragic utterance –

L'âme-en-peine, a piece as violent as the *Passacaille*, yet covering only one page. Again Couperin's irony and his melancholy are interdependent, and that *Les Folies Françoises* is riddled with witty japes only makes this epilogue the more agonizing. This is indeed an apotheosis to the disaster of the Regent's life; a soul in purgatory is redeemed by the tragic grace of Couperin's music.

The association of this suite with the Regent was originally made by Jane Clark, and seems to me convincing. It has however been challenged by my friend Michael Moran, whose knowledge of the period is considerable. He points out that the Regent was not royal in any real sense of succession to the throne, and so wouldn't have been entitled to the Fleur de Lys. An interpretation more in keeping with the literary spirit of the time would, he considers, be to regard the *ordre* as a 'moral lecture' to the young Dauphin, later Louis XV. 'Certainly the 413

Regent's lascivious life may have inspired Couperin to examine the nature of a tormented soul, but surely as a warning to one whose life was before him rather than as a tribute to one whose life was drawing to its close. This is the only *ordre* that concludes on a note of deepest pessimism. To the Dauphin it would have meant that such a dark fate as is contained in *L'âme-en-peine* is inescapable if the passions are allowed to rule reason. If offered to the Regent its unassuaged gloom would have offered no consolation at all, scarcely a helpful gesture from Couperin who was his friend.'

There is a lot to be said for this view; I doubt it only because the music sounds like a heartfelt personal testament rather than a moral lecture.

Ordre XIV in D major and minor

This suite forms a contrast to the thirteenth in a manner that is psychologically revealing at a level deeper than irony. For it deals in its open D major with the open air and the creatures that live in it, at the opposite pole to the passions that make all us humans, not merely a distraught Regent, simultaneously tragic and absurd.

Le Rossignol-en-amour.
La Linote éfarouchée.
Les Fauvétes Plaintives.
Le Rossignol-vainqueur.

> All these bird pieces are quite subtly descriptive, with liquid flourishes for the nightingale and plaintive tweets for the warblers. The linnet doesn't sound particularly scared, though his reiterated rising third suggests a mild agitation. The plaintive warblers anthropomorphically absorb the pathos of the minor key; and all the pieces probably contain amorous in-jokes about human birds. We'll never know what they are, and they don't matter except in so far as they indicate how interdependent Couperin's out-of-doors and in-doors were.

La Julliet. If she is a girl, nothing is known about her, unless she could be Romeo's Juliet irregularly spelled. The month of July was sometimes thus spelled in French literature, so this may be a summer piece, apposite to the birds as well as to

414 *Le Carillon de Cithére.* A Watteauesque paradise evoked in the

tintinnabulations of little bells. Chirruping birds are also emulated, sounding at once like real denizens of nature and like angelic messengers. Always in Couperin there is this equivocation between the artifices we cleverly invent and the dreams we will-lessly dream. In Watteau's painting the beautiful young people embarking for Cytherea are attired in fancy dress: they know that Cytherea, however desirable, is a Never-never-land.

Le Petit-Rien. Significantly the *ordre* ends with this insubstantial two-part invention: which might be human fatuity aurally shrugging its shoulders, or might be a bird cocking a delicate snook at our imbecility, as contrasted with the self-sufficiency of victorious nightingales. Even frightened linnets don't *know* that they're scared by the cat.

Ordre XV in A minor and major

This short *ordre* fuses sensuality and pathos even more subtly than the two previous *ordres* in A. It forms a natural sequence to the two suites that precede it in that whereas the thirteenth (about the Regent) was fundamentally 'introverted' while the fourteenth (concerned with the creatures of the air) was 'extroverted', this fifteenth *ordre* is in equilibrium between introversion and extroversion.

La Régente ou la Minerve. An allemande that dissolves physical gestures into a *tendresse* at once spiritual and *spirituel*. It's a very 'inward' piece that lives up to Couperin's directive *noblement*; and the *sans lenteur* which he adds implies here, as it usually does in Couperin, that the emotion is real, without trace of parody. The quality and character of the music resemble that of the thirteenth *ordre*, which we have seen to be (probably) about the Regent, so one might think that this too is a *pièce Régente*. But the alternative title, *ou la Minerve*, must be feminine – so we have to conclude that this is a portrait of the Regent's wife who has had a notoriously bad press. The Regent himself had little time to spare for her from his debauched cronies and doxies, and christened her Mme Lucifer, as a riposte to her crazy pride. The Regent's mother dismisses her even more vitriolically, remarking that she 'looks older than she is, for she paints beyond all measure, so that she is often quite red. . . . She is so indolent 415 that she will not stir; she would like larks ready roasted to drop into her mouth; she eats and walks slowly, but eats enormously. It is impossible to be more idle than she is. . . . I always compare her to Narcissus, who died of self-admiration. She is so vain as to think she has more sense than her husband, who has a great deal; while her notions are not in the slightest degree elevated.' Could such a creature be the subject of such noble music? Perhaps Couperin recognized traces of the regality she inherited as the daughter of the King by Mme de Montespan, and therefore a sister of the Duc de Maine. Perhaps the inwardness of Couperin's vision was precisely to see things the world couldn't see: that the Regent's wife was of bluer blood than her husband and didn't, even if she was no Minerva except in Couperin's eyes or rather ears, totally deny her birthright. There is no evidence to corroborate Saint-Simon's tittle-tattle that at the age of nineteen she had been 'drunk as a bell-ringer three or four times a week'; and the Duchess of Orléans was temperamentally bound to disapprove of any wife, as distinct from mistress, her son contracted with.

Le Dodo ou l'Amour au Berceau. An introverted piece in a different sense, for this lullaby for Cupid, radiant in the open simplicity of its melody, inwardly sensuous in its harmonic texture, sways us into the realms of sleep. The tune, if not exactly a folk-song, is a variant of 'Orléans, Baugency', much sung and played as a contredanse in Couperin's day. Perhaps the Orléans reference relates the baby to the Regent and therefore to the previous piece. Whoever the child is, Couperin's version of the tune, balanced equally between its major and minor sections, manages to be simultaneously warmly enveloping and pathetically frail: the babe's vulnerability and the mother's solace coexist in a nursery ditty.

L'Evaporée. The word means something between vapid and giddy, in the colloquial sense. Though this unambiguously major and merry piece would seem to belong to the 'extrovert' category it is not quite what it seems: the anonymous young woman's vapidity moves so rapidly and lightly that she too seems insubstantial as a dream.

Muséte de Choisi.

Muséte de Taverni.

416   These two outdoor pieces are also outward-looking in that

they imitate scenes of village life, with dancers and bagpipes. None the less the drones create a dreamy effect
because the hard edges of the tune dissolve into them. I
suspect they evoke childhood memories, for Couperin was
born at Choisy-en-Brie, and there was a Taverny near by.
The Princesse de Conti, one of Couperin's favourite pupils,
had a house at Choisy, so he probably maintained contact
with the haunts of his youth.

Les Vergers Fleüris. Descriptive nature music, of course; but I've
indicated how this marvellous piece, with its summer-
droning bagpipe in the middle section, lulls us into the un-
and sub-consciousness of sleep. Again it may re-evoke
childhood memories, or it may refer to the orchard of
Couperin's country retreat at St Germain-en-Laye. Perhaps, dozing in his St Germain orchard, he hazily recalls the
past.

La Douce et Piquante. An unknown girl, but her warmly gentle
melody seems emotionally in tune with the nature musics
prevalent in the suite. Again, 'external' and 'internal' circumstances are at one: as they are in

La Princesse de Chabeuil ou la Muse de Monaco. A sensuously
tender portrait in which a three-part texture glows through
an interweaving of tied notes with flowing semiquavers.
The Princess, daughter of Antoine I of Monaco, was a pupil
of Couperin, and a letter from the Prince to Couperin,
dated 1722, thanks him for a piece he'd composed specially
for her. More generally he adds: 'A day does not go past
without one of your pieces being played here. . . . She's like
a kitten who plays about with the ornaments that bother
her.' It is comforting to know that even Couperin's contemporaries, nurtured on the idiom, were sometimes thus
bothered. The Prince also advises Couperin to take care of
his ailing health.

Ordre XVI in G major and minor

In this suite G major has the same flavour of innocent sensuousness as it had in the previous *ordres* in this key, only it is more
'grown up' because texturally subtler, and it is counterpoised by
a higher proportion of movements in the minor; these tend,
however, to be gracefully elegiac rather than passionate. 417

Les Graces incomparables ou La Conti. This might be Couperin's pupil, the Mme de Conti who was originally a Bourbon, daughter of the fifth Prince de Condé; on the evidence of the piece previously dedicated to her, Couperin seems to have been fond of her. But the high-flown title of this piece rather suggests that the dedicatee is Marie-Anne, Louis XIV's favourite legitimized daughter by Mme de la Vallière, who married another Conti, Louis-Armand de Bourbon. She was a very special person, known as La Grande Princesse because she was tall by the standards of her time, and exceptionally beautiful, even among a galaxy of women who had little to do except groom themselves. Even the virulent Duchess of Orléans has to admit that 'this is of all the King's daughters the one he loves most. She is by far the most polite and well-bred.' She cannot however resist a sting in the tail, adding that she is 'now totally absorbed by devotion', perhaps Maintenon-induced. 'Now' must have been about the time of the publication of Couperin's luminously majestic allemande, which is certainly of incomparable grace, and a far cry from *La Bourbonnoise*, the earlier piece dedicated to the younger Mme Bourbon-Conti.

L'Himen-Amour. This minor-keyed piece, with its rigid rhythm and strained, arpeggiated minor ninths, makes marriage seem somewhat of a pain, as contrasted with the Princess's gallantry. Even the major-keyed *seconde partie* is, though harmonically open, rhythmically imprisoned. If there is a link by opposites between the two pieces, one might argue that the younger Princesse de Conti, Louise-Elisabeth, would fit the role better than the dowager Princess, daughter of La Vallière. On the whole, however, I opt for La Grande Princesse; after all, Couperin tells us that both pieces are to be played *majestueusement*.

Les Vestales. These vestal virgins return to an innocent G major, but shift more slyly to the minor for their *seconde partie*: in which key they end. One can take the title at its face value, or ironically, for the word *vestale* was sometimes waggishly used of a woman of easy virtue. There is a parody vocal version, *Trois Vestales champêtres et trois Poliçons*, the words of which are sexually dubious. But the music itself, which is to be played *sans lenteur*, is not suspect. The implication may be that the girls have their guileless charm whatever their proclivities.

L'Aimable Thérése. Citron thinks this is the Marquise de Lambert, at whose salon Couperin is known to have played, but Jane Clark's suggestion seems to me both more appealing and more plausible. She identifies her with Thérèse le Noir de la Thorillière, an actress who, according to Campardon's *Les Comédiens du Roi de la Troupe Française,* was as celebrated for her beauty as for her talent. She 'played amorous roles with all the grace and finesse possible'. It was she who, having married the lawyer Florent Dancourt, led him to the theatre and to the successful creation of comedies. Her life was sexually adventurous – as is implicit in her appearance in Couperin's *Trois Vestales champêtres* – but her piece has style, a gallantry apposite to the roles she specialized in on stage. This piece is clearly a minor-keyed complement to *Les Vestales,* itself a keyboard version of *Trois Vestales champêtres.*

Le Drôle de Corps. A character from the burlesque theatre, perhaps grotesquely crippled, for his musical gestures in the canarie he dances are ungainly, and his phrases are 'out of joint'.

La Distraite. Probably another burlesque character; the physical gestures of the whirling scales are grossly exaggerated. So these two burlesque pieces make another major–minor duo.

La Létiville. A jolly but songful piece in a flowing 12 : 8, in three 'real' parts, which can be played on two keyboards. We don't know what the title means; presumably it is someone's name.

Ordre XVII in E minor

This brief suite is in E minor throughout.

La Superbe ou la Forqueray. An allemande far grander than was habitual with Couperin in this key. The music is indeed *superbe,* in a vein of noble pathos rather than of heroic splendour; and was no doubt inspired by the subject, Antoine Forqueray (1671–1745), for he, as well as being *maître de musique* to the Duke of Orléans, was among the finest of bass viol players, and was, with Marais, the greatest composer for his instrument. Though he was not primarily a keyboard composer, some harpsichord music of exceptional quality, arranged by his nephew from his viol pieces, was published after his death, in 1747. Its manner is more overtly forward-looking than Couperin's: rhythmically vigorous and exuberantly textured in the style of Rameau. His D minor suite includes, however, a piece entitled *La Couperin* which, returning the compliment paid to him by Couperin, is delicately tuned to the older man's temperament – and to the key that Charpentier described as '*grave et dévot*'. Couperin's tribute to Forqueray achieves its nobility without countermanding the qualities he habitually found in E minor, for him a key of pathos rather than passion, and of wit rather than humour. Wit is certainly evident in the next piece –

Les Petits Moulins à Vent, which naturalistically imitates windmills while giving them a human dimension in the form of idle chatterboxes.

Les Timbres. A rondeau emulating little bells – which again garner human pathos, especially in the third couplet.

Courante. Here the rhythmic contradictions of the French *courante* are exploited wittily.

Les Petites Chrémiéres de Bagnolet. Another shred of evidence to suggest that the Duchess of Orléans, wife of the Regent, may have had qualities to mollify the Lucifer-like characteristics attributed to her by her husband and mother-in-law. She had a house of her own at Bagnolet, near Paris; Saint-Simon described it in 1717 as 'a large and charming country estate'. This piece, with its lilting, folk-flavoured tune, suggests that the Duchess may have emulated the Duchess of Maine, playing at dairy maids, attired *à la Boucher*.

Ordre XVIII in F minor and major

A large-scale suite, covering a variety of contradictory moods.

Allemande La Verneüil. Henri, the original Duc de Verneuil, was a natural son of Henri IV and of Henriette Balzac d'Estragues. Louis XIV called him uncle, though he was not a blood relation. Charlotte Séguier, daughter of the Chancellor of France, married him as her second husband, and at some point the Bourbons assimilated the title. There was also an actor called Verneuil, who specialized in heroic parts and, as we'll see, there are a number of theatrical pieces later in the *ordre*. None the less this grandly gloomy piece in the 'lugub-

rious' key of F minor sounds like the real, right thing, so I opt for a dedication to one of the Bourbons. Yet the next piece –
La Verneuilléte – prevents our swallowing the grandeur of *La Verneüil* with too owl-faced a solemnity. Though still gravely in F minor, with canonic imitation, the texture of this piece is lighter, its manner (*legèrement et agréablement*) slighter. Presumably it portrays a daughter, a chip off the old block, but young and feminine. And for the next piece –
Sœur Monique – we move to the major to portray another young girl. At its face value the smiling tune, in pastoral F major, images an adolescent nun: Couperin had a daughter who entered the cloisters, and he wrote music for convents. But the word *sœur*, like *vestale*, was used ironically for light ladies, and in a vocal parody the piece is indubitably a love song: 'Ma bergère, ma bergère,/L'amour se sert de vos doux attraits.' Though Couperin wasn't responsible for the parody, there is an equivocal element in the original, as in several of his portraits of young girls. A touch of kitten-like sexuality in the tune doesn't necessarily impugn its innocence. Whether or not Sœur Monique is play-acting slightly, there is a theatrical element in all the remaining pieces, beginning with
Le Turbulent, a very rare title in the masculine. It constitutes a shred of evidence to suggest that the feminine gender in the titles denotes the female sex, but hardly enough to discount the contrary evidence. The case that the singular is used to indicate that it is a portrait of Couperin himself as a child, playing pranks in the organ loft, seems difficult to substantiate; turbulence is not a quality one would expect even from a schoolboy Couperin. I suspect it's a burlesque piece, presenting a turbulent actor-acrobat teetering in clattering F major semiquavers on a trestle stage. The piece is funny, but a little frightening and so not altogether alien to the 'serious' pieces in the suite. At one level it helps us to recognize the gleam in Sister Monica's eye; at another level it prepares us for the switch back to F minor for
L'Atendrissante. A deeply affecting piece in double dotted rhythm, with an element of theatrical exaggeration in the wailing music as well as in the direction *douloureusement*. We don't know who is waiting, piteously appealing, for whom or what, but I think that both the baroque heroics and the 421

incipient Schumannesque romanticism of the music are tempered with defensive irony. In any case its gloom is punctured by

Le Tic-Toc-Choc ou les Maillotins. A brilliantly illustrative piece which whirs clock-like, comically but a little scarily, which is not surprising, given the remorselessness of Time. Maillotin is a diminutive of maillot, a mallet or hammer which was used as a military weapon (in this case Time's battering at us?) but also by builders and carpenters (our refuge against Time?). The 'works' of the clock are equated with the harpsichord's clattering mechanism. Punningly, the piece is also related to the burlesque tradition, for the Maillot family were members of the commedia dell'arte who, after their troupe was disbanded, became jugglers and tightrope dancers at the burlesque shows. The music simulates tight-rope walking no less effectively than it echoes the ticking of clocks. Maillot also means swaddling bands, but this cannot be relevant, even though infants enjoy playing with tick-tocks.

Throughout the suite, as well as within the individual pieces, there is a veering and tacking between disparate moods as well as modes that amounts to a highly sophisticated irony – a 'recognition of other modes of experience that may be possible'. Each stance modifies and comments on the others; and it's typical that the ordre should end with

Le Gaillard-Boîteux. A dance on the burlesque stage by a peg-legged man, his wooden stump bumping in the weirdly notated 2 : 6 (really 6 : 16) metre – which serves as a fair comment on the condition of most of us. In this wonderful suite F minor is used with its traditional associations of gravity and the funereal, while F major is employed not with its pastoral associations, but in Couperin's more personal relationship with theatrical illusion.

Ordre XIX in D minor and major

From this point onward the theatre – especially in its popular manifestations, the commedia dell'arte and the burlesque – exerts an increasing influence on Couperin's work. His acquaintance with the actors, actresses, mimes and dancers of the commedia must have survived, indeed prospered, long after the death of his friend Evaristo Gherardi, director of the company at the Hôtel de Bourgogne. On the general implications of Couperin's interest in the theatre I write in the essay on Couperin and Watteau; here seems the appropriate place to state that we have no evidence as to whether Couperin had any experience as a theatrical musician. He had some acquaintance with 'la vie de château' yet made no contribution to the genre of masque or *ballet de cour*, in the manner represented by the quite elaborate scores of composers from Lully to Campra, Mouret, Destouches and ultimately Rameau. His beautiful *Concert dans le Goût Théatral* proves that he was adept at such music, even though he didn't produce any for practical use in the theatre. Or at least he didn't produce any that has survived, for no doubt much masque music in France as in seventeenth-century England, being regarded as ephemeral, was issued in parts rather than in full score. It is probable, however, that Couperin, concerned as was Watteau with the 'ideality' of theatrical illusion, distilled it into purely instrumental forms instead of projecting it into theatre. This goes for the cultivated music for divertissements and *fêtes champêtres*; I'm less sure about the more socially and spiritually 'low' aspects of burlesque tradition, with which Couperin's affinities were direct. Perhaps he produced music for burlesque shows, which he didn't, since it was of its nature evanescent, bother to write down; or possibly his low characters – beggars, tightrope walkers, acrobats, hurdy-gurdy players, bears and monkeys – were flesh and blood yet at the same time idealizations of human attributes. In some ways they seem to anticipate, in their meticulous precision of texture, the fairground characters who, two hundred years later, precariously hold on for grim life in Erik Satie's cubist ballet, *Parade*. There's a hint of this in the tight two-part writing of the first piece in this *ordre* –

Les Calotins et les Calotines ou la Piéce à tretous, which is explicitly a music of the fair. *Le Régiment des Calottes* was a highly successful comedy presented in 1721 at the fair theatre. The *Calotte* was a secret society of bright young things mostly from the military class. They wore as their insignia a *calotte de plomb et des grélots*, and the purpose of their burlesque regiment was to protest against the growing solemnity of the court. Founded in 1702, they wrote satirical verses and performed burlesque plays. Later, after Couperin's day, they were transformed into a serious military society, which established a sophistical code of honour and instituted courts to try defections therefrom. *Tretous* is not, in these élitist circumstances, an ironic superlative of *tous*, but an old spelling of *tréteaux*; burlesque plays were often acted on an improvised stage of trestles. The fact that these pieces are theatre music, even fair music, naturally affects the mode of performance; they should be rhythmically precise, but perky rather than elegant. As in all the pieces *dans le goût burlesque* gestures should be extravagant.

L'Ingénue.

L'Artiste.

Both these pieces portray theatrical types. *L'Ingénue* is a comic character whose music rates as genuinely *in*genuous. But she's clearly a bit of a minx: as is confirmed by a vocal parody, the words of which are sexually ambiguous. *L'Artiste* is a more serious type, as an artist ought to be; the quasi-polyphonic texture is rich yet lucid, and the music sounds sensuously fulfilled and intellectually stable. There was also a bonnet known as an *artiste*.

Les Culbutes Jacobines. Culbutes means tumbles or somersaults, such as were common in burlesque plays. The *Jacobines* refers to the English community in exile at St Germain-en-Laye. The cavorting of the lines suggests burlesque activity on a stage, though it is not clear if or why Couperin thought the Jacobins funny. His disguising of their name with crosses (*Jxcxbxnxs*) may mean that he regarded them, or they regarded themselves, as a secret society. The music comes out, with its abrupt sequential modulations, as grotesque yet also disturbing, as befits a secret society. The joke would seem to be playful: hush-hush, the Jacobites are exiles, though in France at least they weren't in hiding. Couperin also uses crosses in his pieces about the musicians' union, *Les Fastes de la Grande et Ancienne Mxnxstrxndxsx*. In that case he's laughing at the union members' self-importance.

La Muse-Plantine. There seems to be no theatrical connotation here. Nor, although the piece concerns a professional musician, is there any hint of virtuoso showmanship. Mme de la Plante was described by Titon du Tillet as a harpsichordist who 'combined brilliance and delicacy with a perfect knowledge of composition'; her playing 'astonished the best organists and harpsichordists of Paris' – including Couperin, presumably. The piece, with its quaver figuration swaying over a chromatic bass alternating with sustained pedal notes, is gravely melancholic. Perhaps Couperin also regards *plantine* as an adjective fabricated from *plante*, for the piece slowly unfolds like a flower. This again would be a musical pun on the lady's character.

L'Enjouée. The obvious meaning is the main one: played *très gayement*, the music makes the young woman smirk. She could be an actress: especially since an *enjouée* was also a mouche worn, provocatively, on the cheek.

Book IV

In the fourth and last book, published in 1730 when Couperin was sixty-two, he has left far behind the keyboard suite as an arbitrary collection of pieces; the ordering of the movements and their key relationships are now planned with a lucidity comparable with that of the music's economical texture. Although the book is to contain some of his most profound music, he opens it with a short, light-weight, thin-textured *ordre*.

Ordre XX in G major and minor

The major and minor keys alternate to much the same effect, though more sparely, as in previous suites in this tonality; the 'late' date of the music is implicit only in its rarefied quality.

La Princesse Marie. Marie Leszczynska, fiancée of Louis XIV. She became Queen of France in 1725, and this little piece may have been composed then, as a tribute, or may have been written later, since she was among Couperin's pupils. Her piece is a gavotte, tenderly amiable – though the *troisième partie*, in the minor, reflects her origin by being brusquely *dans le goût Polonois*. Its rather fierce vigour, with displaced accents, is in peasant-like contrast with the gentility of the previous *parties*.

La Boufone. Probably not a female buffoon but a buffoon-like   425 jig in burlesque style. The sequential sevenths at the end mime grotesquely.

Les Chérubins ou l'aimable Lazure. This piece too, sparely in two voices, sounds buffoon-like in its cross accents. The Cherubins are perhaps bonny fruits of love such as sport in theatrical divertissements, their antics being whimsical, even tricksy; the *seconde partie*, in the major, smoothes out the first part's tune beguilingly. We have no clue as to who Lazure may be.

La Croûilli ou la Couperinéte. This tender, almost frail piece in 3 : 8 may be a portrait of Couperin's cousin Marguerite-Louise, the brilliant singer who had, however, died in 1721; or of his daughter Marguerite-Antoinette, who was twenty-one when the piece was published. Charlier thinks it's a portrait of Couperin's little son, who died in infancy and about whom we know nothing. It seems to me more probable and more affecting that it should be a portrait of Couperin himself as a child, when his connection with Croûilly was intimate. This is supported by the *seconde partie* in the major, marked *naïvement*: for in this musette the harpsichord simulates a droning bagpipe, and Couperin adds a *contre-partie* for *viole*, should you have one handy. The effect is hurdy-gurdy-like; and we have noted in reference to earlier pieces that in his country childhood Couperin must have heard such peasant music frequently. The introduction of the *viole* may also be a tribute to Princess Marie, who played the instrument, inexpertly.

La Fine Madelon.

La Douce Janneton.

These two related pieces, one in the minor, the other in the major, are portraits of a famous actress of the Comédie-Française. Jeanne de Beauval, commonly known as Janneton, was equally celebrated for her performances in the plays of Molière and for her promiscuity which, rumour had it, blessed or at least endowed her with twenty-eight children. The first, major-keyed piece is marked *affectueuse-ment*, and may refer to her portrayal of the highly affected Madelon in Molière's *Les Précieuses Ridicules*. The twittery ornaments – especially as played by Blandine Verlet, slightly before the beat – certainly sound *précieux*. The second, minor-keyed piece, marked *plus voluptueusement*, no doubt refers to her amorous propensities: though the still querulous ornaments and the sequential sevenths in the bass suggest that Couperin detected an element of affectation here also. Jeanneton (so spelt) is featured with Fanchon in the vocal canon *La Femme entre deux draps*.

La Sézile. Nicolas Sézile was treasurer of the *Offrandes et Aumones du Roi*. This must be his wife, Angélique Baudet, who seems to have been a serious young woman as compared with la douce Janneton. Whereas the Janneton pieces mince in high register, this piece is scored for *mains croisées* in low register, and flows dreamily, like a duet for two *violes*. Henri Charlier thinks that this piece and (less directly) the two previous pieces are based on or related to the *Petite fugue sur le chromhorne* that forms the second couplet of the Gloria in the *Messe pour les Convents*. The key of both is G major, the mood gentle, with a tune based on a descending scale. This seems slender evidence on which to base a correspondence, especially since the metre is quite distinct.

Les Tambourins. This slight suite ends slightly with this innocent pop music. The three- and five-bar phrases in this bucolic music of low life resist civilized symmetry. The second *air*, in the minor, is spikier than the first, though Couperin tells us that 'on doit toujours finir par le premier' – in Edenic G major. Despite the polished lucidity of their two-part writing these little pieces sound pristine: as timeless as the Provençal peasants the dance came from. Tambourins became increasingly fashionable in the divertissements of Campra, Mouret and Rameau, but no one distilled the sun-baked essence of their folk source more precisely than Couperin.

Ordre XXI in E minor

All the pieces in this short *ordre* are in the minor, and all have the noble pathos or delicate wit that, for Couperin, characterized this tonality.

La Reine des Cœurs. And so, *lentement, et très tendrement*, she is, though she remains anonymous.

La Bondissante. A lively lady, also anonymous, whose vigorous phrases, bounding across the bar-lines, do not surrender elegance; and so prepare us for

La Couperin. A noble and chromatically expressive allemande, which is, we remarked, almost Bachian in its closely wrought texture. It has been claimed as a portrait of Couperin's wife or daughter, but must surely, in its fusion of gracious melancholy with irony and even wit, represent the composer himself in maturity – as contrasted with the childlike *La Couperinéte*.

La Harpée: Pièce dans le Goût de la Harpe. Probably a tribute to a family of actors called De la Harpe, with whom Couperin was acquainted. The figuration is not particularly harp-like.

La Petite Pince-sans-rire. A wry joke, but far from a jape, for the descending chromatics and dissonant suspensions preserve the pathos typical of Couperin's E minor, and the bass is the same as that of *La Couperin*, the composer's eloquent self-portrait.

Ordre XXII in D major and minor

This is a lightweight suite befitting Couperin's merry rather than vainglorious D major.

La Trophée. This piece fulfils Charpentier's description of D major in being '*joyeux et très guérrier*'. But the war is theatrical or athletic rather than military. The bounding leaps and chunky chords of the first part guy sportive exhibitionism. The two sequent *airs*, one major, the other minor, reflect touchingly on victory and defeat.

Le Point du Jour. This discreet allemande could refer, according to Philippe Beaussant, to one of the *cabinets d'eau* at Versailles. There is also a district so named, paradoxically in the west of Paris. But it may merely concern daybreak.

L'Anguille. This eel wriggles in irregular phrases, often in rudimentary two-part canon. Though the piece is vividly descriptive, it's also a hornpipe which *may* characterize a seafaring type, possibly from a burlesque play. Certainly the burlesque theatre is evoked in the next piece –

Le Croc-en-jambe – which is a tumble or trip-up such as was common in farces; there was a notorious one in the popular *La Grande Sophie*. But Couperin's farce is not knockabout; the interrupted cadences, irregular groupings and angular leaps are intellectually witty as well as physically exuberant.

428 *Menuets Croisés*. The cross-hand writing on two keyboards

makes the dance rhythm insubstantial, even illusory, so that the piece is in tune with the jokey character of the suite as a whole. This is consummated in

Les Tours de Passe-passe, for here the cross-hands technique – the left hand picking our the thematic notes in alternation above and below the right hand – itself becomes a kind of leger-demain, since one doesn't know precisely where the tune is coming from. The piece is very elegant, however: Couperin's conjuring tricks (rabbits out of hats, etc.) are not those of a pier magician.

Ordre XXIII in F major

A justly celebrated suite in Couperin's comic-theatrical rather than pastoral F major, which proves capable of a remarkable variety of mood.

L'Audacieuse. This richly-textured piece in consistently thrusting dotted rhythm recalls the old, heroic *grand goût.* But in the context of the suite it may represent an archaically heroic actor rather than a grand lady. In any case it's punctured by the next piece –

Les Tricoteuses. A descriptive piece which also tells a human story. The busy knitters click on 'regardless', through chit-tering semiquavers, until in the last clause dropped stitches (*mailles lâchées*) provoke 'horrendous' diminished sevenths – the slip on the banana skin endemic to our 'human predi-cament'.

L'Arlequine. My original text compares this piece to Watteau's no less famous portrait of Gilles; and I have elaborated on this in the essay on Couperin and Watteau. We don't know whether Couperin ever saw Watteau's painting, though he may well have done. But his immediate models would have been the harlequins he saw on stage, gaily naïve, foolishly pathetic, hiding their fear, as Vicentini put it, behind the mask. Perhaps Couperin was also paying retrospective tri-bute to his friend Evaristo Gherardi. Courville suggests that there was a specific musical source for Couperin's piece in Campra's divertissement, *Les Fêtes Vénitiennes*, first per-formed in 1710, and often repeated. A parallel exists between Campra's *Air pour les Harlequins* and Couperin's piece, though it is not striking enough to suggest 429 plagiarism. Indeed, the similiarity provides a gloss on the difference between genius and however delightful talent in the use of stylistic cliché.

Les Gondoles de Délos. Another abrupt shift of mood. This large-scale and ravishing rondeau is quite complexly organized, incorporating a minor-keyed episode itself in rondeau within the rondeau proper. The title makes a classical reference to the cult of Apollo at Delos, but classical Greece is metamorphosed into Versailles, where gondolas (stored in a complex of buildings known as Little Venice) glided on the canals. We are apt to forget how – at least in Le Nôtre's original conception – water was an essential aspect of Versailles, modifying with its volatile fluidity and shimmering light the geometrical rigour of the designs. The men and women in the gondolas, indulging in what Couperin calls *badinage tendre*, must all be young and beautiful, for the dreamy tune wafts them to Cytherea.

Les Satires: Chèvre-pieds. Again a classical allusion, for the goat-footed satyrs are followers of Dionysus. But they also stomp in the parks of Versailles, like classical statues animated; while in the second part, with its dislocated rhythms and savage dissonances, they foot it on stage, *dans le goût burlesque*.

Ordre XXIV in A minor and major

This suite is the longest in the canon, except for the relatively *ad hoc* third *ordre*. Like the other mature suites in A, it is balanced between the minor, here used austerely and often ironically, and the sensuous, even sensual, major.

Sarabande grave: Les Vieux Seigneurs.
Les Jeunes Seigneurs, cy-devant les Petits Maîtres.
A published collection of the Italian comedies performed at the Hôtel de Bourgogne under the direction of Evaristo Gherardi led to their successful revival in the seventeen-twenties. One of the pieces, Dufresnay's *Les amusemens sérieux et comiques*, contains a passage precisely relevant to these two pieces. The *vieux seigneurs*, courtiers of the old heroic age, dance an archaically stilted *sarabande grave*, working hard to hide their 'irregularities under a smooth exterior'. The *petits maîtres*, the young fops of the new

world, on the other hand, 'like to appear more disorganized than in fact they are'. Fundamentally conventional, they enjoy the pretence of outlandishness: so whereas 'the courtier's speech is uniform and always polite, flattering and insinuating, the speech of the *petit maître* is both high and low, a mixture of the trivial and the sublime, of politeness and coarseness'. *Petits maîtres*, we recognize, still abound in the twentieth century – which provides further evidence of the way in which the precision of Couperin's topicality and locality leads to universality. The descriptions quoted above fit Couperin's music exactly: his *vieux seigneurs* are self-consciously ceremonial, never putting a foot wrong; his *petits maîtres* are fidgety and garrulous, their phrases habitually crossing the bar-lines.

Les Dars-homicides. The fatal darts in this lilting 6 : 8, major-keyed rondeau are presumably Cupid's. The freely canonic imitations hark back to the love chases in earlier baroque opera: for instance, Belinda's two pursuit arias in Purcell's *Dido*.

Les Guirlandes. Another piece in lute style, double dotted. The low registration and the enveloping suspensions recall *L'Enchanteresse* and, since it is to be played *amoureusement* but without self-indulgent *langueur*, this piece too probably weaves a love-spell. The second part in the minor, however, is unexpectedly thin in texture and 'cool' in character, as though trying to escape (*coulament*) from the seductress's coils. Again we find the juxtaposition of disparate moods typical of the mature Couperin. It's evident once more in the transition from this piece to

Les Brinborions. A perky little piece in two voices, which musically exhales the whiff of contempt inherent in the word. Even so the fourth *partie*, in the major, with musette-style scoring, is alluringly sensuous, so there may be more in these geegaws or trifles than meets the casual eye.

La Divine Babiche ou les Amours badins. Babiche is a lap-dog, so this young woman, whoever she may be, is presumably toyed with non-committally. Yet the music is genuinely *voluptueuse* and, since it is to be played *sans langueur*, offers genuine satisfactions.

La Belle Javotte autre fois l'Infante. The girl who was once an Infanta was Louis XIV's first fiancée. This is a pretty, slight, *tendre* gavotte for a pretty, slight, tender girl who was sent 431

packing. I see no reason to believe that the title means that the piece had previously appeared under a different guise. Again, it's typical of this suite and of Couperin's mature art that this tiny, insubstantial gavotte should be followed by the longest piece in Couperin's harpsichord music,

L'Amphibie. A real passacaglia on a massive scale, comparable with the greatest examples of the genre in theatre music, or in Couperin's own trio sonatas. Fundamentally, the ostinato is the familiar scale, falling from the tonic through an octave, though this isn't obvious in the opening statement, which returns rondeau-like from time to time. The scale itself is sometimes inverted and, in the minor variations, chromaticized. The Oneness of the passacaglia's Law embraces an immense range of feeling, from the heroic to the pathetic though not, in this case, from the sublime to the ridiculous. Couperin's frequent directives may indicate that changes of mood should produce changes of tempo, though these should never disrupt the pulse of Time. It has been suggested that the title refers to the piece's wide emotional scope; but its particular significance is surely that contained in Sir Thomas Browne's phrase 'Man is an Amphibian' – meaning that he lives, or should live, simultaneously in worlds of flesh and of spirit. Of their nature passacaglias are always corporeal, even processional; in the greatest of them the body sprouts wings as the melodies spring from the turning earth and the beating pulse, as Time marches on.

Ordre XXV in C major and minor

Though this brief *ordre* begins with a piece not in C, minor or major, but in E flat, which makes the grade as the relative major of C minor. Even so, its effect in context is startling, and wittingly so, for

La Visionnaire can be expected to deal in the extra-ordinary. Desmaret's play *Les Visionnaires*, written in 1637, became immensely popular during the sixteen-nineties, and was the inspiration for Couperin's early trio sonata with the same title. I doubt if there is any connection between the old play and this harpsichord piece: though it is theatrical in being cast in the form of a French heroic overture with a slowly pompous first section, followed by a quick freely canonic dance in two voices, but in duple rather than in the conventional triple time. The 'visionary' effect of this theatrical piece is related to its E flat major tonality, which is rarely found in French baroque music since, in the kinds of meantone tuning favoured, it was a very dangerous key, riddled with wolfish intervals. Through the entire range of his harpsichord music Couperin has no other piece in E flat major, and even in this case he can't bring himself to put more than two flats in the key signature. *La Visionnaire* ought to be played in some kind of contemporary tuning – especially since we're apt to think of E flat major, from its later more equally tempered history in the music of Mozart and Beethoven, as a key Masonically affirmatory or humanistically powerful. Bach and Handel, and other German baroque composers, seem to have regarded E flat major as a 'positive' key, as did Mozart and Beethoven: so the French tunings must have been exceptional.

La Misterieuse. Again there's a touch of the visionary, for the elliptical C major of this piece has nothing in common with the eupeptic C major of the first *ordre*. The tonality here, especially in the second half, is weirdly wavery – which makes me suspect that the title refers to the 'mystery of life' in a general sense, rather than to a mysterious woman. It might be both, of course; *la mistérieuse* was the name of a perfume, which a sphinx-like woman might have favoured.

La Monflambert. Probably Anne Darboulin, who married François de la Monflambert, the King's wine merchant, in 1726. Her swaying, C minor piece is as gravely beautiful as she must have been; its *tendresse* is real, to be played *sans lenteur*.

La Muse Victorieuse. This, the only piece straightforwardly in C major, is rhythmically vigorous, making powerful use of hemiola metres. But this temporal victory is not a summation. Earthly triumph, which this piece represents, seems to be to some degree a denial of vision and mystery – so we're not surprised that the *ordre* should end not here, but with

Les Ombres Errantes. Sad ghosts languishing in limbo, their C minor phrases floating forlornly across the bar-lines. They recall the ghosts of Monteverdi's *Ingrate*, not because Couperin knew Monteverdi's *ballo*, but because one suspects that Couperin's shades are marooned in limbo for the same sin as were Monteverdi's.

433

Ordre XXVI in F sharp minor

That E flat major was a 'difficult' key in terms of tuning was peculiar to the French; F sharp minor, however, was universally regarded as problematical. As the dominant of 'suffering' B minor, F sharp minor became for Bach a key appropriate to 'transcendent' states of ecstasy or pain; with Couperin F sharp minor tends to imply sensuous exploration and/or mystical aspiration. In this suite the sequence of five pieces seems as though pre-ordained.

La Convalescente. A poignant allemande almost certainly portraying Couperin himself, for he had been and still was ill. The music's strong pathos complements the elegiac nobility of *La Couperin*.

Gavotte. 'Simply' a dance, yet personal in its melancholy and related in mood, if not in theme, to the previous piece. This solemn piece is at once a dance and a minature tone-poem.

La Sophie. This may be homage to a woman but was more probably inspired by Dufresnay's popular burlesque play, *La Sophie*, in which the Sophie is a dervish who, in whirling, gets a colossal *croc-en-jambe*! The Sophie was played by the Mezzetin of the Italian Comedy. This is an instance in which historical knowledge may affect performance: if the Sophie is a whirling dervish rather than an elegant lady, the music must move as fast as possible. This makes a difficult piece still more difficult, but the effect is exciting, especially in the two-handed clattering of broken chords towards the end.

L'Epineuse. In the *commedia* Mezzetin's sister-in-law was Spinetta – which provides a link to this beautiful piece. There is a technical joke too, for the six *sharps* in the major section are highly thorny! We've noted that F sharp minor was known to the French lutenists as *le ton de la chèvre* because goats were rampant in its problematical tuning. Michael Moran tells me that there was a lutenist *named* de la Chèvre, who was said to be especially partial to the key of F sharp minor. I suspect however that this, if true, was a fortuitous coincidence rather than an explanation of the phrase *ton de la chèvre*. In the major the key is indeed 'way out', though in this piece the music is unspikey in flavour, and tuning difficulties presumably induce a disturbingly visionary

radiance. This occurs, especially in the major episode, if the
major thirds are true, however dubious the fifths.

La Pantomime. Another piece based on the *commedia dell'arte*,
which, like *L'Arlequine*, plumbs the depths of theatrical
illusion. Couperin's harlequin is grotesque, wide-eyed and
foolish, but magically dreams through his sequential chromatics. The Scaramouche of *La Pantomime* moves puppet-
like through the *grande précision* of his dotted-rhythmed
gestures – which tightly control the pain of the dissonant
sevenths and ninths. So we end with a piece that is not so
much disillusioned as illusionless: from which it draws its
nervous pride and sinewy strength. It's hardly excessive to
say that this Scaramouche comes out as a tragic figure –
which tells us something about theatrical illusion as a prop
for human suffering. Incidentally, there is a passage in one of
the Gherardi plays in which Scaramouche twangs his guitar
while somebody beats time unremittingly on his shoulder.
This may have triggered off Couperin's piece, which imbues
a trivial situation with impassioned dignity. *La Pantomime*
ends the *ordre* because nothing, as a human testament, could
follow it.

Ordre XXVII in B minor

We are not surprised when, for the last suite of all, Couperin
returns to his basic B minor, employing this key of 'reality', as he
had done in the magnificent eighth and deeply subjective thirteenth *ordres*, consistently throughout, with only momentary
modulation. Again he achieves a precarious equilibrium between
externalized artifice and a hermetic world of the spirit. The music
sounds, as it looks, purged.

L'Exquise. An allemande comparable with *La Convalescente* of the
previous suite. I suspect that it pays homage to a spiritual
condition rather than to a young woman. The 'exquisite'
lucidity of texture brings balm to the (B minor) suffering
which is the heart of the human condition.

Les Pavots. There is balm too in this piece about poppies, dispen-
sers of sleep. The *scène de sommeil* of Lullian opera, in which
the hero, buffeted by inimical Fortune and by human malig-
nity, falls asleep and dreams that 'the gods' put right the
chaos created by blundering mortals, is here given a personal

435

interpretation. It is possible that Couperin was granted the boon of sleep by the juice of poppies during his long months of sickness. The piece, levelly flowing in crotchets, wilts *nonchalamment*, sounding infinitely sad.

Les Chinois. Exoticism was a cult at the French court, orientals being scattered over the wall paintings, snuffboxes and mirrors of a Boucher. The fashion was given a fillip by the success in 1707 of Dufresnay's play *Les Amusemens Sérieux et Comiques d'un Siamois*, in which Harlequin appeared disguised as a Chinese doctor! Comic orientals were regularly featured in divertissements, though neither Lully nor Rameau (nor for that matter Purcell across the Channel, with his outrageous Chinamen in *The Fairy Queen*) made any attempt to emulate oriental musics; they couldn't have done, since they'd never heard any, and would have been totally baffled if they had. They equated exoticism with oddity of phrase length, with metrical surprise and changing tempi – as does Couperin in this piece. Yet it comes out in final effect as forlorn rather than funny, and is therefore in tune with the rest of the suite. In particular the *lentement* coda is, after apparent farce, curiously touching, transporting us to a fairyland where contrarious people, even of different race and colour, may live together in harmony. Wish-fulfilment must play a large part in any art that is humanistically based, if only because human beings are imperfect. This must be why the French court, although contemptuous of lesser breeds within, let alone without, the Law, could none the less fantasize about an earthly paradise. Prologues and epilogues to ballets and operas usually took place on Parnassus, for the Golden Age must be just round the corner, even though one hasn't entered and can't quite face it.

Saillie. The word means a leap, a sudden start, a gushing out; or figuratively a shaft of wit. The *saillie* was also a step in a dance called *La Babette*, possibly because it was danced by La Babet. It seems apposite that Couperin's harpsichord music should end with an unpretentious piece stemming equally from the movements of the body and from the play of the mind. There's a restrospective element too in that this piece resembles a movement with the same title in *L'Apothéose de Lully*. The basic theme of Dufresnay's *Les Amusemens* is the union of the French and Italian comedies; in musical terms this motive had moulded Couperin's life's work. Having been born of a social world and of the theatre which is a social medium, Couperin's final music sounds, hardly less than the abstract instrumental works of Bach's last years, *sub specie æternitatis*. To listen to it, still more to play it to ourselves, is to enter the magic circle where

> *Only by the form, the pattern,*
> *Can words or music reach*
> *The stillness, as a Chinese jar still*
> *Moves perpetually in its stillness.*
> *Not the stillness of the violin, while the note lasts,*
> *Not that only, but the co-existence,*
> *Or say that the end precedes the beginning,*
> *And the end and the beginning were always there*
> *Before the beginning and after the end.*
> *And all is always now.*

('Burnt Norton' from *Four Quartets* by T. S. Eliot)

Coda

At the end of this survey of the four volumes of Couperin's harpsichord pieces one further speculation may be broached. This concerns the senses in which, we've suggested, the sequence of pieces constitutes a 'world', a panorama of *la comédie humaine*. That Couperin wanted his *ordres* to be played as totalities, each piece reflecting on the other as they portrayed all sorts and conditions of men and women and of modes and manners, even if within an apparently circumscribed society, seems to me deducible from interior evidence: the more so because there is usually a specific tuning appropriate to each *ordre*. The better one gets to know the music – and I write forty years on after the original book – the more does each element of an *ordre* prove to contribute to the whole; that some pieces are tragic and profound, others slight and frivolous, reflects the nature of human society, which Couperin presents with an impersonality at once passionate and dispassionate. Sometimes particular persons are depicted – and as much entertainment must have been derived from the identification of Couperin's 437 musical portraits as from the identification of the *caractères* in La Bruyère's immensely popular and influential book in which, as in Couperin's music, identity was both sharpened and universalized by the masterly stylization. As a game, this would have appealed most to aristocratic cognoscenti, but theatrical types too are always good for gossip. The actors and actresses, even the lower-class professional musicians who feature in Couperin's rollcall are also a part of the pattern: just as the geographical location varies between court and city and village green.

Title Index of Harpsichord Music

C numbers refer to the thematic catalogue of Couperin's works by Maurice Cauchie.

Gavotte (c) I, 3 (C. 126)
„   (f♯) IV, 26 (C. 478)
„   (g) I, 1 (C. 90)
Le Gazouillement (B♭) II, 6 (C. 170)
Gigue la Milordine (g) I, 1 (C. 91)
Gigue (A) I, 5 (C. 147)
„   (b) II, 8 (C. 190)
Les Gondoles de Délos (F) IV, 23 (C. 462)
Les Graces incomparables, ou La Conti (G) III, 16 (C. 261)
Les Graces Naturéles (C and c) II, 11 (C. 215)
Gris-vêtus. *See* La Marche des Gris-vêtus
Les Guirlandes (A and a) IV, 24 (C. 467)
La Harpée (e) IV, 21 (C. 448)
L'Himen-Amour (g and G) III, 16 (C. 262)
Les Idées Heureuses (d) I, 2 (C. 116)
L'Infante. *See* La Belle Javotte autre fois l'Infante
L'Ingénue (D and d) III, 19 (C. 282)
L'Insinuante (a) II, 9 (C. 199)
L'Intîme, Courante (e) II, 12 (C. 223)
La Jalousie taciturne. *See* Les Folies Françoises, Pt. 11
Les Jeunes Seigneurs, cy-devant les Petits Maîtres (a and A) IV,
    24 (C. 465)
La Julliet (d) III, 14 (C. 250)
Les Juméles (E and e) II, 12 (C. 222)
La Laborieuse, Allemande (d) I, 2 (C. 102)
La Langueur. *See* Les Folies Françoises, Pt. 7
Les Langueurs-Tendres (B♭) II, 6 (C. 169)
Les Laurentines (C and c) I, 3 (C. 131)
La Létiville (G) III, 16 (C. 267)
La Linote éfarouchée (D) III, 14 (C. 247)
Les Lis naissans (b) III, 13 (C. 230)
La Logiviére (A) I, 5 (C. 143)
La Lugubre, Sarabande (c) I, 3 (C. 125)
La Lutine (C) I, 3 (C. 136)
Les Maillotins. *See* Le Tic-Toc-Choc, ou les Maillotins
La Majestueuse, Sarabande (g) I, 1 (C. 89)
La Manon (G) I, 1 (C. 98)
La Marche. *See* Les Pélerines, Pt. 1
La Marche des Gris-vêtus (F) I, 4 (C. 137)
Les Matelotes Provençales (c) I, 3 (C. 134)
La Ménetou (G) II, 7 (C. 176)

Menuet (A) II, 9 (C. 203)
    „   (c) I, 3 (C. 127)
    „   (d) I, 2 (C. 108)
    „   (g) I, 1 (C. 92)
Menuets Croisés (D and d) IV, 22 (C. 456–7)
La Mézangére (d) II, 10 (C. 207)
La Milordine, Gigue (g) I, 1 (C. 91)
La Mimi (d) I, 2 (C. 117)
La Minerve. *See* La Régente ou La Minerve
La Misterieuse (C) IV, 25 (C. 473)
Les Moissonneurs (B♭) II, 6 (C. 168)
La Monflambert (c) IV, 25 (C. 474)
La Morinéte (b) II, 8 (C. 193)
Le Moucheron (B♭), II, 6 (C. 175)
La Muse de Monaco. *See* La Princesse de Chabeuil, ou La Muse
    de Monaco
La Muse Naissante. *See* Les Petits âges, Pt. 1
La Muse-Plantine (d) III, 19 (C. 285)
La Muse Victorieuse (C) IV, 25 (C. 475)
Muséte de Choisi (A and a) III, 15 (C. 256)
Muséte de Taverni (A and a) III, 15 (C. 257)
La Nanète (g) I, 1 (C. 94)
La Nointéle (d and D) II, 10 (C. 209)
Les Nonètes, I, 1
    Pt. 1. Les Blondes (g) (C. 66)
    Pt. 2. Les Brunes (G) (C. 67)
L'Olimpique (A) II, 9 (C. 198)
Les Ombres Errantes (c) IV, 25 (C. 476)
Les Ondes (A) I, 5 (C. 155)
La Pantomime (f♯) IV, 26 (C. 481)
Les Papillons (d) I, 2 (C. 121)
Passacaille (b) II, 8 (C. 192)
Passacaille L'Amphibie (A) IV, 24 (C. 471)
Passepied (d and D) I, 2 (C. 110)
La Pastorelle (G) I, 1 (C. 96)
La Pateline (F) I, 4 (C. 141)
Les Pavots (b) IV, 27 (C. 483)
Les Pélerines (c) I, 3
    Pt. 1. La Marche (C. 128)
    Pt. 2. La Caristade (C. 129)
    Pt. 3. Le Remerciement (C. 130)

Les Vestales (G and g) III, 16 (C. 263)

Les Vieux Galans et les Trésorieres suranées. *See* Les Folies
  Françoises, Pt. 9

Les Vieux Seigneurs, Sarabande grave (a) IV, 24 (C. 464)

La Villers (a and A) I, 5 (C. 152)

La Visionnaire (E♭) IV, 25 (C. 472)

La Virginité. *See* Les Folies Françoises, Pt. 1

La Voluptueuse (d) I, 2 (C. 120)

La Zénobie (c) II, 11 (C. 216)

Periphera, 1986

I

WATTEAU, COUPERIN AND
THE THEATRE

The fairly obvious parallel between Watteau and Couperin referred to intermittently throughout this book seems, forty years later, to be worth deeper investigation. Debussy dedicated his piano *Etudes* to 'F.C.' – 'Couperin, le plus poète de nos clavecinistes dont la tendre mélancholie semble l'adorable écho venu du fond mystérieux des paysages où s'attristent les personnages de Watteau'. Though that is too limited an account of either composer or painter, it is basically on the mark, and it's moving that another great creative artist should, across the centuries, have recognized the kinship.

Often there seems to be providence in the fall of a sparrow. It's fascinating that Chardin, supreme master of the sanctity of common things and of common life, should have been born in the year, 1699, in which Racine, supreme master of the *crises de cœur* of Heroes and (especially) Heroines, died; and that Watteau should have been born, with no less allegorical appropriateness, in the year, 1684, in which Corneille, arch-representative of the *grand siècle*'s *gloire* and *grand goût*, had expired and in which Louis XIV, having married Mme de Maintenon, moved into the twilight of his final phase. Though Watteau died in 1721, only six years later than Louis, and so lived almost all his working life in the King's reign, he was never a servant of the Court, and his art is an intuitive protest against *la gloire*. Of Flemish extraction, he came from Valenciennes, moving to Paris in 1702, at the age of eighteen. He was not at first very successful in seeking his fortune, for he worked long hours, in slavish conditions, for a commercial emporium bartering mass-produced paintings and *objets de piété*, not much more elevated in taste than those evident in the tourist-directed cathedrals of today. In those early years his own painting was little affected by Parisian sophistication. Far from denying his rural heritage, he drew and painted, with 'northern' realism, peasants, soldiers and scenes of low life copied or remembered from his childhood. By hindsight we may detect in the eyes of his *vieux Savoyard* a wistful awareness of vulnerability such as typifies the civilized denizens of his later legendary landscapes. We may also note that the military scenes Watteau painted in early youth, mostly set at Valenciennes, are untouched by *la gloire*. For Louis XIV war created, not merely reflected, the myth of the Roi Soleil. But Watteau sees war never as heroic, occasionally as bloody, more commonly as painfully tedious and tediously painful, negatory of the pitiful pomp to which the scarlet uniforms would testify. The drudgery of the soldier's lot obliterates the dreams that make life supportable. Lights that never were on land or sea may glimmer behind, but cannot irradiate, the geometrical precision of firing squad or tramping infantrymen. Moreover, although on the surface evidence of his best-known pictures Watteau lived in a charmed circle of Beautiful People and hedonistic delights, his world was in fact no bed of roses. During the years 1718–20, when he painted his greatest pictures, France was afflicted with God- or Devil-given plague, while man's own greed or folly was disastrously exploding miniature South Sea Bubbles within the economy on which sensory satisfactions had depended.

If northern realism was to work in harmony with Watteau's dream-world, humanizing the grandiosities of a Le Brun, it did so the more readily because the district around Notre Dame where the young Watteau worked was alive with mountebanks, quacks, jugglers, acrobats, burlesque players and other manufacturers of theatrical illusion. This world Watteau contacted by way of his first important teacher, Claude Gillot, who had been born at Langres in 1673 and was linked to the Old World through having been a pupil of J. B. Corneille, a member of the dynasty that included dramatists, poets and visual artists. Claude Gillot himself was a man of many parts, responsive to the divergent currents within contemporary French art, from most of which Watteau profited to some degree. But there is no question that what most fired Gillot's imagination was the theatre. A frequent visitor to the theatre booths of the fairs, he wrote a number of comedies himself, and aesthetically found himself in designing sets for vaudeville acts, operas and puppet shows. Most touchingly, he drew the mythical characters of the *commedia dell'arte*, being himself a personal friend of actors and actresses in the companies.

In the original version of this book a little of the history of the *commedia* was recounted. Since it harked back beyond the Renaissance to the strolling players of the Middle Ages and beyond them to classical antiquity and to primitive ritual, it is hardly surprising that over the centuries the *commedia* characters have exerted a spell comparable only with that exerted by the characters of Shakespeare. Even people who never enter a theatre know of Harlequin and Columbine, Pierrot and Scaramouche, just as Hamlet is part of the popular imagination. In being masked the *commedia* characters, like those of Greek drama, could be at once individualized human creatures and mythological humours. Pantalone – in his heyday the vigorous Venetian merchant, not a crotchety dotard – has his counterpart in the twentieth-century businessman; the Dottore – obfuscatingly learned and ineffectually loquacious – is the perennial civil servant; Harlequin is the common man whose commonness is, if only in wish-fulfilment, his vitality and who, being amoral rather than immoral, needs no justification for living in the moment. It's this interplay between myth and reality that makes the *commedia* so fascinating; from one point of view, being a popular improvised art springing direct from the texture of living, it must have been naturalistic; from another point of view, being highly sophisticated and offering scope for rhetorical tropes and set speeches, it was as non-realistic as the masks worn by the players. Many of the great Comedians, identifying themselves with a single character throughout their working lives, must – like Japanese kabuki players to the present day – have discovered a myriad of personal quirks beneath the universal type, and must have been hard put to it to decide whether their real or their mythical nature was the deeper truth.

This is why the *commedia* was so responsive to change: the flexibility of the myths is necessary to their persistence. Through the centuries the *commedia*'s civilized awareness of the comedy of the human predicament has re-created its conventions in the light and dark of a changing world: from the incipient romanticism of Watteau's and Couperin's presentation of Pierrot as a semi-divine Fool; to the Enlightened democratization of the types in the plays of Goldoni and the tragi-comic operas of Mozart; to the fully-fledged romanticism of the Pierrots of Chopin and Schumann; to Pierrot's transmogrification by Degas, Cézanne, Picasso, Debussy, Satie, Ravel, Busoni and

Stravinsky into a Maimed Innocent; to Schoenberg's image of *Pierrot Lunaire* as a scapegoat for our guilt; to Samuel Beckett's clowns who, waiting for Godot, relate the *commedia* characters to the comic-pitiful expiration of Christian hope, in a theatrical medium that, like the original *commedia*, allows for improvisation, mime, acrobatics, bawdy, song and dance.

Later in this note we will explore what Watteau (and Couperin) got from the *commedia*. For the moment, let us return to Watteau's early years in Paris, and particularly to his debt to Claude Gillot. He paid him the homage, as was customary in the eighteenth century, of direct imitation; with his help he got to know the theatre at first hand, and discovered that the theatre could be a catalyst between reality and ideality. Raucous low types, rubbing shoulders with classical fauns and satyrs, need not be confined to the market-place, and their idealization was encouraged when Watteau, having quarrelled with Gillot, became a pupil of Claude Audran, the foremost decorator of the age, who had in 1699 been employed to design cartoons for the august Gobelin tapestry school. By the time Watteau went to him, decoration was veering away from the heroic towards a gracious femininity, reflecting the latent revolution in society. Watteau responded to the delicacy of Audran's arabesques, as contrasted with the poster-flat realism he had picked up from Gillot. Still more important, Audran was curator of the Palais de Luxembourg, which housed a cycle of twenty-five paintings commissioned from Rubens by the palace's original owner, Marie de Medici.

The sensuality of Rubens's colour, the vibrancy of his line and action, made an extraordinary impact on the young Watteau, and in turn affected his vision of the flowing, informally arranged Luxembourg Gardens, so contrasted with the geometric symmetries of Versailles. If this was in part 'progressive', it was also regressive in that it re-evoked the volatile and ebullient humanism of the early seventeenth century, before the codifications of absolutism. Here were the roots of Watteau's mythical world – which were enriched when, some years later, he was 'discovered' by Pierre Crozat, a member of an immensely rich family of financiers, who was passionately dedicated to the arts. To Watteau he proved a patron as generous in spiritual as in financial terms, for he allowed the painter to study in detail his
452 superb collection of Renaissance paintings, drawings and

engravings. Henceforth, in Watteau's vision, Raphael, Veronese and (especially) Giorgione complemented Rubens's sensual opulence with their more civilized landscapes in which men and women, usually young, seem in harmony with a beneficent Nature.

Now Watteau was in possession of all the wellsprings of his art: the realism of Low Life; the simultaneous immediacy and illusion of the theatre, especially *commedia dell'arte*; the artifice of rococo design; and the visionary world of the Italian Renaissance and of the early seventeenth century. The interfusion of the genres is manifest in the relation between Watteau's paintings and his drawings. Throughout his working life he drew people, especially actors and actresses, from life, in his strongly exquisite *sanguines*. According to le Comte de Caylus, who wrote a memoir shortly after Watteau's death, he used these sketches as a gallery of portraits to populate his legendary landscapes. He 'possessed cavaliers' and comedians' costumes in which he dressed up such persons as he could find, of either sex, who were capable of posing adequately, and whom he drew in such attitudes as nature dictated, with a ready preference for those that were most simple'.

On this relation between reality and theatrical illusion in Watteau, Sacheverell Sitwell has written movingly in his *Cupid and the Jacaranda*:

> It is not certain whether the scenes take place in life or in the theatre. But the confusion gives beauty. . . . The young women are all dancers and the men are all Mezzetins. Every one of them could be, or is, an actor or a musician, members of the profession, therefore, like the writer, and as such, belonging to a world apart. . . . It gives a shock of surprise to meet his Italian comedians strolling, making love, playing their lutes and mandolins underneath the trees. Watteau has removed them from the theatre or the pierrot's booths, and this is something that had never been done before in either painting or poetry. It was a new race of inhabitants, at once more lively and more romantic than the classical gods and heroes of the statues. More unexpected still, to find comedians lying on the shores of the lake, or in wild overgrown corners of the garden. It is the overlapping of the one life into the other that makes the fascination. . . . We are to imagine that the comedians are lodged in the attics of the château. But soon, in their silks and satins, they become the guests themselves, and we begin to wonder if they have ever danced or acted. These are no longer the

453

'sham emotions' of the theatre, if false they be. Instead it is the same person encountered in another sphere of existence, for that has a dual nature. One is the shadow of life, one the real, and in proximity to either there can be no certainty as to which is which. They intermingle; they haunt each other; they throw their shadow each on each.

So Watteau's art is riddled with paradoxes of identity: Le Nain-like peasants and hurdy-gurdy players may be metamorphosed into Audran-like pseudo-shepherds and shepherdesses, attired in the anachronistic garb of the theatre or the archaistic vestments of the forgotten age of Louis XIII, when d'Urfée's *L'Astrée* (about which the young Couperin composed a trio sonata) had envisaged a pastoral dream-world in which Grace might be identified with Nature. A rustic fête by Watteau such as *L'Accordée du Village* looks at first sight as though it were peopled by ordinary folk – who on closer inspection turn out to be in fancy dress. And this painting was directly inspired by a play of Couperin's and Watteau's friend Florent Dancourt – as was the most famous of all Watteau's visionary paradises, *L'Embarquement pour l'île de Cythère*. Finding his cue in the erotic affirmations of Rubens's or the intense calm of Giorgione's figured landscapes, Watteau muted their qualities with melancholy and regret: a nostalgic desire, perhaps exacerbated by his tuberculous condition, to escape into dream. The effect is totally distinct from that of the models; these visions are moving precisely because one is not sure whether the dressed-up lovers are masquerading because their emotions are possibly superficial and certainly ephemeral, or because they are hiding a hurt imposed on them by life, especially by the civilized necessity to conform. It appears that the second version of *L'Embarquement* is mistitled, since it depicts the lovers not in process of setting out for their paradise but on their point of return to whatever reality they have to live in. This picture, in which elegance masks suffering, is, like many Watteaus, a harbinger of romanticism – which Watteau couldn't have been aware of since it hadn't been invented.

But he must have known that his Pierrot–Gilles, unlike his self-engrossed young people on whose flirtations we *eavesdrop*, looked full into the face of the future, even though incognizant of what he saw. On this wonderful painting I would like again to quote Sacheverell Sitwell:

His pose shows how entirely he is borrowed from the strolling players. He stands with both arms held stiffly to his sides, in the attitude of one of the figures painted on the hoardings. . . . It is the portrait of a young man who was a friend of Watteau, or vaguer than that, the son of a doctor who was one of Watteau's friends. He is the Pierrot of the early years of Louis Quinze, painted, in all probability, in 1720 after Watteau had come back from London, and only five years after the livelong reign of Louis Quatorze had ended. . . . Gilles stands before us in the manner of a dolt or giant, one of the freaks of the fair, ordered to stand still and not to move, but, also, it is the stance or pose of his mental state. And, as well, this is the wooden attitude in which the painters of the fair have rendered him in their incompetence. He is one of the daubs of the fairground: the dolt or zany of the tents. And the miracle of this work of art is the poetry and sensibility imputed to Gilles, despite his expressionless face and the woodenness of his attitude. Gilles has stood there for two hundred years or more, and is never a day older. He is not intended for the light of day, but for the lit airs of the theatre. There is in his mood something equivalent to when we see the full moon burning in broad daylight. It has cleared a space in the firmament, but, all the same, it ought not to be there. He is not a rich man, nor a poor one, nor a member of any serious profession. His father, the doctor, will not approve his means of livelihood, which is hopeless and can lead nowhere. It is not work. It consists in standing about, doing nothing. Take one more look at him, before he burns out in the morning sky! He is like a person who stands quite still, out there, and never moves. Moonstruck, to all intents and purposes, but not looking at us with a silly stare. He is in the sacred trance of poetry, and while it possesses him he cannot move or stir. But as we look at him, he fades out, like the moon going behind a cloud.

This of course is verbal fantasy, which is on the mark in that it uncovers reality within illusion. It's interesting that in many of Watteau's paintings of Italian comedians – consider *L'Amour au Théâtre Italien* – the incipiently romantic Pierrot figure outfaces the tougher Harlequin, who was more alive to the farcical and cruel aspects of the human condition. And it's the same when Watteau approaches his subject from the angle of reality rather than dream – as we can see in another of his late masterpieces, *L'Enseigne de Gersault*, an immense canvas painted for Watteau's picture-dealer friend and originally intended as a *plafond* to be hung over the shop. It is illuminating to compare this naturalis- tic picture with the last of Watteau's fairy-tale *fêtes champêtres*, 455 the *Fêtes Venetiennes* of 1718. Here the idealized lovers elegantly dancing in centre are counterpointed by the realism of the solitary, weary-eyed, black-garbed bagpipe player on the left. The figures have mysterious overtones; yet on close inspection the lover turns out to be Watteau's friend Wlengels, while the (benign or minatory?) bagpiper is Watteau himself. Wlengels' deportment is a trifle staid, subject to social conformity, whereas the woman's is spiritual grace, responsive to the music's lilt. And the ambiguous relationship between 'life' and 'art' is pinpointed by the presence in the décor of classical statues, marble goddesses of the Old World whose effect is itself ambivalent, since they are simultaneously ideals of beauty and the consequence of its ossification.

In *L'Enseigne de Gersault* the equation between art and life works the other way round. It is naturalistic in depicting real people in a real gallery, yet is also poetic and mythic – as to a degree any *good* naturalistic painting must be – in creating through its interplay of form and colour a vision of order and love. It is not easy fully to appreciate the poetry of this painting unless one views it live, for no reproduction can do justice to the colouristic overtones and undertones in which its super-natural dimensions become manifest. But one can detect that it is more than it seems. At first sight it looks like a social genre-picture. Gersault the dealer is holding a large oval portrait; his wife is on the extreme right, displaying a mirror to Mme Julienne. Yet the emphasis on mirrors, which are illusory by nature, is significant, and it isn't long before we notice that Mme Julienne is painted in a pose borrowed from Rubens's *Birth of Louis XIII*, while the dog in the right-hand corner is copied from Rubens's Medici cycle. The closer we look, the more the 'old' world of Louis XIII and the mythical world perceived through the painters Watteau most admired temper the reality of the scene. Most, probably all, of the pictures on the gallery walls have particular relevance to Watteau's realms of sensibility: Rubens offers his sensuality, Van Dyck his aristocratic portraiture, Ruysdael his pastoral landscape, and so on. Moreover we note that – despite naturalistic, even satirical detail, such as the connoisseur who scrutinizes a picture of nude bathers with the help of an eyeglass – Watteau himself is in the dress of a bygone age, while the young woman he turns towards is the model who figures in many of the *fêtes champêtres*, in a typically Arcadian pose. It cannot be an accident

456

that the woman next to her is stuffing into a trunk a Le Brun-style portrait of the King himself! Like that other masterpiece, the portrait of Gilles, this picture – to which Watteau was especially partial – looks into a future the artist did not live to experience.

How subtle is Watteau's equivocation between reality and dream is revealed in one of the most personally moving of his paintings, *Les deux Cousines*: in which a pair of lovers are in intimate communion on the right side of the picture while to their left a girl stands with her back towards us, apparently strolling into lonely twilight. The heart of the picture is not the lovers but the solitary girl, vulnerable in her slender loveliness, apparently shut out from that communion, walking through the gloaming towards a classical statue which again owes its emotional impact to its stony imperviousness. Watteau's statues, as 'frozen music', are simultaneously a goal and a threat: an image of a fabled, motionless classical world in which dreams may find repose, but also of a cessation of life's immediate reality. One can't help thinking of this lonely girl, isolated from love's fulfilment, as in some sense Watteau himself. Yet at the same time she is an actress – a portrait of Helena Balletti, a Flaminia of the Italian comedy group with whom Watteau was best acquainted. So the painting asks Pilate's question: What is Truth? – and offers no answer.

Through all Watteau's equivocations music – most intimately immediate of the arts – suggests an approach to communication and to truth. In his drawings, still more than his paintings, of genteel lute, mandolin and guitar players, of violists or even of the grinders of low hurdy-gurdies, the hands, arms, trunk and the relationship between these corporeal agents and the soul manifest in eyes and mouth, all reveal that Watteau understood and venerated music as the language of love and of 'la Rhétorique des Dieux' – to cite the phrase of Denis Gaultier, master lutenist of that earlier age of Louis Treize, which Watteau idealized. This is evident in the most magical of his musical pictures, *Les Charmes de la vie*, and hardly less so in what appears to be an intimately domestic genre-picture, the tiny *La Leçon de Musique*. Watteau's response to music was naturally complemented by his response to the collateral art of dance: so significant during the *grand siècle* as a synonym for humanly achieved order and grace, and drawn and painted by Watteau with so delicate an awareness of the balance between social conformity and personal expression. We have noted an instance of this in *Fêtes Venetiennes*, and one couldn't imagine a subtler comment on the appeal of the minuet to Watteau's society than his painting of the dancers in *Les plaisirs du Bal*. The elegance of the movement is a small triumph for it is achieved, by civilization, against odds, the dance steps being in duple rhythm, the music in triple!

Given Watteau's profound understanding of music and dance it is only to be expected that there should be parallels between the inner life of painter and musician. Though Couperin lived longer than Watteau, producing much of his finest music after the King's death, he too tended to undermine the pomp and circumstance of the heroic monarch, even though he had worked, without apparent resentment, as his servant. In both painter and composer we find a realistic preoccupation with the low life of peasants, soldiers, beggars, bagpipers and above all burlesque players: all of whom may be alchemized into shepherds and shepherdesses, fauns and satyrs. Both painter and composer are obsessed with the theatre and the problems of identity implicit in it. Vacillation between theatrical masks and people living in 'real' social contexts must imply ambivalence: than which nothing could be more remote from the formalities of the classical baroque. Often in Couperin's music as in Watteau's painting human beings dissolve into 'Nature' by way of techniques that appear to, but in fact do not, dissipate line in colour. The linearity that gives backbone to Watteau's sensuousness is echoed in Couperin's (often two-voiced) music, and in both painter and composer this linearity is more strongly marked in their later work. Watteau's drawings of musicians' hands are particularly revealing in this respect; the later drawings are taut, even painful as compared with the fluid gestures of the earlier work, and there is a comparable tensility in the textures of Couperin's last book of harpsichord pieces. This quality accompanies, in both painter and musician, an element of irony, a 'recognition of other modes of experience that may be possible'. Couperin's characters – Sœur Monique, La Fine Madelon, La Douce Janneton, Les Vestales – are Janus-faced in that the music encourages us to regard them with coexistent melancholy and humour, pathos and wit, tragedy and farce. However refined their elegance, they are far removed from the certitudes of Louis

XIV's absolutism. The most 'modern' elements in Couperin and Watteau paradoxically spring from their retrospection.

During the second half of the seventeenth century these certitudes had gradually hardened into dogma. As head of the Académie and one of its leading theoreticians Louis's state painter Le Brun had conceived of the passions in mechanistic terms, describing precisely how each passion ought to be drawn. His 'Lecture on Expression' of 1667 is firmly based in Cartesian principles and discusses the effect of specific passions on facial expressions and corporeal gestures. Not only is there but one appropriate response; all subsidiary characters in a painting must be related to the expressions of the principal characters in a unity comparable with the relation of human limbs to the trunk. A direct parallel was perceived between this unity and the effects of music, which were the result of a congruence of words with mode, rhythm and harmony. Vocal music, especially theatre music, was the only kind ultimately valid, since it was the only kind conceivable as a language, with codifiable 'meanings'; Lully, the state composer, was considered to have discovered, in his *tragédies lyriques*, a formula through which words, music and dance could be unified with effects that could and should change man's behaviour. If he hadn't exactly rediscovered the forms and principles of classical antiquity, he had at least bypassed the benighted Middle Ages, revealing contemporary France as the direct and successful descendant of Alexandrian Greece. The Sun King, in the garb of Apollo, wore the mantle of Alexander the Great himself. Before long Rameau was to extend this absolutism to purely instrumental music, codifying the effect of keys, intervals and chords in relation to men's thoughts, feelings – and actions.

That goal was not attained, however, without prevarication and even struggle – to which Watteau and Couperin, the two greatest artists of the early years of the century, bear eloquent witness. Their creative equivocation had some theoretical support, for Roger de Piles, in 1708, supporting the Moderns against the Ancients, stresses colour at the expense of line, and goes so far as to recommend that 'un peintre doit persuader les yeux comme un homme éloquent doit toucher le cœur'. The purpose of painting is to generate 'l'Enthousiasme': in describing which de Piles has recourse to a proto-scientific vocabulary that resembles the metaphysical music theory of the previous century. Similar attitudes crop up in the music theory of Charles Perrault, whose mechanistic terminology reflects the influence of Descartes and Mersenne: 'Dans la Musique le beau son et la justesse de la voix charme l'Oreille, les mouvemens gais ou languissans de cette mesme voix selon les differens passions qu'ils expriment, touchent le cœur, et l'harmonie de diverses parties qui se meslent avec ordre et une œconomie admirable sont le plaisir de la raison.' Reason is admitted, at the end, as a consequence of pleasure: a tribute paid to the mind because the heart has been touched. In this sense music is a sweet cheat which is also our highest good. Significantly, de Piles described painting as a *trompe l'œil* which was 'une Musique pour les yeux'.

In the case of Watteau and Couperin, it is not a question of the old values being supplanted, but rather of their being renewed in the light of a changing world. We have noted that for all his mastery of colour Watteau was a superb draughtsman, and have observed that as the refinements of Couperin's timbres and textures grew more subtly sensuous, so his control of musical line grew still more lucidly economical. This balance between scales of value would itself have been anathema to the absolute standards of the Heroic Age: though it has much in common with attitudes current at the French court during the first half of the seventeenth century – the period out of which Watteau certainly, and Couperin probably, created their imaginary worlds. Constantin Huyghens defines the role of music as 'particulièrement et principalement pour charmer l'esprit et l'oreille, et pour faire passer la vie avec un peu de douceur parmi les amertumes qui s'y rencontrent'. Not only the sentiment, but the very cadence of the prose, might be Couperin's: as is evident if we reproduce a passage from the foreword to his fourth book of harpsichord pieces, in the noble calligraphy of the original edition (see page 408).

It is relevant to note that Watteau and Couperin not only worked and paradoxically flourished during the decline of *la gloire*, but were themselves men of frail constitution. Couperin did not die particularly young and it is improbable that his condition was tuberculous. None the less the note of melancholy acerbity and elegiac wryness in his prose no less than in his music suggests that, although successful and apparently well liked, he harboured a hermeticism of spirit parallel to Watteau's near-pathological shyness, if not his prickliness of temperament. 460 Both composer and painter lived in, yet were not quite of, their world, and one cannot but wonder whether they mutually recognized their affinity. Watteau effected his uneasy entry into high society by way of the salon of his patron Pierre Crozat, at whose concerts Couperin and his musician colleagues are known to have performed. Though there is no evidence that Watteau and Couperin met, it is feasible, even probable, that they did. Like many of the greatest artists – one thinks immediately of Bach – they found their roots in a forgotten, perhaps idealized, past; lived vividly in the then contemporary world; and were prophetic of a future they did not survive to experience.

Premonitions of romanticism and of modernism are more patent in Watteau than they are in Couperin; far more than the composer he justifies the comparisons often made between him and a musician of a later generation, Frédéric Chopin. That great composer's sensory harmonic 'palette' evokes mysteries – often suggesting water and light – that carry us on pilgrimage to Cythère, while at the same time his dreams are disciplined by controlled musical line and by a classical sense of tonal architecture. Like Watteau and unlike Couperin, Chopin was consumptive – which may bear on the slightly febrile flush that qualifies his, as it does Watteau's, aristocratic finesse. But although premonitions of romantic futures are less patent in Couperin than in Watteau, they do exist – as must be implicit in the fact that Debussy, whose words were quoted at the head of this essay, dedicated his *Etudes* to Couperin, and at the same time regarded them as (humble) successors to Chopin's *Etudes* opus 10 and opus 25. That is the place where three dreams cross.

II

COUPERIN, LA FONTAINE, AND 'CHARACTER'

Both Couperin and Watteau, we have suggested, fabricated their ideal, visionary world in part from memory of the previous age of Louis XIII, not nostalgically looked back to, but magically reborn. There is a further manifestation of this in the world of visual appearances: for the 'architectural' qualities of Couperin's music have more in common with the gardening of Le Nôtre and the building of the earlier Mansart, François, than with the classical rigour of the later Mansart, who became Louis XIV's state designer, as Lully was his state composer. Both J. H. Mansart and Lully were as fanatically authoritarian as was their master, perhaps because they came of low descent: whereas Le Nôtre (who lived from 1613 to 1700) and François Mansart (born as early as 1598) betrayed a grace and liberality of temperament directly reflected in their art, and echoed by Couperin. Light and elegance suffused the gardens and buildings (remember that volatile water and glinting sunshine); and still suffuses the music that Couperin made partly in homage to that visible world.

If Watteau, Le Nôtre and François Mansart are the visual artists closest to Couperin, we find a similarly retrospective ideality in his closest literary peer, La Fontaine. Born in 1621, he too came of an earlier generation than Couperin. He published his most representative and profound work, the *Fables*, in the very year in which Couperin was born, 1668; and both men came from the same region around Brie, an agrarian community not too far from Paris. Jean's father was of solid bourgeois stock, a civil servant who worked for the department of Water and Forests at his birthplace, Château-Thierry. The poet in adolescence studied theology both at Château-Thierry and in Paris, but abandoned it in his early twenties, seduced by poetry and the theatre. As a literary man he was a late starter, his first published work, a comedy in imitation of Terence, being published when he was thirty-three. He was in his forties when his first truly characteristic poems appeared. These were the *Contes et Nouvelles*, a retelling of medieval and renaissance tales which has a Chaucerian energy and wit, telescoping French history and interweaving social strata from peasant to knight to cleric. The ethos and the aura are recaptured fifty or sixty years later by Couperin's medley of high and low aspects of French life in the sequence of his harpsichord pieces, and – in so far as technical parallels between the arts are feasible – one could say that the 'tone', as manifest in Couperin's ambivalences between wit and pathos, tragedy and farce, fashionable immediacy and elegiac retrospection, is likewise comparable.

But the deepest affinity is, as was hinted in the original text of the book, that between Couperin's later music and La Fontaine's greatest poetry, the *Fables*. Both poet and composer, starting from an empathy with all sorts and conditions of men and with brute beasts and blithe birds, discovered within their humanity 'bright shootes of everlastingnesse' and, now and again, tapped the wellsprings of tragedy. The discreet *pudeur* of both men in dealing with the follies and foibles of our human fables tempers emotion with irony, and warms irony with compassion. Though both came from a privileged world, they create worlds that become curiously classless, and even timeless and placeless. The 'moral' values implicit in La Fontaine's *Fables* complement the 'objectivity' of Couperin's presentation of disparate aspects of experience: flexibilities of imagery and rhythm in the case of the poet, and of rhythm, harmony and texture in the case of the composer, carry apparently trivial scenes and events in the context of real life into an ideal world impervious to Time. It is that which renders men who are apparently hermetic autocrats at the same time modern democrats: not twentieth-century democrats, for the democratic ideal has never been and perhaps never can be fulfilled, but democrats *in essentia*. Here is another instance of the equilibrium between reality and ideality detected in Couperin and Watteau.

In old age La Fontaine, regressing to the enthusiasms of his adolescence, became an austere churchman, repented of the improprieties of his *Contes* and dismissed his *Fables* as *jeux d'esprit*, which in a sense they were. In his adolescence Couperin had started as an ecclesiastical musician, though this was more a familial heritage than a matter of religious conviction. From what little we know of Couperin's library we may gather that he was neither a *dévot* nor an intellectual. He doesn't seem to have read religious or philosophical works, and his acquaintance with the classics, mostly in translation, was small. But his interest in theatre is manifest: he owned sets of Corneille, Racine and Molière, and had an extensive collection of comedies, burlesques, and fictional romances, mostly concerned with and often written in a past age. There is some evidence to suggest that, as one might expect, La Fontaine was his favourite poet, whose spiritual essence he re-created in terms of musical sound. It is possible that Couperin as a youth knew La Fontaine as an old man, for the poet was a member of the congregation of St Gervais during the last, devotional phase of his life (at the same time, incidentally, as Mme de Sevigné, another brilliant writer whose prose has a distinctively Couperinesque flavour). But if Couperin did know La Fontaine, it wasn't the old man, whose conversation Saint-Simon found '*ennuyant*', that he responded to, but the creator of the *Fables*, who had discovered within the texture of everyday life a sanity and sanctity that had together created an art at once *spirituel* and spiritual: just such an art as Couperin was himself later to create, in his chosen medium. Though La Fontaine, dying in his early seventies, wept for his literary sins, Couperin knew, as did the nurse who tended the poet in his last hours, that 'God would never have the courage to damn him.'

Relevant to this is the fact that Couperin did on one occasion set La Fontaine's verses. His *Epitaphe d'un Paresseux*, published in 1711, is a slight *air à boire*, of which both words and music touch, however unpretentiously, on the heart of the experience of poet and composer:

> *Jean s'en alla comme il était venu*
> *Mangeant le fond avec le revenu,*
> *Tint les trésors chose peu nécessaire;*
> *Quant à son temps, bien le sut dispenser:*
> *Deux parts en fit, dont il soulait passer*
> *L'une à dormir, et l'autre à ne rien faire.*

That attitude of *laissez-faire*, in which the delicate rhythm creates the gentlest shrug of the shoulders, is mirrored in Couperin's malleable, minor-keyed tune, in the dialogue 465 between the two male voices and the bass, and in the metre, balanced between verbal inflexion and the civilized symmetries of the dance. The folk-like *naïveté* sounds like a distillation of centuries of French tradition, while the momentary frissons occasioned by the potential identity of sleep and death give to the old-world song its personal immediacy: just this fusion characterizes the maturest and profoundest art of both poet and composer. The little song is not really about an irresponsible hedonism but rather concerns an unblinkered acceptance of the present moment: the state of Being which alone validates the Becoming which is the past and future. This tells us, since Being is atemporal, why Couperin's music and La Fontaine's poetry are, at their best, independent of Time. At the core of the 'ample comédie en cent actes divers/Et dont la scène est l'univers', which might be La Fontaine's description of Couperin's harpsichord pieces, one discovers what the poet has called 'le sombre *plaisir* d'un cœur mélancholique'. Complementarily, the valedictory tone which we have noted in Couperin's prefaces is precisely echoed in the verses La Fontaine penned in his sixty-fourth year:

> *Désormais que ma Muse, aussi bien que mes jours,*
> *Touche de son déclin l'inévitable cours*
> *Et que de ma raison le flambeau va s'éteindre,*
> *Irai-je en consumer les restes à me plaindre,*
> *Et, prodigue d'un temps par la Parque attendu,*
> *Le perdre à regretter celui que j'ai perdu?*

La Fontaine's 'ample comédie en cent actes divers' quoted above links up with Balzac's *Comédie humaine*; and suggests that one cannot fully understand Couperin's music – especially the panoply of his harpsichord pieces – except as multifaceted reflections of a single world. I can think of no other work of the period that creates such an impression of diversity which none the less constitutes an undivided whole. The contemporary obsession with 'character', evident in the diarists of the period such as Mme de Sévigné and Saint-Simon and consummated in the immensely fashionable *Caractères* of La Bruyère, bears directly on Couperin's harpsichord music; if one understood enough about the people and places portrayed in the music one would realize that, although it 'takes all sorts to make a world', each person in each aspect – the most trivial along with the most sublime – is necessary to the other. Michael Moran tells me that this is corroborated by a recent retrospective visit he made to Versailles, where one finds, of course, rooms of imposing dimensions apposite to grand public functions, yet at the same time receives from the many smallish rooms – such as Louis's bedroom and the Pompadour's apartments – an impression of sensitivity and intimacy. The rooms decorated in Louis XIV (rather than Louis XV) style in particular have a refined delicacy that parallels the calligraphy of the engraved music, and which also relates to the psychological depths increasingly revealed through the sequence of the four volumes. Not many players are likely to have the time or patience thoroughly to steep themselves in the literature, memoirs and art of the period, yet it may be that without such intimate knowledge Couperin's music cannot fully uncover its secrets. In the original book I discussed relations between manners and morals, and between music, literature and the visual arts. I now suspect that such relationships extend into minute particularities. There must, for instance, be specific parallels not only between musical textures and engraved calligraphy, but also between musical ornamentation and interior decoration; between musical stylizations and costume; between musical rhythm, including *notes inégales*, and deportment as well as dance; between musical structures and architectural landscape gardening. Though such affinities exist generally throughout the history of civilization, they are manifest in the art of Couperin and his times with peculiar force and consistency. It is stimulating to discover, having revised this book retrospectively in retirement, that there are still so many open questions to a subject I've lived with for so many years. They await exploration: though not, at this date, by me.

III

COUPERIN AND THE MUSETTE

Couperin's relation to popular traditions, intermittently referred to in the commentaries on his secular music, is of some sociological as well as musical interest. Sometimes his references are direct, reminding us that, hyper-civilized creature though he was, he lived in a world small enough to embrace all sorts and conditions of men and women. Especially in pieces reminiscing over his childhood, before he gravitated to high places, he may emulate the sounds of peasant music-making, in no way disguising its raucousness: one thinks of the bagpipes in *La Croûilli ou la Couperinéte*, which may re-evoke his natal village and himself as a boy, and of the *Muséte de Choisi* and the *Muséte de Taverni*, bagpipe pieces set in Couperin country. No less raw in immediacy are his imitations of urban street musics, as droned out by strolling players: one thinks of the hurdy-gurdy-whining old men and cripples, and the fife- and tabor-playing jugglers and acrobats with bears and monkeys, who cavort in *Les Fastes de la Grande et Ancienne Ménestrandise*.

More commonly, however, Couperin idealizes and transfigures bumpkin bucolicism and urbanism (as distinct from urbanity) to hint at a vanished Eden which these highly sophisticated people yearned for – as was noticed in our discussion of the *Musette* with *viole* obbligato in the A major *Concert Royal*, and of harpsichord pieces such as *Les Vergers Fleüris*, *Les Bergeries* and *Les Langueurs-Tendres*, in which the bagpipe drone may be sometimes sounded, sometimes only implied. This idealization had a social manifestation in the contemporaneous metamorphosis of bagpipes – a folk instrument of great antiquity that had graduated into art – and of hurdy-gurdy – a medieval art instrument that had become the provenance of strolling players and thence of peasants – into instruments relished and played by the nobility when they went agrarianly slumming. Among

Couperin's secular vocal pieces the musette *A l'ombre d'un ormeau* stems from this tradition, for he uses the harpsichord as though it were the small bagpipe on which fashionable young ladies currently accompanied their *airs de cour*. The vogue started in the late seventeenth century, flourished throughout Couperin's day, and reached its apex twenty to thirty years after his death. Henri Baton, a lutenist at Versailles contemporary with Couperin (he died in 1728), was one of the first to cash in on the fashion by constructing instruments that combined the French bagpipes (*musette*) with the French hurdy-gurdy (*vielle*); they looked like, and sometimes used the cases of, elegantly decorated guitars, and were avidly acquired by elegantly decorated young men and women who wanted to play at shepherds and shepherdesses. We may see them portrayed in the sensuously exquisite, wistfully melancholic *fêtes champêtres* of Watteau.

Henri Baton was mainly an instrument builder. His son Charles became a virtuoso on the new–old instrument, composed music for it, and encouraged others to follow suit. The first treatise of instruction, Borjon de Scellery's *Traité de la musette*, had been published in Lyons as early as 1672; by the time Jacques Hotteterre's *Méthode pour la musette* appeared in Paris in 1738 the instrument had a substantial genteel literature, with pieces for musette solo or for musette with other instruments or as accompaniment to the voice. The most prolific composers were Baton and Hotteterre themselves and two other musette-making specialists, Esprit-Philippe Chédeville and his younger brother Nicolas. Other composers who contributed to the genre were Bodin de Boismortier, Michel Corrette, Montéclair, Philidor, and the great Jean-Philippe Rameau. Couperin, however, seems not to have written directly for the musette; perhaps his Arcadian idyll was so idealized that he spurned an however sophisticated intrusion of the real thing.

In 1982 an ensemble was formed, under the title of *Les Plaisirs Champêtres* and the direction of Jean-Christophe Maillard, to revive the forgotten instrument and its music; a disc issued in 1983 offers examples of most of the kinds of musette music, and of the work of many of the composers mentioned above. Maillard himself, a classically trained player of wind instruments, is also a scholar and performer in the field of Breton folk music, and is thus qualified to appreciate both the high and the low aspects of the musette. On the disc the piece that comes closest to folk roots is a brief modal *Branles* by the Borjon de Scellery 469 who wrote the first musette tutor. It could be, perhaps is, a folk tune, and the softly penetrative drone and the reedy ululation of the chanter approximate roughly to the sound of our Northumbrian and Irish pipes, which may be affiliated to Breton traditions. Fairly close to this *Branles* in sonority and temper is a charming suite of Bodin de Boismortier, in which the musette is accompanied by a separate drone-playing *vielle* or hurdy-gurdy. The titles of the movements – *allemande, sicilienne, minuet, gaiement* and *chaconne* – pay homage to courtly convention, but the sound of the music is bucolic, *faux-naïf* in being cheerily tuneful and rhythmic, with no harmonic subtleties and a minimum of part-writing. The pieces are technically simple as well as simpleminded, for they are for performance by idle young amateurs. Intended to while away empty moments, they do so delightfully. The contrast with Couperin's *use* of this convention is, however, striking – as one may hear if one relistens to his famous *Forlane* from the fourth *Concert Royal*, preferably in a version in which the melody instruments are oboe (perhaps alternating with flute) and bassoon. This is a low, Provençal dance directly comparable with some of the Boismortier movements, but differing from them in that its melody is marvellously memorable. The Watteauesque poetry of the couplet in the minor, which we have seen to contain the heart of Couperin, is far beyond Boismortier, though this does not invalidate the functional efficacy of his music as entertainment.

A suite for musette solo by Jacques Hotteterre, the leading member of a flute- and musette-playing dynasty, is more expertly composed, as one would expect from the man who wrote the most popular manual of instruction. Whereas Bodin de Boismortier gives his dances courtly ascriptions but produces his lowest music in the aristocratic genres of minuet and chaconne, Hotteterre seeks a politer balance between the instrument's peasant origins and its newfound gentility. The pieces, if still simple, are refined, including arrangements of a fashionable *brunette* with the pertinent title of 'Nous aimons les plaisirs champêtres', and of an air from Lully's *Isis*. We are apt to forget, thinking of Lully as ceremonial composer to le Roi Soleil, that many of his tunes have piquant appeal and were widely disseminated.

In this spiritually incestuous world the Hotteterres were related to the Chédevilles, the other main musette family. The elder Chédeville, Esprit-Philippe, is represented on the disc by two works, one a suite, the other a *concert champêtre*, both using musette in collaboration with French pastoral instruments – flutes, oboes, *violes*. The music charms and enlivens with its 'conversations galantes et amusantes' – as does Nicolas Chédevilles's sonata *Les Pagottes*, which owes its appeal to its very rudimentariness. Its *naïveté* is thus not exactly *'faux'*, though considerable skill may be involved in apparent spontaneity, since the music 'sounds' remarkably well – better than some of the composers, such as Michel Corrette, who had academic background and training. Corrette's *Fantaisie* for musette with a miniature 'concert' is in the three-movement Italian convention, and employs sophisticated Italianate stylizations in slightly quaint liaison with folksy elements of French tradition, ending with a jolly, almost Handelian, jig. It has nothing to do with the baroque fantasia convention.

Corrette didn't die until 1795, and the date of this work is probably later than the other pieces on the disc. Italianism was, of course, an established part of French tradition in less specialized fields than musette music, as the case of Couperin himself proves. In this connection it is interesting that the disc includes a sonata reputedly by Vivaldi, who tried his hand out at most instruments and was especially partial to those of low provenance, such as the mandolin. The ascription of this sonata to him is dubious but feasible: the more so because it includes a note not available on the instrument. Such an error would probably have been avoided by a Frenchman working within the tradition.

Couperin's flirtings with *les plaisirs champêtres* remind us that his many bird pieces are seldom simply imitative – apart from a cornily obvious creature like the cuckoo – but are rather distillations of bird-like characteristics, often with human as well as avian associations. It is interesting that the French fashion for constructing mechanical bird-organs flourished in Couperin's time, reaching its heyday a little later, contemporaneously with the climax to the musette vogue. The bird-organ was in part functional, for it could be used – sometimes attaining a high degree of realism, sometimes tweeting notatable tunes by human composers – to teach caged birds to sing. Couperin's bird pieces, such as *Les Fauvétes Plaintives* or the famous *Le Rossignol-en-amour*, are artful stylizations, recalling contemporary 471 *turlutaines*, as bird-organs were often called, after the crying curlew. There is no sharp distinction between Couperin's twittering bird-choruses and the chattering old women in *Le gazouillement*, the tinkling bells of *Le Carillon de Cithére* or *Les Timbres*, or even the more alarming tintinnabulations of *Le Réveil-matin* and *Le Tic-Toc-Choc*. All suggest not only bird-organs but also the later eighteenth-century musical box, though Couperin's exquisitely artful music is as far beyond a mechanical contrivance as his *Forlane* is beyond the insouciance of a Bodin de Boismortier.

IV

A NOTE ON COUPERIN'S TEMPO DIRECTIVES

Since Couperin is a composer with avowed expressive intentions in his music, especially his harpsichord pieces, it may be pertinent to enquire into his indications as to mood and tempo. The basic information about tempo is, for a baroque composer, implicit in the time signature: most obviously, of course, when the piece is also a dance – allemande, courante, sarabande or whatelse – in which both tempo and mood are traditionally preordained. When Couperin adds an adjectival or adverbial gloss to these technical facts, it may be presumed that he does so purposefully. He infrequently adds words to the 'strict' dance pieces, named according to type; when he does so, it is usually to define a genre – *allemande grave* or *allemande légère*, for instance – though the genre naturally carries with it emotional implications. Elsewhere, however, and especially in his 'portraits', Couperin is fairly liberal with verbal comment, and the words he uses and the frequency with which the terms recur shed light on his imaginative world.

By far his most frequent adjective and adverb are *tendre* and *tendrement*, which occur 51 times, seven of which are enhanced by a *très*, five mollified by his characteristic *sans lenteur*. This tally omits generic distinctions like *sarabande tendre*, but includes an exceptional title like *Badinage tendre* which refers to mood rather than to type. Second in the list comes *légèrement, léger, d'une légèreté* this or the other, which recur 33 times, five times with an additional *très*. *Gayement* or *gai* have 30 entries, three times enhanced with a *très*, once with a *fort*. *Gracieusement* scores 28, five times qualified by a *sans lenteur*; *gravement* reaches 27, three times intensified by a *très*, twice qualified by a *sans lenteur*. *Vivement* has 18 entries, two speeded up by a *très*, one tempered by the addition of '*et fièrement.*' These shade into *vite* or *viste*, with seven references, of which six have an additional *très*; these in turn merge into a few formulae such as '*d'une vivacité modérée*'. 473

Lentement has 11 entries, and a *largo* is used in reference to Italian Corelli. *Noblement* appears ten times, *affectueusement* nine, three and two of these entries being qualified by a *sans lenteur*. *Gaillardement* makes eight joyously gallant appearances, once tamed by a *sans lenteur*; on seven occasions *sans lenteur* serves as the only directive. A few other overtly emotive words make sporadic appearances: *languissamment* and *nonchalamment* four times each; *naïvement* four times, once with a *sans lenteur*; *animé* or *très animé* three times; *fièrement* three times. More extreme terms – *pesamment sans lenteur, délicatement, sans vitesse, voluptueusement sans lenteur, douloureusement, dolamment, impérieusement, amoureusement, audacieusement, galamment, grotesquement* appear only once or twice.

It is evident from the above that Couperin – though he uses the word *moderée* five times only – favours discretion and *pudeur*. It is significant that even when he tells us to play *majestueusement*, usually in reference to some particular grand lord or lady, he in five out of seven references pricks the bubble of pretension with a *sans lenteur*. His solitary *impérieusement* is intended ironically; the four *agréablements*, played *sans lenteur*, forestall emotional indulgence. These subtle verbal equivocations merely reinforce the impression we gain from the music: that an *honnête homme* will confront the most savage lacerations of passion and pain with dignity (as Couperin does in the *Passacaille* or *L'âme-en-peine*); and that complementarily he will enjoy exquisite delights of hedonism *affectueusement, voluptueusement, agréablement* and so on, while never forgetting how precarious is present pleasure. The ability to laugh at oneself, as well as at others, helps towards survival. Though this is manifest in the music, the appended words support it, and for that reason merit this comment.

BIOGRAPHICAL NOTES ON THE PRINCIPAL PERSONS MENTIONED IN THE TEXT

ANGLEBERT, Jean-Henri d' (1635–1691). Composer of clavecin and organ music. Successor to Chambonnières as official clavecinist of the Chambre du Roi.

AULNOY, Mme d' (1650/51–1705). Novelist and writer of fairy tales.

BACH, Carl Philipp Emanuel (1714–1788). ⎫ Discussed in
BACH, Wilhelm Friedemann (1710–1784). ⎬ relation to French
BACH, Johann Sebastian (1685–1750). ⎭ classical tradition.

BACILLY, Bénigne de (?c. 1625–1690). Priest and teacher of singing. *Remarques curieuses sur l'art de bien chanter*, published 1668.

BALBASTRE, Claude-Bénigne (1727–1799). Composer and organist of St-Roch and Notre Dame. Clavecin teacher of Marie-Antoinette.

BALLARD. French family of music printers. The firm flourished from the mid-sixteenth century until the latter years of the eighteenth century.

BENSERADE, Isaac de (1613–1691). Friend of Mazarin and Richelieu: devised ballets.

BERLIOZ, Louis-Hector (1803–1869). Discussed in relation to the classical tradition.

BOËSSET, Antoine (1586–1643). Composer of *ballets de cour* and *airs de cour*. Court musician to Louis XIII.

BOILEAU, Nicolas (1636–1711). Representative of the classical ideal. Continued the work of Malherbe. *Art Poétique*, published 1674.

BOISMORTIER, Joseph Bodin de (1689–1755). Composer of opera-ballets and of concerted music, especially for wind instruments.

BOSSUET, Jacques-Bénigne (1627–1704). Bishop of Meaux and member of the Academy. An authoritarian, famous for his sermons, especially funeral orations.

BOUCHER, François (1703–1770). Painter and decorator of the Regency and of the age of Louis XV.

BOURDALOUE, Louis (1632–1704). Jesuit father, celebrated as a preacher.

BULL, John (?1562/3–1628). English composer, mainly of keyboard music. Organist of Antwerp Cathedral from 1617 until his death.

BUSSY, Roger de Rabutin, comte de (1618–1693). Kinsman and correspondent of Mme de Sévigné.

BUTERNE, Jean-Baptiste (c. 1650–1727). Organist and composer. Pupil of Henri Du Mont. Organist of Chapelle Royale, 1678.

CAIX D'HERVELOIS, Louis de (?1670/80–c. 1760). Bass viol player and composer. In the service of the Duc d'Orléans.

CAMBERT, Robert (c. 1627–1677). Composer of ballets, motets and *airs à boire*. Member of Académie Royale, 1671. Settled in London 1673, where he remained until his death.

CAMPRA, André (1660–1744). Composer of ballets, divertissements and church music. Organist of Toulon Cathedral and later of St Louis des Jésuites and Notre Dame de Paris.

CAPROLI, Carlo (1615/20–1692/5). Italian opera composer called to Paris by Mazarin. Maître de la Musique du Cabinet du Roi, from January to June, 1654.

CARISSIMI, Giacomo (1605–1674). Italian composer of church music, adapting operatic techniques to the oratorio. Worked in Rome, but exerted a great influence on French church music.

CAURROY, François Eustache de (1549–1609). Composer of motets, instrumental fantasias, and *airs de cour*.

CAVALLI, Pier Francesco Caletti-Bruni (1602–1676). Pupil of Monteverdi and choir master of St Mark's, Venice. Composer of operas. *Serse* and *L'Ercole Amante* were produced in Paris in 1660 and 1662.

CESTI, Antonio (1623–1669). Pupil of Carissimi, composer of operas.

CHAMBONNIÈRES, Jacques Champion de (1601/2–1672). Composer of harpsichord music. Of noble birth, he followed his father and grandfather as official organist and clavecinist of the Chambre du Roi. Taught most of the composers of the French clavecin school.

CHAMPAGNE, Philippe de (1602–1674). Painter. Friend of Poussin and associate of Port-Royal.

CHAMPMESLÉ, Marie Desmares (1642–1698). Tragic actress, famous for her portrayals of the heroines of Racine.

CHARDIN, Jean-Baptiste-Siméon (1699–1779). Painter (of bourgeois origin) of scenes from middle-class life; still influenced by the spirit of the classical tradition.

CHARPENTIER, Marc-Antoine (?1645/50–1704). French composer, mainly of church music, who studied in Italy under Carissimi.

CLAUDE GELÉE, le Lorrain (1600–1682). Painter; with Poussin the greatest exponent of the classical tradition. Studied in Rome.

CLÉRAMBAULT, Louis-Nicolas (1676–1749). Composer of clavecin music, organ music, and sacred and secular cantatas. Pupil of J. B. Moreau; organist of St Sulpice.

CLICQUOT, François-Henri (1732–1790). Famous organ builder.

CORELLI, Arcangelo (1653–1713). Italian violinist and composer whose work had great influence in France.

CORNEILLE, Pierre (1606–1684). Creator of the classical ideal in tragedy.

CORNEILLE, Thomas (1625–1709). Younger brother of Pierre. Collaborated with Lully.

COSTELEY, Guillaume de (c. 1530–1606). Composer, especially of chansons for several voices.

COTTE, Robert de (1656–1735). Architect and decorator; designed the organ case and decorations of the Chapelle Royale at Versailles.

COUPERIN, Louis (c. 1626–1661). Composer for harpsichord and organ. Organist of St Gervais. Wrote some ballet music.

COUPERIN, François the elder (1631–after 1708). Brother of Louis. Music teacher and organist.

COUPERIN, Charles (1638–1679). Brother of above. Organist and composer. Succeeded Louis as organist of St Gervais, 1661.

COUPERIN, François le Grand (1668–1733). Son of Charles.

COUPERIN, Marguerite-Louise (c. 1676 or 1679–1728). Daughter of François Couperin the elder. Member of the Musique du Roi. Many of the soprano parts in François Couperin le Grand's motets were written for her. She was also a fine harpsichord player.

COUPERIN, Marie-Anne (1677–?). Sister of Marguerite-Louise. Entered a convent, where she played the organ.

COUPERIN, Nicolas (1680–1748). Brother of above. Organist to the Comte de Toulouse. Succeeded François le Grand as organist of St Gervais.

COUPERIN, Marie-Madeleine (1690–1742). Daughter of François le Grand. Became a nun, and was organist of the Abbey of Maubuisson, having taken the name of Cécile.

COUPERIN, Marguerite-Antoinette (1705–*c*. 1778). Daughter of François le Grand. Became celebrated as a clavecinist and succeeded to some of her father's court appointments. She taught the daughters of Louis XV.

COUPERIN, Armand-Louis (1727–1789). Son of Nicolas. Composer of organ music, harpsichord music, sonatas and motets. Organist of St Gervais, and successively of six other Parisian churches, culminating in Notre Dame. Was also an expert on organ building.

COUPERIN, Pierre-Louis (1755–1789). Son of Armand-Louis. Organist of the Chapelle Royale, St Gervais, Notre Dame, St Jean-en-Grève, and St Merry. Composer of motets.

COUPERIN, Gervais-François (1759–1826). Son of Armand-Louis. Composer of symphonies, sonatas and religious music.

COUPERIN, Nicolas-Louis (1760–18?). Son of Gervais-François.

COUPERIN, Céleste (1793–1860). Daughter of Gervais-François. Last member of the Couperin dynasty. Lived at Beauvais with her mother until 1830, when she moved to Belleville near Paris and gained a living by giving piano and singing lessons.

COUSSER, Johann Siegmund (1660–1727). German composer, especially of operas. Studied with Lully, 1674–1682. Director of the Hamburg opera, 1694.

DAQUIN, Louis-Claude (1694–1772). Composer of harpsichord and organ music. Organist of the Chapelle Royale in 1739, and of Notre Dame de Paris.

DEBUSSY, Achille-Claude (1862–1918). Discussed in relation to the classical tradition.

DESCARTES, Réné (1596–1650). Philosopher and mathematician, educated at the Jesuit College of La Flèche. His works, especially the *Traité des Passions de l'âme*, profoundly influenced every aspect of the culture of the *grand siècle*, including musical theory.

DESTOUCHES, André-Cardinal (1672–1749). Amateur composer of operas and divertissements. A pupil of Campra, he succeeded La Lande as Surintendent de la Musique de Chambre in 1718, and was Inspecteur Général of the Opera from 1713–1728.

DORNEL, Louis-Antoine (c. 1680–after 1756). Organist and composer of concerted music and cantatas.

DOWLAND, John (1563–1626). English or Irish lutenist and composer. Visited France in 1580, and became court musician to Christian IV of Denmark in 1598. Settled in London finally in 1606.

DU MAGE, Pierre (1674–1751). Seventeenth- to eighteenth-century organist and organ composer. Organist of collegiate church of St Quentin, 1703–1713.

DU MONT, Henri de Thier (1610–1684). Organist of St Paul, Paris, 1640, and of the Chapelle Royale, 1663. Important composer of church music, including masses on plainsong themes, a Magnificat, and Cantica sacra for solo voices and continuo. (Published Ballard, 1652 and 1662.)

DUPHLY, Jacques (1715–1789). Harpsichord player and composer.

ERLEBACH, Philipp Heinrich (1657–1714). German composer who studied in Paris the methods of Lully.

FAURÉ, Gabriel-Urbain (1845–1924). French composer, discussed in relation to the classical tradition.

FÉNELON, François de Salignac de la Mothe- (1651–1715). Priest, Archbishop of Cambrai, tutor to the Duc de Bourgogne, author of the *Traité de l'éducation des filles* and *Traité de l'existence de Dieu*. One of the most profoundly religious minds of his time.

FISCHER, Johann Kaspar Ferdinand (c. 1670–1746). Composer of organ, clavecin and concerted music; studied the work of Lully. *Le Journal du Printemps*, 1696.

FONTENELLE, Bernard le Bouvier de (1657–1757). Critic and theorist engaged in the war of the Ancients and Moderns. Collaborated with his uncle Thomas Corneille in ballet and opera.

FORQUERAY, Antoine (1671/2–1745). Bass viol player and composer.

FRANCISQUE, Antoine (c. 1575–1605). Lutenist and composer; *Le Trésor d'Orfée*, published 1596.

FRENEUSE, Lecerf de la Viéville de (1674–1707). Francophile musical theorist. Author of *Comparaison de la musique française et de la musique italienne*.

479

FRESCOBALDI, Girolamo (1583–1643). Italian organist and composer. Organist of St Peter's, Rome, from 1608.

GALLOT, Jacques (Gallot le vieux), (16?–c. 1690). Lutenist and composer.

GALLOT, Jacques (Gallot le jeune), (d. after 1716). Lutenist and composer, son of above.

GARNIER, Gabriel (d. c. 1730). Succeeded Le Bègue as organist of the Chapelle Royale in 1702. Friend of Couperin le Grand.

GAULTIER, Ennemond (1575–1651). Lutenist and composer, teacher of Marie de Médicis and Richelieu.

GAULTIER, Jacques (d. before 1660). Lutenist and composer. Fled to London, 1617, and was attached to the English court until 1647.

GAULTIER, Denis (d. 1672). Cousin of Ennemond Gaultier. The greatest of the lute school.

GIBBONS, Orlando (1583–1625). English composer; discussed as writer of organ music.

GIGAULT, Nicolas (c. 1627–1707). Organist and organ composer, one of the teachers of Lully. Organist of St Martin and St Nicolas des Champs.

GRIGNY, Nicolas de (1672–1703). Pupil of Le Bègue, organist of the Abbey of St Denis, and later of Rheims Cathedral. Composer of organ music, mostly of a liturgical nature.

GUÉDRON, Pierre (?1570/75–1619/20). Composer of ballets and *airs de cour*. Maître de la Musique de la Reine and Surintendant de la Musique du Roi, 1609.

HANDEL, Georg Friedrich (1685–1759). Discussed in relation to French classical tradition.

JACQUET DE LA GUERRE, Elisabeth-Claude (1659–1729). Harpsichordist and composer, protégée of Mme de Montespan, and much admired by Louis XIV. She wrote an opera (*Céphale et Procris*) and other stage works, as well as harpsichord music.

JENKINS, John (1592–1678). English composer and string player. Composer of fantasias for strings and some church music and songs.

JONSON, Ben (1572–1637). English poet, dramatist, and masque writer. Discussed in relation to the French classical tradition.

JOSQUIN des Prés (c. 1440–1521). Flemish composer of religious and secular music.

480 JULLIEN, Gilles (c. 1650/53–1703). Organist and composer.

Organist of Chartres Cathedral; *Livre d'orgue*, published 1690.

LA BARRE, Pierre Chabanceau de (1592–1656). Composer of ballets and *airs de cour*. Organist of the Chapelle Royale.

LA BRUYÈRE, Jean de (1645–1696). Writer of *Les Caractères*. Of bourgeois origin, he became tutor to the family of the Condés, and a friend of Bossuet.

LA FAYETTE, Marie de (1634–1693). Novelist, author of *La Princesse de Clèves*. Friend of La Rochefoucauld.

LA FONTAINE, Jean de (1621–1695). Author of Contes and Fables. Elected to Academy, 1683.

LA LANDE, Michel Richard de (1657–1726). Leading composer of church music in the time of Louis XIV. Also wrote ballets, and divertissements. Organist of St Gervais, St Louis, St Jean-en-Grève, and of the Petit Couvent St Antoine. Maître de la Musique de la Chambre et de la Chapelle.

LAMBERT, Michel (1610–1696). Composer of *airs de cour* and operas. A pupil of de Nyert, he was famous as a teacher of singing. Became Maître de la Musique de Chambre, 1661.

LA POUPLINIÈRE, Alexandre-Jean-Joseph le Riche de (1693–1762). Farmer-general of taxes who acquired an immense fortune and became a patron of music. Supported Rameau, Stamitz and others.

LA ROCHEFOUCAULD, François duc de (1613–1680). Grand seigneur and honnête homme. Writer of *Maximes*. Influenced by Port-Royal, though not himself a Jansenist.

LAWES, William (1602–1645). English composer of Charles I's court. Wrote music for viols, masques, church music, etc.

LE BÈGUE, Nicolas-Antoine (*c.* 1631–1702). Composer of organ and harpsichord music. Pupil of Chambonnières, organist of St Merry and of the Chapelle Royale, 1678.

LE BLANC, Hubert. Author of treatise defending the viols against the encroachments of the violin family.

LEBRUN, Charles (1619–1690). Official court painter. Founded l'Académie Royale de Peinture, 1648, Académie de France à Rome, 1666.

LE CAMUS, Sébastien (*c.* 1610–1677). Composer of *airs de cour*, etc. Maître de la Musique du Roi, 1640.

LECLAIR, Jean-Marie (1697–1764). Composer of operas, violin sonatas, and concertos, etc. One of the greatest figures at the end of the classical tradition. Served as instrumentalist in the Musique du Roi and at the Court of Don Felipe at Chambéry. Visited Holland to meet Locatelli.

LE JEUNE, Claude (1528/30–1600). Franco-Flemish composer of polyphonic music and of *musique mesurée*.

LE NÔTRE, André (1613–1700). Designer of the gardens at Versailles and elsewhere.

LE ROUX, Gaspard (d. 1705/7). Clavecinist and composer of clavecin music, motets and *airs sérieux*.

LE ROY, Adrien (*c.* 1520–1598). Lutenist, theorist, composer and music publisher. Associated with Ballard. Published books on lute playing.

L'HERMITE, Tristan (1601–1655). Lyrical poet and writer of tragedies.

LOUIS XIII (1601–1643). Enthusiastic amateur singer and composer.

LOUIS XIV (reigned 1661–1715).

LOUIS XV (reigned 1715–1774).

LULLY, Jean-Baptiste de (1632–1687). Leading composer of opera and ballet for Louis XIV. Started his career as dancer and violinist in the ballet. Of Florentine origin, he became a strenuous opponent of Italian influence in French music.

MAINTENON, Mme de (1635–1719). Married to Scarron and governess of the children of Mme de Montespan; it is probable that she secretly married Louis XIV. Wrote works of instruction for the school of St Cyr which she directed; and much valuable correspondence.

MALEBRANCHE, Nicolas (1638–1715). Disciple of Descartes. A priest, he identified Reason with the Word of God.

MALHERBE, François de (1555–1628). Poet and theorist; link between Ronsard and the Pléïade, and the classicism of Boileau. Secretary to the duc d'Angoulême.

MANSART, Jules-Hardouin (1646–1708). Official architect to Louis XIV.

MARAIS, Marin (1656–1728). The greatest of the classical composers for the viol; also wrote operas of remarkable interest. Pupil of Lully and chef d'orchestre of the opera (1695).

MARCHAND, Louis (1669–1732). Organist and composer of organ music, greatly celebrated as a virtuoso. Organist of many churches and ultimately of the Chapelle Royale, 1706.

MARPURG, Friedrich Wilhelm (1718–1795). German composer and writer of theoretical works.

482 MATTHESON, Johann (1681–1764). German composer and

theorist.

MAUDUIT, Jacques (1557–1627). Lutenist and member of the Académie de Baïf. Composer of religious music, *chanson-nettes mesurées* and ballets for Louis XIII.

MAUGARS, André (*c.* 1580–*c.* 1645). Violist, politician, and English interpreter to Louis XIII, Musician to Cardinal de Richelieu. Author of a *Réponse faite sur le sentiment de la musique d'Italie*, 1639.

MAZARIN (Giulio Mazarini) (1602–1661). Cardinal, minister of state and patron of music. Introduced many Italian musicians into France, in his enthusiasm for the Italian opera.

MERSENNE, Marin (1588–1648). A Minorite friar, ordained in 1613. Taught philosophy at Nevers, and studied mathematics and music at Paris, with Descartes and the elder Pascal. Wrote important theoretical treatises on music. Corresponded about musical theory with Titelouze and others.

MÉZANGEAU, René (15?–1638). Lutenist and composer.

MIGNARD, Nicolas (1610–1695). Official court painter, especially of portraits.

MOLIÈRE (pseudonym), Jean-Baptiste Poquelin (1622–1673). The greatest comic dramatist of the classical age. Collaborated with Lully in opera-ballet.

MONDONVILLE, Jean-Joseph-Cassanéa de (1711–1772). Composer of operas, opera-ballets, and concerted music especially for violin, on which instrument he was a virtuoso. Wrote works for the Concerts Spirituels from 1737–1770, Surintendant de la Chapelle Royale, 1744. Represented the French national school in the Guerre des Bouffons.

MONTEVERDI, Claudio (1567–1643). Discussed in relation to French tradition.

MOREAU, Jean-Baptiste (1656–1733). Composer, especially of religious music to plays and poems of Racine. Maître de Chapelle at Langres and Dijon.

MOURET, Jean-Joseph (1682–1738). Composer mainly of ballets, orchestral suites, and divertissements for the Italian comedies. Succeeded Philidor as director of the Concerts Spirituels, 1728.

MOUTON, Charles (1626–*c.* 1700). Pupil of Denis Gaultier, the last of the great lutenist school.

MOZART, Wolfgang Amadeus (1756–1791). Discussed in relation to French tradition.

MUFFAT, Georg (1653–1704). Alsatian composer who studied with Lully in Paris, 1665. Organist of Strasbourg Cathedral and later music director at Passau.

MUFFAT, Gottlieb Theophil (1690–1770). Son of above. Composer mainly of organ and harpsichord music.

NIVERS, Guillaume-Gabriel (*c.* 1632–1714). Organist and composer. Organist of St Sulpice and of the Chapelle Royale, 1678.

NOVERRE, Jean-Georges (1727–1810). Ballet dancer and dance theorist.

NYERT, Pierre de (*c.* 1597–1682). Rich amateur musician and teacher of singing. Disciple of the Italians.

PASCAL, Blaise (1623–1662). Mathematician, scientist, writer, and Christian apologist. Later associated with Port-Royal.

PERRAULT, Charles (1628–1703). Author of the *Parallèles des Anciens et des Modernes*, and of fairy tales.

PERRIN, Pierre (*c.* 1620–1675). Poet and founder of the Académie Royale de Musique.

PESCHEUR, Pierre. One of the builders of the organ of St Gervais.

PHILIDOR, André (*c.* 1647–1730). Composer and windplayer for the Ecurie Royale and Librarian of the King's Music.

PINEL, Germain (?–1661). Lutenist and lute composer. Collaborated in *ballets de cour*.

POUSSIN, Nicolas (1594–1665). Greatest painter of the classical age. Studied and worked in Rome.

PURCELL, Henry (1659–1695). Discussed in relation to the French tradition.

QUINAULT, Philippe (1635–1688). Poet and librettist to Lully.

RACINE, Jean (1639–1699). Greatest of the classical writers of tragedy. Associated with Port-Royal.

RAISON, André (before 1650–1719). Organist and organ composer. Celebrated as a virtuoso.

RAMBOUILLET, Catherine, marquise de (1588–1665). Woman of society; established salon in the rue St Thomas du Louvre.

RAMEAU, Jean-Philippe (1683–1764). The last great musical representative of the classical age. Composer of operas, ballets, harpsichord music, concerted music and theoretical treatise on harmony. His operatic work dates from the latter part of his life.

REBEL, Jean-Féry (1666–1747). Violinist, harpsichordist and composer of ballets and concerted music. Pupil of Lully.

RIGAUD, Hyacinthe (1659–1743). Court and society painter, especially of portraits.

ROBERDAY, François (1624–1680). Organist and composer of organ music. Teacher of Lully.

ROSENMÜLLER, Johann (*c.* 1619–1684). German composer of motets, cantatas and sonatas. Worked for some time in Venice.

ROSSI, Luigi (*c.* 1597–1653). Italian opera composer, called to France by Mazarin. His *Orfeo* was performed at the court in 1647.

ROUSSEAU, Jean-Jacques (1712–1778). Referred to as author of *Dissertation sur la musique moderne* and *Dictionnaire de la musique*, 1767.

SAINT-EVREMOND, Charles de St-Denis, sieur de (1614–1703). Critic, letter-writer and man of society. Settled in London, 1661.

SAINT-AMANT, Marc-Antoine Gérard de (1594–1661). Tavern poet and member of the Academy. Wrote sophisticated lyrics, grotesques, and *caprices*.

SAINT-SIMON, Louis, duc de (1675–1755). Member of a noble family, courtier at Versailles. Wrote his famous memoirs of the age of Louis XIV many years after the events described.

SCARLATTI, Alessandro (1660–1725). Italian opera composer.

SCARLATTI, Domenico (1685–1757). Son of above. Composer of harpsichord music and operas. Celebrated as harpsichordist.

SCARRON, Paul (1610–1660). Writer of nouvelles and burlesques.

SCHÜTZ, Heinrich (1585–1672). German composer mainly of church music.

SCUDÉRY, Madeleine de (1607–1701). Novelist; her salon was more bourgeois, and more precious in tone than the Hôtel de Rambouillet.

SÉVIGNÉ, Marquise de (1626–1696). Celebrated as letter writer. Sympathized with the Jansenists.

SIMPSON, Christopher (*c.* 1605–1669). English bass viol player and composer for his instrument. Wrote theoretical works on the *Principles of Practical Musick* and on bass viol playing.

SOREL, Charles (1602–1674). Author of *Histoire comique de Françion*, a picaresque novel, with real contemporary characters disguised among the personae.

STAMITZ, Johann Wenzel Anton (1717–1757). Composer and director of the famous symphony orchestra for the Elector of 485

Mannheim. Visited Paris at the invitation of Le Riche de la Pouplinière.

STAMITZ, Karl (1745–1801). Bohemian composer. Pupil of his father (above), trained in the Mannheim orchestra. Visited Paris in 1770.

SWEELINCK, Jan Pieterszoon (1562–1621). Dutch composer, organist and harpsichordist.

THIBAUT DE COURVILLE, Joachim (d. 1581). Founded with Antoine de Baïf the Académie de poésie et de musique, 1570. Composed *airs de cour*.

THIERRY family. Seventeenth-century organ builders who worked on the organ at St Gervais.

THOMELIN, Jacques-Denis (*c.* 1640–1693). Organist and composer, principal composition teacher to François Couperin. Organist of the Chapelle Royale, 1678. Previously had been organist of St German des Prés and St Jacques de la Boucherie.

TILLET, Evrard Titon du (1677–1762). Amateur of the arts. Author of *Parnasse François*, 1732 (containing memoirs of the Couperins).

TITELOUZE, Jean (1562/3–1633). Founder and perhaps the greatest representative of the classical French organ school. All his music is liturgical. Organist of Rouen Cathedral.

URFÉ, Honoré d' (1568–1625). Author of the pastoral romance *L'Astrée*, known as 'le bréviaire des courtisans' (cf. St François de Sales's *Introduction à la vie dévote*, which was called 'le bréviaire des gens de bien').

VAUGELAS, Charles Favre, baron de (1585–1650). Authority on the language of polite society. *Remarques sur la langue française*, 1647.

VAUVENARGUES, Luc de Clapiers, marquis de (1715–1747). Author of *Introduction à la connoissance de l'Esprit humain*. 'Un cœur stoique et tendre' – halfway between La Rochefoucauld and Pascal.

VOITURE, Vincent (1597–1648). Son of a wine dealer. Wit and writer of society verse for the salons.

WATTEAU, Jean Antoine (1684–1721). The greatest painter among Couperin's immediate contemporaries. Worked in Paris, painting especially the *fête champêtre* and scenes from the Italian comedy.

EDITIONS OF COUPERIN'S WORKS

A   Chamber music
B   Harpsichord music
C   Organ music
D   Sacred vocal music
E   Secular vocal music
F   Theoretical writing

C numbers refer to the *Thematic Index of the Works of François Couperin* by Maurice Cauchie, Monaco, 1949.

Library symbols used

DK-Kk	Copenhagen, Det Kongelige Bibliotek
F-C	Carpentras, Bibliothèque Inguimbertine et Musée de Carpentras
F-LYm	Lyon, Bibliothèque municipale
F-Pc	Paris, Bibliothèque du Conservatoire national de musique
F-Pn	Paris, Bibliothèque nationale
F-V	Versailles, Bibliothèque municipale
GB-Ge	Glasgow, Euing Music Library
GB-Lbm	London, British Library Reference Division
I-Nc	Napoli, Biblioteca del Conservatorio di Musica S. Pietro a Maiella
NL-DHgm	The Hague, Gemeente Museum

Where there are many library locations for the early editions of Couperin's works, the appropriate RISM number is given, RISM being the French acronym for 'International Inventory of Musical Sources'.

There have been two editions of the works of François Couperin.
1 Œuvres complètes; publié par un groupe de musicologues sous

la direction de Maurice Cauchie. Paris, Éditions de l'Oiseau-Lyre, 1932. 12 vols.
In the following list, this edition is referred to thus:
Œuvres complètes.
2 Œuvres complètes; publiées par Maurice Cauchie et revues d'après les sources par Kenneth Gilbert et Davitt Moroney. Monaco, Éditions de l'Oiseau-Lyre, 1980–.

As at 31 July 1986 seven out of the proposed total of twelve volumes have been published. This new edition is not a reissue of the 1932 edition; all the music has been newly revised from the sources and errors corrected, and the six volumes of chamber and vocal music now omit the realization of the figured bass. Also included are fascimile pages, which are helpful as guides to Couperin's own notation.
In the following list, this edition is referred to thus:
Œuvres complètes; rev.

A   Chamber Music

Works published during Couperin's lifetime

1 Concerts royaux
Œuvres complètes VII
Œuvres complètes; rev. IV, 1
Fascimile editions: New York, Broude, 1973; Madrid, Arte Tripharia, 1982.

<blockquote>

Harpsichord (or violin, flute, oboe, viol, and bassoon)

Premier concert	G major and minor (C. 287–92)
Second concert	D major and minor (C. 293–7)
Troisième concert	A major and minor (C. 298–304)
Quatrième concert	E major and minor (C. 305–11)

</blockquote>

Published in a separately paginated sequence at the end of *Troisième livre de pièces de clavecin*. Paris, 1722.

Concerts royaux, für Violine und Basso continuo; hrsg. von F.F. Polnauer.
Mainz, Schott, 1970. (Edition Schott 5780–5783.)
Score and parts.

Concerts royaux I–IV: for flute, oboe, violin, viola da gamba and basso continuo; ed. by D. Lasocki.
London, Musica Rara, 1974.
Score and parts.

2 Les goûts-réünis; ou, Nouveaux concerts à l'usage de toutes lessortes d'instrumens de musique, augmentés d'une grande sonade en trio intitulée Le Parnasse, ou L'apothéose de Corelli, *etc.* Paris, 1724.
F-Pn, F-V; *GB-Ge*; *NL-DHgm*
Œuvres complètes VIII
Œuvres complètes; rev. IV, 2
Facsimile edition: Geneva, Minkoff, 1979.
Facsimile edition: Ann Arbor, Michigan, Early Music Facsimiles, [?1980].

The *concerts* were numbered 5–14 by Couperin himself, who clearly thought of the *Concerts Royaux* as numbers 1–4. Mostly for 1 or 2 treble instruments and bc.

  5 F major (C. 312–16)
  6 B flat major (C. 317–21)
  7 D minor (C. 322–7)
  8 Dans le goût théatral   G major (C. 328–38)
  9 Neuvième concert intitulé Ritratto dell'amore
      E major/E minor (C. 339–46)
 10 A minor (C. 347–50)
 11 G minor (C. 351–8)
 12 Douzième concert, à deux violes ou autres instrumens
      à l'unisson   A major (C. 359–61)
 13 Treizième concert, à 2 instrumens à l'unisson
      G major (C. 362–5)
 14 D minor (C. 366–9)

Les goûts-réünis, or Nouveaux concerts for flute, oboe, violin & basso continuo.
London, Musica Rara, 1975.
Score and parts.

Concerto 6, B-Dur: für Oboe (Violine) und Basso continuo; hrsg. von H. Ruf.
Mainz, Schott, 1970. (Edition Schott 6024.)
Score and parts.

[Concert, 13]
Duo G-Dur . . . für Bassinstrumente (Violoncelli, Viole da gamba, Fagotti); hrsg. von H. Ruf.
Mainz, Schott, 1967.

[Concert, 13]
Duo G-Dur . . . für Querflöten oder Violinen; hrsg. von H. Ruf.
Mainz, Schott, 1967.

3 Le Parnasse, ou L'apothéose de Corelli. Grande sonade en trio. 2 treble instruments and bc. (C. 370–6)
Published in the preceding work.
Œuvres complètes X
Œuvres complètes; rev. IV, 4

L'apothéose de Corelli: for 2 flutes or oboes or violins, and basso continuo; ed. by E. Higginbottom.
London, Musica Rara, 1976.
Score and parts.

4 Concert instrumental sous le titre d'Apothéose, composé à la mémoire immortelle de l'incomparable Monsieur de Lully, par Monsieur Couperin. Paris, 1725. (C. 377–89)
F-Pn, F-Pc; I-Nc; NL-DHgm
Œuvres complètes X
Œuvres complètes; rev. IV, 4
Facsimile edition: Geneva, Minkoff, 1979.
2 flutes, 2 violins, other unspecified instruments, and bc

L'apothéose de Lulli: for 2 flutes/oboes/violins, basses d'archet and b.c.; ed. by E. Higginbottom.
London, Musica Rara, 1976.
Score and parts.

5 Les nations, sonades et suites de simphonies en trio, en quatre livres séparés pour la comodité des académies de musique et des concerts particuliers.
Paris, 1726.
F-Pn

Œuvres complètes IX
Œuvres complètes; rev. IV, 3 (includes complete facsimile parts)
Facsimile edition: Madrid, Arte Tripharia, 1982
2 violins and bc
Premier ordre   La françoise, and suite of 8 dances
E minor (C. 390–8)
Second ordre   L'espagnole, and suite of 10 dances
C minor (C. 399–408)
Troisième ordre   L'impériale, and suite of 9 dances
D minor (C. 409–18)
Quatrième ordre   La piémontoise, and suite of 6 dances
G minor (C. 419–25)
The *sonades* to *ordres* 1, 2 and 4 had at their time of composition (*c.* 1692) different titles, i.e.

La françoise	was called	La pucelle
L'espagnole	was called	La visionnaire
La piémontoise	was called	L'astrée

for further details of which see below.

Les nations: for 2 flutes or oboes or violins, basse d'archet, and basso continuo; ed. by E. Higginbottom.
London, Musica Rara, 1976–7.
Score and parts.

La pucelle, La visionnaire, and L'astrée remain under these titles in a manuscript score: *F-Pn* MS. Vm7 1156, and in a set of parts: *F-LYm* MS. 129949

[La pucelle] (C. 390–8)
Triosonate I, E-moll, für zwei Violinen und Basso continuo; hrsg. von F. F. Polnauer.
Mainz, Schott, 1968. (Edition Schott 5689.)
Score and parts.

[La visionnaire] (C. 399–408)
Triosonate II, C-moll . . . für zwei Violinen und Basso continuo; hrsg. von F. F. Polnauer.
Mainz, Schott, 1968. (Edition Schott 5690.)
Score and parts.

6 Pièces de violes avec la basse chifrée, par Mr F. C. Paris, 1728.
F-Pn
Œuvres complètes X
Œuvres complètes; rev. IV, 4
2 bass viols, bc.
Suite 1   E minor (C. 426–32)
Suite 2   A major (C. 433–6)

[Pièces de violes]
Pièces pour violoncelle et piano; retrouvées, annotées et revisées par C. Bouvet.
Paris, Durand, 1923–4.

Pièces de violes; éd. par L. Robinson.
Paris, Heugel, 1973. (Le pupitre, 51.)
Score and parts.

Works unpublished at Couperin's death

La Steinquerque; 2 violins, bc; B flat major (C. 486)
F-Pn MS. Vm7 1156 (score); *F-LYm* MS. 129949 (parts)
Œuvres complètes X
Œuvres complètes; rev. IV, 4

La superbe   2 violins, bc   A major (C. 487)
F-LYm MS. 129949 (parts)
Œuvres complètes X
Œuvres complètes; rev. IV, 4

La superbe: Trio-sonate in A-dur, für 2 Violinen und Klavier mit Violoncello ad libitum; hrsg. von F. F. Polnauer.
Zurich, Hug, 1966.
Score and parts.

La sultane   2 violins, bass viol, bc   D minor (C. 492)
F-LYm MS. 129949 (parts)
Œuvres complètes X
Œuvres complètes; rev. IV, 4

La sultane: sonade en quatuor (1695) for 2 violins, 2 cellos and continuo; ed. by F. F. Poulnauer.
New York, Fischer, 1968.
Score and parts.

B   Harpsichord Music

1 An allemande and eight preludes, published in *L'art de toucher le clavecin*, 1716/17.
For editions, see section F Theoretical Writings

2 Six pieces originally published in
Pièces choisies pour le clavecin de différents auteurs.
Paris, 1707.
F-Pn
five of which were subsequently included in *Pièces de clavecin (Livre I)*. These are
    Les Abeilles
    Les Nonètes i) Les Blondes
                   ii) Les Brunes
    La Diane
    La Florentine
    La Badine
The other piece is a Sicilienne in G (Œuvres complètes II; Œuvres complètes; rev. II, 1).

3 Pièces de clavecin
Pièces de clavecin . . . premier livre, *etc.*
Paris, 1713.
Library holdings listed RISM C4279–C4287 (C. 86–155)

Second livre de pièces de clavecin, *etc.*
Paris, 1717.
Library holdings listed RISM C4288–C4293 (C. 168–75)

Troisième livre de pièces de clavecin, *etc.*
Paris, 1722.
Library holdings listed RISM C4294–C4297 (C. 230–86)

Quatrième livre de pièces de clavecin, *etc.*
Paris, 1730.

Library holdings listed RISM C4298–C4300 (C. 437–85)

Œuvres complètes II–V
Œuvres complètes; rev. II, 1–4

Facsimile edition: New York, Broude Brothers, 1973.

[Pièces de clavecin]
Couperin's Werke; hrsg. von J. Brahms. Erster Teil.
Clavierstücke, livre I (–2).
Bergedorf, Weissenborn, 1869.

Pièces de clavecin . . . revues par J. Brahms et F. Chrysander.
London, Augener, 1888.

Pièces de clavecin; publiées par M. Cauchie et revues d'après
les sources par T. Dart.
Monaco, Editions de L'Oiseau-Lyre, 1968–71. 4 vols.

Pièces de clavecin; közreadja J. Gat.
Budapest, Editio Musica, 1969–71. 4 vols.

Pièces de clavecin; éd. par K. Gilbert.
Paris, Heugel, 1969–72. 4 vols. (Le pupitre, 21–24.)

C   Organ Music

(C. 1–42)
Pièces d'orgue consistantes en deux messes, l'une à l'usage
ordinaire des paroisses pour les festes solemnelles, l'autre propre
pour les convents de religieux et religieuses, *etc.*
Paris, [*c.* 1690].
Manuscripts *F-V* (*c.* 1689); *F-C* (dated 1690), preceded by an
engraved title-page and privilege.
Œuvres complètes VI
Œuvres complètes; rev. III

Pièces d'orgue; par François Couperin, Sieur de Crouilly.
In Archives des maîtres de l'orgue des XVIe, VXIIe, et XVIIIe
494   siècles, publiées . . . par A. Guilmant . . . avec . . . A. Pirro.

Cinquième volume. Paris. 1904. [Edited from *F-V* only.]
Reprint by Schott (Edition Schott, 1978)
Reprint by Johnson Reprint Corporation (New York, 1972)

I Messe à l'usage ordinaire des paroisses pour les festes solemnelles; révision d'après les manuscripts ou copies de Carpentras, Versailles, Paris (Bibl. de Conservatoire) par N. Dufourcq.
Paris, Editions musicales de la Schola Cantorum et de la Procure générale de musique, [?1963]. (Les grandes heures de l'orgue.)
Plate number S. 5843 P.

II Messe propre pour les convents de religieux et religieuses; révision d'après les manuscripts ou copies de Carpentras, Versailles, Paris (Bibl. de Conservatoire) par N. Dufourcq.
Paris, Editions musicales de la Schola Cantorum et de la Procure générale de musique, [?1964]. (Les grandes heures de l'orgue.)
Plate number S. 5943 P.

D Sacred Vocal Music

Works published during Couperin's lifetime

I Quatre versets d'un motet composé . . . [et] chanté à Versailles . . . mars 1703. On y a joint le verset Qui dat nivem du pseaume Lauda Jerusalem.
Paris, 1703.
F-Pc, F-Pn; *GB-Lbm*
Œuvres complètes XI
Œuvres complètes; rev. V, 1
Facsimile edition: Paris, U.C.P. Publications, 1978.
Settings of Psalm 118, Mirabilia testimonia tua, verses 139–42 (C. 45–8), and Qui dat nivem, verse 16 from Psalm 147 (C. 49)

Verset 11	Tabescere me fecit	S, S (unacc.)
Verset 12	Ignitum eloquium tuum	S, 2 violins, bc
Verset 13	Adolescentulus sum ego	S, 2 flutes, violin, bc
Verset 14	Justitia tua	S, S, SS, bc
Qui dat nivem		S, 2 flutes, violin, bc

2 Sept versets du motet composé de l'ordre du roy . . . et chanté
à Versailles . . . 1704.
Paris, 1704.
F-Pc, F-Pn, F-V; *GB-Lbm*
Œuvres complètes XI
Œuvres complètes; rev. V, 1
Facsimile edition: Paris, U.C.P. Publications, 1978.
Settings from Psalm 84, Benedixisti Domine (C. 50–6)

Verset 4	Converte nos	B, flute, bc
Verset 5	Numquid in aeternum	T, Bar, bc
Verset 7	Ostende nobis	T, violin, bc
Verset 8	Audiam quid loquetur	B, 2 violins, bc
Verset 11	Misericordia et veritas	T, T, bc
Verset 12	Veritas de terra	S, violin, bc
Verset 13	Et enim Dominus	S, 2 oboes, 2 flutes

3 Sept versets du motet composé de l'ordre du roy . . . et chanté
à Versailles . . . 1705.
Paris, 1705.
F-Pc, F-Pn, F-V; *GB-Lbm*
Œuvres complètes XI
Œuvres complètes; rev. V, 1
Facsimile edition: Paris, U.C.P., Publications, 1978.
Settings from Psalm 79, Qui regis Israel (C. 57–63)

Verset 1	Qui regis Israel	T, B, 2 violins, bc
Verset 3	Excita potentiam tuam	T, B, violin, bc
Verset 9	Vineam de Aegypto	B, violin, bc
Verset 10	Dux itineris fuisti	B, 2 flutes, 2 oboes, 2 violins, bc
Verset 11	Operuit montes	S, 2 flutes, violin, bc
Verset 12	Extendit palmites suos	S, 2 flutes, violin, bc
Verset 15	Deus virtutem convertere	T, flute, oboe, bass viol, bc

4 Leçons de ténèbres à une et à deux voix, *etc.* (C. 156–8)
Paris, [between 1713 and 1717].
F-Pc, F-Pn
Œuvres complètes XII
Œuvres complètes; rev. V, 2
Facsimile edition: Paris, U.C.P. Publications, 1978.

1ère leçon	Incipit Lamentatio Jeremiae prophetae	s, bc
2e leçon	Et egressus est a filia	s, bc
3ème leçon	Manum suam misit hostis	s, s, bc

Leçons de ténèbres à une et deux voix; édition par Daniel Vidal. Paris, Heugel, 1968. (Le pupitre, 8.)

Works unpublished at Couperin's death

Manuscript sources

a) *F-Pn Rés. F.* 1679 and 1680. A set of five part-books and one score (formerly St Michael's College, Tenbury, MSS. 1432–1437). For full details see Oboussier, P., 'Couperin Motets at Tenbury', *Proceedings of the Royal Musical Association*, 98, 1971/72, 17–29, and preface to Œuvres complètes; rev. V, 2 (1985).

b) *F-Pn* MS. Vm1 1175. A collection entitled *Recueil de motets de différents autheurs*.

c) *F-Pn* MS. Vm1 1630. A collection compiled by Sebastien de Brossard (1655–1730).

d) *F-V* MS. 18. *Motets de Messieurs Lalande, Nathan, Marchand l'aisné, Couprin, et Dubuisson . . . recueillis par Philidor . . . fait à Versailles en 1697.*

e) *F-V* MS. 59. *Recueil d'elévations à une, deux et trois voix, avec bass chiffrée.*

Modern editions

OC	Œuvres complètes
OCr	Œuvres complètes, rev. V, 2 and Supplement.
NM	Neuf motets; éd. par P. Oboussier.
	Paris, Heugel, 1972. (Le pupitre, 45.)

| Accedo ad te (Dialogus inter Deum et hominem) | T, B, bc |
| a, e, OC XII, OCr V,2 (C. 505) | |

| Ad te levavi oculos meos | B, 2 violins, bc |
| a, NM, OCr Supplement | |

Aspiratio mentis ad Deum (*see* O Jesu amantissime)

| Audite omnes et expancscite | T, 2 violins, bc |
| e, OC XII, OCr V,2 (C. 506) | |

Domine salvum fac regem   S, B, bc
a, NM, OCr Supplement

Exultent superi (Motet for St Suzanne)   S, A, B, 2 violins, bc
a, OCr Supplement

Festiva laetis (Motet for St Anne)   S, T, B, bc
a, e, OC XII, OCr V, 2 (C. 502)

Jucunda vox ecclesiae (Motet for   S, S, B, bc
St Augustin)
a, e, OC XII, OCr V, 2 (C. 504)

Laetentur coeli (Motet for St Barthélemy)   S, S, bc
a, OC XII, OCr V, 2 (C. 501)

Lauda Sion (elevation)   S, S, bc
a, NM, OCr Supplement

Laudate pueri Dominum   S, S, B, 2 violins, bc
a, d, OC XI, OCr V, 1 (C. 488)

Magnificat   S, S, bc
a, e, OC XII, OCr V, 2 (C. 500)

O amor, O gaudium   A, T, B, bc
a, e, OC XII, OCr V, 2 (C. 495)

O Domine quia refugium   B, B, B, bc
a, e, OC XII, OCr V, 2 (C. 503)

O Jesu amantissime   A, T, bc
a, e, OC XII, OCr V, 2 (C. 496)

O Misterium ineffabile (elevation)   S, B, bc
a, e, OC XII, OCr V, 2 (C. 494)

Ornate aras   A, 2 violins, bc
a, OCr Supplement

Precatio ad Deum (see Domine quia
refugium)

Quid retribuam tibi Domine   T, bc
a, d, OC XII, OCr V, 2 (C. 498)

Regina coeli laetare   S, S, bc
498   a, NM, OCr Supplement

Resonent organa (Motet for St Cecilia) a, OCr Supplement	S, B, B, 2 violins, bc
Respice in me a, NM, OCr Supplement	A, bc
Salve regina a, NM, OCr Supplement	A, bc
Salvum me fac Deus a, NM, OCr Supplement	B, 2 violins, 2 flutes, bass viol, bc
Tantum ergo sacramentum a, NM, OCr Supplement	S, S, B, bc
Usquequo Domine a, NM, OCr Supplement	A, bc
Veni sponsa Christi (Motet for St Suzanne) a, c, OC XI, OCr V, 1 (C. 493)	S, A, B, 2 violins, bc
Venite exultemus Domino a, b, e, OC XII, OCr V,2 (C. 497)	S, S, bc
Victoria! Christo resurgenti (Motet for Easter Day) a, e, OC XII, OCr V,2 (C. 499)	S, S, bc

Three of these motets are incomplete. They survive only in manuscript *Rés F.* 1680 at the Bibliothèque nationale (ex mss Tenbury 1432–6): 'Ornate aras', 'Resonent organa', 'Exultent superi'. Although the voice and *basse continue* parts are complete, the two instrumental *dessus* are missing. They will be published in Œuvres complètes rev. in the supplementary volume, with reconstructions.

E   Secular Vocal Music

Works published during Couperin's lifetime

All were published in various volumes entitled *Recueil d'airs sérieux et à boire de différents auteurs*, etc. Paris, 1697–1712

A l'ombre d'un ormeau (Air sérieux)   S, S, bc
Recueil d'airs, 1711. *F-Pn*
Œuvres complètes XI (C. 75)
Œuvres complètes; rev. V, 1

Au temple de l'amour (Air sérieux. Les   S, B, bc
pellerines)
Recueil d'airs, 1712. *F-Pn*
Œuvres complètes XI (C. 82)
Œuvres complètes; rev. V, 1

Dans l'île de Cythère (Les solitaires)   S, B, bc
Recueil d'airs, 1711. *F-Pn*
Œuvres complètes XI (C. 74)
Œuvres complètes; rev. V, 1

Doux liens de mon coeur   S, bc
Recueil d'airs, 1701. *F-Pc, F-Pn*
Œuvres complètes XI (C. 44)
Œuvres complètes; rev. V, 1

Faisons du temps un doux usage (Air   S, S, B, bc
sérieux)
Recueil d'airs, 1712. *F-Pc, F-Pn*
Œuvres complètes XI (C. 81)
Œuvres complètes; rev. V, 1

Il faut aimer (Air sérieux. La pastorelle)   S, bc
Recueil d'airs, 1711. *F-Pn*
Œuvres complètes XI (C. 73)
Œuvres complètes; rev. V, 1
Another versions of this piece, for
harpsichord only, appears in the first book
of *Pièces de clavecin* (1713).

Jean s'en alla comme il étoit venu (Air à   S, B, bc
boire. Epitaphe d'un paresseux)
Recueil d'airs, 1706. *DK-Kk; F-Pc, F-Pn,*
F-T
Œuvres complètes XI (C. 64)
Œuvres complètes; rev. V, 1

Qu'on ne me dise plus que c'est la seule   T, bc
absence

Receuil d'airs, 1697. *F-Pc, F-Pn*
Œuvres complètes XI (C. 43)
Œuvres complètes; rev. V, 1

Zephire, modéré en ces lieux   s, bc
(Air sérieux. Brunete)
Recueil d'airs, 1711. *F-Pn*
Œuvres complètes XI (C. 76–80)
Œuvres complètes; rev. V, 1

Works unpublished at Couperin's death

The first two are contained in a manuscript collection in *F-Pc*,
entitled *Ier recuil d'airs à boire en duô et triô. Trois vestales champêtres*
is contained in a MS. in *F-Pc*, entitled *Recueil de trios de différens*
Auteurs.
All are published in Œuvres complètes XI (Œuvres complètes;
rev. V, 1)

A moy. Tout est perdu (Canon à 3) (C. 491) s, s, s

La femme entre deux draps (Canon à 3)   s, s, s
(C. 490)

Trois vestales champêtres et trois Poliçons s, s, s
(C. 489)

F   Theoretical Writings

1 Règle pour l'accompagnement
  Two manuscripts   *F-Pn*
  Œuvres complètes I
  Œuvres complètes; rev. I

2 L'art de toucher le clavecin
  Published at Paris in two editions of 1716 and 1717.
  First edition   *F-Pc, F-Pn*
  Second edition   Library holdings listed RISM C4301–C4302
  Œuvres complètes I
  Œuvres complètes; rev. I

(Monuments of music and music literature in facsimile. 2nd series, music literature 23).
Facsimile edition: New York, Broude Brothers, 1969.
Facsimile edition: St-Michel-de-Provence [Harmonia Mundi, France], 1972.

L'art de toucher le clavecin . . . hrsg. . . . von A. Linde, etc.
Wiesbaden, Breitkopf & Härtel, 1933
Text in French, German, and English, in parallel columns.

L'art de toucher le clavecin . . . Margery Halford, editor and translator.
Port Washington, Alfred, 1974.
Facsimiles from the original ed. of 1716, with a new translation printed parallel with the texts of the 1716 and 1717 editions.

The foregoing lists some editions of Couperin's music from those contemporary with him to the present day. Virtually all his surviving music is available in published form; and the old Oiseau-Lyre edition was, of course, a major feat of musicography. It restored to the light of day almost all the music of a great but largely forgotten composer, keeping as close to Couperin's original texts as seemed consistent with the production of an edition intelligible to modern readers. Thus Couperin's varied clefs were abandoned, but his idiosyncratic notations for ornaments and phrasing were preserved. The edition was printed, with almost startling legibility, on magnificent paper; if both the typography and the vivid green binding seemed a trifle brash for their subject, one could not question their opulence and munificence; at the time, the price of the set was not excessive.

To the Oiseau-Lyre edition there were two serious objections. The first is that it was a library edition, inconvenient for use on the harpsichord, or even by conductors. No systematic attempt was made to issue the works separately, with parts – so the publication didn't help the dissemination of Couperin's music as much as it might have done. The second objection is that the concerted works were printed with fully realized continuo parts, some of which are dubious in relation to what we know of contemporary practices. Continuo players today can only be

riled by the elaborate realizations proffered for many of the pieces. Even if one finds them aesthetically acceptable (usually I don't) one no longer expects to be thus bullied by a notation so complex that one has to 'read' it as though it were a nineteenth-century score. To have to read continuo parts, often in quite dense polyphony, denies their true function, which is empirically to support the interplay of vocal and/or instrumental lines. This objection may of course be made to many modern editions of many baroque composers; we feel it with peculiar force in reference to Couperin, however, because contemporary editions of his work were of such admirable beauty and lucidity. Almost all of these editions have now been republished in facsimile. When we have played *L'Apothéose de Lully* or *L'Apothéose de Corelli* from facsimiles of the contemporary engravings, using only the notations Couperin scrupulously invented, one can but regard editorial intrusions as at worst sacrilegious, at best supernumerary. After one has lived with the music a while the original notations prompt one, of their visual nature, to do the right things aurally, and I have noted that this applies even to relatively inexperienced students. Ask them to play Couperin's violin parts from heavily edited modern editions, with the ornaments (often wrongly) written out, and their response will be gauchely unconvincing; present them with Couperin's own notations and they will respond in the right spirit – to which the letter may be added with a little application.

The exquisite appearance of Couperin's music so matches its sound that it is an inspiration to play from the eighteenth-century score, and it's remarkable how quickly, thus inspired, one learns to cope with Couperin's five clefs, as his own largely amateur public had to. If one is unwilling to make the effort, however, there are reasonable alternatives. The old Brahms–Chrysander edition, though sometimes inaccurate, manages to preserve much of the elegant lucidity of the original, while modifying the multiple clefs in accord with modern usage. Moreover an entirely satisfactory new edition now exists, that of Kenneth Gilbert, in Heugel's *Le Pupitre* series. Gilbert too alters nothing except the clefs; corrects errors; and provides all the scholarly apparatus that is necessary.

Kenneth Gilbert, in collaboration with Davitt Moroney, is also in charge of the reissue of the complete Oiseau-Lyre edition, long out of print. Seven volumes out of twelve (including the harpsichord pieces) have already appeared (July 1986). They 503 reproduce the handsome Oiseau-Lyre typography, with editorial emendations as appropriate, so that this version is Gilbert's latest, if not finally definitive, presentation of Couperin's harpsichord music. Gilbert and Moroney are also in the process of re-editing the volumes of concerted music and of church music, deleting the Oiseau-Lyre continuo parts, which, as already indicated, tend to distort or even to mislead – the more so since the editorial additions were printed in the same bold type as were Couperin's own notations. What we are left with is Couperin's own melody lines and bass (with figures where he gave them); more important, this revision of the *Œuvres complètes* for the first time takes full account of all the known manuscript sources, some of which have come to light only recently. Critical commentaries and extensive new prefaces contain much new information.

The works of Louis Couperin have been magnificently re-edited for the new Oiseau-Lyre series by Davitt Moroney. The references in the section on Louis Couperin have been modified to accord with this new edition.

BIBLIOGRAPHY

Books and Articles about Couperin

Books

BEAUSSANT, P., *François Couperin*, Paris, 1980

BOUVET, C., *Une dynastie de musiciens français: Les Couperin*, Paris, 1919

BRUNOLD, P., *François Couperin*, translated from the French by J. B. Hanson, Monaco, 1949

CAUCHIE, M. *Thematic Index of the Works of François Couperin*, Monaco, 1949

CENTRE NATIONAL DE LA RECHERCHIE SCIENTIFIQUE, *L'interprétation de la musique française aux XVIIème et XVIIIème siècles* . . . [éd.] par E. Weber, Paris, 1974

CHARLIER, H., *Couperin*, Paris, 1965

CITRON, P., *Couperin*, Paris, 1976

HOFMAN, S., *L'œuvre de clavecin de François Couperin*, Paris, 1961

MAILLARD, J. H. O., *Franciso Couperin y su dinastia*, Madrid, 1978

MELANGES FRANÇOIS COUPERIN, publiées à l'occasion du tricentaire de sa naissance, 1668–1968, Paris, 1968

REIMANN, M. *Untersuchungen zur Formgeschichte der französischen Klavier-Suite mit besonderer Berücksichtigung von Couperin's 'Ordres'*, Regensburg, Bosse, 1940. (Kölner Beiträge zur Musikforschung, 3).

SHAY, E. *Notes inégales and F. Couperin's Messe à l'usage des paroisses*, Ph. D. thesis, University of Cincinatti, 1969

TESSIER, A., *Couperin* (Les Musiciens Célèbres), 1926

TIERSOT, J., *Les Couperins* (Les Maîtres de la Musique), 1926

TURNER, J. E., *Notes inégales: treatises by Bacilly, Loulié, and Démotz; their application to the Mass for the Convents by F. Couperin*, Ph. D. thesis, University of Wisconsin–Madison, 1974

WURTZ, M. H., *The sacred vocal works of F. Couperin*, Ph. D. thesis, Washington University, 1965

Articles in Encyclopaedias

CITRON, P., 'Couperin', *Encyclopédie de la musique*, Paris, 1958, vol. 1, pp. 600–601

DUFOURCQ, N., 'La famiglia Couperin', *Enciclopedia della musica*, Milan, 1963, vol. 1, pp. 565–7

FULLER, D., 'Couperin family', *Encyclopaedia Britannica*, Chicago, 1974, Macropaedia, vol. 5, pp. 217–18

HIGGINBOTTOM, E., 'Couperin', *New Grove Dictionary of Music and Musicians*, London, 1981

MELLERS, W. H., 'Couperin. (Family)', *Grove's Dictionary of Music and Musicians*; 5th edition, London, 1954, vol. 2, pp. 482–99

REIMANN, M., 'Couperin. (Familie)', *Die Musik in Geschichte und Gegenwart*, Kassel, 1952, vol. 2, columns 1711–38

Articles in Periodicals

ANTOINE, M., 'Un acte inédit de François Couperin', *Revue de musicologie*, 37, 1955, 76–7

ANTOINE, M., 'Autour de François Couperin', *Revue de musicologie*, 31, 1952, 109–27

BOUVET, C., 'Trois airs de François Couperin le Grand sur des paroles profanes', *Société Française de Musicologie, Bulletin*, 2(3), 1918, 145–8

CHRYSANDER, F., 'F. Couperin: his four books of harpsichord music', *Monthly Musical Record*, 19(224), 1889, 174–5

CHRYSANDER, F., 'François Couperin', *Monthly Musical Record*, 19, 1889, 25–7

CHRYSANDER, F., 'François Couperin. II. The Champion and Couperin families of harpsichord players', *Monthly Musical Record*, 19, 1889, 29–51 and 77–8.

CHRYSANDER, F., 'The Music of Couperin', *Monthly Musical Record*, 19, 1899, 124–5

CLARK, J., 'Les Folies Françoises', *Early Music*, 8(2), 1980

DART, T., 'On Couperin's harpsichord music', *Musical Times*, 110, 1969, 590–4

DUFOURCQ, N., 'F. Couperin, musicien de la terre, de la ville, de l'église, de la cour', *XVIIe siècle*, 82, 1969, 3–27

FULLER-MAITLAND, J. A., 'The "Méthode" of François Couperin', *Chesterian*, N. S. 8, 1920, 229–33

KIRKPATRICK, R., 'On re-reading Couperin's L'Art de toucher le Clavecin', *Early Music*, 4 (I), 1976, 3–11

MELLERS, W. H., 'The clavecin works of François Couperin', *Music & Letters*, 27, 1946, 233–48

MELLERS, W. H., 'Couperin and his church music', *Musical Times*, 109, 1968 (1504), 522–4

MELLERS, W. H., 'Couperin on the harpsichord', *Musical Times*, 109, 1968 (1509), 1010–11

MELLERS, W. H., 'Couperin's suites for two viols', *Score*, 2, 1950, 10–17

MELLERS, W. H., 'On performing Couperin's harpsichord music', *Listener*, 3 January 1957, p. 37

MELLERS, W. H., 'The organ masses of François Couperin', *Music Review*, 8, 1947, 36–9

OBOUSSIER, P., 'A Couperin discovery', *Musical Times*, 112, 1971, 429–30

OBOUSSIER, P., 'Couperin motets at Tenbury', *Proceedings of the Royal Musical Association*, 98, 1971/72, 17–29

SADIE, S., 'Couperin and the perfection of music', *The Times*, 8 November 1968, p. 13

STEVENS, D., 'Couperin-le-grand', *Music and Musicians*, 17, 1968, 22–3

TESSIER, A., 'Un exemplaire original des Pièces d'orgue de Couperin', *Revue de musicologie*, 10, 1929, 109–17

TESSIER, A., 'Les Messes d'orgue de Couperin', *Revue musicale*, 1924, 37–48

TESSIER, A., 'Les pièces de clavecin de Couperin', *Revue musicale*, 1925, 123–38

TUNLEY, D., 'Couperin and French lyricism', *Musical Times*, 124, 1983, 534–5

Original Texts Relevant to Couperin's Background

BONNET, J., *Histoire de la Musique*, 1725

BURNEY, C., *General History of Music*, 1789

TILLET, Titon du, *Le Parnasse François*, 1732 (Supplements 1743 and 1755)

AULNOY, Mme d', *Contes de Fées*, 1697

BOILEAU, *Art Poétique*, 1674
BOISSUET, *Selected Sermons*
BOURDALOUE, *Selected Sermons*
BUSSY, Rabutin, *Mémoires and correspondence*
CORNEILLE, *Théâtre*
DESCARTES, *Abrégé de la Musique*, 1618
DESCARTES, *Discours de la Méthode*, 1639
DESCARTES, *Traité des Passions de l'Ame*, 1649
FÉNELON, *De l'Education des Filles*, 1687
FÉNELON, *Lettres Spirituelles*, 1718
LA BRUYÈRE, *Caractères*, 1688
LA BRUYÈRE, *The Characters of Jean de la Bruyère*, translated by
    Henri van Laun, 1929
LA FAYETTE, Mme de, *La Princesse de Clèves*, 1678
LA FONTAINE, *Fables*, 1668–1694, and other works
LA ROCHEFOUCAULD, *Maximes*, 1665
MAINTENON, Mme de, *Lettres sur l'éducation des filles*
MAINTENON, Mme de, *Correspondence générale*
MALHERBE, *Oeuvres diverses*
MOLIÈRE, *Théâtre*
NOVERRE, *Lettres sur la danse* 1760
ORLÉANS, LA DUCHESSE D', *Memoirs of the Court of Louis XIV
    and of the Regency*, English translation, 1905
PASCAL, *Les Provinciales*, 1656
PASCAL, *Pensées*
PERRAULT, C., *Le Siècle de Louis XIV*
PERRAULT, C., *Parallèles des Anciens et des Modernes*, 1688
PERRAULT, C., *Histoires ou Contes du Temps Passé*, 1697
RACINE, *Théâtre*
ST-EVREMOND, *Lettre* to the Duke of Buckingham, 1711
SAINT-SIMON, *Historical Memoirs*, translated by Lucy Norton,
    3 volumes, 1967
SAINT-SIMON, *Mémoires sur le Siècle de Louis XIV*
SCARRON, *Jodelet*, 1643, and other works
SCUDÉRY, Mlle de, *Le Grand Cyrus*, 1653
SCUDÉRY, Mlle de, *Clélie*, 1660
SÉVIGNÉ, Mme de, Selections from *Lettres*
SOREL, *Francion*, 1623
TRISTAN l'Hermite, *Poésies*
D'URFÉ, *L'Astrée*, 1607
VAUGELAS, *Remarques sur la langue française*, 1647

VAUVENARGUES, *Introduction à la connoissance de l'esprit humain, suivi de réflexions et de maximes*, 1747
LA DESCRIPTION DE VERSAILLES, Paris, 1694
VOITURE, *Oeuvres Diverses*, 1649
VOLTAIRE, *Histoire du Siècle de Louis XIV*, 1751

Paintings by Poussin, Claude, Le Brun, Watteau, Philippe de Champagne, Chardin, Boucher, etc.

MERIAN, *Topographica Galliae*, vol. I, 1655

Modern Works Relevant to Couperin's Background

CLARK, G. N., *The Seventeenth Century*, 1929; 2nd ed. 1947
DE GONCOURT, Edmond and Jules, *French Eighteenth Century Painters*, English translation, 1948
GOOCH, G. P., *Louis XV: the Monarchy in Decline*, 1956
HUYGHE, René, *Watteau: Les Carnets de dessins*, 1976
HULTON, Paul, *Watteau's Drawings in the British Museum*, 1980
ISHERWOOD, R. M., *Music in the Service of the King: France in the Seventeenth Century*, 1973
LEWIS, W. H., *The Splendid Century: some aspects of French life in the reign of Louis XIV*, 1953
LEWIS, W. H., *The Sunset of the Splendid Century: the life and times of Louis-Auguste de Bourbon, Duc de Maine*, 1955
MCDOUGALL, Dorothy, *Two Royal Domains of France*, 1931
MACKAY, Agnes E., *La Fontaine and his Friends*, 1973
MITFORD, Nancy, *The Sun King*, 1966
OGG, David, *Europe in the Seventeenth Century*, 1938; 8th ed. 1961
PRUNIÈRES, Henri, *Lully*, 1910
PRUNIÈRES, Henri, *Le Ballet de Cour en France*, 1913
PRUNIÈRES, Henri, *L'Opéra Italien en France avant Lully*, 1913
ROLLAND, Romain, *Musiciens d'autrefois*, 1908
SITWELL, Sacheverell, *Cupid and the Jacaranda*
TILLEY, Arthur, *From Montaigne to Molière*, 1923
TILLEY, Arthur, *The Decline of the Age of Louis XIV*, 1929
TURNELL, Martin, Articles on Molière, Racine, Corneille, *La Princesse de Clèves. The Classical Moment*, 1948
WELSFORD, Enid, *The Court Masque*, 1927

Critical and Theoretical Works

Original Texts

D'ALEMBERT, J., *Réflexions sur la Musique*, 1773

D'ALEMBERT, J., *Elémens de la Musique*, 1752

AVISON, C., *An Essay on Musical Expression*, 1752

BONNET, J., *Histoire Générale de la Musique*, 1715 and 1725

BOYVIN, J., *Traité Abrégé de l'accompagnement*, 1715

DE CAHUSAC L., *La Danse Ancienne et Moderne*, 1754

BROSSARD, S., *Dictionnaire de Musique*, 1703

DE CHABANON, M., *Observations sur la musique*, 1779

DE CHASTELLUX, F. J., *Essai sur l'union de la poésie et de la musique*, 1765

CORRETTE, M., *Le Maître de Clavecin*, 1753

FEUILLET, R. A., *Choréographie ou l'art décrire la danse*, English translation, 1710

LACOMBE, *Dictionnaire Portatif des beaux-arts*, 1758

LE BLANC, H., *Défense de la Basse de viole*, 1740

LA VIÉVILLE, Lecerf de, *Comparaison de la musique Italienne et de la musique Française*, 1705

GOUDAR, A., *Le Brigandage de la musique italienne*, 1777

GRÉTRY, A., *Mémoires*, 1795

LOULIÉ, E., *Elémens de la musique*, 1696

MERSENNE, M., *Harmonie Universelle*, 1636

MERSENNE, M., Correspondence (Bibliothèque des Archives de Philosophie)

PERRAULT, C., *Parallèles des Anciens et des Modernes*, 1688

RAGUENET, F., *Parallèles des Italiens et des François*, 1705

RAMEAU, J. P., *Traité de l'harmonie*, 1722

RAMEAU, P., *Le Maître à danser*, 1725

ROUSSEAU, J. J., *Dictionnaire de la Musique*, 1768

ROUSSEAU, J., *Traité de la Viole*, 1687

ST LAMBERT, M. de., *Nouveau Traité de l'accompagnement*, 1707

ST MARD, R. de., *Réflexions sur l'opéra*, 1741

Modern Works

ANTHONY, J. R., *French Baroque Music from Beaujoyeulx to Rameau*, 1973

BORREL, E., *L'Interprétation de la Musique Française de Lully à la Révolution*, 1934

BUKOFZER, M., *Music of the Baroque Era*, 1948

BRENET, M., *Marc-Antoine Charpentier*, 1913

BRUNOLD, P. *L'Orgue de St Gervais*, 1934

CHAMPIGNEULLE, B., *L'Age Classique de la Musique Française*, 1946

CHRYSANDER, Preface to Augener edition of *Clavecin Works of François Couperin*, 1887

DANNREUTHER, E., *Musical Ornamentation*, 1894

DOLMETSCH, A., *The Interpretation of the Music of the Seventeenth and Eighteenth Centuries*, 1916

DONINGTON, Robert, *The Interpretation of Early Music*, 1974

GÉROLD, T., *Le Chant au XVIIième Siècle*, 1921

DE LAURENCIE, L., *Les Violinistes Françaises de Lulli à Viotto*, 1922–4

PINCHERLE, M., *Corelli*, 1933

PIRRO, A., *Les Clavecinistes*, 1924

PRUNIÈRES, Henri, *Nouvelle Histoire de la Musique*, vol. II, 1936

RAUGEL, Felix, *Les Organistes*, 1933

SCHWEITZER, A., *J. S. Bach*, 1911

WESTRUP, J. A., *Purcell*, 1937

The Prefaces to the Oiseau-Lyre edition, 1933; revised edition, 1980–.

The Prefaces to the Heugel editions, 1969–1974.

Musical Scores

D'ANGLEBERT, J., *Keyboard Works*

BACH, C. P. E., *Miscellaneous Keyboard Works*

BACH, J. C., *Miscellaneous Keyboard Works*

BACH, J. S., *Miscellaneous Keyboard Works*

BALBASTRE, Claude, *Pièces de clavecin, d'orgue et de forte piano*

BALLARD, *Collections of Brunettes*

BLAVET, M., *Flute Sonatas and other Concerted Works*

DE BOISMORTIER, J. D., *Concerted Works*

BOUTMY, L., Pieces in *Les Clavicinistes Flamands* (Elewyck)

CAMPRA, A., *L'Europe Galante*

CAMPRA, A., *Les Fêtes Vénitiennes*, and other works

CARISSIMI, G., *Cantatas and Sacred Histories*

DE CHAMBONNIÈRES, J. C., *Keyboard Works*

CHARPENTIER, A., *Cantatas and Sacred Histories*
CLÉRAMBAULT, L. N., *Concerted Works and Cantatas*
CLÉRAMBAULT, L. N., *Organ Works*
CORELLI, A., *Sonatas and Concerti Grossi*
CORRETTE, M., *Concerted Works*
COUPERIN, Armand-Louis, *Selected works for keyboard*, edited by David Fuller, Madison, A–R Editions, 1975, 2 vols. (Recent researches in the music of the pre-classical, classical, and early romantic eras, 1–2)
COUPERIN, Louis, *Keyboard Works*
DAGINCOUR, F., *Pièces pour orgue*
DIEUPART, *Pièces pour clavecin*
DOWLAND, J., *Lute Pieces*
DOWLAND, J., *Ayres*
DUMONT, H., *Motets and Masses*
DUPHLY, *Pièces de Clavecin*
EXPERT, H. (ed.), *Les Maîtres Musiciens de la Renaissance Française*
FIOCCO, J. H., Pieces in *Les Clavecinistes Flamands* (Elewyck)
FISCHER, J. K. F., *Oeuvres complètes pour clavecin et orgue* (E. von Werra)
FISCHER, J. K., *Concerted Works* (Denkmäler der Tonkunst)
FROBERGER, J., *Keyboard Works*
FRESCOBALDI, G., *Keyboard Works*
FUX, J. J., *Concentus Musico-instrumentalis* (Denkmäler der Tonkunst)
GAULTIER, Denis (and other lutenists), *La Rhétorique des Dieux*
GIGAULT, N., *Organ Works*
GRIGNY, N. de, *Organ Works*
GROVLEZ, G. (ed.), Collections of *Les Clavecinistes* (Chester)
HANDEL, G. F., Violin sonatas, keyboard suites, etc.
D'HERVELOIS, Le Caix, *Pièces de Violes*
LECLAIR, J. M., *Livres de Sonates*
LA LANDE, M. de, *Musique pour les Soupers du Roi*
LA LANDE, M. de, *Motets*
LA GUERRE, Elisabeth Claude [Jacquet] de, *Pièces de clavecin*
LE BÈGUE, N., *Organ Works*
LE ROUX, G., *Pièces de Clavecin*
LULLY, J. B., *Theatre and Church Music*
MONDONVILLE, J., *Pièces de Clavecin en Sonates avec Accompagnement de Violon*
MONDONVILLE, J., *Sonates pour le Violon avec la Basse Continue*

MOURET, J. *Suites pour des Violons, des hautbois et des cors de Chasse*

MARAIS, Marin, *Pièces de viole*

MARCHAND, L., *Organ Works*

MARCHAND, L., *Pièces de Clavecin*

MARPURG, *Suites for clavier*

MATTHESON, J., *Suites*

MATTHESON, J., *Les Maîtres du Chant*

MUFFAT, Georg, *Florilegia*

MUFFAT, Gottlieb, *Harpsichord Works*

PURCELL, H., *Trio Sonatas*

RAISON, A., *Organ Works*

RAMEAU, J.-P., *Harpsichord Works*

RAUGEL, Félix (ed.), *Les Maîtres Français de l'Orgue* (Schola Cantorum)

REBEL, F., *Concerted Works*

ROBERDAY, F., *Organ Works*

ROSSI, L., *Cantatas*

SCHÜTZ, H., *Sacred Histories*

TELEMANN, G. P., *Musique de table*

TITELOUZE, J., *Organ Works*

TORCHI (ed.), *L'Arte Musicale in Italia* (Ricordi)

WARLOCK, P. (ed.), Songs from Bataille's *Airs de différents auteurs*, 1608–18 (OUP)

NOTE: This Bibliography aims at including all the more important works, creative and critical, which have been consulted during the writing of this book. It does not claim to be a comprehensive list of all the works which could legitimately be considered relevant to the subject.

Index of Works

515

General Index

References in *italic* type are to illustrations and captions

521